# CRAVE

STEVIE CARTER

ISBN (Paperback): 978-0-6459737-0-9

Editing and Proofreading: Molly Hart of Read between the Smut Editorial Services

Cover Design: Steph Williams of Whirled of Papercraft

Illustrations (Paperback Edition) by @vicdrawss and Stevie Carter

Created with Vellum

# AUTHOR NOTE & CONTENT WARNING

Reader discretion is advised. This book is not intended for those under the age of 18. It contains many distressing and unsettling themes.

If you have any known triggers, it is best not to continue as this series only becomes darker in some parts. I've mentioned many times that I started writing Crave during a particularly dark time. This was an outlet while on the waiting list for therapy — to keep my mind busy and to escape from the real world.

This book is not intended as a reference for healthy sex and relationships and should not be considered one — ever. While these characters are a figment of my imagination, that does not mean I hold their views or condone their actions. They are all morally gray, at best.

**Themes within Crave include, but are not limited to;**

Strong suicidal ideation, suicide attempt, age-gap relationship, on page assault and rape of a main character (nightmare), recollections of statutory rape (therapy), on page death, mentions of nonconsensual surgeries, explicit and on page sexual interactions between characters, general mentions of blood and other medical practices, pregnancy and pregnancy loss (miscarriage), male and female infertility, disordered eating, drug and alcohol use, explicit language, physical abuse and torture, general violence and use of weapons.

Feel free to contact me if you find more along the way.

*— Stevie*

# WELCOME TO CRAVE. DID YOU BRING YOUR MASK?

**Tonight's Setlist**

Billie Eilish - NDA
Isabella LaRosa - Haunted
Mr. Kitty - After Dark
Thornhill - Raw
Halsey - Young God
Cameron Grey - I Want It All
Ocean Grove - When You're This High You Can Say What You Like
Metallica - Sad But True
Bad Omens - What It Cost
Bad Omens - Like A Villain
The Neighborhood - Sweater Weather

*Stitch Up*

***1.*** *To join or close by sewing.*
***2.*** *To manipulate a situation so that someone is placed at a disadvantage or wrongly blamed for something.*
***3.*** *To prank, trick, or deceive (a person), whether or not malice is intended.*

*Stitch*

***1.*** *n. a very funny person.*
***2.*** *n. a sharp pain, usually in the side.*

# PROLOGUE

## THE STRANGER

Sitting in the passenger seat of my pickup truck with my feet on the dashboard, I searched for her through the window. Though it was late, the weather was unseasonably warm, and her car hadn't passed by at the usual time. It could mean only one thing; she was out for a run.

The hill I'd parked on concealed my truck within the tree line, high and steep enough to see her coming from a mile away — literally. Even in the dark, my Gifted eyesight allowed me to watch her from a distance.

If tonight's run were like the others, she'd be recklessly bounding around empty streets for a little over an hour, her scars exposed as if they weren't beacons pointing directly to the horrors of her past.

When I'd started recording her movements, this part of the routine was an opportunity for me to break into her home and confirm her identity.

But like her, the house was a fortress with lethal surprises. I'd not been able to get close without setting off motion lights and cameras. The fence alone was dangerous enough, having sliced my hand open as I tried to climb over it.

There was no way for me to know what her house contained, though I knew I could show up during the early hours of the morning under the guise of needing medical assistance.

But if I did that, she'd recognize me. And I couldn't blow my cover. Not yet. I still had work to do in Bedlam.

Even then, I'd come to accept that I'd have to disappear once my mission was complete and she'd never learn my identity. She'd never learn everything I was doing… was for *her*.

She was trying to move on and had more than enough ghosts from her past to keep her occupied without me adding more to the mix.

*There she is.*

She came into view on the road below, her pale skin glowing in the moonlight. The nocturnal life had claimed what little color her flesh could maintain.

While observing her, I found it impossible to believe she was once the right hand to an unfathomably treacherous man; now one of the most notorious villains the underworld had ever seen.

The public life she once led with him came to an abrupt state of inactivity. No new photos of them had surfaced for years. Her social accounts featured a girl who was a convincing look-alike, but the strategically chosen angles never showed her entire profile.

There were no appearances above ground at her boyfriend's side to make him look more man than a monster. More shocking than that, she hadn't been seen in the underworld; his favorite place to show her off.

She once had everything anyone could ever want, and yet I found her here, hiding out in the mountains, seeming to have given it all up.

It didn't fit the typical MO of someone who had made it to the top. Money and power were difficult to let go of, and no one ever had the guts to leave it all behind.

Especially not someone with her reputation and status.

Once greed's sharp claws grasped the back of your neck, it called the shots, maneuvering you like a puppet toward your next target. Draining, consuming and destroying everyone in your path to feed the monster whose grip only grew tighter as it demanded more. There were few things that could free you of that hold, and I always wondered how she, of all people, found the strength to be released of it.

*No wonder they all think she's dead.*

When whispers of her death reached the mountains, I'd found myself crushed by a distorted sense of relief. I'd believed, like most in the underworld, that she had finally succumbed to the fate of most villains — killed by one of the enemies she and her boyfriend had made along the way.

But perhaps things weren't as they appeared, and she wasn't the content queen of the crime-fueled netherworld we all mistook her for.

Why else would she resurface in disguise, two states north of her domain, no king in sight?

He was coming for her. And the steel and glass castle in the country's grimiest city was awaiting her return.

My back itched, and I straightened to get a better look at her position. The clothing's fabric that I'd chosen for the night's stakeout irritated my skin, distracting me from my musings.

There was no need to follow the girl every night. When I'd discussed it with my trusted people, I'd been told it was unnecessary, that villains weren't worth the trouble and I'd be wasting my time becoming attached to someone destined to meet a messy end.

It didn't deter me, though. She was far too valuable.

She couldn't start a new life without her past skulking in the shadows, primed to drag her back into its murky depths.

And I wasn't the only one following her.

I settled into the driver's seat and released the breaks. The car rolled backward through the trees, only starting up once the tires connected with the road.

Driving without lights at high speed was dangerous, even with my vision, but I couldn't risk being seen until I was closer, unwilling to expose my regular hideout.

The road through the hills zigzagged down the slope and I stole a glance at her each time the trees cleared enough to view the scene below. She was further down the stretch and coming to a bend.

A car rounded the corner in the distance, swiftly closing space between them as she ran in the dark.

As the lights of the pursuers' car illuminated the air around her, she leapt from the side of the road and into the pitch-black pine forest.

Then, she disappeared.

*Smart girl.*

Paranoid with the knowledge she was wanted at Home, she didn't take any chances with the vehicle as it approached from behind.

I rounded the last corner from which she'd jumped, switching my headlights on as I slowed to a reasonable speed.

The other car had come to a stop; its occupants already out and preparing to search. I pulled up behind them and reached for my cap and sunglasses.

One man stood on the side of the road, shining the light from his phone into the forest. Another, beyond the guardrail, paced the shadowy tree line that sloped down and away from us.

They wore dark business suits and had sunglasses on — not the typical attire for residents of these parts.

"Stitch!" the man over the edge called as I killed the ignition. I left the headlights on in hopes they'd be weary of me getting a clear look at their car and its plates.

"It's time to come Home!" the other called to the darkness as I stepped onto the road.

My deep voice traveled over the rumble of their idling car, "You guys need a hand?"

"Nah, we're good," the man on the road responded, his tone defensive as he turned to acknowledge me; the stranger.

He lit a cigarette and blew the smoke across the space between us. The foul smell twisted with the scents of petrol and crushed pine needles as he sized me up. The weather didn't call for the long sleeves of my jacket, the shirt that came high up my neck, the jeans, and the gloves.

Returning the favor, I glared at him through my sunglasses. I wouldn't have needed them as part of my disguise, if not for knowing who these men worked for.

Ensuring I remembered his features for the next time we inevitably met, I noted there was nothing particularly interesting about him. His tanned skin, dark hair, and mustache weren't anything to write home about.

But then, he turned to look at his partner; vaulting himself back over the barrier, and his neck moved in a way that it exposed part of a tattoo. *Find-Bingo*. I didn't need to see the rest.

The other man met us in the glow of my headlights, ignoring me as he opened their trunk. My height allowed me to steal a peek at the contents: ropes, zip ties, plastic sheets. He picked up a heavy torch about the length of his forearm and tossed another to the man still cautiously glaring.

"You sure you don't need help?" I offered, keeping them busy, if only for a few minutes.

*I can hear her.*

These men evidently weren't Gifted or else they would have easily tracked the whispers. She was struggling to keep quiet while calling someone for help on her phone.

"We're fine," the man with dark red hair finally said. He looked over his shoulder and squinted through the pines. "Just looking for… our dog." He almost scrunched his features when referring to her that way.

Despite the girl's position in their world, everyone was aware of her treatment to a degree. She was risking the perilous woods, alone in the dark. Anyone in their right mind would have done the same to avoid being forced to bear her collar.

"I'm happy to help. I know the terrain well," I said, hoping that if they accepted my offer, I could lead them further away from her.

"Thanks, but *no*." He let out a strained laugh and set a hand on his hip, glancing to where she disappeared. "Stitch will come home eventually. She just likes to make things difficult for us."

"That," the other added, continuing to blow smoke around us, "and she can be pretty fucking vicious if she's cornered by the wrong people. Best not to get strangers involved." His words held a warning.

*They want me gone.*

They'd had many opportunities to snatch her, but had either been lazy or were toying with her as a cat would with a mouse. The former wasn't acceptable in their roles, and their boss was becoming restless.

The red-haired man turned away, not wasting another moment to allow her more time to escape. He switched on his torch, and the thick beam of light flooded the ground as he leapt back over the edge.

*Fuck.*

"Be mindful of the bears!" I called after him before turning back to his partner. "I think I saw a couple on the way down."

"Bears?" He dropped the butt of his cigarette and crushed it with his shoe.

"You *are* in the Gray Mountains," I reminded him with a tight laugh. "Bears own these hills."

The way he arched a brow confirmed my warning did as intended — he felt stupid. They hadn't thought of that. And while they were well prepared with the equipment to restrain the girl for the long trip back to her former lover, these men weren't survivors. Not in the sense that she was.

I shrugged, continuing to rope him into a casual conversation. "They're an unusual breed out here. Nocturnal. Night hunters. They don't grant the peace of killing you before they start tearing into your guts."

His skin paled slightly, and his smug features flickered.

"I once saw a pine covered in intestines," I continued with a smirk. "Strung up all over the branches like the feral creatures were decorating for the holidays. Oh, you should be mindful of traps, too. They'll take your legs clean off."

He gulped and cleared his throat. "We'll keep that in mind."

This interaction had been drawn out for as long as I dared, "You two have a good night. Good luck with your dog," I called smoothly, turning to leave.

I pulled around their car as the man with the mustache slammed their trunk shut and rushed to join the other. I drove slowly, continuing in the opposite direction of her house, praying they'd take my reluctance to leave as suspicious.

It could give her a head start if they took the bait, though I hoped it wouldn't lead to anything physical. Those men and I were bound to cross paths again soon, and I couldn't risk being recognized as the one stalling her return to Home.

As I drove toward the nearest town, a black spot appeared on the horizon. It rapidly increased in size as it barreled toward me. If it wasn't for the moon's glow, reflecting on the car's black paint, I would have thought it was a UFO.

"Fuck!" I hissed, angling my face down. I'd moved fast, but even at this speed, there was a good chance the driver would recognize me.

Without its lights on, the car raced by, rocking my truck with the slipstream.

"What a dick." I rolled my eyes, refusing to acknowledge my relief at seeing *that* vigilante. Not all those watching her intended to cause harm, and I had left before the hunt turned graphic.

As I continued on the long roads, devoid of life, headlights appeared in my rear-view mirror. But only for a few moments. The car turned down a road that would lead to the highway.

*Smart move.*

Had those men hung around any longer, they would have made tomorrow's news cycle as another bear attack in the mountains — if any recognizable remains were recovered.

I had no doubt they'd be back again soon.

Proof of life was needed in Bedlam. It was only a matter of time before the girl was snatched and brought before The Collector.

# ONE

## NAMELESS

### JANUARY 3RD

7:45pm

*Early. As always.*

It was a habit I would die with. Always early. Always on time — raised to believe that being late was the height of rudeness. I was also raised to believe the world as we knew it would end and I would live out my days in a steel bunker underground. My parents were… *strange*. Even for this world.

I dropped into a chair facing the door adorned with Dr. Lindsey's nameplate and rubbed my eyes.

*Fuck, don't do that again.*

Pulling my phone from the pocket of my thick jacket, the reflection on the screen confirmed I'd smudged yesterday's eyeliner.

*Was it yesterday's? Probably last week's.*

I used to have a few hundred thousand online followers for my makeup skills alone. At least, I believed I did. Most of them were probably waiting for the inevitable end to any girlfriend of a wealthy man who fell into the role of "online personality" — the moment their comfortable life publicly imploded. Lucky for me, that all happened in private.

*What would they think of me now?*

These days, I barely put in enough effort to ensure I didn't look like a walking corpse.

I scratched along my mirrored hairline, removing the spots of black dye that hadn't washed off in the shower. There was nothing I could do for the bags under my eyes. The last of the concealer I'd dabbed on before leaving the house had done shit-all to hide that I'd barely been getting any sound sleep.

The screen brightened with a message, hiding the scowl of the judgemental bitch squinting back at me;

**Good girl getting your ass out of bed on time.**

A tremor slipped down my spine, pulling my shoulders back and sending a twitch up the side of my neck. He knew I'd want to break his nose for calling me that, and it was a brave move to hope I would forget by the time I saw him at work.

*His paycheque must have cleared, fucking smart ass wouldn't dare otherwise.*

**Need concealer. Don't show up without it.**

**What shade?**

**You fucking kidding me?**

**Did they finally create transparent makeup?**

I replied with the middle finger emoji and he quickly texted again, always fast to ensure we'd be on good terms before the overnight shift together.

**I'm just saying you don't get enough sun. Can we switch to day shifts before we all start looking like the undead?**

I took a deep breath and threw my head back against the wall. The off-white paint was wearing as thin as my patience for this man's jokes.

The air filling my lungs was stale, but clean, likely from relying on air-conditioning all year-round.

The space was familiar, but not comforting. Each time I stepped through the glass doors to this multi-storey medical center, I was reminded of what I left behind. Many years of my life had been dedicated to helping people on a floor much like this. But I was no longer the "fixer" of everything from clothing to open wounds on my parents' property. Or forced to work on Home's medical floor with my colleagues, performing illegal surgeries and administering stolen drugs under the ever-watchful eye of the boss. For the last two years, I'd been doing things on my terms.

The fluorescent bulb above hummed to a migraine-inducing frequency and I squeezed my eyes shut to block out the blinding light.

*You'll fall asleep.*

Drifting off wasn't the problem. I was always tired enough to do that in a matter of seconds and couldn't be trusted with the snooze setting for my alarms. The reason I was waiting for my first one-on-one therapy session was because my paranoia was getting out of hand, and I was tired of hiding knives under every surface in my house. I could never relax enough to escape the ghosts. They followed me wherever I traveled.

*He could be here... watching you right now...*

My eyes opened, darting to the right. The eerie glow came to an abrupt end on the linoleum, revealing nothing in the chasmic darkness of the long hall.

I lifted my phone again to find something to keep my mind busy and settle my pulse. Life on the run meant my fake social accounts provided none of the escape they had in the past. The name wasn't mine, and I used the same profile picture across all of them. The photo wasn't of me, but someone who resembled enough of my general look, though I suspected she was taller. I'd saved it off the internet and hoped life had dealt the girl a better hand than I'd received.

There were hundreds of photos of me that existed from sharing a public life with *him* — my ex.

A news article slipped under my thumb. *Several* articles of the same story I'd watched in bed before I'd convinced myself to get out and face the cold.

"*First Gifted to Run for Governor.*"

It was bound to happen eventually. While I didn't care for above-ground politics, for everyone else, it would be interesting to follow along. The man would get a lot of attention, whether he successfully climbed the political ladder or died trying.

*He'll totally die trying.* I giggled as I clicked the link, tucking my legs up on the uncomfortable chair and angling away from the expanding abyss of the corridor.

It had only been a few decades since the "Gifted" had made themselves known, and as someone in the medical field, I couldn't resist the opportunity to learn more, whether it be factual or straight-up gossip.

There weren't many of them, but enough had been studied before the experiments were scrapped, concluding they were simply "happy accidents" —

sporadic genetic mutations that enhanced some people enough to be considered superhuman, with a rare few bestowed with otherworldly abilities.

A reel of the "First Family" — the same that was shown with any Gifted news — played on the screen. It wasn't the family that immediately came to mind, but the first of *them* to be publicly outed. The moniker, obviously, caused a further divide between those accepting of the newly exposed beings and others who were fiercely patriotic.

The term "Gifted" was coined soon after their existence became public. With one of the country's most prominent televangelists, his wife, and only child, having their true identities revealed by an unknown source.

It was all hastily spun into a positive, and their many millions of devout followers referred to their abilities as "Gifted by God" — *Gifted* for short as time went on. It was a lucky move for the new species, no matter their individual beliefs. Being different in the world usually led to being eradicated out of fear of the unknown. But once the "righteous" religious groups were behind your cause, you were essentially untouchable.

The man of the hour was shown in short clips waving, giving speeches, looking like any other middle-aged politician. He actually looked a little familiar.

*Shit, I've probably met him before.*

I imagined what he might look like with his face half-covered by a mask. Most Gifted seemed human. It was hard to tell who was the real deal and who was faking. Others were something extraordinary.

I sunk further into the chair and texted the article link to my watcher.

**Seen this?**

**Yeah. People are already losing their minds. It'll mean more work for us when shit turns violent. More work = more $$.**

He had a point. Any minor upset in the balance would mean a heavier workload for us.

The Gifted popping up everywhere had brought out extreme reactions across the globe. People became obsessed, many fetishized the beings while others were desperate to be like them. Others took more radical action — hunting them or making their lives a living hell.

On the other end of the spectrum, people like my family — stemming from a long line of doomsday preppers — believed this to be the tipping point for humanity, and completely withdrew from society altogether.

I blinked my vision to clarity, thankful for another text to disrupt the thoughts of my parents.

**Should we take bets now? Hero or Villain?**

**He's in the government. Villain for sure.**

It was always the same headlines in the news. "Heroes" saving the few, "villains" destroying the many and vigilantes in between, not necessarily good or bad, but creating their own kind of chaos.

Some humans snuck into the mix to create more trouble, eager to ride on the glory-filled waves the Gifted stirred, wasting their lives on the fantasies of unobtainable power and uniqueness.

Most Gifted were merely preternatural beings who didn't care for taking sides. Others were trying to live out their lives in peace, creating mayhem simply by existing. I understood them well… to a degree. The desire to disappear and live in peace, out of the spotlight and the public eye. It was the polar opposite to the way I had lived with my ex.

**Still waiting for the therapist?**

**Yep. Shouldn't you be in bed?**

**Yeah. But I couldn't sleep knowing today would be hard enough without bringing him up.**

This wasn't my typical Friday. For the last twelve months, I'd been in the *other* room. Dr Lindsey was best known for assisting with cult deprogramming, relationship breakdowns, and working with domestic violence survivors. Ticking more boxes than I wanted to acknowledge, I'd been sitting in her weekly sessions for the last year before I spoke up about my past. But group therapy, as it turned out, wasn't my thing. Apparently, what I had to say was too fucked up. Or as my psychologist put it: too "triggering and intense" for the others, and it was "best to be discussed in a different setting."

In other words, one-on-one, where I wouldn't disturb an entire room of people trying to escape the horrors of their pasts.

I would never compete with or compare personal trauma, but if only one story of what my ex had done was too much for the group, this doctor was in for an *intense* experience herself with our private sessions.

7.59pm

I tapped the soles of my boots on the linoleum, still waiting. Even from my place around the corner, I could hear the sobs and comforting words from the other's in the group.

*This can't run over time. I've got a call to make.*

I had a strict routine on "the outside" and I needed to stick to it. *Especially* on Fridays. I hadn't seen or heard from my family in twelve years, but it hadn't stopped me from trying to reach out, and Friday nights were my best chance.

They were always in the back of my mind, and I'd be trying to remember their faces when I should've been focusing solely on my patients.

*What would they look like now? Do my brothers have families of their own?*

It was likely that they would, and I'd probably missed every important milestone since running away at sixteen.

My thoughts and my nails anxiously picking at the seat's peeling pleather were interrupted by the clicks of Dr. Lindsey's short heels, echoing as she approached from the other room.

"Katie!" she called in her always-cheery tone. A fake name – one of a few. "I'm so glad you took me up on the offer for some one-on-one time. Come on in."

She unlocked the door, and I hurriedly followed her into the small room.

It was dimly lit, and not as cold and clinical as the hall. The warm tones of the walls and furniture made it cozier.

I lazily threw my body down onto her couch to the right while she sat facing me in a chair, a few feet away on the left. She crossed her stocking-covered legs at her ankles and placed her hands in her lap.

Immediately feeling like a slob, I rearranged my posture to mimic hers. I'd briefly considered dressing better for this appointment. But why bother playing pretend with someone who was going to spend an hour picking my brain? I figured I might as well show up as myself if she was going to learn all of my darkest secrets, week-old gym clothes and all.

I was never taught to sit nicely, be lady-like, and smile politely.

*If I had, how different would I be?*

They were some of the things I needed to learn quickly to survive as a Bedlam socialite, but my upbringing was still deeply embedded within my stubborn bones.

With three older brothers, my parents raised me exactly as they did my siblings. I appreciated that Mom and Dad didn't treat me differently from the boys, it meant I could be as useful to them on the homestead.

I was better than them at some things, which led to many arguments. Not always between my brothers and I, but also with my parents about what I was expected to do with my future. The last time I saw them was during one of those arguments, and I wished every day that night had ended differently.

"After our last group session, I worried you might not come back. Again, I hope I didn't cause you any distress when I interrupted what you were sharing." Dr. Lindsey seemed genuinely concerned as she had the week earlier.

While I understood she was protecting the group, it was obvious she feared cutting me off may have come at the cost of me seeking help altogether.

"That's fair," I nodded and cleared my throat. "I didn't mean to cause any problems. I guess I thought it was about time I finally shared something with the group." Sitting through so many meetings without saying anything was making me feel like a total creep. "I want to get better," I smiled, hoping it didn't look too forced. I didn't smile all that often. It felt weird on my face when I tried.

*Your eyes are too wide, you look insane.*

"Well, that's great to hear." Her smile was sweet, genuine. "You deserve to get better and not be defined by your past relationships as you move on with your new life."

*Relationship,* I corrected her in my head. *We were* "forever."

He took me at sixteen. I escaped at twenty-six. For most of that time, I didn't know how to define the arrangement between us, so for anyone asking, *he* was simply "my ex."

Any brief encounters I'd had with others since leaving Home wouldn't count for anything and could never be considered "relationships." I had no desire to be tied to another person. Not anymore. All I needed was a physical release to tide me over every now and then, until I eventually felt the need for another. Just *enough* so I could move on and get my work done.

Dr. Lindsey reached for the pen and notepad tucked into her chair between the arm and seat cushion. As she glanced at her notes, I looked her over, as I did with everyone I met. I'd seen her many times before in the harsh lighting of the group therapy room, but everything about her seemed softer in this light. Kinder, if possible.

The faint smile lines and the creases on her forehead made me guess she was only a little older than me, maybe in her mid-thirties. Her natural red, wavy hair was always tied into a loose, low bun. She was taller than me, and from what I could gather, she had a great figure, but always wore baggy clothes.

If I saw her on the street, I would assume she was a librarian. Though, psychologist suited her fine, too.

"Last week you mentioned you were trying to come to terms with leaving a cult. And this cult leader 'Eric' had abducted and assaulted you since you were sixteen." She looked at me for confirmation. "One of the reasons I asked you to come to private sessions is because our group is strictly DV support. We try to keep on topic for the sake of those who participate. While I'm certain you absolutely belong in that category, and we'll get you back to the group in time," — she gave me a small, reassuring smile — "I feel we might have more to process before then."

I bobbed my head to acknowledge what she'd said, still caught on the word "assaulted." I needed a moment to take in everything else. It weirdly felt too strong of a word after enduring years of grooming and manipulation.

Was it assault if Eric cared for me? Allowed me to pursue my dreams? Provided everything I needed or wanted for ten years? Did *everything* that happened between us while I was infatuated with him count as assault?

There were moments between us that felt like genuine affection. True connection. But looking back on it, it was all *so* wrong. In reality, the word "assault" barely scratched the surface of what happened back at Home, and that single word instantly had me questioning everything in my life. But I was glad Dr Lindsey wasn't shying away from uncomfortable truths.

"I can see why it's taken you so long to speak up. Ten years living with an abuser and attempting to start over is no easy feat," she praised. "The fact you've not gone back or contacted him at all for the last two years is an enormous achievement in itself. Many people who endure relationships like the one you were in, often return. Some attempt to leave several times with no success.

You're very brave for making the choices you had to, to get out for good. You've got a whole new life to look forward to, and I'm excited to assist you however I can to ensure you live it to the fullest."

While I appreciated the kind and *thoroughly* rehearsed words, I wouldn't call what I did *brave.* I mean, yes, I got out. That part was true. But Dr. Lindsey didn't know I'd given up on life and only "escaped" via a body bag. Whilst I might have lived long enough to drag myself into therapy, my "excitement for life" was severely lacking. Most days, I wished I hadn't woken up after I got out of Home.

I decided not to mention that — yet. I wasn't ready to relive that day and the horrors which my mind had long since locked away to protect what was left of my sanity. It would haunt me forever, and I was convinced no amount of therapy from kind doctors could ever relieve me of my responsibility in the deaths that led to my freedom.

"In our group session, you mentioned you hadn't seen or spoken to your family in twelve years? How about we start there?"

# TWO

## NAMELESS

I left the gym at 11pm after spending a little longer on the treadmill than I'd planned. While therapy hadn't brought up too many ghosts, I still needed to run off the heaviness of my confessions.

I was raised to act as though my mouth were stapled shut. To speak of the way my parents raised their family at the base of the Gray Mountains in isolation from the world made me feel like I'd spilled family secrets that were best left buried.

But the therapist had proven easy to speak to when it was just the two of us, and there was no judgment in that small room. While I was paying for her confidence, it was nice to have someone to talk to about the things that made me most feel like a complete freak, namely eating preserved food older than me and forced into training drills that had us hiding underground for days.

I tugged my jacket a little higher around my neck and slipped my key between my fingers. If the two men in the corner of the gym floor believed I hadn't noticed their staring, they were dead wrong. I was always aware of what was going on around me, and while the walking corpse look *might* be their thing, I highly doubted it.

While the most damning of my scars were covered by my tank top, my left shoulder exposed plenty of raised lines from Eric's favorite knife. I may have been far from Home, but I'd be stupid to think there wouldn't be people out this way who'd recognise me. Two years was a long time for someone like me to still be alive without Eric having me successfully hunted and returned Home. Hunted *or* returned home. My fate depended on how much I'd pissed him off with my dramatic exit.

There was no doubt he had some idea of my location, despite my best efforts to keep off his radar. Suffering from bouts of extreme paranoia, every time something surprised me or caught me off guard, I would try to find the holes in which he could have forced his influence.

*It's probably just my imagination. They're not following me.*

I couldn't risk getting into *another* fight. I'd already been kicked out of four gyms, and there were only so many more between therapy and my house. My fault. I could admit that, at least. I picked fights, always quick to bite, and constantly on the defense.

It wasn't in my nature to get along with strangers. I was raised to view everyone outside of my circle as a threat. I didn't have much of a circle anymore, and if the past was anything to go by, I didn't make great choices about who I let in.

While I hated sharing the gym with people who'd gawk over my ass and hover while I hogged a treadmill, I had to ensure I could still keep up a decent pace during the colder months.

January in this area was rough. Snow fell heavy on the mountains during winter, and the cold air rushed down the slopes to meet the small city below. Most other months were nicer, making it a tolerable trade off. I only had to deal with it long enough to find my family, then I could find somewhere warm to retire. The money was waiting for me, but I wasn't ready to leave until I had closure. I needed to hear it from *them* that I was the embarrassment of the century and that they wouldn't take me back.

My car — a dark gray SUV — was a popular make and model. While I didn't need the space and features of a vehicle this size with being on my own and never participating in outdoor activities, it was inconspicuous. It was also one of the few left in the parking lot, prompting me to do a visual sweep of my surroundings and quickening my pace to reach it.

I had a strict schedule on the outside, just as I did in Bedlam. Only out here, I had to be organized and drive around instead of walking down the hall, where everything I could ever need was ready and waiting for me.

It took much longer in the real world to get my day started. While frustrating, I couldn't complain about having the freedom to choose each of these things. I got to pick which gym I went to, the food I ate, the clothes I wore.

It was a shock to my system for the first few months as I found my feet, out on my own for the first time in my life. But I was grateful to no longer be someone's doll to dress up, show off, and loan out as they saw fit.

Back in the car and out of the cold, I drove to the last stop before my shift. It was close to 10pm, making the skies and roads the same shade of black.

*Time for coffee.*

It was my favorite part of my pre-work routine, and on Fridays, it acted as a reward for working up the guts to make the phone call I was dreading.

I instructed my phone to "Call Mom" as I pulled onto the highway, stupidly hoping for it to start ringing. Maybe I had a thing for putting myself into situations that could only ever end in disappointment.

Straight to voicemail, as always.

Unavailable. *Again.*

"*Fuck*," I hissed, swerving out and around the few cars on the slick road.

You'd think I would have learned by now.

It had been the same routine for the past two years. I'd call, tell her about my week and ask her how the family is going before ending my pathetic, one-sided conversation. Filling her in on the little happening in my life, never to have my call returned.

As far as I knew, and I was basing this off information from when I was sixteen, Mom would drive away from the property to an area with mobile signal, late on Friday nights.

I always tried to call when I knew she'd most likely be handling the phone in hopes to catch her.

While a tedious process on their end, I couldn't blame them for trying to do everything they could to protect their family. Monsters of all sorts were always the leading headlines in the news. As were the Gifted, banding together to banish evil. They were mostly big-city problems and dealt with promptly, but it was no wonder people thought the world was ending.

We lived in a dead zone, just as my "off the grid" prepper parents insisted. They raised us on acres of woodland in a house my grandparents had built by hand. Dad made drastic changes to the house and property as he got lost further down the rabbit hole of his doomsday obsession.

He was prepared for almost anything. The many sheds, tunnels and shelters on our land could attest to that. It was too bad no amount of weapons and stocked bunkers could protect his only daughter from one man.

The house was intentionally hard to find, and though I'd tried searching for it when coming back to the mountain state, even *I* couldn't find its exact location.

It had been a decade between leaving my family and my escape from Bedlam; the landscape had changed too much in that time. I could have sworn I'd found the right location, but there was nothing there. Open land. No house. No crops. No sheds. None of Mom's Royal Velvet sunflowers or Dad's livestock and dogs. No sign of them.

Just… emptiness.

The thought of not knowing where they were made me sick every time they crossed my mind. Mom and I had a great bond, but I must have hurt her beyond forgiveness with my last words.

It just didn't seem like something the God-fearing woman would do; holding a grudge against her child for twelve years over the stupid decisions I'd made.

But here I was, leaving voicemails.

"Hey Mom, it's me. Obviously…" I trailed off, already feeling stupid for having any hope today would be different.

"Umm……" one-sided small talk was so fucking awkward, "I started a new type of therapy this week. Maybe once I sort a few things out, I can come home? I know you're getting these. Probably deleting them without listening… I wanna come home, Mom."

Few things upset me; I was an expert at bottling my feelings. But the rejection I'd faced from my family each week since leaving my criminal life behind had been tough. Had I known what I was getting into, I never would have met with Eric the night I left my family behind.

I cleared my throat to wrap things up.

"Anyway, if you could ple—" *Beep.* Cut off.

I called again, and was met with the voicemail inbox being full.

*Full? What the fuck?*

Mom had *never* let that happen before. She was strict with routinely clearing out messages, relying on her inbox for invitations and updates from others within their circle, plus I'd been calling her every week for two years. There was absolutely no way she'd be so careless with it.

My mind instantly jumped to the worst-case scenario; *Has something happened to her?*

Voice wavering, I ordered my phone to call her again.

Straight to voicemail.

*Weird.*

Did that mean she was on her phone? Creating more space in her inbox at the same time I was calling?

"Mom, call me! Shit!" I hung up and glanced over my shoulder.

Too distracted with the idea that something may have happened to my family, I'd missed my usual exit. The next one wasn't for miles, much closer to my house. There was no point turning around and going that far back for coffee. It would throw my timing off to get some work done before my shift started.

Pouting at the thought of missing out on my favorite sugar-loaded, barely-coffee-resembling beverage, I decided to grab something from the first place I could find at the next exit.

There was absolutely no way I could get through a Friday without caffeine.

# THREE
## NAMELESS

Turning off the highway, I pulled up to a restaurant about twenty minutes from home. It was one of many on a long strip of eateries and bars on both sides of the road. Most were closed for the night, their lightless interiors visible from the street.

This one had a bright sign in the front windows that read "Open 24 Hours." Its dated facade and peeling paint had me worried I'd be laughed at for ordering something resembling my usual.

It looked to be quiet, with no diners visible through the large windows. So long as there was caffeine, it worked for me. Upon closer inspection, it had no drive-through.

*Dammit.* I sunk into the seat and turned the car off. I'd have to get out and interact with *people*.

At my usual place, I would simply speak into a box and coffee would appear at the next window. It was magical. I would take my drink and sit in the car with the heater on to go over a few things on my laptop before heading home to shower and dress for the overnight shift.

I tried Mom's phone again, staving off social interaction for a few more seconds. Straight to voicemail.

*That must mean she's still using her phone and getting my messages.*

It unfairly felt like I was *so* close to receiving proof of life from her, but then nothing. Like every Friday, I got *nothing.*

*Well, today I got rejected, so that's something different. Right?*

It was 10:30pm, still hours before I needed to start work. Hoping it would be warmer in the restaurant and the caffeine would be worth the quick amble in the cold, I dragged my butt out.

With my backpack over one shoulder, I crossed the slick ground to the building. A sprinkle of snowflakes twisted in the air around me; a reminder that I needed to tread lightly.

A bell above me rang loud into the empty restaurant as the door closed, sealing the cold and highway noise on the other side.

It took only moments to scan from the entrance for blind spots in their security camera layout. It was weak, as expected.

I rolled my eyes at the blinking red light on the small white box, pointed my way.

*I might get caught if I wanted to steal the bell, but that's about all it's useful for.*

There was no one to greet me, likely due to minimal staff being on so late in the night.

I could relax a little. With my head still reeling from the voicemail situation, I needed to clear my brain with some mind-numbing work, and the quiet would help.

I peeked around an archway to the right. It led to the dining area I'd seen from the carpark. The space was littered with small square tables and rectangular booths lined along the walls and under the front windows. Leftover decorations from New Year's Eve, just a few nights prior, still hung from the ceiling.

With no one bothering to meet me at the entrance, I helped myself and picked the last booth at the right, the only one without glass beside it.

I slipped into the side that backed against the corner, angling my body to face the dining room. The tops of the seats were short, only high enough to cover my back. I couldn't risk anyone getting a good look at the weird shit I'd be typing for the next couple of hours.

The position gave me the clearest view of the room. I wasn't expecting anyone to follow me, but the men watching me at the gym were a good reminder I could never be too careful.

The dark green, padded leather of the seats weren't as comfortable as those in my car, but it was a fair trade for the warmth. I unzipped my jacket a little and rubbed my hands together, hoping they'd thaw out soon.

With another quick glance around the room I opened my laptop and set to work. My patients trusted me to keep their details discreet, and I didn't disappoint. They weren't *all* bad people. Many were. *Most* were. Some simply had no other options for access to basic healthcare, and I refused to turn anyone away. While I was far from a saint, I was so drawn to helping others, particularly when they were at their worst and bloodiest.

Technically, I was a nurse.

*Was.*

I'd been stripped of my title and qualifications after being unfairly tied to the interference of two bodies I'd never wanted to interact with. My name was all over the incident, and once a couple of nosey cops got involved, I couldn't avoid the penalty.

It was illegal for me to treat my patients, or anyone for that matter. Those who sought me out understood this. It was a mutual agreement between both sides needing to keep off the radar. No one had blown my cover or put me at risk of being discovered by Eric in the eighteen-ish months I'd been operating my business from my house.

I took a deep breath, counted to five, and instantly felt my head clear of the stress from the car. Opening my calendar first to check the schedule for the night, I found only one booking, but that was typical. We tried to keep Friday nights open for the walk-ins. Drunken accidents, bar fights, and overdoses. By the morning, I'd have notes filled with names, treatment details, and payment plans.

Moving on, I checked my inventory trackers, ensuring I had enough supplies for the typical Friday jobs. There was nothing worse than being caught mid stitch-up and not having enough sutures to close a stab wound or to reattach an ear. If my usual Fridays were anything to go by, I'd likely be doing both before sunrise.

*Perfectly stocked, as always.*

Between prepper parents and working with a strict surgeon for ten years, I only bothered with inventory checks to feel good about having one thing in my life under control.

The hairs on my arms and neck abruptly stood on end.

*You're being watched.*

Glancing up from my laptop, I startled. One of the staff was standing at the edge of my table. It was rare someone could sneak up on me, especially someone of his size.

*What is he? Six foot? Maybe a little taller.*

I frowned, trying to work out how the fuck I hadn't seen him coming.

*Maybe I'm losing my touch.*

He matched my expression by frowning back from above.

"You just helped yourself there, huh?" he accused.

"I'm sorry, what?" was all I could think to say after my work was interrupted with an abnormally rude greeting by a server.

"You walked right in and helped yourself to a table." He gestured to where I was sitting, raised his brows, and appeared to wait for me to defend my harmless actions.

He looked annoyed, his voice strained. I could tell it would have been a little deeper if he wasn't so instantly irate with me.

"Umm. Well, no one was around when I walked in. And it's freaking cold. So yeah, I sat down." My tone became more irritated with each word I spoke.

I tried to lower my eyes back to the screen, but there was something about his size and stance that held my gaze. I visually assessed people fast on the daily for threats, injuries, weapons, anything that could interfere with treatment. It was also useful for situations like this.

*Not covered in blood like everyone else I'll be observing tonight.*

I'd already worked out his height. Early-thirties. In perfect health, aside from needing glasses, which honestly, looked ridiculous on him. The lenses magnified his eyes and the clear frames were far too big for the handsome face they sat on. Perhaps they weren't his, looking more like they belonged to a serial killer from the 60s.

*Who am I to judge? I ditched the designer labels years ago.*

He had thick, dark hair. A rich brown that reflected the light with an auburn tint. The undercut it had been styled in was growing out, still shorter at the sides but the longer strands at the top were lazily brushed out of his face, likely starting to get in his way with sudden movements.

Broad shoulders. No facial hair.

*Good thing. It'd be a crime to cover a jawline like that. God, focus!*

He had a name tag. And if it wasn't fake like each I'd given since I was sixteen, his name was Logan.

Other than his face, his deeply tanned arms and neck were all his uniform exposed. The loose red polo shirt and dark jeans showed no tattoos. That raised suspicion. In my world, tattoos were used to gauge how dangerous someone could be and who they worked for. I knew it for a fact, having been branded as one of Bedlam's worst.

If he wasn't disturbing my work so much and trying to accuse me of breaking into an open restaurant, I wouldn't have minded looking at him for a few extra seconds.

He narrowed his eyes.

*What's his problem?*

I didn't have the patience to find out. I needed to send invoices. I tried my best to sound calm, but everything about the phone call had me agitated and quick to snap.

"Am I in some kind of trouble here?" I started. "Or are you going to let me get on with my night? Better yet, are you going to take my *order* like you should have already? Or does this establishment pride itself on starving people instead of serving them?"

I should have stopped there, but being caught staring made me feel like I'd shown weakness.

*All or nothing.* I wouldn't give a shit if I got banned from this place too. There'd have to be somewhere on the way home that served coffee.

"I'm also guessing *you* should have been somewhere around here to ensure weirdos like me don't help themselves to tables without your knowledge?"

He sighed and crossed his arms. "What can I get you?"

"An iced coffee, please," I said without bothering to maintain eye contact between us.

He let out a laugh, startling me with the volume in the otherwise quiet dining room. "You're fucking *joking*, right?"

I couldn't tell if *he* was joking or not and was about done and over the whole fucking day already. And it was still only the early "morning" part of my routine.

Stupidly, I took the bait.

I closed my laptop and folded my hands over the top so I wouldn't clench my fists.

"I am not... *fucking* joking." My voice tightened as I ground the words through my teeth. "Why would I be?"

"You just *complained* about the cold." He unfolded his arms to place his hands on his hips.

That was a shame. They'd looked good that way, and at this rate, were his only redeeming quality, given his attitude. If I were being honest, *all* of him was nice to look at, but I had such a *thing* for a good set of arms.

He raised an open hand towards the entrance of the restaurant. "I'm one hundred percent certain it's snowing again, and you're ordering the coldest drink you can think of?"

I blinked a few times, too confused to speak. When I opened my mouth, he cut me off, berating me further.

"Who drinks coffee at ten forty-five at night? Doesn't that keep you up?"

*God,* it was no wonder they rostered this guy on overnight shifts. He'd probably drive everyone away so the staff wouldn't have much work to do before swapping with those on the morning shift. But who was he to question my drinking habits? Caffeine was the least of my concerns and probably the kindest of the poisons I ingested to function like everyone else.

"Had *you* done *your* job..." I scoffed. "I would've had my coffee fifteen minutes ago! And what's it to you what I drink and when?"

It was like I was fourteen again, arguing with my brothers over nonsense to get a rise out of each other. Pushing buttons until someone snapped.

*But this is a stranger.*

What would happen if I made him snap? Looking at the difference in size between us, I should have been a little smarter about this whole encounter. While I wasn't useless for my size, if it came to him against me, I didn't stand a chance.

*Though... those arms on me.* My imagination ran wild, and I shook my traitorous skull to send away the thoughts of being held too tight in those arms.

He continued his interrogation, "Name three kinds of people who would order coffee at this time of night."

I was glad we were the only people in the room. This man was clearly losing his mind. Witnesses to our exchange would have been awkward.

*Kinds of people?* He was barely making sense.

With an annoyed shrug, I took the bait again. "I dunno… nurses, cops, people who just want *coffee* without being questioned?" Why was I even encouraging this conversation? I bet I could probably order alcohol here until five in the morning, maybe later, but an iced coffee on a cold day was apparently unacceptable. "I'm two of those right now!"

Logan appeared to be lining up his next insane rebuttal until he heard the word *cop*.

*Ha! Maybe now, he'll leave me alone.*

His voice dropped to a normal volume. "Fine, I'll be right back."

I was right about his voice; it was a little deeper, smoother still. Pleasant, when it wasn't having a go at me for no fucking reason.

*What? Was it that easy?*

It was like a switch flipped and he'd come to his senses, realizing what I'd asked for was perfectly reasonable.

Logan began to walk away, but I wasn't done with him for stirring me up. I was no longer calm and in the mood for invoicing. My patients would probably appreciate the delay in knowing how much they owed me anyway.

"Hey, Logan?" When he turned I said, "I want the *biggest* iced coffee this place has to offer. I'm *not* joking," I added quickly.

He walked the few steps back toward the table and leaned with his palms on either side of my laptop, towering over me.

*Funny, that time I heard him approaching just fine.*

I didn't break eye contact or even blink. I was good with confrontation and standing my ground. So much so, it had gotten me most of my scars. Eric always loved to remind me I was reckless and never *fucking learned* from my mistakes.

Logan was good with eye contact too. His face was so close to mine that even in the poor lighting of the restaurant, I could make out the distinct transitions between the green and brown shades of his irises.

I felt self-conscious under his intense gaze. I looked like trash from the minimal effort I'd put into my appearance before leaving the house and had spent a little longer than usual at the gym.

*I bet if I'd looked half decent it wouldn't take much to get him to fuc — Whoa, calm down!* I made a mental note to add "get laid" into the work calendar. It had clearly been too long.

*The bodyguards will get a kick out of that.*

"Honestly," Logan smirked, bearing straight teeth and an unexpectedly charming smile. "I don't think your little body can handle that much."

He was *too* close. His cologne swarmed my senses. The scent was woody, heavy on the amber. I tried not to take an obvious deep breath to fill my head with the hypnotic fragrance as I leaned back into the corner of the booth. And to ensure he didn't take my move as a sign of defeat, I bit again.

"You'd be surprised at what this little body can take." It sounded dirtier than I intended. It was too early for this shit, and I was distracted by the fact he smelled *so fucking good.*

His eyes dropped from mine, and the corners of his mouth twitched, appearing to sense my thoughts as he suppressed a laugh. If the whole exchange wasn't giving me mental whiplash, I wouldn't have minded him hanging around a little longer to have something to look at while I worked.

"I'll take your word for it," he promised, eyes meeting mine again after regaining composure. "Anything else I can get for you?"

I needed to have the last word.

"Yeah, seeing as today *isn't* cold enough, I want extra ice cream," I said with a straight face as I lifted the screen of my laptop, dropping my gaze from his to resist all sudden and bizarre urges to grab his face and pull it to mine.

He laughed as he turned to leave.

"Keep the ice cubes whole!" I called after him, craving something to chew on to calm my nerves.

I silently hoped he wouldn't spit in my drink, but something about the way he looked back over his shoulder told me he wouldn't.

# FOUR

## NAMELESS

10:53pm

Logan returned as I was halfway through itemizing a bill for a shoulder I'd popped back into place. He set a stein glass of what annoyingly looked like the iced coffee of my fucking dreams beside my open laptop. It smelled like *coffee*, not sugar.

"Sorry it took so long," he apologized as he straightened up. "I had to convince the guys at the bar to let me use one of their glasses."

I bit my lip, trying to hold in a laugh.

"Is something wrong?" His tone quickly switched back to being as annoyed as it had earlier. "You *asked* for the biggest."

"It actually looks amazing," I confessed.

The tension in his shoulders dissolved as I took a sip through the straw and gulped the icy liquid. Relief overtook his features, as though he'd expected I'd spit it out.

*Fuck, it's perfect. Maybe I can get through this shitty day.*

"Good?" He watched intently as I took another sip.

"Yep. Why? What did you do to it?" I teased.

His expression quickly twisted as if offended. *Here we go again.*

This guy was like me, quick to snap, and seemed to take things too literally. It was a shame the coffee was so good.

*I might actually have to come back here. Can I force myself out of bed in the middle of the day to avoid his shifts?*

"I didn't do anythi—" he started until I raised my hands.

"I was *joking*. It's perfect. Thank you." I looked back to my screen and opened my notes on a stitch-up I'd performed at the end of the previous night's shift.

I peered over my screen, jumping in my seat when I found he hadn't left.

Apparently, there being no other customers and me complementing a drink were invitations to take the other seat in the booth. The table was narrow, not leaving much space between us, so I straightened up when his knees brushed mine under the surface. I took a deep breath, counted to five, and closed my laptop. *Again*. It looked like I was never going to get paid for my work.

"Can I help you?" I asked when he didn't catch the cue to explain why he'd joined me.

I was starting to doubt *anyone* would be able to help this strange man.

*Should I have sat at the bar instead?* I didn't think caffeine, even the amount he'd given me, would make interacting with him any easier.

"So… which are you?" He raised his eyebrows, looking me up and down.

"What?"

"You said you were two things. Gonna go out on a limb here and say one of those is a *person who wants coffee*." He tipped his head and squinted through the thick lenses of his glasses. "I doubt you're both a cop *and* a nurse."

"Oh." I'd caught up to the conversation in his head that he'd brought me partway into, surprised he was still hung up on what I'd said earlier. "Nurse," I confessed, pulling the glass closer now my laptop was proving useless for the night.

It was technically true. I *was* a nurse.

"Really?" He leaned back in the seat, not that there was much room to do so with his size. His eyes narrowed further as he continued to visually take in every on-edge inch of me.

"You think I look more like a cop?" I mimicked his expression.

"Well… No, I think you're too small to be a cop with all the weird shit they deal with these days. But then," — he blinked away from my stare — "I thought maybe you *were* a cop because you don't look friendly enough to be a nurse." he appeared to have spoken without thinking, and bit his tongue.

A laugh slipped through my cold lips. *Wow, he doesn't hold back.*

Maybe his social skills weren't that of a thirty-plus year old. Like I could talk. Between homeschooling until sixteen and living in a building full of criminals until twenty-six, my ability to discuss anything other than the interesting array of wounds I'd treated was average at best. People only liked to hear so many stories about detached limbs and buckets of pus for so long before it turned them off.

*Maybe I make Logan nervous.* I liked to think I did.

"What makes me not look friendly?" I asked as I took another sip, surprised I sounded a little hurt, and again, encouraging a conversation I didn't want to have. Particularly not with someone who so quickly hit a nerve earlier. Maybe my isolation was starving me of mental stimulation.

"I said, you don't *look* friendly… but I'd also like to add, you don't *talk* nicely either. *For a nurse*," he said with a mischievous shrug.

Another laugh from me, *God, he's not wrong.*

He smiled shyly and muffled a small laugh of his own. "I'm serious. I'm not joking."

His smile caught me off guard. He was actually very cute. It was lucky for him, I didn't like people disrupting my work at the best of times, but with Logan, I unexpectedly didn't mind so much.

*Cute and crazy. Sounds about right for the type I seem to attract.*

"I know. It's true." I smiled back, "My line of nursing isn't *friendly*. Most of my patients are bigger than me and often need serious help. I can't look like a doormat around those people. I wouldn't survive."

"Looking like a doormat would be a strange way to show up at work." He frowned playfully.

*Is he joking?* I wasn't sure. At least the back and forth with him had distracted me from the phone call for a little while.

"What's your name?" he asked, leaning closer.

"Summer," I said without thinking. I should have picked anything else. I'd picked a million fake names before, why didn't I think of one now?

The name was given to me when I left my parents. Or at least close to it. *Sumar* to Eric in private when he was happy with me. *Summer* to the rest of the employees at Home.

Eric had chosen the name himself, explaining that I needed to cut all ties to my family if I wanted to be free and *his*. It made me feel special. I was so young and *so* fucking stupid.

It was Logan's turn to laugh again.

"Is there something funny about my name?" I snapped.

"Shit, you're *serious?*" He smirked. "In that case, it goes perfectly well with your sunny disposition."

*So he does understand jokes?* I knew the name didn't suit me well. It might have, long ago, before I was broken into the life Eric and I had made together.

"Yeah. Now if you don't mind, I really need to get back to it. I've got heaps to do before I leave for work and I have more coffee to drink than I would normally consume in a week." I tipped my head to the glass and could have almost touched the moment Logan realized I was subtly asking him to leave.

"Told you that little body couldn't handle it." He slipped out of the booth to walk away. I couldn't think of a comeback that wasn't going to bring him back to my table, so I let it slide.

Finally, I was left to get my work done, making a quick job of the invoices and paying the bodyguards.

I barely finished the coffee out of spite and left a big tip in hopes it would come across as "the final say." Though, I was sure it'd be lost on Logan.

# FIVE

## SUMMER

While the drive home from the restaurant was short, the change of scenery as I approached my suburb made the distance appear much further. Houses and street lights became sparse as I took the long, winding ascent into the hills.

My house was at the end of a dark court and to the left. I pulled up through the electric gate with eight-foot hedges on either side, greeted by the bright exterior lights saturating every inch of the front yard. No one could hide from me.

Despite setting up in a permanent residence for the last eighteen months, I was technically still on the run. Hiding in plain sight. I'd run as far as I could before staying put to find my family and move on with my life. Although, I was still stuck on the '*finding family*' part of my plan.

I had designed this place with the help of one of my many patients. It was like a miniature version of Home, only not quite as cold. Everything was neat. Orderly. Clean. From the dark hardwood floors that flowed through most of my house, to the flawlessly manicured hedges that had grown tall to conceal iron fences.

The private contractor I hired to make the fence ensured the points along the tops were literally as sharp as knives. The bodyguards and I had only needed to remove two impaled idiots so far. It was oddly satisfying being the one to stitch them up and charge them for my time.

We'd considered letting them bleed out for the fun of it, with the idea they'd be great deterrents for those who'd be dumb enough to climb over. But I was sure my neighbors, though there were none for miles, would have had questions if I left the corpses of wannabe thieves out on display. Besides, they might have attracted bears and other wildlife.

The house itself didn't look like much from the front. A window a few feet to the left of my front door. To the right, a triple garage, then a double attached to that on the far right. I parked in the bay furthest from my house and walked back across the wide pebbled driveway to the front door.

I was visible on at least three cameras as I punched in the code to get inside. I could have taken the internal access doors, but that would mean I'd have to text my watchers that I got in safe, and I wasn't in the mood for the back and forth before they showed up to work in a couple of hours.

I listened for the door to click into place behind me, and set my keys on the hallway's narrow table, a few steps in from the door to the left. Above it was a mirror, in which I got in a quick glance at myself as I moved past it toward my bedroom.

*Hmm. Yeah, not very friendly-looking. Fucking jerk.*

First up was a hot shower, one of two each day. I let the water wash away the bizarre start to my night, then ran a towel over my hair and twisted it into two french braids.

It felt like more than a lifetime ago since Eric taught me how to tie it to his liking. The experience was oddly one of the more deeply intimate moments between us. Though it was practical, and I kept up the habit, he haunted every swift motion my fingers made.

My hair was short enough that the braids left little to grab at my neck. I'd kept it cut and maintained at this length for many years. Long and loose hair was too much of a hazard around some patients.

It was a bonus that it looked like I'd put in some effort once I untied it after the second shower following my shift. Not that anyone ever saw my hair while it looked half decent. I would go straight to bed and essentially start the same day over again.

I threw on a white crew neck T-shirt and tucked it into black, high-waisted jeans. After hooking up the four buttons at the front and slipping on my chunky work boots, I was dressed and ready for another day. Night. *Whatever.*

Opposite the hallway table was the internal access door to the larger of the two garages. I unlocked it with a different code and was greeted by the bright lights I always left on.

The space was well heated year-round. Most of my patients ended up at least half naked while I sutured or treated what their life choices had gifted them.

It was technically the early hours of Saturday morning, but this was my Friday night. Officially, I started work at two-thirty in the morning and would usually finish around six. I'd miss the sunrise most days.

My shifts weren't long, but I could fit in a fair amount of work each night. The pay was obscene for my short interactions with each patient and I had more money than I knew what to do with. There wasn't a need for long hours, just enough time to be available to help those who needed it, and to keep my skills sharp.

A text in the group chat with my bodyguards read, **ETA 5 minutes.**

I sat at my desk in a generic office chair, spinning between the screens displaying the security feeds, mounted on the far wall from which I'd entered. The computer on my desk below and to the left showed the same, updated documents I had barely worked on with all the interruptions at the restaurant.

My calendar showed the booking wasn't until four-thirty. It was a simple checkup on a job I had stitched up the previous week. Everything else for the night would be a surprise.

Two burly men appeared in the camera as they walked up the driveway from the street.

Tony and Ben. Fake names, of course.

Before I interviewed them for their positions as my bodyguards, I had them each pick a new name; for their protection and for mine. They claimed to be cousins, though they looked more like siblings. Either way, it was already more information about them than I cared to know.

They were the same height, both broad with bulky arms and legs, covered in traditional tattoos. I wouldn't be game to mess with them, and hopefully no one else would want to either.

They ate a sickening amount of food in the short hours of their shifts, all to maintain their enormous size. I couldn't imagine how much they ingested in a day, but was grateful they always brought extra food for me, knowing I would often go whole days having consumed only coffee if they didn't.

I eventually worked out what language they spoke to each other. Trying to be polite, I learned a few basic words and phrases so I could understand the jokes they shared that always had them roaring with laughter.

That was a mistake. The bits and pieces I'd put together of their conversations were about what and *who* they did on their days off. I stopped learning in order to give them their privacy and guessed it was the reason they'd spoken in their native tongue around me in the first place.

They were good people. Too good for the likes of me and my work. As far as I could tell anyway, even without knowing their real names.

Despite my lack of knowledge about them, they knew almost *everything* about me. Once hired, I gave them the entire rundown of my past. I felt they deserved to know exactly what they were getting themselves into with the runaway girlfriend of a psychotic crime boss from Bedlam.

I grew to feel safe with them. They were generously compensated for the risk, and were always on time.

*So they fucking should be for how much I pay them.*

It was one of the only things I was strict with.

Their job mostly consisted of sitting around between collecting patients who I couldn't trust with my address, and being the 'muscle' when I needed help with particularly difficult invalids.

They also drove the van while I worked on people in the back if I needed to make urgent house calls, and when they came along with me to my favorite club. They would stand guard while I would act as a nurse for the people who got into trouble on their drunken nights out.

The two men reached the house and helped themselves to the other garage, their deep voices traveling through the connecting door that divided the two spaces. They were taking it upon themselves to ensure the van was stocked. One less job for their boss, and they had consistently proven to do well enough by my standards for me to not have to worry about inspecting their work.

2:35am.

There was a knock on the middle roller door. I hadn't recognized who it was but saw movement on the screens and expected the sound.

With the press of a button on my keyboard, the door lifted and quickly closed behind a man as he stepped inside.

A regular of mine. I sighed. He was a good fit to describe my average patient; male, tall, with a muscular build, aged anywhere between twenty-five and sixty. I tended to many people from all walks of life, but there was something about this type that meant I worked with them the most.

Blood trickled from an open gash where his eyebrow was split. It looked worse than it was; head wounds were always so generous with their gore. I'd likely have him cleaned, stitched, and with pain meds in hand, ready for the next person to walk in before he'd finished telling me how he earned this new wound.

"Sit."

He moved with a laugh to rest in the chair where I treated all my patients. It was like any other dental chair; perfect for lowering my patients to work on their injuries.

I grabbed the sutures, loaded my needle, and began my work.

With my patient gone, the bodyguards joined me in the warm room to keep me company until the next person needing my help arrived.

"How was therapy?" Tony asked as he sat at my computer, inspecting the open calendar to check if more bookings had come through.

"Fun," I grumbled.

"It'll be good for you." Ben folded his arms and leaned on the chair I'd disinfected, quickly hopping off and moving to my stool after I raised my brows at him. He couldn't help himself; it was his favorite chair in the room and he had a terrible habit of touching it the moment it was sterile.

"You think?" My words dripped with heavy sarcasm as I moved to the cabinets. I noted which pain meds I'd given the patient so I could order replacements.

"Maybe it'll improve your mood," Tony teased to break through my snarky attitude.

"No, what'll improve her mood is what popped up on the calendar." Ben laughed at the note I'd added earlier. "Anyone in your sights, boss?"

"Why?" I turned back to face him with a deadpan expression. "Are you offering?"

They laughed, prompting my features to cave under the contagious sound, cracking a smile myself. They knew I was joking; the two of them were way too much like older brothers for me to ever consider it. Though, I might have been a little older than them. Ben, at least, even with how similar the two men looked.

I'd met them on the same night. Ben, with the top half of his face covered by a mask, literally caught me as I tripped down the stairs out the back of the club, saving me from toppling headfirst into the gravel. Me, out of practice in my heels, tumbled into his thick arms as he helped himself back inside after stepping out for a cigarette.

The encounter was short and sweet. Where people used any excuse to get their hands on another's body, he had a good reason for the palm on my butt as he'd held me. But instead of allowing his touch to linger, he rushed to put me down and apologized profusely before disappearing back inside.

Later that night, I'd had my first of many terrifying encounters with a patient. The man I was tending to flew into a rage over his pain before I could begin stitching him up. I stupidly froze, never having had someone scream at me in such a way as I tried to help them. He'd lashed out, hitting me square in the face.

While my hands fumbled to catch the blood pouring from my nose, a man who I thought was the same from earlier came to my rescue. He roughly disposed of the person giving me trouble by knocking him out and dragging his limp body down the alley, leaving him on the street.

Tony was confused as I thanked him for helping me twice in one night. It was then that Ben made himself known again, and I laughed in pained hysterics at my mistake.

I'd offered them jobs on the spot, knowing I couldn't keep working without incidents like that occurring again at some point. They immediately gave false names, as I requested, and I interviewed them the next day while I unpacked the garage, having moved into the newly built house.

My relationships with them were strictly platonic. They'd only ever end up in bed with me if I'd had a meltdown or became so drunk at the club that they felt I needed more of a babysitter than a bodyguard. Had I actually allowed myself to know more about them, I had no doubts I would have loved them like family. I kind of did already. As much as I could in our unconventional situation.

"Nah," Ben shook his head playfully. "Sleeping with the boss isn't in the job description. If you bump up my wage though, it'd be tempting."

I rolled my eyes at him while the time in bed with Eric crossed my mind. Sex was literally in my contract, and I'd been paid well for it.

"I can't imagine what you do with the ridiculous amounts of cash I throw your way now. What the fuck would you do with more of it?"

"Maybe save the money on Ben and buy yourself new toys instead," Tony joked, but there was a hint of seriousness to his tone. It earned another eye roll from me, now thrown in his direction.

"Are you two planning on making fun of me all night?" I whined, already knowing the answer.

"Yep." Ben continued to push his luck. "You seem more lively tonight, we'll take the better mood while we can."

"Maybe it's got something to do with the fact I had *real* coffee," I muttered, leaning over Tony's shoulder to see two more bookings had come through. My night was about to get a whole lot busier.

He laughed and stood from the chair, gesturing to Ben it was time to leave to collect a patient. "Really? Going to kick the sugar-filled bullshit excuse for coffee you're addicted to?"

"Maybe," I said, wondering whether I could put up with someone like Logan again to get my fix every night.

"Oh! Before we go." Ben reached into his pocket and tossed me a thin tube of ivory liquid.

"How much do I owe you?"

"Nothing." He grinned. "Consider it a gift."

I smiled as they left. They didn't know it was my birthday. One of them. The fake one.

# SIX

## SUMMER

### JANUARY 4TH

Saturday was like any other day of the week, only I didn't have to wake up as early. There were no therapy appointments on the weekends, so I went for a run on the long, quiet roads around my house instead of driving out to the gym.

I wasn't as good or as fast as I'd been when I trained every day at Home, but it was the perfect way to clear my mind and ensured I was at least still quick enough to get away in a hurry if — or *when* — I needed to.

Running through my neighborhood alone at night hadn't proven to be dangerous so far. I knew the streets well and had scoped out plenty of places to hide if need be. My main concern was the fauna.

The Gray Mountains were known for being home to a savage breed of bear, though I'd seen none. Even in all the years on my parents' property, we'd never encountered any. It gave me a false sense of security. That maybe the thing everyone feared so much was simply a myth… an imaginary enemy.

The night was cold, almost freezing. It would have been smarter to travel to the gym, but it hadn't snowed for days and I felt claustrophobic with being inside all the time.

Work on Saturday night was the same as Friday, just a few less patients in total. It gave me time to catch up on paperwork and hang out with the bodyguards for a while; my only source of social interaction for the weekend.

Sundays were my forced days off. I would have happily worked every day, but after ten years of no breaks at Home, I was trying to give myself a somewhat normal life. It also wouldn't have been fair for my employees to not have a whole day off each week, and I couldn't trust more people to hire others to fill in for them.

I'd always be on call for the few I trusted with a number to contact me, and could handle those rare, small emergencies on my own.

It was my night to do whatever I wanted. So, naturally, I kept to myself and avoided the outside world. Everything I would consider worth leaving the house for was closed during my waking hours anyway. Sometimes, I watched movies or read medical journals to pass the time, like I used to with an old friend. But mostly, I slept.

As great as weekends were, I always felt relieved when the start of a new work week rolled around.

And first up on Monday night was therapy. Like Friday, I wore gym clothes, but threw on more makeup than last time. It made me appear a *little* less tired, and adding blush on my cheeks made me look like I'd been freshly resuscitated. Funny, I had seen what I looked like after being brought back from near death. It definitely didn't look this good.

The moment I stepped into Dr. Lindsey's office, she looked me over and smiled when I assumed my position on the comfy sofa.

"You look refreshed today," she commented, writing a quick note on her paper. It seemed a little makeup earned me good marks. "Last session, we talked a little about your family."

*Ugh. Here it comes.*

I bit my tongue to stop from reacting. It didn't help. I scowled at the pain.

"How do you feel talking about Eric today? Are you up for that, or would you still like more time?"

I thought about it for a moment. I knew this would have to come up eventually. The complete breakdown of our relationship and my escape were the reasons I sought therapy in the first place, and she knew that. She was only trying to help get me on track to recovery.

His name, Eirik, or Eric, as he'd had it changed so it wouldn't draw attention for simply being foreign. Hearing it spoken out loud made my shoulders roll back and my head involuntarily twitch. The man was mentally inescapable. Speaking his name made me fear he'd appear before me, like it would conjure the devil out of thin air.

To anyone else, Eric would seem incredibly handsome, charismatic, and perhaps a little unstable with his wild ideas. In the earlier years I'd known him, he'd had a contagious excitement and boyish charm, but the pressure of his work and reputation in Bedlam seemed to have driven him mad.

As I grew older under his care, we actually looked like quite the couple. Him, barely changing over the years, and me, transforming from teen to the woman who worshiped the earth he walked on.

"I'm… willing to try."

"Great. Maybe we can start with small details. I'll write a few notes so we can come back and expand on these later when you're ready. Okay?"

"Okay." I shifted on the couch, preparing myself physically before mentally diving into the disturbing depths of my past. Even if I wanted to tell her *everything*, I would have to draw a line somewhere for her safety. "I was sought out by him. Recruited, I guess," I started. "I mentioned Dad liked his prepper conventions and meetups. I often went with him. They were rare trips away from the property, and I couldn't resist a break from the work and the same old scenery. From what I was later told by S—"

Pausing, I realized I couldn't reveal the names of my coworkers. It would give too much away about my identity and those I was once involved with.

"Someone I worked with," I amended. "Eric overheard Dad bragging about my skills."

"What skills are you referring to?" She eyed me curiously.

"Stitching." I shrugged.

"Stitching?" There was a hint of intrigue to her tone. "What did you stitch?"

As I placed my hands on my knees, I suddenly felt like a kid again, excited to ramble on about their favorite hobby.

"Everything!" I replied, a genuine smile curving my lips. "I started with simple things like cross-stitch and repairing clothes. I didn't know it at the time, but it was Mom's way of testing if I was any good before moving me on to animals."

"Animals?" Dr. Lindsey tried to hide a concerned frown.

"Yes. Not live ones or anything gross like that," I explained quickly to put her mind at ease. "Things like pig skins after Dad butchered them. You know, like how tattoo artists practice on skins before moving onto people?"

"Yeah, okay. I know exactly what you mean." She seemed amused by my excitement and clearly relieved I'd clarified the animals were not *alive.* "So where did that lead?"

"I wasn't just good and neat, I was *fast*. The more I practiced, the faster I got. Then I treated my brothers mostly. They were always hurting themselves around the property."

A small laugh escaped me over the memory of the boys, all lined up to be stitched by their little sister after stupidly daring each other to crawl through Dad's new stash of razor wire.

"Have you ever stitched yourself?" she asked.

"Oh. Yeah, I guess a couple of times, when necessary. Despite what I do for work and see every day, I actually have a pretty average pain tolerance."

"That's always the way. So where did it go from there?"

"I became known within our community for my skills. My parents were so proud of that." I could clearly envision their happy faces after the first time I stitched up a neighbor. He would have lost a finger had he needed to drive all the way into town for help. "That's what the argument was about." The smile promptly vanished from my face. "My parents wanted me to stay with them. Like, *forever*. But I was constantly being told I could be a nurse or a doctor by the people I was helping. I guess it got in my head that there might have been more out there for me. I didn't want to be confined to the log house and farm while my brothers were expected to move on to their own land… and make their own families."

"I'm noticing your change in mood here. We can come back to that argument another time. How about we go back to your father bragging about your skills?"

"Yeah, okay." I shook my hands and tried to relax, taking a deep breath and counting to five.

*Clarity* – the trick worked every time.

"Dad was telling his friends about what I'd been doing — the people I'd helped. Eric, under the guise of being a prepper himself, was lurking around to seek out recruits for his… cult."

*Cult* was the closest word I could think of to describe my time in Bedlam when I went looking for a therapist. The way we lived at Home, the initiations, the tattoos and signing our lives over to the boss… there was no better way to summarize it without explicitly telling this woman I was a villain. So, cult it was.

"Eric listened to their conversations. Clearly, I was someone who would be of great value in a group of people cut off from the outside world."

I didn't learn until years later that Eric had traveled to the convention to scope out someone else entirely.

The other he hoped to recruit was immediately forgotten once he set his sights on me. I didn't know if they ever became part of Eric's Collection, or if he never bothered to pursue them again. Lucky for them, if that were the case.

"I moved to Ho—" I cleared my throat. "The cult compound and got to work pretty much straight away."

*Shit, I'm gonna need to make a list of all the things I can't say here.*

*Home.* While the structure portrayed no loving or comforting features worthy of the word, that wasn't Eric's reasoning behind the name. It didn't matter what the place looked like, just the psychological effect a single word could have on someone's mind.

Home was where you were safe. Where your broken pieces were carefully handled by those you trusted to put you back together. It was where your family lived. Family like the father figure many employees were missing before Eric found them.

Not all those I lived with at Home were bad. I mean, they were *all* criminals for being associated with my ex. But they each filled the gaping voids I was left with after leaving my family.

*Convinced to leave them behind.*

*Coerced after being told they wouldn't take me back after what he and I had done…*

*More like what he had done. Fuck, girl, keep your head straight.*

"You told the group that you're a nurse." Dr Lindsey took more notes, pulling me from my thoughts. "How did you go from a girl on a farm stitching pig skins to becoming a practicing nurse?"

*Ha! Does she want twelve years condensed into one hour of therapy?*

I obviously gave her the short version.

"Eric wanted me properly qualified. It made his dealings appear more legitimate if he employed *real* surgeons and nurses. He made special arrangements at the college I chose, as he'd promised. When I was seventeen, I began my studies and was fully qualified at nineteen."

Eric had more money than he knew what to do with. Paying off the college to accept me early didn't cost him much. If the college hadn't accepted the money, he always had other means of making people do what he wanted. I finished the four-year course in just two, thanks to his donation.

"My stitching was great, and my grades for all my classes were perfect. I learned everything I needed to know about human bodies from The S — *a surgeon* – I worked with all day, every day. Getting my nursing degree was one of the easiest things I've ever done." I didn't mean to sound so boastful, but it was true.

"You're still a nurse now. Did you consider further studies? To become a doctor? A surgeon like your mentor?"

"Yes. That's exactly what I hoped to do."

"So, what happened?" She set her papers down on her lap, giving me her full attention.

"Danny." I flinched as his name passed through my lips for the first time in years. I briefly permitted myself to think of him every now and then before locking those memories away.

A sharp pain throbbed beneath the flesh on my back, as though one of the names had been freshly carved, reminding me I didn't *deserve* to think of him.

Dr. Lindsey seemed to sense this wasn't a topic I was ready to talk about.

"I have one more question about Eric before we finish up for today – if that's okay?"

"Yeah."

Eric, sure. I'd tell her anything at this point. Anything to get Danny laying on a cold metal table out of my head.

"You were sixteen when he took you from your family?"

"Yep. Umm. Maybe a few months shy of seventeen."

*As if that makes it any better.*

"How old was Eric?"

"When we met, he told me he was twenty. I didn't question it. I didn't think it was too weird for a twenty-year-old to be *interested* in someone who was *nearly* seventeen." I looked at my hands, trying to remind myself that I wasn't the one in the wrong here, no matter what he'd said in the years that followed. "He was twenty-seven," I finally answered, giving the best number I could think of.

It was quite the age gap, but still not the truth.

When I looked up, Dr. Lindsey wedged her notepad into the gap beside the seat cushion. "You've done well today. We might take it a bit easier next time if this was too much, but I'm proud of you for saying these things out loud."

# SEVEN

## SUMMER

Small snowflakes settled on my jacket as I walked to my car. The cold wind on my skin felt good, as though every exposed pore on my body was taking it in, helping me breathe.

Mentioning Danny made it feel like my lungs would collapse – much like the injuries suffered by the boy on the table beside him.

The trip down my morbid memory lane was a little too much to take with me to the gym. For fear I might actually stop breathing in a room full of strangers, I decided it was best to skip that stop and make up for it after my shift with a run.

"Call Mom," I directed my phone as I pulled my seatbelt on and left the parking lot. It was only Monday, but it was worth a shot. Mentioning the argument and talking about Eric had me missing her so much.

The car stopped, and I looked up to take in my surroundings. I'd pulled up at the restaurant I'd visited the previous week. I must have gone on autopilot to save myself from a complete meltdown. First Danny, then Mom. I rubbed my eyes.

*Fuck, I need coffee.*

Wasn't one-on-one therapy meant to be helping? It was easier to risk being considered a voyeur in group therapy than going through this. I reminded myself with an internal eye roll that healing was "a process." So Dr. Lindsey kept telling me, anyway.

But in this moment, I felt like an open wound, and I didn't want to bleed this stress and panic onto anyone else if I could help it.

I took a deep breath as I sat in my car.

Then another, and entered the restaurant for the second time.

*Shit. I'm here at least an hour earlier than last week.*

I instantly registered the sounds of *many* people from both sides of the entrance as I trudged in from the cold.

The dinner rush was over, but there were still tables filled with people eating dessert or waiting for their plates to be cleared.

My booth from the previous Friday was empty and clean. The server, a different one who was *actually* at the front desk and doing her job, happily took me there when I asked.

After wriggling into the corner, I opened my laptop and stared at the screen.

*It's Monday. I didn't work yesterday. No invoices to catch up on. The garage is stocked. Shit.*

I didn't know what else to do to help clear my head.

Then, yet another server approached my table. Apparently this place had a normal number of staff on during dinner hours. They roughly set an iced coffee on my table. It was in a large, but much more manageable sized glass this time, but I hadn't ordered yet.

"Someone had this sent to your table," she shrugged, sounding bored when I looked up at her for an explanation. "Oh and it came with this," she dropped a folded note beside the glass and turned to walk away.

It read, *"That little body of yours should be able to handle this size."*

*Is he for real?* I suppressed a giggle and took a sip.

I imagined having read Logan's note without understanding the context. What made it worse was that after our first encounter, I had *no* idea if he meant it seriously or if he was trying to crack another joke.

As I sipped at my coffee, I decided this place was ruining me for the over-priced garbage I could pick up at the drive-through. It was better than I remembered. Either that, or I needed it more than last time after having brought up both my best friend and the other man I was trying to shake from my system.

Grabbing my phone from my back pocket, I settled on mindlessly scrolling to pass some time before I left for work.

While I often avoided the news, I couldn't help but skim through trashy articles about which celebrities were dating each other, and which Gifted were dating celebrities. In my old life, I'd easily decipher which of either I knew to be leading double lives as villains, tormenting the city from the underworld.

Turned out it was a slow news day for the gossip writers, and with nothing else to waste time with on my phone, I put it away and began people-watching.

A booth on the opposite side of the room was full of interesting characters. A woman with skin darker than the icy roads outside sat with two others. Her hair was platinum blonde. She could have been my exact opposite, color wise. Even seated, I could tell she wasn't very tall, though her figure was slender.

*Someone should make dolls of her.*

The woman was Gifted. Or a convincing fake. Some, like her, stood out more than others, while most looked like regular people. You'd have to catch them in the act, doing something unusual or extraordinary to learn that they were different. I wondered what her gift could be to make her look that way.

Another at the table who caught my attention was the man sitting with his arm around her shoulders. He was white, though his skin held a warm tan. His bulky frame could have been that of a wrestler. I could see the definition of his muscles under his long-sleeved shirt. It was borderline comical to observe how awkward he looked, trying to fit in the booth with shoulders that wide. Just because he was large, it didn't automatically mean he was Gifted too. But considering the woman he sat beside, he could have been.

My gaze lifted to the sunglasses on his head. They reflected the light of the dining room in an odd way.

I didn't get to observe the other woman sitting across the table from them, only noticing that she was crying, and had a similar pair of sunglasses resting on her red hair. My observations were interrupted by a familiar voice. Was I actually excited to hear it?

"Wow! Looking friendly," Logan did a double take as he found me in my corner.

"What?"

"Last time, I said you didn't look friendly. You do now, though. Not that the unfriendly look was a bad thing. You looked great then too, but now you just look…" He paused and shook his head at himself. "Friendlier."

*Wow, that's a lot of words to not say much at all.*

I took in his features again, noticing he had a cut on his left cheek. Odd though, it was nearly healed, and I'd only seen him three nights earlier. Even if he'd been injured on Friday, the barely-visible yellow bruising was well into the final stages of repair. It spread across his cheekbone and up around his eye. I doubted many people in the room could have picked up on the subtle change in his even skin tone.

*Must have been a decent hit. But how did it heal so fast?*

He was waiting for me to respond, so I rushed with, "Oh yeah, put an ounce of effort in today. Feeling good after a quiet weekend."

He leaned with his palm on the low divider of the booths, blocking out the rest of the space and making it feel like we were alone again. "Yeah? Not coming in after a date or something?"

I nearly spat the coffee. Me, dating, was one of the most hilarious things I'd heard in a while.

"In gym clothes?" I scoffed.

"Well, maybe it was a shit date and you needed to let off some steam afterward."

I laughed, "No, not tonight. Not unless you call reliving traumatic experiences with a therapist a date?"

*Maybe he'll see me as damaged goods and give me some space.*

*Wrong.*

Logan slipped into the booth as he had last time. The scent of his cologne spread to my side of the table, and I smiled as his knees bumped mine again. My reaction would no doubt only encourage him to keep coming back.

"I mean, that wouldn't be very romantic. Unless you have a thing for your therapist. Is it a man or a woman?"

"A woman."

"Well, that works if you're into women. Are you?"

*Was this guy born without a filter between his brain and mouth?*

"Not really. Well, definitely not my therapist."

"I am. Into women – not your therapist," he said with a shy smile, pushing his glasses back up the bridge of his nose with the tip of his middle finger. He tried not to laugh at himself with the way his words seemed to keep tumbling out, unchecked.

"Noted." I tried to keep a straight face too, but that smile of his was contagious.

"Here's something *I've* noted. You didn't drop in over the weekend. I thought maybe there was something wrong with the coffee, and you only drank so much to be polite. Bet you needed to piss so bad when you got to work."

"I did," I admitted. "And my routine is different over the weekends."

*Why am I disclosing this with a stranger?*

"Mine's not," he shrugged. "I'm here almost every night. I've got nothing better to do, so I usually take the shifts everyone hates."

*That sounds lonely.* I filed his comment for later and took a deep breath as I closed my eyes.

"Am I… bothering you?" Logan asked cautiously. Had he asked the first time he sat down the previous week, I would have said yes. But I was enjoying his presence and the way I seemed to make him nervous. And though I'd never admit it, I was growing to like how much my face hurt from smiling.

I opened my eyes to see Logan's disappointed pout. "Oh. No. Just… being suffocated by your cologne, is all," I confessed, trying to work out what other ingredients it had to make it smell *that good.*

*Maybe it's just him.*

He frowned and subtly turned his head, taking a slow draw to gauge the intensity for himself. "Shit, maybe I should ease up on it?"

"God, no!" I said too quickly. "If anything, you should wear *more.* It's… intense. I like it."

He bit his lip to hide his smile, leaning on the table with folded arms as I took another long inhale.

*Fuck, those arms.* I did everything in my power to keep my hands on my side of the table, ignoring all temptation to trace the lightly defined veins traveling up the back of his hands to his forearms.

I couldn't help it, I had to ask, "You've got a cut on your face. Did you have that checked out?"

"Checked out?"

"Yeah. I'm sorry – it's a nurse thing. Did you get it cleaned properly? By the looks of the bruising, it could have been big enough for stitches…"

I'd trailed off, coming to my senses when I noticed I'd reached across the booth for his face. I quickly tore my hand back, cursing it for suddenly exposing its ability to move against my will.

"Oh… no. It's nothing," he said slowly, eyes following my hand as I lowered it. "I heal fast and it's nearly gone anyway."

I knew more than enough about human bodies to know what I was seeing was *not* normal.

*Dammit. He might be Gifted.*

It was a disappointing realization. He was cute and funny. But I couldn't get involved with anyone who was Gifted. Not even for a night.

I didn't know what compelled me to speak my next words. My mind was smart enough to protect me from what he might be, but my mouth had clearly caught the infectious case of *missing filters* that Logan seemed to suffer around me.

"Well, if you find you ever need anything looked at… I can fix nearly everything." I'd just signed up for a nurse's worst fucking nightmare — unexpected questions about bites and rashes for all eternity.

"Thank you, but I wouldn't want to bother you with how often I would need it. If you can fix nearly everything, you must be pretty well trained?"

"Yeah. I studied perioperative nursing in college."

"Oh, shit," his eyes widened with surprise, "So, you work in ORs?"

"Umm…"

Technically I *had* worked in a room that we did operate in… *illegally*. And I was under the instruction of a notorious surgeon, much like a nurse with my training would be… *kind of*.

"I used to. I do much smaller jobs now. I haven't done full-blown surgery in a couple of years."

"Wow, that's impressive. So do you—" Something caught his eye on the other side of the room. "I have to go."

"Okay," I said, surprising even myself with my disappointment.

"The gang and I are heading out. One of our friends… She died a few weeks ago. We haven't had a chance to do anything in her memory yet."

"That's awful. I'm sorry, Logan."

He smiled, but it didn't reach his eyes. "It was nice seeing you again, Summer," he crooned, standing to leave.

"You too."

Logan walked over to the booth I'd been ogling earlier, and the occupants stood as he approached them.

*What an unusual mix of people.*

# EIGHT

## SUMMER

### JANUARY 7TH

Tuesday night. Back at therapy, taking any after-hours appointments Dr. Lindsey had available.

"Okay, Katie," she started as we settled into our regular positions, "during our last session, you mentioned Eric and the age difference between the two of you. Is this something you're comfortable to continue discussing?"

*Anything but Danny? Abso-fucking-lutely!*

"Sure. What about it exactly?"

She took my relaxed response as a cue to dive into the bigger questions playing on her mind.

"After he took you, did your *relationship* start immediately?"

"Surprisingly, no," I told her truthfully. And by the look on her face, she was surprised too. "He didn't have all that much to do with me until I turned nineteen. We started dating soon after that."

Eric had, in an odd way, courted me from my nineteenth birthday. It made little sense at first, having slept together the night I was taken. And then, nothing. For two years.

Eric seemed to have indulged in a moment of weakness when I "chose" to leave the mountains with him. We did nothing other than a handful of public appearances and a little flirting until I'd completed my studies and been initiated. After that point, I was officially his to do with as he pleased.

"Do you know why that is?"

"Well, he was a prominent figure in Be — *the cult.* And while there was quite the age gap, it still made everything look a little less disturbing for him to be dating a nineteen-year-old instead of a sixteen-year-old."

She bobbed her head, still taking notes, "So his image, despite this being a cult and the negative connotations that in itself comes with… it was incredibly important to him?"

"More important than anything."

*More important than me.*

"You say you *dated.* Did you feel you had a choice in the matter?"

Could I admit I was a contractually bound sex toy for one of the biggest names in Bedlam, only for him to essentially ditch his own rules and *almost* fall for me as hard as I'd fallen for him? There was a padded cell at Hartford Asylum waiting with my name on it if I started talking shit like that.

"To a degree. The first year after we made it… *official*, things were intense. Amazing. Like something out of a fairytale." My gaze dropped to my lap, eyes burning over the memories.

Eric and I spent every spare moment of that year together. I was his and he was about as much mine as I could make him. He spoiled me, took me on his business trips to show me and my skills off. I spent every night in his bed on the top floor of Home instead of my own room, many levels below.

While we kept the most intimate of our physical interactions to the privacy of the top floor, the way he touched and kissed me in public that first year was far more ardent than what he'd originally allowed for in his rules. Eric had accused *me* of being confused and blurring the lines between my feelings and obligations, but he wiped those lines away completely once I'd willingly offered myself to be his, contract or not. Forever — as he wanted from me.

"So, despite the difference in age," Dr. Lindsey continued, "and ignoring what he'd done to you in the past, once you were of legal age, did you consider this a consensual relationship?"

I understood she wouldn't see it as consensual, despite my thoughts on the topic. He was an older man that had removed me from my family. Still, I gave her the honest answer.

"Yes. I did. I loved every second of it… in the beginning," I admitted, discounting the night of my Initiation where Eric and I ended up far too drunk before getting into bed together.

*For fuck's sake. You are unbelievable. You'd win gold in mental gymnastics for the way you leap over key parts of how he treated you.*

"But things changed after that first year? What happened to spark such an intense decline if you both seemed so happy?"

I appreciated the way she played along with my fantasies instead of making me feel as pathetic as I knew, deep down, I was.

"Someone important to him died. I was part of the medical team who couldn't save the guy,"— I wrung my fingers in my lap — "I think after that, he held it against me. But we were kind of stuck together for the sake of his image."

*Held it against me. Will you ever stop lying for him?*

Eric was fucking *livid.* Just one day earlier, he'd whispered sweet things in my ear as he fucked me from behind, to the next where he pinned me down in a similar position, arms held behind my back as he hacked the first name into my skin.

Things between us took all sorts of horrific turns that still left me dizzy. For years, I tried to work out how the man seeming so infatuated with me had turned into the monster who made me question my every move and still lurked in my nightmares.

"Traumatic events can often lead to relationship breakdowns. Even in ones that are arranged. *Forced,*" She was carefully choosing words that gently challenged my beliefs and wouldn't scare me off, but I knew everything between Eric and I was *beyond* fucked up. There was nothing normal about it, no matter what I felt for him at any stage. But even years on, those better memories would slip into my head and threaten to unravel any progress I'd made.

"It's a shame you couldn't leave him or seek help." She smiled sadly. "I can imagine that would be impossible within a cult."

I nodded at her. "Yep. Even with things falling apart, Eric was hell-bent on us being together *forever.*"

We ended our session there, leaving me with too many mixed memories of deeply impassioned kisses and screaming matches I'd never won.

# NINE

## SUMMER

There were no more therapy sessions booked for the week, but I was back at the gym each night. It was too cold to run outside and provided the release I needed for the trauma I couldn't talk about.

I went back to the restaurant after each workout, craving the coffee and unable to deny myself the one good thing I could depend on each day.

The company wasn't proving bad either.

Logan worked every night. Some, he had more time to chat. Other nights, his friends were there, and they'd take his attention from me. I didn't mind, I had work to do.

The more I talked to him, the more I worked him out. While Logan was shy at first, he was also a little erratic; too mentally energetic for his mind-numbing job. Overall, he seemed harmless, and I had actually started to look forward to our interactions.

On Thursday, around midnight as I was packing up to leave, Logan mentioned he wouldn't be in the following night.

"Bold of you to assume I'm here for *you* and not the coffee," I teased, looking up from my screen in time to watch him slip into the seat across from mine.

I'd gotten into the habit of lifting my legs out of the way so he wouldn't bump them, then would set my knees between his to give him more room under the table. He seemed to like the closeness, and I didn't mind it either.

"But *I* make the coffee, so really, you're here for both of us."

I bet I looked *stunned.*

"Oh, wow. You just disappear to the kitchen and come back with it. I had no idea *you* were responsible for making it. You'll have to tell me how you get it so perfect." I giggled, closing my laptop.

He gave me a small smile, but almost sounded sad as he asked, "If I did that, would you ever come back?"

My face heated with a blush. I bit my tongue, then quickly changed the subject.

"I won't be in tomorrow either. I have the night off work to… go to a seminar. Out of town."

*Nailed it,* I praised myself. *As if I owe him an explanation.*

"Sounds *fun.*" His tone was sarcastic, which surprised me. Until this point, I'd wondered if sarcasm was lost on him.

"It'll be okay. Gotta keep learning new stuff."

"True. I'll actually be out of town, too. My friends and I… have business to deal with."

"Business?"

Was this "business" going to lead to more fast-healing injuries? That big guy he hung out with looked pretty dodgy, and I'd bet they got up to all sorts of trouble with the Gifted woman.

Logan's frown exposed he'd said too much, and I wasn't about to start digging through his personal life, so I cut it off there. "Well, good luck with that. I gotta get going."

"See you Monday?" he asked hopefully as he left me in the corner.

"Yeah… can't start my day without caffeine."

He'd only made it a few steps away before he spun back.

"Can I," he began, tapping the end of the table with his knuckles and rocking on his feet. He was nervous again, for the first time in days.

"Yeah?" I prompted.

"Have your number?" he finished quickly, as though he had to force the words into the space between us, or else he'd chicken out.

"Oh."

*Fuck.*

I could see why he was acting strange.

*Stranger?*

My skin warmed again, but I didn't want him to know he was having the same effect on me as I was with him.

"I have conditions," I purred to hide my surprise at his request.

"Okay?" he let out a small laugh and seemed to relax at the fact I hadn't immediately declined.

"Please don't call me when you're drunk. I'm a nurse. I have enough to keep me up at night without thinking about what new injuries you'll be acquiring."

"Anything else?"

"Yeah. Photos are fine. But… not the kind you'd send to a nurse for a diagnosis." I widened my eyes playfully in hopes he'd understand.

God, I loved messing with his head, watching the cogs turn inside that gorgeous skull as my meaning sunk in. He arched a brow and grinned once it clicked.

Logan set his phone on the end of the table. "Wait. How old are you, Summer?" He looked me over, trying to work it out for himself.

"Twenty—" I started, and his fingers twitched to retrieve his phone.

"Eight!" I finished with a laugh. "I'm *twenty-eight.*"

Seeming happy with my answer, he flicked the phone across the smooth surface. I tapped in my number and slid it back.

"Have fun at your seminar, nurse."

As I walked to my car, I felt a little lighter than usual, and actually a little sad I wouldn't be seeing him again until Monday.

# TEN

## SUMMER

### JANUARY 10TH

The second Friday of each month was different from the others. I still had to get out of bed, but instead of dragging my ass out, I jumped.

I went for a run in the cold to help settle my nerves and contain the excitement for our quick road trip in the hours to come.

Once back home, I rushed to shower and dress, wearing nothing but black on these nights as they got messier than my time in the garage. My standard button-up black jeans were paired with a black, long-sleeved crew neck, no matter the weather.

These clothes were safe. The tightness held me together. They left me with barely any skin showing — only my hands and face were visible for now.

The club had no real dress code, only one rule — to wear a mask before arriving at the door. That was up for interpretation. The bodyguards and I settled for black masks that covered the top half of our faces. Others covered every inch of their skin. A few bold individuals would occasionally arrive in *only* their masks.

By the time I was dressed, I looked more like I would be robbing the place instead of working there. It made my clothing choice all the more appropriate. Putting some effort into my hair, I added more waves to make it appear a little shorter than if it were straight and hanging around my shoulders. I gently pressed colored contacts over my irises, changing the stark blue enough to seem blue-green, masking my most identifying features.

As much as I loved the club, visiting Crave was one of the greater risks I took in this new life. It was a portal leading directly back to Eric. Too many of his contacts and connections skulked in the shadows. I was genuinely surprised I hadn't already been snatched and dragged back to Bedlam.

*You never know, tonight could be your lucky night!*

Despite the fact I'd be wearing a mask, I put on a full face of makeup. I added plenty of black eyeshadow so it would fill the holes of the mask that surrounded my eyes.

If I didn't have a therapy appointment to attend first, I would have painted around my eyes black, like many of the club's other patrons. I could imagine the notes Dr. Lindsey would write about me, showing up dressed as a raccoon, nine months too early for Halloween.

The bodyguards were waiting for me outside with the van stocked and ready to go. They took me to my session and happily waited for me to be done. They never complained. Their wages were enough to secure their loyalty forever. Possibly longer.

I almost bounced into my therapist's office and made my way to the couch, swinging my legs and tapping on my knees as I waited for her to begin.

She noted my appearance and smiled. "You've got plans for tonight?"

"I do." No one dressed this hot for therapy. At least, I didn't.

"A date?"

I laughed. Why was that the topic of the week? Couldn't a single, twenty-eight-year-old woman, with a business to run and a psychotic ex to hide from, do it alone? Why did I need to drag someone else into my upside-down life? It could all come to a gruesome end at any moment. Why add someone to worry about just so I could have a few normal experiences?

I'd given up on a normal life a long time ago. *All* life, for that matter.

I tried not to let my mind wander to what Eric would do to someone I allowed myself to date, or *love*, other than him.

"No, not a date." I waved my hands, shooing away the visions of my best friend bleeding out.

*Not tonight, thank you, brain. You can keep that shit to yourself.*

"Some friends and I are heading to a club I used to work at. We go once a month."

No lies there. It was always a relief when I didn't have to side-step around every truth. I wanted to be honest with this doctor, but like always, I had to be careful.

"Well, that sounds great! What did you do for work there? Bartending?"

"Actually I was… first-aid." Again, it wasn't quite a lie.

After hitchhiking back to the mountain state following my escape, I made an arrangement with the club owners. I'd met them a few times on my trips with Eric and his cronies, on the odd occasion he had business out this way. It was the kind of place only certain crowds knew about.

The clientele of Crave consisted of vigilantes – Gifted or not – straight-up villains, and those who were desperate to meet or fuck the monsters that haunted their dreams.

The owners worked the bar to keep a close eye on those coming and going. They hated Eric. Most sane people did. The Collector was a harbinger of chaos and death. They preferred he stayed in the big city he loved to torment, like a kid with an ant farm and matches.

I'd always loved the trips to the club and the owners didn't seem to mind me — the young girl on Eric's invisible leash. It was such a drastic change in scenery. Crave wasn't a beautifully boring building with the hospital-like level I was limited to for most of my days. Years.

People didn't seem to think about how villains pulled off such awful stunts. It took an entire team, and I was one of the best on the medical floor for when their plans got fucked up along the way. It didn't allow for much of an opportunity for me to leave with always being on call.

Crave was the opposite of the ER at Home — dirty, grungy. Dark and mysterious with its black walls, low lights, and red carpeted stairways led to what everyone called *"the rooms"*, where people would play out their darkest fantasies.

The reality was that the club was a small part of our lives. Many didn't understand how deadly villainous wildfires like Eric could be, until it was too late. Too many people got burned alive. I wished I meant that figuratively.

It was easy to see the appeal for regular people who wanted to be a part of this world. I'd helped to sell the lifestyle. Above ground, I was the pretty thing on Eric's lap for the gossip columns. In the underworld, I was much more guilty of being a partner in crime, still his to show off, but for my skills to be used as bargaining chips, not just for what we had between us.

The agreement with the owners was to have a small table out the back and out of the way where I could stitch up their patrons. If it meant their customers could come back inside afterward and keep spending money rather than leaving and taking their friends with them to go get fixed up at a hospital. Anna and Kit were happy to have me there. It was how I got on my feet after relying on Eric for far too long.

"Well, I should have thought of that," Dr Lindsey interrupted my musings. "I bet someone like you would be incredibly useful in that setting." She leaned on the arm of her chair, propping her head up with her hand. "Does this happen often, Katie?"

"What?"

"Becoming lost in your mind." She waved her palm in front of her face, "Being distant. Deep in thought."

I smiled and rolled my eyes. "All the time."

She nodded and made *another* note. "Now, I don't mean to pry, but you laughed when I asked if you had a date. Does that still feel like something out of reach for now?"

*Forever*. "I…"

"There's no one you've met recently that you would consider getting to know better?"

I raised a brow. The question was a little *too* well timed. The only new person in my life, if you could call it that, was Logan. While he was great to look at when he thought I was busy working, and he was making me laugh more than anyone had in a long time… I couldn't "consider" him.

*Could I?... Nope.*

I couldn't risk losing the best iced coffees within driving distance from home. But there was something else about the question that gnawed at the base of my brain. It didn't fit her usual style. It felt gossipy, nosey, not helpful.

*Eric? No… Don't let your mind wander. You're already too paranoid.*

I took a deep breath and tried to shake the feeling off, but my thoughts were caught between being hunted via my therapist and the sudden realization that Logan could *ever* be thought of as more than the man who brings me coffee.

*He takes the time to talk.*

*Flirts with me.*

*Hmm. I gave him my number.*

*Oh God, you're fucking useless.*

"No, there's no one even close to that right now." I smiled, hoping I hadn't given away anything in my expression. *She's here to help me, not spy.*

Dr. Lindsey watched me with a subtle smile as the thoughts turned over in my head.

"Maybe there… kind of is… *someone*. I dunno, it's stupid."

"It's not stupid," she reassured me. "What's stopping you from taking things further?"

"Well, for starters, I only gave him my number last night."

"People have done more with less." She let out a little laugh, and I couldn't help but smile too.

"I know," I sighed. "I guess I just still feel too fucked up from… the cult. Trusting people is hard."

"It really can be." She had assumed the position of a wall to bounce my thoughts off instead of telling me what to do. This was evidently one of those moments I had to figure my problem out on my own.

"I've only ever been in a committed relationship with one person. And I don't want that kind of relationship again. I have to protect myself from getting hurt like that *ever* again." She nodded at me while I spoke, still taking notes. "I need someone I can trust. Completely, or it won't work." It was more an admission to me than to her.

"Katie," she interjected, "after what you've been through, I can absolutely see why you would strive for *complete trust.* But that might be something you can never do. Setting a realistic goal like, *trust enough*, might be a start. No one's asking you to commit yourself to this person, just to give them a chance if you're both interested."

"*Trust enough*. I guess we'll see."

"Yes. Now, go enjoy your night out with your friends. I'm sure as a nurse, you've earned a night to let your hair down."

*You have no fucking idea.*

# ELEVEN

## SUMMER

We started our hour-long drive to the club. The bodyguards sat in the front, with me in the back, lying on the chair as I took in the space around me.

The van was originally an ambulance, though the bodyguards helped me make modifications. It was white and nondescript. The stretcher was removed, replaced with an identical chair to the one in the garage. It made it far easier to work on my patients from all angles, especially for moving around their head; where most injuries for my clientele presented during these shifts.

The chair could be removed, if need be. It even had an eject function which would send the whole thing and whoever was causing too much trouble straight out the back of the moving vehicle. I hadn't had a reason to use that feature yet, but between me and the bodyguards, we'd secretly hoped I would need to, one day.

I had a stool of my own, small enough to move around the patient to work on them from various angles. I'd learned the hard way not to use one with wheels, like the one at home in the garage, particularly when the van was in motion.

The shallow drawers and cupboards along the sides were filled with drugs and equipment that both a paramedic and a surgeon would find useful, though I no longer participated in illegal operations. I couldn't bring myself to do it on my own, and my mentor was locked away in my mind with the rest of my past, unable to help me provide those services like we used to.

A sheet of bullet resistant plexiglass separated the back and the seats upfront. I'd seen too many movies where the driver had been taken out, and everyone ended up dead. I'd rather I be the only one at risk in the back. While the cousins were well compensated in danger pay, I would never forgive myself if anything happened to either one of those fucking clowns.

We pulled up to the back of the club, using the dark alley down the right side of the gray brick building. The club was in a large and deserted industrial area, with surrounding warehouses used by arms dealers and drug runners. None of it was my business unless a deal went south and someone showed up in my chair.

Once I was set up, the bodyguards took turns throughout the night to either stay close or to head into the club to meet with friends or drink; they were free to do whatever they wanted. I only asked them not to get too drunk or high to drive in case we needed to leave in a hurry.

Soon, a man was brought out the back with a friend on either side, supporting his weight. He'd suffered quite a hit to the face; the skin along his cheek was split open. The injury looked familiar, or at least, it would have, had the one I was thinking of not healed so quickly.

His friends had barely laid him in the chair before I'd cleaned him of the blood. A few quick pokes of local anesthetic followed so he would soon be much more comfortable.

Then, it was time to stitch. I loaded my needle and stretched out a length of suture. This injury was standard for Friday nights, and I had done this more times than I could ever hope to count. I'd be willing to bet my house that I'd measure the perfect amount of thread every time.

I pierced the skin under his eye socket at one end of the wound, brought the sides together and tied a neat surgeon's knot. The Surgeon himself taught me this move — meeting his almost impossible standards. I thought of my old colleague every time I sewed someone up.

My preferred method was the continuous stitch, and most wounds at Crave fit the requirements. Going against everything I'd been taught in college, I used only my hands, a needle, and thread. With no assistant to help me while I worked, I found the tension I created with my small hands was far better than I could achieve with any bulky forceps or suture holders.

I spun the needle and thread effortlessly. It was as easy as tying shoelaces, and probably looked like I was knitting with my fingers.

While it did get messy – and slippery on occasion – I was strict with hygiene.

Others would think my techniques were archaic, but in my defense, I wasn't solely trained for hospital settings. My lessons continued outside of college hours, where I was taught how to adapt to more… *unsavory* environments. I could seamlessly stitch one of my colleagues in the back of a speeding car while playing a game of chase with the Bedlam PD.

The friends of the man on my chair spoke candidly, as if I weren't even there. Many people did. I'd heard the name floating around the club — *The Nameless Nurse*. I guessed that meant everyone thought I was also *earless*.

Tonight's topic was weapons. Boring as shit. I preferred the juicier gossip; like when politicians were found high and handcuffed to the beds in the rooms upstairs. The things I overheard in this space would be enough to have some of those try-hards in the club running for their lives.

Six stitches were sewn in about as many seconds, not leaving me time to listen to much of the conversation. I was typically faster per stitch on bigger jobs as I built more momentum.

When I was happy the wound wouldn't reopen, I quickly added three extra stitches at the end and tied them off. They made a shape like an arrowhead and were unnecessary. If I had ever been caught doing it in a professional, rather than criminal setting, I would have likely lost my ability to practice even earlier than I had.

It was my way of tagging people, like you would with a shark before releasing it back into the wild. These stitches would only leave the smallest indents in the skin, but if I ever worked on this man again, I would know. I performed a quick backhand bite to ensure the thread was tied off securely.

As always, my patient left happy and amazed at how quickly the time between us was over. At least, his friends were. The injured man was still out of it. After giving his friends strict instructions on how to care for him, and what to do if it looked like a more sinister head injury, I shooed them out of the van and cleaned up, ready for whatever would show up next.

Within minutes, there was another knock on the doors, and a regular poked his head in. I sighed at the sight of him.

"Hey, *you!*" I called. "Come on up."

I didn't know this man's name, at least, not his real one. The bodyguards had done some snooping and told me he went by "Pyro." He hadn't told me that for himself yet, and I was having too much fun picking on him as I tried to get him to tell me of his own accord. You never knew with vigilantes if their titles were something they were proud of, or if the name was given under negative circumstances.

"Busy night?" His deep voice was slightly muffled by the full-faced mask of the skin-tight suit that covered every inch of his body. Many of the characters who were more serious about their criminal careers hid their identity well.

"Always," I responded, patting the chair to prompt him to sit as I pulled up the stool.

This client's suit was... *intense*. While he seemed like a nice guy as I worked on him, his costume was intentionally designed to hold the gazes.

His hands were covered in a deep red fabric. It melded into a burned orange before transitioning into a metallic gold around his shoulders and neck. The same pattern from his feet traveled upward while his mask, mostly red, morphed with the same colors as they descended, meeting with the gold at his neck.

He looked like a giant flame, and I always made fun of him for it. Especially with the confirmation from the bodyguards that he was Gifted, and from what they'd heard, was known for playing with fire. It didn't help that he was so tall, maybe a few inches over six feet.

The height and colors made him stand out like a bloated corpse on an ice rink. Unmissable, yet you'd be smart to keep your distance while you got a good look in. Pyro received plenty of attention, wanted or otherwise, and always ended up in the back of my van when we visited Crave, adorned with a variety of injuries.

"So, what's it tonight, Kindling?" I teased, reaching over to close the doors for privacy. I could only guess I got an eye roll from him under his mask, seamlessly attached to the rest of the material covering his impressively sculpted physique.

Closing the door meant the noises from outside were instantly silenced, leaving the two of us in the quiet space. The bodyguards kept an ear out for me, but I felt safe with those who didn't want their identity uncovered.

It was odd. You'd think those with full suits like Pyro might have been more of a threat, able to hurt or do God knows what and get away with it. No one could identify them.

But during the time I'd worked out of the van and in the garage, regular humans caused more trouble for me. It didn't mean I condoned anything the Gifted got up to, but it went to show that humans were and would always be the real "bad guys" in the end.

He slowly removed the gloves of his suit to reveal his beaten hands. Knuckles swollen and bloody, despite the protection of the fabric. It was a minor injury, and being Gifted meant he'd heal faster than the average human, but then, this man was a little different.

His skin was mottled in color and oddly smooth, almost shiny. Like all of it had been scarred in the past, taking a long time to heal.

Now the bodyguards had confirmed his Gift had something to do with fire, I couldn't help but get a sense that Pyro learned about his abilities through the means of a terrible accident. It seemed to be the way most Gifted discovered their powers.

I cleared my throat, banishing my curiosity and the questions I wanted to ask. I'd been burned too, though not to this extent. Most of those scars were only noticeable if I ever got enough sun for the other parts of my body to hold a pathetic excuse for a tan.

I understood how excruciating even small burns could be, and I couldn't imagine the pain this man had survived.

"Beating people up again?" I asked lightheartedly, gently holding his hands to inspect them.

"You know it," he said with a little too much enthusiasm.

Sighing, I disinfected his knuckles. "I'm beginning to think maybe you keep coming in here to see me." I kept my tone light, not too flirty. From previous interactions with him, he didn't seem interested in picking up anyone at the club; he was just there to pick fights.

Pyro's broad shoulders bounced with a shrug. "Well, I wouldn't be doing it right if I didn't end up here at least once every time I headed out this way."

"You're going to pick on the wrong person at some point," I said, disapproving of his nonchalance.

"I can fend for myself," he promised, intently watching my work on his hands.

"I'm sure you can. But either way, you or the next person stupid enough to fight with you is going to end up here."

He laughed. "That's a good thing though, right? For you, at least. I've seen how much you charge."

"Maybe I should put my prices up for regular offenders," I chuckled as he replaced his gloves.

Though I couldn't see his eyes through the mask, he seemed to look at me for a moment longer than I thought was normal. "Thank you," he said as he bounced out of the chair and opened the door to leave. "I'll catch you next time!"

"I could bet my life on it," I mumbled while cleaning the space of the tools I'd used to treat his injuries.

After seeing a few more people, it was getting close to three in the morning. I took a quick break in the unlit alley, about halfway down the side of the club.

Lowering my phone's brightness so no one would notice the glow, I mindlessly scrolled from my spot on the gravel. I rested my back on the tall wire fence on the property line, resetting my brain for the next round of stitch-ups before I clocked off.

A car pulled up across the road. It only caught my attention as the group clambering out was quite rowdy.

Pushing my body back into the fence and craning my neck to see who was making all the noise, I silently made a bet that at least one of them would be in my chair by the end of the night.

There were four. A mix of full costumes and various degrees of face coverings. Only the biggest names strut around mask free at places like Crave.

The first to come into view was a bulky man, his shoulders so wide I wondered how he could sit next to anyone in the back of a car without either of them hanging out the window. Next, a woman whose skin was so dark I couldn't tell where her sparkly black suit ended. Paired with her platinum hair, it was a dead giveaway I'd seen her before.

My stomach dropped, already predicting what was about to come next.

*Nope.* I looked at my phone. *Just wild coincidences, there's no fucking way.* I internally rolled my eyes at the lies I told myself to keep my head from imploding and tried to force my gaze to stick to the screen of my phone, but it was fruitless. As I glanced to the mouth of the alley, he was there.

*Logan.*

Covered in a dark, almost black suit from head to toe with patches of red highlighting the best parts of his figure. To anyone else, there would be no way to identify the person under the suit at a glance, but it was unmistakable. There was no way I could forget a body I'd stared at for so long.

Standing at a little over six feet, he folded his arms as he leaned against the wall of the building across the street, talking and laughing casually with his friends.

I instantly felt sick as questions started rushing through my head. Had I met him before? Here? Did he come to Crave often? Did he work for *Eric?* Could he be a spy?

Had I been – and I had to admit this in the moment – actually *looking forward* to seeing Logan most nights, only to be playing into another one of Eric's games?

A noise from down the back of the alley disrupted my mental spiral, and I let out a sigh as I found Tony, walking toward me from the direction of the van.

"There's a bartender waiting for you," he announced, extending his hand to help me up to my feet. "You alright? You're looking a little whiter than normal."

"I'm good… trying to…" I glanced over my shoulder. The group had moved on, probably into the club by now. "You know… I don't actually feel too good. How about we leave straight after this job?"

"Whatever you need. We can leave right now." Tony didn't care when we left, he got paid the same either way. But he did care about me, and could sense something was wrong, "I can send her back in?"

"Her?"

*Shit.*

There was only one female bartender at Crave I knew of other than Anna, and Tony knew the owner by name. If I didn't help this woman now, it would only add to the compiling guilt I carried on my back for the part I played in destroying her family.

# TWELVE

## SUMMER

I took a deep breath and stepped up into the van, quickly closing the doors behind me.

"Nessa," I greeted her without eye contact, opening the cupboards in search of my tools. This woman may have hated me, but she wasn't a threat. There was no need to assess her like I did with the rest of the night's patients. She was a little taller than me, with flawless black skin and long hair styled in box braids, twisted into a bun.

Between the two of us, she was always more adventurous with her makeup palette. Back at Home, I would create classic looks on the nights I filmed makeup hauls or was paraded around by Eric. Nessa always picked the brightest shades to get the best contrast with her skin tone, looking every bit the charming daughter of a wealthy mobster.

Not much had changed with our appearances since I'd last seen her. But everything had completely changed between us. It was *far* worse.

I grabbed the tools for treating what I'd already assessed with a glance as a shallow but lengthy cut on her palm.

"Stitch Up," she greeted me, equally cold.

*So that's how we're playing tonight.*

Those of us Initiated into The Collection were given titles. The more I thought about it, the more cult-like it was. We were reborn into chaos, never questioning and ever-loyal to our maniacal creator.

*At least she spoke to you. It's more than you deserve.*

Nessa using my title was a low blow. She knew enough about what I'd endured the day her husband died, but that petty attitude of hers always won out.

"How's the little one?" I continued as if she hadn't just verbally punched me in the gut.

It wasn't her fault she didn't like me, so I tried to be polite. Her relationship with Danny was set up to distract him from me. I was untouchable, someone else's property. Poorly treated property, but still, not to be tampered with by anyone but Eric. Danny broke that rule. Being my best friend and a valuable member of the inner circle, he was given a rare, second chance and was quickly paired with Nessa, the daughter of a crime boss friend of Eric's. They quickly fell for each other. It was equal parts magical and a true fairy tale for them, as it was heartbreaking and soul crushing for me. The couple married within a year of meeting and had a boy soon after. He'd be about eight years old, but that wasn't the child to which I was referring.

"He looks like his Dad." Her cold tone turned icy, and I'd walked right into that one like a fucking moron. If I had stabbed myself with one of the scalpels in the van, it would have hurt less.

We sat in silence as I stitched the two sides of her palm back together. I added my three signature stitches at the end, as if I wouldn't remember Nessa being one of my patients. The scar on her lower abdomen from where her first child emerged had those same three marks. I'd tagged and released her into a completely different world to the one we were in now.

"Thanks for dropping in." I turned away to clean up so the bodyguards and I could leave.

"Really? That's it?" She was understandably mad. We hadn't seen each other in more than two years. I had tried to ensure she and her baby would be taken care of, but that arrangement quickly fell apart when I survived my escape.

When I'd heard the owners of Crave hired her about a year earlier, I was relieved. It was good money and they took care of their staff. She was far away from Bedlam and Home. In the time I'd been working out the back, she was never rostered on. I'd assumed it was on purpose.

"What do you want me to say?" I spun on the stool to face her, leaning with the back of my head on the cupboard behind me. I was so ready for this night to be over. She was the last obstacle between me and my bed.

"I want to know *exactly* what happened in that ER!"

Between caring for an eighteen month old, working late nights at this place, and the horrific loss she'd endured, I was shocked Nessa didn't give up the same way I had. She had much more of a right to than I.

Reaching for the doors and opening the back of the van, I gestured for her to get out.

"Ask your father. I'm sure Eric shared all the details with him."

Nessa gawked in disbelief and stormed out. She turned back once she was on the ground, and attempted to inflict as much pain on me as she lived with each day. Apparently I wasn't dealing with enough.

"You're unworthy of carrying *my* boys' names, but you *do* deserve those fucking scars!" she spat.

Eric's treatment of me was no secret, but it was something no one openly talked about, much like the fact I was sixteen and he hid me for years before he could show me off to the world with less judgment. Apparently, if no one spoke of it, it wasn't happening.

Nessa, now hysterical, resorted to pointing out the obvious. "You've got as much blood on your hands as Eric does."

*This is going nowhere.*

Biting my bottom lip, I nodded and closed the doors in her face. My bodyguards took it as their cue to get moving.

I felt like such a piece of shit.

*You are.*

What did she expect? Every gory detail? The number of bullets or stab wounds in each of their bodies? That they died two minutes and fourteen seconds apart?

She had no idea of the kindness I was providing by sparing her those final moments of the people she — *we* — loved the most.

# THIRTEEN

## SUMMER

We pulled into the furthest garage beside my car, and Tony walked me to the front door. His footsteps didn't sound on the other side of thick timber until the lock clicked into place between us.

I set the alarms, threw my keys at the hallway table, and dragged my tired body down the hall, past my bedroom, the main bathroom and spare bedroom on the left before turning right through the archway, into the open-plan kitchen, living and dining areas. It was a beautiful little house, and was too bad I never really used most of it.

Everything was black, red or white. They were *my* colors. Dark stained floors and black marble bench tops, white walls and red couches. As much as I hated to admit it, it was very much like the areas Eric had allowed me to redesign at Home.

But this was *my* home.

Opening the fridge, bare except for a few bottles of my favorite clear spirits and bottles of water, I behaved and reached for the water.

I tossed it to my bed when I reached my room, then took my clothes off before walking through the wardrobe to the bathroom. As I looked in the mirror I kept my head in place and turned my body to the right.

There they were, hacked like a macabre grocery list. The top five inscriptions in my skin had partially faded over time, particularly the top three, but the bottom four were much clearer. The last two could probably be read from across the room as if they were added yesterday. They were added the day of my escape, and hadn't healed as well as the rest. My upper arms, chest, and torso also had their share of marks. Small scars from burns on my arms, a partially removed tattoo below my right clavicle, cuts from violent patients who got a jab or two in before the sedatives or an arm around their neck took effect. I could hide most of my flaws under a crew neck T-shirt.

These scars were reminders of who I was and where I came from. Most were punishments dealt out by the man I'd loved, put there by Eric to teach me a lesson when he couldn't face the losses he caused, and blamed them on everyone else. In some sick way, they became trophies to us both.

First in view across my left shoulder blade, the name at the top; *Jareth Hanley*. It had been there since I was twenty. The man whose name I carried was barely recognizable when he was placed on one of our metal tables. We were ordered to save him. Threatened that if we couldn't, we'd join him.

I'd never witnessed Eric completely lose his cool until that moment. While I'd only ever been introduced to this friend of his once, he clearly meant a lot to Eric.

We couldn't save him.

Bones pulverized. Organs punctured. My guess was that he'd pissed off a bad crowd, and they destroyed him for it. Even if we could have done anything, it would have been cruel to force him to live a moment longer.

Our team had barely started removing what was left of his bloody clothing before his time of death was called. The four of us who were ordered to save him stood around his body, heads down with our tails between our legs as our punishments came. Eric hit everyone where it hurt most.

For some, it was money taken from the accounts created for us when we officially became employees of Home. For others, it was time added to their contracts.

Contracts weren't negotiable unless we agreed to more time in exchange for something we desperately needed. Most of Eric's employees were recruited under dire circumstances and given an amount of time in years, months, days — however long he needed each of us for specific jobs.

We were given the paper to sign, or *shot* where we stood. It was simple.

To be offered a contract at all meant you were at the end of the line anyway.

Working for Eric, forced or otherwise, provided his employees with money, stable living arrangements, and health care through myself and those I worked with. It oddly didn't feel like such a bad deal, and that added to how bizarre the whole system was.

But I was so young and dumb. Enchanted by how he could give me anything I wanted, though it was mostly his affection that drove me to be such a perfect drone. I was too naive to see he'd simply removed me from the small cage that was the life with my parents, into a slightly bigger, prettier one that was Home.

The contract I signed could only be terminated "in death." I signed it soon after I graduated from college. It was the first of its kind. No guns necessary. I wanted the *forever* he promised.

My punishments were unique. Though we were essentially a couple, both in private and in public to an extent, Eric knew I still desperately sought his approval as equally as he demanded my obedience. It came as a complete shock to both of us when I questioned his treatment of the staff who had absolutely no hope of saving the man. They might as well have been set up for failure.

Eric was absolutely insane, manic and dangerous almost daily, but a lot of that was for show to live up to his reputation. I never once thought I'd actually be on the receiving end of the monster we all thought he was pretending to be.

While clearing the table of Jareth's blood, pain suddenly radiated in my neck before my surroundings blurred and turned dark. I knew my drugs well, and it only took me a moment to realize I was likely hit with strong tranquilizers.

I dropped, and when I woke, I was in Eric's room.

At that point in time, I'd been in the same room just a little over a year earlier, dressing with him for my initiation. He had said sweet things about the way I looked and helped me put my dress on.

Then, a year after an intense and seemingly romantic affair, I found myself regaining consciousness, naked and mutilated in his bed. I was certain more was done to my body than I could see and feel, though the excruciating pain across my left shoulder took precedence over my internal injuries.

Eric may have had me knocked out, but whatever he'd done to me didn't involve painkillers. I couldn't remember if I was conscious for the experience or not, but my nightmares since the event showed a disturbingly clear picture of what my body had endured.

Upon waking, I staggered from the bed across the concrete floors to the bathroom's stone tiles, where I tried to inspect the external damage in the mirror.

The name… Violently hacked into my skin.

Looking down into the double vanity, I spotted a bloody pocket knife in the other sink.

Unbeknownst to me, Eric was sitting beside the bed in his velvet wingback chair. He appeared to be in shock as I ran to him and I climbed onto his lap like the pathetic little pet I was. I'd held his face in my hands, begging him to forgive me as he looked up at me in disbelief.

While he did *kind of* forgive me at first, things had changed between us. The loss of his friend created a deep crack in his already fragile grasp on reality. And as time went on, it became his preferred method of punishment for me.

Eric knew I didn't care about my contract; I was too stupidly loyal and in love with him. And as for the millions accumulating in my bank account, when was I ever going to be permitted to leave Home to spend it?

Deep down, I believed he began to get enjoyment out of what he did to me. Nine names gave him time to experiment and get creative with my conscious state.

Knocked out.

Numbed.

Awake and face down with my hands tied behind my back.

I was so far detached from reality I actually believed I deserved it all. When Eric personally dealt the penalty for being disrespectful or being unable to save those he needed for his Collection, I took it as a sign he was still able to show *something* for me.

With my mind back in my bathroom, I turned the other way and into the shower. The hot water poured from the waterfall shower head, and steam billowed out to fog up every smooth surface. I stayed there for a while, until I remembered that Nessa wasn't the only problem I'd encountered at the club.

*Logan.*

I was certain it was him.

After turning the water off, I threw my hair up in a towel and dug in the drawers of my wardrobe for my favorite pajamas. I had a night of amateur sleuthing ahead of me, and I wanted to be comfortable.

I found the oversized, black band shirt and tossed it on with some black cotton shorts. I could have done without the shorts, the shirt was like a dress on me, hanging around the middle of my thighs and baggy on my shoulders.

But I was nothing, if not practical, and always had terrible visions of being hunted down by Eric's men, having to flee in the middle of the night. I'd seen enough bad movie plots to know the girl traipsing around the forest in her underwear was always the first to be offed.

Content with my attire, I made my way back to the fridge. It glowed with heavy disapproval as I grabbed a half-empty bottle of vodka. I closed the door and paused for a moment before I told the judgemental appliance, "Go fuck yourself."

I practically skipped back to my room before I jumped onto the center of the bed and opened my laptop, typing in the password of the week.

Frozen, my hands hovering above the keyboard, I didn't know where to start. My stomach bubbled with an anxious excitement, like a teen with a crush, about to dig for all the dirt I could find on him. Only I didn't know if I was going to like anything I found.

Vigilantes were dangerous. *Gifted* vigilantes were a whole other category I didn't need to be involved with.

*God, he looked good in that suit.*

I downed a mouthful of vodka and thought about the way the skin-tight fabric clung to his arms when he'd folded them, cursing Tony for interrupting before I got a better look.

*Was it the suit? Or is it because I know who's underneath?* I didn't care, he was hot either way, and I'd already endured enough therapy for one night to bother dissecting my excitement. I just needed to work out if he were a danger to *me*.

I began my search with "Logan" on all the social sites I could think of. It was impossible to narrow things down with no surname. I didn't even know if his first name was real or not. I checked dating apps for local men around his age, only to come up empty. But I did save a few profiles to come back to once I was done cyber-stalking.

With a heavy sigh, I slumped back against the pillows. There was *nothing* on him.

*Maybe try to find the alter ego? What color was the suit? Was it all red? Black and red?* I hadn't been close enough to get a decent look at the pattern, too busy focusing on those damn arms.

The local police reports were next on my checklist, along with news websites and crowdfunding pages for those seeking assistance with paying for funerals and memorials.

If you wanted to find information about anyone who frequented places like Crave, you didn't bother with school fundraisers and animal shelter drives. You followed the chaos instead. The blood and gore, destruction and madness. And that's exactly where I found him.

*Bingo.* The air caught in my lungs.

There were no mugshots. He'd never been caught, but there were a couple of sketches. Enough to confirm I was being served coffee almost every night by a murderous vigilante. A real one, too, not someone dressing up and playing pretend. Logan was undoubtedly one of the Gifted.

The reports I skimmed through mentioned strength and speed, typical and obvious markers for many like him, but I was more curious about what set him apart. This criminal often left no one behind who could talk, so there wasn't much to go on. "Personality shift" was the only clue I found; quoted from an incomplete witness report.

This vigilante was wanted for a multitude of disturbing crimes; the details and blurred crime scene photos were able to turn even my hardened stomach. The felon seemed to have a thing for dealing out justice on his own; almost all of his victims were wanted criminals themselves. But his methods were clearly warped, and he seemed to take on the role of executioner, leaving a string of graphically shredded and unrecognizable bodies between the Gray Mountains and Bedlam.

"Another man from *fucking* Bedlam," I whispered and shook my head in the dark. "I sure have a type." I took another swig from the bottle and continued scrolling to find a name for the masked face.

*Vengeance.*

"Fuck!" I hissed. While I gave myself a second to appreciate that "Vengeance the Vigilante" was one of the least creative names I'd heard floating around my circles, having a name now made everything much more ominous.

A handful of news articles turned into dozens when I searched for "Vengeance." All similar in description, crime and gore.

One article in particular stood out. Well, there were many articles of the *same* story… All of them had a similar title, and the report appeared to be picked up by every news outlet in the country.

"Twenty-three Officers Slaughtered in Bedlam's Worst Massacre." The main suspect was none other than the serial murderer, Vengeance.

The story was familiar, having lived in Bedlam at the time it occurred. Not that I really cared or paid much attention to it. Eric and I were in the midst of our steady downward spiral. And twenty-plus fewer cops on the street meant easier work for us.

*If he only goes after criminals, maybe I won't make the list of casualties.*

My brain was evidently affected by the poison I was ingesting. It took a moment for my dumb ass to remember I was, and always would be, one of the worst criminals to come out of that city. *But then, why cops? Who am I kidding? In Bedlam, most of them are corrupt.*

*He's got a thing for skulls.*

I gulped at the images. I would have been less disturbed if the monster *collected* skulls, but no, he was much more into "popping" them like fucking water balloons. Each of his crime scenes contained a jigsaw of human remains, and for many of those, the misted brain matter was a common feature.

I dropped my head in my hands to focus on my breathing and let my towel unwind from my hair. It fell from my head and onto the laptop screen. I let it sit there, not wanting to see anymore of Vengeance's handiwork as my mind caught up.

It was hard to believe the cute guy I'd been flirting with, who'd shyly asked for my number, was capable of the dismemberments I'd just read about. I needed to see him in this new light, with his cover blown.

*If he has anything to do with Eric… I might have the upper hand for the time being.*

Although, after reading Vengeance's methods, my gut told me Eric would stay away from someone so messy and unrestrained.

"Dammit," I spoke to my empty house. It was still only the early hours of

Saturday morning. I needed to stick to my routine if I didn't want to give Logan any reason to suspect I knew who he was. I also didn't want to appear too eager to see someone who I'd just given my number to. Murderer or not, I didn't want to come across as desperate.

As if the devil himself could sense he was on my mind, my phone lit up on the bed.

I unlocked it to find a handful of explicit images along with the text: **Think your little body could handle this?**

His height and arms weren't the only things he had going for him.

My lips curved with an involuntary smile at the message and the knowledge Logan was thinking of *me* after a night out with his friends.

*Should I send something back?*

I reached for the bottom of my shirt.

*The fuck is wrong with you?* I quickly scolded myself, remembering what I just learned about the body and mind the huge, hard dick in the photos was attached to.

*What would I send? Nudes full of scars? That'd get him going.* I rolled my eyes and sighed. *I've had too much to drink.* It didn't stop me from lifting the bottle again as I swiped back and forth between the photos.

After a moment's thought, I texted back.

**I think you'd be surprised at what this little body can handle.**

I threw my phone across the bed, equally shocked I'd responded after learning his identity and anxious about whether he would message again.

*You don't have definitive proof yet.* Although, that felt like a lie. I was sure it had to be him.

I felt hot and unsettled despite the cool seeping into the house from outside, not knowing what to do with the information I now had to sit on for days before seeing him.

My phone laid face down at the far corner of the bed. It taunted me. Dared me to look again. I couldn't remember the last time I'd received photos of that nature, and was glad he'd acted on the conditions for being able to contact me. I'd had every intention to find someone to play with at the club after my shift, but seeing Nessa totally ruined my mood. More so.

I reached for the phone, ignoring all the red flags life was vigorously waving in my face as I opened the message again. There he was. At least, the only part of him I needed for the moment.

Without taking my eyes off the bright screen, I leaned back to reach into my bedside drawer, fumbling around in the dark for any toys that could come close to his length and girth.

After settling on one of my favorites, I slipped my arm under the sheets and spread my legs. I imagined exploring every inch of Logan's sculpted arms and his hands holding me down as he fucked me.

# FOURTEEN

## SUMMER

### JANUARY 13TH

Sitting through the hour of therapy was painful. I wanted to fast forward to my next stop. But until I figured out time travel, I had to face every minute of my miserable life.

"You seem a little distracted today," Dr. Lindsey squinted at me from her chair.

"Yeah, I am. My weekend was… strange. And I'm really keen to meet up with one of my friends for coffee."

"In that case, how about we finish up early today?" She closed her notebook. "I'm sure seeing your friend will have a more positive impact on your mood than talking when you're not up for it." She smiled, and I believed her. My suspicion about her was dying down.

"You know," she continued as I stood to leave, "I thought, with the way you were dressed tonight that maybe you were headed out. Maybe on a da—"

"A date?" I asked with a laugh as I opened the door. "Good one, doc."

I moved so fast I almost ran through the building's dimly lit entrance, greeted again by the cold air outside. I caught a glimpse of my reflection in my car's tinted window, understanding why her thoughts would have traveled that path.

I didn't bother leaving a message for Mom. She clearly didn't want to talk to me. I was now leaving messages every other day, sometimes multiple. Her voicemail never reached its limit again, and yet, I'd still heard nothing in return.

Despite my eagerness to see Logan, I drove around aimlessly for over an hour. Leaving therapy early hadn't changed the fact I didn't want to show up to a dining room full of people.

It gave me time to clear my head and work myself up for confronting someone I was having confusing feelings about. The less witnesses for outing a killer, the better.

I pulled up at the restaurant, slamming the car door behind me as I made a quick and confident pace to the entrance, each footstep heavy with purpose as I made my way inside.

With skipping the gym and having dressed in normal clothes instead of the activewear I'd worn every time I had visited so far, I was looking more than presentable for the imminent exchange.

I wasn't able to sleep through the anxiety and had been up doing my hair and makeup since five in the evening to make the time go by faster. I wore my black, high-waisted jeans, a tight white crew neck shirt, and the most expensive black heels I owned. They had been thrown on as I left the house in a last minute decision. An attempt to not feel so physically small by comparison.

Logan spotted me as I walked in and did a double take.

"Your table just opened up." He grinned and led me to the empty dining area. I smiled politely, pretending not to have a clue about the double life he led. He seemed excited to see me again, and I had to ignore that I might have been feeling the same.

"Coffee?" he asked as I slipped into my favorite spot in the corner.

"Make it two."

"Thirsty?" He frowned. "Maybe you should try water."

"They're not *both* for me." I swept my gaze up at him, giving him a strong dose of blink-free eye contact.

It took a moment before his expression changed and shoulders dropped. And though he looked disappointed, he left to get my order without any questions.

Within a few minutes, he was back and set the drinks down.

"Logan?" I called as he turned away. My stomach tied itself in knots as he looked over his shoulder.

*Don't be dumb. You've got the upper hand here.*

"You need something else?"

I squared my shoulders and smiled up at him, "Yeah, you."

His head cocked to the side, like a puppy trying to work out where I'd hidden its favorite toy. I gestured to the seat across from me in the booth. Still, no lightbulbs.

"I don't understand…" he lightly shook his head, brows pinched.

"It's *for you.* Is it quiet enough for you to sit for a minute?"

He straightened up a little, looked around and shrugged at the empty restaurant. "We're pretty flat out at the moment, but I'm sure I can stop and chat."

*Is it me, or is he getting better with jokes? He's starting to relax around me. Maybe it'll be easier to get answers out of him.*

"What do you need from me?" His legs moved around mine under the table as he made himself comfortable. He almost smiled as I moved mine between his, assuming our regular position.

"I don't *need* anything."

*Can't I buy him a coffee without an ulterior motive?* I guess I couldn't. I *was* there to try to get information from him. I had no choice but to gauge how much danger I was in while around Logan. I needed to learn if he was working for Eric.

*You're paranoid. Not every person who comes into your life is one of his puppets.*

"I thought it would be nice to have coffee," I tipped my head to the side and smiled again, widening my eyes enough to look cute, hoping I didn't look crazy. "You know, get to know you better since I'm seeing you most days now."

"And my dick." He referred to the photos without missing a beat and took a sip of his drink as I choked on the first mouthful of mine.

"Fuck, that's amazing," he quietly praised himself as he peered into his glass. "Are you okay?" he laughed, folding his arms on the table when he noticed I'd inhaled the liquid.

*Yep, I couldn't forget those arms if I tried.*

I had another weird urge to run my fingers along his smooth skin. The definition on his forearms was enough to make my mind wander.

*God. Focus.*

I cleared my throat. "I'm fine."

When I met his gaze, he was smiling. I'd been caught checking him out. Apparently, subtlety wasn't going to be my strong suit for this encounter.

"You didn't send any pics back. Didn't like what you saw?" His foot tapped under the table, but I couldn't give him the satisfaction of the compliments *that* particular appendage was worthy of. I was on a mission.

"Body image… *issues*," I said, only slightly bending the truth as I played with my straw to avoid his eyes.

I certainly didn't need someone like an unstable vigilante having photographic proof I was one of The Collector's pieces — even with my tattoo mostly removed.

"For real?" He scoffed and looked me over. My turn to smile, though this time, it was entirely involuntary. I took another sip of the freezing cold drink in hopes it would bring the temperature down on my face and neck. "Did you dress up just to have coffee with me, Summer?" He removed his arms from the table, leaning back on the seat to get a wider view of me.

Was he teasing or serious? There was no point in lying to him. Direct communication was the best way through this.

"Yeah. I did," I purred.

His eyebrows flew upward in surprise, like he'd been joking and truly hadn't expected the answer he wanted to hear to be correct.

"W-well, you look real fucking cute." He pushed his glasses back up his nose, fingers quivering as he continued to stammer. "I mean, you *always* look cute, but today you l-look… cuter? Hot, even. Fuck."

Blushing again, I bit my tongue, hard, in hopes it would remove the deep color spreading across my pale skin like wildfire.

*Enough flattery. I'm here for answers.*

"Thank you. How was the trip out of town with your friends?" It was my turn to give him whiplash, and my flirty tone turned a little too cold.

"It was… good." His eyes darted to the side.

"*Business* dealt with?" I made a point of sitting back and keeping my expression flat.

His tapping under the table picked up again. Maybe I was making him anxious, but not because I had discovered his biggest secret. Perhaps it was because I was giving him a little of the attention he may have been wanting from me.

"Yep. How was your seminar? Learn anything cool?" He turned the questioning back on me without giving any details.

"Not really, but I got some practice in." This was feeling too much like an interrogation from both sides. I needed to soften my demeanor or else I'd be stuck with only getting short answers and questioned in defense.

I had to *give* some if I wanted to get some…

*Answers, of course.*

Though I would have taken anything he was willing to give me the moment he sat down and that thick shroud of cologne spread from his side of the table to mine.

Releasing the tension in my shoulders, I tried smiling again. The muscles in my cheeks already ached from trying to hold the foreign expression.

"I actually got to stitch some people up." My confession piqued his interest as I sipped at my drink. Everyone loved graphic nurse stories to some degree, and from what I'd read over the weekend, this man had a thing for *graphic*.

"Yeah?" The tapping stopped as he focused on my lips.

"Yeah. Brows, hands, arms, you name it."

"You mentioned your line of work wasn't *friendly*, much like yourself before you've had caffeine." The guy thought he was a *fucking* comedian. "Do you work with addicts? Or in a psych ward?"

*Time to "give some." This should put his MO to the test.*

"Actually, between you and me." I lowered my voice and set my elbows on the table to lean closer. He did the same, closing more of the small space between us. My pulse picked up as I looked into his hazel eyes. "My work isn't exactly… *legal*." I gave him a playful eye roll as I toyed with the neckline of my shirt.

His expression changed, instantly serious, and his warm eyes turned a little cold. He dropped his gaze, making me think he might not want to know more. If he learned what I did, would that be enough for me to end up like the bodies I'd read about?

"Care to elaborate, Summer?" he asked cautiously, locking his gaze back onto mine.

"Well, technically, I'm not meant to be practicing at all. I was stripped of my license, like, two years ago." He nodded along to my confessions. "And most of my patients are criminals." I paused, waiting for his head to explode. Figuratively, of course, though mine now had a very good chance of doing that if he saw fit.

"Huh. So, after you help criminals, they probably go out and commit more crimes, right?" His voice was a little different, more like a low growl and lacking the smoothness I'd been playing over in my head as I put the pics he'd sent me to good use. Multiple times.

"I mean, what they do with their lives is none of my business once they leave my practice," I said with a nervous laugh as I scratched at my neck.

*Shit. Maybe this was a terrible idea.*

"You have your own practice?"

"Yep." I smiled, perking up at the thought of what my hard work had so far amounted to, even with the possibility it was about to get me slaughtered.

"That can't be legal either if you're not allowed to work as a nurse..."

"Nope."

*Now to really fuck with his mind.*

"I don't only help criminals, though."

He raised a hardened brow. "No?"

"No. I help anyone I can. I'm *unbelievably* talented." I grinned as I held his gaze. Or was he holding mine? Either way, our eyes were fixated on each other's as he took in each word. "And my skills would be wasted if I wasn't putting them to good use every day. I help people who can't afford health care, but I charge the criminals through the nose for treatment. They need more from me, like anonymity, around-the-clock access and other services I shouldn't disclose with you." I narrowed my eyes playfully.

He looked offended, but hey, he was meant to be a regular person without a secret, vigilante life, and I was going to keep treating him like one until he admitted it.

I kept going, almost unable to stop talking and exposing some of my biggest secrets. Saying these things out loud was making my mind feel like it was swirling around in my skull. It was exciting to talk to someone about what

I did without a mask covering half my face or watching every word around my therapist.

"I don't keep much of the money. Like, at all. A lot of it goes to treating good people who would otherwise die without what I can source for them. Many of my patients are here illegally but have committed no crimes and only want a good life for their families. If they ended up in a hospital, their identity would be discovered, and they'd likely be deported. Or worse."

After a moment of watching Logan unpack my ramblings, he finally replied.

"Well, that's a very… *morally* gray area," he said, blinking a few times and seeming equally shocked with his answer as I was. He gave a tight nod, appearing happy with what he'd settled on.

*Morally gray... Is that the deciding factor in who gets brutally wiped out and who lives?* It seemed a very precarious set of scales to determine life or death.

*Whose morals? His alone or society as a whole?* The logic seemed flawed. Nothing could ever be so black and white.

Maybe Logan liked me more than I thought, and he'd jumped some major hurdles to come up with an excuse not to kill me. A fucked up thing for me to think of as *sweet.*

"It is." I pushed my luck a little further. "But it's very rewarding. Totally worth the risk to help others. And to redeem myself… for *my own* past crimes."

"Well, I think it's *awesome.*" Logan threw his hands up as if he couldn't possibly hear anymore without the pretty girl flirting with him being torn to shreds if his mental scales tipped too far to one side.

"So, what about you? Is this your dream job?" I gestured to the space around us. "Ever done anything cool or unusual for a living?"

"Oh, yeah. I was a cop for, like, seven years," he announced smugly. "A detective, specifically. For five of those."

I froze, looking at him with what I could only imagine was a severe case of saucer-sized eyeballs as his admission registered.

Had I just confessed a bunch of serious crimes to someone even more dangerous than I thought? Logan may have seemed socially awkward and missed some cues, but it was obvious this guy wasn't *stupid.* Especially with what I learned he was capable of getting away with *and* keeping two separate lives.

I wouldn't have been surprised if everything he'd shown me was an act to not seem like a threat. Cologne warping my clarity, included.

"Really?" my voice wavered. "Wouldn't have picked it." I finished my drink and pushed the glass to the side, trying my best to keep my exterior calm and like I wasn't internally spiraling into a panic.

"Hey… Do you want to… go out?" he asked.

"What?"

"Out?" He shrugged. "You're all dressed up. I wouldn't want that look to go to waste just sitting here in the same place as always."

"Umm. Sure?" I said as he stood. My mind tried to recover from that sharp turn as I took the hand he extended. The heels made my face much closer to his than it had ever been. Close enough to see the *slightest* mark left from last week's injury.

"I know a place not far from here where we can grab a drink, if you can take any more fluids?" He grinned shyly as I took in his features.

My immature mind forced a giggle out of me. I always put my ability to twist people's words into something dirtier than they intended as a result of constant trauma, particularly during the vital years of my brain's development.

He shook his head and muttered, more to himself than to me, "Does your mind live in the gutter?"

"I'm sorry, let's go." I released his hand, realizing I'd been holding it all that time. I needed answers, not distractions. And he was proving hard enough to focus around at the best of times.

Logan disappeared for a moment while I waited at the entrance. He'd changed out of his work shirt and reappeared in a tighter-fitting white T-shirt that he zipped a jacket over.

The jacket went well with the glasses, looking like something my grandpa would have worn. Its pattern consisted of various gray shades in thick horizontal stripes. Despite it not being particularly attractive, it looked warm.

Good thing, too, because it was still freezing outside.

# FIFTEEN

## SUMMER

It was close to midnight, and we were sitting at a bar down the road we had walked to. Conversation between us was light; the music was too loud for much talking. But we were out and in a new setting, so that was something.

It certainly wasn't how I'd expected the night to play out. I was hoping for some kind of confession from Logan by now, but his charm seemed to have gotten the better of me. I internally scolded myself for getting caught up in cute looks when I should have been looking for threats.

With not much opportunity for chatting, it gave me an excuse to observe him more intently. There was even less space between us as we sat on barstools than we'd had across the table in the booth. We sat similarly to how we did at his work, with his feet resting on the lower bar of my stool and my legs between his.

He smiled a lot. At least, he did when he was around me. Always timidly looking down first before meeting my gaze. The expression reached his eyes every time and warmed his features. His magnified eyes were magnetic, and he was mesmerizing to look at. I hadn't expected someone who was Gifted could be so likable.

He put his hands in his jacket pockets when he seemed nervous, but was expressive with them in the few moments between songs when talking about things that excited him; his friends and his car.

I had to admit that it was actually nice being out together. Though, I was about to ruin it. I had no choice. If Logan had been keeping a double life for years, he'd know better than to slip-up in such a public setting. I needed to get him alone.

After a few drinks that were evidently hitting me much harder than they were him, I had an insane idea. More like a death wish.

As I leaned closer to Logan, I gently cupped the side of his warm face. I drew him over to speak softly in his ear, with just enough volume so there was no chance of mishearing me.

"Do you want to come back to my place?"

He pulled back and gave me a look I couldn't read, thanks to too many drinks on my part.

"You've been drinking," he said firmly, reaching for my hand and placing it down on my leg.

"Yeah, so?" I shrugged, subtly trying to keep my balance on the chair.

"Oh *shit*, you *drove*."

"I have someone who can pick up my car and take it home before I'm there." I pulled my phone from my back pocket and sent Ben a text. "See? Done!" I waved my phone around, not actually giving him the chance to see the conversation between me and the bodyguards.

I'd left Logan no choice now, and could tell by the look on his face that he didn't like being cornered or coerced.

*Neither.* I smiled up at him.

It was cruel, but I still hadn't gotten *any* evidence that this man was a mass murderer. Not even small hints or confessions he was Gifted.

"I will take you home. And make sure *you* get in the house. And that's it," he bargained, continuing to stress as he raked a hand through his hair. "Fuck! I didn't even think about your night shift and that you shouldn't be drinking before work. At this rate, you'll end up stitching someone's hand to their fucking face."

I laughed at the idea of doing that as he grabbed me by the hand to drag me behind him. It was probably only to steady me, but I was glad to be holding hands again. His were so much warmer than mine, and I found myself not wanting to let go this time.

After a few steps outside, I started stumbling in my shoes. It surprised me;

how out of practice I'd become after being quite well trained to walk in all sorts of high heels in the past.

*Goddamn. How strong were those drinks?* I shouldn't have tried to go one-for-one with Logan. I'd consumed things far worse in the past and not felt this wobbly.

*Have I made a mistake?* I entered a brief moment of terrifying clarity, remembering I was likely in the presence of a killer.

Even *I* couldn't believe how stupid I'd been for giving Logan all that information about my work and then drinking with him. For all I knew, I could have been poisoned in his plan to rid the earth of me for my crimes.

When Logan noticed I was struggling to keep up with his longer strides, he stopped and turned to me.

"Do you want me to carry you? You're so slow, you'll be late for work."

The thought of the arms I'd fantasized about *actually* holding me made my skin scorch. I took a small, unsteady step backward, putting my finger to his chest to make him take me seriously as I wobbled.

"I would normally say *no* to something like this—" I started, but was cut off by being thrown over his shoulder. I didn't protest. In fact, I laughed at the feel of the blood rushing to my head while he held my legs tight against his chest.

"This isn't what I had in mind." I clutched the sides of my face, queasy from the world being tipped upside down.

"Well, if I hold you in front of me, and you're sick, I'd get covered," he called over his shoulder. "I'm safer this way with a lightweight like you."

I giggled. "Can't handle vomit?"

He squeezed my legs a little tighter. "Can't handle a lot of things. The gang makes fun of me for it all the time. Call me a germaphobe."

*Really? Those crime scene snaps say otherwise.*

"Okay… that's fair." I sighed, upside down, grateful we didn't have far to travel before I could be put back the right way up.

"Body image issues," he mimicked my excuse from earlier, "I don't know what you're on about. You *feel* amazing."

I realized then that he had a hand on my butt, and concluded I *must* have been poisoned to not notice it sooner. I was surprised he'd touched me three times in one night. Everything between us until this point had been over a table. Bumping legs beneath its surface didn't count.

I giggled again as he grabbed at my ribs to lower me to the ground, already at his car. He gently brushed his hands down from my shoulders and held my wrists to steady me. More contact. His hands were *so* warm.

"You've got a thing for the cold?" he asked, tipping his head to the side. When I didn't give my usual reply, he continued, "Cold drinks, no jacket? You're *freezing*." He almost sounded annoyed, like he was dealing with a stubborn child who refused to dress appropriately for the weather. In his defense, he wasn't far off.

Logan unzipped and took off his jacket to wrap it around me. I couldn't decipher if he was being romantic, or just trying to get me home without any damage. Most likely the latter.

"Imagine if I let a girl named *Summer* freeze to death on my watch." He laughed, shaking his head and keeping a close eye on me while I lowered my body into the passenger seat of his car.

"Don't go anywhere," he told me before closing my door. I couldn't imagine I'd get anywhere fast, drunk and in these heels.

The seat was comfortable, though. The black and red leather was impeccably conditioned. If he really was the vigilante I'd seen at Crave, they seemed to be *his* colors as much as they were mine. There were no back seats, and the entire space smelled strongly of his cologne.

The fragrance was mixed with another I didn't recognize. Perhaps a cleaning compound that would never find its way into my workspace.

*It's coming from the seats.*

I tilted my head to inhale again, confirming the source. It wasn't a chemical product that could be used to remove evidence or hide the handiwork of a deranged murderer. It made me feel a little better. He cared about his car. The chances of me dying in this seat were slim.

Logan disappeared into the restaurant, returning after a few minutes to the driver's seat with coffee in a takeaway cup. It was the hot and boring kind.

"Aww what, why? It's awful," I whined before even tasting it after he'd handed over the cup.

He laughed at the face I pulled when I took a sip. Nausea swirled in the pit of my stomach, and I had a feeling that if I were sick in his car, he'd never speak to me again. Still needing answers, I drank up.

"Because you have work to get to, that's why. Hey, your car's gone," he noted, glancing around the parking lot through the windshield.

*He knows what my car looks like?*

"Told you I had it sorted."

I tapped my address into the car's GPS when he gestured to it, and he started driving in the direction of my home. If Logan really was working for Eric, as one of my weakening theories about him suggested, then I was being incredibly foolish. My house and work were parts of *my* secret identity. I was leading the fox directly to the chicken coop.

"Fucking *dumb* chicken," I whispered out loud by mistake.

"Me or you?" he asked with a confused laugh.

"Me. Getting drunk with a stranger on a work night," I offered, taking a sip of the coffee so I looked a little less insane talking to myself.

"Are we really strangers, Summer? We've known and seen each other nearly every night, for what, almost a few weeks? You know where I work. I now know where you live." He glanced at the GPS, and the hairs on my arms rose in defense. "I'd say that makes us at least a step above strangers."

"I guess." I observed him as he drove, having a difficult time pulling my gaze away, more than when I watched him work and he thought I wasn't looking. "But we don't really *know* anything about each other, do we?"

"That's not true." He frowned, eyes sweeping the road to take in the drastic change of scenery as we left the small city behind. "I know you're a nurse. Or at least, you *were*. I know you're a bitch before coffee. *Iced*-coffee." He tipped his head to the cup in my hands and smiled. "I wouldn't be surprised if that reversed the effects."

"We'll soon find out," I muttered sourly, almost immediately proving his theory.

"I'm also gonna guess you're a loner."

"The fuck is that supposed to mean?"

"Look at you," he offered, chuckling at me as I looked down at my clothes. "No. That's not what I meant. Not *physically*. Physically, you… look great." He shuffled his shoulders against his seat as I drank more coffee to shut myself up. I didn't want to end up dead and left on the side of the road to rot. That, and I needed to hide my blushing at what sounded like *another* compliment.

"I mean, you work weird hours," he explained. "You hang out in empty restaurants."

"Sounds like someone else I know." I raised my eyebrows at him when he looked at me.

"Hey, I have friends," he argued.

"So do I." I elbowed him from my seat, convincing myself the bodyguards could count as friends when I didn't even know their real names.

"What kind of music do you listen to?" He narrowed his eyes as he tried to guess for himself. "I bet it's dark. Moody."

"Oh, no." I shook my head in disgust, "I don't listen to music."

"What?" It was his turn to use my favorite question. He looked at me for far longer than I appreciated while driving well over the speed limit. "C'mon, for real?"

"Yes. Can you watch the damn road?" I pointed out the windshield. "It may be hibernation season, but if we hit a bear, we're fucked!"

"No music at all?"

"Nah, it's all just noise, isn't it?" I shrugged. "Drives my bod-*colleagues* mad that I never play any at work."

Small talk about music was my least favorite kind of mindless chit chat. People couldn't get their heads around the fact that I didn't have a favorite song, band or genre. If anything, the sounds irritated my senses. Danny and I had always listened to music in his car, but my love for it seemed to have died with him.

As we approached my street, I recalled the information I'd found on Logan. I knew he was capable of slaughtering people, and I wondered if I were next… and if he would do it in my home.

It was hard to imagine someone who looked so good and seemed so normal could be capable of creating such horrific crime scenes. But then, I'd seen enough crime documentaries to know better.

The darker, more tired part of my mind decided it didn't really care if I were about to meet my demise.

*Maybe then I can be relieved of everything I'd done.* I sighed as we began the ascent along the winding road.

"Are you okay?" he turned to me, patting my leg before quickly pulling his hand back. He balled it into a fist, as though we'd reached our physical contact quota for the night, and he'd somehow crossed the line.

I sipped my coffee, and instead of telling him my plans to jump out of the moving car to potentially avoid a gruesome death at his hands, I went with, "Yeah, you know that point where you start to sober up and remember how depressing everything is?"

"No, not really. Alcohol doesn't have much of an effect on me."

I raised a brow at his comment.

"I put it down to my size," he added quickly. "It takes more than average for me to start to feel the effects." It would have been a reasonable explanation had I not known what he really was. Alcohol didn't have much of an effect on Gifted. Lucky jerks didn't have to suffer through hangovers like the rest of us.

Logan pulled up on the road, then walked me down the driveway when the high gate moved from our path. He held my hand tight in his after I insisted that I needed it for balance or else I'd kiss the pebbles.

I punched in the code to get in, not caring if he saw; having a stranger enter through this door with me would prompt the bodyguards to reset it once we were inside.

*Still, imagine what your father would say if he ever learns you told a stranger where you live.*

I squared my shoulders and promised myself that if I lived through the night, I would search for my missing sense of self-preservation in the morning.

Turning to Logan, I gave him a look I wouldn't have refused if the roles were reversed.

"Would you like to come in?" I purred.

"No," he said firmly, though the smirk on his face was more suited to my tone than his own. "You're drunk."

*Wow.*

He might have been some insane, aspiring superhero going about everything the wrong way, but he was already more respectful of my ability to consent to anything than Eric had ever been.

I needed to fix this or else our next encounter could be awkward.

I widened my eyes and smiled. "Don't worry, I'm not going to take advantage of you." It cracked what was left of the serious look his features were trying to hold. "I'm serious. Come in, Logan. I'll show you where I work."

"Really?" Curiosity got the better of him, and he stepped inside. "I didn't realize you worked out of your house."

The door clicked into the frame behind us, and he was mine until I unlocked it with the code to leave.

*Or until he kills me and leaves through a broken window. Joke's on him, I guess. Unless he can break through bulletproof glass?*

"Yeah! It's all through there." I nodded toward the internal access door behind him. "Give me a minute?"

I stumbled into my bedroom and through to the wardrobe to kick my shoes off. I tried to line them up neatly on the floor under my hanging clothes, but one kept falling over. Deciding on not having a half-drunken meltdown over the heel's disobedience, I shoved both shoes into an old backpack I'd had stashed away down there since… forever.

Satisfied with having defeated the difficult shoes, I stood and caught a glimpse of myself in the ensuite mirror. Still wearing Logan's jacket, I didn't look as much of a mess as I felt. I took a deep breath, and where it usually cleared my mind and helped me relax, it only made me feel sick.

Knowing it would likely betray me later, I forced my stomach to release its contents into the sink, careful not to get any on the jacket. Though, maybe a bit of vomit would have been an improvement on the pattern.

*I should have done this earlier.*

Already starting to feel steadier on my feet, I rinsed my mouth out with the strongest stuff in my bathroom. Twice.

When I walked out of my room, I made a quick left down the hall, away from Logan as he waited for me. Gifted or not, he'd no doubt heard what happened in there, and being unable to handle my alcohol made me feel weak.

A heavy sigh followed me as I moved further in the opposite direction than I'd promised. The sound of the air leaving his lungs made my eyes roll back with the need to hear it again.

"I'm just grabbing some water!" I called as I made it to the fridge. Two nights of drinking so close together was unlike me, and my stomach was protesting. I hadn't eaten when I woke up, or much at all throughout the days before. All I'd consumed since the late-night sleuthing on my laptop were liquids, too many of those being the drinks at the bar.

As I pulled my head out of the appliance, Logan was standing in the archway to the hall.

"You want one?" I held out a bottle, not confident in my ability to walk it to him without making myself feel worse. He took a few steps toward me, into the kitchen to take it, leaving the hallway behind.

I smiled. He hadn't even wanted to come home with me. He didn't want to be in the house. But now he was as deep into this as I could get him. If I'd been completely sober, would he have come more willingly? Or not at all?

Either way, I still needed to work out how much danger I was in around him, and I'd rather do it here – where my knives were hidden. Of course there were plenty in the unused kitchen, but there was also one under a couch cushion, and others taped to the undersides of the dining and coffee tables.

Too much time alone watching the occasional horror movie, an actual psychopath in my past, and having preppers for parents led to an unhealthy amount of underlying paranoia.

Watching as Logan opened the bottle, I was surprised that in my mental state, I could still make the connections between having traded one cage for another all those years ago, to now potentially trading one killer for another.

*Nah. There's nothing between Logan and I. Flirting and sexting at most. I can't imagine this becoming anything more serious.*

"So, are we going to do this?" he asked, pointing back to the hall, breaking my concentration and bringing my mind back to the kitchen.

I didn't like being ripped out of my head when I was so deeply lost in thought. It made me aware again of how gross I was feeling. That, and I was mildly disappointed he was referring to me showing him where I worked instead of taking him to my bedroom.

Playing up feeling sick a bit more than I actually was, I said, "Just one more minute? I really don't feel okay."

"Maybe you should sit down?" he suggested.

I switched on the lamp beside the window as I stumbled past so the room wasn't in complete darkness, and sat on the largest of two couches, facing away from the kitchen and dining areas and toward the TV that I only used on Sundays.

I rested my back on the left side, sitting over the cushion where the knife was hidden and lifted my hands to my face to steady the room.

"I'm gonna stay here until the room stops spinning, if you'd like to join me?" I called to Logan, who still hadn't moved from beside the dining table.

He made a point of sitting as far away as possible from me on the same piece of furniture, but there was still only two feet between us. I folded my legs on the couch and angled my body to face him, further closing the space.

After a moment of trying to gather my thoughts, he broke the silence first.

"Do you always throw up on first dates?"

I shot him a cold look before my foggy head registered he was teasing me again. Looking down, I played with the zip on his jacket to avoid eye contact, buying a few more seconds to process his question.

*He thought this was a date?*

He had asked me out.

I accepted.

We went somewhere together.

*Oh shit.*

I looked up at him through my lashes and matched his playful tone. "Is that what you call this? A date? I thought we were just grabbing drinks."

He hid his disappointment well, but I was too good at reading people. At least, I was… when not in such a drunken stupor, that is.

That shy smile reappeared. "I guess it doesn't count if you weren't aware it was happening."

*If only that applied to everything in life.* Dark memories flashed in my mind; visions of being tied up in a blood-soaked bed.

"I'll be more direct next time," he promised.

*Next time.* I smiled and looked down at my hands, they were so warm now. The jacket might have been ugly, but I suddenly didn't want to give it back.

"Logan… I don't… date," I admitted.

"At all?"

*More disappointment?*

"Not at all," I answered quietly. "I was with someone for a long time. It ended… *terribly*. I can't imagine ever letting someone get that close to me again."

"Did he cheat on you?" It was a fair assumption, but Eric could barely be bothered with me, let alone chasing other people.

"No. At least, I don't *think* so. We weren't really… together… not by my choice at least." How could my past be put into simple words? Logan gave me the time to arrange my thoughts. "I was actually trying to move on a couple of years ago. Start a new life with the help of a friend of mine. But he caught wind of our plan. I believe he put my best friend in a situation they couldn't escape from… It didn't work out."

Danny was being brought up a lot lately. I needed to accept that I could only hold off being haunted for so long.

*Might as well keep saying the name until he appears like a fucking urban legend.*

"Your ex sounds like a dick." Logan nudged my knee with his.

I laughed at his attempt to lighten the mood, doing my best to ignore those lifeless faces on cold tables that insisted on sitting in the back of my mind.

"Yeah. He was… Is – if he's still around. Thankfully, I've had no contact from him for nearly two years. I feel like I'm starting to have my own life for the first time. Dating hasn't worked its way into that yet." I played with the zip again. The metallic clicking against my nails helped fill the heavy silence.

"Were you young when you got together?"

"*I* was sixteen when I left my family to live with *his*."

"So what, like, high school sweethearts that didn't work out over time?"

"Not exactly." I bit back my smile, unable to suppress the reaction over the thought of what my ex might have been like as a teen. "He was… *much* older. And I didn't actually go to high school."

"Then how'd you get smart enough to become a surgical nurse?" Thankful for the subject change, I looked up at Logan and shrugged. "I dunno. I studied hard. And maybe I'm just smart." I wasn't feeling particularly smart in this moment. A vigilante sitting on my couch, knives under cushions, and coming down from too much booze. "What about you? Do you date often?" I steered the conversation to focus on him.

"Not really, too busy." He sighed, and my eyes involuntarily closed for a beat at the sound.

"Really?" I pried. "What do you get up to other than your late shifts?"

"Fighting crime." His tone indicated he was making a joke, but I knew the truth, so I giggled to hide my suspicions. "I spend a lot of time with my friends," he clarified.

"And… what do they do?"

"Construction," he answered quickly.

"Construction? The whole group?" I snorted. "Even the doll?"

"Doll?"

"Ah, blondie," I elaborated. "Perfect hair. Looks like a doll I would have begged my parents for as a kid."

There were no dolls on the farm. Knives, bows, rifles, sure. But dainty dolls inspiring me to be anything other than the child who would be left with the property once my parents passed? Not a fucking chance.

"Oh. Harrison. She might be small and pretty, but you'd be surprised at what she's capable of."

Internally, I bet that I would be. What kind of name was Harrison? Maybe her surname, if it wasn't fake.

"Well, that explains most of the look of the group, I guess—"

"Are you feeling better?" he interrupted, making me wonder if he actually cared or if he was trying to redirect my thoughts away from what he got up to in his spare time.

"I am." I had another question on my mind and jumped right to it. "Do you have a family?"

He was a man in his thirties, statistically speaking there was a fair chance he'd been married. Maybe he had kids. Though, his car said otherwise and the thought of him being a parent mildly disturbed me. Could Logan really be running around in the night, decimating people and popping skulls before returning home to play the role of loving father?

"Not anymore." His answer was short to mask the sadness in his voice. It gave me a little hope he hadn't killed them, but I wasn't going to push him for more on that yet.

"Favorite food?" I continued. The string of questions felt like a childish game, but I'd never been in a position to do this with anyone, and I'd lost such a large portion of my youth to crime and contracts.

"Hmm…" He narrowed his eyes and shrugged. "That's a tough one. I'll eat just about anything. Maybe pizza. What's yours?"

"Coffee," I answered with a shrug, as if the answer wasn't already obvious.

"That's a *drink*," he argued.

"It comes from *beans*. It counts. Plus, it's all I consume some days, so I need to say it's food or else my body will discover how terribly I treat it."

That got another laugh out of him. Maybe it was the last of the alcohol leaving my system, but the sound made me feel warm. It wasn't maniacal, evil or directed at me with the intention of making me feel powerless. I wanted to keep hearing it.

I checked the clock above the doorway to the hall.

2:15am

*Damn.*

"I should get ready for work."

"Do I have to leave?" he asked, disappointment in his tone again.

*I thought you didn't want to be here in the first place?*

"No, I still haven't shown you around. Here, I won't need this."

Instead of unzipping the jacket, I pulled it over my head. The friction of the fabrics lifted my shirt, no higher than a couple of ribs. Even in the dim light of the living room, a few permanent souvenirs from my time at Home would have been on display.

Logan didn't say anything, but I was sure he would have seen them. I threw the jacket at him excitedly. "Let's go!"

# SIXTEEN

## SUMMER

I tapped in the code for the garage, and the door swung open. I gestured for Logan to enter first, but he was hesitant, so I brushed past confidently.

The room was bright and warm like always. I didn't have much to prepare as I tended to tidy and prep at the end of my previous shift after recording my patient notes.

*Always prepared.* Another positive thing that seemed to hang around from my childhood.

This space was sacred to me. My methods and habits were borderline religious. In complete contrast to my time at Home, *I* was the one who made the rules, and I was in control of who I treated and when.

To bring Logan into this room meant I would have to stop fucking around with his moral compass for the time being and get myself in the right frame of mind. I wasn't about to bring the games and wild theories into my workspace where it could distract me.

As Logan took a few steps in, I held my hand up, signaling for him to stop. He froze, eyeing me with caution.

*Time to start treating him like the person you suspect he is. Just don't let your drunk ass give too much away.*

"If you value your privacy, I suggest you don't take another step."

He tensed and clenched his fists. Understandable, as what I'd said came out like a threat. I pointed to the ceiling and smiled to soften my words.

"Constant surveillance." He looked up to see the camera I was pointing to. "Like I said, I work with all sorts of people. I need to take every precaution I can to stay alive."

He nodded, then grinned. "So, you're happy for me to have never existed here?" I didn't quite know where he was going with that, but it made me a little nervous. Was my simple act enough for him to clue on to why I'd bother to protect his identity?

"I guess. That is the *only* blind spot." I warned him.

From the other side of the room, I kicked the stool on wheels in his direction so he could get comfortable in "his spot."

With only minutes left before the start of my shift, I double checked and straightened the tools on the small table beside the chair, awaiting my first patient for the night.

Logan spun in circles on the stool a few times before the cabinets on the walls caught his attention. They were shallow and backlit to view the contents through the glass doors and stretched from floor to ceiling, covering almost the entire length of the back wall of the room. Each was locked with similar keypads to the other doors in my house, ensuring it was as difficult as possible for people to steal from me.

He was reading the labels on bottles and containers. There'd have to be millions of dollars' worth of drugs in those cabinets. I stocked everything from mild painkillers and antibiotics to things I'd whipped up by special request that could do horrendous internal damage in the wrong hands. Or the right hands. I guessed it depended on whether or not you were on the receiving end of their effects.

"How do you come by all of these?" He pointed to the hundreds, if not thousands of pills and liquids in front of him, no doubt hoisting me up to the top of his hit list as he read what some of them could do.

I laughed. "It's probably best you don't know."

I witnessed his struggle not to argue as he decided between trying to be a regular person who would agree with me and a criminal who'd love that kind of information. Whether he wanted to know to justify killing me or as a resource of his own, I didn't know.

*If I tell him who my supplier is, would they turn up dead? Even if these illegal drugs are used to treat good people? Then how will I care for my patients?*

"Fair enough," he settled on, blinking a couple of times. "So… do you shower in here?" he nodded to the open shower, further down the wall toward the roller doors and backing onto the wall we'd entered through.

I laughed and leaned my hip on the chair, a move that would have earned Ben a glare from me. I was too caught off guard by the question to notice what I'd done. "No. I use it to wash patients."

He scrunched his nose. "You *wash* them?"

I rolled my eyes and listed the reasons people might need to shower under my care. "Chemical spills, large burns, infections…"

"Okay. Makes sense." Logan smiled to himself, and I wondered if he was thinking about me showering. It made me a little self conscious, despite the amount of clothing I wore that left almost *everything* to the imagination.

Both mine and his eyes darted to a movement on the monitors displaying the security feeds, and I began to think those glasses were part of a costume. With what I knew of people like him, *Logan* could very well be the disguise and Vengeance could have been his true identity.

"My bodyguards," I spat quickly, not wanting him to react to feeling cornered.

"You've got… bodyguards?"

"They're here to remove anyone who causes trouble." By the way Logan's eyes narrowed, I believed he got my message, but switched to a lighter tone so he wouldn't get too hung up on my meaning. "With me being so small, it's the smart thing to do."

With a tap of a button on my keyboard, the door lifted to reveal Ben and Tony. They stepped in and the door closed quickly, sealing the four of us in the room together.

"Who the fuck is this?" Ben asked, slipping a hand into his pocket and squaring his shoulders defensively when he spotted Logan. Tony, beside his cousin, folded his arms and glared at the stranger. They'd never walked into the garage and seen me with anyone that they weren't aware was booked in or had been brought to me.

"Calm down," I said with my back to them, checking my table again. "I know you two would have seen him enter the house with me. Meet Logan."

Tony elbowed Ben and gave him one of those looks they only shared between themselves. "Ohhhh," he smiled.

*Fuck. Here we go.*

"The guy with the coffee." Ben nodded, exposing the fact I'd had private conversations with them about Logan between patients over the past few weeks.

*Assholes!*

Those two truly were stand-ins for my brothers. Making jokes at my expense, teasing me and trying to embarrass me whenever they could. It was all in good fun, and some days, I only got out of bed knowing I'd have their company for a few hours in my solitary life.

"Okay guys, time to leave," I said. While I was fine with them teasing me, I still didn't know how much I could trust Logan to have him join this particular circle.

"No, wait, wait," Tony chimed in.

*Ugh. They're going to ruin everything.*

"Logan, she doesn't shut up about the coffee. We have a theory it's code for something else," Tony continued as he rocked on his feet, hands also in his pockets now that he'd relaxed enough to unfold his arms.

*Oh my god.* Much like my brothers, they didn't know when to stop, and at this point, Logan was laughing along with them.

*Great to see he's getting comfortable.*

"Nah, it's just coffee," he timidly reassured them. Then something devilish flashed behind those hazel eyes. "That's all she's let me fill her with so far."

The cousins *loved* that, their roaring laughter ricocheted throughout the enclosed space; more fuel for them to make fun of me later.

*So far?! Does he really think that way about me? Oh, come on, Summer.* I internally argued with myself as I tried to ignore them. *Why else would he send you those pics?*

There'd be no way I'd be letting Logan "fill me" with *anything* if he were suddenly going to be besties with those two.

*Admit it. You kind of want him to.* My eyes dropped to Logan's hands and narrowed in thought, wondering if I'd picked the right sized vibrator. Tony, elbowing my ribs, snapped me out of my focus.

"Get out!" I growled at them, trying to pinpoint the moment where I was suddenly left on the outside of this new comedy trio forming right before my eyes.

"Really?" Tony stopped laughing enough to talk again, ignoring my demands and continuing his discussion with my guest. "We've seen the photos, man. We were hoping she'd have jumped on that by now. It'd put her in a better mood."

More laughter as I rubbed my brow and bit my lip to suppress the smile trying to break through.

The bodyguards took it as their cue to shut up. They immediately stopped poking fun and raised their hands as they often did when they realized they were pushing my boundaries.

"We brought you food," Ben said, holding out a paper bag like a peace offering that I snatched from his hand, his arm extended as though he feared what I would do to the limb if he got too close.

"Thank you. Now, go."

They turned and ducked under the door as it lifted. It was just after two-thirty, and they had someone to pick up and bring back by three-fifteen. As the door rolled down, their laughter picked up again, and I couldn't contain my smile. It was an infectious sound, even when it was aimed at me.

Logan began to roll my way.

"Stay in your corner." I snipped, annoyed at him for getting along too well with *my* staff. It was also a reminder he'd be exposed if he moved any closer.

"I was only playing along with them." He grinned and turned back to the cupboards. "They seem like great guys… but I wouldn't want to get on their bad side."

He had a point, and it annoyed me more. The best way to make friends with those two was through humor. He'd done well and was clearly more fun to be around than me.

"So, Summer… you talk about me?" He had a dumb smirk on his face. It was annoyingly cute. Logan was enjoying himself too much. I tried not to smile back, not wanting to give him the satisfaction of an answer.

Unfortunately for me, that was just as bad as straight-up confirmation I'd mentioned him more than a few times.

"I keep them… *informed.* About everything, really. So they know what I'm up to in case I show up dead." I held his gaze for a few seconds before reaching into the bag I'd taken from Ben.

My head hurt, feeling like I'd already endured a whole day and still had a full night's work ahead of me. I ate, offering Logan some of the food, but he refused, saying I "clearly needed it more" after being sick earlier. I didn't fight him on it. I hardly ate as it was, and whatever Ben brought for me was too good to share.

While I never questioned the bodyguards about their personal lives, I was sure neither of them could be responsible for all the amazing flavors that kept me alive between coffee stops, unable to imagine them cooking.

A few minutes before the cousins were due back with my first patient of the night, Logan was still trying to get back on my good side from across the room.

"So… no dirty jokes, huh?"

I sighed and slumped in my desk chair, done with eating and feeling a little better for adding food to the poison I'd consumed earlier.

"Jokes are fine. Great, even. I'm not, like, a prude. I have older brothers. My poor Christian parents were oblivious to the things they talked about in front of me." That, and all the men I'd hung around at Home weren't angels. I learned plenty of things from my conversations with them that I'd acted out to keep the boss content. "I dunno. I guess my sex life is enough of a joke as it is without purposefully making fun of it." I let out a small laugh at how pathetic I was.

"Hits a nerve?"

"Hits *all* the nerves." A joke of my own. There was so much nerve and tissue damage on my back from Eric's many masterpieces.

"Noted." Logan didn't sound bothered by my inability to laugh at myself as he spun back to the shelves to continue examining the bottles. I wondered if he understood the notes on them. He hadn't asked about a single one.

I'd never been so thankful for the bodyguards to arrive again, breaking the silence. They guided a regular patient of mine in before leaving me to my work, knowing I was completely safe with this man.

"Who's this?" my patient asked cautiously, nodding to Logan as I helped him into the chair. At least he hadn't sworn like Ben, not that my own language was that of a princess, but I tried to tone it down while around my patients.

"My apprentice."

He gave me a disbelieving look. I'd known this man for a while now, enough for him to sense when I was lying. Brian and I met at Crave when his daughter came to me for help at my table outside. She had sprained her ankle, cutting her night of clubbing short. I'd waited with her on the curb for her father to arrive, ensuring she safely got out of the dingy industrial area.

Brian was thankful I'd kept an eye on his daughter, unhappy with her for being out in such a shady part of town. He and I talked for a little while, and I learned he had just been diagnosed with cancer, having to pass his carpentry business onto his sons prematurely as the diagnosis was looking grim.

His family had helped me fix up my house when I'd bought it. We traded renovations for me arranging for him to see one of my contacts who could provide him with chemo, off the books.

His family was more than happy to exchange their work on my house for healthcare if it meant they could receive the treatment he needed without going into extreme debt from medical bills they'd never have a hope of paying off.

Once my house was completed, I still paid them generously. While I'd only wanted his family to be financially stable as he recovered, it had bought their loyalty; a common theme amongst many of the people I worked with.

It made me wonder how much thought Logan — *Vengeance* — put into people's individual situations before deeming them worthy of death.

"Fine. He's my date. Apparently." I gave Brian a wink.

"He's not good enough for you." He smiled as I wiped the inside of his elbow with isopropyl alcohol, taking a deep breath to inhale the scent.

I giggled. "You don't even know him."

It was funny how I picked up people along the way in life who filled the roles I desperately needed around me. Brian was acting like a disapproving father.

"I don't care, no one's good enough for you."

I smiled and took his blood. Dad would have no doubt said something similar.

"I can hear you both," Logan piped up from his place in the corner.

"Good." My patient laughed as I labeled the vials.

Brian hadn't been in remission for long, and I had him seeing me regularly. He might have been worthy of Vengeance's hit list for coming to me for illegal treatment, but to me, he was a precious gem worth protecting.

When we were done, he tried to offer me money, and I refused, just as we did every time he visited. I sent him out the door with Ben to be safely taken back to his family.

3:30am

We'd reached the time of night where things always took a turn. Much like when there was a full moon, there seemed to be a time where things got wilder than normal for no apparent reason.

Another known patient of mine arrived; Ross. Not in need of help for himself but for his brother. I didn't appreciate people bringing strangers to my house without being told prior, and I knew from the moment they walked in that this man was going to cause trouble.

While I was excellent at appearing calm, jobs like this still scared me to some degree. I was only human, and smaller than almost all of the people who walked through my doors. I looked over to Logan and mouthed "blind spot," needing him to know I didn't want him to get involved when this inevitably turned ugly.

Logan nodded, face stoic as he observed the man's behavior.

I turned back to my unexpected invalid, Alan. Late forties. A little on the larger side, unlike the stickfigure his brother resembled. He was already in an erratic state, shouting and swearing from the pain inflicted by a large cut down his back.

Apparently, he'd mouthed off at someone while drunk, and when he turned away, he was slashed with a broken bottle. It was one of the most believable stories I'd ever heard in my workspace, seeming exactly like something he would do, considering the names he was calling me before I'd even started working on him.

If I wanted or needed to, I could refuse to help the patients. The bodyguards would be thrilled to ensure he was properly *taken care of.* But something never sat well with leaving anyone to suffer if I could help them. I'd always experienced a deeper calling to heal, regardless of how I was treated or how much money I could be offered to hurt someone.

Logan kept his eyes on me, probably looking for any sign I couldn't handle someone like this.

With the help of his brother, I managed to get Alan to sit on the chair with his legs hanging over the side, facing the garage doors and away from me.

My *date* would see everything from this angle. I was glad he could see, I wasn't nervous or self conscious about my skills. I was *the best*.

I'd been shown off and lent out to the world's most notorious villains, those willing to pay the right price, and I never disappointed.

With a pair of scissors, I removed Alan's shirt, starting yet another argument about me damaging it; as if the *giant* cut in the fabric from the bottle was of absolutely no concern to him.

I took a deep breath to clear my head of the nonsense he was spouting and set to work, poking him several times with local anesthetic. I was no stranger to how much that stung, but I didn't feel bad for any discomfort it caused him. He was being a dick and would be numb soon anyway.

Once his pain subsided, he was a little more bearable and the name calling died down, only throwing a "stupid bitch" and "dumb slut" at me every now and then. The words slipped off my scarred skin. I had a different, tattooed name that haunted me when I was alone. Plus, I was a far fit from either of those descriptors.

After cleaning the wound, I ensured there were no glass fragments hiding in his open flesh that would cause him trouble later. I'd be happy to never see this man again, and needed to be thorough.

I tied my first stitch at the top of his shoulder blade to the right of his spine. My hands moved quickly, fingers gently guiding the needle under and over the skin.

When I was younger, I liked to pretend I was a spider, spinning a web across the large pieces of dead pigs. I used to hold my work high above my head, proudly showing it off to my father while he tied ropes in the pine canopies, setting traps.

Before long, I was done.

Forty stitches in about thirty-three seconds. Well, forty-three, counting the extras I added to tag him. It wasn't a bad job, but I think the alcohol had slowed me down a little.

I unlocked one of the cabinets and retrieved a small bottle of antibiotics and another of painkillers.

Despite what I had done for him, Alan argued he wanted stronger pain relief. But I didn't cave. When people started talking like that, I needed to assume they'd abuse the meds and would be back for more, knowing I stocked the good stuff.

Ross was kind enough to thank me before leaving and paid for my work. They were ushered down the driveway by Tony, who would no doubt have words with him about bringing strangers in without giving us a heads up first.

I turned to Logan. "Hopefully, that's all for tonight," I said as I washed blood off my hands at a small sink by the shower.

"We're not going to talk about *that?*"

His tone made me brace for the lecture on working with dangerous people. It was one of the leading reasons I didn't care or make time for men in my life. The last thing I needed was someone breathing down my neck, telling me I couldn't do my work the way I wanted. I wasn't stupid, I knew the risks.

"Talk about *what?*"

"That was unbelievable!" It was my turn to tip my head to the side in confusion as he continued, "I've never seen anyone get stitched up that fast."

"Well… I'm pretty good at what I do."

"I'll say. Wait, you're not secretly one of those superheroes? Are you… Gifted?"

I snorted at how far it was from the truth, especially since I'd spent all night trying to get him to confess that *he* was Gifted.

"Nah, didn't think so." He laughed, though he looked a little disappointed again. "You're way too cool to be one of those losers."

That was something I could agree with. I hated the idea of superheroes. For the most part, the Gifted had proven to be all show and no substance.

While I didn't think villains and vigilantes were much better, there was something about the Gifted who were treated like Gods that made my eyes roll so far into the back of my head I'd hoped they'd get stuck. I didn't want to see another news article about how *wonderful* they were.

They created more chaos and caused more deaths than most in the underworld combined, and everyone turned a blind eye because "they're amazing" and "they tried." I'd patched many people up from the disasters they'd caused during my time in Bedlam. Big cities seemed to draw out more of the strange characters. Thankfully, I hadn't come across too many since moving back to the mountain state. Just a few at Crave, and now my *date*.

No other patients showed for the night, and I was grateful for the break; my head was pounding from not having enough water after all those drinks.

We said goodbye to the bodyguards as their shift ended. And feeling relatively safe to be alone with Logan again, I turned the camera off in the garage so he could freely move about the room.

I unlocked the cabinets containing the more interesting drugs, and let him help himself to pull them out to read the fine print on the labels. Though, I kept a close eye on him to make sure he didn't pocket anything while he thought I wasn't looking.

Each bottle had all the information you'd find if it were bought from a pharmacy, but also another, printed sticker. My notes. What they could and couldn't be mixed with to avoid nasty side effects, what to mix them with to inflict pain to extract information, and how much would cause an overdose.

We'd used the same method back at Home, only we also included which drugs had the reverse effect for overdose. I believed I'd once had that information used against me. In one of my attempts to escape, I'd taken a bunch of pills and hadn't planned on waking up.

*But here I am.*

"This one seems pretty intense," Logan stated, reading the notes of one small bottle filled with a clear liquid. "What would you use this for?"

I removed it from his warm hand to read the label for myself. My eyes darted to his, and I gnawed my lip when I realized what it was.

"It helps with… *extracting* information."

"What? Do you torture people or something?" His tone was serious, but he couldn't hide the flicker of excitement in his eyes. I didn't want him to think I was anything like the monster he was meant to be. And if I was, wouldn't he use that as an excuse to kill *me*? That didn't seem fair.

"I've… done what I've had to… to stay alive," I explained with a sad smile. "Not everything has been as ethical as I care to admit."

I hoped he wouldn't read too much into that. I'd wanted to avoid using my ex's money, and had done some pretty dodgy shit to quickly earn a decent amount of cash after settling out this way. Those millions still sat mostly untouched, waiting to be spent on whatever I desired. But it was tainted with death, and I was certain the account was being closely watched.

"I think you're kind of amazing, Summer," Logan said softly as he took the bottle back and returned it to the shelf.

"Only *kind of?*" I teased. He smiled and turned back to the cupboard.

While he busied himself with reading, I sat at my computer and recorded a video, as I did at the end of each shift. A quick recount of who I'd treated and how. Writing all of those details was exhausting and tedious. Saying it aloud helped me remember each part of the night as I talked through the steps.

"Captain's log?" Logan joked when I finished.

"Yep." I giggled as I switched everything off and spun in my chair to face him. "Time for bed."

"So… my cue to leave?" He gave me a look I interpreted as *"I'll stay if you ask me to"* and my stomach knotted in response. I didn't know what it was about him, but I found myself *liking* Logan enough to not throw the weeks of becoming acquainted away on one night of sex.

*It's probably just the coffee.*

"Yeah." I said, surprised at the disappointment in my voice. I walked him to the front door through the hall, unlocking it with the code before he slipped past me, free of the trap I'd set for him.

"That was a long night. No wonder you're in such a mood before coffee," he said, forcing another giggle from me as he turned back at the doorway.

He leaned to one side of the frame with his arms folded. Even with the sleeves of his jacket being loose and not giving me much to look at, I could use my imagination. I'd seen enough of those limbs as I watched him work to memorize every inch.

*Focus for a few more seconds. You can think about that when you're in bed.*

"Well, thank you for ensuring I got home safe—" I flinched, startled by his sudden movement.

My hand was instantly on his chest; my open palm pressed hard below his neck to keep the space between us. He seemed impressed at my speed before his expression sobered.

My breathing sped up, my chest heaving as panic set in. My stance and wide eyes were both too telling as to why a person would react in such a way, to something as simple as a kiss.

*You're damaged goods. A guy can't even try to kiss you without you freaking out.* I took a deep breath to settle my nerves. And then another, focusing on his thumping pulse beneath my fingers.

"I'm sorry, Summer. I should have asked," Logan frowned, shaking his head at himself.

He slowly reached for my hand, pulled it away from his warm body, and lowered it to my side. My breathing slowed, and the familiar heat returned to my skin, only this time it was from feeling stupid for overreacting.

*Maybe I am safe with him. It's still too early to tell.*

My therapist's words came to mind as we stood there silently, eyes still locked. "You deserve to get better and not be defined by your past relationships as you move on with your new life."

*Is this really any better? From supervillain to murderous vigilante?*

I stepped closer, up on my toes, and tipped my face to kiss him. Logan instantly leaned down to close the gap from our height difference. His lips were soft and warm, a stark contrast to what I'd known for years.

With his mouth on mine, his hands brushed down my arms before moving under them, around my waist and on my back to pull me closer. It was a normal move in anyone's eyes, but I could *not* be touched there.

Breaking off the kiss, I stepped back into the safety of my house, gently shaking my head at him.

"I need to get to sleep," I finally said, suddenly unable to hold my usual eye contact.

"Well, goodnight, nurse." He bit his lip to suppress the wide smile creeping across his features, and I could barely stop mine from doing the same over the way he'd called me *nurse*. He turned to walk away.

The sun was rising, lighting up the front yard with a few thin rays as they crept over the high hedges.

When he was halfway to the street, Logan spun and called to me.

"If you ask me, that turned out to be a great first date. Even with you vomiting halfway through. Will I see you tonight?"

I rolled my eyes and nodded as I shut the door.

After double-checking the house and garages were locked, I collapsed on my bed, crashing too fast from the adrenaline-inducing kiss leaving my system to bother with showering.

As I drifted off, an annoying thought crept into my mind.

*I've revealed so much in one night… and learned absolutely nothing about him.*

# SEVENTEEN

## SUMMER

### JANUARY 14TH

I'd never been as excited for therapy as I was on Tuesday night.

I slept well. Deeply, for a change. And dreamed of Logan — mostly about his arms and the way he'd tried to hold me close as he kissed me. I woke up in a particularly good mood. So much so that I texted "Good morning" to the bodyguards. They promptly messaged back, asking if I'd been abducted or if it was a coded call for help.

Dr. Lindsey instantly noticed the change in my demeanor. "Coffee with the friend was exactly what you needed?" she probed, opening her notebook.

I nodded, trying to wipe the stupid smile from my face as I wriggled to get comfortable in the chair.

"Was it more than coffee?" That question was a bit *too* probe-y.

"It was… a really good night," I confessed, ignoring my final thoughts before slipping into unconsciousness in the early hours of the morning.

*When was the last time I felt like this? Have I ever felt like this?* I wanted to enjoy the buzz while it lasted.

With a small nod and seeming to extract the question directly from my head, she asked, "Have you ever felt like this about anyone before?"

I almost said "No," but then, another man came to mind.

My chest released a staggered breath, the air immediately sucked from my lungs. I couldn't refill them.

Such a simple, innocent question had shattered my calm, taking all the good from the previous night with it.

The abrupt change to my posture and breathing shocked the kind doctor. "I'm sorry, Katie —" she started, but my mind was no longer in the room to hear what else she'd said. Her voice was distant, rapidly moving further away from me.

*Oh, God. Please, not now.* I pleaded with the room not to fade, for the couch to hold me and not reveal where my mind threatened to take me.

*Not the boys*, I begged my fading vision to spare me the sight of a recurring dream; one brother, covered in blood, the others screaming at me. But my panic attacks didn't make deals.

I was ripped from the couch and thrown into the depths of my subconscious, to a place that had been locked away for years. My last day with Eric.

I covered my eyes with my hands, hunching over where the couch should have been, trying to keep the ghosts out of view as they appeared around me. I cried for air, suffocating with the guilt of being unable to save their lives. The deceased were always so ravenous for the oxygen in my body, desperate for it to fill their own.

My hands dropped to the cushion below, gripping it tight as I tried to breathe. When I opened my eyes, I was back at Home.

The smell of our ER was comforting. Clean and sterile. If stainless steel had a smell, I would have turned it into perfume and filled all of Home with the fragrance.

Being a perfectionist, I spent too much time laying out my tools, lining them up in the order of how I believed we would need them for an incoming emergency.

It wasn't clear who our next patients were, but I was certain I knew.

I felt so calm.

*This is just a memory. A vision? You were a fucking wreck before they'd even been wheeled in. If you were this calm, you might've had a chance at saving them.*

Everything felt off, blurry around the edges as the scene played out. Each time I tried to focus on something specific in the room, it would warp and disappear, fading into darkness.

There was a sound. The ambulances pulled up outside, and the doors of the ER instantly burst open. Two stretchers were wheeled in, but I couldn't see who was on them.

My mind jumped ahead, unable to relive the horror unfolding in front of me.

"Dead on arrival," someone announced behind me as I stood in the center of the room. I couldn't tell where the voice came from, but they had decided my best friend was beyond repair without even allowing me to do everything in my power to bring him back.

I looked at my hands. They were covered in blood.

*Whose?*

It wasn't just on my hands; it was on my face. My clothes. The fabric was saturated and sticking to my skin.

It was everywhere. It poured down the sides of the metal tables. I was standing in a pool of it. *Their* blood. The shoes I'd worn for my workout in the gym were soaked, deep red.

Pulled by an invisible force, I was shoved over to the second table and instantly climbed up. My knees rested in the warm liquid beside a body as I frantically started chest compressions.

*Surely, I could save one of them?*

I stopped breathing, and I wasn't allowing myself any oxygen until the body under my hands took some for themselves.

Pulled forward in time again, I became dizzy with the sensation. My head spun as I tried to fill in the missing pieces.

Suddenly, I was screaming at Eric the moment he entered the room and threw a scalpel, slicing the side of his face.

And then it all went black.

My body sluggishly rolled over. The unusually heavy feeling in my arms prompted me to wake up. I hurriedly searched for my phone in the dark. It was plugged in to charge on the bedside table. I tapped the screen to see the time, but it was too bright to look at, the light made me squint as I tried to read the blurred numbers.

"It's about three in the morning," a familiar voice informed me.

*3am? I missed gym, and work, and... Oh no, coffee!*

I dropped my phone back to the table and searched the room for the voice. The only light source was the dim glow from the TV on my dresser, beside the door for the walk-in and ensuite. As my eyes narrowed at the screen, I tried to make sense of what it was playing.

*Infomercials? Was I watching something and fell asleep?* I couldn't remember how I'd gotten to bed and cautiously sat up to look at the other side for clues.

I screamed when a hulking mass reached out and grabbed my arm.

The voice laughed. "I know, I know. Not the man you were hoping for."

"God, you gave me a *fucking* heart attack!" I hissed, slapping the arm before throwing myself angrily onto my back.

"I gave *you* a heart attack?" Tony snorted. He was the more dramatic of the two bodyguards when it came to scolding me for my actions. I immediately knew by his tone I was in for one of his signature lectures.

Ben never dared speaking to me this way, and sometimes, it made me worry I'd hired someone too soft for the job.

"You know that girl I was telling you and Ben about," he started, lying beside me in the dark. "The one with the *huge...*" He cupped his hands at his chest.

I rolled my eyes, hoping he could see my expression. He was dramatic *and* descriptive.

"Uh-huh." With my face in my hands, I hoped that if I tried hard enough, I could go back to reliving nightmares and not have to listen to this week's episode of *Tony's Sexual Conquests* — a show I was graced with literally on a weekly basis.

"I finally... *finally,*" he emphasized, throwing his arms in the air before letting them fall to our sides. "*This* deep in her." — more hand and body actions, in case I wasn't already aware of what he was implying.

I pulled my pillow over my head. He paused.

"Are you done?" I asked, voice muffled.

"When I get a phone call," he ignored me, continuing with his story, "from a number you *specifically* stated was, under *no* circumstances, to be ignored. I was *under* one of the best circumstances I've had all year. I had to throw her off to answer the call, informed that the boss was out. Unresponsive." He'd quickly flipped from joker to stressed. "When I got there, your therapist was threatening to call an ambulance. For *you,* boss. You've made it clear how much of a complete and absolute *no* that is."

I removed my pillow and rolled over to throw my arm across his chest, hugging him. I could barely see him in the dark, but I'd known Tony long enough to sense he'd experienced one of those times where he was truly earning his pay.

"I'm flattered I'm your number one emergency contact for therapy. But I'd rather deal with the more frequent calls like the ones Ben gets."

"I'm sorry," I whispered. "Who the fuck sedated me?"

His gulp was audible. "I did. On the drive home. You wouldn't stop screaming about blood."

"You're either a very good employee or very fucking stupid."

He rolled on his side to face me, propping his head up with his hand. I wriggled back a bit and returned my head to my pillow. We were friendly, but not *so* friendly we felt the need to be up in each other's faces in bed.

"While you plan my severance…" He huffed. "wanna tell me what happened?"

"It was like a complete… *break*. I was back at Home. I saw… *everything* from that last day all over again."

Ben and Tony had nothing to do with my life in Bedlam, and were the only people not in that emergency room who I'd told of those events.

"Is everything taken care of?" I asked, remembering the patients I was meant to see during the shift I'd missed.

"Of course it is." He waved his hand as if the damage control was a piece of cake. "Ben contacted the bookings to reschedule and I sent out the texts that we were closed."

"Thank you."

"Oh, and Ben swung by Logan's work to let him know you wouldn't make it tonight, so he wouldn't come looking for you when you didn't show."

"Ugh." I pulled the pillow back over my face. "Do you think he was nice to him?" I asked from the place I was planning to spend the rest of the day, drowning in my pool of embarrassment.

"Yeah, I reckon he would've been. The guy left a good impression. Is it serious between you two?"

When I didn't answer, he lifted the pillow to peek at me.

"It can't be," I answered.

"Don't be like that. You've come pretty far in two years. There's still hope for you yet."

"Yeah, maybe *one day*." I wanted the attention off me. "You know it's only January, right?"

"What's that got to do with anything?"

"I'm sure you'll be *under* plenty more circumstances before the year is out."

He laughed. "Yeah, you're right. I've already got someone else lined up for tonight. Unless you plan on having another meltdown? Maybe I should keep my clothes on this time. I wasted a good minute trying to find my shirt after your therapist called."

"Oh my God, will you stop?" I pleaded.

"Why? You don't want to hear all the details of the night you ruined?" he teased. "Maybe you'd rather hear about the blender I just ordered."

"What?" My eyes darted to the TV. "Tell me you're not ordering dumb shit off the TV again?"

"What the fuck else am I meant to do while I wait for you to sleep off your meds. *Or pills. And booze*."

I glared at him, equally pissed with having my own habits made fun of.

He grinned. "It comes with a set of knives. You want them?"

I huffed, "*Everything* you order comes with knives! What am I meant to do with *more* knives? I don't think I even own proper cutlery. I only have drawers. Full. Of. Knives!"

"Well, you're the prepper. You've always said you can never have too many. And I've seen how good you throw them." He shrugged as he rolled off the mattress to stand, leaving me alone in my bed.

"I'll throw them at *you* if you keep wasting your wage on stupid shit."

"You'd know more about the other things I spend it on if you ever let us talk about what we do outside of work," he chided, moving for the hallway.

"Tony?" I called as he reached the door. "I kissed Logan."

"*Seriously?*"

"Yeah." I giggled, unable to hide my excitement.

The bodyguards were aware I would occasionally take someone up to the rooms at Crave for *much more* than kissing, but bringing someone to my house and planning on seeing them more than once was something I hadn't done with anyone before.

"Want us to look into him for you?"

"Nah, I've got it covered." I rolled over to sleep off the rest of whatever I'd been sedated with.

"I'll be on the couch if you need me."

He'd be my babysitter until he deemed me fit to be alone again.

# EIGHTEEN

SUMMER

## JANUARY 15TH

Night rolled around again, and this time, I was dreading therapy. Dr. Lindsey had given Tony strict instructions to return me the following day at my normal time.

*I'm going to get fucking committed. Again.*

Sitting on the couch with my head down as if I'd done something wrong, I wasn't at all feeling in the mood for talking. But I didn't have another option. I needed to keep this up and get through the trauma of Home if I was going to try to live a normal life.

Dr. Lindsey started off by apologizing, ensuring I was okay, blah, blah, blah. I drifted in and out for a bit, still a little groggy despite having slept through most of the day until Tony woke me up to feed me. I hadn't wanted to eat, but he bargained with me; I could drive myself to therapy and then to the gym before stopping for coffee, unescorted, if I cleared my plate of whatever he'd brought for me. I agreed and earned my freedom.

*Freedom*, I scoffed at the notion. *I may be free in a sense, but they track my car.*

"So… I think we've come to a point where we can't make any further progress unless we speak about Danny." She grimaced.

That smacked me right back into the present.

"How about Eric?" I offered snidely. "Still *plenty* to talk about there. We haven't touched on my initiation into the cult yet." I wagged my eyebrows, tempting her with disturbing stories I was sure she'd love to dissect.

"I understand this is very difficult for you. If you answer me one simple question about Danny, we will leave it at that for now and move back to Eric. Can you do that for me?"

Nodding once, I hoped the question would have a short answer, and that I didn't need to go into any detail.

"Your relationship with Danny. Overall, was it good or bad?"

"Good."

*Thank God.* A simple answer I could give without an ounce of hesitation. No one-way ticket to Sedation Station.

"Back to Eric then. In one of your previous visits, you mentioned you met him at a… convention?" She flipped through her notes before she looked up at me, eyes peering over the many pages she was accumulating on my past with just a few visits. "Would you like to tell me more?"

"Sure," I lied and began unenthusiastically telling the story. "It was a small event. Held in a town hall a few hours away from the family home. These people aren't known for trips to the big city. Almost everyone attending stayed in local motels within walking distance…"

"Did you meet him in the hall?" she pushed when I trailed off.

"No. Umm. I actually, *literally*, ran into him outside our motel room. He appeared disoriented when he bumped into me. He was seeking medical help. But it was all a lie." I started picking at one of my thumbnails, feeling stupid all over again to have fallen for it. It added to my bad mood.

"He was injured?"

"Yes, a deep gash on his forearm. Self-inflicted."

She bobbed her head as she took more notes. "So he sought you out after hearing your father talk about your skills. Do you believe this was his way of putting those skills to the test?"

"Absolutely. Once I'd apologized for bumping into him, he explained he was on the way to the motel office for first aid. I…" God, I felt stupid admitting it. "Offered to help. The cut was clean and simple to work with. I told him I was also attending the convention and could fix him up in no time."

It was mostly the truth. Eric and I had literally run into each other. Only we hadn't rushed into the exchange where I offered to stitch him up. He was frozen with shock, staring at my features in awe and swallowing hard before regaining enough composure to speak. Even then, it was a broken mix of English and a language I'd never heard before.

That particular part of the memory always stood out in my mind. No one had ever looked at me that way. It was a type of attention I'd never received. And I liked it.

"How did he respond to your offer?"

"Very eager. I assumed it was because he was hurt and wanted to get it fixed quickly." I thought back to the pain on his features as he emerged from the fixation on my face and held his heavily tattooed arm out for me to inspect.

"Then, what happened?" She pulled me back from my thoughts of the rest of Eric's ink, the hundreds of tattoos hidden beneath his clothes.

"He led me to his room. Told me he had a first-aid kit there, but didn't know how to stitch himself up on his own. All the high-quality equipment was there in preparation for me… inevitably stupid enough to go with him." I sneered as my body sunk into the chair, tired of how dumb I felt as I brought up these events.

"Remember, what happened as a result of this is not your fault. You were a child. A young girl, kind enough to help a stranger." Dr. Lindsey's voice was firm.

I nodded and continued, "Once we were in his room, I stitched him up. It was quick. Not as quick as I can do today, but he was impressed."

The feelings of pride in my work and disgust at my naivety swirled in my stomach.

"Do you need a moment?" she asked, treating me with caution after our previous session took such a sharp nosedive.

"I'm okay. Nothing happened then," I hurriedly explained. "It wasn't like *that*, not until later."

"Breathe for a moment."

After a few motions I continued, "I left after that. But then I kept seeing him over the next few days to check on the wound, redress it. The night before we left, I made one more check as we wouldn't be seeing each other again."

*Or so I thought.*

Eric never had any intention of letting me go so easily.

"He and I spent hours in his room, just… talking. He asked a lot about *me* and what life was like with my parents and brothers. He asked me what I wanted to do with myself. I told him I wanted to be a nurse, but he said I could do so much better."

The memories of all the compliments and praise to lure me in swarmed my mind. Those were the foundations of our relationship, but they quickly turned to Eric depriving me of more than my parents ever could on our isolated property.

"That's when he told me he owned a major company in Bedlam and asked if I would ever consider leaving this state behind. To go pursue my dreams. With him."

"In Bedlam?"

*Fuck.* I hadn't mentioned the city to her before. "Yeah. A lie, to a degree. There were businesses attached to the cult."

"What did you say to his offer?"

I exhaled a sharp laugh, "I told him I was desperate to get out of this place. That my future had been decided for me and I fucking hated it. It wasn't much of a life to look forward to. I couldn't even go to be a nurse in a hospital somewhere. The most I'd end up doing would be patching up the community's cuts and scrapes. I wanted adventure and my own money. My own name."

*I got all of that. Maybe I should have been more careful about what I wished for.*

"He promised I could have all of those things, and more, with him. He told me he *needed* me, and I would be doing great things, helping people."

"What happened then?"

"I got… drunk. That night… in his room. I didn't mean to. We were up so late talking and he offered me alcohol. I took it. My dad and brothers weren't missing me. It was the last night of the event, and everyone would have been out late to celebrate, knowing they wouldn't see each other again for a while."

My parents were *so* strict. I may have only been sixteen at the time, but I was already aware of the things I was missing out on in the real world and took the first opportunity that came my way to have any normal experiences.

Dr Lindsey sat quietly to not disturb my momentum.

"We kissed. It felt…" I wanted to say *wrong*, but the attention I received from Eric was just *something else*, so I confessed and said, "Good. A few hours later, I woke up on his bed and realized how late it was and left to get back to my room."

"You woke up on the bed? Had anything happened there?" I knew where she was going with this.

"I… *think so*. I'm not perfectly sure." I grabbed at my fingers and cracked my knuckles, distracting myself from the words as they tumbled from my mouth. The blurred memories of my first kiss. Eric's lips on mine. Being pulled onto his lap. Replacing clothes. But nothing distinct in-between. "I felt… odd. But I thought it might have been from the alcohol."

She took more notes. *She'll have enough for a fucking book at this rate.*

"Then?"

"Then… I saw him in the morning as we were leaving. We exchanged numbers and he said he would send for me within the week. I *wanted* to go with him – to Bedlam. Between the affection and the promises and him seeing my potential… I told Eric I would wait for his instructions to leave."

"But your family caught on?" she recalled from the times I'd mentioned the argument between my parents and I.

I rolled my eyes. "Yes. My eldest brother, James." I loved him the most, but he was raised to be fiercely protective of his younger siblings. I couldn't so much as breathe in the wrong direction without him eyeing me.

"He saw Eric and I talking and claimed to have… *heard us*… in Eric's room together. He must have brought it to my parents' attention a few days after we got home. I was texting Eric back and forth on the family mobile that I'd snuck out of their room and they… read everything. They interrogated me, as parents of teens try to, anyway. I turned it into an argument about me wanting to go study in the city when I turned eighteen."

"How did they take that news?"

"As awful as expected. That night was… one of the worst. I told Mom I wanted to be nothing like her. That she was weak for letting Dad call all the shots for the house, farm, what us kids could and couldn't do." I wiped at a few stray tears. "I told her I wanted a life I could be proud of, without stopping for a second to consider the fact she was perfectly happy and proud of who she was."

"That was the last night you saw them, wasn't it?"

"Yes. I have bits in my memory missing. I remember packing my bag, but I don't remember leaving. It was all very chaotic. I somehow got to the hotel that Eric had arranged to meet me at, but there was a fire."

"A fire?" She frowned with surprise by the dramatic turn of events.

"Yeah, something faulty in the building. The whole thing went up."

"How did you escape?"

"That's another missing piece. All I know is Eric was there and he risked his life to get me out. Next thing I knew, I was at a different hotel with him, halfway to the city. He saved me. I felt such a strong sense of… *owing,* I guess. So when he made his advances, I didn't stop him."

I couldn't refuse even if I'd wanted to. When I woke up, I asked Eric if I could call my parents. He'd told me they'd already made contact with him through the number I'd left in their phone and explained that he'd sent them photos of me, asleep in his bed, to prove I was safe. They hadn't taken it well, and I couldn't blame them for their reaction. My singed clothes had been removed, and I found myself naked beneath the sheets.

They'd told him they were done with me. That I was an embarrassment to the family and my actions were unforgivable. I was Eric's problem now.

"On this occasion… do you believe it may have perhaps been…" she paused, but continued when I frowned, not understanding where she was going, "Rape?"

"*Rape?* No! We had sex."

"Katie." The firm voice had returned. "You were *sixteen*, he was twenty-seven. You were taken from your family and felt you *owed* him. There's *nothing* balanced in that relationship."

*Shit.*

"We…" I started to argue, but settled for throwing my hands up, letting them fall back to my sides on the couch with a defeated *thud.* "Yes. Fine."

She granted me a pause to let that sink in. "I know it's hard to admit, but you did it." Her voice sounded proud as I looked up at the ceiling, like we'd made some amazing breakthrough. I didn't feel like I had. I just felt fucking raw.

"Now," she said, "care to talk about something that makes you feel good?"

"Sure." I folded my arms and slouched further down into the couch, feeling like I'd been mentally violated and absolutely nothing would make me feel okay.

"Want to talk about Danny?"

I narrowed my eyes at her.

*What a sneaky bitch.*

# NINETEEN

## SUMMER

This session had already felt long enough, but thanks to Dr. Lindsey and Tony conspiring behind my back, I was booked in for a double.

I made a mental note to pop one of Tony's tires or cut his brakes when he arrived for the night's shift, but quickly settled for texting him a single emoji of a middle finger. He promptly replied with a winking face blowing kisses.

After everything I'd exposed, talking about my best friend actually seemed like a nice idea. We had many good years before it all ended horrifically.

"How did you meet Danny?" She smiled as she pushed her glasses up, always sliding down from referring to the pages of notes in her lap. Her tone set the mood for this discussion as light and happy. I went along with it while I could.

"Through work in the cult, actually." I grinned at the memory, and began recounting our time together. Though, for the therapist, I left out some details. "He was hired to… do deliveries."

It wasn't a lie, I just left out the part where the deliveries were of weapons, drugs, bribes, and cadavers on the odd occasion.

Danny was gorgeous. I had a crush on him before I even got to know him.

He was at least five inches taller than me, with richly tanned skin and the darkest brown, almond-shaped eyes. His straight, black hair was usually kept short, though he went through phases of growing it out. His high cheekbones only made him look more handsome as he got older.

We knew each other for a total of eight years, and over that time, he covered himself in tattoos. He was probably part of the reason I found tattooed people more trustworthy. Eric excluded, of course.

While I'd thought my childhood was unfair, it was nothing compared to my friend's.

Danny's mom died of cancer when he was little, and he was the only child to a father who couldn't safely process the grief of his wife. His dad turned to drugs and alcohol, leaving Danny to care for them both. He cracked under the pressure, dropping out of school and leaving his father behind, determined to start a better life for himself.

By the time he was eighteen, he found his way into Eric's employment. Though he was the same age as me, he quickly surpassed me in rank, proving his worth and living up to the title bestowed upon him at Initiation.

We got along like flies on a corpse, having the same sick sense of humor and being fairly immature in some areas due to our upbringing. Though, he was far more street smart and better with people than me.

It was something he learned through being exposed to his father's drug habits, which I could never experience on a piece of remote land with only my family for company.

I started college at seventeen, and Danny was there for the last year of the two years of my studies. Part of his contract was to ensure I got to and from the campus safely each day. He would drop me at the door and was always there to pick me up without missing a beat.

He and I had the same taste in music and would try our best to embarrass each other as we sang loudly with the windows down in Bedlam's gridlocked traffic.

Everything with him was fun. Light. My memories of him seemed to have a warm shining filter over them.

My favorite memory of him would always be the day I took my final class. I had completed my college courses fast and was set to graduate along with my peers. Thanks to The Surgeon's constant guidance and sharing of skills in my time at Home, I'd received top marks across the board.

I excitedly ran from the building, and he was there, waiting for me in the carpark. He beamed with pride as I ran to him. When I slammed my body into his, he hugged me tight, lifting me from the ground, spinning around, shouting, "You did it, girl!" over and over, not giving a fuck about the looks we received from those around us.

We, and a small group of friends from Home, were given permission to leave the premises for the night to celebrate. It was a rare wish of mine to be granted. Eric had to give a little every now and then for me to not become so miserable in my cage, and it was only early days for him to be gaining my trust while my contract was being drafted.

We stayed out drinking, dancing, and partying until the early hours of the morning.

Danny walked me to my room upon our return to Home, a few doors down from his apartment as I hadn't yet been banished to the medical floor. He told me for the millionth time how proud he was of my achievement.

As we hugged goodnight, he kissed me, and I kissed him back. Then, nothing. He didn't expect anything more of me; he just looked at me as if I was some kind of magical creature that brought him joy, and I felt exactly the same for him.

We said goodnight and parted ways.

A few days later, Danny attended my graduation, sitting among the front rows and cheering the loudest when I made the walk. The others from Home, Eric included, lurked somewhere in the back, unwilling to be seen.

In the days that followed, I hadn't been able to see Danny. There was too much work to do, and he was no longer required to chaperone me to and from classes.

A date was swiftly set for my initiation into Eric's inner circle. Although the boss and I were "dating" with a handful of public appearances under our belt to give the magazines something to focus on, things hadn't progressed between us. He hadn't made any real advances. It was confusing, and I didn't understand where we stood.

I'd had every intention of asking Danny to be my secret date for the big occasion. We'd likely be hanging out together for the whole night, anyway. But when we finally had a moment alone, there was an obvious change to him.

He told me he'd met someone.

It fucking *stung*.

Danny didn't sound too enthusiastic about her at the time, and when he mentioned her name, I recalled she was the daughter of one of Eric's closest criminal associates.

Anything between Danny and I was immediately over. Eric must have had spies watching the night we were out and made quick work to separate us. I was meant to be *his*. I hadn't seen my contract yet, but suddenly had a clear idea of what was to become of me.

Danny married at nineteen. Later that same year, and soon after turning twenty, he and Nessa had their first child — a baby boy I delivered with The Surgeon. It was a bittersweet moment.

The safe arrival of a perfect little person was as much a celebration in the dirty underworld as it was above ground. But seeing everyone celebrate them was just… *hard.*

They'd named their baby Michael, Mikey for short. Unbeknownst to Nessa, it was my middle brother's name.

It made me wonder if Danny had ever dreamed of a future between us involving children before his life was snapped in a new direction, leading him far away from me.

After much debate between the new parents, I was named my new favorite human's godmother. I spoiled that child with whatever I could. Mostly love, as I had nowhere else to place it where it would be returned.

Mikey was always under my feet in my room or on the medical floor, usually trashing the place, but I could never be mad. He was perfect. And looked exactly like his father.

The couple went on to have two more babies that didn't make it to term. In the end, Nessa was expecting their fourth. I later found out after escaping from Home that it was another boy, though I'd never met him, and likely never would.

"He sounds like an amazing friend," my therapist commented as my mind traveled back to her office. I felt lighter having told her of some of my most precious memories of the first man I ever loved.

"He was the best." I sighed, holding on to those good times tight, scared that they would float away and I'd forget their sweet faces.

"Each time he's been mentioned, you've spoken about him in past tense. I'll admit, I'm cautious to ask why after you've shared so much."

"He died."

"I'm so sorry, Katie. How awful for his wife and children."

*Child,* I corrected her in my head.

# TWENTY
## SUMMER

Though therapy was intense, I still felt the need to get back into my regular routine.

My next stop was the gym, where I spent every second on the treadmill, ensuring I ran long enough to put distance between myself and those haunting me.

When I arrived at the restaurant, it was closer to midnight than I'd planned. After working out, I'd sat in my car for a while, feeling all sorts of anxious and awful for not having shown up the night before, as Logan expected.

Whether he was going to lead to my demise or not, I stood him up while being sedated like a rabid animal, and I wanted to make things right.

Ben told him I was called away for an emergency, not that I had instead been collected, sobbing and unable to breathe from the floor of my therapist's office.

I couldn't remember doing or saying anything that would warrant being knocked out, only my brain cracking open after a single, spoken word and filtered snippets of the worst day of my life.

*So far, anyway.* With my track record, I was sure life still had greater disasters for me yet.

As I helped myself through the archway to the dining area, Logan appeared from behind the wall that led to the kitchen. He froze.

"Hi," I said quietly when he didn't start moving again.

"Coffee?"

"Yeah."

"Your table's free." He grinned, tipping his head to the desolate row of booths.

I sat, unsure how we could pick up from where we left. The plan to see him the day before had felt so natural after having spent the night shift at my house together. To have that momentum interrupted now gave everything an odd feel.

Logan returned with two coffees. That was a good sign, at least. Without knowing what to say to get us started, I took a sip and hoped the words would form.

He was staring at me from his side of the table, foot tapping on the ground, as if he also didn't know where to begin. His gaze burned my skin as I looked around for something to talk about to break the silence.

"You're okay." I couldn't work out if it were a statement or a question. "One of your—" He paused. "*Ben* came by and told me you had to go to some emergency? You look… *really* tired. Was it a long night?"

"Yeah," I lied, hoping the single word covered all bases. But then I was instantly annoyed. Everything between us was becoming based on nothing but lies. I felt agitated, thinking I'd made the wrong decision and wasn't ready to face Logan after such a rough twenty-four hours. "No, actually… I didn't. He was covering for me."

"Oh, okay…"

"I…"

He sighed when I didn't continue, "You're seeing someone else?"

"What? No." I scowled up at him. To me, it felt like quite the leap to come to that conclusion, but I understood it from his point of view. He didn't have another explanation.

"You can be honest with me, Summer. I'd never even asked if you were," he tried to reassure me with a despondent smile. "I'm not gonna be weird and freak out about it."

It was an odd relief to hear him say he wouldn't react badly to me being with someone else. Particularly after I suspected Eric had the "someone else" killed off in what was most definitely a "freakout."

As I watched Logan lean back in his seat, preparing for me to cut ties with him, I decided to put an end to some of the lies. I wouldn't have been able to keep up with so many new ones each time I met with him, and I planned on continuing to meet with him.

*To work out if he's dangerous, right?* My brain questioned my motives. *Sure.* I lied to myself.

"I had a… bad therapy session," I admitted with a flat tone, watching for his reaction to me being so broken.

"Oh?" His posture straightened.

*Who doesn't like to know what leads others to therapy?*

"Yeah. Like, a full-blown meltdown." A laugh slipped out, despite me not thinking it was all that funny.

"Really?" He seemed amused that I was finding my own deteriorating mental health a joke.

"Yeah," I laughed again, a little more genuine, thinking about how it must have looked to be carried out of my therapist's office and put to bed by Tony. I would have seemed like a rag doll in his arms, and the gentle giant would have treated me like one as he ensured I was safely tucked in to sleep off my sedatives.

"There she is," Logan said quietly, more to himself than to me at the sound of my laughter. I sensed my face and neck were turning red, and his eyes dropped to observe the change in color as he leaned a little closer.

"So… how bad are we talking, nurse?" he teased. "They knock you out?"

"Yeah. Tony did after he peeled me off the floor. I woke up in bed beside him at, like, three in the morning. He had to monitor me like a damn child for the whole fucking day."

Logan laughed. "I bet he gave you hell for that."

"He was more pissed off that I interrupted him and some girl having sex." I started to giggle uncontrollably, covering my mouth with the sleeve of my gym jacket, which only made Logan laugh harder. The sound melted the last of the remaining stress from therapy.

"Well, that sounds like a rough night."

"Yeah, I've had some bad ones, but it was definitely up there." I sat back, too, feeling at ease now I seemed to have cleared things up with him.

"Hey, you wanna have some fun tonight?" He raised his brows, and a glint of excitement flashed in those hazel eyes.

I so desperately wanted to tell him *yes* without knowing exactly what he meant by "fun."

"I wish I could," I started.

"Work," he answered for me. "I'm gonna have to get used to your nocturnal life. Pretty sure there's a freak or two out there wearing bat wings, running around at all hours. They'd make perfect friends for a loner like you."

He had me laughing again, and it wasn't lost on me that he implied we'd be spending more time together.

"Wouldn't you be missed here?" I gestured to the dining room, worried I would end up getting the poor guy fired if we made a habit of running off when he should have been working, "You already left early on Monday to take me out."

"Nah, I have an arrangement with the owners." He shrugged. "They're fine with me coming and going so long as it's not too busy. Which, as you know by now, it's pretty dead from this time onward."

*Convenient.* I looked around at the empty room. *Maybe that means he'll be up for visiting my house at all hours of the night... To spend time with me while I work, of course.*

He looked down at his hands, seeming to play with his next words before he spoke. "You've still got a bit of time before you need to head off. Do you wanna meet my friends before you go?"

"Really?" It sounded like a big step. He'd met my bodyguards, and I guessed they were as close as I had to friends, or even family until I could find the rest of mine. "Yeah... okay."

"Come on, then."

When he stood, I followed his lead and walked behind him. He guided me to the entrance of the restaurant, and straight through to the other side, under another large archway. I hadn't set foot in this part of the building before, always turning right instead of left.

The room was dimly lit, with many booths to the right, along the wall that shared the arch. The seats could fit larger groups than those in the dining room. A lengthy bar with high stools was on the opposite wall.

We walked to the last booth where the familiar group were seated. I suddenly felt underdressed in my gym clothes. I hadn't put much effort into how I looked and was still coming around from sedation. I made a note to do so well with my appearance next time that they wouldn't recognize me and would think Logan had found himself a major upgrade from the zombie I too-often resembled.

His friends appeared to have already been drinking for some time and were the only group in the bar. They were *loud.*

As we reached the table, Harrison stood, rushing to greet us. She was even more beautiful up close. I had noted how dark her skin was the other times I'd seen her, but it was different as she stood directly in front of me.

It resembled the result of heavy blackout tattoos, only it continued to places like in her nostrils, ears and the nail beds of her hands — areas that likely wouldn't be inked.

It was enough to convince me she was most definitely Gifted. As she moved, her skin sparkled, covered in millions of silver dots, visible depending on how the low light of the bar touched her body. She resembled a galaxy, and was absolutely mesmerizing.

"The doll," she introduced herself, holding her hand out to shake mine. I took it and flashed Logan a quick look.

"Did he tell you—"

"Oh yeah, he's *terrible* at keeping things to himself." She rolled her eyes, sparkling like faceted diamonds, and smiled as she lowered her voice. "And I agree with you, I think I'd make the fucking *coolest* doll."

The man behind her, still seated in the booth, let out a muffled laugh as he sipped from a beer bottle. I recognized him immediately — unusually broad shoulders, a huge, fit and bulky frame. I was surprised he could fit in the booth at all.

"What are you laughing at?" she snapped, returning to the seat beside him.

"Just thinking about the type of *doll* you'd be," he teased her, and she slapped his arm. I doubted he even felt her small hand hit him.

"The type *you* wouldn't be able to keep your hands off," she countered, leaning in to kiss him.

"So, that's Harrison and Tommy," Logan shook his head at them, "*on* again this week, by the looks of it. And this is Jackie." He gestured to a woman sitting opposite the others.

Jackie waved and smiled shyly. She appeared to be around my age, looking a little younger than the others, though Harrison's age was hard to pick.

If Jackie was the other woman I'd barely caught a glimpse of at the club, she was taller than me, curvier too. Her hair was dark copper and hung long around her waist, straight for the most part, but twisted into loose curls at the end. The small smatter of freckles across her nose made me believe her hair was naturally that color.

We sat with them. Me, beside Harrison, and Logan sitting on the opposite side with Jackie. He immediately reached across the table to hold my hand, and I took his without a second thought.

We'd had many interactions with each other, but I guessed the kiss two nights ago and him being reassured I wasn't seeing anyone else meant we were moving on to things like holding hands.

It was such a simple thing he offered without hesitation. I could barely focus on the conversation at the table as he mindlessly traced my knuckles, gently rolling his thumb over them while he spoke with his friends.

The only hands I'd ever held in public were all part of my role and, to a degree, always had an underlying level of threat if I didn't behave as expected. Unless taking my hand to help me out of expensive cars while I wore absurdly high heels counted for anything, I'd never been shown much *real* affection outside of Home.

As I quietly witnessed the interactions between Logan and his friends, I found that they were an odd bunch of individuals, but got along like family. They were kind and quickly included me, making jokes at Logan's expense to get me to laugh and help me relax. It was nice to have the tables turned after he and my bodyguards got on better than I thought they ever could with meeting just once.

"So, what do you get up to for fun?" I queried when we'd been sitting with them for some time. It was an innocent enough question to ask the group.

"We hang around here a lot," Tommy answered, not giving me much insight into their secretive double lives.

"Sometimes, we hit up a club a while away from here," Harrison offered. Logan shot her a look from across the table. It was subtle, and I only noticed because I was looking for it.

"Yeah? Which one?" I pushed.

"You wouldn't know it" Logan said, shaking his head and not meeting my eyes as he peered into his glass.

"Maybe we should take her sometime?" Harrison kicked Logan under the table. He clenched his jaw. She liked trouble. And I instantly liked her.

"Logan mentioned you're a surgical nurse?" Jackie asked from across the table, eyes darting anxiously between them.

"Yeah, going on ten years." I smiled proudly through the lie.

"I bet you've seen some crazy shit," Tommy commented as Logan pushed another beer bottle in his direction.

"I guess." It was a comment everyone made when they learned what I did for a living, and I tried not to think of the long list of *crazy* I'd encountered in that time.

"What's the most messed up thing you've seen?" Jackie asked. Evidently, hanging around this potential, Gifted murderer had desensitized her and removed her filter, too.

"Oh, well…" There were too many examples I could give. I swallowed hard at the thought of the instances that led to each of the names on my back.

*I'm not ready for this, I lost my fucking mind yesterday. The sedatives might not even be completely out of my system.*

Having mentioned Danny and disclosing the first time in which Eric had physically taken advantage of me during the *one* therapy session made me too raw to create the coherent thoughts to answer her.

Logan squeezed my hand, bringing me back to the booth. "Don't ask dumb shit like that, Jack." He elbowed her playfully, but his expression as he observed my reaction was heavy with concern.

I blinked a few times to set my mind straight as Harrison turned on the seat to face me, completely blocking Tommy behind her.

"Have we met before? I *swear* I've seen you somewhere. You look *so* familiar." She narrowed her pretty eyes and studied my face. "It's been driving me mad since you walked in."

"I don't think so." I tried to laugh her off. "I'm sure I'd remember meeting someone like you."

*Fuck, does she recognize me?*

My makeup tutorials and clothing hauls were still all over the internet.

Though, I'd noticed the comments had been disabled. Too many viewers were asking where I'd gone.

Harrison shrugged. "If you say so. You wanna come to the bar with me to grab another drink?"

A quick glance at my phone made my heart drop. I was hoping she would be the one to spill more information than Logan about who *they* were before she worked out who *I* was.

"I actually need to go. It was great meeting you all," I told them as I shuffled off the seat.

"I'm sure we'll see you again soon." Harrison eyed Logan as she spoke to me. She seemed to love making him squirm. "Logan keeps telling us what a wonderful addition you'd make to our little gang."

I smiled at the thought and waved goodbye, pretending not to know exactly what she was talking about. A group of vigilantes would certainly find a quick-stitching nurse as useful as everyone else who had tried to acquire me for their team.

Logan walked me to the entrance before I stopped and turned to him.

"Your friends are cool," I told him, though Harrison made me a little worried his affection towards me was a trick to get me to sign up to be a private caretaker for a small group of criminals.

"Do you really have to go? Stay a little longer?" he pleaded, easing my concerns about being used a little. "You don't start work for a while."

"I've set time aside for inventory checks tonight," I explained. Between a man kissing me, being knocked out after therapy, and now having to repeatedly banish ghosts from my mind, life was feeling a little out of control.

Counting, ordering, and stocking my supplies was black and white. I desperately needed it to reset my mind.

"I'll come with you then. I can help."

"How about after your shift?" I suggested. "Head on over when you're finished here. I'll be done with work by then and we can… hang out?"

"Okay, I'll finish up around six. See you then?"

When Logan leaned in to kiss me, it didn't set off any defensive reactions.

Neither did his hands on my butt as he pulled me closer.

*That's concerning.* I noted my comfort in his closeness and the fact he might have been learning where he could touch me that wouldn't cause me to move away.

"Oh, come on!" Tommy called over the back of their booth, breaking us out of the moment.

"See you later," I promised, and turned to leave.

# TWENTY-ONE

## SUMMER

I showered and dressed for work when I got home, then made a quick job of taking inventory.

Thankfully, my shift for the night was an easy one. I removed the cast of a teen whose parents were undocumented. I supplied antibiotics for a little girl who had an ear infection. I only gave two stitches all night – five if I counted my tag – on a child who had found their father's hunting knives. I would have felt bad about tagging a kid, but then, I could be worse. I could be like the father who left unsupervised knives around the house.

Not even *my* dad did that, and he'd bought me my first weapon the day I was born. It gave me a very… *unique* sense of what made a good parent.

The night was peaceful, particularly after the way the previous day had played out. Without anything gang-related or severely horrific, it reminded me of why I wanted to become a nurse in the first place. Helping others came so naturally to me, and despite my "unfriendly" appearance, I was capable of being gentle and kind. I wished I could have offered myself some of that same kindness.

At the end of my shift, I recorded the video to document patients, notes and ideas, then switched everything off. As I sat back in my chair, it swiveled slowly to the left.

I scanned the cabinets and patient chair as they came into view. Taking a deep breath at the sights around me, I was content in the moment. It was a rare luxury to relax enough to feel this way. Escaping Eric, starting life over. It was all paying off.

*6:20am*

My phone vibrated on the desk.

Someone was outside. The bodyguards had left for the night, so it could only be one other person.

"Super hearing?" Logan asked with a smirk as I caught him reaching up to knock, not letting go of the idea I could be one of those Gifted super-freaks like himself.

I held up the phone. "Saw you coming."

He didn't look too bothered by that. Logan was, after all, just a regular guy, dropping in to see a friend. I wasn't supposed to know the potential threat he posed each time I met with him.

*What the fuck am I doing?*

The cold air swept across my skin and swirled into the hall behind me. I stepped aside for him to get into the house, and had a strong desire to be wrapped in his jacket again.

As we walked the hall, Logan took in more of his surroundings in the light of the rising sun.

*The glasses could be real then, no super-vision with this one?*

The idea completely threw me. The Gifted seemed to have a standard list of superhuman abilities. Perfect vision, excellent hearing, super strength, quick healing and godlike reflexes. A few also had extra Gifts, like he apparently might, contributing in some way to his graphic killing sprees. Though, I was struggling with the idea that Logan was as menacing as the police and witness accounts stated.

"What's through there?" he asked, nodding to the door at the far end of the hall, opposite the front door.

"Oh. Laundry."

"And… How many bedrooms?"

"Two…"

"Do you live alone?" he asked as we neared the end of the hall, turning back to look at me with his hands in his pockets and brows raised, anticipating my answer.

My eyes widened, and I gulped.

*He really is scoping out the house. Should I tell him I have a roommate? Would he be less likely to hurt me here if he thinks someone might catch him in the act?*

His shoulders drooped a little as he read my reaction, realizing how suspicious his inquiries were beginning to sound.

"Cameras, codes," he offered. "You don't feel safe in your own home?"

*Maybe I've got him all wrong?*

"You've seen for yourself what I do for work." I shrugged away some of the tightness in my shoulders. "There are people out there who… *want me.* For my skills. I can never be too careful."

*Skills. Body.* It was never clear which Eric needed more once he laid eyes on the girl whose father was so boastful about her *skills.*

"The bodyguards are here all the time," I lied, hoping he wouldn't be so quick to work out how much time I spent on my own.

He nodded as he turned from me. "If this is what your house is like, I bet your Wi-Fi password is eighty characters long."

I giggled. "It's actually only six. It's one, zero, capital D, one, lowercase N, three, if that's your way of asking for it."

"Iodine? You nerd." Amused, he shook his head as we arrived at the kitchen and retrieved his phone from his pocket. "It was, and thank you."

"I literally have nothing to offer you except water. Or vodka?" I told him with my head in the fridge. "Might be a bit early in the day for that. Although, we've just both finished work?"

"Water is fine," he called over his shoulder, looking about again and inspecting the small, round dining table in the space opposite the kitchen, untouched since the day I assembled it. I was certain he'd already checked out the place on the first night I invited him in. Maybe he was looking for changes?

*Or ways to kill me.*

Perhaps Logan was trying to learn more about me, just as I was with him. Surely I was starting to raise suspicions too.

*Or you know, maybe he likes you and wants to know more about you? Could that even be possible?*

Harrison's final words were playing on my mind, that maybe Logan's interest was purely for recruiting purposes.

"Here." I tossed him a bottle that he caught, having barely seen which direction it came from. He looked at it before his eyes darted to mine. "Wow, good catch." I laughed to hide my shock.

He smirked. "Yeah. I'd… give that a nine."

If he wasn't going to be upfront about the other half of his identity, I could use our alone time to run a few little tests of my own.

When I moved to the couch to sit down, he took that as his cue to do the same. Kicking my boots off and tucking my legs underneath me, I turned to face him as I propped my head up with my hand on the back cushion.

He sunk comfortably into the space beside me, not making an effort to keep much distance between us this time now I was sober.

"How was the rest of your night?"

"Good." He smiled, sharing nothing as he opened the bottle and took a long sip. "My friends really like you."

"Yeah?"

"Yeah, Harrison is keen to meet up again. But I think she'd try to run away with you if I gave her half a chance. Don't get me wrong… she and Tommy are together. Well, at least, they are this week. On again one week, off again the next." He shrugged. "She just likes you a lot."

I couldn't hide my smile. It'd been so long since I was brought into an established group of friends and couldn't imagine I had much left in the way of social skills after two lonesome years. Having three brothers and only male colleagues at Home, I was left without a well-rounded set of friendships.

"How was work?" he asked.

"Fine. Nothing too wild tonight. It was nice."

Logan reached over and touched my leg, smiling at me from across the couch. He seemed relieved to hear that I wasn't in some kind of danger after he'd had a small taste of what I do for a living.

"All kids tonight. Which is rare," I continued, observing his hand as the warmth from his palm seeped through my jeans and into my skin. "They're nicer to deal with than the others who come to me."

He began playing with the seam of the fabric above my knee. The way his fingers ran up and down the small space may have been a mindless action to him, but it had me transfixed.

*First hand holding and kissing me goodbye, now this? What is he playing at?*

"You like working with kids?" His smooth voice broke my concentration on his fingers.

"Most of the time. So long as the injuries aren't too severe. I struggle with seeing little ones in pain," I explained as my mind betrayed me for the millionth time, showing flashes from my past where I held a small body close to mine, begging for them to wake up.

"Do you think you'll ever have kids?" he asked. It seemed a very personal question for what might have been a second attempt at a date. At least, I assumed it was. I wouldn't know what a second date would look like, considering the closest to first dates for me were quick trips to the rooms at Crave with people I had no intention of ever seeing again.

The answer would likely bring down the mood, but I was determined to not have every conversation riddled with lies.

"I don't think so. I… I probably can't even have kids," I admitted, eyes still glued to the way his fingers were rubbing my leg.

*Maybe his Gift has something to do with hypnotic hands.* I almost smiled, but then I remembered the photos I'd seen of the damage these hands could do.

"Have you… *tried?*" he asked cautiously.

I giggled and looked up. His head tipped to the side while he waited for my answer. The question made it sound like he was asking whether I'd ever had sex, not if I'd purposefully tried to create another person.

"Not intentionally." I bit my lip, pausing at the memory of being questioned by cops after a physical assessment.

They were the ones to bluntly inform me I'd had "two or more dodgy abortions" based on the internal damage. I wasn't aware of any such procedures, but whoever performed them wasn't very skilled, and had left me with a mess.

"A few *botched removals* have likely sealed my fate." I struggled to look away from his curious frown.

"You didn't want them?"

"I honestly didn't even know they existed." Breaking the eye contact, I stared off into the room in search of words that could even begin to explain some of the more disturbing parts of my past.

"My ex, Eric, was *controlling*." I gave the understatement of the century. "He was very much involved in all of what happened to this." I gestured at my entire body. "From what I ate, to how I looked… They were removed before I'd found out I was pregnant. I learned about them after I left him."

I cracked my knuckles, hoping the popping sounds would flush the thoughts of Eric away.

Logan was so painfully unaware of what was going on beneath my clothes as I sat beside him. I wondered if a man who healed so quickly would find my scarred body to be disturbing.

"How exactly does someone get away with doing that?" His hand stopped moving, features troubled as I met his eyes. It was exactly the look I wanted to avoid. I didn't want anyone feeling bad for me when I willingly did so much wrong in the years of mine and Eric's villainous reign over Bedlam.

"Umm… to put it simply, I was… part of a cult. For many years. I haven't been living out this way for long." I stuck to my story for therapy to keep track of the lies I couldn't avoid. "Cult leaders seem to have their own set of rules."

"That's… fucked up, Summer."

I shrugged. "You said you were a cop? Then you know what it's like these days. People can get away with nearly anything."

My words weren't far from the truth. With more time passing since the Gifted made themselves known, their numbers were growing and many were trying to make it big, whether they be good or evil. Authorities at all levels struggled with tiptoeing the line between controlling those who were different and the moral treatment of beings who were still essentially human.

"I was married… a long time ago." His hand started moving again, his heat seeming greater than before. I was grateful he took a turn at sharing something to take the attention from the morbid information I'd let slip. "We tried to have kids. But nothing stuck. In the end, it was decided there was something wrong with me. So, we gave up to spare us the pain… and the debt."

"Married?" I echoed, immediately assuming the mystery woman was a regular human.

As far as anyone knew, if two Gifted people had a child, there was a one hundred percent chance it would also be Gifted. Though, if Gifted tried to have children with regular humans, it didn't work out. *Many* had tried, but there were no successful outcomes. None lasted past a few weeks gestation.

As a nurse, and someone interested in the research, it was fascinating, but also incredibly sad. With the Gifted still far and few between, at least the registered ones, it left for many couples trying to have children who simply could not. *Ever*.

The only good thing to come of it was that no women, Gifted or otherwise, were forced into being used as incubators for armies of superhuman beings. Many unethical studies were exposed, but from those, it was scientifically concluded we couldn't mix.

A worldwide surrogacy ban for all people took effect the year I was born, and adoption wasn't a possibility in most states for unregistered Gifted citizens. I didn't think for a second that Logan was registered on any list, except for maybe the country's "most wanted."

*Should I check that? I'd bet what's left of my mind, he's on it.*

Our conversation left me with questions about Logan's family, curious to know if both his parents were Gifted, or if he were a happy accident. I couldn't ask, still not meant to know he was one of them in the first place.

"Yeah. We were young and dumb," he continued with a sad smile. "Married straight out of the academy. We rushed into it, but we were happy."

"Did not having kids change that?" The awful question tumbled from my mouth before I could catch it.

"Nah. She passed a few years ago. I moved out here to get away from everything that reminded me of what we had."

While the discussion had taken a dark turn, I was too intrigued with getting inside his head to lighten the mood.

"Where did you work before coming to the mountains?"

"Bedlam. Messed up place."

"Yeah, completely."

He sighed. "Turned off yet, nurse? Don't want to hear anymore? I've got too much baggage."

"Ha!" I snorted. "I've got more baggage than a fucking airport."

"What? *More* than being in a cult? I doubt that," he challenged, moving his hand from my leg to push his glasses back up the bridge of his nose. He rested his arm along the back of the couch, further closing the space between us. "Tell me a bit about your baggage, if you've got so much."

I scratched at my neck and tucked the hair that slipped from my braid behind my ear, keeping an eye on how close his hand had moved to me *and* the cushion where I hid the knife.

"Ah. Okay. Well." I shifted uncomfortably, not knowing exactly how much was safe to reveal to a murderous criminal. "I have three brothers."

"Three? Damn. I only have one sister and she interferes enough with my life."

It wasn't lost on me that he'd previously said he'd had no family. Maybe he only meant no wife and kids. Hearing about a sister and knowing he was a sibling was something I hadn't expected to learn.

*It could be more lies.*

He looked at me expectantly, as if I would share something similar. Instead, I offered more of the truth.

"Yep. James, Michael, and John." I recalled them in order of age.

"My dad's name w—is James," Logan said with a smile.

"For real? James is my favorite. He's the eldest and always treated me the least like I was a waste of space."

I wondered if they ever thought about the little sister who followed them around the property, stitched them up and loved them dearly. Even John, sometimes. Had they seen my rise to power? Or had my family been isolated enough to not witness the monster their youngest had become?

"They haven't spoken to me since I was sixteen. Same with my parents."

I rested my head on the back of the couch, not realizing that I was leaning on Logan's wrist until his fingers began gently toying with my hair. I found it mildly concerning that the sensation didn't make me jump from the couch, knife in hand.

"That's rough," he offered as I stared off into the room again, trying not to draw attention to his touch in case it made him stop.

"It is. We were so close growing up. Not that we had much of a choice. We were homeschooled together. Being primed to take over my parents' land and to run the property. Or I was, at least. The boys were free to move out to their own spaces. But still, I've heard nothing from any of them since I escaped. I've tried to contact Mom, but I think they're done with me. For good."

"You mentioned sixteen last time, too. Does this have anything to do with the ex?"

I leaned into his hand a little more and rolled my body to face him.

"It has everything to do with him. I guess they don't want anything to do with me after what I did…"

"Surely, what you did at that age couldn't have led to a lifelong shun?"

"I dunno. Would you ever talk to your sixteen-year-old daughter again if she ran away with a stranger, nearly double her age?" I slipped my hand under my head so I could hold his now that he'd stopped stroking my hair.

Relief caught my tears when he didn't pull his hand away. Logan was proving to be very affectionate where words failed him, and I wanted to take it where I could.

It'd been so long since a man had touched me without expecting something in return. I could only remember the one kiss from Danny. Everything else in my life seemed to have strings and contracts attached.

"I would," Logan said as matter-of-fact, squeezing my hand in his.

Something about his tone made me believe him, especially after hearing how much he'd wanted kids in his past life. I imagined he would have taken all the bad with the good. My parents must have seen things differently, with them being able to have four children in as many years.

"It's their loss, Summer. How about we watch a movie or something?" he suggested when I didn't respond, too lost in my head again. "We don't have to be so serious every time we're alone."

"You've got time to stay?" My question held more excitement than I believed it could carry with being so tired from a double therapy session and a full night's work.

"I don't start work until late tonight." He shrugged.

"Okay, give me a sec."

I left to grab a blanket from the dresser in the spare room, and he picked a movie he claimed to have seen a thousand times. I'd never heard of it, but he swore everyone had and it was his favorite.

As I curled up on the couch beside him, Logan lifted his arm; an invitation for me to sink into his side before he wrapped it around me. I covered us both with the blanket, though we didn't really need it with the amount of body heat he created in the jacket.

As we settled into place, I realized that no one had held me like that in my whole life. His warmth and the softness of his jacket on my cheek and neck were a comfort I'd never experienced. As the movie started, I listened to his breathing and heartbeat, unable to stop counting as it pulsed under my ear.

He'd picked an action movie, and the longer we watched, the more I could imagine him performing the terrible deeds of the antihero and myself having to clean up the mess. Maybe that's where our lives were headed if we kept this up.

Logan rocked my shoulder, bringing me back from the sleep I was steadily drifting into.

"This is my favorite part." He spoke softly, resting his cheek on my head. It took me a moment to catch up with the story. The main character's girlfriend had broken up with him. She'd said some code word they'd agreed on to signal she was in danger and needed him to rescue her; that she still loved him. "What would yours be?" he asked, rubbing my arm under the blanket.

"My what be?" I mumbled, still trying to follow along and fighting my heavy eyelids.

"If you were in trouble. What would you say so I'd know you needed saving?"

I smiled at the idea. It was cute, and could very well be useful at some point if we had any kind of future together.

*What a fucked-up fairytale that would be.*

Ignoring my internal comment, I pondered on it for a moment. "Same situation? I'm leaving you? Bad guy is taking me away?" I lifted my head from his chest to look up at him.

"Sure."

I shrugged. "I'd tell you I'm taking your jacket."

It was all I could think of, and the feel of it on my skin made me think I would probably end up stealing it at some point anyway. He'd already let me wear it once and part of me hoped he would again.

He laughed. "But it's my favorite."

"All the more reason to say I'm taking it."

"You've got a good point, nurse."

Logan straightened on the couch and reached to grab me at my ribs, pulling me onto his lap so I faced him with my knees at either side of his hips. The position gave me a little more height. My face was level with his, and even closer than before we'd kissed at the door.

"I mean, I don't ever expect you to need to use codes with me, Summer."

"I know," I laughed, playing along with his game. "But I'm sticking with the jacket."

Resting my forehead on his, I looked into his eyes through the thick lenses of the glasses, taking note of the colors and the subtle transitions between them.

I pressed my lips to his.

Neither of us expected me to make the first move. I'd caught him by surprise. I'd caught *myself* by surprise. Relief washed away my nerves as he parted his lips and kissed me back.

The longer we kissed, the heavier our breathing became, making me giggle when I noticed after a few minutes that we'd fogged up his glasses. I removed them from his face, gently folded the arms and placed them beside us on the couch. I returned my hands to his arms, and Logan watched intently as I grabbed and squeezed from his forearms up to his shoulders, taking in their shape and firmness under the soft fabric of the jacket. When one of my hands reached the back of his neck, I drew him in to kiss me again.

Not noticing how carried away I'd gotten as I sat on his lap, I found myself leaning into his body. With our torsos connected from the chest down, my hips rolled, pressing my crotch against his.

If I didn't know my broken body so well, I could have sworn I was getting wet at the thought of things between us moving further.

Logan seemed to be on the same wavelength, shifting to take off the jacket.

And his shirt.

*Oh, fuck!*

I was so excited at the sight of him shirtless I almost felt sick.

Logan's arms were a small preview at what was under his clothing. Every muscle on his body was softly defined. He clearly wasn't going for the body-builder look like Tommy, but it was obvious he had to be working out frequently to maintain the appearance.

I was snapped from my observing trance by his quick moving fingers; aimed for the bottom of my shirt.

"No! Wait!" I exclaimed. "I can't!" His hands immediately let go when I pushed them away.

"You don't want—? Fuck, I'm sorry." He ran a hand through his hair, keeping it from touching me again. "I'm… *completely* misreading things here."

"No, I *want* to. I just… can't."

It was unfair. Surely he'd think of my scarred skin as repulsive. Especially now I had the knowledge he looked *that fucking good* under his clothes.

"Body image issues?" he teased, but looked worried as he repeated the excuse from the night of our first date.

"I've got scars," I admitted, sitting back on his lap. Taking note of how incredibly *hard* he felt underneath me, I hated myself for not being able to put what I'd seen in the pics he'd sent me to good use. "Like, *heaps*. Bad ones."

He raised his eyebrows and inspected the small amounts of skin that were visible, likely realizing in all the times he'd seen me, I'd been covered up just as much, if not more.

"You hide them well."

He also mustn't have seen them the other night when I removed his jacket, adding me to the confused bandwagon with the confirmation that his vision wasn't consistent with the other things I'd been noticing about him.

"Yeah. They tend to raise a lot of questions I'm not willing to answer."

The room suddenly felt too bright. Too exposing.

*Damn this nocturnal life*. It was close to nine in the morning. Streaks of warm sun rays had spread across the floor from the window.

Taking a deep breath and settling on making do with what we had, I grabbed his jacket, zipped it up and pulled it over my head. It was big enough that I could use it like a tent to take my shirt and bra off underneath without him seeing anything. I dropped them to the floor and pulled my arms through the sleeves.

"This is the best I can do for now, if you'll take it?" I offered, feeling so fucking stupid, but also not ready for this opportunity to be physical with each other to end.

"If that's what it takes." He smiled, and some of my embarrassment dissolved. "It'll be like my eyes are closed."

His acceptance without making fun of me was enough to get me kissing him again. Logan slowly slipped his hands under the jacket. Holding my waist first, still covered by my jeans, he pulled me close so that I was grinding against his erection when my hips moved.

"Can I?" he asked, pausing before touching bare skin. I nodded, mouth on his, my hands in his hair. "Say the word… and I'll stop," he promised, breaking the kiss to glide his lips down my neck while his hands moved higher up my body. My ribs, my breasts and my shoulders were all touched by his *hot* hands. His fingers left warm trails over every inch of skin they explored. I may not have wanted him to see my scars, but Logan's soft strokes over each raised cut and piece of dented flesh brought me a sense of peace that almost made me reconsider the jacket. He pulled me closer so my chest leaned on his, sadly through the fabric. I hoped one day soon that all of my skin could be pressed against his. I wanted my entire body to be touched by that same warmth in his palms.

He groaned against my neck, grip tightening to squeeze my ribs. The guttural rumble came from deep within his chest and vibrated under my palms; a reaction to me pressing harder on his thick shaft.

Logan's lips returned to mine and his hands moved higher on my back, just below the list. I froze, and he pulled his face from mine.

He asked in a whisper, "Need me to stop?"

"I don't *want* you to."

"But do you *need* me to?"

I thought about it for a second. "No. But this is about as far as I can go for now."

"So I can keep kissing you?" His mouth moved to my jawline and neck, my pulse throbbing under scorching lips as they gently brushed my skin.

"Yes." I smiled at his eagerness as he pulled me closer again.

"Okay… just so we're completely clear… *no* sex?"

I gasped and set my hands on his chest, pushing away. The way he asked so openly had my skin feeling hot all over.

*Does he really want to move this fast?*

I didn't like the idea that he might view me as "easy" with this only being the second time we were alone together.

"You don't…" He eyed me curiously. "*Feel* that?"

"Feel what?" I giggled, sure he was referring to something other than his dick. Would he really be so lame and try to use an excuse like "the spark" to get in my pants?

*If I'd taken the meds, it'd probably work.*

But my nearest bottle of pills was too far, stashed in the bathroom cupboard. I didn't want to kill the mood by running off for the drugs I needed to be intimate with anyone. It wasn't very discreet.

"It's nothing." Curiosity quickly evaporated into unease as Logan shook his head.

"Maybe not yet? Does this even count as a second date? You're so eager to have your way with me and move on?" I tried to sound playful, but the words tumbled out with a hint of hysteria.

"That's okay. I'm in no rush." With what I felt pushing up against me as I sat in his lap, that had to be a lie.

Narrowing my eyes and taking a deep breath, I tested his statement.

"If you're really not in a rush, would you get checked for me? STDs and all that? I handle a lot of bodily fluids and get tested regularly… despite the lack of sexual partners lining up to fuck the nurse who hangs around half-naked men most days."

I may have been equally eager to get his clothes off as he was with me and mine, but this would buy me some time and allow me to be more prepared with the right resources for the next time we got so close.

"Of course, Summer. Consider it done. Is that all?"

*So quick to please me.*

I raised a suspicious brow and shook my head. "No, it's not. I honestly have a lot of…" I hated that I had no choice but to admit it. "*Problems* with sex."

"That's *okay*," he assured me again, brushing a loose strand of hair from in front of my eyes.

"I've just…" I paused, trying to form an explanation that wouldn't scare him away. I didn't want him thinking I was too damaged to bother trying again. "I've never been in control over much of my life. Any of it. Especially the physical stuff until after I escaped the cult."

Logan gave me a wide-eyed look that told me he understood what I was saying, even with my codes and vagueness. He leaned back into the couch, putting more space between us.

"The same ex you mentioned? The guy from the cult?"

"Yep."

"He raped you?"

I always preferred it when people were direct with me, but having Logan ask so brazenly made me think again that his people skills were lacking. Maybe he didn't care for excuses and mind games. I put it down to him having been a cop in the past.

Either way, I felt like I was having an out-of-body experience as we kept on the subject. It wasn't like me to open up and freely discuss these things with anyone. My therapist could attest to my unwillingness to share.

But there was something about the way Logan held me, listened to me. I really was, stupidly, starting to feel safe with him. That, and him, still being topless beneath me, had my head swimming.

"Umm… yes," I admitted to both of us. "It's something I'm still struggling to come to terms with."

Logan tipped his head again, slowly. I imagined that his moral scales were set to the idea of Eric and not me. He took a deep breath, his expression troubled again as he looked me over, on his lap and hiding in his jacket. My safety barrier.

"Is there anything else I should know?" His tone had turned a little cold.

"The scars. They were his doing."

He raised a hardened brow, jaw flexing as his breathing picked back up again. If it wasn't such a disturbing exchange of information, I would have seen this potential overprotectiveness as a bit of a turn on.

"He sometimes drugged me, knocked me out," I continued, apparently taking a page out of Logan's book and abandoning the filter between my brain and my mouth. "He'd use belts around my hands. Sometimes around my neck. I'd be out cold *most* of the time when he cut me. He was kind enough to do that at least."

*Might as well dig this hole deeper.* Although, at this point, I didn't feel like I had much of a choice in whether I kept sharing. It all spilled out of my mouth.

*Was that mouthwash filled with emetics?* I had to work that out later, too busy vomiting secrets to discover the source of my atypical veracity.

"I'd wake up bloody and…" I played with the zip of the jacket, my eyes stinging with tears. "Almost always completely naked. Our relationship didn't involve a normal sex life. It kind of did… in the beginning. It mostly consisted of him starving me of affection, sometimes for months. Even then, what happened most nights between us wasn't *completely* consensual. The physical stuff was… always done on his terms."

Logan set his hands on my thighs, as though he was trying to ground the two of us.

"That's a lot," he finally said, features softening as he took more deep breaths.

"I know, *I'm sorry.*" I covered my mouth with a trembling hand. "I don't know why I even said any of that. I'm not good at this." I internally scolded myself for ever thinking I could try to move past the one-night stand phase of my body's escape from Eric. My mind would never be free of him.

Logan gently shook his head. "Don't apologize for something done *to you.* That'd be like me apologizing for having a dead wife, it's ridiculous."

*We certainly are a damaged pair.* My head was down, and my eyes were stinging again now I was done with disclosing some of the darkness of my past. I felt dirty for having brought any of it up.

*This is why you don't date. You can't. You're too fucked up, even for a murderous vigilante. What does that say about YOU?*

Logan lifted my face with his knuckle, and I looked away as I blinked out tears. I hadn't cried often since leaving Home. I was condemned to sit deep within my well of grief, unable to reach up to the places where my tears were stored.

Thoughts of "little" things like Eric pinning me to his bed and hacking into my body rarely made me cry. There were other things from my past that haunted me so much more, but Logan was having an unusual effect on me, acting like a floating device so I could say these things without drowning in panic. Oddly, I felt safer with him than with Dr. Lindsey.

"I'm broken," I whispered, both to him and at the fact I was trusting a killer with any of my secrets.

"Aren't we all?" he said, more to himself than to me. "What do you need?" He released his grip on my legs. I wished he hadn't done that, it was the only thing holding me together.

"A lobotomy," I answered with a teary eye roll.

"Don't try to make me laugh." I could hear the smile in his voice. "What a waste that would be. Besides, you already look like a zombie half the time."

"Honestly, I think I need sleep," I confessed with a small laugh.

"That's probably a good idea. I'll get going." He reached for his shirt and glasses, putting them back on and lifting me to the floor as he stood from the couch.

Logan planted a kiss on the top of my head and turned to leave.

"You don't want your jacket back?"

He looked me up and down with a lazy smile. "Nah, you look real cute in it. Bring it with you tonight."

"You're not worried I'll steal it?" I teased.

His smile turned shy. "It's not the only thing I'm worried someone like you might steal, Summer."

The warmth returned to my cheeks – he didn't know enough about my past for that to be anything but more flirting.

Logan cleared his throat and blinked away, but couldn't hide the nerves as he jokingly accused, "I have a nice car. For all I know, all that hypnotic kissing was the distraction you needed for the bodyguards to make off with it."

I laughed. "Which would you miss more? Car or jacket?"

He shrugged. "Well that depends, would you be in either when it goes missing?"

*How can he be the vigilante I've read about? Are these parts of him real?*

"You should stay."

I had no idea *what* I was thinking, and guessed I just didn't want him to leave after having told him so much. What if he went asking around about who I was, who my "ex" was? He'd likely get himself killed. It wasn't hard to put two and two together once you started looking into "Summer and Eric." Ever a quick internet search would easily produce hundreds of photos and gossip columns from our many years together.

"Stay?"

"I don't know if I feel like being alone. After all that." I gestured to where we'd been sitting. That seemed to be enough for him to make up his mind.

"Sure. You want me to sleep on the couch?" He started to walk back, but I blocked him from stepping around me with my palms on his chest.

"I'd be okay… with you in my room?" I was pushing my luck. "We'll *just* be sleeping."

"Only if that makes *you* happy, Summer."

We made our way down the hall together, and as we reached the room, I drew the blackout curtains so the space plunged into enough darkness to sleep. Logan remained in the doorway with his arms folded, leaning on the frame.

He narrowed his eyes at the bed. "This will make or break us, nurse."

"What?" *Maybe he totally misunderstood. He probably thinks you changed your mind and still want to fuck him.*

I mean, I *did* want to. *Really* wanted to. But after everything I shared about Eric I was in the wrong headspace. It was possible to change that if I needed to, my pills were in the ensuite – just a few steps through the wardrobe.

"The bed. Which side do you sleep on?" he asked as he stepped into the room.

I failed to hide my relieved sigh. "Umm, the side by the door."

"I *knew it*." He pretended to be disappointed as he playfully shook his head and shrugged. "I guess it can't work between us. That's *my* side of the bed."

"Maybe you'll have to suck it up and let me have my spot. And when I sleep over at your place, I'll sleep on the other side."

"When, eh?" He chuckled, then instantly turned serious. "I'll cut you a deal, Summer."

"Okay?" I asked, trying not to give him the satisfaction of a giggle as I played along.

"I'll have the side closest to the door," he said firmly, standing at the side of the bed, folding his arms again as he waited for me to accept.

"That's it? That's not a *deal*, that's a statement," I countered.

"Fine, I'll throw in the disposal of any monsters that disturb our sleep. I can't get to them fast enough to protect you if you're blocking my way. And I absolutely cannot risk having them take you first."

I laughed. "Monsters? Like what? Villains? Gifted?"

"There's an epidemic." He struggled to keep a straight face, eyes wide behind his glasses as he waited for my permission.

"You'll keep me safe?" While I gave him a playful eye roll, the idea of that sounded nicer than I'd ever admit.

"I swear it, Summer."

"Fine!" I agreed with a sigh, and he immediately dropped down to the mattress in the place he'd claimed.

I collapsed on the bed beside him and turned away in a huff. Logan pulled me into his chest, and I wriggled my body into his as he wrapped his arms around me.

It was comforting to have someone in the house who was there for *me*. Not because I'd employed them or they needed me to treat their injuries.

"Logan?"

"Mmm?"

"How are you meant to fend off monsters if you're facing this way?"

"Shh," he whispered. "I didn't think that part through. Get some sleep. I'll come up with a good enough excuse to keep *my* side."

I drifted into a deep sleep, knowing that he was there, holding me, and protecting me from monsters like himself.

# TWENTY-TWO

SUMMER

## FEBRUARY 4TH

*It's just a dream.*

I knew it was, I'd seen this before. But I needed the reminder each time I traveled to this place. It wasn't based on my most horrific memories. It were as though my mind knew I couldn't deal with the very worst, so it settled for *second worst* to fuck with my sleep. Come to think of it, I had a lot of second-worsts that my sleeping brain liked to cycle through as I tried to rest.

In this particular instance, I stood in a dark room, the details around me were too black and blurred to define the shapes except for Eric, standing in front of me with his low bed to my left.

"I'm sorry, Eric!" I screamed for the millionth time, wiping streams of tears and snot from my face. There was nothing I could do but let this recurring nightmare play itself out around me. Sometimes I was in my own body, other times I watched our exchange from above. This time I seemed to be graced with a mixture of both.

Eric, a few feet in front of me, shook his head, too enraged to express his disappointment, barely able to bark a few orders at me. His pale, angled features scrunched with fury.

"*Get on the bed!*" his smooth voice had disappeared, replaced by a demanding, rough growl and giving me the highest word count to leave his mouth since I'd woken on the cold concrete floor of his bedroom. I'd been sedated, and brought to the seventy-fourth floor for him to decide what my first punishment would be.

Everything had been perfect between us up until this point. I'd always behaved and done exactly what was expected of me. In return, he praised my work and worshiped my body. Though, clearly not my mouth, and the way I'd talked back to him in front of my equals.

Eric may have appreciated my physical appearance, but the way I spoke was often too much for him. So much so, he ensured my contract included specific clauses about where I was allowed to speak candidly.

In my dreamy state, I was still madly in love with the man standing before me. Witnessing how enraged I'd made him made my heart ache.

"Eric, *please*," I begged, ignoring his demand, "We all tried. Did you *see* him? There was nothing left of him. We *couldn't* save him!"

"Take your clothes *off*."

We were only going to go in circles. There was no winning with him. So I obeyed, unable to imagine anything too bad would happen. I believed Eric had treated me well since he and I agreed to start the private affair, just over a year prior to the event this particular nightmare was based on. But with therapy and a shit-tonne of hindsight, these graphic hallucinations had revealed themselves to be the sharp tips of the icebergs that lurked beneath the murky depths of my denial.

I'd barely stripped down to my underwear before Eric roughly grabbed my arm and pulled me onto the bed. At this point, I'd assumed he wanted to let off some steam. He'd often used me as the tool to help bring him back to a better and more stable mood.

He tore my bra from my body before grabbing a fistful of hair at the base of my neck, shoving my face into the sheets as he mounted me from behind, still fully clothed himself.

With his knees, my arms were pinned down at my sides. Eric may have been tall and lean, but the man was far stronger than me. It didn't stop me from trying to break free, struggling against him to no avail. He sat on my back, applying his full weight. I could hardly breathe. Something wasn't right, my movements had never been so restricted.

As my dream progressed, I was granted a better view, my mind showing me the scene from the side of the bed, looking over us. Having my subconscious travel to this dark place so many times, I could almost completely detach from how horrific the memory was. It had desensitized me enough to observe and critique Eric's work.

*He's about to start.*

The version of me, held down, couldn't see the knife Eric had produced from his pocket. He flipped it open and raised it high above his head, then brought it down with both hands, hard into my left shoulder blade.

With my mind having put the pieces together over time, I didn't believe Eric had originally intended on adding the names to my skin. It truly seemed as though he were planning on stabbing me to death.

*Here comes another one.* I braced myself, watching on, wishing he'd have gone straight for my throat to end me there. It would have saved me the suffering of what would come in the years to follow.

He repeated the move a handful of times before the more theatric part of his own fucked up mind kicked in and he began hacking the name of the dead man into my flesh.

*Messy, but he gets better with time.*

His hands, covered in my blood, trembled from the adrenaline and shock of his actions.

My body writhed, and I screamed in complete agony beneath him. Blood oozed from the wounds, flowing over my sides and up to my hairline, soaking the sheets beneath me.

I couldn't see what tool he used, nor did I know why he had resorted to such extreme violence. Not even twelve hours earlier, we'd been moaning each other's names under the same set of sheets before we kissed each other goodbye to start our separate work days.

"It was our *only* chance, Sumar." he sniveled, slicing the last letter of the name as he moved lower on my body. My arms were released, only I didn't move.

Eric rolled me over, knees still at either side of my hips so I couldn't escape, not that I had the willpower to do so.

My skin was saturated, red and slick with my blood. It covered my chin, neck, chest and stomach as I tried to reach up to him with what little strength I had left.

"I'm sorry," I tried to say, but it barely came out as a broken whisper, muffled as I became overcome with shock.

"It's *not enough*, Sumar." he cried, holding my face tight in his hands, his forehead pressed to mine, "Do you *want* to die? *To leave me again?*"

"No…" I groaned from the pain, unable to move from both the damage to my back and from Eric holding me down.

"I tried to *save you,* darling." Eric was so far into his blind rage, there was no level of depravity too deep for him to stoop.

"Summer?" A voice called to me. It didn't match the scene.

*It's just a dream.* I watched on, unable to turn away as Eric removed my underwear and untied his belt.

"Summer!"

Eric forced himself into my bloodied body, wrapping his hands tight around my neck as he began to thrust.

"Summer, I'm here. You're okay."

The voice wasn't mine, choking without a fight under Eric's grip. It wasn't Eric's, yelling that I deserved to die if I didn't want to be with him forever. For the second time that day, I slipped into another state of unconsciousness and became completely unresponsive.

*No wonder my mind is such a fucking mess. How many times did he render me unconscious over all our years in bed together?*

"*Summer!*"

The voice distracted me too much from what played out in front of my eyes. I hadn't noticed Eric was done with my body, looking more like a mutilated corpse as he abandoned me in a pool of blood and stumbled to the bathroom to begin his lament over what he'd done.

Everything around me grew blurry, and lighter the longer I searched for what had stirred me.

"Summer, wake up. Come back to me." The voice sounded a little worried, I didn't like hearing it that way.

When I opened my eyes, I found Logan's — free of his glasses and looking back into mine. I blinked a few times while I tried to work out where we were.

"I think you were having a nightmare," he said quietly, brows pinched with concern as we laid in bed with our bodies turned to face each other. His warm fingers softly brushed the hair that had unraveled from my braids, swirling it around my ear as I wiped tears from my face.

"Oh," I whispered as the heat of his hand on my skin brought me back to the safety of my bedroom, "Yeah, that happens a lot."

"I've noticed. This isn't the first time I've had to wake you."

"Ugh. I'm sorry," I whined and rolled to my back, glaring up at the ceiling, "How often?"

"Every couple of nights."

I sighed. "If I'm disturbing your sleep too much, I'll understand if you don't want to sleep over anymore." I secretly hoped he wouldn't take my offer. Even with the knowledge that Logan was likely a wanted criminal, I had been feeling safe enough to fall asleep beside him.

Every night.

For almost *two weeks*.

The warmth he brought to the bed had me more eager to get under the covers than I'd ever been. It was quite the feat considering the bed was already my favorite place to hide from the world. His presence gave me more solid rest than I'd had in two years. My last decent sleep before meeting him had been the night I'd spent locked in a padded room, and I never thought I'd ever feel that secure again.

"Don't you worry about me," he shrugged. "I usually just put another movie on and go right back to sleep."

I smiled and rolled over to search for my phone on the bedside table to check the time: 10:30 am

It was a Tuesday, mid morning. I'd only been asleep for a few hours. We'd planned on waking soon for our first attempt at spending the day together, rather than me waking up earlier in the night or trying to go out after our shifts when we both needed the rest.

"What should we do today?" Logan asked, pulling me over to his side of *my* bed and wrapping me in his arms from behind.

"Hmm," I answered, still sleepy, "I don't know… but I think I know what *you* want to do." I giggled, pushing my butt back against his body to feel him throbbing, and growing harder as I pulled the sheets up around us.

Logan put his hand up the back of my shirt, moving it around the front to gently brush his fingers down my chest and stomach. He'd been getting more handsy as the days went on, and I was happy about it. So long as I was completely covered, under the bedlinen, *and* in my pajamas.

Things between us hadn't physically progressed all that much, though it was obvious we both wanted it to.

The reasons why we hadn't had sex yet were piling up and I couldn't decide which was taking the lead.

Was it me? Too mentally fucked up by Eric and the work he'd made of my body. Or the fact I was almost certain the seemingly sweet man, kissing my neck and roughly grabbing my hips from behind as I woke each morning, was *Vengeance*, serial murderer?

I'd done a little more research into the vigilante between his visits. Vengeance currently sat comfortably in sixth position on the country's most wanted list. It was an impressive achievement, considering the other names he was competing with. Either way, I was playing with fire, and it was only a matter of time before I got severely burned.

We'd spent every "night" in my bed together since the first time he'd stayed over. Logan didn't seem too bothered by our arrangement so far. He wasn't pushy. If anything, it made me more comfortable around the man I should have found absolutely terrifying.

"Oh!" he hissed excitedly in my ear, putting an abrupt end to the groping I enjoyed, "If we've got the whole day together, we can go see the movie I was telling you about?"

*Ah, yes.* I held my breath so I wouldn't groan.

The new, absurdly graphic movie he was so keen to see. Another that would no doubt soon be added to his rotation of intense thrillers, slashers and action films he'd play on the TV in my bedroom for us to fall asleep to in the early hours of each day. His taste in movies should have been enough of an indicator to his alter ego. I was surprised the man's identity hadn't been discovered before.

*Or maybe it has, and he's killed everyone who learned it before you.*

"Yeah, okay." I agreed, closing my eyes again, not ready to leave the heat he created to get up and face the cold.

"Can we stop by my apartment first? I need to shave and grab clean clothes." He'd been crashing in my bed in his boxers, wearing his already worn clothes for the trip back to his own home in the morning, where he'd shower and dress for the parts of his day I wasn't privy to.

"Sure!" I said a little too enthusiastically. The chance to see how he lived and whether Vengeance casually stored trophies of his kills around the house was too much of a good opportunity to pass up.

*He could also be leading you away from the safety of your home to slaughter you for your own crimes.*

*Shit.*

Careful to ensure my favorite, oversized band shirt covered every inch of my damaged flesh before I moved, I left the bed for the wardrobe and closed the door behind me as I switched the light on.

*Out to see a movie.* I flipped through my hanging clothes. *So it's another date, right?*

I picked out a deep red velvet dress. It was loose fitting but had a turtle neck and long, tight sleeves, perfect for the cold weather. I grabbed a pair of thick black leggings and my chunky black work boots to go with it.

Head to toe in dark shades. Just another habit I brought into my new life after being dressed up like a doll in nothing but black or red for years.

I quickly threw on a basic face at the bathroom mirror to complete the outfit, and so I didn't look too tired with giving up my sleeping hours to spend time with Logan.

Taking my braids out from the night before to reveal a mess of waves, I quickly parted them roughly with my fingers. It was as good as it could get with it being almost the middle of my "night."

As I turned to leave the bathroom, I spun back to the mirror and pulled it at the base to reveal the shallow cupboard behind. I grabbed the bottle of my favorite pills and stuffed them into a small clutch.

Moving back to the bedroom, ready to leave, I opened the walk-in door to catch Logan still propped up on the pillows in bed, scrolling on his phone. His eyes darted to me for a second before they rushed back to his screen.

"Ugh," he whined, "You look *so* fucking good. Red really suits you."

*So I've been told.*

"Then why not look for longer than half a second?" I glanced down at my dress, wondering if he was lying and I actually looked ridiculous. He'd seen me in nothing but jeans, white shirts, pajamas and gym wear since we'd met. I'd hoped putting in some effort deserved a little more than a split second of his attention.

He dropped his phone on his bare chest and sighed as his eyes met mine.

"Summer… I peeked," he admitted.

My jaw dropped, and my heart exploded into a frantic rhythm. Logan quickly sat up and raised his hands in defense.

"Not at *you,*" he hurriedly explained, "Not while you were getting dressed. I wouldn't *dare* cross that line."

That didn't make me feel better, I had no idea what the fuck he was talking about. We'd built up a weird kind of trust over the past few weeks with him sleeping in my house, and it was swiftly vanishing with the thought of him spying on me.

*Aren't you trying to do the same to him?*

If he didn't mean *me,* I could only assume that he'd found something else. Maybe something about my own secret identity that I wasn't ready to share with him.

Logan learning my role in the underworld would absolutely have my murder by his hands bumping him up another place on that most wanted list.

*Imagine the shitstorm Eric would face if he could never prove you were still alive.* It disturbed me to admit I found the thought a little exciting.

"Then *what* did you peek at?"

He scratched at his neck, guilt smeared across his face. "The drawer."

"*Drawer?*" He couldn't have found my safe, it was too well hidden. "What drawer?"

He tipped his head to the bedside table. With Logan having taken what was originally *my* side of my bed, I hadn't thought to relocate the toys at any point in the few weeks since switching to the other side.

"Oh!" I laughed. Relief quickly swept over me, but my neck and face burned with embarrassment. I was grateful the neckline of the dress was so high, he'd only see about half of what he made me feel. "But *that's* a line you're okay with crossing?"

He grimaced at my response.

I arched a brow at him from the end of the bed, "So… Does what you found make you uncomfortable?"

"Quite the opposite, actually," he said, a little too smoothly.

I felt hot all over again. The tension boiling between us had to bubble over at some point, and with the pills in my bag I was finally prepared for it.

"Well… We should get going, right?" I asked, breaking the intense eye contact between us and moving for the door.

"Yeah, just give me another minute." He sighed and leaned back onto the pillows, unlocking his phone again to continue scrolling.

"Something wrong?" I frowned, wondering what could have possibly been keeping him from seeing a movie that sounded like it was written *specifically* for him.

"Nothing wrong… just… *rock hard* at the thought of you using any of them on yourself," he confessed with a strained laugh. "Looking at all the awful shit in the news to replace the thoughts and calm me down."

"Well I'm going to grab some water while you get dressed." I told him, giggling as I made my way down the hall to grab a bottle from the fridge.

Once I heard the light to my bedroom being switched off, I made my way back to meet Logan at the front door. He started pulling his jacket on, but missed the hole for the sleeve as he tried to guide his arm through it, *twice*, distracted by watching me as I walked towards him.

I slowed my steps to give him a better look. "Ready to go, *now?*"

Seeming unable to form words, he nodded, hungrily taking me in and suppressing a grin as I typed the code to open the front door.

Everything he'd seen while snooping through my stuff seemed to have sparked a new hope. Maybe he thought our sleepovers were destined to be a little more fun at some point.

"So…" he started as we crossed the driveway in the cool air, headed for his car on the street. "Which one is your favorite?"

*God, just take him back inside. You've got the pills in your bag. What are you waiting for?*

I *knew* he'd see my blushing out in the daylight. It would be a permanent feature on my skin at the rate we were already going for the day.

"I'm quite partial to the blue one." I confessed, not adding it had been my go-to since the night he'd sent me pictures of himself.

He gnawed his lip as we got into his car, turning the key and sitting quietly for a second while the adorably dumb smile from the hallway crept across his face again.

"Go on, ask," I encouraged him, sensing he had at least one more question about the contents of the bedside drawer playing on his mind.

He turned the car around and started to drive down the winding street before he settled on what he most wanted to know, "Was… was one made of *glass?*" his eyes darted from the road to me, seeming too shy to maintain eye contact while asking such bold questions.

"Yep." I confessed, giggling again, "I've got a bit of a thing for heat."

*If his hands and body are so hot, surely that means every part of him is the same?*

My stomach tightened a little over the thought.

*He's ruined me for coffee, what if he does the same with my vibrators?*

"Would you…" he cleared his throat. "If we get past… what we're doing now… do you think you would ever be…" He trailed off, but I got the gist.

"Logan… are you trying to ask if I'll let you use them on me some day?" I gasped and raised my eyebrows at him, keeping my expression dead serious.

He turned to me, eyes wide with alarm, no doubt concerned he'd crossed another line with me again so soon. I shouldn't have been so mean, but I let him squirm for a second.

"Sounds fun." I purred, pleased that I'd had the sense to bring the pills along.

Logan nodded again, seeming at another loss for words. I wondered if his head was full of the same fantasies as mine.

He eventually composed himself enough for normal conversation the closer we drove to his apartment, twenty minutes in the opposite direction of the restaurant.

I felt a little guilty learning he drove an extra hour by the time he got to his job, every day, just so we could sleep in the same bed. *Just* sleep. *For weeks.*

We took the elevator up to his floor and he unlocked the door to his home, holding it open for me to step into the space.

The view was impressive from the wall opposite the entrance. It was almost entirely made of glass, and led to a balcony with a low couch. He lived in the nicer part of town, and while it wasn't a city full of skyscrapers, there were taller buildings like this one that had a fantastic view of the Gray Mountains in the distance. I could almost pick the exact slopes I grew up under, even from being over an hour's drive away.

"You like the view?" he noted when he caught me staring, "It's even better when the sun sets."

"It's really pretty," I said and turned away, not allowing myself to get upset on our first full day together, "I used to live much closer to them when I was a kid."

I continued scoping the room for signs of danger. There was nothing but wall to my left, and immediately to my right was the kitchen. Most of it against the wall that shared the front door. A small narrow island divided the space between the kitchen and living area with a TV, couch, and three seater dining table behind it. There was a hallway, further to the right that Logan led me to.

"My bedroom is in there. Help yourself," he gestured to the closed door on the left as he took the right to the bathroom. There was one more door, further down the hall, closed to hide its secrets.

"My roommate's," he told me.

*Funny. He's taken his glasses off and can still see me looking at it from so far away.*

"What are they like?"

"My roommate? She's nosey as fuck. So don't leave anything here. You'll either never get it back, or she'll hound me with questions about it," he said mindlessly, focusing on applying shaving cream.

It was an odd thing to say, and I wondered if she was more than just a roommate. Maybe a girlfriend, and I was unknowingly crossing *all sorts* of lines with this man.

He noted my confusion in the reflection as I leaned against his door across the hall.

"She's my sister," he chuckled, reaching for a razor on the bench, "I moved in with her after I left Bedlam. She and her husband had just split, so we decided to stick together for a while. It wasn't meant to be this permanent, but we've been here for a few years."

Deciding that sounded fairly truthful, I nodded and turned to open his bedroom door. The room was average sized, made to feel a little smaller by the king bed, its head leaning on the right wall. A door to the same balcony I noted earlier was directly across from me, with more views of the mountains. To my immediate left was a walk-in, its door slightly ajar. A dresser with a TV on it shared the wall with the frame I'd walked through. I took note of the height to the drop beyond the glass as I stepped closer.

*Way too high for any chance of surviving the fall if things turn deadly between us.*

"Can I go through *your* stuff?" I called as I sat on the bed, quickly slipping one of the pills in my mouth and swallowing it dry. Now I'd scoped out the place for any immediate threats, I needed to take the edge off for more amateur sleuthing.

The pill's fast-acting effects already had me thinking the reason we'd made a stop here wasn't only to freshen up for our day out.

Being alone in his apartment made me wonder if Logan would see the opportunity as I did. Maybe he thought the change of scenery would make me want to take things further between us. He didn't know I'd have him *anywhere* under the right conditions.

*Does he want to fuck me? Or kill me?* I sighed. I still didn't know, but was glad to already be feeling less anxious over either option.

As Logan ran the water in the bathroom, I considered running back to the kitchen, using the sound as cover to grab a knife. But the bathroom door was wide open and he would see me with eyes that had proven to be observant enough for one day.

"Ahh, yeah? I guess," he called back.

He should have seen it coming, or at least known I'd have a peek after he'd rummaged through my toy collection.

Regardless of his answer, I shamefully had to admit that I *really* wanted to poke through his things to look for proof of who he really was.

*What if you find the suit? What then? Confront a killer in his own home? You're a fucking moron.*

"I'm not going to find anything *dirty* in these drawers?" I asked, hoping I sounded teasing and not too tense as I quietly pried one open. Grabbing one of several, identical bottles of cologne in the top drawer, I popped the lid off and inhaled deeply.

"I *wash* my clothes before I put them away," he said, prompting an eye roll from me. Even with concentrating on his face, there was playful sarcasm in his tone.

The water ran again while I flipped through neatly folded T-shirts, athletic wear, and underwear. Everything was kept so orderly. *Too* neat. I could have guessed he was a Gifted serial killer from inspecting the stacks of identically folded shirts alone. Eric kept his clothes just as neat, and seeing everything this way made my skin crawl.

"That's what my phone is for," he laughed, still on the subject of me finding porn or anything along those lines in his room.

Stepping lightly on the floorboards, I made my way to the door of his walk-in and pushed it open. It swung without a sound to reveal an enormous mess of clothes and shoes spread all over the floor, hangers tangled, and a small wash basket overflowing. I exhaled heavily at the sight. It was like two different people shared the space.

*Maybe he knew he'd bring me back at some point and stuffed everything in there? Or maybe to bring someone else here? It's not like we're dating. Not officially. I don't even know what we are. Adults having PG rated sleepovers?*

I couldn't contain my smile at the chaotic space.

*At least now he seems a little more normal.*

I crept over to the only bedside table in the room, knowing that's where I kept some of my secrets and hoping it'd be where I'd find his.

Two ring boxes greeted me as I pulled it open, one larger than the other. I grabbed and opened the bigger of the two to reveal a men's wedding band. It was made of white gold, and had a date from around ten years prior engraved on the inside.

*Too personal, put it back. This isn't what you're looking for!*

I reached for the other box and flipped the top. Two, much smaller, white gold bands. One laced with diamonds with the same date etched into the delicate metal.

My hand trembled as I snapped the box shut, feeling guilty for having gone that far. I just wanted something to trip him up on his cover, not to dig through his entire, heartbreaking backstory.

As if I were possessed after replacing the boxes, my hands moved to a small stack of photos at the bottom of the drawer. Lifting them from their place, I noticed a police badge stashed beneath them.

*At least that lines up with what he's shared with me so far. Maybe I'll finally learn his surname.*

I flipped through the photos. Logan appeared in almost every one of them, most with another woman. She was *beautiful.* Tanned skin, brown hair and eyes, radiant smile. By the looks of their height difference, even if she were wearing heels, she would have been far taller than me.

*The wife,* I concluded, not feeling anything but heartache for the gorgeous, younger version of Logan in the photos, knowing the beautiful couple wouldn't be together for as long as they'd planned.

While she was stunning, the only thing about her that made me self conscious was that I might not be Logan's typical type. Perhaps I was just a look to tick off his *"fuck-it list"* — much like what Tony was doing.

I looked through more of the photos in my hands. Wedding photos. Logan — *unbearably* handsome in a tux. He looked so happy standing beside the picturesque bride in white. Their wedding party contained the familiar faces of his friends. Tommy, his best man and Harrison amongst others as bridesmaids.

One of the women had almost identically-dark skin to Harrison, only hers held a warm glow, not the tattooed tone with starry sparkles. As her ice-blue eyes held mine, I wondered how one group of friends could be so insanely good-looking. I tried to work out which of the women might be Logan's sister, but found no clues.

Another picture showed who I could only guess were his parents, beaming with pride on their son's big day.

With every new photo I viewed, it became harder for me to believe Logan could be a monster in any sense of the word. He looked like a normal man, trying to have a normal life, like so many of the Gifted.

Hands suddenly wrapped around mine, and the photos were gently pried from them. I should have known he was coming, the strong scent of his heavy cologne had reached my nostrils before I'd seen him, but I'd sabotaged my own reaction times with relaxants.

"I thought you'd gone *too* quiet in here." He smiled timidly, replacing the photos and closing the drawer before he sat beside me. He'd changed. Similar dark jeans to what he typically wore, his shirt was black with long sleeves, pushed up to his elbows, the soft fabric sat *tight* on his body.

"I'm *so* sorry, Logan, I went too far. That's *none* of my business—"

"I'm not upset you saw them." He gently shook his head and smiled sadly. "I just don't want you to feel weird about all of this. It's the past, it can't be changed. It's just something I've had to bring into every attempt at a relationship since. You get it though right? With you having been married too?"

"Wait, *what?*" I snorted.

"In the cult? With your ex?" he tried to clarify, squinting at me through his lenses.

"Oh. No." I tried to suppress a laugh, "No. Uh-uh. Eric and I were *never* married."

"Oh. Wow — I just assumed," he placed his hand on my leg, "With you being sixteen and there for what, *ten years?* I thought he would have arranged for that to happen early on."

"You'd think — but no. It wasn't part of my contract."

"Contract?"

*Fuck!* I'd let that slip. If Logan really was from Bedlam and hung around dodgy places like Crave, there was a good chance he might have heard the rumors about my ex and his methods for having us sign our lives over.

"Ah, yeah, you know. Just the arrangement of it all. Whatever. But *no*, I've never been married." I hoped my doped up ramblings didn't give too much away.

My admission made Logan look more sad for me, like I was dating someone with a whole past life and I'd not experienced as many things. I didn't appreciate that look. I'd experienced far more than what the average person endured, and I wasn't in the mood to be pitied.

"Does that…" I started, "Does that bother you?"

"No," he reassured me with a small smile, "I just thought maybe it was common ground between us, you know? It doesn't seem fair. I've done everything by choice and you've had none of that. Only to leave a cult and end up spending time with someone like me."

We had far more common ground than he knew. Crave covered plenty of ground, figuratively and literally. The world we were a part of. Bedlam. I wanted to tell him we weren't so different, but couldn't.

"Someone like you? It doesn't bother me that you lived and enjoyed life before I came along." I elbowed him playfully, "I mean, I might have, had there been like, a crazy ex to deal with — like what you're getting on my end of whatever this is between us."

"Are you over him?"

"Are you over her?"

"I asked first," he said, pushing me like I'd elbowed him, only with far more force. I gripped the mattress tight to not fly off the bed.

"Fine," I rolled my eyes, "Yes. I'm *over* Eric. Maybe not in the normal way. My mind is *completely fucked* and he's left me with literal scars. But there was no reciprocated love there."

*Just me, completely pathetic and wishing for years he would feel the same for me.* I swallowed hard as I looked down.

Logan bobbed his head, taking it as his cue to share. He was getting better with cues.

"I'm over Millie, I guess. In the sense that I can move on. I *know* she'd find a way to haunt me if I didn't at least try to keep living a normal life."

His comment about haunting made me try to suppress another laugh. I was *constantly* haunted by my past. The increasing number of similarities between myself and the serial slaughterer who had me alone in his home were starting to scare me.

"What's so funny?" he asked, turning his body to face mine. He gently used the fingers of both hands on my collarbone to push me back to lie on the bed.

"We're just such a *fucking* mess."

He was all smiles when he moved on all fours over me. I sunk into his pillows, dropping my legs to the sides for him to rest his hips on mine.

"Too messy?" Logan teased, trying to keep a straight face as he leveled his eyes with mine, "No good? We should give up now, shouldn't we? Before shit gets too serious between us."

"Yep. I'm no good for you. Far too broken." My voice wavered with excited anticipation when he leaned down to kiss me. I grabbed at the nape of his neck, his mouth on mine as he lowered himself onto me. Using one of his arms to hold himself up just a little to not *completely* crush me, he ran the other hand up the side of my face and into my hair, holding my head in place.

Everything with him was soft. Well, that was a lie. I could feel him, *hard* again, rubbing against me through his jeans when I lifted my legs to wrap them around his waist.

Logan's *actions* with me were soft. Gentle touches, light kisses. His fingers traced my ear and jawline as he moved his hand lower to grope at my breast through my dress.

Overcome with the effects of the pill, I became more lightheaded in the cloud of cologne as he moved his mouth to my neck. My breathing became heavier at the feel of his warm lips brushing against my skin.

Despite the chill in the air, sweat formed along the edges of Logan's hairline. I rolled my hands up his sides and around to his back, digging my fingertips into his shoulder blades. The move made him work harder at my neck, and he used his hand to pull the fabric of my dress away so he could have better access to more of my bare skin.

Leaving one hand at the back of his head, encouraging him to stay in place, I reached between us to undo his belt with the other. Sufficiently drugged, all I could focus on was *finally* getting him inside me.

"Oh! You want me *now?*" he asked excitedly, taking note of my eagerness to undress him.

"Yeah. *Now.*" I moaned.

Logan leaned back on his knees, hands sliding up my legs and under my dress, firmly gripping the top of my leggings and ready to remove them.

"Can I?" he asked just as eagerly as my hands moved.

"Yes! Do it!" I exclaimed as I looked up at him.

His eyes darted between mine. Something I couldn't read flashed across his features as he observed me from above. Logan let go of my clothing and dropped down over me, hands at either side of my head on the pillow so our faces returned to being only a few inches apart.

"Have you…?" he started, squinting at me and lifting his glasses to rest them on his head. His hazel eyes oddly had a darker tinge to them in the lighting of his room as he inspected my face. "We're gonna be late. We can always come back to this," he said quickly, replacing his glasses and moving to sit at the side of the bed, catching his breath and fixing his belt.

"What?" I snapped as I sat up, shocked at being rejected after he'd been all hands with me in bed just an hour or so earlier, asking me about toys and whether he could use them on me. What had he seen that could stop him so suddenly?

"We… haven't eaten anything today."

"Wouldn't that just slow us down?" I asked, trying not to sound too hurt.

"I think it'd do the opposite," he said, clearly not believing his own lie, but followed it up with what sounded like a very truthful statement, "The things I want to do to you, nurse. You're gonna need all the energy you can get."

"Is that so?" I laughed. The rejection stung a little less, but plain ol' confusion set firmly in its place.

"Yep. Come on, let's go," he demanded as he moved to the door, zipping his jacket up over his shirt, signifying the moment between us was completely over. I sighed and tore myself off the bed through the heavy weight of disappointment.

"I just need to fix up my hair." I told him as I paused by the bathroom.

"Okay," he called, and kept moving toward the front door.

I ran to the mirror and roughly brushed my fingers through my waves. I looked fine, but that wasn't what I was really there for. Leaning closer to my reflection, I examined my eyes in a bid to find what made him so abruptly change his mind. My pupils were dilated a little more than normal, and not quite as reactive to light as they should be, a typical side effect of what I'd taken.

*Fuck. How could I have been so stupid? Of course he'd see that if he's Gifted.*

The glasses, again, had me thrown completely off his scent. They *had* to be fake, and he was a wolf in sheep's clothing. But then, he'd just chosen to not have sex with me while I was high.

No matter how hard I tried to understand Logan, I just couldn't place the danger — or if there was any to begin with.

I left the bathroom to meet him at the door as he held it open for me, locking it behind us before we made our way down to his car.

# TWENTY-THREE

## SUMMER

"Pizza okay with you?" Logan asked when we walked by a quiet restaurant.

"Pizza is perfect." I lied, not really caring for any food at this time of the day. I'd never been a midnight-snack kind of person in my upside down life.

We were seated, and in spite of my protest that I wasn't hungry and would have been fine with my glass of water, Logan ordered the largest pizza on the menu. I let him choose the toppings, unable to remember the last time I'd eaten this specific food. He'd mentioned it was one of his favorites, and he seemed well-versed in its myriad of ingredients.

"How do you not know what's good on pizza?" He asked after a few minutes of chatting while waiting for our food, hung up on something that really wasn't all that important to me.

I shrugged, "I don't eat out much. Or order food much. Tony and Ben usually bring me whatever they're having and I just hope for the best."

Logan chuckled, "Well, lucky you've got them or you'd starve."

"Probably." I agreed, no trace of a joke on my end.

"So what'd you do before you had them to keep you alive?"

"Oh." *Shit. How do I even begin to explain that?* "Do you think I'm so hopeless I couldn't feed myself?"

"With what I've seen so far, yeah." He rolled his eyes, grinning as our food arrived. He grabbed a slice of the enormous dough circle between us. "But by the sounds of it, there was a gap between leaving the cult and finding those two."

After reluctantly choosing the smallest slice, I dragged it onto my plate and began pulling small pieces off with my fingers rather than lifting it to bite. The piece was bigger than my face. I'd eaten less in a whole week.

"I lived with some friends for a while." I explained, "They kept me fed and alive while my house got built."

"You haven't mentioned them before. Do you see them anymore?" he asked between mouthfuls. This was starting to feel like another interrogation.

*It's a date, you're meant to be learning things about each other. Besides, you've been interrogated before and it was nothing like this. That cop was nowhere near as hot. And his partner was a total fucking jerk.*

"I see them about once a month. At least I try to, I get pretty busy with work."

He nodded and grabbed another slice while I quietly picked at mine. I was glad he didn't ask too much more on it. Those "friends" were the owners of Crave. If I mentioned them by name, Logan might have put the pieces together.

While I was growing more certain the man sitting across from me, inhaling slice after slice of pizza, probably wasn't working as a spy for my villainous ex, I still needed to protect those I cared about.

Anna had found me on the side of the road in the desert on the way back from one of her trips to Bedlam for the more *exotic* stock. The barkeeper and her husband took a great risk to themselves and their business for hiding me. They offered me a place to stay while I worked on earning enough money to support myself for the first time in my life.

"Do you ever worry about how dangerous your job is?" Logan's tone was adorably protective. I didn't need his protection, but I liked the way it made me feel.

"Sometimes, but that's what the bodyguards are for."

"I mean, you don't worry you'll get caught?"

"Are you planning on dobbing me in?" I purred.

"No," he smiled and dropped his eyes from mine as he took another bite, "But surely you've thought about it?"

"All the time," I admitted with a shrug, "But I guess no matter what happens to me, it'll never be as bad as my time at Ho—" I cleared my throat. "In the cult. It's worth the risk."

I shuffled on my seat and put another small piece in my mouth, hoping if I were too busy chewing, I wouldn't fuck up and say something that would give too many of my own secrets away.

The pills not only helped me relax enough to be intimate, but they also had the terrible side effect of making me too chatty in my unwound state.

"What about you?" I spun the conversation back on him. "I know you were a cop, but have you ever done anything worth being locked away for?"

"I've never been caught for any of the things I've done." he laughed, then quickly explained himself when he noted my wide eyes, "Graffiti, mostly. Dumb shit as a teen with Tommy. We never got caught."

"I see." I giggled. He was kind of telling the truth, Vengeance had never been caught before, and with the condition he left people in, he likely never would.

"Well, I can't say I was so lucky. Though I was only locked up for like, a day."

I couldn't count how many slices he was up to at this point, but that piece nearly went down whole.

"What? You've been in *jail?*"

His reaction made me laugh. "Why? If I admit to it, will you stop sleeping over? An ex-cop can't share a bed with a criminal?" I searched his eyes for a deeper reaction to my words, and hoped he wouldn't be so hypocritical.

It was true, I'd been locked up overnight while my plea deal was being finalized. I would *still* have been locked up had I not taken it. Or worse, Eric would have pulled the strings of his indebted political puppets to get me out early, and I'd be back at Home, forever bound.

"No… I just… wouldn't have picked it."

"Well… I mean, you've seen what I do for a living. None of that is… *legal.* Things catch up to everyone eventually. I've had my turn of taking the fall for dodgy work." I explained, keeping the details of my best friend's death to myself. I couldn't risk Danny's ghost joining us for our date. He made a terrible habit of appearing at the worst of times.

Logan sat back in his chair, probably wondering when his crime sprees would come back to bite him now I'd planted the thought in his head.

My shoulders tensed as I braced for it — the question. *What did you do?* But it didn't come. If he knew, would it end in my gruesome death? Maybe he thought it would, and didn't want to risk it.

"Should we go?" He asked, "The movie starts soon."

"Sure." I agreed, abandoning the rest of my slice and wiping my hands.

Logan looked at my plate, "H-how many slices did you eat?"

"This is my first." I said as I looked down at the half eaten piece, proud I'd eaten more than I thought I could.

"Are you fucking kidding me?"

I shrugged, "You know I don't eat a lot."

"Yeah, but…" he shook his head.

I didn't know much about modern-day Gifted people, but all that extra strength, speed and quick repair had to come from somewhere. I guessed it was likely linked to a higher calorie intake than regular humans.

The way he'd eaten so mindlessly as we talked without so much as breathing between slices of pizza made me think he might still be hungry, even after essentially eating the entire thing himself.

*Maybe he would have eaten more if given the chance.*

"Carb-loading?" I teased.

"Something like that." He frowned at my plate, as if it were the ceramic's fault he'd fucked up.

"So, do you work out often?" I widened my eyes as I spoke, hopeful that playing flirty would distract him from me cluing onto his secrets and make me look too dumb to work it out.

We hadn't had the chance to talk much about what he got up to during the hours we were apart anyway, so my question shouldn't have raised any suspicion.

So far I'd learned he worked for a good portion of his time away from me, but there were also the times he was out with his friends, and I was eager to know what the group got up to during the times they weren't at Crave. Plus when I'd snooped through his clothes earlier, I noticed about half of them would have been suitable for wearing during workouts.

"Yeah… when I can."

"I thought that might have been the case."

Logan folded his arms across his chest and looked down again as he smiled, appearing a little self-conscious,"What makes you say that?"

"Oh come on. How many times have I seen you with your shirt off?" I kicked him playfully under the table, "And your arms…"

"What about them?" he hurried to inspect the limbs as if I'd just announced they were flawed. He didn't seem to think too highly of his own looks. But then, neither did I, no matter what the gossip columns of Bedlam's favorite magazines said about me.

I shrugged and toyed with the high neck of my dress as I leaned with my elbows on the table, "They've just quickly become my favorite thing."

He swallowed hard before giving me a sly smile. "So, nurse… when do I get to see *you* with your shirt off?"

A nervous laugh spluttered up my throat. "You had your chance earlier and didn't take it." I reminded him as I sipped at my water.

He narrowed his eyes a little and sighed. "Come on, let's go."

"Want me to pay for this?"

"Are you kidding? You ate *one* piece! Not even. There's no way you're paying for it."

"Fine." I argued, "But I'm paying for the movie."

# TWENTY-FOUR

## SUMMER

Logan didn't fight me on buying tickets when we arrived at the cinema. I convinced him to get the largest tub of popcorn, still thinking he could have eaten much more than what I'd seen him consume at lunch.

We entered the dark and completely empty theater with Logan quickly guiding me to the back row.

*At least if he wants to try anything here I can run to the bathroom to take another pill.* Though, the first one still hadn't completely worn off, and I was still a little out of it as we took our seats.

But *no*.

Not only did *one* other person join us, choosing the seat *directly* in front of mine like she had no other fucking options, but Logan was most *definitely* there to see the movie.

He took in every detail like he had back at my house with the films he'd claimed to have seen a million times. It was kind of adorable, and I found I was more interested in watching him than what played on the screen.

He quickly became so consumed by the story I could have stripped all of my clothes off and I don't believe he would have noticed. It was tempting. But even with being high, I still didn't have that kind of confidence with someone else in the room with us.

Despite the theater being so large, I oddly felt a little confined. The heavy fabric of the curtained walls was far from our seats, yet every time I glanced their way, they seemed to have moved a little closer.

Logan eventually noticed me staring at him, and if it wasn't so dark, I could have sworn I'd finally made *him* blush.

"What?" The question was muffled by a mouthful of popcorn.

"So… you were a cop and you're *obsessed* with shit like this?" I whispered, trying to work out exactly where Logan ended and Vengeance started as yet *another* car exploded on screen.

"Yeah…" he shrugged with a small smile and turned back.

"Have you thought about going back to it? Crime out this way isn't as bad as it is in Bedlam. It might even be easy work by comparison."

Seven years seemed like a long time for someone to commit to their career, only to give it all up. Was someone like Vengeance subjected to the same hauntings everyone with similar professions eventually experienced?

I found it an unlikely theory, considering the crime scenes he created on his own were probably worse than what he'd seen, even as a cop on an average day in Bedlam.

He shook his head and whispered back without taking his eyes off the action, "I'm just not sure I'm the right fit for it anymore."

*Right fit?* I guessed someone who turned people he perceived to be guilty into piles of gory goop wasn't exactly the stable mind they were looking for in the police force. Even with the present day chaos the Gifted contributed to their workload, Logan could be a loose cannon.

*They had to have all been guilty of something.* I recalled the headline my handsome date would go down in history for — all those slaughtered officers. If he were a cop at the time, how did he slip through the cracks undetected? I should have grabbed the badge instead of the photos when snooping through his room, positive that learning his full name would have helped me uncover more of his secrets.

"Do you miss it, Logan?"

"Yeah. Sometimes. I dunno, I like my life as it is now. Popcorn?" he asked, tipping the enormous bucket my way. I took a few pieces off the top and ate them slowly, one piece at a time as I thought about what other information I could extract from him while he was in this movie-induced trance.

"Really? You are *totally* content with what you do?" I pushed, unable to believe someone like him could happily give up the action he was so addicted to, only to wait on tables and sit around in an empty restaurant most nights while all the fun happened elsewhere.

Logan forcefully tore his eyes from the screen and turned his head to me, "Yeah. I get to do my own thing most of the time. Can you imagine if I were still a cop, though?" he elbowed me and turned back, "You and I would make a fucking cool team."

I laughed at the deeper meaning. Vengeance paired up with a nurse. It would be a similar arrangement to the work I'd once done for a crime boss who hired me to stitch up a man while one of his goons simultaneously sliced him for information.

I could never do that again.

Besides, Logan and his friends seemed to have quite the cozy team image going for themselves, and I didn't know if I could ever fit in with them.

"What about you?" he asked as he looked at me again, his own questions evidently burning hot enough in his mind to abandon the movie for another moment, "Are you happy with what you do now? Even though it's not helping with OR stuff and surgery? You get to call the shots in your own home... Would you ever go back? Not to Eric or the cult I mean—"

"I know what you mean, and yeah, I'm happy wi—"

"Shh!" The woman in front of us cut me off.

"Shh, *yourself*." I hissed back.

"*Summer*." Logan chuckled, tipping the popcorn to me. I grabbed a few more pieces from much deeper in the bucket than I had just moments ago.

"Fuck her." I whispered as I chewed, annoyed at having our momentum broken.

"Who do you relate to most?" I asked after a few minutes passed, "The good guys or the bad guys?"

Logan spun to face me again, squinting behind his glasses as I gave him the most innocent smile I could force across my features. It was lucky we were in the dark, innocent wasn't something I pulled off all that well anymore.

"I guess it depends on their motives," he frowned, eyes dropping to the bucket between us, "Any half decent bad guy is relatable in some way, right? Makes you wonder if they're really all that bad." Something about my question bothered him. Logan's voice grew more dour as he continued. "*Good guys* usually aren't *that* good. What do they really change or save? They get just as many, if not *more* people killed, and are hailed as heroes. It's *fucking stupid.*"

Goosebumps rolled in a wave from my arm beside him and over the rest of my body. The woman in front of us felt it too, I noticed her tense, even in the dark.

*The cinema is freezing, right?* I sighed and forced myself to face the reality of the situation. *God you're fucking stupid, you KNOW it had something to do with him.*

Going against all internal warnings, I reached for Logan's hand and squeezed it as my other pulled at the high neckline of my dress. I felt like I was suffocating, the fabric suddenly too tight and the walls were too close. I swear they drew nearer every time I glanced to either side of the room.

"Yeah, *fucking stupid.*" I agreed.

"Shh!" the woman hissed again. I kicked the back of her chair.

"Summer!" Logan let out a hushed laugh, "You'll get us thrown out."

"I'm sorry!" I huffed. Whatever he'd done had me instantly on edge. "I don't know what got into me."

"So, nurse… you've seen some crazy shit," he started, oblivious to my struggle to stay calm, "Could someone survive that?" he nodded to the screen where someone was just whacked across the head with a baseball bat.

My giggles were laced with mild hysterics, "Yeah, he'd probably be fine. Tell me, is the way they use handguns in movies realistic at all?"

He frowned at the screen, "Nah, not really. I have to disassociate pretty hard when watching movies like this. Like Jackie does when she…" he cut himself short on revealing more of the gang's secrets, "How about that guy?"

I watched as someone was torn in half by the villain, "Ugh… maybe not that guy."

"Yeah, probably not," he agreed with a smirk. Had he done something similar to a human body? I had the unnerving realization that I didn't actually care to know if he had. I was enjoying our time together a little too much. Far more than I'd planned.

*Fuck, you're weak. You don't just go for shitty men, you fall for fucking monsters. You never learn. Eric always said you never learned from your mistakes.* I swallowed hard and dropped my eyes from the screen.

"Hey, are you alright?" Logan asked, squeezing my hand, still in his.

"Yeah, I—" My eyes flicked up at the action to see a man being stabbed. I counted the times the knife entered his body, central to his chest.

*Eleven. If it stays at eleven I'll be fine. I'm just on edge, I need to fucking relax. Have those curtains moved closer AGAIN?*

The character on screen was stabbed once more and collapsed to the ground. A laugh escaped my lungs and I threw my hands up in defeat. It seemed it was my body's only way of stopping itself from bursting into tears, though it made me look just as crazy.

"Will you *shut up?*" the woman in the row below spun around in her chair to glare up at me.

"*Excuse me*?" I looked down to her in the dark, not really able to make out many of her features and still giggling from my state of madness at the scene that threatened to cause sedation-worthy flashbacks.

"Shut up!" she demanded, "I'm trying to watch!"

Leaning forward, I grabbed the back of her chair tight in my hands and dropped my face to hers.

"So are we. If you can't take the commentary, then maybe you should *fuck off.*"

"Why the fuck are you even laughing?" she snapped back, "It's *not* funny."

"When you see shit that's *too fucking close* to real life, it kinda does make it a little funny." I sat back in my chair and folded my arms, not taking my eyes from hers.

"Summer?" Logan tried to chime in.

The woman looked at me like I was too crazy to push further and turned around in her seat.

*Smart move. Why, Danny? Why now?* That man just wouldn't rest in *fucking peace*. There was always something to remind me of him. *Fucking inescapable, no matter what I try.*

I hadn't noticed Logan trying to pry my hand from my folded arms and became annoyed at the sensation of being grabbed at.

"*What?*" I shouted.

"Maybe we should go?"

"And miss your movie?"

"You know I'm just going to end up watching it every night in bed. I just wanted to spend time with you," he assured me.

"Okay. Yeah, let's go."

Just as we got to the end of our row and started down the steps, the woman, now behind us, couldn't let us leave without making a comment.

"*Fucking psycho,*" she mumbled.

Laughing as I turned back to her, I called out, "Oh I'm a *fucking psycho*, am I? That's a title I can live up to." I tore the popcorn bucket from Logan's hand, and before he could register my actions, I tossed it into the air and hit it hard as it came back down. It flew several feet in front of us before the remainder of its contents rained down on her and the surrounding seats.

"What the *fuck* is wrong with you!" she screeched, standing up.

"A lot, to be honest—" I let out a squeal as the room flipped upside down. Logan had picked me up and thrown me over his shoulder, carrying me out of the room and into the bright light of the foyer. He didn't set me down until we were out on the street.

"I'd hate to see what you'd do in a full room if you're willing to pick fights with the *only* other person in there. No wait, maybe I *would* like to see that," he laughed, grabbing my hand tight to lead me further away from the theater. I had no doubt he was trying to move me away fast before she followed us or I considered going back in there myself.

"I didn't need you to *carry* me out of there," I growled, and the second his grip lessened, I removed my hand from his. "Now I probably just look more crazy."

"Fuck what she thinks," he laughed again, placing his hands in his pockets as he walked beside me, "And you kind of *are* crazy. What got into you back there? Are you always so much of a troublemaker when you're out in public?"

"I'm *not*." I promised, hoping it wouldn't deter him from spending more time with me. I was once an expert at perfect public behavior. Clearly, no longer having threats hanging over my head made me relax a little too much.

"I don't know… you didn't feel it suddenly get real cold in there? I think that and the movie was just a bit much."

He sidestepped straight around my comment on the temperature, "You've never reacted that way to any of the others."

"Let's be honest, Logan. I'm usually asleep while you're watching them."

He laughed, "Yeah, fair enough."

"It was only a matter of time before I saw an exact replica of the fucked up shit I've seen."

"Wait, so, you saw that kind of thing in the cult? I wouldn't have thought you'd been exposed to so much violence."

*Shit.*

"I think you'd be surprised at what happens behind closed doors in places like where I was. I'm sorry I ruined the end of your movie." I apologized, completely embarrassed by acting out in front of him. I usually saved that behavior for bars and gyms, not quiet theaters, not that I'd ever been before. "I don't even know *how* to act in places like that." The words of my thoughts slipped out by mistake.

*Maybe this is why I don't go out. Or date.*

"No way. You made it much more entertaining." His hand grabbed mine again, swinging them between us as we made our way back to his car. I didn't let go this time, feeling better now I'd calmed down. "Hold up, what did you mean by that?" He'd stopped moving and pulled on me so I'd turn back to face him, "You've been to a cinema before, right?"

"Nope. That was the first time."

His mouth popped open with surprise.

"So what?" I demanded with a frustrated shrug, adding *defensive* to the list of overwhelming emotions a single day off had forced upon me, "D'you think I was allowed days out of the cult to go do normal shit? I lived in the fucking *woods* as a kid. And I haven't had time for things like this since escaping. I've been spending all my time trying to get my life together."

"I just…" he frowned, "Don't feel like I'm the right person for you to be experiencing *firsts* with."

"Why? Shouldn't it be up to *me* who I choose to do these things with? Can you tell me what is so wrong with *you*, that you shouldn't be the one?"

It was a question for both of us. Not only wanting him to admit he was more than just *Logan*, but also for me to actually produce any evidence at all that this man was no good for me.

He shook his head, "What else haven't you done that I should know about?"

"How long have you got?"

"Summer, I'm serious," he sighed, though he was smiling.

I shrugged again, "I don't know. Probably heaps. But — don't give me that look!" I scolded him for looking sad for me, "I've done plenty, okay? More than the average person could hope to dream of. Just maybe not normal shit like *dating* and *seeing movies*." I rolled my eyes and pulled him along again. "If it makes you feel any better, maybe think of the fact that I'm *choosing* to do things with you. I never had the autonomy to do something as simple as that in the past."

Logan tugged me sideways to kiss the top of my head. I guessed it was his way to show he appreciated what I was getting at before he said, "We should get something to eat."

"Are you kidding? I don't think I can eat much more today. Maybe not even this week."

"Home then?" he suggested, "You should probably get back to sleep for a couple of hours before you have to get up for therapy."

"Yeah, I guess."

"Unless… there's something else you'd rather do?"

We hadn't set foot through my front door before Logan's hands were running up the backs of my legs to lift me. He held me off the ground and against his body as I wrapped my limbs around him.

The door softly closed behind us as I roughly kissed his jaw and mouth while he carried me further into the hallway of my house.

He reached behind his back, and I couldn't work out why until I felt a tugging at my hand. My clutch was suddenly ripped from my grip and tossed like a frisbee down the length of the hall. I was surprised it didn't break through the laundry door with the force of its connection.

*Fuck, he's onto me. I can't do this without the pills.*

Logan dropped me to the bed, crawling on top of me as I resisted the urge to wriggle backwards, not wanting to move away from him and *desperately* praying I'd find a way to match his energy. But I knew I couldn't.

I kissed him when his mouth met mine again, reaching for his face with trembling hands.

*You'll be fine without them.* The more realistic part of my mind kicked in with, *No. No. I can't do this!*

He stopped, and lifted himself, hands on the bed and arms extended to give me space. His brows tied over the sight of my wide eyes, "Something's wrong."

"Logan, I can't. I–"

"You don't have to explain yourself to me. If you can't, you can't."

"Surely you're getting sick of this by now?" I frustratedly blinked back tears at how ridiculous I was being, sure this absurdly patient man was ready to give up on the idea of us ever getting further than kissing.

"If I was, I wouldn't be here," he reassured me, "You wanted to earlier. It's fine to change your mind. I'm sure you'll want to again when you're ready." He rolled over, grabbing my hand as he laid beside me and holding it tight while he steadied his breathing.

"You're too good to me," I wiped my eyes and laughed, though the sound came out choked and miserable.

"I wouldn't say I'm *good.* Do you really think I'd be able to enjoy myself if you weren't into it? Let alone even start doing *anything* with you if you didn't want to?" he rolled over, propping his head up on his hand and looking down at me.

"It's all I knew for a long time."

"Well, that's *not* how it's going to be between us. You either want me, completely, or it doesn't happen. *At all.*"

There were no words to describe the conflicting feelings I had for Logan. Surely someone who treated me this way couldn't be *that* bad?

Don't get me wrong, the act of not having sex with me when I didn't want to didn't *instantly* make him a perfect person. It certainly didn't absolve him of all he might have done, and *would* do in the future as the masked criminal I was trying to uncover. That would be ridiculous. *Right?*

I reached for his face and gently traced the edge of his jaw with my fingertips, unable to tell him exactly what I was thinking, but I hoped the touch showed in some way that I appreciated what he was saying.

"Can I ask you something?" he said quietly, eyes closed and leaning into the feel of my skin lightly brushing his.

"Of course." I bit my lip, suppressing a smile at how peaceful he looked for those few seconds before he opened his eyes and frowned.

"Have you slept with other people since you left the cult?"

"Umm…"

"Don't think on it, just answer," he pleaded softly.

"Yeah. A couple."

He let out a heavy sigh. "Good."

"Good?"

"Yeah. Good. If you hadn't, then I guess we'd be dealing with bigger things. You *can.* You just won't… with me?" He started out strong in his revelation until he got to the end, now seeming to be worried that I didn't see him in that way.

"I want to. *With you.*" I reassured him, "I just haven't worked out how to have sex with you and then see you again." I giggled, embarrassed I'd said it out loud.

He laughed as I sat up. "What does that even mean?"

"Well… I didn't exactly plan on liking you *this* much, Logan," I confessed, a little annoyed for not sticking with my original plan.

Although I did, in a way. There were no signs of Logan working with Eric as far as I could tell. And apparently that was a good enough excuse for me to think the job was done.

The corners of his mouth slowly turned up, and he gently shook his head, "Neither. But there's just… something about you…" he scowled, looking me over.

The way his eyes devoured every inch of my frame made me feel hot and bothered all over again. My poor body couldn't keep up with the jumbled up signals I'd been throwing at both of us all day.

I grabbed one of the pillows from behind him and threw it in his face.

"Why?" He laughed as he sat up, wrapping his arms around the pillow, still giving me space. I didn't want it. I wanted to *be* the pillow. In his lap and wrapped tight in *those* arms. But I was set on not giving him any more reasons in one day to think I wasn't worth his time.

"Because I feel weird when you look at me like that," I whined. "I'd rather you just look at me like you want to fuck me. Then we do, and then we get on with our lives. Like everyone else I've slept with since I left. But you *don't*. And I don't know what that means."

"Are you worried I'll hang around? We've gone too far, even without the physical side for you to just drop me like a one night stand? Oh my God, Summer!" he exclaimed, eyes wide behind his glasses as he made fun of me, "Are you worried you'll fall for me if we take things further?"

I knew he was teasing, he had to have been onto me with the pills and knew the reason we hadn't had sex yet would involve them in some way. Before I could open my mouth to argue, I was hit in the face with the pillow.

"Fair's fair," he shrugged at my shocked expression before lifting his hand up to catch another I'd tried to throw at him."You won't win this fight, nurse."

"What makes you say that?" The small part of me that still had some sense of self preservation was still trying to force him to slip up with his Gift in front of me.

"I'm just too good. You'll have to ask my sister one day. I nearly killed her play-fighting when we were kids." He chuckled at a memory we didn't share and he pulled his phone from his pocket, sighing as he read a text, "Harrison needs me. Are you gonna be okay if I leave for a bit?"

"I'll be fine." I said, watching as he replied to the message before pocketing the phone.

"I'll be back later."

"You don't have to come back." I said, hating that I'd even thought the words before they came out of my mouth. Giving him an *out* if he needed it — to get away from someone as fucked up as me who just seemed to be wasting his time.

"But I *want* to." He leaned in to give me a quick kiss on my forehead. "If I can respect your *autonomy*, Summer, can you at least try to do the same for mine?" he said smoothly as he walked backwards to the bedroom door.

I rolled my eyes. "Yes."

"Good. Then I'll be back later. Wait—" his gaze darted to the drawer beside my bed, "Think of me while I'm gone, nurse?"

"I already do."

His expression was playfully pained as he sighed and turned to leave.

# TWENTY-FIVE

## SUMMER

### FEBRUARY 12TH

Therapy. Again.

*I should just move into this damn building.*

Dr. Lindsey shuffled to get comfortable, looking over her notes as she pushed her glasses up the bridge of her nose.

Each time I observed someone touch their glasses that way, I held in a smile, envisioning Logan doing the same thing. I couldn't get him out of my head. To be fair, he was beside me in bed every night, and I spent most of my spare time with him.

Still, he was taking up a lot of space in my mind, more since our day together the week earlier. It was hard to believe I felt so much for someone I was unfairly holding at arm's length.

*That and he's, you know, likely a dangerous vigilante. Or have you completely forgotten about that?*

"Okay Katie. We've been doing well," she grinned over the papers. "There's obviously still a lot of gaps and things you're not quite ready to share, but you've been painting quite a detailed picture of your life."

I tried not to snicker at the heavily censored, "detailed" version of everything I'd given her so far.

"If you're up for it, we could discuss the type of abuse you endured during your time in the cult… and maybe work on strategies to process that?"

"Oh, we're ready for something like this?" I sat up straight, eager to hear her ideas. It could be the ticket to being more comfortable around Logan without the layers of clothing and the darkness as my crutches.

"I think so, we'll just take it one step at a time. You've mentioned sexual abuse spanning many years," she swept her hand across the paper on her lap as if to emphasise a timeline.

"Yeah, and physical too," I added, not meaning to interrupt her.

"Other than the sexual acts?"

"Yeah."

"Katie, I can help you with that too if you… elaborate?"

"Oh, for sure." I stood and untucked my white shirt with the intention of lifting it up. I was in my work clothes, having woken up early and already gone for a run when Logan left at sunset.

"Oh! No!" Dr. Lindsey threw her hands up. "There's no need for that *at all.* You *never* have to expose any part of yourself to me. In fact it's probably bordering on completely inappropriate," she explained with an embarrassed smile, the words tumbling from her mouth.

"Shit, I'm sorry." I said, feeling hot and stupid as I scurried back into position on the couch.

"There's no need to apologize."

"I just thought it would be… like, *helpful.* If you saw what he'd done to me?" I narrowed my eyes, cheeks growing warmer still as I tried to explain.

"I understand. You can describe it to me if you wish," she offered, interlocking her fingers on her lap and rearranging herself in her seat, seeming quite discomposed at the threat of one of her patients almost stripping in front of her.

I took a deep breath. The idea of showing her my scars didn't bother me like it did with Logan.

She was a doctor, there to help me. Not a love interest, who'd want to flip me over in bed at some point, only to be greeted with a list of names of other men.

*And a boy.*

I waved my hand to the side of my face, pushing the memories back into the dark where they belonged.

"I'm… covered in scars." I started with my hands on my knees, not knowing how to arrange these words. Showing her would have been so much easier.

"Oh?" she said, leaning a little closer.

"Eric used to give out… *punishments* to people at Ho— in the cult."

She tipped her head to the side, "Did he do the same to anyone else?"

"Not exactly. He'd punish people in different ways. Taking money. They'd owe him favors and all that," I was purposefully vague about the concept of our contracts. "Mine were always physical. I was the only one who he treated *this* way." I hovered my hands over my torso and motioned downward, gesturing at what was underneath my shirt.

"Do you have any insight as to why? Why he would think to do this to *you*, specifically? Not *why* in a sense of what you did to deserve it. I'll make it clear now that his actions were *his own* choosing, and likely a reflection of his own issues. You did nothing to deserve being treated so terribly that it resulted in scarring your body."

My eyes welled up unexpectedly. Her statement was kind, but I didn't believe it. I couldn't. Terrible things happened at Home, and I played a part in so many of them.

"It started as part of our arrangement. That I was to *be his*. It was all for show, like so much of him. He was always rough with me in bed, but it evolved into much more abuse than I ever expected as part of the role."

She nodded slowly, "You say an *act*. Was Eric perhaps using you to hide he was…"

"What, like, hiding *deviant behavior?*" I asked with an involuntary laugh. "No. Eric…" I frowned, trying to work out the best way to describe his preferences without giving too much away. As far as I knew, I was the youngest he'd taken to bed for some time, he wasn't in the habit of luring children into Bedlam. "I wouldn't know what to call Eric if I had to put a label on it. I honestly think people bore him. He makes no attachments. They're just a means to an end. He doesn't care who they are, just what they can do for him. But he knew he needed to be seen as *desirable* to round out his public image. That's what I, the pretty thing on his arm, was for. Other than my stitching of course. Just a bonus that I was a girl he could get double the work from, I guess."

While this was something I truly needed help with processing, I just couldn't bring myself to be *entirely* truthful. It hurt too much, and some scars weren't physical.

What hurt most was that he'd chosen *me* to be with him for the rest of my life, and that life so quickly turned miserable.

I had loved Eric more than anything. There wasn't a single person in all of Home more devout to our leader than I had been. If he kept treating me the way he had in our first year together, there was no question that I'd still be proudly curled up in his lap, fulfilling all of my villainous duties.

But after the first time Eric carved a name into my skin, he was in as much shock at his own behavior as I'd been, unable to believe he'd snapped and been pushed so far that he'd almost murdered me.

At first, he seemed too scared to touch me again, but he regained confidence over a short time, with more names to be added over the next six years as he decorated my skin.

He threw himself further into work and secretive deals, excluding me from things where he typically would have had me at his side or on his knee. I continued to do everything I could to bring us back together. And in the moments we were, there was none of the same tenderness in his words or actions. Not that he was ever a very *gentle* person.

We fell into an unstable routine. He'd be distant, and I'd act out to get his attention, always reaching the point where I'd push him too far, not caring that I was risking my life. I loved him and I was lost without him.

Whenever he was driven over the edge, and one of our own were lost, it'd be *my* fault. Regardless of whether I was on the team in charge of saving them or they died in the streets. He would tell me they *"died for me"* not so much *"because of me."*

It only added to my perception of Eric losing his mind over time. The worst of his maniacal decline was only ever shown to me, and the few others who managed to wholly piss him off. Though, those lucky pieces of shit would end up dead, and I'd just keep living through one carving after another.

To everyone else, he was business as usual. People's fears were only made more valid with the rumors and whispers of what he was willing to do to me in private — the girl he apparently loved. Imagine what he could do to others he didn't care for? They didn't want to be on the receiving end to find out.

Between the major events that added names to my back, we'd argued plenty. Eric gained enjoyment from biting back and studying me as I fell apart, desperate for his affection. I felt more like an experiment than a living being to him while he observed how far he could push me in return.

He'd eventually give me the attention I'd begged for, though mostly in the form of his hands around my neck as he fucked me. His only need for me was a physical release, his focus no longer being so much to retrain me to be the perfect partner for the rest of my life.

I took it willingly at first. Missing him enough to take whatever I could get. He'd explained to me early on that breath play was his favorite kink, and that I was safe in his hands. But the play, originally intended for my pleasure, turned to torture over time. It was terrifying. Choked and taunted, he'd dare me to die in his hands.

I'd wanted to.

Once Eric learned I'd found a way to slip out of consciousness faster, hoping I'd never wake up, he moved onto experimenting with ways to keep me around for longer. He'd loop his belt tight around my neck, allowing me just enough air to drag out the experience as he saw fit, getting off to my suffering. He seemed to receive true elation in my transition from struggling under his grip to slipping away.

My unconscious body left him to do as he pleased while I was quiet and no longer causing him trouble. I guess, in those moments, I was the girl he'd always wanted me to be.

Dr. Lindsey sat back and folded an arm across her chest, holding her jaw between her thumb and fingers as she took it all in, the notepad balancing on her lap.

"It wasn't always that way. Like I've said, it happened over time. But after his friend died it just… kind of started then and kept going. He still had his physical needs…" I trailed off, too numb and my throat too swollen with sadness to reveal anything more.

"Do these scars Eric has left you with interfere with your everyday life?"

"I mean, I've got some decent nerve damage," I shrugged. "But I can move fine and they don't hurt anymore."

"I meant more along the lines of relationships. Do they interfere with trusting people? Being intimate?"

"Oh. Absolutely. There's this guy I've been seeing. I really like him. A lot. But I can't bring myself to show him or get too physical with him. Not yet. Maybe if he hangs around long enough, I'll be able to trust him completely with something like that," I said with a shaky laugh.

"Trust *enough*."

"Yeah," I sighed. "Trust enough."

"Could this be the friend… you met up with for coffee?"

"Yep," I narrowed my eyes. "Why?"

Dr. Lindsey shrugged, a small smile pulling at the corners of her mouth, "Your mood has been a little different since that night."

I tried not to roll my eyes at what the bodyguards would make of that comment.

# TWENTY-SIX

## SUMMER

With my phone in hand, I left my therapist's office and started dialing Mom's number as I walked to my car.

*Voicemail, what a surprise.*

"Mom," I slipped into the driver's seat and closed the door with a loud *thud,* ensuring the cool air stayed on the other side. "Just checking in. Making sure you're all okay." I turned the key and placed my phone into its holder so I could steer without it taking valuable space from my small hands. "I'm kind of seeing someone… I think." I tried to offer some of my life to her in hopes she'd take an interest in her daughter and finally return my call. "Anyway… Call me?"

I hung up, and tried not to let the crushing weight on my chest lead to tears. So much of my life revolved around the people I loved rejecting me. It wasn't easy to keep all the hurt locked away, but now wasn't the appropriate time to let it out.

It wasn't long before I pulled up to Logan's work, excited to see him. I'd arrived a little earlier than usual, having driven straight to the restaurant after therapy.

The air buzzed with many voices, the spaces to both the left and right of the entrance were bustling with people.

I was greeted by an unexpected face.

"Jackie, hi!" I called as she approached with a smile.

"Hey! He's not here," her copper brows pinched together, "But I thought I'd see if you wanted to hang out with me until you need to leave for work?"

"Oh, sure!" I shrugged, trying to remember if Logan had said anything about being too busy to meet up. "Are the others here?"

*This could be a chance to get some answers out of all his friends while he's not around.*

"No, just me I'm afraid," she said with a sad laugh.

"Well, that's still perfect!" I tried not to sound disappointed. Jackie seemed to be the quieter member of the group, but I was sure I could still work on her for insight into their secrets.

She smiled, seeming relieved I hadn't rejected her offer, "Wanna grab a drink?"

"Like, at the bar? The coffee will no doubt be garbage without Logan." I pouted at the idea of missing out on my caffeine hit before work.

"Yeah, sure!" she said excitedly, and I followed her to the left. We found two empty bar stools at the very end and across from the booth where I'd first met the group. The room was loud, but not as rowdy as the bar Logan had taken me to.

"So, what do you do?" I started my interrogation with a seemingly harmless question disguised as small talk when we took our seats. The stool was so *ridiculously* high I needed to use the bench of the bar to hoist myself up.

*It's NOT because I'm ridiculously short,* I stubbornly reassured myself.

"I'm in IT," she said with a smile. "Surveillance, specifically. It's a pretty cool job, not as cool as yours though."

"Ha! Yeah I guess. But I can imagine yours involves a whole lot less half-naked people than mine."

"You'd think," she said with a giggle, and I couldn't help but laugh with her as she waved the bartender over and ordered our drinks.

"Can you…" I paused, wondering if it were inappropriate to ask a favor from someone I barely knew. "Track cell phones?"

Jackie raised a brow. "Got an ex you want to keep tabs on? Sorry!" She shook her head at herself. "That's none of my business."

"No." *I know exactly where he would be.* "I've been trying to get a hold of my family for a while."

She nodded. "Logan mentioned that, but told us not to bring that up, too. Said it was a sore spot."

"It is. I guess I'm out of ideas on how to find them."

"Here," she handed over her phone, and I almost gasped at the familiar set of ice-blue eyes. The woman in the photo of Jackie's wallpaper was the same I'd seen in Logan's wedding pictures. "Add the number," she instructed. "I'll see what I can find."

"Thank you," I passed the phone back. "So, where is everyone tonight?"

"They're actually out because of me," she gave another sad smile as she pulled her long hair over one shoulder, winding it around her hand before letting it drop. Admiring the deep red shine in the dim lighting of the bar, I couldn't pull my gaze away while it slowly unraveled.

"Oh?" I prompted, swiveling a little on my chair from side to side.

"Yeah. My wife, Celeste… I don't know if Logan has ever mentioned her. She passed a couple of months ago. They're meeting the detectives on the case while they're in town. Dealing with the details I can't stomach."

I placed my hand on her arm and gave it a squeeze, "Jackie, that's awful."

Our drinks arrived, and she took a mouthful of hers before patting my hand and smiling. I noticed for the first time that the expression never met her eyes.

"It's getting easier. Kind of. Not really," she exhaled another sad laugh. "But I've got great friends. They're helping me get through it."

The thought of what a strange group they were made me grin as I dropped my hand. And as much as I wanted to believe her, I couldn't help but worry they were out causing trouble somewhere.

Logan and Harrison were clearly Gifted. Tommy, I was still undecided on. Those three were clearly the 'muscle'. Maybe Jackie was the 'brains'.

Looking her over, I concluded she must be human. It would be why they'd leave her behind when they disappeared, she was too vulnerable and weak.

*Like me.* I huffed sourly, lifted my glass, and froze. The familiar burn of its contents slammed hard into my nostrils. Whiskey. Eric's drink of choice. I took a sip to be polite, ignoring the memory it sparked — his tongue on mine, only seconds after signing my contract. Gently, I placed my glass down with absolutely no intention of ever touching it again.

To top off the invasive vision, a hand suddenly pressed on my lower spine. Logan had touched me there plenty of times, but I instantly knew by the size and temperature that this *wasn't* his. I threw my shoulders back in disgust, instantly irate over a stranger thinking they could put their hands on me.

"The fuck?" I started, spinning my seat around. A man I didn't recognise stood in front of me, another beside him. "Can I *help you?*" I snapped, still trying to shake off the shape of his palm as if it were a filthy imprint on my skin.

He was much taller than me, even as I sat on the bar stool, but that wasn't a particularly impressive feat. Blonde, bulky, probably in his late twenties. A few tattoos were visible around the tops of his arms, under the short sleeves of his T-shirt. They appeared meaningless, like he would have picked them moments before having them added to his body. Quite the contrast to the carefully chosen ink in my world.

His friend was almost a clone, a little shorter with darker hair. He had a scar that disrupted his right eyebrow. The indents in his skin from where it had been stitched in the past were visible, but I knew instantly that it wasn't my work. Jackie turned to face them too.

"Can I buy you a drink?" he asked, unfazed by my reaction or bitter expression.

"No. Thank you. I've got one," I pointed with my thumb over my shoulder at the barely-touched liquid sitting on the bar.

"What about you, then?" his friend asked, turning the attention from me to Jackie. We glanced at each other and I snorted. Knowing that Jackie was still in the depths of grieving the loss of her *wife* made the whole situation even more ridiculous.

"No, thank you," she said much more politely than I'd bothered to.

"C'mon," the first guy said to me, clearly unable to take a fucking hint.

I leaned back with my elbows on the bar and tipped my head to the side. Grinning maniacally, I locked my eyes on his and heavily enunciated my next words, "No. *Thank you.*"

He scowled, seeming not to appreciate the rejection or my demeanor.

I could feel it already — Ben was going to get a call. He would need to bring one of the fake IDs we hadn't yet used to bail me out for the trouble I was about to get into.

Flirting with danger was a specialty of mine. The man standing in front of me couldn't inflict anywhere near as much pain as I'd been dealt in the past. It made me reckless, as though Eric had set the standard for the awful shit my body could endure, and it was way too fucking high.

"You don't have to be such a cunt about it," he gritted through his teeth.

I did *not* like that word. I swore plenty, but even I tended not to use it. And being called it pissed me off.

I'd encountered many people in the past who'd used it to describe me, some lovingly — like a nickname. But for those dumb enough to coat it with venom before spitting it my way — Eric made sure they would be long decomposed in the places the Finders had dumped their bodies.

I laughed as the man took his first step away from us. "The only *cunt* here is the guy who handles rejection like a toddler."

"The fuck did you call me?"

I couldn't stand people who weren't able to take as much as they dished out.

Rolling my eyes, I shifted to spin back to the bar, but not before he spat in my direction as he walked away. He must have had a deity watching over him, the glob of saliva missed me and splattered on the floor. For that, I wouldn't remove his tongue.

Leaning closer to Jackie, I asked, "Does spitting at someone count as assault in this state?"

"Yeah… I think so, why? Wait!" she started, but I'd already moved, kicking him in the back of the leg.

It wasn't a hard kick, and he barely wobbled, but it was enough for him to turn back. I hopped off the stool and put myself between the man and Jackie, not wanting him to mistake her for the one who'd touched him.

"*Summer!*" she hissed from behind. I detected an amused note in her voice.

"The fuck is your problem?" he growled.

I folded my arms and glared up at him. "I don't appreciate being called a cunt for not accepting your sad attempt at a pick up."

"Well you are one, so *fuck off*." He poked me in the chest, making me sway on my feet.

"That's twice now," I purred, "Spitting, touching me. Is there anything else you want to do while you still can?"

"You've got quite the mouth on you. Maybe you should keep it shut."

*I'm so sorry, Ben.*

My giggle was taunting, "Or else, what?"

He took the bait and stepped closer, lowering his voice, "Or you might learn that I know a few ways to fill it that'll keep you quiet."

Like many before him, he was writing me off as little and weak. He shook his head at me when I took a step back to size him up.

Too bad for him, I understood human anatomy well enough to pick the places that'd have a man on the ground within seconds.

My intention wasn't to only drop him, though. No, I wanted to do something that would last a little longer so he'd remember the pretty face that was about to bruise us both.

I took one step towards him and he grabbed my arms tight. I'd had enough of him touching me. Using his grip to steady myself, I placed my boot on his knee to lift my face closer to his.

I threw my head back, then slammed the top of my forehead into the soft part of his nose.

He immediately released his painful hold. Thankfully, I expected his reaction and landed on my feet. I turned back to quickly push myself up on the barstool beside Jackie.

My pain would set in later, but by the sounds of the man behind me and his friend's furious meltdown, the blood would have already been gushing from his nose.

It was a dirty move, and I only used it sparingly. The Surgeon had scolded me, much like my parents did, when I told him how I used the trick on John when we were in our early teens. It was just so *fucking* satisfying and effective. So long as I wasn't on the receiving end, of course, like when James taught me how to do it properly.

Surge attributed my many head injuries to my reckless behavior. And although Eric had always insisted my brain showed no signs of lasting trauma, I'd been doubting that since the moment I invited Logan into my house.

"You're *wild*." Jackie laughed, downing the last of her drink and seeming completely unbothered by what I'd done. I guessed that's what happened when you hung out with the Gifted too often.

Sticking my fingers in the drink, I fished out the largest ice cube and pressed it to my hairline. A hit like that would leave at least a small mark.

"Ladies," the bartender leaned on the bench in front of us. "Gonna have to ask you to leave."

Jackie and I giggled as we hopped off the stools, stepping around the red speckles on the floor.

"One night," I sighed as cool air whipped at our faces when we reached the parking lot. The weather was starting to change, not so many freezing nights, but still cold. I worried Logan's sudden disappearance meant he wouldn't make it in time to get into bed together. I'd grown dependent on his warmth to fall asleep. "The *one* fucking night Logan's not here and I get into a fight at his work."

Jackie smiled and shook her head, "I get what he sees in you, Summer. You're a lot like Celeste. And you're a lot like *him*."

*I wouldn't know.*

I still knew so little about Logan. Maybe the cut on his face was from a similar incident.

I tossed the last of the ice cube to the ground and asked, "Do you need a ride?"

"No, I'm good," she said, checking her phone, "N-Harrison just texted she and Tommy are on their way."

"Too bad I'll miss them."

"Yeah. They're going to lose their minds when they hear what you did." Her small smile stretched to a mischievous grin as she slipped her phone into her pocket.

"Ugh. I can't imagine Logan will be too impressed." *Then again, maybe he would be.* I couldn't hide my smile at the thought of him finding out more about the type of person *I* was. The good and bad.

"I won't tell him," Jackie elbowed me. "I'll leave that confession for you."

"Well, I should go." It felt like another inventory check was the best way to calm down before my shift.

"I'll let you know if I find anything on the number!" she called as I left for my car.

The drive home was short as I replayed what I'd done at the bar over and over in my head, trying to justify my awful decision, no matter how good it felt.

I was meant to *help* people, not hurt people.

Maybe I needed to have a break every now and then for what was left of my sanity. I wasn't one of the *good guys*. I never had been.

A familiar car on the street made my heart skip a beat. After pulling into my garage I quickly walked across the driveway to meet Logan, waiting at my door. The bright security lights shone warmly around us, and I was too excited to see him to bother asking how he'd gotten over the fence.

"Been here long?" I asked, pulling my phone from my back pocket to see the notification he'd arrived about ten minutes earlier.

"Not long," he said, totally unable to lie about it.

"Good. I had drinks with Jackie after therapy. Well, I had some of *one* drink with Jackie." I beamed as the head butt replayed in my mind.

He raised a cautious brow. "You did?"

"Yeah. It was nice to spend some time with her. She told me you guys were seeing some cop about her wife?"

The tension in his shoulders melted at the mention of his cover story. "Yeah. It was rough. Hey, I got something for you."

I was too intrigued by what he held between us on his open palm to push my questioning further.

Logan placed a small metal container in my hand. I turned it over and unscrewed the lid. It was a candle. It wasn't something I'd expect him to pick for me, but then I lifted it to my nose.

"Iodine?" I whispered, and hurriedly tipped it upside down to read the label. "Antiseptic." I laughed at the fragrance's description, "This is fucking *perfect*. Thank you." My tone was a stark contrast to my earlier *"thank you"* to that jerk at the bar.

"You like it?" he smiled shyly, one hand in the pocket of his jacket while the other pushed his glasses back up his nose.

"I love it." I promised, holding it to my nose again. It oddly reminded me of Home, but in a good way. More of the medical floor where I worked with The Surgeon and not only the ghost laden ER.

While it was a shame my crippling fear of fire would never allow me to light the candle in my house, I liked the idea of keeping it close by to smell and remember that he'd picked such a thoughtful present.

"You were on my mind," he rocked on his feet. "You're *always* on my mind, Summer."

I lifted my eyes from my gift to meet his, and the familiar warmth I *constantly* experienced around Logan spread from my chest and up to my face.

"Nurse… Do you wanna do this? For a while?"

"Do what? Stand outside in the cold?" I laughed and tipped my head to the side, biting my lip at his contagious nerves.

He stepped closer, blocking the lights from my eyes so I could see his face a little better.

"Life? Us? Together?"

"Is that your way of asking me to be your girlfriend?" I teased.

He threw his head back and sighed. "I'm thirty-one, nurse. Don't you think we're a bit beyond the words *girlfriend* and *boyfriend?*" he held his breath, waiting for my response.

"Nope. I've never really had a boyfriend." I frowned at the candle in my hands. Of all the gifts I'd ever been given, it was already my favorite. It was so *me*. Not sparkly things to be paraded around in or to shut me up when I whined for attention.

"Okay then," he started with a smirk. "Summer, will you be my girlfriend?"

"No." I walked past him to unlock the door.

"*What?* Why not?"

"I'm *kidding*. I've never really had the chance to turn anyone down, either." I giggled, placing the candle and my keys on the hall table while he stood in the doorway. "Yes, Logan. I'll be your girlfriend." I reached for his hand to pull him into the house.

"What happened here?" he frowned, softly brushing his thumb across my hairline.

"It's nothing." I grabbed at the fabric on either side of his zip and tore him down to kiss me.

# TWENTY-SEVEN

LOGAN

## FEBRUARY 12TH

I'd been sleeping in Summer's room, in her bed and beside her, for weeks. The odd arrangement had quickly become a comfortable routine for us. She'd stop in at work for coffee, where we'd act like we weren't sleeping beside each other every night. I'd try to leave her to get her work done, but always found myself gravitating towards the little nurse as she hid behind her laptop, scowling at the screen. She never seemed bothered when I joined her in the booth, so long as I brought more coffee.

She'd leave for work, and when I finished up in the early hours of the morning, I'd swing by in time for her to be packing up from her shift. We'd then watch movies she should have already seen, but hadn't due to years in the cult and general detachment from the outside world.

Sometimes we'd skip that step and immediately slip into bed, exhausted from our separate lives, barely seeing each other before our eyes closed. Many times we'd used the last of our energy under the sheets to feel each other up with all light blocked from the room.

She was getting close to letting me feel every inch of her, and I was eager to give her more than a few inches of me.

I'd typically wake earlier in the evening than Summer, and would spend a few extra minutes in bed to savor the silence of the house; a relief for my heightened senses.

There was barely a noise on her isolated property, only the quiet hum of the kitchen fridge and the others for medication in the garage. And *her*.

Soft, shallow rushes of air and a steady beat behind her ribs. I'd watch her sleep, ensuring she would always take her next breath, finding myself grateful each time her chest rose and fell that I hadn't fucked up yet.

What a waste it would be to remove a face as pretty as hers from existence.

Her thick lashes and pale pink lips were always hidden beneath strands of silky black hair. In those moments she reminded me of the movies my sister loved when we were kids – one of many featuring comatose princesses. Like them, Summer would stir if I kissed her, but I hated disturbing her peace when she wasn't being tormented by nightmares.

Everything about her was quiet. Peaceful and orderly. From the way she spoke when it was just the two of us, seeming to let the guard down that she kept up for the outside world, to how she mindlessly straightened her medical tools three times before she used them.

Even her stomach rarely made a noise, which I found fucking weird. I was glad she couldn't hear like me – mine would have woken her up like a fire alarm, and I didn't want the woman, barely interested in food, to feel bad that I was starving by the time I woke her to let me out. Like a house cat, scratching at the door for freedom.

I'd kiss her cold lips goodbye, and she'd promise we'd meet at the restaurant after she finished with therapy and the gym. Then I'd drive away, always praying she'd show up – that nothing would happen to her in our hours apart and that she wouldn't do anything to upset the fragile balance we were teetering on.

Summer was guilty of plenty, yet innocent of so many terrible things done to her. But her treatment in the past wasn't enough to completely absolve her of all she'd done. Each time I woke beside her, I feared I'd open my eyes to a mangled corpse.

It was almost impossible to bend the rules after she so easily confessed to her crimes. But the fucked up part of my Gift that forced me to set the scales straight must have decided to wait and see what else she was capable of, 'cause

I kept waking up every day to a recognisable human figure, my hands *not* covered in her blood.

There was *something* about her that was making me turn my back on the very nature of my existence, drawing all pieces of me to her. I couldn't work out what it was, all I knew was that I needed to hang around long enough to find out what made Summer so different.

It was only early days for us, and certainly not a normal relationship by any means. I'd tried "normal" in the past and it had ended in more death than I was capable of accepting I'd caused.

Not that Summer understood normal anyway – she had nothing to compare us to other than cruelty and abuse. While it set the bar awfully low for me, I was trying to make her as happy in the time we spent together as she was making me.

Though, I had to keep things from her. I couldn't tell her what I was, and I was certain she still had plenty more secrets of her own. I just took each day as it came, hoping we'd survive each other. Mostly, I hoped she'd survive me.

Especially *now,* with the little nurse having just agreed to be my girlfriend.

Summer started to back up as she stood on her toes to kiss me. Instead of breaking away as I feared she would, she grabbed handfuls of my jacket instead, pulling me further into the hall.

The door clicked softly into place behind us as we reached the kitchen, mouths still hard at work as I held her tight by the arms to keep us close. She didn't know I'd spied on the code to get out of the house, but I reveled in the idea of it being only the two of us, locked up together and unable to leave until we were done with each other – not that we'd gotten that far.

After rounding the couch in the dark, shitty eyesight not yet adjusted to the lack of light, I let go of her for a moment to feel my way down onto the seat.

I reached for her hand, and she quickly kicked her shoes off as I pulled her down with me. Her knees sunk into the cushion at either side of my hips, and her heart audibly throbbed at an equal pace to mine. She parted her legs further, lowering herself so our bodies connected.

I reached for the sides of her face to pull her in to kiss me again, and she did the same with one hand at the back of my neck, the other brushing the hair away from my forehead. Her cool skin against mine, always hot, was an arousing contrast that made me crave her entirely naked body pressed to mine.

As our lips met again, I sensed this kiss was *different*. It had more force and purpose than any of the others we'd shared so far.

*Oh fuck, it's really happening?*

My excitement dipped for a second, wondering if she would change her mind about us being physical… again… at the last second. But the sound of my jacket being unzipped brought me back to her. I shrugged my shoulders out of the warmth as her hands rushed to grip my exposed arms. She had such a *thing* for them.

I took my glasses off and folded them quickly, tossing them across the couch. They were of no use to me in the dark anyway.

With a hand on the back of her neck to lock her face with mine, I lowered the other to begin working at the buttons of her jeans, deciding in the moment that Summer must have *specifically* picked this style as another way to protect herself.

Focusing on her mouth while subtly working on one button after another while her hips rolled was like trying to blindly break into a *fucking* chastity belt. Our breathing grew heavier with each one successfully unhooked.

*Finally.*

With that hurdle out of the way, I slipped my hand inside the jeans, under her. The angle was awkward for my wrist, but I wasn't going to let anything deter me while she was okay with me getting this close.

Summer was warm, the wetness from her body's need to be touched had soaked through the last piece of fabric separating us. I tugged it aside. She held her breath, then released the softest sigh.

My fingers had barely brushed her clit when her hand roughly gripped my forearm. I stopped, brow tightening with the need to frown. I opened my eyes to look up at her.

"No?" I cleared my throat, attempting to mask the disbelief in my voice.

"I can't," she smiled down at me, skin flushing warm.

I pulled my hand out of her jeans, grabbed her hips tight and tried to clear my mind of all the things I wanted to do to her.

We were both so eager for each other's bodies, I was sure her reservations wouldn't hold forever. There had already been too many times we'd come *so close* to fucking.

The tension between us would have been unbearable, the teasing and rejections not worth my time if she didn't have such a bizarre hold over me. I needed to be patient until she was ready. And *not high*.

It was painfully obvious once I'd seen her eyes that she'd taken something when I'd met her in my room at the apartment. After taking a pause, eager and about to tear her clothes off, I could *see* and *hear* the changes in her.

Those pupils were unresponsive, and her heart rate faster than how it typically sounded when I got her all worked up. I couldn't touch her even if I'd wanted to, my own rules wouldn't allow it. I wasn't an exception to them. No one could be.

*She kind of is, though. For some reason.* I squinted at the blurred woman, still alive after so many weeks of revealing her secrets to me.

*We're getting close. It'll happen when she's ready.*

"But that doesn't mean *you* can't," she continued, shifting to hold my shoulders.

Summer lifted herself enough to slip her feet to the ground and parted my knees when she dropped to hers on the floor between them. She swiftly reached for the button of my jeans and pulled the zip. Her meaning sunk in as she grabbed my dick, throbbing for her, and guided it with icy hands through the front of my boxers. Her eyes widened, pupils flared.

Was she surprised? Disappointed? I doubted the latter. I may have been self-conscious about many things, but the size of my dick wasn't one of them.

She traced thick veins with slender fingers, her small hands making me look even bigger.

I'd been curious about what I might look like in her mouth. I'd been envisioning those blue eyes rolling back as she choked on the length.

The air caught in my throat as she moistened her lips with her tongue and tucked her jet black hair behind her ears.

Holding close to the base with her right hand, she gripped my thigh with her left and positioned herself to lower her mouth around me.

I exhaled an unrestrained sigh at the unexpected warmth of the cold woman's mouth, and watched as her head began to bob up and down, using her hand to work what couldn't fit in with the rest.

My head slowly rolled to rest on the back of the couch and I squeezed my eyes shut at the sensation of her tongue swirling the head of my dick. She started taking the length deeper to her throat, leaving me with barely enough sense to wonder what had prompted her to take this leap.

After a few minutes of our heavy breathing and the occasional groan from me being the only sounds in the house, I asked, "You sure you don't want to get on?"

I internally hoped she'd reject my offer. I was far too close to coming to give her much of a good time if she decided to let me inside her now.

Summer lifted her head, and I looked up as she started smiling with my dick still in her mouth. Her lips, glistening with saliva, were a darker shade of pink from the friction of her work.

"Finish in my mouth," she spoke quietly, but her tone was demanding, almost begging, and her eyes on mine were wide with excitement.

Fuck, I *wanted* to. But this woman had a complicated history she'd only shared small parts of with me. I couldn't have her convincing herself to do these things in a bid to keep me around – I was already hers.

"You're sure?" I asked. Her head jerked back a fraction and she blinked a few times.

I'd believed every word she'd said to me the first night I'd slept over. I detected no lies when she spilled *those* dark secrets, and since then, I'd been noticing so many little things about her.

Summer was like a cat on edge, always overly aware of her surroundings, particularly of people standing behind her and noting the exits for quick getaways.

She consistently reacted to certain scenes in movies. Stab wounds in particular made her heart race, though I was yet to learn if she found them exciting or terrifying.

I'd wanted to bring these things up with her, but one night she'd flinched, caught by surprise when I reached across the couch to brush hair from her neck. The sharp recoil she tried to mask with a shrug gave me enough of the answers I needed for now – the years of abuse she'd endured still had their claws deep within almost every aspect of her existence.

"I'm sure, Logan. I *want* this." She set herself back to it with more vigor, seeming to take my questions as an admission that I wasn't going to last much longer.

My body melted further into the couch, and my head rolled back again as I reached for hers. I cautiously threaded my fingers in her hair at the sides, caving to the intense urge to grab her skull and push her down. The move didn't trigger a negative response, though her motions paused for a split-second before she sighed at my touch and started again. With my dick now reaching her tonsils, the last thing I needed was to startle her.

I pushed my luck a little further; bucking my hips in time with her movements. The scent of salty tears when I pushed a little too deep almost made me slow down to check on her, but she showed no signs of needing to stop.

I noticed Summer's other hand wasn't on my leg anymore.

With my eyes still closed, I focused solely on her and every motion she made; the way her head moved at a steady pace, her hand gripping a little tighter, and the pressure of her tongue.

There was a subtle noise – friction against fabric.

*Fuck, is she playing with herself?*

A small moan slipped through the lips around my cock and vibrated along my shaft as she *finally* gave a taste of the sounds she could make for me.

*Shit, maybe I should warn her?*

But it was too late. I couldn't hold on any longer. She'd upped the speed and I'd already begun pulsing *hard* in her mouth.

The release was more intense than I'd anticipated, and far more satisfying than any I'd made on my own since I'd mapped out her body under my jacket on the first night she'd let me touch her all over.

"*Fuck.*" My eyes rolled back as her throat contracted to swallow the load. Her thumb – gliding up my cock to drain every drop – made it twitch against her tongue, already craving more.

Summer tucked me back into my boxers and I shifted to replace my jeans as she looped her buttons. She wiped her mouth of our combined fluids with the back of her hand, and I grabbed it, turning her palm up to bite the ball of her thumb as I caught my breath. I didn't know where else to place my desire to wrap my hands around her ribs to crush them. To do *anything* to hear that moan again.

Biting her lip, she smiled at me from above.

"Ow." Her breathy whimper, and gripping my shoulder with her other hand made me release my bite. As she returned to my lap, I kissed the place on her palm with deep marks from my teeth.

"Fuck. I'm sorry, Summer."

She giggled and turned her body, rearranging her legs so they rested across mine. Her ass slipped over my right thigh and onto the couch as she leaned with her back on the high arm.

Placings my hands on her legs, I ran my thumbs across the seams of her jeans, replaying all that'd just happened over and over in my head so I wouldn't forget a second of it.

"Was… was that… okay?" she asked with another giggle, setting her elbow on the back of the couch near my head to prop hers on her hand. She smiled, but her eyes were scanning my features more intently than typical. She took in every move I made, seeming desperate for some kind of approval over her actions.

"That was… *fucking phenomenal.*" I blurted out. I couldn't tell her it was the perfect distraction from the lead that had left the gang with more questions than answers. How would the little healer take the news that I was constantly making more work for people like her? *If* the suspects survived my questioning.

Summer bit her lip again and shyly looked away, focusing somewhere outside the glass wall. The moon rays bounced off a small structure near the back of the property, adding a little light to the dark space around us.

I reached for my glasses and slipped them back on to get a better look at her. She seemed so calm as she stared off into the darkness.

Not wanting to ruin the mood, especially after what she'd done, I tried to stop them, but still couldn't help but let the next words leave my mind.

"While that was… *incredible*," I swallowed hard, determined to work this woman out *before* we moved on to fucking, sure that if we were to ever have sex I'd never have a clear thought pass through my mind again. "I gotta ask… You were okay with doing that, but you're still not ready for–"

"Nope." Her eyes darted to mine and she forced a small smile. "I just need to be a little more organized. You keep springing this on me," she said with a laugh that I felt through her body with her legs still over mine.

"You want me to like, text you half an hour before I start thinking about you?" I teased, and she rolled her eyes at me, "It'd be too hard, Summer. You're always on my mind," I confessed for the second time.

She smiled again with a little more sincerity and brushed the fingers of her free hand slowly down the front of my shirt.

"How bad was it?" I asked, unable to stop myself again. Apparently she'd sucked my fucking brain out and I now lacked the ability to preserve this relationship when it'd only just properly started. "That you can't feel safe with me? Even now?"

I never assumed asking her out would instantly lead to us taking things further, but I'd hoped that being her "boyfriend" would mean she could begin to trust me a little more to freely share the details of her past.

Summer looked out the window again, her gaze becoming unfocused. I was desperate for answers, but I didn't quite have a full hold on her mind without the eye contact.

"Bad," she whispered, hand pausing on my chest, "The things he did to me when we were alone… that was where he showed me who he really was… and it was *dark*," she shared of her own volition, more than I often allowed.

*She does feel safe with me.*

"You know I'd never…" I started, but had to accept my words were just that – *words*. She'd probably heard them all before. I'd taken countless statements from people who'd been abused by their partners. Many of them were victims who would either show up again for the same reasons in the future, or turn up dead. I needed to *show* Summer she could trust me. At least, the part of me I could control.

"I know," she said, "I just like you… a lot. I don't want to ruin my first attempt at *normal*."

*Normal, that's all I've ever wanted.*

Seeming to sense the small dip in my mood, she lifted her cold hand to the side of my face, then glanced over the back of the couch. Her expression went blank. Her heart skipped a beat. Her mild panic set off my internal alarms; the hairs on my arms and neck stood on end and my hearing heightened to listen for anything that could be behind us.

"Shit. I gotta get to work!" She jumped off my lap, facing the TV to slip on her boots.

*The clock.* I sighed, replacing the air in my lungs with a deep breath. *No danger. Just out of time.*

I straightened on the couch, sitting up to sneak in a quick slap across her ass while her middle was level with my chest. She shifted her weight from one foot to the other when I moved, making me miss my mark.

"Ugh. Five out of ten," I huffed, slumping back into the cushions.

She spun quickly, looking down at me with an amused frown, "Did you just… grade yourself hitting my butt?"

My eyes darted to the side. *Fuck, have I crossed a line?*

"Yep."

"Well in that case," she folded her arms, "I'd give it a *four*."

Arching a brow, I stood to tower over her small frame. Leaning down so our eyes were level, faces only an inch apart, I whispered, "*Run*."

Summer's eyes widened, and she quickly darted around me to escape. I rushed after her, and she let out a high-pitched squeal as she rounded the doorway to the hall too quickly. The time it took her to steady herself was her downfall, I'd caught up and slapped her again, getting a decent *crack* as my hand connected with the black jeans tightly wrapping her ass.

"Ow!" she laughed and spun to shove me. I grabbed her by the arms and pinned them to her sides.

"How was that, then?" I demanded while I walked her backwards, trying not to laugh at how much she struggled to release herself from my grip. Humans were comically weak. I gave her a little room to wriggle, recalling she'd been forcefully bound in the past. I needed her to know this kind of play between us would always be safe. "Give me a better score and I'll let you go, nurse."

She rolled her eyes and bit her tongue to hide her smile, but she couldn't hide the way her pulse thumped with more force in her wrists as I held them. I fucking loved how she reacted when I referred to her that way.

"A six," she offered in a cool tone.

My jaw dropped. "Six? Jesus. Do I need to put you through a *fucking wall* to get a ten?"

She giggled when I let go and continued down the hall, tapping in the code to unlock the garage for me before moving to the bedroom. I heard her reach the bathroom as I entered her workspace. Two bulky figures had already let themselves in for their shift.

Ben folded his arms and Tony raised his eyebrows upon my entrance. I was never entirely sure if I should feel threatened by them. They were fun, but loyal only to Summer.

I cleared my throat. "Hey, guys."

"Fill her up yet?" Tony asked, fracturing Ben's attempt at a serious glare. He sucked in a laugh and adjusted his posture.

"N–… not quite. Just… enough." I stammered from the corner, my chair in the blind spot was always waiting for me, even on the nights I didn't make it home in time to watch her work. I didn't know what to tell them, but I assumed it was in my best interest to *not* discuss what I'd just done with their boss's mouth.

They exchanged a look, leaving me no choice but to guess they were brothers. I often glanced at my sister in the same way, both of us knowing what the other meant without needing to say anything.

For a moment, I wished my Gift was to read minds. But then, even knowing what little I did of these two, I'd probably regret peeking into their heads.

Tony cocked his head with a sly grin, "Tried calling her a *good girl*?"

"Umm. No." I lowered my voice, "Why? Should I? Does she like that?"

Praise kinks were simple. Straightforward. It was something I could do for Summer if that's what she wanted. There were others I had to steer clear of that might risk crossing the lines I was bound to.

The idea of calling her a "good girl" wasn't as much a turn on as the idea of working out *all* of Summer's quirks and desires now that things had taken a physical turn between us.

"Don't be a dick," Ben elbowed him, "He's got a pretty face, imagine what she'll do to it."

"So, no?"

Tony sighed. "The last time someone called her that, it took two men our size to restrain the feral little shit before Ben showed up to collect her." He may have been calling Summer names, but I sensed nothing but adoration. Maybe even pride.

Ben pursed his lips and shook his head. "Ugh. The blood. Poor fucker took a dumbbell straight to the nose. I've never seen someone so small do so much damage to another human."

Tony squinted at the ceiling, "Was that the third or fourth gym she got kicked out of? I'm losing track."

"Why does she bother with gyms?" I laughed, trying to picture the divine carnage. Summer had a spare room in her house, I'd peeked in there while she slept. It only contained more unused furniture. She could have filled it with gym equipment if she found it so hard to get along with others.

They looked at each other, seeming to decide this was a harmless piece of information they could share with me.

Tony answered, "She only uses them when it snows. She'll take running outside over being confined any day."

*So she gets kicked out of like, almost one per month,* I noted with a smirk. *Who the fuck am I dating?*

Their statements gave me a little relief. It explained why Summer would show up to meet me at work earlier some nights. I'd first suspected that I wasn't the only stop after therapy. But I couldn't ask for fear of looking as possessive as I felt about the little nurse.

The bodyguards grinned in unison when Summer walked in, hair neatly braided and ready for work.

"The fuck are you clowns smiling about?" she glared at them.

Ben shook his head at Tony, and they moved to pick up the first patient of the night.

Summer turned the glare on me. "What did you say?"

I threw my hands up in defense. "Nothing!"

"*Just enough,*" Tony called out as the door closed behind them. Their laughter filled the cool air outside.

My phone buzzed in my pocket, the perfect excuse to not meet Summer's scowl with her bodyguards trying to throw me under the bus.

It was a text from my sister; **Your girlfriend is WILD. Hurry up and tell her before I do.**

"So… drinks with Jackie. Did anything interesting happen?" I tried to not sound too concerned, but I needed to know what went on in my absence.

Summer spun on the spot by her desk, "Why? Got secrets you don't want her to spill?"

“No,” I laughed through the lie, “But *you* might.” I raised my brows and she froze.

“Oh!” she exhaled an anxious laugh, tapping the top of her head where I noticed what looked like a bruise was starting to bloom under her pale skin. “Bumped my head?”

“Summer?” I probed, a little concerned I might’ve been blown by someone with a mild concussion. And that *same* someone was about to be left in charge of other people’s health for the next few hours.

“We were just having fun,” she cleared her throat and turned back to her table, checking for the third time it was ready for when a patient walked through the door.

“Fun?”

“Yeah, the kind where Ben gets called to bail me out,” she giggled and sat in the chair at the computer.

My phone vibrated again. The message was from Summer, a prompt to download an app.

“What’s it for?” I asked.

“It’ll give you the codes.”

“Codes?” I didn’t know if she was trying to distract me, but I could no longer focus on my questioning.

“Yeah. For the house. Garage. Computer too. Just in case,” she explained, then arched a brow, “The *gate*. Codes change daily to get in the front door, remember it in the morning ‘cause the app only shows you once for the day. The one to get outside is *always* the same.” She narrowed her eyes at me. “So I can make a fast getaway… from the monsters…”

“Why?” I asked, shocked she trusted me with this much information.

She shrugged, blushing as she turned back to the screen. “You’re my boyfriend now. Or has what I did on the couch made you forget? I trust you, Logan… Enough.”

# TWENTY-EIGHT

LOGAN

## FEBRUARY 13TH

A woman's scream tore me from the depths of sleep.

*Summer?*

I knew it was her before I'd opened my eyes. Though, I'd never heard her make that sound before. I was certain what I wanted to do to that little body wouldn't make my girlfriend's screams sound anything like the one ringing through the house.

It was the sound of pain. Not the fun kind.

My hand flew to her place beside me. She wasn't in bed. The room was naturally dark; the blackout curtains still raised. She'd still be at work. I wasn't usually asleep at this time of the night, but I'd been out with the gang following new lead's on Echo's killer.

When I'd arrived at Summer's house, I was exhausted from spending the night *extracting* information from someone we'd believed was in contact with Celeste the day she died. It was another dead end and I, like the others, just wanted to sleep off the gutting disappointment.

I was at the garage door in seconds, clothes on and typing in the code Summer trusted me with. There was shouting – the voices of two people echoed on the other side.

When I shouldered the door open, Summer's wide eyes darted to mine. She raised her right hand, warning me to stay in the place where she let me watch her work. I'd gone fourteen years without my cover blown. I couldn't imagine showing up in some of her security footage for a few seconds would expose me to the world, but I appreciated that she cared enough to hide me.

Though, it did make me wonder how much she was onto my secrets. But surely if she knew who I was, it'd be over between us? I couldn't dream up a scenario where Summer was aware of my identity and she wasn't dead.

Had my little nurse signaled for me to help her, the man in the garage, responsible for half the shouting I'd heard, would have already been torn to unrecognizable pieces. My girlfriend's pretty, pale face would be decorated with the bloody splatters of the invalid dumb enough to upset her.

I observed him. He looked familiar. He'd been here before, a few weeks earlier on the first night she'd let me in the house.

*Alan. Remember that for later.*

He rambled incoherently. Possibly drunk, or high. Maybe both, judging by his erratic pulse and wide pupils as he shouted about the painkillers Summer had given him not being strong enough. He didn't deserve to have that injury treated by her in the first place, yet he had the balls to return and demand more of her. I made a mental note to hang his sack from one of the pines. Maybe small birds would put them to good use. Maybe it would finally lure out one of those bears everyone was so scared of.

There was space between Summer and Alan – more than ten feet. He must have backed off a bit since the scream, but the scalpel he thrust threateningly towards her dripped red. I inhaled deeply. Blood.

*He'd better fucking hope it's his.* I scanned the room. *Where the fuck are the bodyguards?*

Summer shouted back, calling him all sorts of deliciously crude names I'd never heard her speak. I couldn't contain my grin as the string of profanities left her mouth. Those lips were on mine just hours earlier, when she'd kissed me goodnight and I'd left her to work while I went to bed.

She was small, at least in comparison to me, but the way she held herself when she worked with scum like Alan was impressive.

I hadn't known for long about what she did for work, but I'd hated it the moment she confessed, and not only because of the risk from my internal call to kill her.

I would never think to prevent Summer from doing what she loved, but knowing most of the people she cared for were also worthy of death at my hands was unbelievably difficult to ignore.

While she and the drunken asshole exchanged more vicious words, I set my hands in my pockets and looked her over.

*Why'd you scream?*

She was still on her feet, her stance confident. Pale, but the normal kind for her, so I wasn't worried she was at risk of collapse.

She was wearing what she wore to work every day, reminding me of a cartoon character when I'd first seen her wardrobe. Multiples of the same high-waisted black jeans and plain white T-shirts to cover the body she still didn't want me or anyone else to see.

Summer told me she was comfortable in the tight-fitting clothes as they didn't leave anything for unruly patients to grab ahold of. While it was sensible, I was dying for the moment she decided I was worthy of tearing them completely from her figure.

My mind burned with curiosity over what she could possibly be hiding. I constantly caught myself fantasizing during the long hours at work. But it was still a subject best left alone until she felt safe enough to show me. It might set me on a new path to kill the man who'd hurt her, and I was far from done with getting to know the nurse.

It was painfully difficult to focus on anything else in the room with how the fabric hugged her curves. Every button on those jeans pulled tighter at her waist, further emphasizing her wide hips and heart-shaped ass.

I'd been spending so much time reading the labels of bottles in the cabinets and her clever little notes on each one as a way to distract myself from her bewitching presence. I'd memorized the names and dosages as a distraction from the idea of bending her over the chair she used for treating patients.

The fact she wore white surprised me. She looked good in those shirts, and even with my shitty eyesight, I could see through the thin fabric enough to know which bra she'd put on before her shift.

The amount of blood and gore I'd witnessed her work with made me think it would've been more practical to wear something darker – much like the suit I wore when dismembering morons like the one spouting verbal abuse at my girlfriend.

A sick part of my mind toyed with the thought that maybe she *liked* the contrast of the red blood on white created by the end of each night, just as much as part of me, disturbingly, enjoyed seeing her covered in it. Red looked so fucking good on her. Clothes or claret; I didn't care.

The man raged on as Summer turned to her desk, only briefly having her back to him as she ripped open the top drawer.

In that split second, I saw the blood. It seeped through the light fabric on her left side.

It explained the bloody scalpel. He'd cut her. Caused her to bleed. Neither of the other people in the room had any idea Alan's fate was sealed. In my eyes, he was as good as dead.

An exhilarating idea flashed in my mind – tearing the hand that held the scalpel from the rest of his arm. But only for a second. I couldn't allow my mind to get carried away with those plans until Summer was safe.

The cut to her rib cage was about halfway between her underarm and hip. A little closer towards her back than her chest. Even with my limited medical skills, I knew it would be a bitch to close it up.

The sight of her injury was enough for me to start moving for him, but then I caught a glimpse of what Summer had pulled from the drawer.

*A gun? No, two.*

She instantly tossed one in my direction. I caught it effortlessly. Without hesitating, I lifted my arm to aim directly at his head.

*Ten out of ten,* I praised myself, hoping Summer hadn't seen my flawless catch. I'd already slipped up with too many little things around her. She'd surely be putting the pieces together soon if I didn't do a better job of controlling my actions.

Shooting wasn't my usual method of disposal, but if it was what she needed from me, I was *more* than willing. I could already see the contents of Alan's skull dripping from the roof.

The gun wasn't one I recognised – a rare occurrence with my history. It was too light. Whatever it was, it couldn't have been loaded. Probably a good thing with Summer tossing them about the room like confetti.

In the moment it took for me to inspect the weapon, she'd pointed hers at him.

I found it amusing that she was cautious about me being caught on camera, but happy to throw me a gun and implicate her boyfriend in what could very well end up a murder.

*I couldn't ask for a more perfect partner.* Even the darkest parts of my Gift would have to approve of Summer and drop the idea of ever killing her.

My thoughts on wanting her to be mine forever were cut short.

Her shot was superbly aimed; the projectile lodged deep into the right side of his neck. The sight of the scene unfolding before me had my heart racing. I closed my eyes and breathed in slowly, holding the darkness at bay and keeping myself from making a wreck of the man dropping heavily to the concrete floor.

*She's so fucking perfect.* I opened my eyes to admire the woman, capable of disposing of her own threats.

"Camera's off!" she called, trying to twist her torso to get a better look at the wound. It was an awkward part of the body to see, and each time she moved, blood spread further through the shirt.

When I stepped up to the body, I spotted the tranq dart and sighed. It was clever. Between the moment she pulled the gun from the drawer, to shooting, there was no way for him to know his life *wasn't* about to end. The little nurse was capable of putting a deep fear into people, but allowed them to live.

*Fuck, she's too good for me,* I told myself for the millionth time.

I would finish the job later. We'd say our goodbyes sometime in the next few days and I would hunt him down.

Jackie would help with locating him. Tommy would come along to keep me company and to ensure I didn't get sloppy with the evidence as I came down from the kill.

Summer wouldn't ever *want* to know what I did during my time without her. Not even my best friend could stomach the mess I made, and he'd seen far more than the others.

A pained cry drew my focus from Alan's ugly face. Summer sat at the computer, holding her side and bracing herself on the desk. The scent of her perspiration reached my senses, and my ears were flooded with the sound of her heart beat. It was too fast, and her skin was beginning to turn too white, even for her.

I rushed across the room, scooped her up and laid her on the same, reclined chair where she treated those unworthy of what her skilled hands achieved each night. Far too many of them like the man out cold on the floor. Too many of them like *me*.

I inspected the injury, confirming it was too far around Summer's side to reach it herself.

I was going to have to stitch her up.

# TWENTY-NINE

## SUMMER

It stung. *So fucking bad.* I'd been sliced and cut so many times, but I'd never become used to the feeling. And while it would have been nice not to be in so much agony as the gash across my ribs generously decorated my white shirt, I reminded myself that it was a *good* thing. To allow myself to be used to this pain would be to completely give up. To be irreparably broken.

My breathing was labored, and I could sense I was starting to panic. The adrenaline from having shot at a patient had worn off and the guilt was starting to sit heavy in my stomach.

Logan stood over me, assessing the damage as I laid on the chair. His warm hands were gentle on the area around the wound, exposed through the hole in my shirt.

"I'm gonna need something to calm down before I black out," I ordered, voice wavering, "That shelf." I pointed across the room and told him the code for the cabinet. He retrieved the pills I needed and I swallowed one. Then another before he snatched the bottle from my hand and threw it out of reach.

*Damn him and his obsession with these fucking shelves.*

He was learning too much, and now denying me a good buzz from taking too many before I worked out *how the fuck* I was meant to stitch myself up.

My metal table, always set with the tools I needed for the night, was by my head. I reached over and grabbed a needle, loading it with the thread, bloody hands trembling.

"What the fuck do you think you're doing?" he demanded, voice high with shock. He'd been calm as he entered the room, took what could have been a *real* gun without hesitating and watched me shoot someone in the neck. But *now* he had a problem with what I was doing? What did that say about him? Or about what Logan thought I was going to do to my patient?

"I'm gonna…" I gestured toward the open wound as if it wasn't completely obvious that I needed to close it.

"No you're not!" he said, like it was the stupidest idea he'd ever heard.

"Fuck, Logan, I can't go to a hospital!"

"*I'm* gonna do it."

"What?"

He sat on the stool and wheeled himself as close as he could. My shorter legs were clearly an advantage when maneuvering around those who needed help.

Logan adjusted the height of my chair so it was lower to the ground, giving him a better view from above.

"I don't think you should–" I started, but he ignored me and rolled me on my side, giving him easier access to the hole in my body.

I was facing him, kind of. The view from my position was mostly under his arms and chest. I wasn't going to complain about the scenery, especially with a double dose of the pills kicking in.

"You need to take your shirt off." He wasn't being unreasonable. I would have already had his shirt off and thrown across the room if the roles were reversed. For a moment, the meds and thoughts of undressing him were almost enough for the pain to subside entirely.

He gave me a stern look and repeated, "You *need* to take your shirt off. Maybe your bra too. It's too close, and I don't want to get it caught on the needle."

"Absolutely not!" I shouted, thinking I'd said that in my mind, but had snapped at him instead.

"Summer," he tipped his torso to the side for his face to be level with mine, "Let me help you. The sooner I close this up, the better."

He wasn't wrong, and it annoyed me he was making the most sense between us. That was *my* job.

We compromised; he could cut my shirt and I would move my bra up and out of the way as much as needed so he could get it over with.

After telling him where I kept the antiseptic, I soon felt small, uncomfortable pricks around the cut as I took deep, shaky breaths. My head started to feel like it was floating. The pain eased more by the second and the pills to stop the panic attack made me feel a little loopy.

"Have you ever done this before?" I asked, "Or am I about to have another hack job added to this canvas?"

"Only a couple of times." Was he dropping his cover? Too concerned about me to keep up the act? The thought made me smile. "You know, people slicing their fingers at work all the time," he added.

*Nice save.*

"And… my Mom w—is a doctor," he confessed, giving me a little more of himself. "She tried to teach me and my sister stuff like this. Said it would come in handy one day. Not that we ever really listened. I would have paid more attention, had I known I'd end up with someone like you." He chuckled, though it was tight with stress.

"Was or is?" I asked, too high to stop myself from pointing out his slip-up. He didn't respond. "Well I hope you listened *enough* to not butcher me like that jerk."

I hadn't noticed Logan was already stitching until he pulled a little too hard, making my body rock.

"Slow down if you need to," I whispered tiredly to him. "I know I'm fast, but tension is far more important than speed. I'm not going anywhere." I let the side of my head drop to the chair and loosened the tightness in my shoulders. I was in safe hands.

*Surely he wouldn't bother stitching me up if he ever planned on killing me?*

I believed if Logan were going to dispose of me, he would have done it while my guard was down – either while I slept or when he had his hands wrapped around my skull the previous night as I blew him on the couch.

Though, from the praise I'd received for my skills in the past, part of me believed he may have simply wanted me to finish getting him off before deciding my fate. Had he passed up the perfect opportunity to redecorate the living area with my brain?

The garage was so quiet. The only sounds were his loud, steady breaths as he focused. From where I laid I had a good view of his chest, and tried not to think too hard about what he looked like shirtless. My mind wandered to thoughts of how I could get him to breathe like this again. I loved the sound, and added the noises in my mind to those he'd made on the couch, already on repeat in my head.

We kept getting so carried away almost every night before we fell asleep together. I wanted him *so* bad. But after what happened in his apartment I knew I couldn't get away with drugging myself to relax enough about the fucked up mess under my clothes.

*It's a shame his arms are over my body, busily sewing my side back together instead of around me as I ride him.* I huffed out a sigh and closed my eyes.

When I opened them after a few minutes, I noted that Logan had started to sweat. The room was warm, as always, and he'd been thrown into a role he wasn't trained for. He smelled *so* good.

The heavy scent of his cologne was stronger than usual as it mixed with his sweat, suffocating my senses and increasing the intense urge to throw all insecurities out the window and pull him onto me. At this point I didn't care if he'd even finished stitching, I just wanted him.

*Whoa, easy. At least sit through this before getting carried away and fucking with an open wound, you know how messy that can get.*

I tried my best to keep my eyes open so my thoughts wouldn't run away each time I closed them, but I didn't have much luck. The pills I'd taken were the same I stocked in my bathroom. I also kept some in my backpack. I even had a stash at Crave for when all signs were pointing to a quick trip upstairs to one of *the rooms* with some hot stranger I'd never see again.

I'd taken to self-medicating in my early days at Home, when I realized I was too scared to convincingly fulfill the physical stipulations of my contract. They were addictive, and I continued with the awful habit after I left Bedlam behind. They helped me relax enough for my body and mind to agree that I was *allowed* to give in to physical urges every now and then.

I was confident when *alone* with the stash of toys I kept in the bedside drawer, but being physical with another *entire* body which included eyeballs that wanted to see me naked was something I still found incredibly daunting.

*Did I really think I could ever have a normal sex life after escaping him?* I rolled my eyes at myself.

It took Logan about twenty minutes to finish with what would have taken me a few seconds. While I would have eventually worked out a way to do it on my own, there was something sweet about him trying to care for me.

A gentle hand rested on my head, "I'm done."

"Can I see?"

Logan grabbed a mirror I kept in a drawer of my desk and angled it so I could inspect his work.

It wasn't bad. Not perfect, but my standards were far too high. He'd used a different method to me, which took me by surprise.

*Interrupted stitches, no wonder he was so slow.*

Perhaps watching me work had made him uncomfortable with trying to replicate my moves, knowing his own would never compare. Or maybe it's how he was taught by his mother who either "was" or "is" around.

Either way, I didn't mind, and was glad I didn't have to work out how to stitch it up myself in such an awkward spot. My shoulder and neck tensed at the thought of the cramp I would have gotten from twisting to reach it.

"It's really good," I finally told him, making sure my tone sounded as impressed as I felt.

Logan smiled shyly, "It'll do the job," he rolled back to extend and stretch his legs while getting a better view of me. "Summer… can I ask about the sca—"

"No."

He sighed. I hated the disappointed sigh when I was the one to draw it out of him, but I also kind of loved it. And I wanted to learn how to make him do the opposite of that noise. I'd only started to work it out by using my mouth.

*I wonder what noises he'd make if I used my—*

"So what if you've got a few scars?"

"No." I said again. More annoyed now that my thoughts had been interrupted.

"Honestly, if you just showed me, it'd all be over with. I can feel them when I hold you in bed, they don't bother me at all."

"No." I sat up so our faces were level, only a few feet apart.

"I've already seen some. It's *just* skin."

There were others, healed long ago in the area he'd stitched. They would have been unmissable in the bright lights of the garage, no matter the state of his eyes and the usefulness of those glasses. But they weren't the worst of the damage.

I hooked my foot around one of the bars of his stool and quickly jerked him toward me. His reflexes were flawless, not even becoming slightly unsteady at the motion that would have made anyone else topple backwards.

"*No.*" I told him firmly, then leaned closer to kiss him. He kissed me back.

*It's time to do this.*

My mind was finally clear of the chaos, torment, ghosts and blood. The pills ensured I could only think of *him.*

Logan placed his bloody hands on my thighs, moving them up to around my hips and under my shirt. I didn't fight him, I still had the safety of the torn fabric to hide beneath.

I wrapped my legs around him, and with my hands on his shoulders, pulled myself from the reclined chair and onto his lap.

His lips moved from my mouth to my neck, and my breathing became heavy. I held him there, obsessed with the warmth on my skin as I roughly ran my hands through his sweaty hair.

Logan abruptly stopped. I pulled his head up to look at him for a clue as to why we weren't already undoing belts and buttons. Wasn't this the moment he'd been waiting for as much as I had?

"It's my turn to say 'no', Summer."

"What?"

"You're *high* right now," he shook his head while he caught his breath. "You would have had one hell of an adrenaline rush. You were *just* sliced open *and* stitched up." He pointed out the obvious as I frowned at how close those words sounded like the name I once proudly flaunted around Bedlam.

"I *want* to," he reassured me, "God, I want you, nurse. You have *no* fucking idea."

"I have *some* idea," I teased and bounced a little on his lap to grind on him, hard and throbbing through our clothing. *Too* much clothing. I wanted to take it all off. Forget the questions about the scars, I'd happily strip in front of him on the double dose I'd taken if he kissed my neck like that again.

He gave me a knowing look before giving another signature sigh. If he kept doing that, I couldn't listen to him. My self-control had become minimal at best and he made it so much harder to focus.

*Fuck it. I won't.*

I decided against listening to Logan. I may have been a little foggy, but I was *conscious.* Who the hell was he to decide what I could and couldn't do with my body? I was done with having others control me.

Grabbing handfuls of his shirt, I pulled him into another kiss. When his lips parted again I found myself grateful to be sitting on him, worried my legs would give out at any sign that he wanted me.

The force with which his mouth moved on mine and his hands firmly grabbing at my hips were the green lights I needed to start lifting his shirt. My palms rolling over the smooth skin of his back prompted him to pull me higher onto his lap, bringing our bodies closer together. His actions made my head swim and my body anticipate the pleasure to come.

*See? I knew he wouldn't refuse me after making it clear for weeks that he needs to fuck me as much as I NEED to fuck him.*

Logan shifted to stand up, and I tightened my legs around him.

*Where are we going? The bedroom?*

Nowhere.

He dropped me roughly to sit on the patient chair and turned from me to walk to the door, replacing his shirt as he went.

I tried to think of reasons he could be leaving. What would he return with? Did he have something in the bedroom he wanted to use? I knew he liked the look of my toy collection, but couldn't imagine he'd be reaching for them during our first time.

He'd already sent me the perfectly clean results from the tests I'd asked him to get done. So unless he was retrieving some kind of protection we didn't really need, I was at a complete loss as to why he'd break our momentum.

"W-where are you going?" I called, voice quivering with excitement as he reached the door to the hall. He opened it before turning around.

"I'm going *out.*" He looked unhappy. The way his brow furrowed made his hazel eyes appear far darker than I'd ever seen.

"Why?"

Was it not obvious enough that I didn't want him to leave?

*How much more of a hint does he need? Maybe I should just take my clothes off.*

"I'm not *him!*" he shouted,"I will *never* do what he did to you!"

"I know—" I started to argue, shocked he'd bring Eric up at a time like this.

"*Do* you though? 'Cause you seem to think I'm okay with *fucking someone* who can't *possibly* make a clear decision after what just happened." When Logan put it like that, I could see how it all looked. Tears pooled in my eyes and I tried to blink them away. "You told me he drugged you, Summer," he kept going, voice growing colder with each word, "How would this *be any better?*"

*It isn't.* I bit my tongue. *But I'm not capable of doing any better.*

When I didn't reply, he turned to leave.

"Will I see you tomorrow?" I called after him, wiping my eyes and glad he was too far into the house to see me crying. I could hear him in my bedroom, pulling his shoes on.

"No. I'll be out with the gang, we've got somewhere to be." I was happy to bet "somewhere" would be Crave.

"Saturday, then?"

"Maybe."

His car keys scraped the surface of the hallway table before he helped himself out the front door. I didn't move from the chair, I only glanced around the room, trying to work out what the fuck had happened between us. Everything seemed to be going so well.

And then I ruined it.

I startled as the roller door lifted and the familiar footfalls of Ben and Tony stepped in behind me. "What are you doing back here?"

I'd sent them home nearly an hour ago. With no more bookings and the rest of the night looking to be quiet, I'd hoped to get a few more hours of sleep in the arms of my Gifted hot water bottle.

"Got pinged." Tony answered, "Saw movement outside the house the second we got home. Fucker must have snuck through the gate as we left."

I'd completely forgotten about Alan, and turned on the chair to get a look at him — still out cold on the floor. That tranq wouldn't wear off for hours.

"We also saw Logan leave," Ben teased, prodding the man on the floor with his foot. "The fuck did you get up to with this guy?"

"I'm gonna need you two to deal with that," I said without turning to look at them.

"Did he hurt you?" Ben asked, noticing the blood on my side and torn shirt as he rounded the chair. When I didn't answer, he carefully tried again, "Boss, do we need to take care of *anyone else?*"

"Oh god, no." I pulled myself out of the terrible cloud Logan left me to deal with on my own. "I need to shower." I stood from the chair, clutching my side, the sudden move sparking sharp pain.

"Righto, Boss," Ben called after me.

When I turned to close the hallway door, Tony was blocking it.

"What?" I snapped, not in the mood to explain why he and Ben were on unconscious-body-duty.

He knew me well enough to not push me when I was in too much of a bad mood, and instead of checking on me like he wanted to, he grinned and went with, "Ben's complaining about the money again, says you don't pay us enough."

Ben's laughter echoed in the garage before a weak giggle slipped through my sniffles, "Tell him he can go fuck himself."

I left them and headed to my bathroom to wash another day away.

Logan made it clear he wouldn't be coming back for at least a few days.

I'd be counting down the seconds until we left for Crave the following night.

# THIRTY

SUMMER

## FEBRUARY 14TH

My favorite night of the month had finally arrived. We would soon be heading out to the club, and I had bigger plans than simply stitching drunkards up for decent cash.

I was falling too fast for Logan, even knowing his lies and secret identity. He hadn't returned after our argument, as promised. I'd had a whole day to think straight without his arms around me and the intoxicating cologne fogging up my head.

The plan was to confront him at Crave. At least, more directly than I'd tried so far.

Like I had for my previous trip to the club, I put more effort into my hair and makeup, not wanting to look stupid if my mask were to come off at any point during the night.

As I finished putting loose waves through my hair, I slipped my contacts into place over my irises. This set was particularly deceptive, with just enough color to make my eyes look more green than blue, but still clear enough to see my pupils reacting to light. Many visitors to the club wore others which didn't allow for that, and faking eye color was a dead giveaway that they were trying to throw off their scent.

At least, it was obvious to me. But I had a knack for noticing those minute details in people who were playing pretend. Unfortunately, it seemed Logan did too.

I dressed in black. Only this time I wore a full, matte, leather catsuit that clung to my frame and looked especially good around my butt and hips. It was surprisingly comfortable, and still allowed me the movement to get my work done.

Most importantly, it covered any identifying scars.

There were too many people who frequented Crave from Bedlam for the biggest night of the month, and there were already enough rumors circulating about me that I didn't need to unintentionally confirm while preoccupied with unmasking my boyfriend.

*Boyfriend? You're fucking delusional. He's so done with you. You fucked it up after only a few days of being his girlfriend.* My inner monologue had been particularly harsh since Logan left me in the garage.

I had the tendency to spiral after messing something up. My mistakes often led to me blacking out with an expensive leather belt around my neck following my arguments with Eric. I didn't believe Logan would ever hurt me, but having him so upset with me was punishment enough.

*See? Delusional. He's Vengeance. It's gotta be in his nature to hurt people. God, you're so fucking stupid.*

After slipping on my favorite heels, I secured my mask and caught a look at myself in the hallway mirror as I left. I looked *good.* Hopefully irresistible. I'd have to wait and see.

After driving the hour to the club with the bodyguards and setting up the van, it was time to get some work done. I'd hoped to head inside to see if Logan and his friends had arrived, but was immediately thrown into stitching up a head wound.

By the time I'd reached the halfway point through my shift, there were still no signs of the gang, and as the minutes ticked by I started to feel like I was losing my confidence in confronting him at all.

"Hey!" A familiar voice called through the back doors of the van as I cleaned my bloody tools and organized new ones for whoever was lucky enough to sit in my chair next.

"Hey!" I called back. "Burning Man!"

He laughed, stepping up beside me and closing the doors. "Okay, that's gotta be one of your worst so far."

I shrugged and reached for the supplies I typically needed for the vigilante in red and gold. "Well, you won't tell me your name, so I have to keep guessing."

"You're probably running out of ideas by now?" he asked, getting comfortable on the chair.

"Kind of, yeah. There's only so many names that can go with a suit like this," I gestured to the body of the man who's name I'd learned over a month ago.

"It's Pyro," he said quietly.

"Get out! How the fuck did I not think of that?" I laughed, having asked the same question to the bodyguards while they'd cackled like hyenas at me when they revealed his name.

Another *lame* vigilante name. At least Pyro was actually Gifted, not playing pretend like many of the others, currently trying to impress and hook up within the concrete walls of Crave.

Pyro, as the bodyguards informed me, was more of a troublemaker than I'd first realized. He'd been moving between the Gray Mountains and Bedlam for almost as long as I'd been away from Home. He picked fights and caused chaos everywhere he went, all with the intention of catching the eye of the big crime bosses, hoping to be recruited.

A literal career criminal. They were everywhere. I would know, having once been on display to show how much fun could be had in Bedlam as part of Eric's Collection.

Pyro tugged at the arm of his skin-tight suit, pulling it away from the gloved portion I typically worked on and revealing his forearm instead. Like the flesh I'd seen on his hands, it was covered in scars from burns, recovered long over time.

I quickly glanced at, but blinked away from the many vertical lines closer to his wrist. They were almost healed, and none of my business unless he spoke about them. I had to be strong in my job. I knew better than to get attached to my patients, but learning this seemingly easy-going man had such viciously hacked self-harm scars made my eyes burn a little.

There was a shallow gash in his forearm I hadn't noticed through the suit, likely because so much of his costume was metallic red.

"Nice," I cleared my throat and began cleaning the wound, "What does the other guy look like? Will he be in here next?"

Pyro laughed again and shook his head. "I think they had to take him elsewhere."

"You could at least leave them in a state where I get paid to fix them."

"I'll try harder next time." he promised, watching me tie off the last stitch in his skin.

"Good. You're all done. But I'm sure I'll see you again soon."

"Wait, you know my name now." he cocked his head, appearing to eye my face through his mask. "Don't I get to know yours?"

"That's not how this works, buddy," I stood to clean up, "I can't be a nameless nurse for my safety if I go handing it out to every weirdo like you."

"I bet it's something pretty. Ellie? Hallie? Summer? Maybe Lana?" he rattled the names off quickly, and I hoped he didn't notice me react to any in particular. His tone wasn't teasing or flirty. And if he were interested in impressing the bigger bosses of the underworld, there was a good chance he'd know the name Eric had given me. Either of them.

*Send him away. Others have worked it out before and Eric's only sent the Finders once.*

I turned to him, smiling politely. "Okay, Pyro. Time to leave. You've officially overstayed your welcome and I'm due for a drink."

"I'm just messing with you. You're smart not to say."

"You're damn right I am." I kept my tone light so it didn't sound as though his guesses had bothered me.

"Catch you next time." he said, jumping to the ground.

"I'm taking a break!" I called around the side of the van to whichever of the bodyguards was earning their paycheck. Taking a deep breath to clear my head, I exhaled slowly and found my quiet spot in the alley.

In the shadows, I leaned against the brick wall of the club. It vibrated against my shoulder as I skimmed over trashy gossip articles. I smiled, glad I was no longer one of the girls in the photos that the columns tore to shreds or praised, depending on what they wore or how much their weight had changed. It cleared my head of the patients I'd already seen. Bloody noses, head injuries, cuts and grazes. The club was a rough place on the nights when people from all over came together. People like Pyro, purposefully causing trouble certainly didn't help.

Then, *they* pulled up. Loud and excited to get in the club — the same group I'd seen the month before clambered out of their car across the street. As I slowly crept through the dark towards the road to get a better view, someone from further down the alley called them over.

*Shit!*

There was nowhere for me to go as the group quickly headed my way. I turned to face the back of the alley and leaned on the wall again.

Dressed in black and standing in the dark helped me blend in a little. They would definitely see me, with at least two of them being Gifted, but I hoped I didn't look like I was worth giving a second glance while I pretended to be getting some air like anyone else would.

*With the way I look in this suit? Are you fucking kidding me? I should have picked something else.*

Their footsteps grew closer. Both women chatted excitedly. They walked right past, just as I'd hoped. There was no reason for them to interact with a stranger.

Once they were a few steps ahead, I allowed myself a glance. *He* was there.

God he looked so fucking *good* in that suit. It tightly wrapped every inch of the perfect body I'd been seeing *most* of in bed every night.

It wasn't fair. Why did I have to get involved with someone so deliciously treacherous?

Seeing Logan had my heart rate picking up. There'd been no contact between us since he left my house, and I was still upset over what he'd said.

*Is it over between us? It could be.*

I had no idea what a functioning adult relationship was meant to look like outside of my parents, and it had been so long since I'd been exposed to that.

My gaze lingered on his butt and a sigh slipped from my lungs. He didn't stop walking, but turned to glance over his shoulder.

Our eyes locked. At least, I think they did. I couldn't see his eyes through the black spaces of the mask covering them. I swallowed hard and quickly dropped my gaze to my phone as he continued moving with the group.

*Did he recognise me?*

Did it matter? Even if he did, he couldn't say anything.

I was just a nurse, protecting my identity whilst working at a club packed with villains. He, on the other hand, would need to admit who he was to be able to mention my being there.

I had the upper hand again.

*Maybe I will mess with him tonight after all.* The thought helped me regain a little of the confidence I'd lost before they arrived.

Moving as quietly as my heels allowed on the gravel, I crept up the alley to watch the group enter the club through the back door, near the parked van.

As the door closed, I settled on my decision. I would make the most of the night if there was a chance of it being our last.

# THIRTY-ONE

## SUMMER

The end of my shift approached fast, and while the club would still be open for hours after I was done, even I had a limit on how much I could handle in one night.

Sometimes we went straight home, but I'd often try to join in on the chaos to unwind. In my pre-boyfriend days, I'd occasionally pop some pills and hop on one of the poles to find someone to play with. But not tonight.

There was a knock on the back of the van as I cleaned up after my last patient. I opened the doors, assuming it was either Tony or Ben bringing my first drink now my steady hands were off duty.

It was him. *Vengeance*. The man in the vigilante suit who I was certain was my boyfriend.

"I was told you're the one to see if I needed help?" His voice was clear enough for me to understand, but sounded slightly off, muffled in some way by the suit. For a moment, I wasn't sure if I had the right guy, but then noticed I was taking in an abnormally long breath, inhaling the cologne that swirled the space between us.

"What do you need?" I asked, my heart skipping a beat before the pace quickened.

"I've got a cut on my back, I can't see it to know how bad it is." He tried looking over his shoulder as he stepped up inside with me, his height forcing him to hunch over in the space.

"Come sit down, then." I ordered, guiding him to sit on my stool. I needed access to his back, not for him to have it pressed against the chair.

I stood behind him to make a quick assessment of the injury. Taking full advantage of the situation and the closeness, I spent a little extra time gently gliding my fingers across his shoulder to down and around the wound. He tensed, and suppressed what almost sounded like a sigh at my touch.

"How did this happen?" I asked quietly, trying not to use too many words, sure he'd recognise my voice – if he hadn't already.

"No fucking idea. It's pretty wild in there tonight. I think it was done with broken glass."

*Liar.* I rolled my eyes behind his back.

The cut was too neat for jagged glass, and likely the work of an incredibly sharp knife. I would know, and it was insulting he thought I wouldn't notice the difference.

Now I'd touched the suit, I knew for a fact there wasn't a chance glass could slice through it. It was high quality stuff, far rarer to source than the inferior fabric of Pyro's suit. I'd made many orders with the same material in the past for Home's goons to wear on their missions to create chaos throughout Bedlam. Eric had arranged for some of my clothing to be made from the same if he were particularly distrusting of the people we were traveling to see.

While I'd discovered his identity, I was at a total loss for how Logan could have obtained the costume on his wage. Last I checked, a custom design in his size would easily cost upwards of a million dollars.

And I would bet the twelve million in my bank account that Logan had gotten one or more of his friends to help him create the injury so he'd have an excuse to come to me and confirm my identity.

I didn't care much for the money. Maybe I should have bet on my ability to digest caffeine, it meant so much more to me.

In the light of the van, I took note of the distinct pattern of the fabric. The base was a deep black, no light reflected from it, making it perfect for stalking in the dark. Textured hexagons covered every inch in blood red, black, and others that transitioned seamlessly between the two, depending where on the suit they were placed.

Areas like his shoulders and neck were darker, whereas spaces like his pecs and forearms had more red to them. I couldn't deny how much I liked the design. I had a thing for those colors, and the placement in each area enhanced the look of the remarkable body the fabric was fortunate enough to encase.

Now that we both seemed to be playing the same game, I wanted to make this interaction between us as difficult as possible for Logan.

Instead of moving behind him to stitch, I leaned over from the front. Standing between his legs with my chest pressed to the left of his neck, the rest of my body brushed against his as I worked.

Thankfully, the cut was closer to the top of his shoulder, or else I'd be working upside down, much like the position he'd put me in when he carried me to his car on our first date.

With each time I leaned over, his posture tightened, and I could have sworn he shook his head slightly at the amount of physical contact I ensured we were making.

*Is he as tempted to grope me as I am to take off that mask?*

I had to give him credit, I knew how good I looked in my disguise and yet, he kept his hands to himself. It made me grateful I had a good enough excuse to be touching him all over. I wasn't so confident in my ability to control myself around him.

A low growl rumbled up his throat as I injected the anesthetic. I stored the sound in my mind for later, hoping I could find a way to get him to do it again, with or without the pain.

*If he ever lets you get this close again.*

The wound needed only a few stitches, taking me just seconds to close before I added the extra three at the top end, near his shoulder; another shark tagged and ready for release into our pestilent ocean.

Without his knowledge, I also threw a few quick weaves over the slice in the fabric to patch up the suit.

"I heard you were fast," he complimented my work when I sat on the patient chair and handed him my payment details.

"You heard right. You're all done. And if you don't mind, I'm ready to *finally* have a drink."

He cocked his head to the side and leaned back on the stool. "How about I grab you one, *nurse?*"

I gulped, heart racing at the way he called me "nurse." It was appropriate, considering the circumstances. He wasn't meant to know my name and I was *the nurse*. But it was all in the way he said it; crooned low in the same tone he always used when we were away from the club.

*Don't do it,* I internally begged. But he did it – he folded his arms.

*Fuck. Those fucking arms. What is he playing at?*

I arched a brow at the masked face. "You wanna buy me a drink?"

"Yeah. Unless you've got a date waiting inside for you?"

I giggled. "A date?" *Maybe he's testing you too.*

"It *is* Valentine's Day."

"It is?"

I hadn't paid attention to the date. And if I were being honest, I'd grown to hate every big event and holiday as time went on at Home. But this relationship, though it may have already been over, was new.

*Could we change that, together?*

He shrugged. "Someone like you shouldn't be out here patching up villains all night."

"Someone like me?" *The weak, human girlfriend?*

"Someone who looks as hot as you do. Working. While everyone else gets to have all the fun in there."

The catsuit suddenly felt like a sauna. I needed to change the subject. I swallowed hard to hide my nerves at the way he seemed to be eyeing every inch of me through his mask.

"Do you consider yourself to be one of those villains?"

His head tipped back slightly, and I could only guess he was squinting in thought. "Wouldn't you?"

*Twenty-three police officers. That's more than enough for villain status.*

"I don't judge my patients on their appearances. And I don't like labels."

He sighed. "Neither do I."

"I would never have guessed something as lame as Valentine's Day would mean anything to a *vigilante*." I teased, making a point of not calling him a villain as I hopped off the chair to toss the last of the bloody gauze into the trash can beside the cupboards.

"Vigilantes can't be romantic?" Logan's familiar, anxious laugh made me smile.

"I've never known one to be."

"We should change that."

*Fuck, it's like, a million degrees in here.*

"I couldn't think of a better way to end my night," I purred, laying the enthusiasm on thick as I looked down at him, barely suppressing the urge to pull at the neck of my clothing so I could breathe. I hoped he felt at least a little jealous, and that he might still be oblivious to the fact I knew *exactly* who he was.

As he stepped out of the van, he turned and held out a hand to help me down. I declined and jumped to the gravel, silently thanking my ankles for giving me a flawless landing while in heels. If that didn't have him second guessing who I was after seeing me try to walk in them on our date, nothing would.

We headed inside. The dark space with flashing lights was packed to the brim with hundreds of people.

Entering through the back meant we needed to cross the dance floor to reach the bar. I maneuvered through the maze of criminals, the beat of the music pulsing through my entire body. It was so intense, I often joked with the bodyguards that if someone's heart ever stopped, we'd only have to drag them inside to use the floor in place of a defibrillator.

We arrived at the bar where I made eye contact with Kit. He was quick to recognise me, and ignored the others shouting over the music for his attention.

"Usual?" he called.

"Please." I smiled at him.

I loved Kit. He was tall, tanned and fit, with thick black hair and the darkest brown eyes I'd ever seen. Arms, and likely much more, covered in tattoos. The complete opposite of his wife, making them an even cuter couple in my opinion. If he were much younger, and single, I wouldn't turn him down for a ride in one of the rooms. But our relationship was strictly platonic – more like family after he and Anna took me in.

Vengeance leaned against the bar, arms folded and facing the floor.

"Nothing for you?" I asked, giving him doe-eyes from under my disguise.

He shook his head and pointed to his mask before looking back to the sea of bodies. Since he was missing out on my interaction with Kit, I nodded to my friend. He winked and quickly made my drink, handing it to me before turning away to take someone else's order.

The drink was served in a martini glass; a bright red liquid with small flecks of white.

As I reached for the drink Vengeance spun and slammed his hand over the top.

"It's spiked," he warned, loud enough in my ear to hear him over the music.

Even with the overwhelming noise of the club, I could detect the concern.

"I *know*." I shooed his hand away and downed the drink in one mouthful. I was there to have fun, and since I couldn't do that as *Summer*, I had to do it as my alter ego.

Well, *one* of them.

I bet Logan wouldn't touch me now he'd caught me on the pills again, but I didn't care. He was mine to torment, and I was sure I'd find a way to change his mind.

After placing my glass down I grabbed his arm and pulled him in the direction of the dance floor. I wasn't much of a dancer, but you didn't need to be at Crave. All that mattered was your ability to move to soul-splintering bass lines before finding your way upstairs to make decisions that would haunt you in the days to come, only to have you running back in a month's time in hopes you'd find your masked partner.

Or a better one.

We were instantly surrounded by bodies in motion, with no space for light to pass between them. Limbs and tongues intertwined, the others around us moved in a hypnotic rhythm. The pill Kit had crushed into my drink quickly took effect. It was dizzying, and lifted the darkness weighing on my mind.

As we made our way deeper into the ocean of masks and costumes, Vengeance pulled at my wrist to turn to him. His hands swiftly slipped under my arms and down to my butt to draw me closer, ensuring I was guarded from the movements of others and so I'd focus solely on him without floating away.

My hands rubbed over every inch of his body, and he gave into temptation, doing the same to me. The suit was smooth under my grip as I squeezed at his arms, and if it weren't for that *fucking mask* on his face I would have had his mouth on mine.

He roughly gripped at the place on my ribs where I'd been stitched, and I bit my lip, trying not to cry out in pain. Did he intend on hurting me so I'd give him more clues to my identity?

As my lips brushed over his, concealed by the fabric, his gloved fingers pulled at the zip below my neck, low enough to expose a little cleavage. It was as close to removing clothing as I would allow on the floor. I grabbed his hand and guided him toward the stairs that led to the rooms.

*Surely after all the times we've come close to having sex, he won't turn down the opportunity? Not in a place like this?*

Virtues and morals stampeded for the exits at Crave. The club was known for allowing people of all kinds to explore their darkest fantasies with strangers. He'd be insane to turn down anyone, especially his girlfriend, about to offer to get him off with whatever ideas he mightn't ever let surface in the bedroom at home.

Three steps up and I felt resistance as he pulled at my arm, turning me to him again. With the additional height of my shoes on the stairs, our faces were level. While he looked directly at me I still had to fight with the mask to guess at what the expression underneath might be.

"It's Valentine's Day." I reminded him, "I promise it'll be one you'll never forget." My stomach tied in knots as his face dropped from mine before looking up at me again. Mask or not, Logan couldn't hide that shy smile from me. "Come play with me!" I demanded in an excited whisper, widening my eyes and tugging on his gloved hand. He shook his head and started to back away. "Why?" I tried not to sound as hurt as I had when he left me in the garage, but his refusal made my chest ache.

He shrugged. "I've got a girl at home."

Giving him my best attempt at a polite smile while enduring the hot sting of rejection, I nodded and dropped his arm, not understanding why I felt so envious of this "girl" when he was referring to me.

I knew I was being ridiculous by feeling so upset. Maybe I just so badly wanted to fuck him while he wore the suit. I doubted there would be another chance to get close to *Vengeance* again. At least not until next month.

Why was he hellbent on keeping this secret? Even now?

He walked away, leaving me alone on the dim staircase. Moving up more steps to the landing, I threw myself down on a low, velvet couch. I tried not to think too much of its history as I brushed white powder from the arm and slouched into the cushions.

There were more stairs in front of me that led to the top level. I shook my head at the thought of the many STDs I would inspect and treat in a month's time from what was happening behind all those closed doors. Even with that grim thought, I felt like I was missing out.

Still mentally buoyant from the pill I'd consumed and having touched so much of Logan, my body ached for his.

I scrolled on my phone in the dark, waiting for my buzz to wear off before collecting the cousins from whatever mischief they were getting involved in. My head was too foggy to read much, and I barely noticed someone was climbing the stairs, not paying them much attention until they sat right beside me.

Vengeance.

"Changed your mind?" I asked hopefully, shoving my phone down the top of my suit and twisting my body to face him. I lifted my leg over his, my knees settling at either side of him. Unable to resist touching, I ran my fingertips from his shoulders and down his arms before moving back up to his neck, trying to find the gaps in the suit to remove his mask. I didn't want to take it off completely, just enough so I could kiss him. Two days without Logan's scolding lips on mine already felt like a lifetime.

"I think you're in some kind of danger." His tone was serious.

"What do you mean?" the playfulness in my voice faltered as I took in the details of his mask. The black patches over his eyes were smooth. Not made of the same material, but also not reflective like glasses.

*Glasses. How do you cope without your glasses?*

I didn't have the mental capacity to work it out.

"I overheard some men outside," he roughly grabbed my shoulders, forcing me to stop focusing on his arms, "They were saying *stitch up*. Made me think they might be looking for a nurse. They're from out of town. I think they're from Bedlam."

My stomach dropped, and the hairs on my arms stood on end.

"Did one have red hair?" I demanded, "Maybe another had dark brown? Business suits? Sunglasses?"

The masked man beneath me nodded.

"*Fuck,* he's found me." The words barely left my lips, strangled by a panicked whisper, "They're here to take me back."

A lump formed in my throat and my hands began to shake at the thought I could be moments away from seeing Eric.

Vengeance pushed me off his lap and seized my arm, tearing me up the stairs and through one of the hallways on the upper level. There were countless doors on either side he could have dragged me through to hide, but he led me to a glass door at the very end. It opened onto a small balcony, likely put to use by people who needed a cigarette after whatever feats they'd performed in the rooms.

"Wait! You don't expect me to jump?" I shrieked, nearly toppling over the railing from having stopped so quickly after running. Vengeance grabbed me firm around the waist, steadying me. Being on the top floor only made us about four stories high, but I wasn't Gifted like him.

He laughed, "God no, they'd be finding bits of you for weeks." He scooped me up in his arms and held me tight against his chest.

*What if I've made a mistake? Too distracted to see the signs that this could be the moment I get handed over and whisked back to hell?*

"Close your eyes, nurse." He told me. I obeyed, placing far too much trust in a vigilante to save me from a villain.

With his forehead pressed to mine, he took a step back, then swiftly leapt over the edge, landing hard on the ground below. It made my jump from the van in heels look like I'd taken the first, wobbly steps of a foal.

The van pulled up behind me as he gently set me down. "I told your friends you might need to make a quick getaway."

"Umm… Thank you?" was all I could get out, dizzy from having fallen four stories.

The doors at the back opened and Tony roughly grabbed my arm to pull me up. Vengeance slammed the doors in my face as the van began to move.

"This place is full of freaks, but he doesn't seem too bad." My bodyguard commented as he sat on the stool.

"You have no fucking idea." I dramatically fell backward onto the patient chair beside him, "Eric's onto me again."

He reached for my hand and squeezed it. "Bound to happen at some point, right, *Stitch?*"

"Yeah," I sighed, staring up at the roof of the van. "I guess I was stupid to hope he wouldn't send Finders after me again so soon."

# THIRTY-TWO

## LOGAN

"Come play with me!" Her voice was clear over the obnoxiously loud music as she pulled at my arm to take me upstairs.

Fuck, I *wanted* to.

Even with the color of her eyes slightly off and her face half covered, I knew it was her. I thought I'd been imagining things in the alley. The woman scrolling on her phone in the dark had so many similarities, but I left it at that – similarities. Not *her*.

But I was in denial. And I'd grabbed that ass enough times to know better.

Summer didn't do much of anything above the books and she worked with shady patients, but for her to even *know* about Crave, let alone *work* at the club was out of the question.

Or so I'd thought.

She was eagerly awaiting my reply, eyes wide and a flirty sway to her shoulders.

Offering herself to me in a place like the club meant she was just as, if not *more* keen than I was to take things further between us. As if her excited perspiration wasn't enough to get me rethinking my stance on the rooms, her scent mingled with the heavy notes of her perfume; almond, jasmine, vanilla. The hypnotic concoction made me want to fuck her in whichever room she picked.

But I couldn't do that here.

I didn't care for the idea of fucking *anyone* in this filthy place, with not so much as completing my way up the staircase in all the years I'd visited. Besides, I couldn't imagine anything long-term would be possible between us if the physical side of it started in masks and lies.

I wanted *Summer*, not the nameless nurse. After everything I *hadn't* shared with her, I felt I owed her my *real* self when she was ready, not the killer in the suit.

What would she expect me to do? Text her the next day to meet and make up after our fight, pretending like I hadn't already fucked her?

*Shit. How much does she already know about me? Does she know what I'm capable of?*

There was no way I could take a step further without confirming my identity and totally blowing my cover. Or was it already gone? And for how long?

If she knew my identity, still let me in her house every night, *and* slept beside me, did it mean she could *accept* me for who I was?

Surely she'd have outed me if she couldn't. Or at the very least, broken it off between us.

Unless of course, she had no idea, and just wanted to fuck the tall, faceless guy in the suit like many who had tried their luck before her.

But my gut told me that wasn't the case.

If she were asking me, *Logan*, to go upstairs, then I was in far more trouble with her than I realized. Only the gang knew the truth about Vengeance. Everyone who'd known me before I moved to the mountains was under the assumption I was dead. Not even my wife, after seven years of marriage, had put the pieces together and worked it out. Though, she probably learned that news during her final moments as she was murdered in our bedroom.

Summer and I had barely known each other for a couple of months – she couldn't have known. I shook my head and backed away. I needed air. I needed space to think.

"Why?" she asked, voice thick with disappointment.

Maybe she wanted to make up as much as I did after how we left things at her house. But I couldn't do *anything* with her for the night. It didn't matter that I wanted to, I'd caught her popping pills. *Again*.

"I've got a girl at home."

It was the best I could do. It was true, mostly. I *did* have someone who maybe *should* have been at home instead of standing on the dingy staircase in a club full of criminals, asking me to take her upstairs for *kind-of* anonymous sex.

The visions of me bending her over the end of a bed were almost enticing enough to lock us in one of the rooms, take my mask off and share my secrets with the woman who apparently still had *many* of her own.

Summer forced a polite smile and nodded, taking my rejection well. Still, I hated making her feel that way.

*I'll find a way to make up with her and we'll work out how to try this again, preferably anywhere outside the walls of Crave.*

I left her on the stairs without looking back. She was too tempting. The way she'd stitched me in the van, making a point of standing between my legs and leaning with her tits on my neck – all those invitations to touch her. I'd struggled to reject them.

Having had every inch of her body rubbing against mine on the dance floor left me feeling as though she was imprinted all over the skin under my suit.

I stepped out the front of the club for some air, and to make sure Jackie's car still had tires for me to drive them all home later.

Crave was in one of the dodgiest parts of town. It *had* to be. It was a deterrent for those too scared and weak to play with the big names that passed through the doors and down into the criminal underworld.

It was a portal directly to hell, with me being one of the many demons lurking in its shadowy corners. It made Summer being there all the more unbelievable. I may not have known everything about her, but I didn't believe for a second that she belonged in this moral sinkhole.

"Have you seen a girl, about this tall, probably stitching people up?" a red-haired man in sunglasses and a business suit asked the group of smokers leaning on the wall to the other side of the club's entrance.

"Ah, not tonight," a masked woman answered, "But there's sometimes one out the back? Are you hurt?"

"No. Just looking for an old friend." He sighed and moved to enter the club. I listened to his movements for a little longer after he walked through the doors, trying to separate his voice and footsteps from the pulsing music and gyrating bodies that the solid walls contained.

"Go start the interview." He spoke to someone a few paces in from the entry.

"Without you?" Another voice responded. "The guy's unstable."

"You'll be fine. Just don't piss him off. I'll keep searching. The boss will lose his fucking mind if we manage to get a new recruit *and* snatch Stitch Up —" His voice faded as he moved further away.

Whoever he was, he seemed more business-like than someone simply finding an *old friend*. I'd seen him once or twice before, about a year prior with a large group of people, no doubt escorting one of Bedlam's biggest through Crave. Not that I'd paid too much attention at the time, they all had the same look.

I was left with two choices. One; I could leave the woman I knew was Summer, *my girlfriend*, to deal with him in a place where no one would give a second glance at a woman being snatched and disappearing. Or two; I could potentially ruin what was left of my cover and get her out of here.

*Like I even have to think about it.*

Keeping my identity undiscovered had always been top priority, but the idea of Summer being in danger made her safety take a firm lead.

Silently, I skulked down the shadowed alley to where the packed up van waited and the two bodyguards were smoking. Even with their masks on, there was no doubt they were Tony and Ben.

"I think someone from out of town is looking for the nurse," I called to them, keeping my distance so I didn't appear to be a threat.

"The fuck you talking about?" One of them called back, flicking the end of his cigarette to the ground and crushing it into the gravel.

"Some dodgy looking piece of shit in a business suit out the front was asking about her." I shrugged as they looked at each other. I tried not to sound like I cared too much about the nurse, but the look they exchanged told me I needed to get to her – now.

"*Fuck*, where is she?" The other asked.

"I know where she is. Or where I left her at least… I can get her out." I offered.

"Why should we trust you with her?" the first stepped closer to me. I would have been nervous, had I not been Gifted and known who they were.

Both men were close to my height and much wider in the shoulders than me. I worked out often, but they were far more committed to the offensive look. They may have been jokers at Summer's house, but didn't fuck around with her well-being in the garage, or at Crave either it seemed. I actually felt a little better about her being at the club, knowing she brought these two along with her.

"You shouldn't." I admitted, "But if you want my help, I need to move. He mentioned something about a stitch up? Could they be looking for her to do a dodgy job on a big name?"

I had a million questions running through my head about Summer and what else she got up to that led her to places like Crave.

The second got in the driver's seat while the first spoke low, hurriedly explaining, "No. They're here to take her to Bedlam. If that happens we'll never see her again. Go get her. Where do you want us?"

"If she's close to where I left her, then meet us under the balcony around the other side." I called back, leaping up the stairs and into the club.

The music immediately sent painful tremors through my heightened senses. Sound waves collided with my bones as I began the search for my little nurse. I brushed past the man who was looking for her out the front, and a few others with a similar appearance, heading in the direction I'd come from.

Climbing the stairs, I prayed she hadn't found someone else to visit one of the rooms with, and that I wouldn't need to pry her off the dick of a more willing participant than I'd proven to be.

We'd not discussed if either of us were open to seeing other people. I'd assumed she wouldn't have had the time between her work and how often we were together. Now I'd seen her in the club, I really had no idea who I was dealing with.

Spotting her on a couch at the staircase landing gave me more relief than I wanted to admit.

Climbing the steep stairs in two bounds, I rushed to sit beside her, not knowing how to tell her she needed to get the fuck out of here without completely giving away my identity.

"Changed your mind?" she asked, mood and heartbeat instantly picking up as she shoved her phone into the top of her suit and turned her body. She lifted her leg over both of mine, abruptly sitting on my lap.

*Oh, shit.*

My eyes dropped to her cleavage. I wanted to *be* that phone. I wanted to grab at her ribs again to make her moan like she had earlier.

Summer ran her hands up and down my arms, taking note of the colors in my suit, her palms gently brushing the textured fabric.

Maybe it was because she was high, but she seemed fixated on the pattern. The light touch of her fingertips moving from my shoulders, over my pecs and lower to my stomach made me want to throw her over my shoulder and take her to the backseat of Jackie's car.

*Fuck. I need to focus.*

"I think you're in some kind of danger," I told her, grateful my voice didn't do something stupid, like break mid-sentence at being caught off guard with her jumping on me so eagerly.

"What do you mean?" she squinted at my face, but my mask gave nothing away.

Gently batting one of her hands away when she searched for the join in the fabric near my neck, I had to risk saying more to her. "I overheard some men outside," I grabbed her shoulders in an attempt to show her I wasn't fucking around. It prompted her to stop playing with my arms and take me seriously.

"They were saying *stitch up*." I explained, "They're from out of town. I think they're from Bedlam."

"Did one of them have red hair? Maybe another had dark brown? Business suits? Sunglasses?" What little color her skin held instantly drained as I nodded, relieved she was finally listening to me. "*Fuck,* he's found me." her voice wavered, eyes growing rounder under her mask, "They're here to take me back." The thumping behind her ribcage rapidly accelerated. I always kept tabs on her heartbeat, but had never once heard it like this around me.

*Fear. She fears for her life. Wait... Now? Not when we're alone? And she knows who I am?*

That was something I needed to shelve and come back to later. The surprising thought was threatening to distract me further when she needed me to keep her safe.

Without another word, I pushed her off me and pulled her up the stairs by the arm. We ran, with me dragging her through the hallway that I hoped would lead to the balcony I'd seen several times from below. Thankfully, I was right, and hadn't wasted precious seconds of time for her to escape.

"Wait! You don't expect me to jump?" she screamed when I stopped to judge the distance to the ground, grabbing her around the waist so she didn't topple clean over the railing as she lost balance in her heels.

I laughed and scooped her up in my arms. "God no, they'd be finding bits of you for weeks."

She trembled in my hold, suddenly looking so small. It was hard to believe this was the same woman who'd sworn at and shot her patient. The threats of her ex appearing had rattled her to the core.

*Is that who she dreams of?*

The same tremors in her limbs often appeared when she cried in her sleep.

Her irises, blue-green with the contacts I could see right through, darted between mine.

"Close your eyes, nurse," I told her. She gave a shaky nod and squeezed her blackened eyelids shut. I lifted her a little higher against my chest and rested my brow on hers. She exhaled the breath she'd been holding, and her trembling eased.

I took a step back, sucked in a deep breath and jumped over the edge to the gravel below.

*Nine out of ten, a little wobbly on the landing.*

I hoped she would have given me a better score. I was a little tempted to ask for one, and would have, had it not so quickly become a running joke between us.

The van pulled up behind Summer as I set her down and inspected her, making sure she wasn't hurt and was able to balance after the rush of the fall. As my eyes passed over her leather-wrapped figure I still couldn't believe that the woman I'd been in bed with for weeks was standing in front of me, in her own disguise and at one of the shadiest places from home to Bedlam.

I couldn't deny how *fucking hot* the thought was; the two of us being a part of the same world, as dangerous as it was already proving to be with people hunting her.

She could be everything. My girlfriend, part of the gang. A medic to us if she wanted as we took out the scum of the earth, under the radar with the tips our detective contact would throw to us on occasion.

There was hardly a better life to imagine. At least, not one with a Gifted and a human sticking together.

*She's already one of us, look at her. Just tell her.*

I considered removing my mask and leaving with her. The others could find their own way home.

"I told your friends you might need to make a quick getaway." I said, instead of confessing.

*I'd be stupid to tell her.*

I swallowed over the disappointment. If she didn't know my secret and went looking for answers after finding out it was me in the suit, I couldn't imagine I'd ever see her again. I was just another monster she should have been running from.

"Umm… Thank you?" she blinked a few times, still looking a little dizzy from being ripped through the club and essentially thrown from the top of the building.

As fast as the doors at the back of the van opened, one of the bodyguards grabbed her by the arm and pulled her up into the vehicle. He gave me a small nod as I pushed the doors shut and they peeled off.

I listened for the van on the streets for as long as possible, before they were too far to hear with the distance between us. They weren't intercepted as far as I could tell, allowing me to let out a long breath as I dropped the tension in my shoulders. I could relax, knowing she was moving further away by the second from the men who were looking for her.

"Hey!" Someone called to me as they rounded the corner at the back of the club, "Have you seen a girl about this tall?" He used his hand for a guide. "Black hair, smart mouth, can stitch someone up in a few seconds."

He got her height and descriptors amusingly accurate, making me think he might have known Summer well. It made him all the more dangerous if he were a part of the life she didn't want to return to.

"Nah, sorry. Never seen her."

I glanced back at him as I climbed the steps, spotting a gun under his jacket.

*What kind of cult has people carrying weapons into a place like Crave?*

Could Summer have been involved in a gang? Not the kind like my small group of friends, but one that warranted her fear of being taken back to its leader?

Cults, of course, were dangerous in their own way. I'd dealt with a particularly disturbing one in the past, and while they destroyed lives, the leader hadn't needed to use weapons to subjugate mindless followers. Not physical weapons, anyway.

Everything Summer told me about her time in Bedlam could easily tick all the same boxes for the mob or a cartel. Being a nurse within the group and being exposed to so much gore suddenly made perfect sense. Crimes related to those groups were often messy, brutal, the kind that would lead to the reactions I'd been witnessing in her for myself.

*What else is she hiding?*

# THIRTY-THREE

## LOGAN

I squeezed onto a barstool between Jackie and Nova.

"I'm dating the nurse!" I announced, still adrenalised from helping Summer escape and learning her secret identity. For now, I ignored the fact that mine was also likely out in the open, too.

Jackie giggled, "Yeah, we know."

"Nice gal," Tommy added from the other side of Nova, playing along with Jackie's teasing, "You introduced us already, remember?"

"Did you hit your fucking head or something?" Nova sipped at her drink and laughed. The skin of her hand around the glass sparkled like a galaxy under the flashing lights of the club.

"No, dickheads." I sighed at them. "*The* nurse. The one who stitches people up, *here*."

Nova spun so fast on her stool she nearly toppled off.

"So… what? You're not seeing Summer anymore? I thought that had potential with you introducing her to us." She took another sip with much less enthusiasm than the first.

"No." I shook my head again in frustration and tried to explain, "I mean, yes. Summer *is* the nurse."

"What?" Nova gasped, and the others gawked at me, eyeballs threatening to pop out of their skulls. "That hot little minx working out the back of the club? That's *Summer*?"

The man behind the bar cleared his throat loud enough for us to glance up and see him frowning at us.

*Shit, we shouldn't be saying her name in this place.*

"Fuck, how'd you land *that?*" Tommy reached around the women between us to lightly punch my arm.

"Did you have any idea?" Jackie asked, tone as impressed as Tommy's.

"No idea until we walked past her outside." I admitted, lowering my voice enough to not attract the attention of the bartender. "Her bodyguards were here too."

"So is that the reason you got me to slice you up?" Nova shoved me, grin wide and sparkling, "You wanted to spy on your girlfriend? Have some *alone time* in the van together?" Her giggles were cut off by Jackie snorting at her.

"You mean you cut him without even knowing why?"

"Are you really surprised, Jack?" Tommy sighed, downing the last mouthful from a beer bottle, "You know what they're like."

"Okay you two, our table just opened up, leave us for a minute." Nova commanded. Tommy and Jackie hopped up to quickly claim our usual spot to the left of the floor.

"Does this mean it's happening?" Nova squealed, turning her body and committing me to a conversation I didn't want to have. "She can join our little gang? Between whatever weird shit she gets up to in her garage and here?"

"*No.*" I groaned, knowing this was just the start of a barrage of questions about to come my way.

"How serious are you about her?" She spoke in an excited whisper. Our Gifted hearing allowed us to have much quieter conversations than when the others were involved. "If you tell her, can we finally hang out with her?" She pleaded, "We won't need to watch *everything* we say. Jackie is useless at calling me Harrison, she even told me she nearly slipped up in front of Summer."

I didn't understand why Nova bothered with a secret identity. She wasn't on the run, but she insisted on being called by her maiden name, not the one carefully chosen by her parents. Just one look at her and you knew she was different. Special.

"And Tommy." She rolled her eyes, though she smiled when his name passed through her inky lips, "You know it's only a matter of time before he says something damning."

"I'm… fairly serious… I think. I dunno, I don't want to tell her I'm Gifted and for it to fuck everything up between us."

"But you didn't tell Millie… and that didn't end well," she mumbled. Nova hated bringing up my late wife as much as I hated her doing so. "This could be a chance for everything to be *completely* different."

"You really think so? She'll just be another human getting caught up in Gifted lives. They all end up dead."

She couldn't see my expression through the mask, but reached over and squeezed my arm like she had her mother's enhanced vision.

"You like her a lot. And she *surely* knows, Lo- *Vengeance*." She quickly corrected herself. We rarely talked about personal things like this at places like Crave, and she especially didn't care for talking to me in my alter ego's state of mind. "There's no way Sum— *she* hasn't figured it out if she works here. I saw you two earlier, she wanted you *so bad*. Why didn't you take her upstairs?"

"We haven't quite… gotten *there* yet. I didn't want our first time to be *here* of all places." I mistakenly admitted, knowing how much her glittery brain was about to read into my every word. I didn't know if her brain was *actually* glittery, but whenever she got on my nerves, I threatened to pop her skull so we could all find out.

"You mean to say you *haven't fucked her?*" her eyes narrowed behind the useless mask she wore. I hadn't introduced anyone I'd been dating or fucking, in years. My friends knew I'd given up on the idea of committing myself to anyone again after what went down in Bedlam. "It's been *weeks* since you started sleeping over at her place. Like, two *months* since you met her. That's unlike you." She bounced excitedly on her barstool, then froze and slapped my arm.

"Ow!" I hissed. "What the fuck?"

"You're in love with her!" She accused, hitting me again.

*Fuck, am I?*

"Don't be fucking stupid. I barely know her." I tried to speak firm, but only ended up sounding confused, wondering at which point my obsession with Summer had evolved into infatuation.

Nova laughed, "Deny it all you like. I know you too well." I couldn't deny that, she could read me like a fucking book. It was infuriating.

I'd never expected to start over with anyone new, no matter how much the gang pushed me to try again. It sounded tedious and exhausting after everything I'd lost. I was content with the idea of living out the rest of my days avoiding capture for the gore I smeared across the country.

*At least, I thought I was...*

I sighed and leaned with one arm on the bar to support my head on my hand, wishing I didn't need to be sober to drive the others home. Nova always seemed to spark the awful desire in me to consume obscene amounts of alcohol. Though, nothing behind the bar would actually work for me, I'd need something much stronger.

"You *promised* you'd tell me if you were ever falling for someone. If she means that much to you, we don't want everyone getting acquainted without the right protection," she gently tapped my temple with her index finger.

"I know. It's not like I planned for this to happen." I rolled my eyes. She couldn't see my face, but I hoped she got the gesture as my head moved. "I've got *it* under control."

"You say that, but you keep moving *up* the list, not down. She'll be safer if we're all around," Nova said uneasily, sipping the last of her drink as she waved at the bartender for another. "You need to go fuck the nurse. *Now*." She stood from her barstool, new drink in hand.

"What?"

"You've fallen for her without even knowing if you're *physically* compatible! That's not okay," she giggled. "You need to do it now before you're in too deep for us to save you."

I thought about it for a moment before shaking my head. "Not tonight."

"Come on! It's Valentine's Day! Don't pretend like you can't hear everything that's going on up there."

"Oh, I hear plenty." I grimaced under the mask. There were more moans and pieces of furniture being rocked in the rooms than typical.

"Where is she?" Nova looked around the crowded room as if she expected to find Summer amongst the horde of disguised criminals.

"Home. Someone was looking for her. Her ex, I think. I jumped with her in my arms from the roof to get her out of here." I said as we moved to join Jackie and Tommy, waiting for us in the booth.

"Oooo, so you rescued the girl? I knew the fun side of you was still in there somewhere." She nudged my ribs playfully, but the sadness in her tone couldn't be hidden from me, not even with the migraine-inducing music she bounced along to. "If she's waiting for you at home it sounds like the perfect opportunity to get things started."

"It does. But we're not even talking at the moment." Me again, admitting things that would only stoke her gossip-fuelled fire.

"Oh, for fuck's sake, Vengeance! Fix it! Go do something that'll get the nurse's heart racing and seize that *fucking moment* before someone else does. If she hangs around places like this, I'm sure she's got a list of people who'd happily meet up with her at a moment's notice. Fuck, put me on the damn list," she laughed as we reached the edge of the crowd.

"You'd like that wouldn't you?"

Nova knew no boundaries, and *privacy* wasn't a word she understood.

"Who wouldn't? She's hot as fuck, and from what I've heard, she gives great head." She shrugged and side-stepped through the gap of the circular couch, rounding the low table in the center to straddle Tommy's lap.

"Does everything I say to Tommy go through his ears and straight to your head?" I accused, tugging at the thick, black curtain that encircled the booth, pulling it enough so I couldn't be seen from the floor as I sat on the opposite side.

While I preferred closing them entirely, Jackie was spinning on the pole at the center of the table, and I didn't want to interfere with her finding someone to temporarily relieve her pain.

As she wrapped her legs around the metal, I prayed for the millionth time this place was thoroughly cleaned at the end of each night. With what went on upstairs and on these couches, I could have easily been covered in forty people's worth of DNA each time the gang and I visited the club.

"You know it." Nova grinned at the man beneath her, holding his face between glittery hands as she drew him in for a kiss. It was the risk of sharing anything with Tommy. I couldn't tell him a fucking thing without him spilling everything to Nova the second they were alone.

"You gonna fix things with the nurse?" She asked when she resurfaced.

"I'll see her tomorrow." I promised, observing the floor and its occupants through the gap in the curtains. I didn't want to spend another night without Summer, but I needed to give her space to clear her head of the night's events. I didn't want her to feel obligated or pressured to thank me for getting her out of the club before she was found, and I couldn't stand the thought of upsetting her again by rejecting her before those pills were out of her system.

"Tommy, are you up for hunting tomorrow night? I need to take care of something before I see Summer."

"Human or animal?" he asked, not really bothered either way. He was too busy to give a fuck, groping Nova's tits and ass like Jackie and I weren't even there.

I laughed at his question. There was only one thing I hunted.

"Human."

# THIRTY-FOUR

SUMMER

## FEBRUARY 15TH

As I woke on Saturday night, the events from Crave ran through my mind, a mixture of nausea and excitement flowing through me.

Logan said he had 'a girl back home'. Unless he were able to juggle multiple girlfriends *and* a double life, it *had* to be me. I tallied up the amount of hours we'd been spending together each day, and let myself relax about there not being other people on the side.

I wouldn't have minded much, but he didn't seem like the sharing type. And I was okay with that, so long as it was something we had equal expectations of.

"Should I text him?" I asked the ceiling.

Waking up cold and alone in bed for the second night in a row had sucked. Stupidly thinking of this as a challenge, I was too stubborn to cave first. Besides, *he* was the one who had walked out on *me*.

The thought of Logan's mind reeling from seeing me at Crave was a little too satisfying. He'd have questions that desperately needed answers, but he couldn't have them unless he shared his own secrets.

*At least he'll know how I've been feeling.*

The weather was still cold, but it hadn't snowed. I forced myself to go for a run to clear my head, and the following hours melded into a typical Saturday at work. Lots of quick stitch jobs, just how I liked it. Thankfully, no unruly patients.

6:25am

At the end of our shift, Ben and Tony joined me in the garage after dropping my last visitor home.

"Breakfast?" Tony held up a brown paper bag.

"More like dinner for us, isn't it?" I smiled and took it. I couldn't remember the last time I'd eaten, and they'd probably noticed my mood was a whole new level of awful since Logan stopped dropping in. Not to mention the stress from nearly being *found* at the club.

The cousins had brought me cheeseburgers, and while all food made my stomach squirm to some degree, I welcomed the greasiness after days of mixed emotions, pills and alcohol.

"So, where's Logan?" Ben pried as he perched himself on the patient chair beside me, dumping a heavy bag of his own beside him on the seat. His eyes darted to mine when he realized I had *just* cleaned it.

"I dunno." I narrowed my eyes at him playfully, deciding not to bite one of the hands that fed me, even if he did just create more work for his boss. "All he said for tonight when I asked him if we were seeing each other was, *maybe*. And that was two nights ago." I spoke between bites.

Tony, sitting on Logan's stool, gave Ben one of those looks they shared between themselves.

"What? You think it's over?" I snapped at them, taking another bite in hopes it would rapidly improve my mood so they wouldn't cop too much of my foul attitude. Especially after they'd been kind enough to bring food and spend time with me so that my only interactions for the day weren't solely with grumbling patients.

"Nah, we don't think so," Tony said with a smirk.

"Did you guys argue or something?" Ben asked, as if he didn't already know from the way Logan stormed out and my own demeanor as they'd found me alone in the garage. Well, not quite *alone* — I'd had the body of an unconscious man for company.

"Yeah. Kind of. I was being dumb," I curtly admitted, folding my legs up on the chair and letting it spin around slowly while I took more bites.

"That's unlike you," Tony said.

"What? Dumb? Ha!" I scoffed, "All I seem to do is dumb shit at the moment. Did Ben tell you what I did at the bar?" I asked him with my eyebrows raised.

"Yep. Would have killed to see that," Tony laughed through a mouthful.

"I'm surprised I didn't get a call about that one." Ben shook his head.

I'd been behaving for a while, and he'd probably started to relax about needing to bail me out at all hours of the night. Day. Either way, he found it to be the most stressful part of an otherwise easy job.

Tony nodded. "Might need to tone it down for a while if Eric was behind those guys looking for you at Crave. Leaving a fresh trail of broken noses will only have him narrow down your location."

"Yeah," Ben agreed, peeling open *another* wrapper. I didn't bother counting how many burgers they could eat in one sitting anymore, both men were bottomless pits. "We were on a three month good behavior streak. Here I was, thinking maybe Logan had calmed you down."

"Maybe something's changed." I said mindlessly as I spun around again, wondering whether Eric was after me for something new, or if he were just desperate for his missing piece to come back and join The Collection. Maybe his bed just wasn't the same without me in it, unconscious and bloodied up.

"Either way, we'll be more careful," Tony promised, "So… you and Logan?"

I gave him a sad smile. "I tried to fuck him," I admitted, prompting them to look at each other again before they looked back at me.

"You mean you haven't yet?" Ben demanded, seeming annoyed. It was unlike him. He typically enjoyed hearing about what I'd gotten up to in the past, knowing I'd be in a better mood for at least a few days before the inevitable decline.

"No. Why?" I snapped. Tony held his hand out to Ben, already digging through his wallet for cash. "Are you two taking fucking *bets* on my sex life now?"

Tony shrugged as he pocketed the money and reached for another burger. "What's stopping you, boss?"

"Well, kind of nothing now. I tried the other night but he didn't want me while I was high on painkillers and relaxants." I kept the part about me also trying again at the club to preserve Logan's identity.

"That's a good thing though, right?" Ben asked, "It's a far cry from how you've been treated in the past."

I sighed, "Yep. Literally the opposite." They gave each other another look I didn't have a hope of understanding. "I'm gonna head in for the night."

I stood from my chair and handed Ben the bag with the remaining food I hadn't touched, feeling the need to scrub my body raw after talking about Eric and barely referring to what he'd done to me.

After saying goodnight to the bodyguards, I headed for the shower, and couldn't help but think of Logan as I stood under the hot water. Everything warm reminded me of him.

*God, those arms.*

The way we'd touched at Crave. How he pressed his body against mine. The way he'd kept me safe.

*He can't be a villain, at least not in the sense that I know. Though, vigilante is often no better.*

I'd still heard no word from him. God only knew what he and the others were up to. It's not like I could text any of them and get a straight answer, I didn't have any of their numbers and they'd all probably cover for him anyway. They could never be my friends in the way they were his for as long as he kept these secrets.

*Could things ever be perfect between us? It's a relationship based on lies. Surely we were doomed from the start.*

As I stepped out of the water there was a knock at the door. A notification on my phone confirmed there was movement outside, but the bodyguards were long gone.

I checked the cameras, and there he was. Logan.

I hurriedly ruffled a towel through my hair before wrapping it around my body and making my way to the front door.

My fingers trembled with nerves as I turned the handle and hoped desperately that he hadn't come to break up with me. Especially not while I wore nothing but a towel.

As Logan stood under the harsh security lighting, I couldn't quite pick his expression. Relieved I opened the door? Excited to see me? Cautious to not say anything about Crave?

"Summer…" he finally spoke, voice shaking, "I need your help."

"What?" I narrowed my eyes, glad we were at least saying words to each other, but still mad about our last interactions in the garage, and now, on top of everything, cautious about what he may have learned about *me* in the time we were apart.

He casually pointed to the right side of his lower abdomen. I'd been so focused on his face I hadn't looked down. His white T-shirt was soaked with blood.

"God, Logan! Why the fuck are you standing there? Get inside!"

I rushed to the other door, hand shaking through the code and shouldering it open the moment it unlocked.

The second we were in the garage I ordered him to take his shirt off. Whatever the injury was under the fabric had to be *big* and I needed to see it immediately.

*Is this something I can handle on my own? Should I take him to a hospital?* I started to doubt my abilities at the sight of so much blood on someone I cared for – I couldn't lose anyone else.

As he took the shirt off I hunched over to assess the damage. This time his injury was unmistakably caused by glass. It looked like something from a cartoon. The wound was circular in shape, consisting of many holes from where jagged pieces had pierced his skin. I hoped none were so deep that they'd punctured anything vital.

*He's Gifted,* I tried to remind myself through the panic. *Even if it's deep he'll likely be okay. Probably. Maybe?*

"Fuck, Logan," I gasped as I touched his skin. There was something in addition to the blood. Another fluid. I tried to inspect it further but it was clear and completely odorless, though his hands carried the faint scent of bleach.

*Chemical?*

I couldn't tell by looking at it. Too many dangerous things ticked those boxes. There was no time to sit around, working out what one single glass bottle on the planet could have possibly contained when used to stab my boyfriend, not while he was at risk of bleeding to death in front of me.

I needed the wound cleaned. I couldn't stitch him closed to seal whatever that stuff was inside and have it potentially eat away at his organs.

"Shower," I demanded, unable to form any other words. We both fumbled to undo his belt, hands and fingers becoming tangled as I pulled it through the loops of his jeans and tossed it to the floor. He smiled at the energy I used to throw it.

*Smiling? How is he so fucking calm? Probably already delirious and dying of blood loss.*

Logan stepped into the shower and I instructed him on how to feel for any leftover glass while he rinsed his skin clean. Watching as the water ran over his body, it suddenly occurred to me this was the first time I'd seen him *completely* naked.

Between the photos he'd sent, our time on the couch, in bed, *and* seeing him in the skin tight suit, there really weren't many blanks to fill. I tried not to get distracted now that I had tangible access to the whole picture, but the sight of his chiseled limbs and bare ass forced an ill-timed burst of visuals through my frantic mind.

The thoughts of him earlier in my bathroom and seeing him now twisted my stomach into tight knots. I needed to calm down. Logan needed me to *focus*. If anything happened to him, I'd have another name added to the long list on my skin.

He wrapped his lower half in the towel I handed to him, and he pulled it down a little to clear the injury of the material for me to work on, revealing his V-cut abs.

Still too panicked to talk, I pushed him to sit on the chair in the same position he'd dropped me in just days earlier.

We'd changed roles – it was my turn to stitch him. I hoped we wouldn't make a habit out of this.

*If he lives.*

I rushed to grab anesthetic from the cabinets and quickly poked him several times around the wound.

I didn't wait long enough, the area would have only been partially numbed, but I needed to start before it could take full effect for fear of him losing too much blood. The towel's edge had already soaked through, deep red.

*He's GIFTED,* I tried to remind myself again, but I wasn't paying mind to the voice in my head. I didn't need it distracting me. I couldn't lose him.

As I rolled the stool over, I remembered I was also still wearing *only a towel* and pulled my legs closed. I wished I were still in my practical work clothes so I didn't have to worry about something as ridiculous as sitting 'properly' at a time like this.

The cleaned wounds were free of any debris, all punctures were clear of the unknown liquid and looking safe to close up. I loaded my needle and began stitching.

Logan made a noise as I pierced his skin. We locked eyes. It was *very much* like what I'd extracted from him outside of Crave. Again, I hoped I'd hear it in the future, though, maybe without him being in *this* much pain.

I took a deep breath, needing to banish the sound from my head. It was hard enough to focus with him so calmly leaning back on his palms with his legs apart.

Another deep breath.

One more for clarity.

*Shit, I can't stitch like normal.*

The wounds had too much space between them, but my hands still moved quickly as I weaved him back together. Over and under the skin, I ensured each interrupted stitch was so neat that his body would look just as perfect once he healed.

I snipped the last piece of excess thread and slammed my needle down on the chair, taking a breath for the first time since touching him. I closed my eyes and lifted my hands to my head, holding it together, not caring about Logan's blood on my fingers that I brushed over my temples and through my hair.

I felt sick. Light-headed. I hadn't even remembered the extra stitches, I just needed him to be okay.

Breathing heavily, I opened my eyes to look up at him.

"That was like, two minutes!" he sounded thoroughly impressed as he caught his own breath.

In amongst my complete hysteria, I felt myself smiling. I was glad he was happy with my work, and now things were calming down, I could replay the last few minutes and all the ways I got to touch his warm skin.

"Two minutes and fourteen seconds, twenty-six stitches." I felt a dizzy spell coming on, and held tight to the sides of the stool, hoping he'd catch me if I fell off.

*Two minutes and fourteen seconds.* The time replayed itself in my mind before I violently shook my head to clear it of those two lifeless bodies.

"I might've been able to stitch faster, had you given me a heads up that *my boyfriend* was on his way, about to fucking *bleed out* in my house."

"I know, I should have called," he huffed, poking at a few of the flawlessly tied sutures, "Hey, you don't usually stitch this way."

"There were too many individual punctures. If I sewed them up my regular way, it'd look like a spider weaved you back together." I giggled, and he smiled at me.

"So…" The way he tilted his head to the side and looked at me had my stomach in knots again. His face was free of his glasses and his wet hair was slicked back from his face. It made him look different. "I'm still your boyfriend?"

"I guess," I said, suddenly very aware of the state of us and the bright lights in the garage. Both of us in towels.

*God, he looks so fucking good in a towel.*

Abruptly standing, I moved to the cabinets before turning back to him, putting some space between us as I forced air into my lungs and cleared my head of the parts of the encounter that would haunt me. Particularly the thought of losing him… *In my house.*

Logan stood from the chair and stalked towards me, I matched his steps by walking backwards. It seemed he'd suddenly remembered the towels too. I didn't want to move away from him, but if our bodies were to touch in any way, I'd *want* him. And I wasn't prepared for it.

"I can't," I whispered as he towered over me, my back up against one of the glass doors where I stored the antibiotics.

If I were to breathe any deeper, my chest would touch his ribs. I was still wrapped up, but the thought of our skin *finally* connecting was enough for me to mindlessly reach out and run my fingers along the edge of his bloody towel, just below his abs.

*All self control washed down the drain along with his blood, apparently.*

"You're safe with me, Summer." There was a desperate note in his voice as his gaze followed my fingers. "But I can wait."

"How much longer?"

"However long you need."

There was no pressure in his words, only reassurance that what he felt for me was more intense than any excuse I could come up with to keep putting off the inevitable.

"Logan, I'm… *way* too fucked up for this." My cold skin suddenly felt like it was burning hot, embarrassed again by having to acknowledge the permanent damage to my body and mind.

He sighed and leaned closer to breathe in my ear, "I think you might be just the right amount of fucked up for *me*."

The soft caress of his breath tumbled down my neck and my knees almost gave out. What did he mean by that? Did his comment have anything to do with seeing me at Crave?

He planted a kiss on the top of my head and stepped back to turn away. I expected more of a fight, but he'd proven to be better than that. He wouldn't try to trick or coerce me into anything I wasn't fully committed to. I loved that about him, but kind of hated it too. I caught his arm and pulled him back.

Logan stood over me, looking down into my eyes with a hungry excitement.

"Changed your mind?" he asked, though he already knew the answer.

I got up on my toes to bridge the gap between us, but he wouldn't close it. It was a kind of torture I wasn't familiar with, knowing I could have whatever I wanted, I just had to say the word.

Looking smug as he lowered his face a little closer to mine, still out of my reach, he asked, "Do you *want* me?" His tone was teasing, his smile widened. He leaned down to place a hand on each of my thighs, slowly moving them up to the edge of my towel. "I *need* to hear you say it, nurse."

"God, I fucking *want you*, Logan."

With his palms at my butt, he lifted me from the floor and I wrapped my legs around him. In what felt like a blink, he'd carried me through the open door to the dark hallway and set me on the narrow table, the perfect height to keep our faces close.

His warm lips on my mouth moved to gently brush my jawline. The sensation of our temperature differences was almost enough to distract me from the moment he picked his angle. He paused when I sucked in a sharp breath and asked, "Can I?"

My nails clawed his shoulders like the lap bar of a roller coaster. He was the only thing I could hold onto to keep me from falling from the terrifying heights of doubt in my ability to go through with this.

"Yes."

A mix of panic and anxious excitement throbbed through my entire body while one hand guided his dick and the other rested on my lower, towel-covered back as he brought us closer together. Logan's eyes fluttered closed and he barely mouthed the word "fuck" as he opened them to watch me take him.

He was *warmer* than I expected. The heat as he pushed a little deeper spread through my core, yet there was no pain, even without the assistance of the pills to help me relax.

"God, you're wet, Summer," he spoke in a heavy sigh. My body tensed, and I felt hot again. "It's a *good* thing, perfect even." he reassured me, resting both his palms on my hips.

I dropped my shoulders and unclenched my jaw. I was well versed in what human bodies *should* do during moments like this. But I'd never had a partner in which I was comfortable enough for *my* body to respond as it should. At least not without the help of drugs or alcohol.

Even as I blew Logan on the couch, I'd assumed the small amount of whiskey I'd had at the bar contributed to these foreign reactions.

*This is what it's meant to be like. You're allowed to feel like this about someone else.*

He pulled me closer so that I was on the edge of the table, away from the mirror behind me. With one hand at the middle of my back, he braced himself on the wall with the other.

He pressed his lips to my forehead and started moving, slowly at first. I lifted my legs around him again, and they tightened at the sensation of him sliding further inside me.

My body gradually accepted his size, but at one point, I questioned whether *my little body* really could handle so much of my vigilante. I was no stranger to fucking men on the *larger* side, but it had been years since I'd had sex without a high to numb the stretch. My exhale was heavy with relief as the discomfort quickly eased and I began to enjoy the feel of his steady pace.

After a few minutes of appreciating his rhythm, I realized things were moving along much faster for me than they were for the man gently lifting my face. His tongue teased my mouth open for me to kiss him.

*Kissing during sex? I forgot that's allowed.* I was glad it was, I'd never felt so connected to another being than when his tongue met mine.

Logan's moves weren't quite *for him*. He could have been done by now if he'd wanted. The long, smooth strokes and the angle he picked were all about hitting spots I hadn't really cared to take the time to explore with others.

As I clung to him, I found I was making sounds that'd never escaped me before. True pleasure. Not forced, doped-up moans to please someone else.

My hands, gripping Logan's back and neck combined with my legs – still tight at his waist – were all the motivation he needed to keep his cadence from faltering.

"Want me to stop?" he teased, angling his face to look down at me as he picked up the pace, "It's too much? Need a break, nurse?"

"What? *No!* God, don't stop now!" I whined, roughly grabbing at his hips to do whatever I could to drive him *deeper.* I leaned back against the mirror, lifting my legs so my knees pressed against the sides of his ribs. Logan looked down and clenched his lip between his teeth. He liked what he saw, and so did I when I dared to peek at the thick appendage; glistening with my wetness each time he pulled out before thrusting at the angle that made me see stars.

I blinked hard and tried to focus on the dick liquifying my fucking mind, but instead, noticed for the first time that Logan's perfectly sculpted body was almost *entirely* hairless. I didn't have the mental capacity to ask why as my fingers wandered the divide between his pecs and abs.

My head rolled back, knocking against the mirror as I squeezed my eyes shut. The towel suddenly felt too tight across my chest, restricting my lung's need to expand to take deeper breaths. Maybe it was a good thing – I didn't want to get too carried away and disappear. Not now. I didn't want this to end.

"Should I pull out?" he offered between heavy breaths. "When I'm close."

"*No!* I want to feel it. I want *all of you.*"

"Then *let it go* for me, Summer," he growled low in my ear. The change to his voice sent a wave of goosebumps up my arms. The hand at my waist dipped between my legs, his thumb rubbing my clit. "*Fuck.* You're already there. I can *feel* it."

I inhaled sharp and moved a hand to cover my mouth, but Logan grabbed my arm and pinned it above my head, seeming enthralled by the sound of me enjoying him and not allowing me to hide it.

"That's it," he crooned, scolding lips pressed to my forehead as his thumb continued in slower motions. "Go again. Come for me, nurse."

My mouth popped open to argue. Once was enough of a victory without the pills, but every inch his fingers touched was burning with an addictive heat I couldn't get enough of.

"God, *Logan!*" I moaned as he angled his head to suck at my neck. Every thrust seemed to melt my spine a little more. The lingering sensitivity tumbled into another orgasm, and I believed I could literally float away.

Until he bit me.

It wasn't sharp enough to break my skin, but I hoped it left a mark. I wanted proof this moment between us was real.

Logan's teeth sunk further into my flesh, forcing another moan that started in pain but it quickly dissolved into pleasure. It was enough for him to join me over the edge.

The satisfying sensation of his strong pulse inside me added to the intensity of the whole event, like we'd truly achieved something together.

Though he wouldn't have known it, this was a monumental step in my freedom from the diamond-studded collar I'd worn around my neck for ten years, never once allowing anyone to come in me without protection since escaping Home.

Logan's movements slowed to a stop, and my mind traveled back to my body. I brushed my lips along his left collarbone and my hand behind his shoulder found a faint indent in his skin. I froze, then traced the mark again.

Three small dots at the top. Almost completely healed already, just one day later.

Though the stitches were removed, it gave me all the confirmation I needed – I'd caught my shark.

I should have been scared, but I felt nothing but complete elation. Both at what we'd just done and at the fact that I truly believed Logan wasn't a danger to me at all, and maybe he never had been.

"I need…" I whispered, not knowing how to finish the sentence. I reached for his neck and gently ran my hands through the beads of warm liquid coating the surface of his skin.

Logan was *covered* in sweat, and I had a bizarre urge for it to be all over me, to be completely doused in the warmth his body created. He was still inside me but I pulled him closer again, annoyed that my towel, now patchy with his blood, still stood in the way of all our skin touching.

Logan held my face and kissed me again before wrapping his arms around me, holding me close as I raked my fingers through his hair and down his arms.

He groaned when he pulled out, and rested his head on my shoulder to catch his breath. My eyes threatened to roll back.

*That's the sound.*

It was an almost identical noise to when I'd stitched him.

"Was that so bad?" He kissed his way along my collarbone and up my neck before lifting his face to be level with mine, still breathing heavily, cracking jokes already.

"No." I suppressed a smile, looking away from him and admitting it to both of us, "I never, for a second, thought it would be."

When he moved to kiss me again he grabbed the top of my towel to pull it off, but I slapped his hand away.

"Summer," he pleaded softly.

"I still don't think I can."

"Now is as good a time as ever." He gave me a lazy smile and gestured to himself. I couldn't remember when his towel had come off. The garage?

Logan had a point. His mood seemed so euphoric at what had just transpired between us that maybe it wouldn't scare him away like it could at any other time.

"I got you," he promised, grabbing my hand when I hopped off the table. I dropped the few inches to the floor on wobbly legs. The fingers of his other hand cautiously moved back to where the edges of my towel met on my chest. Gently, he unfolded them, letting it drop to the ground. Every part of my mind screamed at me to scoop it back up and run away.

In addition to what Logan had stitched up a few nights ago, I had many more scars across my torso. Four deep divots on my lower abdomen from surgery. Some random scribbles from when Eric became bored waiting for me to wake up, eager to show me the latest masterpiece in my aching flesh.

There were the patchy remnants of a tattoo, just below my right collarbone. I was yet to have it completely removed, and it was illegible now, but it once read "Stitch Up" in an ornate font. It was a gift from Eric, performed during my Initiation, to which he had a smaller matching version amongst his many tattoos.

Logan's eyes darted to the mirror behind me, then back to my face, waiting until I gave him permission to get a proper look at the places I wanted to hide the most.

Nodding as my eyes dropped to the floor, he gently pushed at my shoulders with his fingertips to spin me around, holding onto them with warm hands once I turned away from him. I guessed that was his way of ensuring I wasn't left feeling alone.

Despite the reassuring touch, I still felt like a complete freak on display.

Logan brushed my damp hair to the side and over my shoulder, revealing the entire list. I was glad some were so faded that the full effect of what had been done to my body wasn't being seen by someone who really seemed to care for me.

Nine names. There was no way he wouldn't have questions. And would he recognise the other marks for what they were? The stab wounds?

Logan's reflection in the mirror was troubled as he took it all in. I held back tears when his darkening eyes passed over every mark on my skin.

No one but Eric had seen my body in its entirety. I'd been his property since I was sixteen.

Anyone else I'd tried to be intimate with hadn't been around long enough to get to a point where they'd need to see me completely naked. It was all quickies at the club or in dark alleys behind bars. Not in my house. And certainly not with someone who referred to himself as my *boyfriend*.

Logan spun me back to face him, pulling me close and his eyes away from my body.

The show was over.

"It's a lot, but it's no deal breaker." It sounded like another joke, and I tried to take it as one.

I stepped back, my eyes searching his for any signs of repulsion or judgment. But Logan appeared both tired and relaxed, like nothing could phase him in the moment. I wished I could have read every thought in his head now he'd finally seen the damage.

"Come shower with me." It was more a gentle demand than an invitation as he picked up the towel and tossed it into my arms. "Watch your step, though." he called back, making his way to the ensuite.

Looking down, I noticed after having stood there for a few minutes that I'd started to leave quite a mess. I was amazed I hadn't noticed it earlier.

With the adrenaline of sewing him back together and the moves he was using on me, protection was the last thing on my mind. Not that we needed it with incompatible DNA, but my timber floors might have appreciated it.

Much like him, Logan's cum was hot in temperature. *Hot* in the amount too. I'd never seen anyone produce a sample of this volume. He'd nearly drowned me on the couch a few nights earlier, but I'd thought I was just out of practice.

"Do you always make this much?" I teased, pointing to my legs as we stepped under the hot water for the first time together.

"Yeah," he admitted proudly, "Why? D'you enjoy being filled like that, nurse?"

I giggled. "I think I do *now*."

"Give it a few hours and I can make just as much again." He laughed, though he seemed a little self-conscious before returning to playful, "Twice in one day and you'll have no friction between those thighs."

"Yeah? And what about three times?" I purred, feeling heated at the thought of repeating what we'd done, over and over.

He frowned in thought. "I don't think I've unleashed that *inside* anyone three times in a single day." He shrugged, grinned down at me and flicked water at my blushing face. "I do this a lot, too." He timidly pointed to his neck, though he was referring to the mark he'd left on mine.

I reached for the skin that still throbbed, and for once, didn't flinch when Logan raised his hand. He gently cuffed my neck, thumb pressed against my jaw to tip my head to the side for him to inspect the site.

His eyes turned dark with concern. "Was it too much?"

"No." I shook my head as he let go, wondering if he really cared about a bite after he'd finally seen what else I'd endured.

"I have questions," he stated as I rubbed where he'd bitten, "About what I saw."

"I'm sure you do."

"I'm not going to swamp you with them, though. I want you to tell me when you're ready."

"*Really*?" Curiosity would have gotten the better of me if our roles were reversed.

"Yes. Really," he said with a cautious smile, "I've seen a lot, Summer. But nothing *quite* like what you've been through. I only want you to share when you feel safe enough to do so."

I blinked away more tears. I could have gotten away with crying in the shower, but I was still unsure what Logan's vision was like without his glasses.

"Okay," I agreed, "While we're on the topic of sharing…" I anxiously bit my lip, prompting his silence as he waited for my confession, "You're only the second person to see me completely naked."

His posture softened and he nodded, "I could have guessed."

"How?"

"No one with a body like yours would be so self-conscious–" he stopped, taking the hint with a small laugh when I flicked water in *his* face. Compliments on my bare form weren't something I was ready for.

I tried to keep my tone light, still recovering from the shock of being so comfortable with him that we were now naked *and* showering together. "There's nothing you're desperate to know right now?"

"Honestly… this caught my attention." His fingertips gently traced what was left of the tattoo.

"You can ask."

"Was it your ex's name?"

"No. But close. I guess it was my… pet name."

"It's a big deal to remove something like that. I can't imagine what you've been through, but you're making it *incredibly* hard for me to not think that you might be a superhero," he laughed, brushing wet hair back from his face. The sound forced a smile across my lips, and he pulled me against his body under the water, kissing me again.

The sun had risen on Sunday morning before we climbed into bed. Together again. Only *different*.

It was my day off to try to be normal; it didn't matter that I'd be spending most of it sleeping beside him. Logan had already let his boss know he wouldn't be coming in to work, but only after I'd dropped subtle reminders that he was "only human" and was *just* stabbed. His cover required time off to heal, but it would probably only take a day or two.

I wondered what lies he'd use over the coming weeks to convince me that he didn't need my help to tend to the injury and to not remove his shirt again, so soon after getting a first taste of what we could do with our clothes off.

As I laid naked in bed, wrapped in his warm limbs under the sheets, it occurred to me that I was so far down this rabbit hole with Logan, I hadn't asked how he'd been stabbed in the first place.

*Was it another self-inflicted injury to get us talking again? That's fucked up. But why does part of me find it so hot?*

I closed my eyes, listening to his steady breathing behind me. My mind was too hazy from the adrenaline crash and endorphins to care that this relationship had taken such a serious turn.

It had started out just weeks ago with me trying to work out if I were in any danger around Logan.

Now I was having sex with a mass-killer.

# THIRTY-FIVE

SUMMER

## MARCH 9TH

"So, who's idea was it to go out to dinner?" I asked Logan while glaring at the clothes in my wardrobe, deciding on what to wear.

It was a Sunday evening, so whoever chose the day for our outing knew I didn't have to rush off to work, giving us plenty of time to get to know each other.

"Harrison's," he sighed at the opposite side of the walk-in, flipping over and over again through the handful of his shirts I'd made space for.

"Did I leave my gray shirt here? The one with the comic book characters on it?"

"Ahh… no?" I answered without looking at him. *Of course he'd notice that one's missing.* I bit my lip to hide my guilt. He didn't need to know how fucking weird I could be. Not yet, anyway.

Logan roughly pulled on a black, long-sleeved shirt and pushed the sleeves to his elbows. I didn't know if he did it because it was comfortable, or because he knew how much I loved being able to see those arms. Either way, I wasn't complaining.

He rubbed his eyes under his glasses before turning to me. He was nervous. Not the fun kind that I still brought out in him by being too bold with my flirtations or when I agreed to try new things in bed he'd jokingly suggest or subtly hint at.

It was the kind of nervousness caused by him knowing he'd held out on letting me get to know his friends for as long as he could, and we were about to meet with three other people who could potentially spill his secrets.

*I'll have to thank Harrison for this later.*

I smiled as I picked out a long, flowing black dress. It had thin straps, so I grabbed a light jacket to wear with it to keep my back covered.

Buying clothes that I thought would look great on me during late night, vodka-fuelled, online shopping sprees was a terrible habit of mine. They'd arrive and I *would* look fucking great, only to remember I couldn't freely wear them outside the house without finding ways to cover up the scarred skin they revealed.

This piece at least, showed off my legs a little through the sheer skirt of the lower half. I hung it on the towel rack in the bathroom until I was ready to put it on.

Turning to the vanity drawers, I retrieved the full-coverage foundation I used to cover up what was left of my tattoo on the odd occasion where my clothes revealed more of my chest.

Harrison, excited as I was to see her, was too observant, and the remaining patches of my tattoo and its placement were like neon signs pointing to my identity. And with the way she and Logan got along, it likely wasn't something she'd consider keeping from him.

"Out of… pure curiosity," Logan warned me before one of his questions about my past was about to arise. He never pushed too much for details. It actually helped me share more with him, knowing it was always on my terms. "Wouldn't it be easier to finish getting it removed instead of having to cover it up?" He leaned on the frame of the bathroom door and nodded to my hand working the sponge across my collarbone.

"Yeah, it would," I admitted, pulling my dress from the hanger, "But it hurts like a bitch and I've been putting it off because it's uncomfortable for like, a week when my shirts rub on it."

"Fair enough." He intently watched my every move as I slipped the dress on before turning away. I pulled my hair to the side for him to tug the short zip up the back. He pulled it slowly, gently grabbed my shoulders when he was done and pressed a scolding kiss on my left shoulder blade. It had been a month since he'd first seen me naked, and I hardly hesitated with taking my clothes off around him anymore. There was barely an inch of me that those lips hadn't touched.

"Oh, I've got something for you!" I said, stepping away before we became distracted with removing the clothes we'd just put on. I reached for the bottom drawer under the sink where I pulled out a box and handed it to him.

He opened it and smiled at the black, glass cologne bottle, "So, firstly, thank you."

"But?" I giggled, sensing it was coming.

"*But* you've snooped through my things. You know I've got bottles of this stuff lined up for when I run out."

"I know," I slipped on my jacket and stepped into my shoes, growing a few inches in height for my face to be a little closer to his. "But now you've got one *here*." Logan cocked his head, frowning, so I explained, "You're spending so much time here. Maybe you should bring more stuff over than just a few extra shirts and your toothbrush?"

"Whoa, slow down," he said with a smirk, opening the bottle to douse himself in the strong fragrance, "Someone might think you want to keep me around forever if you start saying shit like that."

"Would that *someone* be you?" I teased, arching a brow at him and trying to keep a straight face. He kissed me and grabbed my hand to leave.

We took my car, and arrived at a restaurant where Tommy and Harrison were waiting outside for us.

"Our table is ready!" Jackie called as she appeared in the doorway, rushing over to greet me with a hug. She seemed a little more spritely than she'd been the last few times I'd seen her. Not that Logan had ever given me enough time to talk to her in private to really see how she was coping, but I was hopeful this first night out as a group would mean things could change.

"You can take your jacket off, it's fucking hot in here." Harrison fanned herself with sparkly hands as she took her seat at the round table.

"Oh, I'm fine," I said, taking my seat next to Logan, who thankfully separated us.

Jackie was on my other side and Tommy sat across from me, holding Harrison's hand on the table between them.

While everyone dressed nice for dinner, Jackie and Tommy wore sunglasses on their heads again. It was an odd and unnecessary accessory for the time of night. They certainly didn't coordinate with the cute dress, boots and jacket the woman beside me was wearing.

Thinking back to our drinks at the bar at Logan's work, it might have been the only time I'd actually seen her without them. That was also the only time I'd seen her without Logan and Harrison present. I wondered if the glasses had anything to do with the two Gifted beings in the group. I was still unsure about *what* Tommy was.

*He's big... and I'm sure those arms could do some damage, but I'm still not sold on him being Gifted.* Tommy's eyes widened a little when he noticed my staring. I quickly dropped my gaze to a menu.

We ordered our food and, much like my boyfriend, Harrison seemed to have a thing for pizza. Though she and Logan ordered the same, they refused to share — even when Logan left a few pieces, he wouldn't give them up when Harrison tried to take them. I barely picked at a salad while the remaining two at the table also devoured heavily carb-laden meals.

Once I'd argued with Logan that I was, in fact, finished with my food and had no intention of eating another bite, I spotted a slight exchange of raised eyebrows between him and Tommy.

"Be right back," Logan patted my leg under the table and stood to leave.

"Something wrong?" I asked, ensuring my smile hid that I'd witnessed their subtle interaction.

"Nah," he shook his head and returned the smile before it faltered a little, "Just need to step outside for a second."

"Yeah, uh, need a smoke," Tommy blurted out as he stood.

"I didn't know you smoked, Tommy," I playfully narrowed my eyes at him. I'd never noticed his need to duck out at any time in the few interactions we'd had. And he'd been drinking every time. I'd hung around a lot of smokers at Home, and they all seemed to burn through many more when there was alcohol involved.

"Yeah!" Harrison's tone was sour as she joined me in glaring. "Taken it up again, have you, babe?"

"I... well..." Tommy shrugged and rushed to follow Logan, already walking to the entrance and giving his friend the perfect escape.

Harrison turned to me and rolled her eyes before smoothly sliding herself over to Logan's chair. She leaned on the table with her elbow to prop her head up. Jackie, already sitting beside me, turned on her chair.

Both women cornered me in a way, though I didn't feel too anxious about it. I couldn't imagine they'd pose any actual danger to me. They probably just wanted to know more about the woman suddenly taking up most of their friend's spare time.

"So," Harrison purred, "You and Logan."

"What about us?" I giggled at her immediate jump to the topic.

"How'd you two meet?" Jackie queried from the left. "He hasn't told us. You just kind of... *appeared.*"

"Oh," I said, surprised Logan hadn't already told them. Harrison seemed like the type who wouldn't have let him get away without sharing those kinds of details, "He yelled at me at his work."

"Romantic," Harrison laughed, "Yet, it still worked on you?"

"Well, I kind of yelled back."

"There you have it, perfect for each other," Jackie teased, taking a sip from her glass.

"What is it that draws you to him, Summer?" Harrison tipped her head, playfully widening her faceted eyes at me, "Or do you have a thing for being yelled at?"

"Umm." My skin heated with a blush from being put on the spot and having my mind immediately jump to all the time we'd been spending in bed together.

And on the couches.

In the car.

My bathroom.

Since the first night I'd shared my body with Logan, things had taken a very... *physical* leap for us. Like we were catching up on the month we'd wanted each other. And then some.

There was something addictive about our bodies connecting. The intoxicating warmth he created. It almost had my eyes rolling to the back of my head at the mere thought.

But I had an idea that my growing obsession with Logan stemmed from the way he treated me. We were equals in bed. Equal in everything. That wasn't something I understood at first.

I wasn't a doll to dress up and play pretend with in public, making everyone wish they were me. Only to head back to the top of the tower to be pushed to the edge, hauled back and abused so often I'd believed it was love. Like a mouse tormented by a cat, knowing it was in death's grasp, but kept playing along until the deadly feline showed enough mercy to put it out of its misery.

Only Eric never granted me that kindness.

And I wasn't scared of Logan.

I often reminded myself that I *should* have been. My defenses were far too low when I snuggled up on the couch beside a killer. My vigilante may have tried to joke about me wanting to keep him around forever, but the idea of that really didn't sound too bad.

*Fuck. My vigilante?*

"We're just… having fun together," I settled on.

Harrison frowned at my answer. "That's all? Just fun?"

"Well, I guess."

What did she want me to say? That I might be –

"Falling for him?" she teased, sparkly eyes observing for reactions to her question. It made me wonder if part of her Gift included something to do with mind reading.

As though Logan could hear our conversation across the restaurant, over the voices of dozens of chattering diners and through the glass window, his eyes met mine. Giving me one of those lazy smiles before looking away, he made my stomach feel like it'd detached itself from my digestive tract and was about to claw up my throat.

*Butterflies, you idiot. He gives you butterflies when he looks at you that way.*

My skin sweltered enough for me to regret my clothing choice.

"You two are spending *a lot* of time together," she continued, "I'm sure it's not *all* being spent in bed. He doesn't usually care to let people hang around so long."

"I might be…" I swallowed hard at the heavy admission and immediately tried to cover it up, "I mean, look at him. Who wouldn't want to spend as much time as they could with someone like that while they've got the chance?"

"You don't give yourself enough credit," Harrison scoffed. "You're far hotter than he is."

Jackie elbowed me from the other side. "I guess I see what you mean. There's barely been a man that I've found even mildly attractive since… forever. But I guess Logan would be one of the few." She squinted at him through the window, scrunching up her freckled nose in thought.

"It's the height," Harrison said sourly, "It's a pussy magnet. Women can't seem to get past it. He gets plenty of attention from men too. It doesn't matter what he looks like, so long as he's *that* tall."

"Have you and he… *ever?*" I queried, playfully kicking her under the table and trying to decipher if she was jealous of the attention Logan received or jealous because *she* wanted his attention.

"God, *no!* The giant dork isn't my type."

"Dork?" I snapped.

"I mean – the glasses. Don't they make him look ridiculous?" she giggled, "Not that he cares what they look like. They're only *meant* to be temporary, but he could try a *little* harder."

*Temporary?*

Knowing that Logan should have Gifted sight had stopped some of my theories from aligning.

Perhaps he'd suffered some intense damage that required him to heal over time, but I couldn't comprehend what could hurt someone like him so much that he'd need to wear them for longer than a few days.

*Pyro…*

My burned patient's condition provided more evidence that the Gifted could sustain long-lasting trauma.

*But why doesn't Logan seem to need the glasses ALL the time? And why have his other injuries healed? What could possibly cause so much harm?*

"How long have you known Logan?" I asked.

"Forever."

"Tommy too?"

"No. But I actually met him through Logan. They've been best friends since high school."

That lined up with something he'd already told me; about him and Tommy never getting caught for what they got up to as kids. I could relax a little, learning that Logan was actually telling me some truths amongst the tall stories.

*And the stories he omits completely.*

"If you've know him that long, have you ever noticed that he heals–"

"So!" Harrison interrupted, "Let's talk exes!"

"Ugh, why?" Jackie groaned, "Give the girl a fucking break."

"I just want to get all the dirt on Summer while we're unsupervised," Harrison confessed, making the three of us laugh.

"I'm gonna need another drink." I grabbed my glass and downed the last of the liquid, reaching for the jug to refill it.

Jackie giggled, "There's not even any booze in that."

"Yeah, well… Gotta keep hydrated for this interrogation."

"Okay, I'll settle down," Harrison promised. "We're just a bit protective of him."

I smiled, unable to imagine anyone of either Logan's size or reputation would ever need people like the short sparkly woman and the cute redhead on my other side to protect *him*.

It was sweet.

*Tommy, though.*

I still couldn't work him out. He'd barely said a word all night, but each time my gaze passed over the restaurant windows, he was animated as he spoke to Logan. No cigarettes of any type were visible in either man's hand.

*Maybe he just doesn't like you. He might sense his best friend is falling for a liar.*

"So," she started again, "First boyfriend?"

*Oh shit. If she hears one word about Eric she'll know who I am for sure.*

"Logan," I admitted, grimacing at how that sounded. Twenty-eight years old and only counting the month we'd been dating as my first proper relationship. The first in which I'd freely agreed to, anyway.

"What?" she snorted, "Come on, tell me the truth. There's no way *anyone* would want him as their first. He's too much of an end-game kind of guy. You're meant to have fun before you find someone like him."

"Mm-hmm," Jackie piped up, leaning over to stick her fork in the salad I'd abandoned, "Mr Serious, wants to settle down. Dreams of a big family. At least he used to…"

"He's getting better." Harrison shot her a defensive look. "Coming out of his shell again. Not spending so much time in his own head."

"You're right." Jackie smiled sadly.

"So?" Harrison said, looking eager for me to change my answer as she redirected the topic.

I blinked a few times, recovering from the idea that Logan still might want all of those things. Things he couldn't have with me.

*You want the truth?*

"Well… as a kid I was raised on a secluded piece of land by preppers in the mountains. From there, I was part of a cult from the time I was sixteen. I only escaped a couple of years ago. There haven't been many chances to date anyone between all of that."

As far as the world knew, Summer had simply appeared in Bedlam at age nineteen. Depending on which journalists hated me that week, I either clung to the first millionaire I could find to fund my lifestyle, or fell madly in love with the man trying to make it big in the city.

Eric's wealth had grown exponentially since then, as did the farce that was our public relationship.

"A cult?" Jackie asked, giving Harrison a warning look, signaling to her friend that she'd gone too far with the questioning.

Harrison could barely lift her jaw from the floor, "Well, no wonder you don't like pizza! You've never lived in the real world."

"It's not that I don't like *pizza specifically*," I growled in defense. "Who said I didn't? I just haven't eaten it many times before. Like most of this stuff," I gestured to the table.

"Then what the fuck *did* you eat?" she looked me over like I'd told her I wasn't born on Earth. At least she seemed to have dropped the questioning about relationships for the time being.

"Whatever we slaughtered on the farm. Or what was brought to me in the cult." I shrugged like the answers were obvious, but Harrison shook her head as though she couldn't understand the words coming out of my mouth.

"*Please*," she hissed in a low voice, "Please tell me Logan wasn't your *first?*"

I choked and nearly spat my mouthful of water across the table, laughing as I cleared my throat,"No. No, no, I'd had plenty of experience in *that* department before I met him. I had a partner in the cult. But it was… *arranged*. So, I guess I try not to count that."

"And since *leaving* the cult?" she probed. Her questioning felt very much like Logan's had, only I wasn't feeling as relaxed as I had when spilling my secrets to him.

"A few others. Nothing serious." I frowned, not feeling this was the kind of discussion I wanted to be having out at dinner and in public with a woman I was barely acquainted with.

For all I knew, she could have been storing our entire conversation in her mind to repeat to Logan. While most of it was things I'd already told him, I didn't feel like he needed to be presented with a full list of the people I'd fucked before we met. I would never have expected the same from him.

"Speaking of families," Jackie interjected with a tone that suggested she was trying to save me from Harrison's prying, "I looked into the cell number you gave me."

"Yeah?" I gasped."Anything?"

Jackie grimaced, and my heart sunk. "It's active. There's a mailbox attached to the number. It's empty."

*So they* are *ignoring me?*

"What are we talking about?" Logan asked, nudging Harrison roughly on the shoulder to push her out of his seat as he and Tommy returned to the table.

"My family… and ex-boyfriends."

Logan didn't bother hiding his glare at Harrison and protectively gripped my thigh under the table. While I still hadn't shared *all* of the gory details with him, he knew enough of what went on with my ex to know it wasn't fit for dinner conversation.

"Back to talk our ears off?" I said to Tommy to break the tension between the two Gifted people to my right.

He smiled and shook his head, not gracing me with an answer.

*Why does he hate me?*

I knew I wasn't going to be everyone's taste, but I felt like making a good impression with the best friend was important. And I was failing.

After the plates were cleared, I tried my best not to stare with bewilderment as Harrison devoured two desserts and considered a third.

*Does she not care to try to look normal, though, impossible with her skin? Or does she simply have a major sweet tooth?* It was entertaining to watch either way.

Jackie and I kept the conversation light between us with Logan joining in while Tommy grew quieter still, seeming to shrink silently in his chair as he sat opposite to me.

It was late by the time we said our goodbyes and the others made their way towards their own cars.

Logan turned to me before we reached mine and asked, "Stay at mine tonight?"

"What? Really?" I hadn't spent the night at his apartment before. "Just after I told you to bring more things over to mine?"

"It's late. My place is like, a minute from here. I can grab things to take to yours when we wake up."

"Will your sister be there?" I asked, hoping I'd finally get to meet her.

"Nah. I told her I wanted the space tonight."

*Damn.*

Seeing his sister might have given me more of an idea of his Gift's origin. At this point I wondered if she was real.

His plan was spur of the moment, but I had my backpack in the car with my laptop and spare clothes that I took with me to the gym. I doubted the kind of sleepover we'd have at his apartment would be much different to what we'd been doing almost every night at my house. I could survive the night without my pajamas.

"Sounds great," I agreed.

# THIRTY-SIX

SUMMER

## MARCH 10TH

We arrived at Logan's apartment a little after midnight.

After dropping my backpack by the front door, we ran to his room, stripping down to our underwear as we prepared to climb into his bed together for the first time.

"Oh, no you don't!" I shoved him when he moved for the side closest to the door.

"I hoped you wouldn't remember." he sighed and rolled across the bed to the far side, complying with his end of the deal we'd made the first night he'd slept in my room.

"Well, I did." I giggled, "And how the fuck would I be able to see the TV from behind you? Your shoulders are too wide."

"Too wide?" he scoffed, "I've never heard you complain about them before. You won't be watching anyway, you'll be sleeping."

"Yeah, but I want you *behind* me." I pulled the covers over my shoulder and turned towards the TV. He moved into position, his hot chest pressing against my back as he picked a movie. "And I'm *not* complaining."

Violence and gore splashed across the screen, and I fell asleep faster than anticipated. Not as eager as I thought I would have been to play around in his room for the first time with the knowledge I wouldn't be rejected like I had during our previous visit.

Maybe the rejection from my family was sitting too heavy in the back of my mind, and knowing they'd instantly disown me — again — for falling for a Gifted vigilante had further dampened my mood.

As the hours passed, my stomach ached. I tossed and turned, disturbing my sleep and Logan's many times throughout the night.

Once the sun was up and the room grew brighter, I gave up on trying to get back to sleep. With my eyes still closed, I felt for Logan in the bed beside me. I rolled into him and lifted his arm to wrap it around myself, nuzzling my forehead against his neck. My movement caused him to stir, and he pulled me into a tighter hug.

"What should we do today?" he asked through a yawn.

"*Nothing*."

I pulled the displaced sheets around us and brushed my lips along his jawline. I still felt a little off, but wanted to make the most of our time alone together in the apartment.

He sighed in my favorite way; the heavy exhale a reaction to my touch and suggestions rather than me driving him mad. Though, I loved doing *that* too.

Logan walked his fingers over my hip and around my back to unclip my bra, pulling it from my breasts before lowering his hands to hastily remove my underwear. I kicked them off from around my ankles, flicking them behind me under the sheets. They fell heavily to the floor, and I was too distracted by Logan's hand moving between my legs to register the sound.

"You're a *mess*," he chuckled excitedly in my ear. "Were you dreaming of me, nurse?"

"Always." I giggled, surprised at the way his fingers slipped inside me with *too much* ease.

"Wait that's… a-are you sure you want—"

"Yes!"

Logan's lips were at my neck as he rolled to his back. With his hands tight at my ribs, he pulled me with him so that I was on top. Lifting me a little under the sheets, he began my guided descent around his hard dick, slowly lowering me to ensure I could comfortably consume every rigid inch.

His right hand lost its grip and slipped up my ribs, causing me to drop. The motion forced him to glide in too deep, too quick.

"*Ouch!*" I hissed.

"Fuck, *sorry!* Hold up… Summer?"

My eyes flew open in search of what bothered him. I blinked several times to take in the brightness of the room, not used to waking up while being doused by so much sunlight.

Logan looked up at me, eyes wide. As my gaze dropped to our bodies, I gasped in surprise.

"Oh. Oh, shit." I pulled my legs together to lift myself and wriggled back to sit on his thighs. His dick, still standing tall between us, was completely covered in bright red blood. "Shit," I said again, brushing my hair out of my eyes. My hands started to shake and I let out a nervous laugh, "I'm so sorry, Logan. I wasn't expecting–"

He cut me off, waving his bloody hands at me before swiftly turning them around. His pupils flared, inspecting the red coating his palms and fingers before he dropped them to look at my ribs — and everywhere else he'd touched.

Logan's bloody handprints were all over my body.

"Don't be sorry." His laugh was tight. "I guess I wasn't expecting to see *so much*."

It was a fair comment, there was *a lot*. I leaned to peek over the edge of the bed. The underwear I'd kicked out in a rush were dark, saturated.

"Oh, God." I whispered as I looked down at us.

"Are you… okay?" he asked, always quick to ensure anything new between us wasn't too much for me to handle.

"Are *you* okay?" I scoffed incredulously, "You're handling this better than I am! It doesn't bother you?"

I couldn't imagine *any* amount of bodily fluids would bother the man who redecorated the homes of his victims with their innards. But me, filling his bed and covering him with it? It might have been a different story.

"God, Summer," he chuckled again, gently placing his warm hands on my legs, sticky with the drying blood, "I'd have no business playing with female anatomy if I didn't understand how it works."

My lips curved with a smile at his comment. "It's just… a lot." It was far more than typical for me in such a short time.

"This hasn't happened since we started dating. I thought maybe with what you'd told me about your past that you weren't able to…" his brows tied together as he eyed the scars on my lower abdomen.

"Oh, like, ovulate? I still *can*. It's fairly sporadic. And pretty graphic. Always has been. Sometimes too close together, sometimes five weeks go by before I notice this hasn't happened for a while. You've seen how well I take care of myself," I frowned at my gruesomely decorated body, "It's just another thing about me that's a complete fucking mess."

"Oh," he gulped, "Wait, so does that mean… you *can* get pregnant?" The warm undertones of his skin rapidly paled.

Blood and gore – no problem for Vengeance. The thought of knocking up his girlfriend, though impossible between us? Terrifying, apparently.

"From what I've been told about *the damage*, I might not be able to… make them stick." I immediately bit my tongue at my word choice.

Logan had mentioned he and his wife couldn't "make anything stick" between them, and they'd gone further than simply *trying* and traveled the unsuccessful IVF route.

He nodded, appearing to add a mental note to the many others he stored within his inner *Summer* file.

The color returned to his skin on a smirk. "Should we clean ourselves up? Maybe we can finish this in the shower?"

While giggling at his enthusiasm, the cramps that matched the carnage suddenly kicked in. I squeezed my eyes shut, my hands rushing to clutch my stomach.

"Or not," he winced, observing me with concern. He reached up with a bloody hand to firmly hold the arm at my abdomen. "What can I do?"

"I'm fine." I groaned, holding my breath through the pain.

"You're *not*. Tell the bodyguards you're skipping work tonight. I want to keep you here."

"Why?"

He moved from underneath me to leave the bed, looking back as he reached the bedroom door. "I just... need to make sure you're okay," he shrugged, but seemed a little distressed as he took in the sight of me, covered in blood as I kneeled in his bed.

"Why wouldn't I be?"

*He surely doesn't think...* I tried to banish the thought entirely. But now he'd planted the idea in my mind, my breathing started to pick up in pace. *Could it really be?*

"C-can you pass me my bag?" My voice wavered, "It's by the door."

Logan retrieved it before reluctantly leaving for the shower without me – but only after I insisted several times that I was fine to be left alone.

With my phone, I took photos of the sheets, *some* parts of my body, and my underwear on the floor. I texted them to one of the others in my circle.

Since moving back to the mountain state and starting my work, I'd caught the attention of a few other doctors and specialists who worked similarly to me. While none of them had their degrees stripped like I had, they were all of the same mindset – that everyone deserves proper health care.

They each did all sorts of jobs under the radar, like the oncologist I'd arranged to see Brian. We shared patients when necessary, passing them between each other, depending on who could help them best.

She replied immediately.

**Is this yours or a patient's?**

This doctor always made time for my questions, never leaving me hanging for answers. I'd been seeing her for about a year to assess and monitor the damage from my years at Home.

**Mine. As heavy as after my last surgery.**

I messaged back, referring to one of the times I'd almost bled out in Eric's room. More specifically, after one of my botched abortions under the guise of him caring for me.

**Is there a chance you're pregnant?**

I flinched at the text, not wanting my theories and Logan's concern to be confirmed by someone who actually *knew* what they were looking at.

Logan and I had spent enough time naked together for it to be a possibility. But even if there was a chance he could get me pregnant, we both knew it wouldn't last. Our genetics simply couldn't mix.

Though he hadn't confessed he was Gifted, I was now terrified that I might be getting served with an awful dose of our incompatibility, so early into our relationship. And in his fucking apartment of all places. Maybe after all the secrets I'd been keeping, I'd forgotten how eager reality was waiting around every corner to ruin things between us.

**He's Gifted.**

I watched as she stopped and started typing three times before I received:

**Come see me tonight. It WILL eventually happen if you're not careful with him.**

"Baby? You're too quiet," Logan called from the shower.

"I'm fine," I stuffed the evidence in my bag so he wouldn't have to see any more of it. But handling it all, and the heavy, metallic scent only made my hands tremble. "Does your sister have a pet or something?"

"No. Why?"

"My bag wasn't zipped up all the way when you gave it to me."

He sighed, and not the fun way. I didn't know what that meant, but he'd mentioned his sister was nosey. Could she have been home some time during the hours we were asleep? Would she have *really* touched my stuff?

I sent the bodyguards a message to cancel my work for the night, and another, privately to Tony with a time to pick me up from the apartment.

Thankfully, Logan's room wasn't carpeted like mine, and before he'd finished in the shower, I'd cleaned the blood from the floor and found new sheets in his chaotic walk-in to remake the bed.

Swapping with him to shower, I spent far longer in there than planned. The scalding hot water seemed to be the only thing to ease the sharp aches in my lower back.

He stayed in the bathroom to keep an eye on me, mindlessly tapping on the bench with nerves and humming a tune I couldn't recognise.

"Help yourself to whatever my sister has here. It's the least she can do having snooped through your stuff." He was still mad at the mystery woman as he kneeled on the floor, rummaging through the cupboard under the sink in search of pads and tampons. It seemed to be another excuse to stay close to me — I could have found them on my own.

"I thought you were joking when you said she's nosey."

"Oh no, she's the fucking *worst*," he looked me over while I stood under the water, trying my best to resist the urge to hug my abdomen in front of him. "It's getting heavier, Summer."

I glanced down at the tiled floor to see more diluted red swirling the drain. I closed my eyes and shook my head. Dealing with bloody patients… piece of cake. But my own blood? Always a shocking surprise.

"Hospital?" He offered with his forehead pressed to the other side of the glass. His hazel irises had turned dark with worry.

I thought about it for a moment. "I… I *can't*."

I had none of my fake ID's with me, and I had every suspicion that using my real name would flag the Finders. I'd be a sitting duck, bleeding out as Eric's henchman scoured the hospital floors.

Logan raked an anxious hand through his hair and nodded without pushing for an explanation – a benefit to dating a vigilante who probably avoided anywhere that would require him to use any form of legal identification.

"I'll be fine." I tried to smile to ease his nerves as my insides continued tearing themselves apart. "Give me a few more minutes?"

He left to give me space, but when I opened the bathroom door I found him again, leaning on his door frame across the hall. He held out his jacket.

"What's this for?"

The days were too warm to wear what had quickly become my favorite piece of his clothing. Even with its inability to show off Logan's body underneath, the soft fabric always smelled like him and gave me a comfort I couldn't find anywhere else.

When I didn't take it, he zipped it up and pulled it over my head. I slipped my arms through the sleeves.

*He's trying to care for you. Let him.*

The idea was foreign to me. If I were ever unwell in the past, I was sent to my room and cared for by my colleagues until I was in a good enough state to return to work or the seventy-fourth floor.

"Come back to bed," Logan said as he took my hand and dragged me along behind him. He watched me intently while I tried not to show any signs I was still aching as we settled under the fresh sheets, the others already removed from the room.

He turned the TV on to play another of his movies, but his eyes never left mine.

We laid facing each other in silence. Logan brushed the damp hair from my face, tucking it behind my ear. His hazel eyes shifted to an even deeper brown as they searched mine for answers.

To help ease his mind, I broke the silence, "Can we stay in bed all day? All night? Can I move in? I'll be like another piece of furniture in your room. We'll see how long it takes for your sister to notice." I bit my lip to keep it from trembling.

"Yeah," he agreed with a sad smile, gently wiping panicked tears from my cheeks with his warm fingers. "Anything you want, nurse."

"All I want right now, is *you*." I rolled over, pushing my back into his chest so he'd hold me.

"I'm not going anywhere, Summer." His words against my ear were hushed with the heaviness of a final promise. I relaxed into the safety of his arms, tightly wrapping me as he buried his face in my hair.

The sounds of the movie lulled me into an uncomfortable sleep. I held my stomach, reminding myself that while the pain might have been similar to what I'd felt in the past, it wasn't caused by Eric this time.

*Just my own fucking stupidity.*

# THIRTY-SEVEN

## SUMMER

"Summer?" Logan gently rocked my shoulder to wake me, "Tony's here to pick you up."

I sat up in bed, disoriented by the missing time and the dark.

*Did I sleep all day?*

"Your things are packed. I've got your clothes here," he continued as I rubbed my eyes, "He mentioned he's taking you to a doctor. Baby, I can't help but feel that's something *I* should be doing."

"I'm sure it's nothing," I tried to reassure him while I talked myself into removing his jacket and reached for the clean clothes he'd found in my backpack.

"If it's not?"

"Then…" I shrugged, pulling on leggings and a loose shirt. I couldn't think about that right now. "We'll try to be more careful so we don't have to deal with this again. Besides, the doctor I'm seeing is like me."

"I don't know if that makes me feel better, or more concerned." He gave me a tired smile and pulled me along.

"She takes patients privately in her home at all hours like I do. Doesn't appreciate strangers where she can help it. Only her work is a little more specific than mine. I've been seeing her since I found her for…" I looked down as we reached the front door, "You know, the internal stuff. Monitoring the mess."

He bobbed his head in understanding and opened the door to reveal Tony, waiting to take me. "I'll meet you at home when you're done?"

"Home?" My mood picked up a little at the way he'd so casually said it.

"*Your* home." He kissed my forehead goodbye.

"Let yourself in if I'm not back by the time you get there." I told him as we left.

"Sounds like things are getting serious," Tony teased me after the doors to the elevator closed.

"What?"

"He's got the codes, boss. Calling it home. You're okay with him being there without you."

*Hmm.*

"Yeah… I guess it is."

"And now this…" he tipped his head to my stomach.

"Whatever this is, it wasn't intentional."

"Can't imagine it would've been," he lowered his voice. "I'll be kind for now, boss, but once this is over, I'll lecture you like you do with me."

"You sleep with someone new every few days!" I argued as we stepped out of the lift and through the front doors to the street. "I remind you for your own safety. This is different. This is–" I paused, glaring at my reflection in the passenger window.

"Serious? Long term? It's a *good* thing," Tony reassured me while I shook my head at myself, "It's like you're growing up."

I dropped into the seat with a huff, wriggling to get comfortable on the towels I'd asked him to bring for the two hour trip.

"You know almost better than anyone what I've done. You think that stuff wasn't *grown up?*"

"Yeah, I know. But this is different. This is all your doing," he elaborated, turning the car around to begin the long drive.

*He's right. This is all your fault.*

"I think I'm about to ruin everything." I said after spending most of the drive in silent pain.

"Why?" he asked, patting my leg for the hundredth time when I brought my knees up to my chest. I wanted to curl up, but there was no avoiding the aches, no matter my position.

"Would you stay with someone if you got them pregnant a few months after meeting them?"

"Fuck no," he laughed, "I'd *definitely* call it quits."

I had no idea if he was serious or not. As much as I liked to think I knew him well enough to know if his words were true, I really didn't. And I didn't want to question his answer and accidentally learn more about him.

"But Logan's different, right? He's *obsessed* with you, boss. You say it hasn't been long but… the way he watches you work. You don't see it. It's *intense*. I think he could replace both of us. But don't let Ben know I even put the idea in your head."

*Do they suspect he's Gifted?*

It was late in the night by the time we'd arrived. I was a little sad that I'd never seen the house in the daylight. It was enormous, and stretched along the width of the block in a picturesque suburb full of similarly designed structures.

Tony drove through the high gates as they opened, parking on the driveway.

"Do you want me to come with you?" he offered, going above and beyond his job description.

"Nah," I got out of the car, "This is something I need to deal with on my own."

The front door opened when I lifted my hand to knock. She was as careful as me, and had probably seen us coming from before we'd even arrived at the gate.

"Summer," she greeted me with a warm smile.

"Hey, Dr. Reynolds."

"Come on in," she stepped aside, gesturing for me to enter her home.

Most of the lights were off, but down the long hall to the right, past the many sitting rooms and fancily decorated living areas, the light to her office was on and waiting for us.

I followed her, taking in the details of her outfit as she walked ahead. Dr.

Reynolds was about my height and had a similar frame. Her dark hair had gray streaks through it, a few more than the last time I'd seen her.

She wore a black, knee-length dress with a high front and back, and sleeves down to her elbows. Her heels were short, but by the way she confidently strode the hall, I guessed she would have worn others that were much higher when she were younger.

Though I couldn't pick her age exactly, I would have guessed she was in her late sixties, and I hoped I would look half as good as her if I were ever permitted to live that long.

Dr. Reynolds turned and waited for me to enter the room. She turned the lights down low, knowing from my previous visits that I was far better at being a nurse than I was as a patient.

I kept my garage in a minimalist state, storing only what was absolutely necessary. Being surrounded by all the equipment in her office not only reminded me a little too much of the ER at Home, but also seemed to surface experiences I'd long since tried to drown. Particularly those of waking up post-op, alone, and confused.

I'd never wanted to come to Dr. Reynolds in the first place. After all I'd been through at Home, I would have been happy for no one to ever touch me again, and had avoided seeking any help for what was left of my reproductive organs for too long before I'd found her. It only took me a few visits before I felt comfortable enough to tell her all about what Eric and I had done together.

*What he had done to me.*

"How's the husband?" I tried to make small-talk as she settled at her desk.

"He's well." Her smile, even with being married for almost a year, was still timid over the thought of him. "Have you got your medication with you?" she asked, gesturing for me to sit on the examination bed.

*Fuck!* "No. I've been off it for a while."

"That's impressive. But how did you find yourself in this situation if you're not taking them? Immaculate conception?"

"I feel safe with my boyfriend," I admitted, grinning involuntarily, "There hasn't been any need for the extra help."

"Well, that's *good* for you." She smiled and grabbed a tablet from her desk to pull up my records, "You didn't want him here with you?"

"No. I told him it's nothing."

"So, with him being Gifted, are you protecting him from what it could be? Or yourself from his reaction?"

She was too fucking smart, and always saw straight through my bullshit.

I sighed. "Both."

"If he's Gifted, like you say, then he'd know this is something that happens all too often. Why not have him here?"

"It's too early for us. We've only been dating for a little over a month." *Can people even survive a grenade like this thrown at their relationship so early?* "And... He's got a history. Wanted kids in the past." *And he might still want them now.* Jackie's comment about Logan wanting a big family in the past made my eyes sting. "I think this would be too much for him. Besides, he hasn't admitted to me that he's Gifted."

"Well, that sounds... unnecessarily complicated."

"You're telling me." I said with another sigh as she motioned for me to lie down. "I have a question... about Gifted men." I began pulling clothing down, and up.

"I've worked with many, maybe I can help," she offered, squirting warm gel across my abdomen.

"This one I'm dating... he runs hot. Like, *hot*. Even his... fluids," I giggled in spite of how exposed and uncomfortable I felt, "If he were with a Gifted woman, do you think that'd affect his chances of having kids?"

She laughed too, "Gifted really do seem a lot like us, Summer. But their mutations can be vast evolutionary leaps. If he's as *hot* as you say," – she smiled mischievously at me – "I'm sure it's all part of his evolved state. Without any reason to believe there are other issues, or a sample of his *fluids*, I can only assume everything is in working order. Especially with *you* here right now."

*I guess she's right.* I stared at the ceiling, avoiding the screen like my life depended on it. If something between us had tried to blend, it would be proof enough that Logan wasn't shooting blanks and his deceased wife was definitely a regular human.

I spent the next few minutes with my eyes closed and trying to steady my breathing as Dr. Reynolds rushed through the necessary examinations to determine how much trouble I'd gotten into this time.

Once she was done, I sat up and covered my face with my hands. I focused on her words, hoping with each one that passed through my ears, it would expel one of the sensations of her checkups. Particularly the heat of her hands on my stomach.

While I enjoyed the warmth Logan placed on my skin, it felt wrong feeling something similar, warmer in fact, from someone else.

"Well, everything seems to be okay," she said, "And if the bleeding has slowed, then I don't believe there's anymore cause for concern."

"So? What was it?" I dropped my hands to grip the edge of the bed, bracing for what I already guessed she would say.

"I'm sorry, Summer. You've likely miscarried. Very early days. Too early for a heartbeat."

*Just as expected for getting involved with Gifted men*

I sucked in a sharp breath as the diagnosis hit me like a fucking train, but while upsetting, I felt an odd sense of relief. This was brutal, but at least I was present for it this time, held in the arms of someone who cared for me.

Not given a chance by mismatched genetics, sure, but not ordered to be removed by a madman without my knowledge like the others before it. That had to count for something.

Dr. Reynolds took my blood while I thought about what the fuck I was meant to tell Logan when I got home.

"Your body has been through enough, and while it's all looking *mostly healed,* I still wouldn't recommend putting yourself through multiple losses with this man to keep up an act. It'll take an awful toll on you, Summer. Both physically and mentally. No Gifted man is worth that."

"Wait… Mostly healed?"

"Yes!" She exclaimed, taping a cotton ball to my arm, "Things are looking *much* better than your original scans."

"What? Are you saying if I actually *wanted* kids, I could have them now?"

The revelation was startling, having all but convinced myself that children could *never* be a part of my future.

I couldn't stand the thought of bringing any into my world after having lost so much. My life was too fucked up to entertain the notion, and I had no doubt Eric would hunt me down until the end of time. It wasn't a safe existence to add offspring to.

*But I've just gained back something Eric stole from me.* I smiled at the thought. There were no words for the peace her news brought me. I may have still been scarred externally, but knowing some of the internal damage I'd been left with had been erased was some of the best news I'd ever heard in my life.

"Maybe," she said. "It's something we can look into when you find yourself a viable partner. Or if the two of you want to look into other options."

*Fuck.*

There was no way I could consider a Gifted vigilante a "viable partner" and with how hard Logan had tried to have his own children, those other options weren't likely to be considered.

*Gees, do you hear yourself? Do you really think you and Logan will be together long enough to seriously think about things like this?*

"Are you still in group therapy?" Dr. Reynolds asked, grabbing a tissue from the box on her desk and blowing her nose before offering one to me.

"One-on-one now," I answered mindlessly, taking one, though I didn't need it. I was stuck in one of those numb moments, being given too much information that I didn't know how to react to yet.

"Good. You're going to need it. Your mood will probably dip over the next few days. You need to take care of yourself."

"Okay." I said, hearing her, but not really listening.

"I'll see you next time," she patted my leg. "Hopefully for something a little more positive."

# THIRTY-EIGHT

## SUMMER

Tony dropped me at home in the early hours of the morning, promptly leaving when he noticed my vigilante waiting in the doorway.

I ran into Logan's open arms and he lifted me, holding me tight as he carried me into the hallway and kicking the door closed behind us.

"Good news?" he set me down, eyeing the cotton taped to my arm as his warm hands squeezed mine.

"Kind of," I grinned, "I'm not sure if it's *good* exactly."

He blinked twice and his features lit up. "You're *pregnant?*" He roughly grabbed my shoulders to hold me at arms length, looking me up and down. His pupils rapidly dilated, eyes wide with excitement behind his glasses.

*He's excited? What the fuck?*

"What? *No!*" I shook my head, "Hold up, you think that'd be *good* news?"

"Well," he let me go and stuffed his in his pockets, "N-no. I don't know. Your mood took me by surprise."

"Logan, we've known each other for like, a few months." I said with a shaky laugh, "And you told me you can't have kids. Did you not mean that?"

He scratched at his neck as he thought of an answer for me, though I already knew what he should have been saying. I scowled up at him.

*YOU'RE GIFTED, just fucking admit it!*

"I… probably *was*." I said to fill the silence, shuffling on the spot and feeling exposed with all the space between us.

"*Was?* What does that mean?" His eyes darted between mine, begging for clarification, but they darkened with his mood before I'd even answered.

"You *know* what that means." I found myself not wanting to say it. It'd been surprisingly hard enough to hear it.

Would the vigilante I'd become so attached to decide that my body's refusal to carry his offspring was enough of an excuse to put me on his hit list? It seemed unfair, but then I still hadn't completely worked him out.

"Summer, we're adults." His voice, completely void of the excitement it contained just a moment ago, was now low and defeated. "Don't fuck around with things like this between us. Be straight with me."

I unwillingly repeated the news, "She thinks I miscarried. Early." I swallowed hard after the words left my mouth, wishing I also had pockets to stuff my hands into. I craved the pressure of my tight work clothes over what I currently wore. "That's likely what all the bleeding was. I'll know for sure in a few days. I'm sorry." My voice was quieter than I intended. Having seen his reaction to the possibility I was carrying his child had capsized any confidence I'd brought home with me.

Logan's features softened and he shook his head, "Please don't apologize. I just got… carried away at the thought that maybe…"

"Something stuck?" I offered with a frown, disapproving of my word choice again.

"Yeah," he said with a heavy exhale, reaching for me to take his hand. He sat on the end of the bed while I left for the walk-in. "I know we haven't been together long… But if it were to happen, not that it can… *clearly*." He roughly rubbed the side of his face with his hand. "I'd be *okay* with it, Summer."

"Okay with it?" I echoed in disbelief as I took my clothes off.

"It's not like we *planned* on it. But if it *could* happen."

The subject, as I'd suspected, was too much for him. I'd cruelly given him some kind of hope that the thing he'd wanted so desperately in the past could be brought into what we had now.

I couldn't believe how well he'd instantly accepted the idea, believing Tony's answer would have been much more acceptable for only having known Logan for a couple of months.

Standing naked except for my underwear in the wardrobe, I turned from him to hide. An intense wave of disappointment crashed into my chest; the awful realization that as much as Logan might be worried he couldn't give me something, I equally couldn't give it to him – no matter how long we were together, or what we could end up feeling for each other.

*I knew we couldn't handle something like this.* I already regretted telling him at all.

"I need to… process this," he said as he met me in the walk-in, "Do you want me to call Tony and have him come back and stay with you?"

I didn't like the sound of that. What on Earth would a murderous vigilante do in order to process soul-crushing news?

"You don't want to do that *with me?*" I wiped my face to hide my tears. The thought of him running out on me while I still hadn't "processed" anything had the mood swings I wasn't ready for kicking in prematurely.

Logan leaned with his head against the doorframe of the walk-in, looking up at the light, "I'll stay if you want me." I detected the slightest waver in his voice.

"I *want you* to stay with me."

"You're sure?" he asked with a sad smile.

"I don't understand how to deal with any of this, Logan. The other times this happened I woke up *alone* and operated on without having any idea of what'd been done to me. I got so depressed I tried to–" I choked at the thought of the seventy-four storey drop I should have taken to spare us both this pain.

*Danny wouldn't have died a month later,* I internally beat myself up with more thoughts of how damaging my existence was for those I cared about.

Logan took a long draw through his nose with his eyes closed, "You deserve better than this, Summer. I can't cope with knowing I've brought you so much pain. More of the same." His eyes flickered to the surgical scars on my abdomen.

"This is *not* the same. We weren't careful. We fucked up. You're not leaving me to bleed out on my own, that's a pretty fucking good start."

He frowned, though the tension in his shoulders eased. "You really wanna work through this?"

"I don't think things between us should end over a mistake. How else are people meant to see if they can make it if they let the first hurdle take them out?"

He swallowed hard and bobbed his head, seeming to agree, but still not giving me enough closure.

"Hey! Look at me," I pleaded. I reached for his arms, still tight across his chest. His eyes finally dropped to mine, revealing more hurt than I was prepared to see. "Logan, if you need an out, then take this one. I won't hold it over you. This isn't a minor thing for a couple to go through."

"I'm not looking for an out, Summer. Do you really think I'd give you up by choice? I'm offering *you* one."

"Well you can file your offer under dumb deals I want no part in."

"Then I'm not leaving," he promised, stripping down to his boxers before he reached for me, "I want to give you space from me if you need it. After what I've just put you through…"

"What *we* put me through," I corrected him, taking his hands and relieved he seemed just as clingy as I felt, "This was as much my doing." I knew the risks and still took them as we got carried away.

Logan lifted me so I could wrap my arms and legs around his body before he sat on the end of the bed again with me on his lap. I hugged him tight and spoke into his ear through another wave of runaway tears, "Jokes on you though, apparently I'm going to be a moody bitch for the next few days."

"More so?" he said with a small laugh before his voice turned sad, "A few days… What exactly are you planning on doing for that amount of time? Surely not working? Let me take care of you."

I took a deep breath, trying to calm myself without any luck now that I could hear he was also struggling to hold himself together, "I was thinking of spending the week in bed, crying and eating pizza. Does that sound okay?"

"Really, nurse?"

"Not really, you know me well enough by now to know I'm not eating pizza." I admitted, getting a small laugh out of him as I buried my head in the curve of his neck. I inhaled deeply to take in the last of the day's cologne. It was instantly calming.

After rubbing his eyes under his glasses he grabbed my shoulders again to straighten me on his lap.

"So… Wanna tell me the good news?"

"It's nothing exciting," I promised with a shrug, "I'm not quite as damaged as I'd been when I left the cult. Internally anyway. Mentally, physically in other ways – still fucked up."

He smiled and held me tight again, "That really *is* good news."

I broke out of the hug before I became comfortable enough to start crying again.

"Pizza?"

"It's like, three in the morning, babe." He shook his head at me, but if my running theories on him were correct, he could probably eat absurd amounts of food at any time of day.

"It's evening in my upside down days," I countered, "There's a place not far from here that's open all night. They deliver. I found it after I learned how obsessed *you* are with it."

"You'll learn to love it," he promised, laughing at the way I scrunched my features. He kissed me on the nose before shifting so we could both get under the covers.

Logan turned the TV on as I searched on my phone for a website I'd bookmarked.

"So we're really going to do this?" he asked, wrapping an arm around my shoulders. "Pizza and crying in bed for the week?"

"Yep. We can swap sometimes if you want," I said, handing him my phone so he could pick what we were – mostly what he was – going to eat. "I should probably eat at some point over that many days."

We ignored the movie, spending the time in bed silently holding hands as we waited for our food to arrive, both of us still shocked by the events of the day.

Logan elaborated on what he and his wife went through during their years of failed IVF. He didn't speak much about her specifically, which made me a little sad. I wouldn't have minded hearing more about her to fill in the gaps and to learn more about Logan through the way he spoke of her.

He shared enough for me to understand why he jumped to the conclusion that I was pregnant.

I *was*. *Had been*, as confirmed by the blood results to come in the following days. The miscarriage between us was a step further than they'd ever experienced, though it carried the same crushing disappointment, and we'd carelessly put him through it all over again.

Logan took the week off work to stay with me, barely leaving the bed, where we spent most of our time talking or sleeping. It was the longest break we'd had from each other's bodies since our first time in the hallway. Sexually, anyway. His hands rarely left mine and he was always within reach when I needed him.

It was nice, but I was glad it didn't have to last forever. I was eager to reconnect with him again in that sense, worried he might have seen this as a sign we shouldn't be physical with each other anymore.

Thankfully, he didn't. And once I'd recovered, we quickly became reacquainted and made up for lost time.

The event, though heavy on our minds, seemed to bring about a new level of intimacy between us. We were a little more open and honest with each other about our situation… and what could never be.

# THIRTY-NINE

## SUMMER

### MARCH 12TH

Dr. Lindsey observed me from her armchair, "You seemed very eager to get a session in this week. What's troubling you, Katie?"

Where the fuck was I meant to start?

Dr. Reynolds had warned that my mood would be unpredictable with my body expelling the hormones it no longer needed. She wasn't wrong.

The previous week had been rough.

Logan, not leaving my side was a comfort I grew a little too dependent on. I didn't know what to do with myself once we both needed to go back to work and our normal routine – the double lives of a Gifted vigilante and a woman with just as many secrets.

I'd been feeling numb, yet, like a complete fucking wreck at the same time.

But I didn't want to bring up the miscarriage with Dr. Lindsey, it was still too… raw.

"I think I'm a bit depressed. More so. Just… really down again." I confessed that part, at least.

She gave me a small, understanding smile. "It's not surprising you're feeling this way. After all you've been through, even with it being nearly two years since leaving the cult, these emotions sometimes stay with us consistently

– or reappear whenever it suits them. Your scores today," she continued, glancing over the questionnaire she'd given me to gauge my mental state before we started our discussion, "don't concern me so much that I feel like you're a risk to yourself. But that's not for me to decide." She looked up, brows raised.

*She's waiting for you to give her an indication of how likely it is that you never show up to therapy again.*

"Oh. Shit. No," I started, "I've felt *way* worse than this. This is… a downer I guess. I tend to pick back up. I'm not feeling like I'd kill myself or something – if that's what you're asking?"

"That's *exactly* what I'm asking." Another sad smile pulled at her features. I felt awful that Dr. Lindsey had *me* for a patient. I was so beyond fixing. I couldn't be made whole again. But I'd learned to tread the dark waters my mind often tried to drown me in. This latest obstacle in my life would be no different.

"I know when I'm at the point of no return," I reassured her. "I've been there twice." I hated admitting it. It made me feel weak. And I was so fucking tired of feeling weak and powerless.

"Is this something you'd like to talk about?"

"Sure." I agreed, "Maybe just *one* of those times, though. The other is… still too much for me to think about sometimes."

"Of course. Whatever you're comfortable with."

The day I escaped Home didn't end how I'd intended it to. It was one of my darkest memories and the atrocity of what I'd tried to do to myself didn't sink in until I'd left Bedlam. And it *still* wasn't enough to escape Eric forever.

*Just another thing you failed at.*

"About a year before I left the cult, things seemed to start going downhill. More than usual." I squinted at the broken memories, the missing time, the aches my body carried, both from Eric and from unknown sources that I had no recollection of receiving.

For months, I woke up with bruises on my face and body, bumps from impacts to my head, all without any explanation. I slept far more than usual, but put that down to my mood.

Eric had all but banished me to the medical floor, no longer allowing me to reside with him on his level at all. I'd only slept in his room a handful of times over that final year, and for half of those, he hadn't even been at Home. Too busy with meetings he no longer saw me as stable enough to bring along.

I wasn't coping, and there was no way for me to get the help I needed.

"I was denied medication for my depression," I explained as I picked at my nails. "Eric didn't like the idea of me being drugged while I worked for him."

"That seems a little odd. You'd think he'd want you in top form for what was expected of you. Helping patients, etcetera."

"Yeah, you'd think. Sometimes, I felt it was another way to control me. He'd make me feel good for a little while and then I was a mess the second he was done with me. He wouldn't need to work so much to wear me down to that point again."

It was another example of why I felt like I was nothing more than an experiment to Eric. That year was the longest stretch of time he'd made me suffer without giving me a break. I was the toy he liked to push, to see how far a human could go before they crumbled. And I crumbled plenty. Cookies in a demonically-possessed blender would have held themselves together better than I had.

*Yet you survived, that's gotta mean something.*

"What toll did being kept in that emotional state take on you?" she asked, pen at the ready to start taking notes.

## Two Years Prior

Cold air whipped hair into my eyes and chilled the bare skin of my arms and face as it swirled around me.

I laid on the cold concrete ledge on the roof of Home. The top of the building – flat and graveled – didn't quite have the same finesse as the rest of the menacing black structure.

There wasn't much to look at from my position. The tops of the few skyscrapers that were taller than Home, encircled my view of the night sky, dulled with pollution. Occasionally, one of the Gifted would fly past. No matter how many years I'd spent in the city, the sight of them was always surprising.

To my left, the gate and tall wire fence were a few feet away, meant to keep people from having access to the ledge.

Lucky for me, the gate was never locked. I'd been on the roof since sunset, making a habit over the last week or so to come up here every night after my shift, working up the guts to move closer to the edge before talking myself over.

Danny had come the previous night, begging me to move back to him and away from the drop, promising that he was trying to find a way for us and his family to leave Home forever. I'd believed him. He was the one who's promises I could believe.

*That's not true.* I looked up at the few stars whose light could penetrate the thick smog. *Eric has kept every promise he's ever made, you just don't appreciate what that means.*

Hot tears rolled down the sides of my face, growing colder the further they moved from my eyes. The sensation surprised me – I'd been crying for hours, and couldn't believe I had anything left inside me for fresh tears.

My back had grown stiff from the uncomfortable ledge and my body ached all over from the surgery I'd had just a few days prior. Like the surgery before it, it was only meant to be minor, but the pain was becoming unbearable, and I wasn't allowed any painkillers. My fever was high, and I was certain I had an infection.

Surge still hadn't returned from wherever he'd disappeared to, but was due to come back during the night. Once he saw me, he'd convince Eric that I couldn't possibly remain in this state.

The torn pages of a book in my left hand flitted in the breeze. I'd anxiously ripped little pieces of the medical studies I'd been reading, letting them fall from my trembling fingers like snowflakes when I'd sat with my legs dangling over the side of the building.

I missed the snow. I missed the stars. I missed the mountain slopes I'd played on as a child.

My right arm swung heavily over the sidewalk, seventy-four stories below. If I rolled my body slightly to the side, I could slip down to meet both the cold concrete and eternal darkness.

It would have been more comforting and kind than the man whose voice floated through the air to greet me.

"Summer," Eric called from the gate, "Get back inside."

A demand. Not a devastated plea to save the woman he loved. That wasn't who I was. He didn't love me. From day one I was told that he never would. But I stupidly saw it as a challenge, so sure the man I gave everything to would reward me with something as simple and natural as loving me in return.

*But he doesn't. And never will.*

I didn't respond to Eric's order, I only blinked away more tears from heavy eyelids that had been rubbed all afternoon and well into the night.

"Summer," his hypnotic voice turned a little softer and he slowly paced towards me. What started as a shadowy figure at my left revealed the man I loved as he stepped into the city's glow.

With his hands in the pockets of his suit pants, he looked out at the buildings rather than allowing his gaze to fall to the mess of a human at waist height as she laid on the edge, trying to convince her body to roll over and be done with it.

Eric hadn't come to the roof to pry me down any other time. Something about the state of me over the previous days must have had him taking my moods more seriously. But it was too late.

I looked up at him, drinking in his exposed forearms, covered in ink, and the dark suit, perfectly tailored to his body. His handsome face had high cheekbones and angled features, tight with disapproval. None of him loved me in return. It was torture.

I'd followed my contract to the letter, all in hopes it would spark something other than cruelty behind his actions, and that the version of this man I'd fallen so hard for would find his way back to me.

What did I receive instead?

I was tortured and mutilated, hurt and controlled.

As I rolled to the side, my center of gravity shifted to pull me from the ledge. I closed my eyes. I didn't want to look death in the face as it rushed to greet me.

Sharp hands gripped my arm and ripped me from the fall, throwing me to the gravel against the fence.

Eric let out a sharp breath and adjusted the sleeves on his shirt from the sudden move that kept me from the release I sorely craved.

I cried in pain, holding my stomach as I stood.

"I knew you were becoming unstable, but this is ludicrous, Summer."

My mind was made up – I'd had enough of him. I took a step towards the drop, but Eric grabbed me again before I could move further, as though I were that predictable.

With his hand at my neck he roughly pushed me against the fence, and held me there, green eyes livid as they pierced mine before he let me go. It was a warning that I'd be in for far worse than being thrown around if I tried again.

"Of all nights?" he asked, dark brows weighted by disappointment, "We have plans."

"I don't want to go out tonight, Eric." I whimpered with my head down, wiping more tears from my eyes and brushing the hair from my face to tuck it behind my ears. It was a futile act; the wind kept blowing it back in my face.

"It's our *anniversary*. How would it look if my sweet Summer were found, a mangled corpse on the sidewalk, on a night like this?"

Like always, he cared only about how my death would affect his image. I should have thrown myself off sooner, before the sun set, so passers-by could have used the better lighting to see what was left of me.

"Can't we stay in?" I begged, "Who even cares if we're not seen tonight? I don't give a fuck anymore, Eric."

"Summer, I *need* you. Our time together isn't over. It won't be for a long time yet," he smiled down at me, gently stroking the side of my face.

I closed my eyes and threw a filter over his words before I let them sink in, making them sound more like he was begging me to *live*, to *stay* with him because he *loved me*, not because he'd invested years into our cover.

"I just want to sleep." I cried, desperate to return to the room that had become more like a cell. Having spent so much time in my small apartment, I'd grown to depend on it for safety, almost unable to recall how to act when free of its walls.

"We leave in two hours," he continued, ignoring my pleas. "Get ready in my room. I'll be keeping an eye on you."

Eric held the gate open as I trudged through, and instructed a Finder waiting by the door that I was *never* to have access to the roof again.

We made the short trip in the elevator down to his floor, me walking ahead of him, shoulders slumped and upset with myself for the missed opportunity.

Eric silently watched over me while I showered. He impatiently leaned on the vanity, dressed and ready to leave as I cried on the floor under the hot water for longer than my short time frame to get ready allowed.

He dried my hair as I applied my makeup to his standard, ensuring my swollen, red eyes didn't stand out so much before he helped me into my dress.

It was beautiful, as always.

The velvet was red, Eric's preferred color on me when we were seen above ground together. The straight skirt had a high slit in the side, and the top had long sleeves with squared shoulders. The back reached high at my neck but the front plunged low between my breasts. The material was, as always, cleverly cut to hide my scars and concealed all but the last black letter of my tattoo.

It had only been a few months since Eric added the seventh name to my skin, leaving less options for revealing clothing as time between us passed. I feared one day I might have to be covered from head to toe. He hadn't touched my face yet, but I'd already had to cover my neck several times for trips out of Home.

Eric tied a black, corseted belt tight around my waist, emphasizing my figure. The thin straps criss-crossed from side to side, tiptoeing the border between Summer and Stitch up.

It was fitting for the night, being Eric's unwilling submissive, playing out the role I was contractually obliged to fulfill.

Once dressed and made up, Eric stood back to give me an approving nod. It made my knees weak, and the thoughts of falling from the roof were expelled from my mind. Though, only for a few moments.

He held his arm out for me to take, receiving no usual smile from me as I used him for balance to step into my favorite heels before he dragged me back to the elevator.

We were driven to his favorite restaurant. We ate. He drank a little while I restrained from taking his glass to drown my sorrows, numb my pain, and to work up the courage to tell Eric exactly what I thought of him.

"I have a gift for you," he said with a small smile, retrieving a box from his jacket that could only contain jewelry. He gently pushed it across the table. I plastered the expected smile across my face, took the box and waited for the predictable flashes of paparazzi cameras.

I opened the box to reveal an exquisite set of diamond earrings most girls would have traded their souls for.

"Happy anniversary," Eric said quietly as I inspected the new pieces that would reside in his room, not my own, for the next time he needed me to dress up.

"Oh, Eric," I laid the appreciation on *thick* while no one was within earshot, "What am I ever going to do with *another* pair of earrings." I snapped the box shut with one hand.

His jaw clenched ever so subtly.

"They're beautiful," I said, slipping back into survival-mode outside the safety of his bedroom, "Thank you, Eric."

He gave me another approving nod as our plates were cleared.

I was tired, crashing hard from the adrenaline from nearly plunging to my death, and from how raw I felt from crying all day. There was something wrong with me, more than just not feeling well from surgery, but I couldn't pick it.

Tears pooled along my lashes, surprising me again that I had anything left to give.

"Not now, Summer, save it for Home," Eric warned under his breath.

*Fuck it.*

I was done with pretending. Done with him sitting across the table, playing out his role as the perfect boyfriend, only for him to hurt me later when we went to bed.

While we were in public Eric wanted to *sell it.* He wanted everyone to believe we were *hopelessly* in love with each other. It was our fucking anniversary and I wanted to give everyone a good show while he had no choice but to play along for our *precious* image's sake.

"Ten years," I said quietly, "I'd have thought celebrating a decade since I came to Bedlam would have called for a more lively celebration."

"Seven years to the public, darling," he reminded me curtly. Others couldn't know I counted the time before he started to show me off, when I was still underage. Still a *child.* "I believe what we've done tonight is about as lively as I can allow for the girl who threatens me with her demise."

I stood from the table, startling him with my sudden movement as I sidestepped around it. Sitting on his lap, I quickly pulled his mouth to mine. When he kissed me in return, my spine seemed to melt away one vertebrae at a time.

Eric *knew* he had to do it. How would it look if he rejected a kiss from his doting girlfriend of *seven* years on their anniversary?

He hadn't kissed me this way in public for years, never leaving me so much as an ounce of space for improvisation in my actions to potentially blemish his appearance.

Eric barely even kissed me at all in his room anymore, and *never* during sex. He believed kissing showed too much affection, and was at fault for me getting my wires crossed, making me stray too far from my place.

"You're pushing your luck, Summer," he spoke low in my ear, keeping his smile up to ensure those watching wouldn't catch on to how much of a fucking sham our relationship had become.

"If you think," I stood, repositioning to straddle him on the chair. The high slit in the dress worked to my advantage and showed off more skin than he cared for me to display outside of his floor at the top of the tower. "For even a second," I whispered in his ear as I kissed his neck, leaving lip-shaped smudges from my red lipstick on his pale skin, "That I give even the *slightest* fuck about what you'll do to me after what I tried to do on the roof, you are *very* much mistaken, my love." I ran my tongue along his smooth jawline, and raked my fingers through his hair, daring to ruffle each perfectly brushed strand before lifting my face to meet his eyes.

"Save this for Home."

"No." I smiled at him, eyes blurring with more tears. "You want to give me something for our anniversary, Eric? Give me something fucking *real. Anything*." I begged with my lips at his ear. "Because right now there is *nothing* I want more from you than to terminate my contract and throw me from the *fucking roof yourself*."

Eric pulled his face back a few inches. He must have taken my words and expression as truth because he gently drew me closer by the back of my neck to kiss me again.

The feel of his lips on mine was intoxicating, even if only to stop my threats. I lightly rocked my hips on his lap, not giving a fuck about who saw us.

*This'll give them something to write about,* I internally rolled my eyes as I broke off the kiss.

"I love you, Eric." I held his face tight in my cold hands with my forehead pressed hard to his, "So *fucking* much."

"I know you do, darling," was the best reply he ever offered, no matter how terribly I was falling apart over him.

He tipped his head to the side and gave me what could have almost been mistaken for a distressed look. My sadness was one of the few things that could get Eric to feel *anything*.

The fact that he couldn't even fake an "I love you" for the sake of our facade drove away what little sanity I had left.

I could always replay the moment later in my mind, replacing his words with what I needed to hear until I found a substitute for the roof, but instead, I decided to push my luck even further.

"Say it," I demanded in a whimper, sitting back on his lap and playing with the buttons on his shirt. "I need to hear it. Say it here, I know it's not true, but please, Eric, give me *something*." I wiped the few drops from my cheeks that were brave enough to show themselves in public.

"No, Summer. Let's go home. You've done well tonight. There's no need for this to continue." He shifted underneath me to stand.

"No. Not yet, give me a few more minutes," I pleaded, aware that I was the one who hadn't wanted to go out in the first place.

"This is proving to be too much for you," Eric said sternly as he stood, dropping me roughly to my feet from his lap.

We sat in silence together on the back seat for the short drive to Home. I could barely keep my eyes open from how heavy they were from the crying and the pain of being refused a few moments break of Eric's rules.

We arrived back in the dimly lit room on the top floor, most of the low light coming from the glow of the city on the other side of the enormous glass wall. I tossed the new earrings into a drawer of the wardrobe, watching them tumble and settle in amongst all the other gifts he'd given me over my decade of service to him.

Eric helped me out of my dress before I undid his belt and tossed the belt to the bed. He'd want to use it on me later.

Slipping off my underwear, I made my way to what used to be my side of his bed, ready to feel *anything* he was willing to give, just to keep me going for another day.

I paused at the sight of them on the floor, even in the low lighting I could see they were dark with blood. Looking down, my legs were covered in patches from where the fabric rubbed against my skin as I'd taken them off. And I was losing more — thick lines of it rushed down my glowing limbs to the concrete floor.

"Oh, shit," I whispered, trying to make sense of the sight.

I'd researched my recent procedure, and trusted Eric to pick a competent surgeon when my friend asked to be removed from the team. While the incisions in my abdomen weren't as I expected, the bleeding was *definitely* not in accordance with what was typical post-op.

Emerging naked from the bathroom, Eric stood behind me, drawing in my perfume as his lips grazed from my shoulder to my ear.

"What's wrong?" he slid his hands under my arms, lightly brushing his fingers down my collarbone and over my breasts before settling them lower to firmly hold my waist. I tipped my head to the floor, and he pulled away. "Not tonight, then," he sighed, moving to his side of the bed.

"What? It's never stopped you before. Why now? I need this Eric!" my voice was shrill with desperation, "Like you said, *of all nights!*"

He turned back, reaching for and holding my arms tight. When he opened his mouth to argue, he paused, eyes widening as I whimpered in pain and clutched my stomach.

"This is different, Summer. You need to see The Surgeon, he should be back by now. I've let this go on for long enough, you need the proper treatment to recover from this. I don't think you can do it on your own."

"The fuck are you talking about? It's nothing!" I reached for the belt, snatching it up and forcibly stuffing it into his hand. "*Do it.*" I demanded, "I need it Eric, *please*. I need something, I can't keep going on like this."

*My God, more tears?*

Eric took a step back, genuine concern crossing his face like he was having some kind of horrific revelation. "I think… I've pushed you too far, darling."

"No!" I screamed at him, "I'm fine, *please*," I cried *again*. Sobbing, *again*. I couldn't catch a fucking break from these tears.

"I need you to wait here." he turned to his wardrobe, reaching for the rarely-worn-in-front-of-anyone sweatpants and tight, black T-shirt. They were the clothes he often wore in his private gym, away from the rest of us. No one would see him this late in the night when only making the short trip to his office on the same floor.

"Eric!" I called as he rushed for the door. He looked at me with a frown as I stood above the expanding pool of my blood. "Don't leave me. I don't want to be alone. *I need you.*"

He swallowed hard, shook his head and continued on his path, phone to his ear as he exited the room. I was left in the cold space with nothing but silence and misery hanging around my head like a thick fog.

*He doesn't give a fuck about you. He never has. Do it now.*

I stumbled to the bathroom. The knife he used to carve the names into my skin would be in the cupboards under the sink.

Finding it in amongst the towels, I thought to grab one of those too, and wrapped it around my body. I wasn't sure who was going to find me, and thought that even though I'd be dead, I still didn't want to be found naked on the chance one of my friends walked in.

The tub was cold against my upper spine as I settled into the empty space. I made quick work of key veins, poking the point of the blade under the skin of my wrists, my thighs and at my neck before tossing the knife across the room. It tumbled over the stone tiles to settle somewhere beside the shower behind me.

The warmth of the blood was my only comfort as it drained from my body, making the porcelain tub a little less icy under my bare legs. I tried not to smile at the thought of Eric being the one to find me later.

Leaning back and resting my head on the bath's high edge, I noticed that stars had started to dance before my eyes. Darkness bled into my peripherals, slowly at first, swirling like a fog before it consumed my vision entirely – just as it often seemed to before I blacked out.

*Happy anniversary, Eric.* I closed my eyes, grateful it would be our last.

"And then what happened?" Dr. Lindsey asked, a grim look on her face as her notebook balanced on her lap, barely touched as she carefully observed me.

"Then I woke up in Eric's bed a few hours later. Untouched. Well, dressed in pajamas of sorts but not touched in any other way."

I'd been dragged from the bathroom, cleaned up and stitched, bandaged and tucked beneath silk sheets. The Surgeon stood above me, looking absolutely devastated over my actions.

Eric sat at my side with a hand on my leg, waiting for me to wake up.

"And Eric's reaction?"

"Genuine relief to see that I was alive. He asked a lot about how I was feeling."

"And… how *were* you feeling, having survived that?"

"It's going to sound fucked up." I warned her with a sad smile, "But I felt a bizarre sense of… relief? I felt normal, for a bit. Like what I'd done had taken my craziness away, and I was able to function again for a little while."

With each passing year at Home, Eric dragged me further into the deep end of his all-consuming insanity. He often darkly joked about killing himself in hopes it would finally clear his mind so he could start anew. For most of our relationship I'd wished he would find a way to do that, in hopes he'd return the man I fell so hard for.

Maybe that's what I almost did.

# FORTY

LOGAN

## APRIL 11TH

"I'm working at a club tonight!" Summer said with an excited bounce as she put makeup on in her bathroom.

"Really?" I asked, trying to sound surprised while I rolled my hands down her back to grab her hips, giving them a tight squeeze. I slapped her ass while she leaned over the sink and turned back to the wardrobe; an attempt to control myself around her. If I touched her any more than that, I'd be tempted to take off what little she had on. Then we'd both be late. I'd make sure of it.

"How was that?"

"Hmm. A seven. At most," she mumbled, concentration shifting back to working on her eyes after rolling them with a grin at my reflection.

How was I meant to respond to the news of her job for the night?

She'd been doing this a lot since I got her safely out of Crave. Little words or looks over the last two months of us trying to live our secret lives in each other's presence.

So many invitations for me to expose my secrets. But I wasn't taking any of them.

She had no doubt read about what I was by now, and all of the horrific things I was capable of. She didn't need the confirmation that she was dating a murderer. Even if all of my jobs were justified.

I didn't just kill and move on, I destroyed and displayed. It was the opposite to what she did for a living. Summer deserved better than me, and I didn't want her to work that out.

*Would she ever sleep next to me or with me again if I actually confirmed it all? Would hearing it directly from me be too much?*

"Trialing something new." She was back on topic, not letting me out of this conversation so easily, "Maybe I'll do it more often if it works out."

Dropping hints about Crave was her boldest move yet, but still, I wasn't going to bite.

*At least, not anything but her neck.*

I eyed her from behind for a few seconds longer, noting the freshly bruised impressions from my teeth before grabbing one of my shirts from the walk-in. Leaving her marked gave me a little relief, though it wouldn't mean shit at a place like Crave.

"Working the poles?" I called from the bedroom while I dressed to leave, hoping I'd piss her off enough to stop her tempting me for one day.

It worked.

"What? No! I'll be *helping people*," she stormed out of the bathroom and poked me in the chest, adorably mad that I'd ever suggest my little nurse wouldn't be there to work her magic, "Tending to injuries. All that amazing shit I do on the daily."

"Hope it goes well. I gotta get going." I checked my phone for the time, "See you when I get home?" I bit my lip, hard.

*Shit, I nearly said it.*

Wasn't it the perfect time? Saying "I love you" after a goodbye seemed like the natural follow up. Still, it didn't quite feel right with me leaving to dress in disguise for a night of lies.

"Sure." Summer said, still glaring, but then broke the act to step up on her toes to kiss me.

"Babe?" She called as I rounded the doorway. I leaned back to look at her, and could feel the warmth from her blush across the room. She chewed at her tongue before settling on, "Say hi to your friends for me."

*That wasn't what she wanted to say.*

"Okay, nurse."

It was a typical Friday at the club; busy, too loud, and late by the time we got there. The gang and I had gotten caught up following another lead on Echo.

When nothing came from our information, we were all feeling pretty fucking low and had planned on heading to Crave anyway to keep an eye on Summer. My friends were growing more desperate to include her, always arguing that she was already one of us. They wanted her to know their own identities. But I couldn't let them.

We sat in our usual booth on the edge of the dance floor. When I picked my spot on the couch I brushed traces of white powder onto the floor, caught in the fabric instead of up someone's nose. I laughed at the thought of how upside down my life had become since leaving Bedlam. Ex-cop, now villain. I'd traded dusting for fingerprints to wiping cocaine from couch cushions.

The floor before us was full of bodies, and would only grow more crowded as it got later. Sitting between Nova and Jackie as Tommy fetched their drinks, I searched the room for my girlfriend. Summer wasn't outside by the time we'd arrived, but the van was still there. She'd finished up for the night and must have headed inside for a drink, but I hadn't seen her at the bar as we walked past.

*Fuck, I hope she's not upstairs.*

As I watched the crowd moving to another song that would no doubt be stuck on loop in my head for days, I wondered if she'd be spiking her drinks again. Would I be fucking Crave's nameless nurse when I got home? Or would I ruin her buzz by rejecting her if she were high. The pills seemed harmless, just strong relaxants that made her a little loopy.

Still, I didn't like the idea of her needing them to fuck me. That's *if* Summer was still taking them. If she were drugging herself at home, she was doing a good job of hiding it. Over our months together I'd kept a close eye on everything she did when things were looking to become physical between us. But here, without being able to see every move and hear every sound like I could in her house, I had no idea what the little nurse could be up to.

As one of my favorite songs started playing, I found her. On a fucking pole in the center of the floor. It was surely a punishment for my earlier comment.

Summer wasn't alone, there was another with her. I didn't know the other woman, but recognised her as one of the staff I'd seen on the odd occasion at the bar. They seemed to be getting along; laughing and spinning.

The taller woman had neatly braided hair, and her neon yellow makeup stood out in striking contrast to her skin. They were talking, but I was too far away to hear their conversation.

Nova leaned in to speak to me. "Will you go grab her off that pole and take her upstairs already?"

"What?"

"You're undressing Summer and eye-fucking her from here," she tipped her head in my peripheral, smiling at the way I couldn't tear my gaze from my girlfriend. "Do us all a favor and do it in private. At least before someone else does."

Her comment made my eye twitch. I couldn't just *go* to Summer. If I connected with her in any way in the club other than for medical attention, she'd have all the confirmation she needed.

It was bad enough I'd gotten Nova to slice me up to get into the van and confirm the nurse's identity.

And Tommy, taking an impressive hit at my stomach with a bottle of whatever the fuck we'd found at the abandoned shed after I'd made quick work of Alan, all in order for me to work up the guts to talk to Summer and make things right between us.

*God, what the fuck is wrong with me?*

All these lies and secrets made me feel so immature. I couldn't believe the roundabout ways I was trying to communicate with someone I slept beside every night. I'd never acted like this in the past.

*I might have been better at keeping secrets back then. Or could this be some kind of self-sabotage, and I really do want her to know?*

"Admit it, Logan," Nova spoke so softly that only I could hear her, "She'd fit in perfectly with us."

A lump formed in my throat as I watched Summer lift herself up on the pole, mesmerized by her sloppy moves.

What started as the hot little nurse being a good distraction to get me through the long and lonely hours of the late night shift had quickly turned into so much more. She picked on me as good as I gave it to her. She was funny, sarcastic, she swore a lot, but I never would have guessed things could get *this* intense between us. I'd fallen for her faster than she stitched people up.

We'd already endured and survived things that would have made others give up on the idea of being together. The thought of including her in the vigilante life my friends and I led was quickly pulled from the table.

While I didn't feel like I had to pretend *too much* around Summer, I couldn't drag her down into this hellish existence with me. Not when she was still trying so hard to escape the clutches of her own personal demons from the past.

Aside from not telling my girlfriend about being Gifted, I was able to share more about myself than I had ever bothered with anyone else since I met my wife. But just like Summer, I'd never shared all my secrets with Millie. Maybe it was the reason we lasted so long… Maybe it was the reason she died.

Either way, Nova had been accusing me of not learning from my mistakes of the past, but this wasn't one of them. My girlfriend was human, and I needed to protect her from all that posed a threat to her fragile life – my secrets included.

The other woman stepped down from the pole's platform, leaving Summer spinning by herself. Another tick sparked in my mind as I watched her move. She wasn't as hopeless as I'd been led to believe. Just when I thought I had most of Summer figured out, I'd see something new, and she'd have my mind spinning – much like she was on that piece of metal.

*I wonder how many hours she's spent on a pole to work that out?*

She leaned back, looking relaxed under her mask as she stretched, only holding on with her legs.

*I'm never gonna be able to listen to this song again without wishing I were that pole.*

Summer suddenly flipped herself right-way up and made eyes with someone on the floor.

This place had weird rituals, and I'd watched this happen plenty of times. If someone on a pole made enough eye-contact with another, they'd disappear together. Off to play out what their boring lives wouldn't allow them to do at home.

A large man by the bar had caught her attention. She moved directly to him through the crowd before they made their way to the stairs.

It was one of her bodyguards.

*This is a fucking joke, right?* I tensed at the sight of him wrapping an arm around her shoulders.

She must have known I was there, and was messing with my head to force me to reveal my identity. I had to admit, it was tempting. Though, it'd likely be through the means of removing someone's limbs, and I didn't think she'd appreciate me murdering her staff.

"Are you going to–" Nova started, throwing her arms up after watching my girlfriend leave with another man.

"Yes, I'm *fucking going*, Nova." I snapped, already moving to stand.

I kept my distance as I followed the pair, allowing them to get out of sight so they wouldn't see me if they looked over their shoulders. My hearing easily picked up their movements – her heels alongside his heavy footsteps. I could sense which direction they turned at the top of the stairs and the paths they took through the hallways.

My heart raced as my Gift kicked in. With each step, I moved more silently across the floor, stalking them down a hall filled with doors at either side. I would never have thought she and either of the bodyguards were interested in each other, and tried to come up with a plan to confront her. But it all felt so wrong.

*What am I doing here, anyway? Invading her privacy? Catching her cheating?*

My blood burned hot as I reached the door Summer and the man had closed behind them. It wasn't like the others, this one was sturdier and labeled "staff."

There was no need to lean on the timber to hear the noises coming from the other side. The music downstairs was loud, anyone without Gifted hearing would have needed to go into the room to hear their voices, but I heard plenty from my place in the hall.

"Oh my god!" Summer exclaimed through what sounded like tears. Her voice instantly had me on edge at the thought he might be hurting her, whether she wanted him to or not.

"He looks *exactly* like his dad!" she gasped.

*Well, that's a fucking odd thing for her to say to the bodyguard.*

"Isn't he perfect?" said another woman's voice, also emotional.

While I had no idea what I was spying on, I felt confident enough to conclude that Summer probably wasn't fucking her bodyguard. But curiosity got the better of me, and I moved closer to lean my shoulder on the frame with my eyes closed.

"How old is he now?" Summer asked.

"He'll be two in three months."

I could hear a child. The sound wasn't clear, likely videos being played on someone's phone. That was confirmed when the exact noises were repeated over again.

The tightness in my shoulders eased at the relief that no one had actually brought a minor into Crave. Even this place, fucked as it may be, was still strict with admitting only those of drinking age. The idea of what a young mind would witness in the club would be enough for Vengeance to redecorate some of these rooms.

"Thank you for showing me," Summer said, her voice somber.

"It was the least I could do–"

"The *least* you could do is *leave* and never come back." Summer interrupted. They laughed, and a man did too.

*The bodyguard? Is she not completely safe with this woman?*

Without more information, I couldn't work out if this were a friendly relationship. The only people Summer had introduced me to were Tony and Ben. As far as I knew, she had no other friends and still made weekly, unanswered calls to her family.

"Do you think you'll have any of your own? Ben told me you were dating!" the woman probed. It was a polite enough question on the surface, but from my past experiences and Summer's recent loss, I knew it was usually answered lightly to hide the hurt.

Summer politely responded, "Maybe. I don't know. I can't though, not after what happened. Losing *them* was too much."

*Losing them? Who? Does Summer want a family of her own one day? I can't make that happen.*

My mouth suddenly turned dry. Did Summer not mean it? All those times she'd reassured me that the news of her body's repair hadn't changed her stance on wanting kids? What would that mean for our future?

As the women said their goodbyes I took it as my cue to vanish. I didn't want to be caught eavesdropping, unable to think of a good enough excuse to be spying on Summer. I wasn't supposed to know the identity of the nameless nurse in the first place.

I ducked into a vacant room across the hallway and closed the door. It wasn't as well made as the staff door, no one seemed to give a shit if noise traveled in the halls. The music blocked enough of the sounds people made in this place.

Still, Gifted ears picked up on too much. Mine, more than anyones.

The space before me was no bigger than my bedroom. A neatly made, seemingly-clean bed to one side, small armchairs with a low table between them on the other. Everything was dark, shades of grays and blacks. Purposely chosen to hide the assortment of bodily fluids that would be spilled onto the fibers. It seemed a pretty standard, safe room in comparison to what I'd heard Crave provided in other areas for its clientele.

*I'd hate to see what a UV light could reveal in here. I'd bet anything it would light up like a cave full of fucking glowworms.* I tried not to touch anything. If I could have, I would have levitated to avoid the carpet beneath my feet.

Summer's footsteps sounded outside, along with Tony's or Ben's as I folded my arms and I focused on their voices. The other woman had mentioned Ben, but I couldn't be sure what time she spoke to him to gather her intel on my girlfriend.

"That went better than last time," the bodyguard sighed.

Summer stopped outside my door, and her steps changed direction as she turned to him.

"You'd hope so, considering I just gave her *four million dollars*," the pair laughed.

"Hey, that's not going to affect our pay, is it?"

*Definitely Ben.*

"Oh, shut up. As if I don't pay you enough already," she snorted before lowering her voice. "Why did you tell her about Logan?"

*She said it. My name. In Crave.* I felt like I'd won a bet with her having undeniably revealed her identity, but I couldn't do anything about it. What would I do? Pop out of the room and blow what remained of my rapidly deteriorating cover?

"Just making smalltalk. Besides, you sound more trustworthy with your name not attached to Eric, especially with Nessa."

"You've got me there," she admitted. "Hopefully, we won't see her for a while… I think we should leave. I'm still a bit drunk and dizzy. And the noises from these rooms are making me miss him."

The bodyguard laughed, "Keen to get home and play on a different pole?" The sounds of her heels and giggles leaving quickly down the hall left me in the dark room with more questions than answers.

Once they made their way downstairs, I left to get back to the gang. But not before someone else emerged from one of the rooms, closer to the stairs. Their gaze followed Summer and the bodyguard, now out of my sight, too focused on them to notice me creeping up from behind.

Pyro. Unmistakeable and unmissable in his stupid fucking suit. He leaned over the railing to catch one last glimpse at her. Unlucky for him, I was far quieter on my feet than any other Gifted I knew, and he *still* hadn't seen me coming from deeper down the hall.

There was something about the way he watched her move that I didn't like. If I were being honest, I didn't like the way *anyone* watched Summer move, but he seemed to be stalking her, like me.

*You realize how fucked up that is? Maybe I should push him over the railing.* I toyed with the idea, but settled instead for scaring the shit out of him.

"What are you doing up here?" I asked, causing him to startle and his heart rate to spike. He spun and crossed his arms defensively. He was a little taller than me, and well built from what the suit revealed as it clung tight to every inch of his frame, same as mine.

We'd be a good match, physically, if we were ever caught in a fight, but I could relax with the advantage of my fucked-up mind. If I needed to, I'd decimate him.

"Same as everyone else," he kept his tone even as I mimicked his stance. I couldn't see his expression behind the mask, but I could tell he was sizing me up, looking me over and assessing the danger like I'd already done with him.

It'd been years since I'd seen Pyro, barely catching glimpses of the suit as he, rightfully, tried to avoid me at all costs after what went down in Bedlam.

He shrugged, "Found an easy fuck."

I didn't like the insinuation that he thought I'd spent time in the rooms, but I couldn't correct him. What was I supposed to say? That I was there to spy on my girlfriend who had just left with another man?

There were plenty of rumors about Vengeance, most of them true. And I was happy to let them circulate for my reputation's sake, but I didn't like the idea of adding "cuck" to the list of things I allegedly was.

"You got a thing for the nurse?" I tipped my head to the stairs, keeping Pyro's attention so she could safely leave Crave while I figured out what the fuck he wanted with *my* little nurse.

*Probably the same as anyone else would want with someone like Summer in a place like this.*

His deep laugh surprised me, "Nah. I'm not dumb enough to get involved with the likes of her."

"The fuck is that supposed to mean?" I demanded a little too defensively for someone who wasn't meant to know her at all.

Pyro looked at me for a few seconds longer than I felt was normal. I couldn't read his face to see what he thought of my clipped reaction.

"If she is who I think she is… she's a troublemaker." He turned to take the stairs down to the bar and called over his shoulder, "You might want to ease up on the cologne, man. I could smell you coming from a mile away."

*Right*, I rolled my eyes, *If that were the case, I wouldn't have been able to sneak up on you.*

I didn't stop him from leaving. I didn't push him for answers. It would have only given him leverage over me if he knew I gave a shit about Summer and her past.

"You good?" Nova raised her eyebrows above the edge of her mask upon my return to the couch.

"Yep," I said absentmindedly, sinking into the cushions beside her.

"Take your nurse upstairs and give her that little needle of yours?" she laughed and took a sip from her tall glass.

I shot her a look that she couldn't see, but she knew me well enough to know it was there.

"Clearly not!" she rolled her eyes, "You wouldn't be in such a terrible mood if you had."

I ignored her while I replayed pieces of the exchange upstairs.

*Where would Summer get four million dollars? Was she paying the other woman off?*

There were too many questions I couldn't ask.

*This is what you get for not being honest with her.*

We left an hour after Summer and the bodyguards. It gave her time to play pretend. To get home, undress from what she'd worn at the club and to be waiting for me to return from my night out with friends.

With my suit stashed in my car on the street, I was ready to play the role of "regular boyfriend."

# FORTY-ONE

## LOGAN

Summer greeted me at the door in her pajamas, an oversized shirt and tight shorts. Her hair was still damp from showering away any traces of Crave.

"Work went well," she said as she let me in. "How's the gang?"

I wasn't in the mood for her games or questions. Seeing her playing around on the pole, giggling with the other woman, taking her bodyguard upstairs – though nothing happened between them – it all made my stomach scorch with jealousy.

With every ounce of my being, I *hated* that I had the intense urge to lock Summer away, where she would be mine to play with, forever. The thought of her with anyone else was enough to drive me more insane than I already was.

I knew it was unhealthy. And while I liked to blame the darker parts of my subconscious for my insecurities and the danger they posed when I got out of control, it was something I was aware I should have been working on.

Things between us had moved fast after our night in the hallway. She'd clearly pushed aside any remaining reservations about what she thought she knew about me.

Over the last two months, we'd spent more time breathing heavily and sweating over each other than talking, save the week she spent recovering from my cursed collateral.

Having had my share of intimate partners before and after my marriage, I thought I knew myself well enough to not be surprised by what Summer brought to the bedroom – and everywhere else she'd have me.

Summer had known no more than three positions – trained to *take it*, not participate. But I couldn't have that. I needed that same fire, determination and stubbornness she showed with everything else she set her mind to. And once she understood that, that she meant more to me than just someone to fuck and dump loads in, and that I wasn't going to disappear when I was done with her, she'd become more relaxed.

The little nurse was mesmerizing, though desperate to get things right to please me. It was a habit she'd brought from her past. I hated its origin, and quickly brought balance to the fears of inexperience and inadequacy with the praise and affection she deserved and seemed to *crave* from me.

I'd watched as she grew more confident in her body and with mine, using my dick, my hands, and my mouth as tools in whatever new ways she was willing to explore.

My new favorite thing was to let her get herself close to coming, then taking over when her moans and her cool body on mine became too much for me. I'd take the reins to throw her over our finish line. Not literally, though, she wasn't opposed to being tossed around when I got carried away.

The thought of anyone else seeing this side to her after the months of work we'd put in together brought out that dark, possessive side of me that tiptoed the edge of my blackouts. Only there was no one to kill; just the jealous rage I needed to restrain, hoping I could keep it from destroying what we had.

As the front door closed behind me I asked, "Is it just us, Summer?"

She glanced over her shoulder at the lightless hallway, brows pulling together as she looked up at me, "Umm, well I'd hope so, considering how much effort I put into ensuring this place can't be broken into."

I couldn't hold back the sigh at her unbearably innocent response, "That's not what I meant. Are there *other people?* Or is it just us?"

She registered my meaning that time, and her posture slouched as though my question were actually a confession, "God, Logan. I assumed once you asked me out that things were exclusive between us."

"It has been on my end."

"Mine too."

"At this rate, I don't think there ever could be anyone else." I spoke my thoughts by mistake, but didn't mind her hearing that if it meant I could banish the idea of me being unfaithful that I hadn't intended on planting in her mind.

"Really? I've got that much of a hold on you? Ruined you for anyone else?" The playful questions tumbled from her mouth as her heart skipped a beat.

*You have no idea, little nurse...*

I pushed Summer's shoulders with my fingers, not so much that it hurt, but enough for her to take a step back. I pushed her again, angling her closer to the bedroom door. The look in her eyes instantly changed from mild concern at my actions to complete understanding.

"Get on the bed." I demanded, voice low as I towered over her.

My mood instantly lightened when more of the tipsy giggles I'd heard earlier in the night escaped her lungs and she ran for the room.

Within seconds we were undressed and Summer was on her back, pulling on the arms she loved so much until I was on top of *and* inside her. It hadn't taken many fucks between us for her to gain comfort in stripping down with me. I'd quickly become attuned to her needs, and she'd done the same in return.

Every inch of her bare skin's friction on mine created a sensation I could only liken to striking a match. Exhilarating. Dangerous.

"Harder, baby. *Please!*" She wrapped her legs around my hips as I moved, gasping against my shoulder as her back arched. A hand grabbed at the nape of my neck while the other clawed at my back when I hit all the spots that got her moaning.

"Fuck, Logan! Don't you dare stop!"

My fingers dug deep into soft flesh as I lifted her ass off the bed to support her weight as I upped the speed. "Jesus, Summer, I'm gonna need to stop if you keep that shit up!"

I could have come from her noises alone — always sounding as though she were on the verge of pained cries, whining for me to fuck that pussy *harder* and begging to have it overflowing with my cum. But I couldn't. At least, not to the extent I wanted to. I constantly needed to remind myself as I got close that Summer was *human*. Fragile.

It didn't help that she knew how much I loved hearing her moan. The way she wrapped my name on her tongue with the sounds of her pleasure as it passed through her lips had my eyes threatening to permanently roll back.

Her voice carried a desperation for my touch like no one else had ever shown. I was yet to decide if it were everything I could hope for, or if it were my imagination playing into the fact that I had a dire *need* to be wanted by her. In either case, it made for a dicey combination that no good could come from. I was bound to hurt her eventually, either through rough sex or by removing these limbs, tied tight around my waist and gripping my arms.

There was *something* about Summer. She might have looked like a zombie most of the time, but the woman radiated with a weird kind of life I was instantly drawn to.

I'd said it before, and thought it a million times – I just couldn't put my finger on what it was that made her so unique. Figuratively speaking, of course, though my fingers had explored every inch of her in my search for answers.

People speak of sparks, like lightning or static when they make a physical connection with someone for the first time. With her, I'd experienced something similar. A magnetic pull since the moment I'd held her hand to help her out of the booth at work. A subtle hum. An addictive energy.

Tommy, the avid truth teller, had cautiously admitted he understood how I felt about her when I tried to describe it to him. He agreed she was different, and had a buzzing air about her that he couldn't explain. And though I knew he'd never act on it, his confession ignited the switch at the base of my brain that had me yearning to eliminate any competition, best friend included.

The inside of my head may have been a fucking disaster, but I knew I wasn't insane with feeling these particular possessive instincts. I'd observed the way the bodyguards looked at her. It wasn't lust they had, but a pure desire to protect when they were in her immediate presence.

Nova had made comments too, though she'd fuck anything with a heartbeat if given the chance. Jackie was too smart to share her thoughts, not wanting to set me off.

There was enough evidence across the board that Summer had a bizarre, gravitational draw on those around her. It was inescapable, and I was completely captivated.

As my dick was still rearranging her organs, she cried, "Harder!" and fuck, *how could you say no to that?*

Caving as I gave her a little more of what she wanted, I warned, “Any harder and I’ll split you in half.”

“Do it!” She giggled, taunting me. Tempting me.

*You fucking tease. You know why I can’t.*

This woman’s death certificate wouldn’t be adorned with any of my usual means of killing. If she asked again, “Fucked to pieces” would be her cause of death.

I nudged her knees with my elbows, encouraging her to drop them further to her sides. She resisted, another taunting grin smeared across her pretty face. I squeezed her a little harder, melting that smug look right off her features.

“Come on, baby,” my tone was equally taunting, calling her bluff as her eyelids fluttered closed, “You can take it.”

Of course she could, I had her wetter than the hosed-down concrete after one of my kills, and that wasn’t the concern here. Once I started driving *that* deep she knew she was out of time. My thrusts, combined with rubbing her swollen clit would have her coming when she’d rather drag out the experience.

I was never far behind, made more turned on by the fact Summer told me she’d once done everything in her power for her sexual encounters of the past to be over with as fast as possible.

She didn’t understand what that did to me, to my mind. It only gave way to more primal thoughts – that she was *mine*, and only I could make her feel this way.

With a breathy moan, she spread wide.

I bit my tongue at the sight of her on display for me.

*God-fucking-dammit! I will slaughter those fucking bodyguards for putting the urge to call her a good girl in my head.*

I clenched my jaw until I tasted blood. Summer probably couldn’t hurt me all that much if I slipped up. If anything, I was more worried I’d blurt out that I loved her or something equally and unfathomably cringeworthy that’d have her drying up and running for her life; like proposing during sex.

“*Fuck*,” I groaned, “you’re so fucking beautiful.”

She smiled, but couldn’t form a response. She loved compliments, but would only accept them for her clothes and hair. So I made the difficult point of holding out until she was naked to give them to her.

"God, *Logan!*" Her voice was strained as though she were balancing on the edge, one thrust away from rushing headfirst into the depths of diversion.

The light from the hall blazed painfully bright as my pupils widened rapidly with the thrill of bringing her pleasure. My senses quickly adapted and I focused solely on her, writhing beneath me. She sucked in a sharp breath – the cue she was there.

"Come for me, nurse." I demanded in a low growl, closing my eyes for just a second to revel in the moment she began rhythmically tightening around my dick. I opened them again to observe the veins pulsing at her neck and in her wrists as her heart thundered louder behind her tits.

She squeezed her eyes shut, bit her lip and spread those legs wider, releasing the hold on my hips so I could move with longer strokes and a little more force.

"Let go of that lip, baby" I ordered, "You don't have neighbors." She did, but not for miles. And I wanted them to hear her.

The way Summer obeyed had me aching to release the load she was dying to feel inside her. I wasn't much into bossing anyone around in bed, but it was fun with her. She trusted my ideas and direction were safe and almost entirely for her benefit.

*Her lips are turning blue.*

"*Breathe*." She always needed reminders to *fucking breathe* as if the motions didn't come naturally to her. Maybe she was waiting for permission. Either way, I wasn't going to deny her oxygen or myself the way my cock twitched at the sharp, shuddering inhale she took as her short nails raked my chest.

The unrestrained sounds of her climax made me grab her tighter, fuck her harder. The chorus of short breaths dissolved my mood, melting the jealousy and banishing the darkness that would always threaten to take her from me.

It almost felt wrong to have such an intense affect on another being. The good kind of wrong. So long as I kept the number of kills down, I had an almost boundless amount of strength and stamina by comparison. Both of which I used wholly to my advantage, making Summer's mind unravel and limbs tremble with a euphoria she'd never find with a normal human.

The sight of her enjoying me so much had me so close to coming, and she knew it.

"Your turn?" Her eyes widened excitedly. To my relief, her pupils reacted exactly as they should.

*Three out of ten. Should have checked that before we started.*

"Nah, I'm not done with you yet, nurse." I pulled out, admiring her lazy smile as she recovered from what would have undoubtedly been one of the best orgasms I'd given her.

*So far.*

I flipped her over so fast she giggled at the head rush as I slowly slid back in. She arched again, up towards me this time.

Thrusting through her gasp, I wiped the flow of sweat from my brow with the back of my hand. A pointless move, as always, it was instantly replaced with more.

Summer let out more of the sounds I lived for, partially muffled by her face being pushed into the sheets. I gripped around her ribs with hands that wanted nothing more than to *squeeze* and she groaned from the pressure between my palms, burying her face further into the bedding.

But I needed to hear more. I wanted her pleasured screams to be the warning that she now had a standard no one else could hope to match. I let go to grab both of her arms, pulling them together in my firm grip at her back to lift her. Not quite hard enough to hurt her as I moved, but tight enough to ensure I wouldn't send her flying over the edge of the bed.

Out of all the new things she'd been so willing to test out with our bodies, I'd never restrained her movements in *this* position.

Apparently there was a reason for that.

Her noises suddenly cut off.

I froze between motions and asked, "Is this okay? Summer?"

No response.

I pulled out again and rolled her over. She immediately tried to cover her face.

"Did I hurt you?" I hovered over her with my hands on the bed at either side of her body, not touching her until she gave me any sign she was okay. I worried for a moment that my Gifted strength had in fact, dialed up while I was too busy enjoying the feeling of her to notice. "Baby, this is why we have a safe word. If *anything* becomes too much, you *need* to use it."

"I know. It's nothing. I'm fine."

I dropped to lean back against the pillows, giving her as much space in the bed as I could while I caught my breath and she wiped away tears.

"You're *not* fine. Please don't lie to me." Rich, coming from me, and I knew it. "Tell me what's wrong?"

She sat up and grabbed the sheets, roughly bunching them around her body. Whatever changed her mood had also snatched away some of that confidence we'd worked so hard on. She wiped more tears away with her fingers as I placed my hand on her sheet-covered leg, relieved when she didn't push me away.

"I think I… got a bit distracted. Mom didn't answer again and… I saw someone at my job tonight that brought up a lot of things I don't really let myself think about."

My heart sank as I recalled the conversation I'd eavesdropped on.

*She wants a family. You can't give that to her. And she'd know exactly why if she's worked out you're Gifted.*

Summer would often become lost in her head, and in the times I pried her away from her paralyzing thoughts, she'd tell me that she hoped her parents and brothers were safe. They didn't deserve her worry for them – not after Jackie filled me in on what she'd found. I didn't want Summer to learn they were ignoring her calls, but it didn't feel right to hide that. I let Jackie break the news when she insisted, reminding me that I was already keeping enough secrets from Summer.

*Does she cling to the idea of finding them because we can't make a family? Is that why she's covered up?*

My eyes flickered lower. Her stomach and the marks from non-consensual surgeries were always the first to be hidden. Some days they seemed to bother her around me more than the ones on her back.

What made this whole situation so much more agonizing was that Summer was ovulating. Years of helping Millie track her cycles and reading temperatures meant I should have known better. Summer's body barely changed by a degree, but to someone who spent so much time inside her, she might as well have been on fire.

I'd completely overlooked the signs last time, believing that getting her pregnant was entirely impossible.

I barely allowed myself to think about the miscarriage. It hurt too much, and I'd only sensed it secondhand. Invasive images often entered my head; of how I'd held Summer for hours with my chest pressed against her back, my scolding palm on her lower abdomen.

Weeks later, I could still sense phantom contractions like those that had trembled beneath my hand when pain ripped through my little nurse's body and she lost more blood from our incompatible creation being expelled.

*It's a good thing I didn't finish. The last thing we need are more reminders that I can't give her everything she deserves.*

"My mind… slipped… somewhere else… I…" she started out alright, but suddenly wasn't able to speak between uncontrolled breaths.

"Hey, hold up. Stop talking." I gripped her arms tight. "You're starting to panic."

I recognised the sound immediately. Between me and the others in the group, we'd had our share of horrific experiences that led us all to feel the same. The most recent being Jackie, when I held her hand as we identified the body of her wife.

"I'll get you some water." I rushed from the room, throwing on my boxers and a shirt as I made my way down the hall, trying to make myself useful. As far as I knew, there was nothing I could do to help Summer as she sunk into wherever her mind wanted to hold her hostage. But I could sit it out beside her.

I returned to the bedroom, only to find it empty. A quick glance through the wardrobe where the bathroom light was shining revealed she'd replaced her underwear and bra. From behind, I watched Summer inspect her reflection before opening the large, hinged mirror. It revealed what appeared to be a very well-stocked bathroom cabinet. No surprise, knowing her.

But she didn't seem to have the strength to grab what she needed, and placed her hands back down by the sink. She swayed on her feet for a moment, then leaned against the wall beside the toilet, unable to hold herself up.

I was at her side, bracing her weight to soften the fall before her ass hit the tiles. The bathroom wasn't huge, but had proven *many* times it could accommodate the both of us.

As I kneeled in front of her with the shower to my back, I put the bottled water down and held her damp face, lifting it to mine to check her eyes and listen to her pulse. Her staggered breaths made it sound like she was drowning as she cried and struggled to breathe.

"What can I do?" I asked quietly, feeling absolutely useless while she fell apart in front of me.

"I feel like… I'm going… to pass out…"

"That's okay, I'm here. I'm not going to let anything happen to you. Maybe I should take you to the bed." I moved in to lift her.

"No!" She pushed my hands away. "I need my meds… They're above the sink." I jumped up to the cabinet and frantically looked at the bottles for anything I recognised, finding one containing the same pills she'd taken the night I stitched her up. They seemed to work well then. "Not those ones… there's a different… bottle… and syringes."

I shot her a confused look as her eyes pleaded for my help from below. It sounded far more serious than any anti-anxiety meds I knew about for a standard panic attack.

When I found the bottle, I dropped back to the floor. It was the only one in the cabinet needing a syringe to access the clear liquid it contained. There was no name or ingredients, just the dosages and Summer's notes.

"Right, zero point eight coming up." I said confidently after squinting without the help of my glasses to read the numbers on the label.

"No, no, do *three* point eight," she demanded, squeezing her eyes shut, thumbs pressed into her temples and knees tucked up to her chin.

"Are you out of your *fucking mind?*" The words escaped with no filter. I didn't like mind games at the best of times, and certainly wasn't in the mood for her to be messing with me with something so dangerous.

I read the bottle again.

"In your notes, your *own* words, it states that three point eight is literally point two of a mil away from an overdose." I pointed to exactly what I was seeing. My eyesight may have been fucked, but I was sure I was reading it correctly. She didn't open her eyes, she only nodded. "I can't do that, Summer." I couldn't be having sex with her one minute and injecting her with unknown substances the next.

*What if this kills her?*

Obviously, part of me was worried about how that would make me look, my girlfriend showing up dead and covered in the DNA of a man who was *also* meant to be dead. But *most* of me wanted to know what this meant for us moving forward. Would this become part of our routine? I needed to know what caused such a massive meltdown so we wouldn't end up in the same position again.

*It was the position that got you here in the first place.*

I glanced at the bed and tried to think back to what we were doing that set off the whole ordeal to begin with.

"Then give it to me!" she snatched the bottle and tried to read the measurements on the syringe in her trembling hand.

I snatched it back, "God, at least let me measure it if you're so sure this won't fucking kill you! Arm or leg?"

I took a deep breath, mentally preparing to jab her. I couldn't recall a time where I'd injected anyone with a syringe other than Summer when I stitched her up, and I hadn't liked having to do it then either. Millie had handled the innumerable IVF injections on her own, thinking I couldn't stomach it. In reality, it was the guilt that made me sick; putting her through so much, when deep down, I knew the outcome we chased would always be impossible.

Summer ripped the needle from my hand and instantly buried the point into the side of her neck.

I watched with shock as she squeezed her eyes shut tight, pushing the end of the syringe for the liquid to disappear beneath her skin.

I roughly grabbed her jaw, tipping her face to mine. She flinched at the sudden move and tried to knock my hand away, but I didn't budge, too focused on her vitals and waiting for her to succumb to the effects of the unnamed poison.

*Fuck, I can't lose her.*

The unbearable thought had my pulse racing at an equal sprint to hers as I peered into her eyes, searching for even the smallest sign that she was about to leave me.

*Don't you dare fucking die on me, nurse.*

It took a moment for whatever it was to set in. Her breathing became steady again and she began looking around the room as if her vision was improving.

Something about my expression upset her.

"Your eyes," she whispered, her own welling up.

I knew exactly what she meant; the color change. The way black bled from the center to consume the warmth, replacing it with the cold stare of the killer.

Forget the poison. I was, and always would be the most dangerous thing in the room.

The benefit to having hazel eyes was that no one really thought too much about the changes. My friends knew better. And I never wanted Summer to experience the same terror they did when the changes kicked in. I blinked away from her gaze and my hold on her eased. She lifted both her cold hands, prying at my fingers with one while the other reached for my face.

"I'm sorry." I cleared my throat, annoyed that my fear took too strong a hold over my ability to be gentle with her.

"I'm gonna be okay," she reassured me, seeing right through me, "It wasn't fair to ask that of you."

"I think… this might be something we *need* to talk about."

"It's nothing. I'm fine," she said, perking up.

"What the fuck is this?" I held the bottle between us. Reading the label again for any sign of what it could contain.

"Something I made myself," she smiled proudly in her new state, but I was still catching up from what I'd just witnessed and couldn't share the feeling.

"That doesn't make me feel better *at all*," I told her honestly, pulling her up to stand with me."Get on the bed." The words held none of the same playfulness they'd carried when I'd come home.

She stumbled across the floor, propped up her pillows and slipped under the sheets, patting the space beside her for me to join as I switched off the bathroom light. I stood my ground at the end of the mattress, folding my arms in a bid to resist the woman I so desperately wanted to protect. What set off her mental descent enough for her to resort to shooting up to avoid the darkness?

"What's wrong?" she seemed upset that I wasn't eagerly jumping straight back into bed with her.

"You're fucking joking, right?"

The room was dark, still a few hours from the sun rising, but I could see the hurt my tone inflicted.

"I'm a little lost."

*That stuff must be fucking with her ability to think clearly. More than the pills.*

"Could that be because you've injected yourself with some mystery liquid?"

She giggled at me, mind no doubt having made its way back to the gutter. I shook my head at her.

"It's for when I'm at my worst and I can't get back. It's *only* for emergencies." I got the sense she was playing it down so that I wouldn't think this was so serious. But I wasn't buying it.

"What does it do?"

"Rips me right out of tunnel vision and panic attacks so I don't black out. It *acts like* a mild sedative to calm my body but it's also very much like a burst of adrenaline to keep me awake and alert. To… escape." She bit at her lip, gaze falling to her lap.

I rounded the bed, dropping to my knees on the carpet and reaching for her shaking hands. She clung to me so tight, like she was afraid I'd disappear. Was she embarrassed by this? Scared of how I could react?

"I was going to bring you back to bed. I would have kept you safe."

"I know. I'm sorry." Her silly mood had dissipated, and an air of sadness emitted from her slouch as she softly brushed her thumbs over my knuckles. "But I *can't* black out."

"Can't or won't?" I was trying to be patient with her. I believed this wasn't something she'd ever intended for me to see, and I didn't want to upset her into silence.

"Both." She answered truthfully.

*Don't start,* I warned myself. *If you start now you won't be able to stop and she'll end up dead.*

I closed my eyes as I asked my next question, hoping it'd be a strong enough barrier to give Summer the freedom to answer me on her own terms. "Baby, what are you trying to escape from?"

"*Him.*"

*That's not enough, little nurse. I need to know more.*

"What happens when you black out?" I probed, feeling like a cop again, only now I was questioning my girlfriend and I really hated having to do it.

"It's when I see them all. The faces of everyone I've let down. They hang around for a while before I wake up. Sometimes it's worse than that. Since I escaped… there's a shadow… talking to me. It's awful." A shiver tumbled down her spine. She cocked her head to the side, nodding towards her back as her eyes shone in the dark. "I'd always wake in his room. Sometimes, I'd get a new addition."

"Baby, help me understand how we got here." I didn't feel I was being unreasonable, I couldn't protect her if I didn't have enough information. "What set it off? You seemed fine, we were having fun?" I gestured to the bed, "I was, at least, I didn't mean for–"

"It's nothing to do with you!" She cut me off, roughly rubbing her eyes with her fingers. "You did *nothing* wrong, Logan. This is what I meant when I warned you about me having *problems* with sex. Something about the position brought up things I've tried to forget."

It suddenly made sense. The way she froze. The panic. The position had triggered a response. A flashback?

*That was the position he'd bind her in.*

My lungs burned. I took long breaths to settle my pulse, barely keeping the darkness from consuming my vision.

*I wonder if she knows she has PTSD?*

Summer often shared her small breakthroughs from therapy, but this might have been something her therapist knew she was too stubborn to accept.

"Why not take the other pills, the same ones you–" *Took in my apartment before I rejected you? Had in the spiked drink at the club?* "had in the garage when I stitched you up?"

*Good save, ten out of ten.*

"Yeah, *those* ones," she said snidely, making my self-appointed score feel a little too high for the tone she took with me. Both our covers were truly blown, but neither of us would admit it. "They're only good if I take them *before* I have sex. Gets me in a good headspace. Relaxed enough so it doesn't hurt so much. But since we've been doing *this,*" – she patted the space beside her again – "I actually haven't taken any."

"Any?" I climbed up to sit against the pillows, pulling her over to sit between my legs. I switched the bedside lamp on to get a better look at her skin.

"Nope. None," she smiled over her shoulder.

It was clearly something she was proud of, and I wished I could have felt happier for her. Summer was as broken as I was, and constantly exposed more of her pieces every time we were together. I wished I were better at returning the favor. She deserved better.

"Do I… *hurt* you?" I asked, suddenly worried that she still might actually *need* the pills, but wasn't taking them purely because I would reject her if I sensed she was drugging herself.

"Fishing for compliments, babe?"

"No." I rolled my eyes at her.

"Yes. But no. It's nothing I can't handle. I love it when you get a bit carried away," she softly giggled, voice turning quiet as she continued. "I started taking them soon after I was… initiated into the cult. I couldn't sleep with him without them. I'd be too tense. If I didn't take them, it'd hurt. Not the fun kind of 'not being able to walk properly the next day', you know?"

I had a vague idea of what she meant by that, and instantly felt bad for questioning her. I'd only wanted for her to be safe, not to make her feel like she needed to share the graphic details if she wasn't ready.

"I care about you, Summer." I spoke low against her ear, "I hope you'll trust me enough one day to not have to do any of these things." As I brushed my fingers down the length of her arm she took my hand and I squeezed hers. The intense warmth in mine transferred to her cold fingers. "It's easy to see that they're all names." I looked over the scars again, mostly visible with her wearing only a bra.

I'd seen them plenty of times, but always averted my eyes. It was a difficult thing to do, removing my gaze when all I wanted to do was take in every inch of her.

But they hurt to look at, and morbid curiosity had to wait until I was done watching my dick be consumed by one of the few parts of my girlfriend's body that held any warmth.

The question constantly ate at my mind; Why would a woman have so many men's names hacked into her skin?

And it wasn't just names. There were numerous jagged lines from where a blade impaled her shoulder. And another I wasn't willing to mention; a small circular divot to the left of her spine, level with her heart. It couldn't be what I thought it was.

I knew it'd break her heart and confidence if I alluded to how much they disturbed me. They weren't repulsive at all, they were only marked skin. But the thought of the pain she'd endured turned my stomach; me, the guy who'd detached his share of digestive tracts.

I'd seen people die of lesser injuries to hers. I'd slaughtered people with less violence. I couldn't imagine someone like Summer could ever do anything worthy of being treated so terribly.

*She's a criminal. I still don't know everything she's done.*

I needed to remind myself of that fact frequently, often forgetting my girlfriend wasn't meant to be alive after those first confessions, months ago.

I lightly kissed the back of her neck, brushing my lips over her shoulder and some of the scars. "I'm guessing they're not notches in your belt?"

"No," she laughed, then her head dropped, "They're the names of people whose deaths I played a part in."

I hated not giving her a choice but to admit it. But with everything she shared with me, the more her story came together.

Whatever Summer injected herself with made her more talkative than normal, I needed to get out what I could while I had the chance and she had the freewill to do so without any added influence from me.

"So, Eric carved the names… Did… Did *you* kill these people?"

*Is she far more like me than I realized?*

"No. I'm a nurse. I don't intentionally *hurt people*. They died because… I couldn't save them." She lifted her face to blink back more tears.

"To punish you, then?"

"I deserved it," she whispered after a pause.

"No. There's no fucking way anyone deserves something like *this*." When she didn't say anything, I kept pushing, "The last two are still clear. And their surnames are the same. Were they related? Daniel Reyes and Michael Reyes?"

She leaned forward with her chest to her knees and I gently traced their names with my fingers, hoping the touch would remind her that her body wasn't doomed to be treated horrifically forever.

"They died the day I escaped. It was the tipping point."

"Do you want to tell me about it?"

She'd mentioned "escape" in the past when talking about leaving the "cult." Whatever happened that day was something she held onto deep inside, flinching whenever parts of it tried to resurface.

"I've only told the bodyguards about what happened that day. They've helped with the panic attacks in the past. Tony especially. He's spent almost as much time in this bed as you have," she giggled and turned to read my expression. "To make sure I was okay," she reassured me, knowing I was pathetic enough to need to hear it. "I can't even talk about these things in therapy without him being called to collect me."

"You know, I really do think you've been lying this whole time." I teased, banishing the mental image of the enormous bodyguard and my little nurse in bed together.

Her eyes widened, "What?"

"Everything I've learned about you, Summer. You still sound like you might actually be Gifted."

She laughed, but *fuck*, I wished it were true. "Ha! God help the world if I'm here to try to make it a better place."

"I'm serious." I said, though I was laughing too, "I bet you've got a badass origin story and everything." I was content enough with what she'd told me, and she didn't seem to be dying from the *mystery liquid*, so I pulled her into my arms and hugged her from behind, kissing the top of her head as she leaned into me. "How long before those meds will allow you to get some sleep?"

"*Hours*," she sighed, "What did you have in mind?"

My mind dashed to the table in the hall, but I wouldn't be touching her again now that I *knew* for certain she had drugs in her system. There were rules, and I stuck to them. We'd already been on the verge of crossing a major line the moment I walked in the door and she was still a little tipsy.

*Look at where that got us.*

I shook my head and swallowed over my nerves. What I was about to request could risk her death by my hands.

"I want to hear your origin story."

I wasn't giving her much of a choice, but things had now taken a more serious turn between us. If I were going to be a permanent part of Summer's life, she would have to share these things with me eventually, just as I hoped she would give me the chance to share all of my darkest moments if I could ever force myself to face them.

"Okay."

She rearranged herself to sit back on the pillows, eyes darting across the room as if the ghosts of the people she carried with her were appearing in the space around us.

"Wait there," I left the bed for the wardrobe and pulled my jacket from its hanger. After throwing it around her shoulders I waited until she pulled her arms through the sleeves before I zipped up the front.

"Sharing your security blanket again?" she tried to tease, but her lip quivered at the gesture.

"Something like that." I admitted, climbing into bed beside her.

Summer slipped beneath the covers and I followed as she rolled her body towards me. With the side of her face resting on my chest and my arm under her head, she pulled the blankets high around our bodies, sealing us in the space together.

She started by explaining how she met Eric at sixteen. After some prying, she admitted he was twenty-seven at the time. Even then, I could tell it wasn't the truth.

It made me glad I'd made a point of confirming her age before taking things further. The three year age-gap between us was far more reasonable than the ten-plus between them, especially with her still being a minor at the time he began grooming her.

She only ever referred to Eric by his first name. While I had the feeling he was much more than "Eric" the "cult leader." I could only push her so many times during a conversation like this, and I just wanted her to keep talking. Besides, if I had a name, I'd hunt for him like I'd hunted other deadly pharisees in the past. Maybe she knew that, so she left out small details.

*Small details, big lies.*

Like I could fucking talk. With most of what she knew about me being half-truths, I had no right to demand every awful detail of her past.

Though, not everything she told me was dark. Her mood lightened as she spoke of her training, her short time in college.

*Danny.*

If he were still alive I don't believe she would have ever given me a second glance on the night we met. I shouldn't have been jealous of a dead man, but she spoke so fondly of him. I was glad she had him in her life for a while. He seemed to be one of the only good things she had in the long years she was held captive.

She mentioned a surgeon who treated her like his own child, passing on all of his knowledge so she could be the very best in what seemed like Eric's collection of carefully chosen henchmen.

We came to a point in her story where she had no choice but to tell me about her last day at the place she referred to as "Home."

"I can't tell you what happened after that day, not yet." Her tone on the topic made me anxious that she might slip back into panic.

"That's alright," I held her tighter against my body. "Just tell me what you can."

I could feel the tears leaving her eyes, slipping across my skin. I wanted to kiss them away but had a feeling it helped her to not have to look directly at me as she shared her story.

She gave her face another wipe and tied her arms around my waist.

"A little over two years ago…"

# FORTY-TWO

## STITCH UP

### TWO YEARS EARLIER

I wiped the sweat from my forehead as I walked the hall of my floor. The ominous black building we called Home wasn't the tallest skyscraper in the heart of Bedlam City, but it certainly stood out.

I peered out the window-wall, my stomach giving me a warning backflip when I stepped too close to the edge. Having just finished my workout in the gym, my legs were still a little wobbly from the hour-long run, and while the glass separated me and the fall, the height always had me on edge.

I froze – startled by the obnoxious alarm in the ER. It echoed across the thirty-seventh floor, so loud my head filled with the ring. I wanted to tear my ears off to stop the pain shooting through my senses.

We weren't expecting any jobs, not that we really had proper days off, but an emergency in the daylight and at this time of the early evening was highly unlikely.

I picked up my pace. The ER was located at the other end of the floor, far from the gym and by the elevators so patients could be wheeled directly in to start our work without delay.

I almost ran straight past The Surgeon's room, but held my arm out just in time. I gripped the doorframe, pulling myself to a halt before leaning back to poke my head in. He was permitted a door, unlike me, but always left it propped open so I could come and go, to talk to and annoy him as I pleased.

"Hey, you hearing that? Or have your ears finally given out, old man?"

"Yes, I heard," he grumbled from the couch, his face buried in a book. "I ignore it. We had no work booked today."

The Surgeon was in his sixties and had lived in Bedlam for a fair amount of his adult life. While he didn't share much about his past with me, and as hard as he tried, I could tell his English was still a little broken at times.

"Well, we're both *fucked* if something big comes in and we're not ready for it."

"Such dirty language for a young lady," he laughed, standing to walk with me to the ER.

He was a tall man with dark hair and wide shoulders, and incredibly fit for his age. There wasn't much to do for those of us who didn't have permission to leave Home as we pleased, so we spent a lot of time on our bodies to pass the years and to keep Eric reassured we were in top shape for any job – whether it be medical, or in my case, for what we got up to in his room.

"If my daughter spoke like that I would–" The Surgeon gestured a back-handing motion.

"Well, lucky for me and your outdated parenting methods, I'm only your *work daughter*," I teased, rolling my eyes up at him as I skipped down the linoleum under the buzzing fluorescents. My shoes made an awful, ear piercing sound as they connected with the flooring that I knew would get another rise out of him.

We arrived at our workspace – a corner room with double doors on each of the walls that led to the hall, wrapping around on two sides.

Due to the doors' placements, everything inside was set at a diagonal angle, treating the room as though it were diamond shaped, rather than square.

The space was so large that having the two metal tables in the center of the room on an angle still left ample room for us and our team to move around the patients when we used them to operate.

In the corner at the back of the room stood 'the drawers' or coolers for storing the dead family members that we couldn't save. Thankfully, for my skin's sake, we didn't need to use them very often.

Across from that, the final and opposite corner was the point where the two halls met. It was a big enough space for Surge and I to share a corner desk there. As Surge reached the desk, he turned the alarm off and checked his computer – information on our imminent job had already started to come through.

"Two males. Multiple wounds. Both critical." He read the little we'd been offered in a grim tone.

"Ahh, what? You're kidding?"

This was not the quiet day that I'd planned. Surge and I were always on call, but I was tired from working out and was hoping to collapse on my couch and watch TV for a while.

"That's all it says, daughter."

"That can't be right," I argued. "Was *anything* in the calendar today?"

"No," he growled, no doubt mad his reading had been interrupted indefinitely. We were always informed in advance of the jobs Eric's crews or our associate's people were sent on for us to organize a full team in the ER. None of us liked surprises.

With only the two of us there for the injuries described, though vague, we were in for a shit-show. We could rely a little on the paramedics bringing these two patients in, but a skilled response unit would have been preferred.

"No bank robberies?" I asked.

"No."

"Heists?"

"No." Surge tried not to smile.

"Thefts?" I was running out of synonyms.

"You're asking the same thing, daughter." Amusement seeped through his otherwise cranky tone while I narrowed my eyes in thought. I paused by the cabinets on the wall, staring at the innumerable number of medications.

"Has anyone left Home for the day?"

Not everyone lived on the premises permanently, there were people Eric could trust to be loyal enough to come back, though I clearly wasn't one of them. The last time I'd been out of Home was for mine and Eric's anniversary about a month earlier, and I couldn't remember a time before that.

I'd earned an around-the-clock ban from leaving the building with anyone, Eric included, for acting up too many times in a short period. Though, I couldn't remember most of the things I'd done that were so wrong, I could only recall that I'd tried to jump from the roof after my latest surgery.

Eric passed it off as a "break" for me from all the "strenuous travel" we'd been doing. All lies of course. And I wasn't stupid, I knew he was trying to keep me contained to the medical floor while I recovered from my latest mental slip. Not a break from work though, that just never happened.

"Danny left about forty minutes ago to collect Mikey," The Surgeon offered from his seat.

"Well that's normal, he always does that on Tuesday. It's not sitting well with me, though. What info have we got again?"

"Two males. Multiple wounds. Both critical."

"Two males." I echoed quietly. That part played on my mind. Not "adult" males like we would usually see. A tremor ran from the top of my spine down to my hands. I breathed in and counted, just as The Surgeon taught me when I first arrived at Home and struggled to adjust to my new life. "Danny mentioned he'd asked for extra work with the new little one on the way. You don't think the boss is sending him out on dodgy little side quests without the proper protection, do you?" I didn't know if I was asking Surge or myself.

Either way, The Surgeon didn't respond.

"Surge? He wouldn't?"

But we both knew Eric would.

Danny asking for overtime wasn't just for the new baby. He was trying to save enough money to run with his family. And me.

Yes, it was an awkward plan to escape Home with someone I once believed loved me, along with his wife and children. But once we were free, our plan was to part ways. I'd leave him and the memories between us behind while he got to live happily ever after with the sweet little family he'd made for himself.

*Has Eric learned of our plans?*

He had ways of knowing everything. Another shiver slipped down my spine. I pulled my shoulders back, trying to move away from the sensation. My mind ruined my body's calm for the second time in just a few minutes. I needed to pull it together.

"Whatever is coming, we need to prepare." Surge was right.

I moved about the ER with ease, collecting tools, medications, IVs, and everything I thought we could possibly need with the very little information we'd been given.

The large metal platforms in the center of the room stood cold and waiting.

They weren't your average operating theater tables. We were all business, no comfort in this space. We had to keep things clean and completely sterile. Everything we did at Home was illegal, after all, and we absolutely couldn't leave any evidence that could be traced back to Eric.

While I wondered who would be placed on them in the next few minutes, I wheeled a small table between them and set up our tools. I lined up my scalpels and needles, threading them in preparation.

My head shot up, and I looked to The Surgeon as my ears registered the first of distant sirens.

As with everything in this city, Eric had an underlying influence. We had many of our own people as paramedics, cops, politicians, you name it.

Only our family and associates were brought back to Home while everyone else would be dumped at the doors of the regular hospitals to bleed out in the overwhelmed waiting rooms of Bedlam.

Nausea swirled in my stomach as the sirens became louder, clearer. I envisioned the roads they would be taking to get to us, and knew the point at which they would turn the noises off to silently slip into Home's basement levels.

The Surgeon broke my concentration, "You're almost as good as me now, daughter. You can handle anything that comes through those doors."

I nodded, acknowledging his words. He was great at pep talks before absolute fucking disaster.

As I inspected and straightened the scalpels on the table between the beds, the sirens outside abruptly stopped.

It would only take two minutes and forty-three seconds for them to get to our floor. I started the countdown in my head, swallowing hard as I closed my eyes. I bounced up and down on my feet and shook my hands to rid myself of the nerves, preparing my mind for whatever was coming.

The elevator *dinged* when it reached our floor. Stretchers were wheeled out as I reached the end of my internal timer.

*Anyone but them,* I prayed. *Please. Anyone but them.*

The doors burst open. Two people, as promised, were rushed into the room. Four paramedics instantly joined our ER team of two. They would have to do.

*You didn't pray hard enough.*

My heart dropped at the sight of Danny on the left, his six year old son on the right, their bodies swiftly transferred onto the cold tables.

"You get the boy," The Surgeon called.

As always, I did as he told me. There wasn't a moment to argue, though I desperately wanted to get my eyes on Danny to assess him. But I couldn't do it at the risk of wasting what precious moments his son had left.

I scrambled with the paramedics to remove Mikey's shirt to view the damage, my back to The Surgeon and his team as they did the same to Danny.

The boy had been shot. Two holes. No exit wounds.

One on the right side of his chest through his ribcage, the other on the lower left of his abdomen. I clenched my jaw to control my shock as I glanced at his sweet little face. His beautiful dark skin, a perfect mix between his gorgeous parents.

Straight, dark hair like his father. Eyes closed and not making a sound. Nothing like the state he was normally in when he visited our floor to terrorize the cupboards with his small hands, always in search of The Surgeon's stash of his favorite sweets.

*He was born in this room. Don't you dare let him die here.*

Grabbing my tools, I set to work on removing the bullet that would have, without a doubt, collapsed the child's lung.

It was an injury that had a terrible survival rate, even with my skilled hands and The Surgeon's knowledge. My priority was to at least have him rid of the bullet and clearing the blood that took up the space his lung needed before it could be re-inflated.

A second pair of familiar hands began to work on removing the bullet from the other wound across the small body. We couldn't begin to tend to much of the damage until both pieces of cold lead were out.

*The Surgeon?*

I did a double take, instantly furious as I looked up at him.

"*You* should be with Danny." I snapped, pissed that I was pulled from my focus.

He glanced at what was happening behind me. My surroundings suddenly expanded from just me and the damaged lung, to what was happening on the other table.

"That's not a flatline?" I demanded an answer as the sound that too often led to receiving wounds of my own rung loud through the room. The Surgeon didn't answer, but his somber expression gave the truth away.

"Daniel Reyes," a wavering voice spoke behind me, "Dead on arrival. Time of death, 4:12pm."

It had been called. Over. *Done.*

He was gone.

I nearly laughed as I rubbed the side of my head with a bloody hand. This had to be some kind of sick prank.

The sky could have broken apart and fallen to the ground outside and I would have shrugged my shoulders and moved on. It would be nothing, just another fucking day in Bedlam by comparison to what I was trying to process with those few words.

Spinning on the spot between the tables, I finally turned to see my friend.

Daring my feet to move, I stepped closer, sharply sucking in an involuntarily breath at the sight of the corpse.

Danny's shirt, cut to access the damage, was one of the many band shirts he owned. At that moment, I remembered it wasn't his favorite. Thankfully, that one had been safely stored in my room for years.

His deeply tanned skin had already begun to drain of its warm undertones.

Seeing him this way was surreal, as though it were a joke, and this corpse couldn't have possibly been the man who'd done everything in his power to help me survive the years at Home.

"Danny?" I whispered as I touched his forehead, immediately snapping my hand back when his lifeless head rolled to the side.

My chest heaved as I tried to swallow air, certain I would black out before my eyes even tried to pass over his exposed chest.

*Holes. Stab wounds. Too many.* I racked my brain for answers as to how a simple job could have gone so terribly wrong.

*Eleven? Twelve? In one person?* It was such a violent display of rage aimed at the heart I'd once occupied. I never got a more accurate count, settling on twelve as it was too difficult to decipher blood from injury as it pooled on his skin, no longer flowing with the vigor it would have if he were still alive.

*This had to be Eric. No, don't think like that now. You need to focus.*

Danny couldn't be saved. Anyone with eyesight could have seen that it was impossible. The metallic smell of blood and the bright red that surrounded his body suddenly infiltrated my senses.

The only person who'd dared show me any *real* love in this place was gone. No goodbyes. No last words between us.

And his son was moments from joining him.

One of the paramedics pulled me away from my best friend. The chance to say any more to him was taken as my body was turned back to the other table.

"Up, daughter!" The Surgeon shouted. I didn't need to be told twice.

I climbed up and instantly settled into position with my knees beside Mikey's body. I was the best choice for chest compressions for a person of his size. My small frame could fit beside him on the cold surface, and I was strong enough to bring him back if his body would allow it.

The paramedic assisting to resuscitate the boy moved aside, and an Ambu bag was removed from his face, revealing the red at his mouth that I refused to believe was blood.

Everything felt fuzzy, my vision blurred. I could sense my mind trying to protect itself from the horror unfolding before my eyes. The more I pushed down on Mikey's chest, the more liquid flowed over my hands. It was too much loss for a little body. For *any* body. My actions were doing no good – just pushing more blood from him like water from a sponge in a tight grip.

But I kept going. I couldn't save Danny, so I had to do whatever I could for his child.

My hearing dropped in and out, able to acknowledge some words from the others in the room before nothing but a loud ringing set in, only for that to dip and allow me to catch more spoken fragments.

I didn't dare stop compressions until one of the paramedics tried to pull me down. I hadn't even heard the time of death being called. My head swirled at the height of the table as I teetered on the verge of collapse.

"Mikey?" I smiled, calling his name as I grabbed his small shoulders in my bloody hands, "You have to wake up, baby. Open your eyes for me!"

I shook him in disbelief. The kid *never* slept soundly. He should have been awake and running around the room, our own little tornado.

"Mikey? Mikey!" I called again, louder as my voice cracked and my mind fractured in front of everyone in the room. "Come on, please. *Please!*" I screamed at his sweet, sleeping face between my hands, smearing more red across his beautiful, resting features.

I lifted him into my arms and held him tight. Heat from his blood seeped into my clothes as I breathed in the sweet smell of his hair and cradled his face against my neck. In the six short years we'd spent together, it was the only memory I had where Mikey didn't wrap his skinny arms around my neck to hug me back.

I pushed away the hands of the others like a rabid animal fighting for scraps, and screamed at them to let him stay with me. I just wanted to hold onto him for a little longer. Forever – if it could bring him back to life.

At that moment, Eric walked through the doors behind me.

My blood boiled at the sound of him speaking so casually after one of our own just had their body hacked apart. Danny was part of *The Collection*. He was *family*.

Nothing should have been calm. We *should* have already been making deals with devils bigger than Eric himself to find vengeance. The loss of Postal's life warranted Bedlam being tipped on its fucking head until those who'd taken him had been found and served the same fate. Worse. I'd do it myself if I had to.

*Unless he was behind it…*

I kissed Mikey's cheek and lowered him gently to the table. As I traced his nose and lips with my fingers, I promised I would see him again soon.

I jumped down to the floor and immediately threw something across the room with more force than I'd ever possessed. Apparently, I'd gotten my hands on a scalpel, but I couldn't remember reaching for one.

The blade zipped through the air, hit the wall above the desk and clattered to the floor. But it had slipped close enough to Eric to leave a deep cut along his cheekbone. Not a bad throw, considering my vision was obscured by the tears I couldn't control.

Hysterical was an understatement. I fucking *screamed* at Eric.

"You did this!" I threw my accusation vehemently across the ER in front of everyone, "You can't stand the thought that someone could actually care for me! You have taken *everything* from me!"

I sounded like a child throwing a tantrum, and had every intention to keep at it while I still had the mental capacity to string words together.

I had just lost two of the people I loved most in my absolute *fucking mess* of a life, and I wasn't going to let him get away with what he'd done.

"Stitch Up," Eric warned, voice smooth and controlled despite the scene before him and the cut to his heartbreakingly perfect face.

"Oh, what are you going to do?" I snorted, throwing my arms out. Neurotic laughter escaped the lungs I wished I could have swapped with the boy, growing colder by the second on the table behind me. "Add another name!"

Eric simply waved his hand and the room cleared out, or so I thought. By the time the room emptied he'd clenched his jaw, nostrils flaring over the way I'd spoken in front of the other employees.

He didn't care how I spoke in private. He'd grown to get enjoyment out of it, but I'd fucked up terribly for slipping up with an audience of my equals.

It didn't matter who I was to him, on the thirty-seventh floor, I was nothing more than a disobedient drone who needed to be put back in their place.

"Are you done?" he asked, regaining composure over his features.

"With you? Yes," I spat, voice shuddering with rage. "I'm *fucking done!*"

"Your contract says otherwise." He cocked his head curiously, taking in my tears and bloody clothes.

"Fuck your contract, Eric. *Fuck you!*" I pointed at him from my spot, halfway across the room. "I would rather *die* than spend another minute in this fucking nightmare with you. *I hate you!*" I screamed, more tears betraying me, and still feeling childlike. I was amazed I hadn't blacked out from the shock I was rapidly sinking into.

"Summer–"

I wasn't hearing it. I was done listening to his sweet voice when it suited him to pull me down from the edge, only to subject me to more years of control and hurt. I was done being the body whose heart and mind wasn't good enough to love in return.

I shook my head violently to stop his words from entering my ears. Before I could steady myself, I was moving in on him, no weapons this time, I didn't need them. I was no longer scared of the monster in front of me.

I'd caught the madness Eric brought into the world and he was *finally* going to experience it firsthand. I was confident I could take his head clean off with my bare hands.

The way his eyes widened showed he believed it too.

My legs suddenly stopped moving forward as a sharp pain pierced through my back and into my chest. Stars instantly disrupted my sight, and everything began to grow dark around the edges.

*A dart? Through the chest?*

The ground rushed up to meet me as I dropped to my knees.

I tried to steady my breath, but the air entering my body didn't sound as it should. Eric's expression was pained when I looked up at him.

"You've been pushed too far. You haven't had enough rest."

The words were similar to what he'd said on our anniversary. The ache in my chest radiated through my entire torso. It wasn't like any tranq I'd felt in the past.

Eric hunched down in front of me as the darkness continued to engulf my peripherals.

"It destroys me to put you down like a *fucking animal*, Summer. But you're a danger to us all in this state."

Eric rarely swore, and each time I was the cause behind it, I wanted an award for breaking the man's perfect poise.

He reached out to tip my face up to his, steadying my failing body in his grip, "It's almost over, darling" he promised, though I had no idea what he meant, or if I was even hearing him correctly. "Once we're done, we'll go back to the way things were." It was a promise I didn't understand. "Take her to my room."

I hit the floor of the ER, hard, knowing I wouldn't want to wake up to see my newest gift from Eric.

# FORTY-THREE

SUMMER

## MAY 5TH

Sharing more of my darkest secrets with Logan seemed to have changed something between us again. I could trust him, enough. More than enough. Though, I didn't think this was exactly what my therapist meant.

While I had no doubt Logan was one of the most deadly criminals in the country, I'd been having an incredibly hard time reminding myself of that fact. I just couldn't see him as anyone other than the boyfriend I was falling for.

It also left me thinking that the vigilante must have decided my actions weren't terrible enough to make me worthy of death at his hands. If I was, I'd be dead already, long ago. It was a weird kind of relief, knowing that my partner didn't plan on murdering me.

*You sure know how to pick 'em.*

We'd been dating for three months, and I was still loving every second with him. Though, this arrangement didn't come without its challenges.

Watching everything I said proved to be more difficult with each passing day.

Logan ignored all my attempts at encouraging him to open up, often trying to contain a smile or throwing an eye roll my way when I pushed a little too hard.

He'd started changing up his shifts at work so he finished by nine each night, typically meeting me at the gym after therapy if I hadn't already gone for a run.

We'd work out together, but I could barely concentrate on the treadmill while watching him do *anything* with his arms. Once he started dripping with sweat and it mixed with the scent of his cologne, my eyes were permanently rolled to the back of my head.

Logan would watch me as I got ready for work in my room each night. I'd found it unnerving at first, the way his eyes darkened and always looking like he wanted to devour me. He behaved as obsessed with me as I felt for him.

I'd set up in the garage for my shift, and he would follow me around most nights. Brushing his fingers down my spine, smacking my butt and demanding I give him better grades while I giggled at his disappointment, never awarding him the perfect ten.

He'd whisper in my ear, lips at my neck, pleading with me to go back into the house with him as I tried to focus on my routine.

It had worked a couple of times, and for the first time in my adult life, I'd been late to work *twice* thanks to his bad influence.

Logan would stay with me for my first patient of the night, despite the safety of Tony and Ben's presence.

If there were ever an easy stitching job, I'd set up closer to his blind spot so I could teach him my methods and let him practice some suturing. All under the guise, of course, that he worked for me. I couldn't trust many of my clients with the knowledge that I had a boyfriend.

The word "boyfriend" still felt dumb to use by this point. I was twenty-eight, he was thirty-one, words like that seemed more suited to juveniles. But with how hard and fast I was falling for Logan, maybe the words were a better fit than I'd originally thought.

After a quick kiss goodnight in the hallway, out of the bodyguards' sight and having my clothes tugged at to join him, Logan would go to bed.

*My* bed. A man in *my* bed. Every single night. For nearly four months.

Who had I become?

Admittedly, I felt safer knowing he was there. If I needed help during a shift, he would come.

It both excited me and made me fear for my patients.

Rumors were circulating about Alan's disappearance. He'd allegedly gone missing two days after I'd shot him in the neck with the tranquilizer. While the drugs I'd used were intense, the same that I assumed Eric had used on me many times, they weren't strong enough to kill a grown man.

There was something incredibly disturbing about the thought that Logan could have been behind his disappearance. More disturbing still, was the fact I actually found comfort in the idea of my boyfriend being so protective of me.

Foolishly, I'd begun to believe he and I could actually have a future together, and if that were the case, there was more than his identity that I needed to protect.

I tried to avoid sensitive topics instead of hitting them straight on like I'd originally planned in my attempts to have him reveal his alter ego. I treated him like a person I wanted to be with long term, entirely dropping the idea that he could be a deranged predator, lurking in my own home.

As I set up for work, I asked Logan not to join me for my first patient.

He pouted over our regular routine being disrupted. "Why?"

"Um… it's something I'd rather deal with without an audience." It was the best lie I could come up with after checking the schedule for the night and discovering who had booked in to see me.

"Summer…"

We'd been around each other so much he could tell when I wasn't being entirely honest with him.

*Good thing I've seen through his lies since the start.*

"I have a female patient coming in for a checkup. I don't think she'd appreciate you being here." I gave him a quick, hopefully convincing smile.

"Fair enough," he bobbed his head, catching my meaning. "I'll come in for the second one then?"

"If you're still awake." I agreed, not making eye contact with him.

Logan left for the bedroom, and a few minutes later I greeted a couple walking through my door as it lifted to accept them into the warm room.

"Hello, Summer," the man, Leo, called cheerfully as he guided his wife to the patient chair. Mia. The woman didn't speak any English. It made me wish

I'd gone to a real school and learned multiple languages as a child. It would have made my job so much easier.

We made do with expressions and *very* basic words, but Leo did a fair amount of the translating between us.

They were a beautiful couple. Perfectly tanned skin, straight black hair, high cheekbones. I couldn't help but think of Danny every time they visited, which wasn't often as Mia was being cared for by Dr. Reynolds, properly trained in obstetrics. They'd booked in with me for a check up while Reynolds was away.

I liked to think they looked like the parents Danny had described, before his mother died, and before his father gave up.

Danny was the reason I tried so hard to care for everyone, no matter their circumstances.

With Eric, what mattered most was treating family from Home and the wealthy underground contacts who were willing to pay for our skills.

I had often wondered if Danny's mother had better access to care, would she have survived? She could have been there for her son, and even though we likely wouldn't have met as a result, the world would have been better off for having him in it.

I asked Logan not to join us for a few reasons. Not only for Mia's comfort and privacy, being one of the few females I tended to, but because this particular topic seemed to be the only sore spot in our relationship so far.

*Aside from the fact, of course, that my boyfriend is living a double life he's pretending I'm not completely aware of.*

Over the previous months, it had been a subject that occasionally surfaced in our conversations. Logan revealed a little more of himself and his desires each time, enough for me to risk it all by testing the waters.

About a week earlier, in bed, I'd stupidly moaned a comment about wanting Logan to put a baby in me. It was all in the heat of the moment. I was on top of him, he was grabbing my ribs with just the right amount of pressure so that it hurt *and* had my head spinning as I fucked him. The words tumbled out before I could catch them.

It felt wrong, especially after the hurt we'd experienced with the miscarriage, but it was *so fucking hot* at the time. Not just for me. In fact, more so for him.

To my surprise and relief, Logan *wanted* to hear it. His reaction was indescribably intense, practically *begging* me to keep it up as he grabbed me harder to force himself deeper, groaning *loud* as he came, filling me with false potential.

He then immediately made me regret it.

For the three days that followed, he wouldn't touch me. He wanted to, though. It made his attempt at self control around me adorably painful while he questioned me until he was satisfied I meant nothing by my comment. He eventually believed that I'd said it *just for fun* and only for teasing to get him off; not that I had some deep desire to have children that he could never give me.

He'd become so hung up on the topic, and because of his reaction, I didn't want to expose Logan to a happy family.

*Especially* not this one.

I took all of Mia's measurements and blood samples. Watching on with an unexpected pang of jealousy as she and Leo looked lovingly at each other, listening to their unborn child's heartbeat on a small Doppler I had on hand.

*Don't be fucking stupid, you don't want one. They're just cute together.*

I sent the information to Reynolds so she'd be kept up to date upon her return.

We then talked for a while, mostly about their living arrangements and the chaos of sharing a house with in-laws – something I'd likely and thankfully never have to deal with.

Leo translated well, and quick enough for Mia and I to be laughing along together. I could have talked to them all night. In fact, time had gotten away from us and they'd been with me for ages.

There was a knock at the hallway as the door rolled up for them to leave.

"Boyfriend," I said to Mia and she gave me a knowing look.

"You can come in," I called as I waved goodbye to the adorable couple, watching them leave to enjoy their last few weeks before their world would be turned upside down.

Logan walked in just in time to see them go, and Mia gave me another look behind her husband's back that I understood all too well. It was the "Holy shit, he's so fuckable" look. I winked at her and pressed the key to close the door.

I'd seen plenty of people give Logan that stare during our times out in public, both at his work and at the gym together.

My stomach turned every time I noticed people looked at him that way. It planted the idea that one day, he'd realize he was dating a corpse when he could have had literally anyone else. To my relief, he actually seemed oblivious to it.

It was his turn to give me a look.

"Don't," I warned him.

He narrowed his eyes. "Don't what?"

"Don't *start*. It took me three days to get you back in me again. I don't think I can deal with you depriving me of that kind of oxygen for so long."

He smiled for a beat, but then his seriousness on the topic set back in.

"Can you *honestly* tell me you don't want that, Summer?"

I sighed. *Here we fucking go again.*

"Fuck no, she's miserable," I shrugged. "She's been sick for eight months straight and then gets rewarded with a *person* that she'll have to take care of *forever*. What a fucking joke." It got a small laugh out of him, and I took a deep breath before continuing. "You need to drop this at some point. Please? You seem to be forgetting that even if there was a chance I wanted a baby, all of *this*," — I gestured to my lower abdomen — "Is still pretty fucked up. I don't know who did the procedures, but I don't think they were even kind enough to use coat hangers."

"You're vulgar," he said with a small smile.

"You fucking love it," I said with a straight face.

His shoulders sagged. "I just don't want you to change your mind in five years time."

I knew why he kept pushing this. He and *I* couldn't have kids. That had already been proven. But there would *always* be the chance either of us could, so long as it were with someone else. I couldn't overlook the fact he was choosing me, just as much as I'd chosen him.

"You're planning on keeping me around that long?" I teased.

"Longer, if you'll have me." he shrugged playfully but the words were laced with his signature sincerity that made my skin burn.

"You know… if I didn't know any better, I'd say you've got some kind of breeder fetish. Maybe you should see my therapist." I joked to break his intense gaze. "And your mom, a doctor, me a nurse. Maybe throw in an Oedipus complex too."

He shook his head, laughing as I made fun of him. Still not taking, or maybe completely ignoring the hint I was done with this discussion in a desperate attempt to preserve our sex life.

"It's more than that, isn't it?" he asked, "Your cycle might still be a mess, but you know you're healing over time. One loss doesn't mean it's over for you."

I snorted at his comment. "Mess" was an understatement. I was bleeding like a stuck pig.

"It's technically three now," I whispered snidely, forgetting he'd hear me, "At least."

"What makes you so opposed to the idea of having a family?"

*Fucking cops and their incessant questions. Old habits die hard, I guess.*

"What, are you pretending you're my therapist now?" I tried to joke again but he didn't laugh. I threw my hands up in defeat. "Mikey."

"Fuck, Summer. I'm sorry–"

"You *asked*."

"Losing him was enough for you to dismiss the idea completely?" He just couldn't fucking help but keep up with the questioning.

"Have you ever had a child *die* in your arms, Logan?"

"No," he said quietly, looking miserable for the pain he was causing me by bringing it up. He shoved his hands in his jacket pockets. It was obvious he wanted to close the space in the garage between us. I could tell he wanted to hold me and banish the thoughts he'd forced my mind to dig up, but he was also set on getting straight answers from me for his own peace of mind about what our future could entail.

"He wasn't even my kid," I continued in hopes it'd get him off my back, "I loved him like he was, though. I can *never* get attached to someone like that again." I threw the remaining tools in my hand to the desk, not wanting to deal with them either right now. "My ex was cruel," I said, only barely changing the subject as I straightened my chair. "I probably would have been dumb enough to have kids with him if it were an option. I can't imagine how he would have treated them if they survived, and I never would have left him. Forced sterilization was probably the best gift he ever gave me in all our years together." I folded my arms and looked up at Logan, still looking regretful.

"Summer—"

"Forget copper for a seventh anniversary present, he practically arranged a hysterectomy."

"Summer!"

"*I'm sorry*," I groaned, "That was all… very dark."

Logan went quiet, lost in thought. I didn't want him to be in his own mind for too long or he might decide to leave, and I wouldn't get my daily dose of him inside me.

"They're both Gifted," I whispered, tipping my head in the direction of the couple who'd just left.

"What? *Really?*"

"Yup. They come to me when they need to, but are usually cared for by the other doctor who's better in the baby department."

He cocked a curious eyebrow. "Unregistered?"

"Of course."

Mia and Leo didn't want their baby's first weeks to be filled with questions and all of them being put on stupid lists. While I wasn't particularly fond of the Gifted in general, I didn't believe it was fair for them to be put on public registers like predators when they hadn't done anything wrong. I was happy to treat them, so long as they weren't a threat to me.

Logan folded his arms, and it seemed his train of thought had switched tracks. "What Gift are they hoping for?"

I smiled at his excitement. He was my boyfriend, but that didn't mean I could tell him *all* the secrets. I'd already disclosed enough private information about the couple to distract him from my own reproductive predicaments.

Besides, Gifts weren't, as far as we knew, directly passed down to offspring. Those who randomly mutated had the standard Gifts – essentially heavily enhanced humans. The child of two Gifted folk, however, would have drastically more powerful abilities, and they could be anything. There weren't enough of them registered to look back through previous generations to see if the same Gifts presented in families more than once.

I eyed the man in front of me, wishing I could ask him if his parents were also Gifted.

"Happy and healthy. Isn't that the best *Gift* they could ask for?"

He smiled and nodded, finally taking one of my hints, "Are you done for the night?" he asked, eyes darting to the roller door.

"Umm. I still have a few hours to take any walk-ins."

"Can the guys let you know if anyone shows up?"

"Yeah," I murmured as he pressed his lips to mine and lifted me from the floor, "Why?" I asked, pretending not to know and wrapping my legs around his waist.

"I already put towels down." His brows rose with hope.

"How many?" I rolled my eyes playfully, though the whole ordeal was making me a little self-conscious. This was the second time I'd menstruated since the miscarriage. The first had Logan in a panic, and I'd offered for him to track it with me so he wouldn't jump to the conclusion I was miscarrying each time. He'd rejected the idea, explaining that he'd tracked enough cycles to last a lifetime.

Though… for this second period, there were days he had stealthily snuck more sugar into my coffee, thinking I, of all people, wouldn't notice something had changed. While he probably did it in hopes it would put me in a better mood, it backfired terribly. I didn't appreciate the tampering with my favorite consumable.

This time, Logan hinted it was about to start before my insides had begun tearing themselves to shreds. I had no choice but to believe it had something to do with being Gifted, and I couldn't ask how he knew.

Logan wasn't at all opposed to having sex while I bled, but blood play of any kind didn't appeal to him quite as much as other kinks. He enjoyed it in the moment, admiring his bloody handprints all over my pale flesh.

But by the time we were done, his hazel eyes always seemed a little dark with uncertainty over his actions, and he would move for the shower faster than typical to wash it away.

Like every time I believed I had Logan all worked out, it left me confused. The scenes I'd discovered on the internet of his graphic work made me think he'd spent more time around blood than I did – an impressive feat considering it was all I was exposed to some nights. Maybe it was *my* blood that bothered him? And perhaps it was because he associated it with my pain? A fucked up thing to find romantic.

"Four. Three didn't cut it last time," he grinned, and I was glad to see his usual enthusiasm had entirely overthrown his anxiety, "You bleed like a fucking mob hit."

"Yeah… You know, I'm surprised you're not more into it," I teased, "I end up looking like most of the people in your favorite movies. I would have thought a blood fetish would be right up your alley."

"*You know*," he mimicked my tone before dropping his voice to a low growl in my ear, "As much as you like to make fun of what gets *me* off, Summer. I've seen the way you *beg for* my cum. You've got a fetish of your own."

"You gonna make fun of me for it?" I pouted.

"No," he gently shook his face in mine, eyes on my lips as he seemed to anticipate the smile I couldn't hide from him, "But I'll have you so full of it and fucked so hard by the end of the night, you'll forget your own name, *nurse*."

"Is that a promise, Logan?" I giggled as he carried me to my room, happy that this conversation hadn't earned me another three day ban from his body.

# FORTY-FOUR

## SUMMER

### JUNE 13TH

Apart from the time we were in bed together or working, Logan and I were still only spending some, *very limited* time with his friends. They seemed to enjoy having me around, knowing I was aware, to some degree, of all of their double lives.

It seemed to piss Harrison off the most. She dropped as many hints as me, constantly met with Logan's warning glares to shut up.

I wondered if things kept progressing with Logan, would I be included in their secrets in the future? Was he ever planning on telling me, or did he believe he could keep that side of him from me, forever? It didn't feel like something we could keep up long term and it didn't feel fair.

I wanted all of him. Even if that meant he had to be honest about the gruesome things he'd done. But I decided I just needed to continue being patient with Logan, believing him to be worth the wait.

I found it amusing; the way his friends knew that I was the one stitching people up at Crave, but unable to communicate with me while we were there. I would get my work done out the back of the club and head inside, strutting straight past the vigilante who'd rejected me on the stairs.

Sitting with his group of friends, Logan poorly hid behind the curtains around a couch while I drank with the bodyguards at the bar. Their collective gaze was almost tangible, boring into the back of my head.

It gave me an odd sense of safety, having all of them there, plus Tony and Ben. With Eric's Finders knowing I frequented the club, having so many allies close by helped me to relax a little more than I probably should have allowed. While I'd done many questionable things in my twenty-eight years of life, I certainly wasn't dumb enough to believe I'd ever be completely untouchable.

It also made for incredibly awkward interactions I didn't need an audience for, especially not from my killer boyfriend who had jealous tendencies I couldn't resist playing with.

"Another?" Kit called as I swung side to side on a barstool. The bodyguards sat to my right, the stool to my other side empty, allowing us to talk more candidly over the volume of the music.

"Yes, please!" I replied, rewarding myself for the amount of gore I'd dealt with for another shift. I was well beyond the point of feeling tipsy, though I'd only had one drink. Kit gave me a look I could barely understand through the holes of my mask. "Oh! You can throw them out." I told him, referring to my stash of pills behind the bar that I hadn't needed for months. He raised his eyebrows and nodded in response.

"That good, is he?" Ben asked from under his mask on the other side of Tony.

I giggled as Tony answered for me, "She'll let us know if she ever leaves her bedroom for air."

Ben rolled his eyes and smiled.

"Sumar?" A voice whispered in my ear. I startled, jumping back a little on my stool and bumping into the chest it belonged to.

There were only two people who pronounced my name that way, and the other was Eric when we were alone. While my ex had lost it over time, this younger voice was still delectably thick with an accent.

"Matty?" I exclaimed, spinning to greet the familiar face. Though disappointingly, half of it was hidden behind his mask.

He leaned on the bar behind me with his hand, bringing his short mess of blonde hair and face full of piercings closer to mine.

"If I knew the nameless nurse still worked here, I would visit Crave more frequently."

My eyes swept up and over his arm, covered by the sleeve of a tight black shirt. Although the fabric left little to the imagination, it concealed a limb I'd gotten to know every inch of after brushing up against it for an entire night, nearly two years prior.

"Who the fuck is this?" Tony asked, tone only mildly defensive for his image's sake when I showed no signs of being bothered by the stranger.

"Remember the job I told you about," I asked without unlocking my eyes from those of the masked man in front of me, "The one with the trafficker?"

Tony quickly turned to Ben for them to give each other one of those looks I couldn't work out at the best of times. I especially couldn't decipher their code after consuming one of my favorite drinks that Kit had made a little on the strong side.

The story was one of their favorites from my time before I hired them.

After leaving Home, I'd refused to touch the millions in my account until it was absolutely necessary.

Word of mouth spread about the nameless nurse out the back of Crave, and it wasn't long before I consistently made decent money. I gave a large cut to Anna and Kit once I'd started earning enough to feed and clothe myself. They protested at first, but I insisted they take it, if only for the risk to their lives for allowing Eric's missing piece to hide out with them.

As the first few months ticked on, I wasn't earning enough for the complete independence I desired.

That opportunity came when a short, round man in a pinstripe suit approached me at my table beside the stairs that led to the back door of the club. He'd recognised my work as something only Stitch Up herself could perform, having hired me to work on his wife multiple times in the past.

Terrified at my identity's discovery and certain he would cart me straight back to Bedlam to hand me over to Eric, I instead learned the two men didn't get along. He simply wanted my fast hands for an upcoming job.

While he was very polite when he spoke in his low, smooth voice, pacing back and forth on the crunching gravel in the dark, I couldn't help but feel a little threatened as his four bodyguards surrounded me at my table.

He offered me two-hundred thousand dollars for *one* night's work. I couldn't refuse. I needed the cash and honestly didn't know if turning him down was an option while being encircled by his men. The big names in the crime world truly did have a thing for theatrics.

On the night I was needed, I skipped work at Crave and was picked up from the back of the club to be dropped at his mansion, closer to the mountains. With my first-aid kit in hand and a bag over my head, I was left at the front door to be patted down by one of the bodyguards.

My job for the night was simple – assisting with torture to extract information. While I had strong feelings that what I participated in was *extremely wrong*, the man under the knife was a well known trafficker, specializing in sourcing young girls of a similar age to mine when I'd first met Eric.

After learning that, it didn't take much for me to happily stitch the cuts alongside the bodyguard who had *way* too much fun slicing him up.

Nothing too deep – just enough carnage for confessions. And no painkillers as I stitched him.

While it was oddly satisfying in a way, those screams still rung in my head every now and then.

Matthias, the bodyguard working the blade, had been a delightful distraction from the harrowing sounds. He and I spent much of the night making eyes and giggling as we steadied each other, slipping on the blood as it pooled on glossy white tiles.

He and I made quite a good pair. Both in torture and *almost* physically. During one of our breaks we were caught by the boss's wife in one of the many spare rooms of the mansion. She'd burst into the space as our tongues were down each other's throats and hands scrambling to reach enough of a state of undress with the intention to fuck. Both of us were riding a rapturous high. A combination of the intensity of the work and from my pills we'd taken together.

His boss offered me a job. Apparently unbothered by our actions and paying no mind to his wife's echoing shrieks about the blood we'd traipsed through her beautiful home and smeared on the bed that we barely used to its full potential.

The boss had hoped my instant *connection* with Matthias would be enough of an incentive to convince me to stay and continue our work together on a full-time basis.

While it would have been absurdly quick and easy money, I begrudgingly said no for the sake of my soul and lost the opportunity to find out what else Matthias' quick hands could achieve after the small taste I experienced before the interruption.

I'd learned to be content with what I'd missed out on. That kind of work would have put me into another situation too much like Home.

A new cage in a sense, and I'd barely had a taste of being free.

The boss reluctantly accepted my refusal, evidently not taking a page out of Eric's book where I'd be tricked, forced or held at gunpoint to take his offer. For that, I suggested I help him in any other ways he needed that didn't involve me purposely hurting anyone.

He accepted my conditions, and I'd visited the mansion a few times since, tending to his bodyguards' injuries or to his children when they were unwell.

I became a trusted name in their house once his wife forgave me for the mess we'd made, further spreading the word of my skills.

"Are you out this way for work or pleasure?" I purred, unable to hide my smile at the memories of our unjustly short time together.

"I guess that depends," his pierced lips parted with a hungry grin, "What can you and I accomplish before the boss calls me to leave?"

"She has a boyfriend, *Tatta,*" Ben growled.

*Am I hearing things or does Ben sound a little too defensive? Does he actually like Logan that much?*

While I would never ask – because I didn't want to know – I'd suspected Logan was spending time with the bodyguards behind my back.

There wasn't a chance I'd dream of doing anything with Matthias now that I was in a relationship, but I thought it might be fun to have him hang around a little longer to get a rise out of the vigilante spying on me.

Obviously, not so much fun that the unsuspecting Matty ended up dead. My hopes were purely to tempt Logan enough so we wouldn't have to keep up this act. *And* so that he wouldn't have to do such a shitty job of pretending not to stare at me through the curtains of their couch, undoubtedly trying to listen in from across the space as I flirted with another man.

Matthias shook his head mischievously before his pierced brows pinched together, playfully begging, "*Please,* tell me it's not true, Sumar?"

He was known for being dramatic, both with words and actions. From the little I knew about him, English wasn't his first or even second language. The accent that wrapped each word he spoke made them a little more deliberate and impassioned.

"It's true."

"Ugh," he laughed softly, "It is not fair. We never got to finish what we started." He bit at one of his many lip rings and lowered his voice. "I still remember how you tasted on my fingers when we were–"

"That's *enough*," Tony warned, though his composure was breaking with a grin at the part of the story I didn't want him to learn. It'd only be more ammunition for the two of them to pick on me later.

Matthias sighed and narrowed his eyes at the bodyguard, then made a point of slowly studying my masked face and lowering his gaze to my chest.

"I see you have men of your own to protect you now. A good idea after how I met you. If someone spoke to my boss the way I do with you, I'd have to remove their tongue. Speaking of," – he arched a brow above the edge of his mask, unable to help himself even immediately after acknowledging the trouble he could get himself into – "I often recall the way yours felt on mine."

A giggle escaped me, "I'm sorry, Matty. *Truly*. Maybe if you wanted more you should have found me sooner."

"You know my work must come first," he said with another dramatic sigh. "Although… those sounds you made could have had even *me* reassessing my priorities."

Ben cleared his throat to catch Matthias's attention, pulling him out of his tunnel vision, firmly fixated on me. While he was intense and straight forward, this man didn't pose any danger. Unless of course, my Gifted boyfriend saw this flirtatious exchange as enough of a reason to dispose of the two of us.

The face behind the mask quickly twisted with a frown. It seemed play time had come to an end. "We need to talk, Sumar."

Ben and Tony hesitated to leave us. They didn't go far, just to different stools on the other side of the bar where they could still keep an eye on me.

Matthias smirked at them over my head, "How serious is it? I can't make you forget your boyfriend if we head upstairs?" he asked, though his mischievous smile turned a little disappointed, seeming to already know my answer.

Letting out a sigh of my own, I gave up on the offer I would have taken without a second thought if I wasn't so obsessed with the man sitting insurmountably tense on the couch. Logan's body seemed so rigid; he likely would have stayed in the same position had the piece of furniture been removed from beneath his body.

I giggled. "I'd say it's getting pretty serious."

"It's nice to hear it. But begging you to play wasn't my only reason for speaking with you." He took a seat on Tony's stool beside me, using his foot on my calf to spin me for us to face each other.

I knew he wanted to be handsy with me, but he wouldn't dare unless I agreed.

Being my first *truly* consensual experience with anyone since leaving Home, I learned that once Matthias got started, he didn't leave much of your mind intact to form the words to get him to stop. Though, the screams of his boss's wife eventually became enough to pierce through his seemingly unshakable focus on my pleasure.

It was a damn shame. We'd only gotten far enough for Matthias to break the hold Eric had firmly pulled over my mind; years of poisoning me with the idea that I could never come for anyone else and that my body could only be his, *forever*. That brainwashing quickly became unraveled with just a few strokes of this masked man's incredibly skilled fingers.

Had I taken his boss's offer, who knows what we could have achieved together?

"What is it?" I asked him, curious to learn what he could know that I didn't already.

"The boss has information for me to pass to you," he spoke as quietly as the music allowed, "There's a *collection* of rumors passing through Bedlam. It spreads like wildfire. Too many believe Stitch Up is dead. With you not showing that flawless face of yours in that filthy town for so long, that *reptile* is finding himself under immense pressure."

"Fuck," I whined, ignoring the compliments I would have once accepted along with his invitation to go upstairs. I took a sip from the drink I'd abandoned on the bar to ease my nerves, but the sweetness only made me feel nauseous.

"We've heard he plans to come to the mountains soon," Matthias continued. "I have no doubt his intention is to find you."

"That sounds about right. A few months ago there were Finders here looking for me."

"How long have you been with your boyfriend?" he changed the subject, gnawing at the bar through his tongue that I'd once been well acquainted with.

"A few months."

"And he remains breathing? Having won the heart of Sumar, the lost monarch of Bedlam's underworld? He's a lucky man."

More of my giggles erupted at the combination of his drama and my stomach turning. "You and your words," I shook my groggy head at him. "Thank you for the warning."

"I fear I won't see you again," he said sadly, but followed it up with a teasing, "It's a shame my words are not enough to get you in one of the rooms – to put both our fast hands to good use." He leaned closer to kiss my cheek goodbye, whispering, "Stay safe, Sumar," before leaving me alone at the bar with my thoughts.

A woman's voice from the stool behind me was a welcomed distraction from the visions of Eric and his eagerness to take me back to Home.

"He was cute!"

"Yeah, he really is," I admitted before turning and realizing the woman beside me was Jackie, come to spy on me a little closer than Logan could get away with while disguised as Vengeance.

"If I were you, I would have taken him upstairs."

*Liar.*

*I* would have had a far better chance at getting her in one of the rooms than Matthias.

I smiled at her from under my mask, knowing my next words would drive Logan insane when she repeated them to him after I left, "Help yourself. From personal experience, he'll have you coming undone within seconds. Multiple times if you're as lucky as I was." I slipped off the high stool and motioned for the bodyguards to leave. "But… believe it or not, I think I've actually found something better." I added for Logan's sake, giving Jackie a sly smile as I walked away from the bar.

# FORTY-FIVE

## SUMMER

As I got comfortable on the patient chair in the back of the van for the long ride home, my phone buzzed with a text.

**Stay over at mine tonight?**

Something about it felt a little off, but exciting. Logan hadn't invited me to stay over at his apartment for months. We'd continued to stop in on occasion, always finding it empty and never staying too long, seeming to avoid his sister.

I guessed he was also trying to avoid the space and the trauma it held while we were still so newly dating. Perhaps enough time had passed for him to be okay with seeing me there again.

*Maybe he's sick of your shit and is finally going to dispose of you.* I quickly countered the thought with, *Or maybe what Jackie recounted has him wanting to take things further with me so I don't take Matthias up on his offers. Things between us have been going well, maybe he's okay with me meeting his sister?*

"Can you two drop me at Logan's on your way home?" I called to the bodyguards.

They waited outside my house while I quickly showered, changed and packed a bag to stay the night. I could have driven, but with how awful I felt from the drink at the club, I knew they wouldn't mind if it ensured my safe arrival.

When we pulled up, it was still dark outside, but close to 6 am with the late night at Crave and the trip home. The cool morning air as the weather prepared itself for a perfectly clear day softly brushed my skin when I stepped out of the car and waved goodbye to Tony and Ben.

The door to the foyer immediately unlocked when I pressed the number for Logan's apartment. As I entered the elevator, I checked my reflection in the mirrored walls.

I looked tired. I was so exhausted from work that I had to fight to keep my eyes open for the whole ride over. I wore different jeans than usual, still tight but smattered with holes around my knees and thighs. My black shirt was buttoned almost to the top of its sheer fabric, revealing the lacy bra underneath.

My scars would be visible to a degree, but I figured with the time of day, there wouldn't be much chance of being seen by anyone who would understand their origin.

*He's having a weird effect on me,* I eyed my reflection, barely bothered by the patchy remnants of my tattoo that were visible through the shirt.

Logan waited for me, drinking in my outfit and movements while he leaned on the doorframe, arms folded as I approached from the lift.

"Are you finally sick of my place?" I teased when he leaned down to greet me with a kiss.

"No. But I thought the change of scenery would be nice," he grabbed me by the hand and led me inside. I dropped my bag by the door as he guided me to the balcony.

There wasn't much space outside, enough room for the outdoor couch he pulled me onto. He covered us with a heavy blanket before pulling my legs over his and wrapping an arm around my shoulders.

"What's all this for?"

"Well, I told you the mountains look amazing when the sun sets. But your life is upside down and you sleep through it every day."

I straightened up and squeezed his hand. "So we're watching the sunrise? I'd take that over a sunset any day."

"Why's that?" He smiled at my enthusiasm.

I shrugged, "Sunrise brings warmth. Life. I seem to lack both of those things. I'm not nocturnal by choice, it's just safer this way."

He kissed my forehead and pulled me closer to his side.

We sat comfortably in each other's quiet presence for a few moments before the mountains began to glow, and I asked him, "Have you ever thought about getting piercings?" I contained my urge to giggle as his body tensed.

"That's a… random question."

"What about tattoos? I think you'd look hot, *more so*." I turned my face up to meet his frown and smiled at him, pulling the blanket a little tighter around my shoulders before quietly asking with doe-eyes, "Is there something you want to tell me, Logan?"

*Will he finally admit it?*

Sighing as he looked into my eyes, he shyly dropped his gaze before responding, "Nothing I can say without looking like a fool for rushing things with you, Summer."

*The fuck does that mean? Rushing? Is he referring to telling me about him being Gifted? Fuck, hold up… Does he love me?*

Logan leaned in to kiss my stunned and barely responsive lips as my mind spun in either direction his thoughts could have traveled with my question.

I snapped out of my surprise in time to kiss him back before he pulled away.

My heartbeat quickened at the thought that he might actually feel that way about me. No one had ever told me they loved me before, aside from my parents. And brothers – when they were forced to.

"The sunrise is that way," he tipped his head and bit his lip to hide the smile trying to spread its way across his features, "You're going to miss it if you're looking at me."

"But what if I just want to look at you?" my question tumbled out, voice faint with confusion over his feelings for me.

"Suit yourself," he shook his head, self-conscious with me not being able to take my eyes from his face, "I was hoping you'd point out where you lived."

"What?"

"The mountains. You said you lived closer when you were a kid. Unless you lived on the other side?"

"Oh!" I finally pulled my focus to the distant terrain and pointed in the general direction of the one I'd once lived below. "Over there."

"What was it like? A family of preppers in the woods… It sounds like the *complete* opposite to my childhood."

I giggled, "It was wild. But fun. My brothers and I always got up to trouble."

He arched his brow. "Troublemakers?"

"All of us. We were always wandering around, setting traps in the woods, climbing trees. All sorts of mischief."

"I'd never pick you for someone who got up to mischief," he mumbled sarcastically.

I gasped with pretend offense. "What is that supposed to mean?"

He shrugged, biting back a grin. "Still nothing from them?"

"Nothing."

"We'll find them," he promised, pulling me in again.

The weight of the night's events; the work, the news from Matthias, Logan's borderline confession to either being a serial killer or falling for me – it all caught up to my tired body as we watched the sun drench the mountains on the horizon.

I briefly woke up hours later in Logan's bed. Head aching and stomach swirling as I suffered a mild moment of panic when discovering I was stripped down to my underwear. It took a minute to remember that it was *me* who had sleepily removed my clothing before climbing under the covers.

*He's not Eric,* I reminded myself for the millionth time. *Just a different kind of monster I'm still trying to work out. A monster who might love me. Is that even possible?*

I sighed as I tossed in the bed. While I appreciated the free drinks, I would have been happy for Kit to be lighter on the liquor if it meant I didn't have to suffer for it later.

Slipping out from under the sheets, I crept to the bedroom door. I'd only made it one step into the hallway before Logan rolled over to begin his adorably protective search for me.

"Nurse?"

"I'm just going to the bathroom." I whispered back, unable to understand his mumbled reply as he rolled over to go back to sleep, knowing I was safe.

I barely made it to the bathroom in time. As I reached the sink my body expelled the bright red liquid that'd been bothering it so much.

While the color would have made anyone else concerned, I'd lost enough of these drinks to be familiar with the shade to know my insides were intact.

I'd also vomited enough blood in the past to know this pinkish-red wasn't caused by anything sinister.

After leaning on the vanity for a few minutes, I straightened up and turned the tap on, washing the evidence of my inability to hold my booze down the drain.

That's when I heard them. Moaning. Heavy breathing. The unmistakable sound of people having sex in the apartment.

*Oh my god, Logan's sister must be home.*

I stifled a giggle with my palm. Sure that she wouldn't want to meet me for the first time by bothering her and whoever she had in the bedroom, I thought it best that I got back to bed and wait until later in the morning before making myself known.

As I approached the hall to get back to Logan's room, the noises became clearer.

"*Tommy!*" A woman's voice moaned.

*Wait, what?*

"*Tommy?*" I hissed out loud by mistake.

The voices immediately fell silent. I backed into the bathroom, turning the light off and closing the door most of the way so I could still peak down the hallway.

Tommy emerged from the room at the end of the hall, quickly closing the door and scurrying toward the kitchen — clearly demonstrating the actions of someone trying to *sneak out* of the apartment.

I pressed my back against the bathroom wall as he bustled past, then slipped out behind him. It was comical observing a man of his size trying to sneak anywhere. His height and size didn't exactly allow for any kind of soundless subtlety.

As I followed him, I covered the noise of my actions with his, moving lightly to match his heavy steps. When he opened the front door, I took a few extra long paces to catch up and pushed him out into the hallway, quickly ripping the door closed behind us.

"Summer!" he started with his hands up, shirt in one hand and barely zipped up jeans threatening to drop and reveal more than I cared to see of my boyfriend's best friend.

"Don't, *Summer* me," I snapped, mocking his defensive stance, "What the fuck were you doing in there?"

The enormous man blushed as though he were embarrassed to say the words. "You're sleeping with *Logan's sister?*"

"Yes," he settled on after a long pause, like he actually had to think hard about his answer.

*Like he doesn't know who he's fucking! What is he playing at?*

"Does *Harrison* know?" I felt a sudden pang in my chest for the sparkling woman who seemed to truly love this man. Even with them constantly being on and off and Logan telling me that Harrison openly admitted she'd been with others in the past during their breaks.

Tommy frowned, again, like he didn't know how to answer my question, "Yes?"

As though a lightbulb suddenly exploded in my skull and lit up the dim hall around us, I realized that I had *finally found it* – the weakest link in the group.

My sights may have been set on Jackie at first, but only because she was human. Harrison seemed like the kind of person who would tell me everything if it weren't for Logan's constant glares at her, and for some reason, she seemed to truly respect his dumb decision enough to keep his secrets.

But all along, it was Tommy. The one in the group I thought maybe didn't like me as much as the others, rarely having spoken to me over the months Logan and I had been dating. And we'd *never* been left together unsupervised.

"Does Logan know about the two of you?" I hissed.

Tommy raked a hand through his hair before opening his mouth to answer.

"Don't you dare," I grit through my teeth, "You tell me more than *YES!* Give me real answers!" He shook his head at me and gulped. "My god man, what is wrong with you? *TALK!*"

"Summer?"

The unexpected sound of Logan's smooth voice from behind nearly made me jump out of my skin. I hadn't heard his approach or the door opening with my voice too loud in the quiet hall. I huffed, annoyed that my opportunity to get any more answers out of Tommy was gone.

Logan leaned on the doorframe with his arms across his chest as I turned to look up at him. He glanced down at my body before smirking at me, then up at Tommy, with whom he exchanged a small nod.

I knew *that* look. I'd been at the center of it a million times when I dressed up and played pretend in public with Eric, or when the Finders caught me sneaking up to the boss's room wearing next to nothing. The subtle glance between them was a silent comment on my body.

"Shit!" I gasped when I looked down, forgetting in my haste to chase Tommy out of the apartment that I was still only in the bra and underwear that I'd worn to bed.

"Whatcha doin' out here, baby?" Logan's voice was high with false surprise as he nudged his glasses up the bridge of his nose, "Almost naked and with *my best friend?*" He'd likely heard every word of the exchange between myself and Tommy, and knew it was completely innocent.

*At least it was on my end.*

What about the other woman in her room, hiding out in the apartment while Tommy took the brunt of my interrogation?

I pushed past Logan and stormed back to his bedroom, slamming the door shut behind me. I ran to his bed, ripping the sheet from its place to wrap myself in it with only my head poking out at the top.

Within seconds the door opened again, and Logan kneeled in front of me as I sat on the edge of the mattress.

"Summer, *breathe,*" he ordered gently, looking up at me with wide eyes and hands on my sheet-covered hips to ground me.

I obeyed, not realizing I hadn't been taking in air since the moment it occurred to me that Tommy likely saw *all of my scars*.

"It's okay," he tried reassuring me for the wrong reasons, "Yes, I know about Tommy and my sister. He and Harrison are adults. They have their own… *conditions* on what happens when they're not together."

"It's not… enough…" I wheezed, referring to the air I couldn't take in, though Logan thought I was still talking about his friends.

"I mean, it's not *for me*. I don't really get it," he chuckled, "But they do what works for them."

"He… saw…" I pulled the sheet tighter around my shoulders, prompting Logan to remove his focus from my eyes. Everything seemed to click as his gaze dropped to my tightly wrapped body.

"Shit, *Summer!*"

My body went limp, and all the light left the room. I was left in the dark.

No ghosts.

Alone.

But not for long.

"Hey! There she is." Logan exhaled a relieved sigh when I moved my head from under his chin to look up at him.

As I made sense of the space around us, I found myself on the bed and in Logan's lap. His arms were tied around my body and I was leaning on his chest, still wrapped in the sheet.

"How long was I out?"

"Honestly, like, a few seconds," he smiled down at me. "I'd barely gotten comfortable before your breathing sounded normal again."

"Seconds? Not like, an hour? More?" I'd never been out for such a short amount of time. Eric used to get *bored* waiting for me to regain consciousness.

"No. *Seconds*. I had you the whole time, like I said I would. You're safe with me, Summer."

Removing myself from his arms and the bedding, I turned to face him. As I kneeled on the mattress between his legs I tried to speak, but my breathing was becoming erratic and I couldn't seem to form words.

He reached out to brush hair behind my ear. "You still sound a bit off, maybe you should try to get back to sleep."

"I don't plan on going back to sleep any time soon." I smiled, finding my voice.

"No?" his eyes darted to the side, not understanding my meaning, "Why? Summer!" he swiftly grabbed my hand when I reached for the bottom of his shirt.

"Take it off."

He laughed, "What? *No*, you should rest."

"No," I shook my head. I needed him to understand what this meant to me. "I want you. *Now*. Logan, *I haven't taken anything*. No pills, no *mystery liquid.* I woke up… safe. Not hurt. *You kept me safe*." My breath shuddered unexpectedly.

"Of course I did. I would *never* let anything happen to you." He gently wiped tears from my cheeks with his thumbs. I hadn't realized I was crying. Probably because I couldn't recall having once cried from relief in my entire life.

"I know. I *trust* you."

He didn't stop me when I reached for his shirt again, pulling it over his head as he unclipped my bra. He grabbed me tight by the ribs to pull me higher onto his lap, and I tied my legs around him so I could lean with my chest on his, holding his face in my cold hands.

"How much do you trust me, nurse?" he asked with his lips on mine. While his tone may have sounded playful, I could sense the deeper weight to his question.

I looked into his hazel eyes and gave him the most truthful answer I'd spoken since we'd met; "*Completely*."

# FORTY-SIX

SUMMER

## JUNE 25TH

6pm

I woke earlier than usual. The heat of the day and the intensity of the sunlight outside made it harder to get a full *night's* rest, even with the thick curtains over my bedroom window.

Before getting out of bed, I sent Logan a text to let him know I was awake. He wasn't demanding to know my every move – I just wanted his attention.

As much as I loved that he worked all afternoon and into the night so he could sleep lightly and listen out for me during my shifts, I was missing him and the full days we used to spend together. Even if most of it was spent sleeping beside each other.

I was sure he'd eventually come to terms with the risk of me being attacked by one of my patients. But I had to be patient with his overprotectiveness while he learned more about me. He'd eventually work out how little of his protection I needed.

**Dream of me?**

He replied to my text within seconds, as though he were waiting for me to wake up. He might have been, and the thought only tempered the heat of the room.

*He's not even in the damn house and he's making me blush.* I smiled and texted back.

**Always.**

It wasn't a lie. I *had* been dreaming of him. Over the months we'd been together, I'd found more of my nightmares were replaced by simple dreams. Not all of them were good. My subconscious still tried to remind me that Logan wasn't the perfect man I'd often catch myself believing he was.

But *most* of them were good.

Like the one I'd just woken from that left me aching for him and tempted to reach for the toys in my drawer. The warmer weather must have been playing tricks on my mind while I slept, surrounding me in a similar heat to what Logan's body often did as he moved above me… beneath me… behind me.

*Fuck, I need to go for a run.* I needed to clear my head of him until he got home. Then I could put some of the dream's creativity to good use.

As I got up to dress in my leggings and a loose singlet, I texted Logan with a few of the details of my dream, to which he swiftly responded;

**Stay in bed, I'll be there in five.**

I knew he was joking. He'd been trying to finish as many full shifts as possible at work so he could either take time off with me, or disappear with his friends.

**Gym?** He messaged as I parted my hair for braiding.

**Going for a run instead. Come straight home?**

The sun was setting as I tied my shoes, and the air had barely begun to cool when I stepped outside. The gate moved aside for me to leave as Logan replied with a winking emoji.

I turned right at the end of my driveway and began to move. The crickets chirping loudly were my only company for the miles I covered while the sunlight gradually vanished behind me.

I'd been making better time and keeping a more consistent pace than I ever used to before I'd met Logan. His influence with ensuring I ate frequently and survived on more than coffee seemed to be doing wonders for my energy levels, though I'd never admit it.

As the road veered to the right, a car began approaching from behind. The glow of the head lights softly illuminated the night air around me, growing sharper as it neared.

I'd lived in the area for long enough to recognise the sound cars generally made when traveling at the posted speed. So, when I heard this one begin to slow as I came into view, my stomach dropped.

It was still a fair way behind, but would catch up within seconds.

I had to think fast.

It could have been my imagination and I was about to make a complete fool of myself, but I went with my gut. I grabbed the guard rail at the edge of the road with one hand, and used the momentum from my jog to hurl my body down to the rough ground below.

Twigs and fallen pine needles crunched under my weight as I shuffled further down the slope to where the tree line became more dense. With trembling hands I turned my phone's brightness down and called Tony.

"Boss?" He answered immediately. Did he ever sleep? It was still hours before he needed to wake for the night's shift.

"I'm probably overreacting–"

"Don't talk. Send your location." The sound of car keys being snatched up off a hard surface and many voices passed through to my ear as he called, "Ben!"

The car on the road above pulled to a stop where I'd vanished from sight. The familiar sound of its heavy doors opening and footsteps on the road made me freeze.

*Finders? Out here?*

With my back pressed against the thick base of a tall pine, my fingers scrambled to send Tony my location.

Ben's response in the background made me smile through the panic rising in my chest, "Overtime? Of all nights? It's gonna cost her."

I steadied my breathing and covered my mouth as one of my pursuers made the same jump over the edge. Foliage crackled under their steps where they paced the tree line.

"Stitch?" A man's voice called.

*Fuck! Simon?*

"*It's time to come Home!*" called another familiar voice.

As I prepared to run through the woods, another car pulled up behind theirs.

"Give me a sign you're still there," Tony demanded. I tapped the phone a few times with my nails. "Good. Fuck, boss, we're further away than usual."

I squeezed my eyes shut, trying to listen to what was happening on the road above. One car with two Finders – survivable. I could outrun them in this fairly familiar area.

But two cars, with the potential of not one, but possibly five more people after me? I didn't like my chances. They could spread out and surround me from all angles. I'd be taken. Just like that, in the dark. Gone. Never to see Logan or the bodyguards again.

*And all because I wanted to run this damned horniness off. I should have just stayed in bed until he got home.*

The occupants of the car shone torches from their phones. Soft light bounced off the trunks to either side of me.

"Breathe," Tony instructed through the phone. I let out the air in my lungs, not realizing I'd been holding it for so long.

The deep voice of a stranger flowed down through the dark, asking if the Finders were having car trouble. I could have laughed with relief at the confirmation that a whole team hadn't been sent to hunt me down.

*Not yet. He's closing in on you.*

The two men insisted they didn't need help, with Simon stating, "We're fine. Just looking for our… dog."

*Fuck you, Simon!* I wanted to throw a rock at his head. Eric didn't keep pets, but I was sure a dog would have been treated far better than I ever had.

"Call him." Tony said to Ben.

"On it."

*Call who?*

The Finders had upgraded to torches, and the light cut through the night like a glowing knife.

There was an abandoned house at the bottom of the hill. If I could make it that far, I could hide there until the bodyguards arrived. I may have spent years dressing up in the city, but I was trained far better to survive the Gray Mountains than these members of my former family.

"Logan?" Ben's voice sounded as a call of his own was answered.

Then, Tony hung up on me.

# FORTY-SEVEN

## LOGAN

Work; boring. Breaks; also boring. But this was necessary. I needed the menial job and the little it paid. I couldn't fund my criminal life solely on voluntary vigilante work and the little remaining inheritance that couldn't be touched without my sister's assistance.

I was dead – *legally* speaking. So working overnight for cash at a dingy restaurant on the side of the highway seemed the best solution to my unemployment problems. The owners knew *what* I was. Not *who* I was. They were happy to have me. A man of my size, Gifted and an ex-cop.

They didn't pry into my past, they just liked the idea that I could keep their staff safe during the night. Even out in the mountains, there were still plenty of freaks and psychos this far from major cities who enjoyed terrorizing the locals.

Their best mode of defense was to hire one.

The restaurant had only been held up once since I was hired, and I believed I'd sent enough of a message for it to not happen again. It hadn't ended well for those who tried to rob the bar. And while I'd scared them off, it ended poorer still when I caught them trying to sneak in for a second round.

Sometimes, I wondered if my victims had families. Mother's searching for their missing children. Loving spouses wondering how they could have been left behind. There were times when I wondered if I were really doing any good by removing these pieces of shit, or if I were simply creating more villains in those who'd seek vengeance for the ones they'd lost. I had to shove those thoughts away. I couldn't dwell on shit like that, it would only drive me more insane.

When I told the owners I needed to change my shifts, their disappointment was palpable. But my priorities had changed. There were more important things to worry about than the lives of those I worked with.

There was *her*.

Stars started to appear in the evening sky as I leaned on the brick wall, out the back by the door to the kitchen. The weather was warm. Uncomfortable. Small beads of sweat built at the edge of my hairline and under the arms of my glasses.

It would have been more pleasant inside, but I preferred to come to this space to clear my mind before heading back to the dining room, where I'd take orders and my brain would rot a little more from boredom.

The song I had on repeat started playing in my ears again. I knew why I was drawn to it. It was dark, depressing. Not my usual taste in music, but sometimes, I needed a break from keeping up the calm facade that was barely held together by the duct tape made of the little patience I had left for this place and its people.

Sometimes I just liked to disappear into the fucked up depths of my mind. It freed me from the hours of tedious repetition until we chased our next lead or I could go home and busy myself with the body and mind of the woman I could never get enough of.

This song seemed to speak to me. I kind of hated that it did. It spoke of division. Alter egos. Blame. I would have sent it to Summer – it could have subtly given her a little insight as to what went on inside my head. But my girlfriend, being the fucking weirdo that she was, didn't seem to care for any music at all.

She'd either lie about listening to it, or impatiently sit through a song as I watched her to make sure she heard it. When it was over, she'd give a polite shrug and tell me she liked it to spare my feelings, but she could never recall a single word or beat. I'd even sent her the song we danced to at Crave and she barely reacted at all. It was disappointing. I'd hoped it would get her heart racing.

Another of the employees came stumbling out into the alley, tearing my concentration from the lyrics. *Two* employees. One of the recently hired cooks was pulled along by a woman on the waitstaff. She spun to him, held his face in her hands and drew him down to kiss her.

I could understand why they were doing this. Their lives were no doubt as boring as mine had been until a few months ago. Quick fucks with near-strangers and work drama were about all that kept this place from being burned down by its miserable employees.

*If I were still a cop, I could arrest them.* I smirked at the idea.

Such a petty crime. Essentially harmless until the cook would learn the waitress had done the same with every other new employee for however long she'd been working here.

She'd tried with me too, but I wasn't interested.

The moment she stepped into the staffroom where I was dressing for my shift, I could immediately smell the STD she carried at the time. And the idea of fucking *anyone* in the dirty alley beside the dumpsters sat far below my hygiene standards. She took my rejection way too personally and had barely spoken to me since.

I turned my music up to dull the sound of the cook pinning the woman to the brick wall. Even without looking at them, I could tell he was tugging down his pants enough to get his dick out to fuck her beneath the short skirt of the uniform. With the volume maxed out, I still couldn't block out the woeful attempt she made at faking her enjoyment. She had none of that animalistic enthusiasm I'd experience each night I went home to *her*.

Pulling my phone from my pocket, I checked the time: *5:55pm*.

She still wouldn't be up for a while, but my mood instantly picked up at the thought of her. There wasn't a day that she'd message later than 7:01pm to let me know she was awake. It was all part of the routine for us, and I think I loved it more than she did.

I closed my eyes, trying to focus on the music and not the scent of cigarette smoke as it swirled the air around me. It'd been years since I quit, but each time this odor exited someone's lungs on a heavy exhale my fingers twitched with the need to carry out the entire ritual.

My eyes darted to my phone before the first buzz from a text was complete. It was her, an hour early. My sight sharpened at the thought that something might be wrong, making it impossible to read the text with my glasses on.

What could have the zombie rising from the dead sooner than usual? To take an hour of sleep from Summer was like trying to pull teeth. I fucking hated pulling teeth, but evidence didn't dispose of itself.

**I'm up!** It read, with the red lips emoji. I let out a sigh of relief at her usual greeting, and that she was safe.

**Dream of me?**

**Always.**

The noises of the other two in the alley, talking softly as they shared the cigarette, all but dissipated as the sound of my heartbeat drowned them out.

Summer had an effect on me I hadn't experienced in years. I liked it – but it still scared me. It'd only break me so much more if either of us ever fucked up.

**Yeah? Tell me.**

**It was too dirty.**

**No such thing. Tell me.**

If I were being honest, it would have been fine knowing she'd slept peacefully in the hours I couldn't be by her side, but intrigue took a firm hold over my mind now she'd hinted at the theme of her subconscious's creation.

**I dreamed you were tearing my clothes off in front of the bathroom mirror. Fucking me from behind.**

I loved it when she came right out and said it, no guessing or dancing around the topic. I didn't have the patience for that. All I wanted were the details so my mind could use it as fuel, to get creative with all the ways I could make those dreams a reality.

She continued; **You held my ribs so tight I think one of them broke. And when you were done filling me with that HOT cum, I got on my knees to suck it off your hard dick. You pushed it so far down my throat I thought I would die.**

Fuck, I loved this side of her.

**Stay in bed, I'll be there in five.**

My shift didn't end for a couple of hours, but if she asked, I'd risk losing my job to be there.

*If I leave right now, I could be there in a few minutes to rail her in front of our reflections.*

My dick throbbed in my jeans and I closed my eyes again. I tried to think of *anything* but fucking that hot little body from behind. It didn't work, all I could envision were Summer's blue eyes, and the way they looked up at me from below, rolling to the back of her skull while I gently played with her hair as she blew me.

For the sake of the diners who'd be at eye level with a hard-on, I thought about my latest kill. There was nothing like hosing brain matter from walls to soften things up.

**Gym?** I texted her, switching the subject to something less provocative. Though, if we planned on meeting up to workout, I wouldn't be able to keep my hands off her once that ass was bouncing on a treadmill. My stomach pinched in jealous knots at the thought of how many people I glared into retreat the last time we were there. I wasn't the only one hypnotized by the way all the best parts of her jiggled.

**Going for a run instead. Come straight home?**

It made sense. The weather was perfect for it. And while I hated the idea of her running around, alone on the roads that would soon be pitch-black as the sun set, I had to give her the space to do what she wanted.

I messaged back a winky face that I hoped would send her pulse into a sprint at the thought of what I might do to her when I arrived.

*Ten out of ten,* I praised myself. *Good move for a normal boyfriend. Not too possessive.*

I trudged back inside, ignoring the call of surprise from the cook and waitress who wouldn't have had a chance of detecting me in the growing shadows of my hiding place. I made my way through to the bar, keeping my headphones in to soften the sounds of the metal and ceramics clashing in the kitchen.

The gang was already waiting for me. When I sat in the booth across from Jackie, she slipped a hand into her bag, retrieving the sunglasses to put them on her head. Subtlety wasn't her strong suit.

"I preferred your later shifts," Nova huffed beside me as I finally removed the music from my skull.

"So did I. But it's better this way." Leaning with my jaw on my palm, I automatically scanned the room for threats – a habit I would die with. We all preferred the quiet of the late night work, but the noise of the bar's patrons and the music blaring from the jukebox was a good trade-off for better coverage as we spoke.

"Any new leads?" Jackie asked hopefully.

"Nah." I hated being the one to constantly disappoint her. "Reid has been hard to get a hold of."

We were hitting nothing but dead ends. Resources were scarce enough as it was without me hounding my old partner for information.

Echo may have been useful in her field, but with the condition her corpse had been discovered, she was quickly written off as a junkie and not worth any department's time.

It was a fucking insult to her memory. Half her injuries were ignored and not noted in the reports Reid risked a promotion to share with me – much to his new partner's disgust.

But Echo was *different.* And humans didn't appreciate police efforts being divvied up for helping Gifted when they'd rather see it used for locking them up.

There was only so much I could do for my friend's widow. I wished everyday that I could do more.

Jackie nodded, and to my surprise, gave an almost genuine smile. "Well, I've got some news for *you.*"

"Yeah?" Worse than having no leads on her wife's death, was the fact that I'd asked her for a favor.

"Still no name… But from the little I gathered, he's just some bodyguard. *They* worked together once. Just *once.*"

I'd asked her to look into the man we'd spied Summer speaking with at Crave. It was reasonable to suss out *anyone* who visited the club, but my intentions weren't pure in this case. While I was adamant about giving Summer the time and space to tell me about her past, I had no intention of offering that same kindness to the characters she interacted with along the way.

I wanted to know how much of a threat this guy could be, not to Summer's life, but to my comfortable position between her legs.

*Just some bodyguard.*

Jackie meant well, but as far as my cover story went, I was *just some busboy*. A far less appealing title when seeking out a mate.

*Zero out of ten. Back to shitty, jealous boyfriend.*

"It sounded like more than *once,*" I countered snidely, and Tommy, quiet until this moment as he sat across from Nova, nearly spat his beer trying to hold in a laugh.

"Whatever he did to her certainly left an impression," he agreed.

Jackie's face flushed pink and she blinked away from my gaze. I hated that my friends rarely made eye contact with me for longer than a few seconds.

"It really did sound like they had a lot of fun." The muttered words under her breath sent a feverish ripple outward from my chest and under every inch of my skin.

Nova elbowed me, sensing the heatwave for herself, "I'm sure you do *just fine*. The guy hinted at taking her upstairs several times and she *still* showed up at the apartment. The girl's obsessed with you." Her words were a little comforting, it sure seemed Summer and I felt the same about each other.

"But he's human?" I asked Jackie.

"As far as I can tell, yeah." That made me sigh. He was better suited to Summer in ways I could never be. "And while I was digging through his past, I looked into… Bedlam cults."

Tommy jumped in his seat, startled by the mouthful of liquid Nova spurted across the table.

"The fuck are you looking into cults for?" she demanded of Jackie, whose skin paled as she scrambled to come up with an answer.

I interjected before Nova made a scene, "I okayed it. You all know Summer was part of a cult."

"You don't think Summer had anything to do with *his* people, do you?"

"Nah. Not *him*."

Jackie found her voice and added, "The Manip — *that* cult is still disbanded. No activity. And there are so many others active right now it'd be hard to know which Summer was a part of without more specific information."

I nodded, putting an end to the discussion.

As my friends got back to their conversation, I allowed my mind to wander a little. I thought of her texts and counted down the minutes until my shift was over so I could leave this shithole behind for another day.

We ordered food. I ate more than all of them combined while a couple of the staff behind the bar eyed me with hostility. It wasn't clear if they knew I was Gifted, but it always seemed to bother them that I got away with doing next to nothing during my long hours.

It was hard to be different in this town. Though it was big, people still knew each other within their smaller communities. They talked. And the general population here weren't known for their kindness to those who stood out.

Things were wildly different in Bedlam. I could have gone shopping for groceries in the suit. I could have strut down the busy streets holding my girlfriend's hand, wrapped head to toe in black and red and no one would've given a shit. We'd look just like everyone else.

*Except, you know, that suit can no longer be seen in Bedlam. Not after what you did.*

"You've got your appetite back." Jackie giggled while I hardly said a word, too busy shoveling food in my face and lost in my own head.

"Never lost it. Had to slow some healing."

Even then, the holes in my stomach had healed suspiciously fast and there was barely a mark from the injury that should have left plenty of scars. Summer never said anything in the few times she insisted on checking and redressing my wounds. I was glad she hadn't. I'd been too moody with being hangry all the time and was worried I'd slip up.

Lucky for us, once Summer took my shirt off and her hands were all over me, we quickly became too distracted for her to bother with the questioning.

Nova rolled her eyes at me. "It's getting old, Logan. How can you expect to have a normal life if you keep so much from her? She should be here with us."

"She's usually still asleep at this time of night." A weak argument, at best.

"You know that's not what I meant. I've been meaning to ask… Does Summer have a tattoo?"

*This woman and her inability to mind her own fucking business.*

"Nah… Why?" I narrowed my eyes at her, and she did the same back to me. Like me, she seemed to sense lies a mile away.

Nova bounced her shoulders with a shrug. "I dunno, I guess she seems like the type to have *at least* one."

"At least." Jackie agreed with a shy smirk, "Something cute. My guess would be on her ass."

"Oh!" Nova clapped as an idea popped into her head, "Or something even hotter, like her inner thigh? Like Cel—" she suddenly bit her tongue and shook her head.

Celeste was one of the few women Nova *hadn't* slept with during the "breaks" between her and Tommy. She barely respected boundaries, but friend's wives were thankfully off the table. With her and Jackie being so close since we all moved out this way, it didn't surprise me at all Nova had pried that kind of information from her new best friend.

I cleared my throat in a bid to redirect the discussion. Though, unable to think of anything fast enough, the topic was still firmly set on my girlfriend's body, "What's with the questions about Summer and tattoos?"

I knew exactly why she asked, but I wanted the distraction for Jackie's sake. Tattoos were like ignited flares, guiding all attention, wanted or otherwise, to people's pasts. Nova was still suspicious that Summer's history was far more interesting than my little nurse led on.

That was obvious, but I wasn't about to ruin everything by treating my girlfriend like a suspect and demanding more answers from her about a time when we weren't together.

Nova's sparkly orbs widened at Tommy, prompting him to answer for her, "Nova and I were trying to guess what she might have."

"Yeah?" I arched a brow at his smug face. Lying so blatantly was a daring move for someone who knew what I could do to them for being dishonest. "You've seen her wearing next to nothing," I accused. "Do you remember noticing anything then?" I didn't mean for my question to come up on such a harsh growl from deep within my chest.

Tommy lifted his eyes to the ceiling, squinting to avoid my gaze entirely. "Honestly, I got a little distracted by…" he paused, smart enough to catch himself before he gave away secrets that weren't his to share – for once. I had no doubt he'd tell Nova eventually, especially now he'd alluded to knowing something she didn't.

I wasn't bothered that Tommy had seen Summer *almost* naked. He'd seen me tear enough limbs from sockets to know better than to think about touching her. I was more upset for Summer's sake. She always put so much effort into ensuring the scars were never seen.

I barely noticed them anymore, but with Tommy only seeing her once, I understood it could be an unsettling sight to take in.

That tight body of hers had been treated like a fucking pin cushion. Maybe more like a knife block, with all those scarred stab wounds.

Nova gasped. "*You* got to see Summer *naked?* Why didn't you tell me! And what were you distracted by?"

"Not *entirely* naked," he corrected her with his hands up.

Nova's hand flew to her mouth. "So? Does she look as good as we imagined?"

"*Better.*" Tommy gestured to his chest and widened his eyes a little, like he had no self control. His eyes darted to mine in apology. I couldn't be mad at that comment. And I couldn't recall which bra Summer wore that night, but it must have been one I'd never seen her wear before. It did an exceptional job of pushing her tits together.

"But no tattoos?" Nova asked, still hung up on the ink.

"*None*." I lied. Kind of. Whatever remained of the one under Summer's collarbone could barely count for a tattoo anymore.

"I mean, you *are* fucking blind," Nova sighed, "Maybe you've missed it."

"Missed it?" I snorted, grabbing a few, uneaten fries from Jackie's plate to toss them at Nova's sparkly face. "I've practically turned the woman inside out on a nightly basis, for *months*. If she had any, I'd know." A smile over another thought of the texts fractured my frustration with Nova. She tossed one back, and I caught it between my teeth.

My friends eyed each other, grinning like juveniles that had deciphered a dirty joke. I shouldn't have been so defensive about their teasing. They were happy for me. It was something I was sure they all believed they'd never feel again.

"I gotta go. I'll catch you guys later." I told them as I stood with only minutes left before I was free to leave.

When I reached the kitchen, my hands moved on autopilot. Tamping coffee grounds, filling a cup with ice and milk. While it wasn't typically my job to make iced coffees in the past, I trusted no one else with anything Summer would be consuming.

Instead of a double shot, I made it a triple, knowing she'd need the spike with what I planned on doing to her before she started work for the night.

As I searched for a lid for the cup, my phone vibrated in my pocket. I never attached names to my contacts *just in case* anything ever happened to me or my phone went missing.

Nova's name was simply a star emoji. Tommy, the chef. Jackie and I were equally excited when I could finally add a redhead to her number.

Summer was the peach, to which she'd raised an unamused eyebrow when she first noticed. I'd told her it was my favorite "Summer" fruit, but really, I hadn't settled on one for her until I spotted her in the alley at Crave. The shape of her ass in that leather suit had clouded my mind for days.

She quickly found it cute when I promised I'd assigned everyone with a picture and not a name. I hadn't thought how that might look at first, and reassured her I wasn't hiding her from anyone – that she wasn't just a fuck on the side.

Sometimes I worried this whole system made me look illiterate, but I texted her plenty for her mind not to travel down that path.

*Just the path of overlooking so many abnormal things about our relationship in order to keep up our acts instead.*

The number on the screen had nothing assigned to it, but I recognised it immediately. This wasn't a connection I was comfortable with keeping from her, but it seemed that having it was about to pay off.

"Hey. What's–"

"Logan?" Ben's voice was strained, annoyed. Mine was about to be too, with all that fucking noise in the background on his end. Dozens of voices, music playing, people singing, Tony's stressed out huffing as he listened in.

"Mhmm?" I asked with my eyes shut tight, pressing the phone between the side of my face and my shoulder. I finished attaching a lid to the cup and jammed a straw through the top.

"Summer's being followed."

My stomach dropped. *Is this it? The moment she disappears?* I had no doubt Summer was being watched after the things she'd told me and finding that assholes like Pyro were spying on her.

But to have her followed out in the secluded hills in the dark? Had I been too distracted with her to notice that someone's grasp was constricting around her?

Maybe I'd gotten everything wrong with switching up the hours at work. It felt like the right thing to do at the time. She'd been assaulted *during* work hours – it made sense for me to be around when she treated patients, even with the bodyguards around. I was a far better source of protection than either of them.

*This woman needs a full-time babysitter,* I sighed.

"Explain."

"Tony could hear the voices of two men saying her name when she called for help."

*Why the fuck didn't she call me?*

"Where is she?" I spoke low and tried to steady my breathing, I needed to stay in control.

"Sending her location now."

My phone buzzed against my ear, and I pulled it away to open the map as I stepped out of the building. She was on the move. In the middle of a fucking forest.

*Of course*, I rolled my eyes, *God forbid she be followed somewhere a little less dangerous.*

Summer wasn't stupid. She'd know how to use the woods to her advantage and might lose her pursuers without my help, so long as they weren't also raised by paranoid preppers.

If anything, I felt more concern for those accused of following her. If I found them before they found her… *Fuck, should I wear the suit?*

"It's my daughter's birthday," Ben said, "We're not as close as we usually are."

"So, you want me to do your job for you?" I laughed as the engine of my car roared to life.

"I wouldn't call if we didn't think anything of it–" he started to defend himself, sounding disappointed.

"I'll find her." I reassured him. The guy might have been a joker, but took his job seriously, and the one time he was unavailable, shit didn't go to plan. "Though I can imagine she'll be pissed with you for involving me."

"Please tell me you've got coffee?"

I shook the cup so the ice cubes rattled against the plastic. He laughed as I placed it in the cup holder and silently prayed it wouldn't spill with the limits I was about to push my car to.

"I might live to see another day," he sighed, "Text me when you find her? Make sure she knows it's *you* coming. The boss tends to bite when she's scared." He hung up.

*The fuck does that mean?*

I should have been more focused on the road as I raced past the other cars in the pitch-black of the sloping terrain, but the thought that Summer could ever be the "biter" between us was a good distraction from the thoughts of what I might be about to find – if I found her at all.

# FORTY-EIGHT

## SUMMER

*Are you fucking kidding me?* I internally screamed. *They're sending my boyfriend?*

I shouldn't have been so livid; Logan was due to finish work for the night and they must have had a valid reason for them to even consider bringing him into this.

To learn Ben had Logan's number was a surprising piece of information I needed to shelve to be pissed about later. It didn't sit well with me.

Were my suspicions warranted? Were they spending time together behind my back? What did they talk about? Were they giving more of my secrets away to Logan when I wasn't ready to share them?

From the road above, the deep voice of the stranger wished the Finders luck before they got back in their car and drove away.

The sound of car doors closing and the engine rumbling as they continued down the road only gave me a brief sense of relief.

Eric's men might not have known the exact location of my house, but I didn't like the odds now they'd appeared on one of my regular routes.

Taking a deep breath, I surveyed the dark woods and took my first step in the opposite direction of my street, not wanting to lead more foxes to the chicken coop.

Though clouds were rolling in, I found enough flickering stars through the pine canopy to determine the direction of the abandoned house.

*Fuck. Please don't let me stumble across any wild animals,* I begged the night as I trudged through the undergrowth with absolutely no way to defend myself.

*Maybe I should carry a scalpel when I leave the house.* I quickly decided that running with a knife on the uneven ground probably wasn't one of my brightest ideas.

The air became eerily still. There were no sounds except for my footfalls on the dirt. It only made me more anxious. If there were eyes on me, their owners were exceptionally still while they observed my escape.

With each step, the earth released an enchanting scent. Crushed pine and bark. Healthy, damp soil. It smelled like home. The home of my childhood, not the sterile glass tank in the city.

The abandoned house appeared ahead of me. Empty. Gloomy. Falling apart. It was in a far worse condition than the last time I'd passed through, evidently not fairing well through each winter without being maintained and properly weatherproofed.

The forest began to thin, and waist-high grass engulfed my lower half as I trekked over the property line and into the overgrown yard.

*God, I hope there's no old traps.*

I dragged my feet and shone the useless light from my phone around to ensure I wouldn't step into any steel jaws that would have me needing much more than a few stitches.

Bear traps were obviously something I didn't want to encounter, but worse than that would be a fucking *bear* while chained up and bleeding out.

"Ouch!" I hissed and looked down. My leggings glistened in the moonlight as I bent in half to inspect my leg. Parting the grass to my right, I found the source of my injury – large chunks of rusty metal, hidden deep within the grass. Probably old car parts left to rot along with the house.

"Ugh." I whined and held the torch over the wound to get a better look, glad I was smart enough to stay up to date with all my shots. The cut stretched a few inches in a curved line, midway between my knee and ankle. I couldn't decide if it needed stitches until I got back to my garage, and I didn't have the tools on hand to tend to it. With no other options, I kept moving.

The sound of a car startled me. Its engine rang loud in the distance on the dirt road that led to the house. Thinking that the Finders must have turned back to continue their search, I turned my light off and ran for my fucking life.

The door to the crumbling structure was locked, but the timber was weak and fractured from decay. I shouldered it hard and exhaled with relief as it cracked open. Splinters of wood fell to the floor as I hurriedly closed it behind me.

The entire house would've been no larger than my kitchen and living areas combined. The small stove and bench took up the far wall, totally dilapidated. What remained of a bed sagged to my right. Last I checked, the outhouse outside was long reclaimed by nature.

There was nowhere to hide. This place would be suitable for shelter when waiting to be picked up, but with actually being *followed* here, it wasn't the best choice on my route for playing hide and seek with Eric's henchmen.

*I could lie down in the grass. Whole fucking car parts are getting away with hiding out there,* I rolled my eyes at myself for having gotten sliced up on a simple jog around the block.

*Fuck. I guess this is it then.* I roughly dropped to sit in the center of the room, facing the door I'd come through as I rolled the fabric of my leggings up to assess the damage. The cut was deep and it hurt to move, the short run to the house had me hobbling.

*Really?* I wiped the blood from my fingers on my shirt. *You're really going to sit here and sulk over a cut on your leg and let Simon drag you back to Eric? Better yet, why don't you just lie on your back right here on the floor and wait for Eric to come have his way with you?*

My thoughts pissed me off enough to push my palms on the dirty floor, lifting myself to stand. I knew what waited for me in Bedlam, and it was worth dying to avoid. The Finders would have strict instructions to return me in a near perfect state, but like all villains, they'd put their life above mine if that's what it came to – as I would do with my own.

The ache in my leg made me limp as I moved for the rotting bench in search of anything I could use to defend myself. The Finders would have guns, but they'd have to use their hands if they expected me to get into a car with them.

I wrenched open a drawer that had almost sealed itself shut and cautiously fumbled through the splinters and metal pieces within. Cutlery. Spoons. Nothing sharp enough to keep space between me and my imminent captors.

The second drawer was harder to open. I grabbed the handle with both hands and used my aching leg to push against the cabinet. The handle snapped clean off under my weight and sent me toppling to the ground.

I glared up at the drawer, and as I were about to start spewing profanities at the inanimate piece of rotting furniture, I noticed it'd budged a little. Grabbing one of the spoons from the top drawer, I wedged it into the gap before kicking its long handle with my uninjured leg. This time, it opened.

"Fuck, yeah!" I exclaimed at the sight of knives and cleavers. Old. Rusty. "Even better." I smiled, grabbing two in each hand then ambling back to the center of the room.

As the car approached the house, it sounded familiar, though not in the same way as Simon's had.

*There's no fucking way,* I frowned, *It's a trick. A coincidence.*

With Eric, anything was possible.

The vehicle skidded to a stop before shutting off. I took a deep breath to calm my nerves and rearranged the knives, leaving one in my right hand, fingers carefully pinching the handle.

Footsteps approached the house as I took another breath and held it in my lungs. Ignoring the pain in my leg, I squared my shoulders and positioned my stance for the throw.

"*Elbow to ear,*" Dad's voice spoke in my mind as I raised my arm. "*Aim through your target, baby girl. You'll be better than James in no time.*"

I doubted my father ever believed that I'd one day be throwing knives at the goons of the man I'd run away with. Or that the skills ingrained into my routine since toddlerhood ended up being puppeteered by one of Bedlam's worst.

As the heavy paces outside came to a stop, the moon slipped behind thick clouds above, plunging my surroundings into complete darkness. My other senses instantly heightened where my vision failed.

*Only one?* I noted there were no other sounds outside the crumbling structure. Just the grass, roughly rustling in the breeze. It wasn't typical of Finders to be hunting solo.

The door snapped from its hinges and fell flat to the floor, sending a cloud of dust into the night air between me and whoever was on the other side.

Hesitation wasn't an option. Only survival. I threw the knife.

My aim was flawless, and I couldn't miss a target of the shadowy figure's size, but the fucker effortlessly weaved out of its path. The blade audibly zipped past their right cheek and into the darkness, landing far in the distance.

*Great,* I huffed, *If I manage to escape this Finder, I'll now have another sharp object out there that wants to fuck up my night.*

The figure took a slow step toward me and I snapped back into position, second blade at the ready.

"Fuck, baby! Did you really just throw a *knife* at me?" The voice was shocked. Maybe a little impressed.

"Logan?"

The silhouette shuffled, then the room suddenly illuminated with the light from his phone. I immediately straightened up and dropped the knives, as if that could hide them. They clattered around my feet as I tried my best to look innocent.

You know, just hanging out in a deserted shack in bear infested woods like I would any other summer night. No biggie.

"The fuck are you doing out here, nurse?" The question was right, but his tone was wrong. He should have been concerned, scolding me for reckless behavior, not arching a brow and smirking down at the sight of me surrounded by rusty projectiles.

"I-I… umm." I stammered as the moonlight crept back over the house. What was I meant to tell him? *I'm running from my insane ex's men through the forest?*

He stepped over the door and took in what he could of our surroundings through his glasses. He was lucky I'd nearly done the same with how weak the door had become, or else we'd have another awkward, my-boyfriend-is-clearly-Gifted moment that we'd have to sidestep around.

*Though, surely we're having one of those moments right now? How the fuck did he dodge the knife with his poor eyesight?*

"Wow, what a dump," Logan said before looking back at me. "Come here often?" he teased, slipping his phone back in his pocket and casually handing me an iced coffee in a takeaway cup from his other hand. Bringing me my favorite drink when he came home was one of the only perks to his shifts being so different to mine.

"No…" I replied with wide eyes, accepting the cup, "God, how fast were you driving? It's only been a few minutes since Ben called you."

"Fast enough," he shrugged dismissively. "I was about to head over anyway."

"You could have killed someone. *Yourself*."

He shook his head and sighed, "You don't need to worry about me. I clearly need to worry about you, though. You're bleeding."

*I'd love to know how he spotted that in the dark.*

"You've got blood on your shirt, nurse."

*Nice save.*

"It's just a scratch." I twisted my leg to inspect the mess it was making of my shoe and the dirt floor.

"Yeah," he agreed with an eye roll, "What'd you get scratched by? A helicopter blade?"

I sighed, "Fine. Can you grab the kit I left in your car?"

Logan's car was my latest victim in my mission to stock the planet with first aid kits.

*Mom would be proud.*

I smiled sadly as he returned with the small black pouch. I sat on the floor and unrolled it beside my hip, picking out what I needed to clean up my leg while Logan dropped to the ground on my right.

"Ben told me you were being followed?" All playful looks from his arrival were replaced with concern now he knew I was injured and not simply playing a deadly game of hide and seek.

"Is that *all* he said?"

Logan narrowed his eyes behind the thick lenses, watching my lips as I sipped at the coffee. "Yeah. He told me some guys were bothering you while you were out on your run. And that he and Tony were further away than normal and couldn't get to you as fast as I could," he explained while I disinfected my wound.

"That's pretty much it," I lied, tossing bloody gauze to the floor to begin loading a needle for the cut. "They were slowing down, calling out shit to me."

"So you thought it was best to run through the woods to hide out in *Tetanus Town* until someone came to your rescue?"

I giggled, "*Tetanus Town* seemed like a better option than being snatched by weirdos in the dark. And I didn't need rescuing… I can take care of myself," I protested stubbornly, forgetting the fact that I was the one who'd called the bodyguards for help in the first place.

It seemed Logan hadn't forgotten, he nodded along to my whining, grin amused.

"Wait, there's no anesthetic here. Should we do this at home?" he grabbed the phone from my hand, using the light to double check the contents of the kit between us.

"Nah, it'll only need three stitches. I'd rather get it over and done with." I told him as I worked out which position to hold my leg, "And I don't want to bleed all through your car. Hold the light up for me."

"As considerate as that is," he grimaced, holding the phone for me. "I really don't want you to be hurting just so–"

My pained groan interrupted him as I started my first stitch. Biting my lip, I focused on my breathing and swiftly sewed myself back together. It fucking hurt, but three small stitches were nothing when I'd had full names carved into me without the luxury of being numbed every time.

Logan shook his head and took the used needle from my hand once I'd finished tying off my work and rolled it up with the rest of the kit.

"You shouldn't have done that. I could have gotten you home in thirty seconds."

"Yeah, but I just got stitched in like, four, so…" I shrugged and stretched my leg out to twist it to the side, wondering if this cut would grace me with another scar. Apparently I didn't have enough already.

"Is it completely fucked up that the sounds you just made had me thinking about those texts you sent earlier?" He picked up my coffee and took a sip.

I laughed and snatched my drink back, "Not really. I think I make similar noises when you're squeezing my ribs."

"Mmm," he sighed and leaned back on his palms, looking me over as I mimicked his position, "That'd explain it. You've never told me why you like it so much." He frowned and took my drink again.

"I can't like it without an explanation?" I raised an eyebrow and ripped my coffee from his hand to get more in my system before he could drink it all.

"Nothing is that simple with you, Summer."

I sighed and took another sip, "I think it's part of the way I've been conditioned."

He frowned at my confession. Logan understood me and all the quirks I brought into this relationship, but it bothered him when something he enjoyed came from dark origins.

"Not in the way you think. I've never had anyone grab me the way you do. The *pain* is what I'm referring to. I enjoy it." I admitted, eyes dropping to his arms as they held him in his upright position. Even with the torch from my phone doing a shit job of lighting the space, the veins in his arms made mine want to give out from supporting my weight. "It's fun. You won't hurt me, I know it's safe with you. And I know you love it too, so don't get stroppy about it."

"I love it, do I?" He lifted an arm to elbow me. "Maybe I only do it to keep you happy."

"*Bullshit.* You get as much enjoyment out of it as I do."

"Uh-huh, *sure* I do." His tone was laced with sarcasm, but he couldn't hide the shy smile.

"One moan from me and you break out in sweat. Two moans and you're–" I held my phone closer to his face. "You're sweating just thinking about it!" I cackled as he turned away from me. "Aww, I'm *teasing*," I pouted. "I'm not lying, but I am teasing. Now that you're done playing *hero* and coming to my rescue, can we leave?"

The slight shake of his head as I said the word *hero* wasn't lost on me.

"All I did was bring the tools," he grumbled, though a sly smile crossed his features, "You just stitched yourself up and will no doubt insist you're fine to start work in a few hours. And you say you're *not* Gifted."

I often wondered what wild theories Logan had about me. The running joke about me being Gifted wasn't getting old for him. It sadly made me think some part of him truly wished that I were. Maybe then, he would have been more honest with me, not having to worry about his weak, human girlfriend. Maybe then, he could have the family he wanted.

I blinked back tears as he stood to dust himself off.

"You wanna act out that dream when we get home?" he asked, reaching out to help me up.

"That depends. Have you got a vigilante suit?" I tried to pull myself up with his hand, but his grip released and I fell hard to the floor. I let out a sharp laugh as the pain from my butt hitting the solid ground shot up my spine.

"Ouch!"

"*Shit*, sorry," he cleared his throat and grabbed both of my hands to pull me up again. "That was… part of your *dream?*" he asked cautiously once I was safely on my feet.

"Oh, did I leave out that detail?" I purred, widening my eyes as I looked up at him.

"Yeah… you did." He folded his arms, like he always did to protect himself from whatever new way I would try to tempt him into telling me the truth.

"It was a pretty hot dream, Logan." I kept up the sultry tone and tilted my head, clawing at the hem of his shirt.

"From the details you *did* share with me, it sounded… fun." He watched my hands moving under his shirt to trace the defined lines of his lower abs. All the working out we'd been doing together had turned his body into something I couldn't keep my hands off. More so than before.

I pushed my luck a little further – though I knew there was no chance he would suddenly reveal his dark side just to make one of my dirty dreams a reality. "It'd be *more* fun… if we could find you a suit."

"Maybe we should get one for *you*," he countered, gently grabbing my hands to pull them out from under the fabric and his body away from me. "But first, we should get you home so you can check that cut under better lighting."

Logan demonstrated an absurd amount of self control when it came to keeping this secret. Even if it meant he needed to pretend he didn't want me.

It was both fun to tease him and *incredibly* difficult not to become frustrated with his rejections. Though, it never lasted long, just until he was sure I wouldn't bring it up again. For a while, anyway.

"A suit *for me?*" I gasped playfully, ignoring his concern in hopes I'd be able to keep him on the topic for a little longer. "I wouldn't say no."

He narrowed his eyes. "No?"

"What colors do you think would work best on me? Are you thinking skin-tight? How long do you think I could wear it before you'd start trying to rip it off?" I bounced on the spot, reaching for his arms to pull them around me.

Logan sighed at my string of questions, unable to ignore them or hide his smirk. "Hmm, red. Yes… and maybe two seconds," he chuckled, taking the bait and gripping my butt tight in his palms.

"Really, red? Not *black* and red?"

Pushed too far again, he arched a brow and released his hold.

"No? You don't like the sound of that?" I continued, eyes still wide as I feigned innocence to taunt him, "You know they're my colors. It'd match my favorite shoes. And it'd go well with your car."

The tension in his jaw and shoulders eased a little. "You've got a point. Maybe we *should* find a way to get you one. What I'd give to see the fabric of one of those suits wrapped tight over *your* ass."

He took a step back without taking his eyes from mine and scooped up the kit. Then the world instantly turned upside down.

"You could have warned me!" I squealed as Logan carried me over his shoulder to his car.

"You didn't see me coming? I was right in front of you," he laughed, opening the passenger door to set me down on the seat.

"*No,*" I grumbled at another sly display of the Gifted skills he wouldn't admit to having.

"Wait here, I'll get your bag." He disappeared into the darkness of the house.

"What? What bag? I didn't bring a bag!"

"This isn't yours?" He reappeared in the doorway, holding up what appeared to be a brand new backpack in one hand.

*It's not mine, but I know exactly what that is.*

My heart jumped with panic, though it didn't need to. This area was known for hosting a wide range of preppers. It would have been stupid of me to think I'd be the only one to see this run-down shack as a stop along the path to safety.

"I went for a run, I wasn't bugging out." I glared at the bag as Logan sat in the driver's seat and handed it to me.

"What's bugging out?" he asked, craning his neck to view the items as I rummaged through them.

"It's a prepper thing. Whoever this belongs to would have hidden it here in case shit hits the fan. It's a terrible structure for a long-term hideout, but secluded enough for hiding a seventy-two hour kit."

Logan blinked a few times and shook his head, like I was no longer speaking a language he understood.

"We're gonna leave this here," I told him, replacing the bottled water, packets and small jars of food and a torch with far better lighting than what my phone had provided.

I held up a knife and inspected it with a sigh.

*That would have been handy.*

I shoved it angrily into the bag, then remembered that the person I'd thrown the rusty blades at was my boyfriend, who came to save me from my hunters.

"Really, why?" he asked when I handed it all back to him.

"I'm not about to steal from another prepper. What a dick move."

"Fair enough," he agreed, getting out again to put the bag back where he found it.

With the way Logan drove along the dark roads to my house, his estimate of thirty seconds wasn't too far off.

Once in the garage, I sat on the patient chair to get a better look at the mess I'd made of my leg.

Logan cleaned it up for me, careful to move around the stitches as he closely inspected my neat work. He looked like he wanted to ask something. My guess was he wanted to know about the three missing stitches I placed on everyone else – him included.

"I hope we don't make a habit of this," he chuckled, tossing bloody wipes into the bin.

"Of what?"

"Being covered in each other's blood," he held up his hands for me to see the patches of red on his fingers from having tended to *another* of my injuries.

"You know, for the one who's *not* the nurse in this relationship, you've dealt with far more of mine than I have of yours." I frowned at how wrong that felt as he moved to the sink to clean up. I was meant to be the fixer, yet Logan kept putting *me* back together.

"I'm sure there'll be plenty of opportunities for us to even the score," he said with a smirk when he turned back, his smile growing wider when my skin flushed pink.

While I may have been constantly pushing him to admit he was Gifted, Logan had been doing the same with me in a way, but with a different topic.

Little hints were always being dropped that he seemed to like the idea of us being together long-term. But, as with me trying to get a confession out of him, I'd quickly find a way to change the subject. "Forever" would always be a terrifying concept to me.

"Should we numb you up?" he asked, unlocking the cabinet where I stored the anesthetic, "I can imagine you're in more pain than you're letting on."

"Sure," I sighed, rubbing my temples to stave off the pain building behind my eyes. I watched him move with ease about my garage. He'd become as confident in the space as me. "Can you grab me something for my head, too? I've got a headache."

"Another one?" he reached for a different shelf to grab a bottle of pills, tossing them to me before moving to another in search of a syringe.

"Yeah… Wait, I think these might be too strong." I threw them back.

Logan caught the bottle and reread the label, "They're pretty weak as it is, you sure you want something else?"

"Yep." I'd been getting headaches on and off for weeks, worried it was a delayed side effect of my sudden withdrawal from the other pills I'd evidently been abusing too frequently.

He passed me a different bottle and I took one pill – only one – then gave the rest back. *Seven* might have been more fitting for the pain in my head and the throbbing ache on the side of my leg, but I was set on not forming any new dependencies.

*Who are you?*

I wasn't sure if I should have been proud or upset with the person I'd become with so many of my changes stemming from this relationship.

"Summer… With you being followed on your run. We've never really talked about…"

*The night you saved me from the Finders at Crave? The warnings you've likely overheard from others? The fact that I'm now being stalked so close to where I live?*

"The fact that the *cult* might want you back," he finished.

*Another nice save, babe. Ten out of ten.* I giggled.

"Don't laugh," he scolded, but smiled as he sat beside me and measured the liquid with the syringe, "I'm serious. I've… encountered my share of cults in the past. And if you were… placed with the *leader*… Don't you worry he'll come after you at some point? The things you know and have seen would surely…"

"Put a price on my head?" I scoffed, "My fence is made of knives, Logan. I have cameras surrounding the house and have two of the largest men I could find, on call – except for tonight apparently. Of course I'm worried – ow! *Deeper!*"

"What?" His eyes rushed to mine, hand frozen at the sound I'd made.

"The needle. It should hurt less if you *go deeper*," I explained, "And you accuse me of having a dirty mind all the time. Have those texts still got you distracted?" He laughed, shaking his head clear of the noise so he could focus on finishing the job. "Did you rush to find me in the forest to fuck me or because I could have been in danger?"

He sighed and packed up the tools, "I was worried about you, baby. The thought of you going missing scared me." His honesty made me feel bad for having teased him.

"Scared you?"

"Yeah. Don't know if you've noticed, but you've kind of grown on me, nurse. I'd miss you if you were gone."

"I've noticed," I said quietly, believing every word as I reached for his hand.

"What… What are *you* scared of?" he asked, wheeling the stool close enough so he could hold my hand in both of his with his lips resting on my knuckles, like he was hiding behind them while he waited for my answer.

I thought about it for a moment. There were so many things that scared me, but there was one thing I had truly come to love and never wanted to live without since leaving Bedlam behind.

"Losing my ability to *choose*." I finally settled on.

The answer seemed simple, though it was anything but. At first I'd been happy to have choices over which of the many gyms I could get myself kicked out of. Now, I was grateful for bigger things; who I chose to be, which name I used, where I slept and *who* I slept with.

"I think I've made some pretty good choices since moving out this way." I smiled at him as I slipped off the chair.

"We'll keep you safe, Summer."

I wasn't sure if he meant himself and the bodyguards, or maybe his group of vigilante friends. Perhaps he meant just the two of us. After my run-in with the Finders, I'd accept any of those options.

"I can keep myself safe."

He rolled his eyes and shoved me as he stood, "Fucking superheroes… always so stubborn."

I ignored Logan's mutters like he insisted on doing when I hinted at him being Gifted and pulled my phone from my pocket to check the time. "We've still got hours before I start work."

"Is there something you want to do before you start?" he asked, pushing his glasses back up his nose with his middle finger.

"Well… *I* don't have any vigilante suits." I pouted, grabbing his hand and paying no mind to his frown at the emphasis on my words. "But I *do* have some tight clothes I don't really care for anymore… would you like to practice tearing things from my body for when I do get one?"

He closed his eyes and exhaled heavily, "Tell me you're not joking?"

"I'm not," I purred, deciding I was willing to sacrifice the catsuit I'd worn when stitching him up at Crave.

*The fact that it's leather might actually slow him down enough to give me more than two seconds before he's got me completely naked.*

"Oh! Can I do it from behind while you're facing the mirror like you dreamed about?"

"Are you referring to *doing* me? Or ripping my clothes?" I grinned at his enthusiasm and yelped when he threw me over his shoulder again.

"Both."

# FORTY-NINE

SUMMER

## JULY 11TH

It had been five months.

Almost six, if I counted the time Logan spent sleeping over before we started dating.

He and I had firmly established quite the happy little routine together. To anyone on the outside, we might have actually looked like a normal couple, still in the early days of discovering who we were as a pair.

Only we weren't normal. And my boyfriend was still adamant about hiding his identity as a Gifted serial killer. Not that I could really talk, with lying about big chunks of my past in order to stay off his hit list.

Despite my willingness to share *many* things about my complicated past, Logan still wouldn't speak too deeply about his – the wife he'd lost in particular. Losing her must have been a huge part of who he'd become in the time since her passing, or else I believed he would have found other ways to be a little more open with me.

It was awful that innocent people had died to make the man I'd fallen for. But then, how many people died to make me who I'd become? *Far too many.*

The loss of our loved ones were enormous weights we both carried into this relationship, and there were surely only going to be more added to both of our *lists* over time. And while I tried not to think about that fact, I guess it always sat on the forefront of Logan's mind too, and could have been one of the reasons he wasn't diving into the terrifying depths of complete honesty with me.

It hurt that he hadn't, but I still believed he'd have to tell me one day.

Until then, we were a recipe for disaster. And, as delicious as it was, I never intended for things to go this far between us.

I had to admit, I loved every second of our weird life together. Things were comfortable. Maybe *too* comfortable. One of us would have to fuck it up eventually, whether he killed me or my ex came back to haunt us, the seemingly sweet stability we were experiencing could implode at any time.

Having a typical *Summer* moment, I knew exactly how to set us down the path to ruin what we had. Only now, it wasn't going to be the same as the time Eric's friend died under my bloody hands, sparking his violent decline into madness. Instead, I was going to tell Logan how I felt about him. Just as dangerous in its own way. *Truly fucking terrifying.*

Under the lamp in the dark living area of my house, sitting on the couch and reading through medical equipment catalogs, I paused and peeked over the top to observe my boyfriend.

He was watching one of his favorite, gore-filled action movies for the hundredth time, wearing what was without a doubt, *our* favorite jacket. The light from the TV occasionally bounced from the lenses of the dorky glasses that framed his perfect profile.

He looked comfortable, reclined in the cushions and chuckling along at the horror unfolding on the screen.

Even I had started to enjoy his movies that, between our life experiences, we knew were incredibly inaccurate for the most part.

"I love you, Logan." I whispered over the pages.

He sharply turned in a rare moment of being released from his fixation on a movie, eyes wide with shock.

*Is it too early? Even after five months of dating? Is he capable of love with the carnage he creates? Fuck. I've totally misread his signs.*

He gulped and cleared his throat, "W-wow. *Really,* Summer?"

The reaction instantly made me feel heated and stupid. I ducked behind the catalog as if that could make him and the moment disappear.

Logan snatched the book from my hands and let it fall to the floor. His expression was unreadable, but with the way he stared, those cogs in his skull must have been turning at full speed to come up with a better response for me.

"*Never mind!*" I snapped, grabbing the crumpled pages from the floor and returning to my hiding place. I sunk further into the cushion and tried to locate the paragraph I'd been reading.

Logan crawled over me, his hands on the seat at either side of my hips, his face behind the catalog. I couldn't ignore him, so I dropped the pages to reveal his annoyingly handsome face as he grinned at me.

"What?"

"I'm sorry," he started, but I didn't want to hear it now that I was feeling embarrassed.

When I tried to straighten up to get off the couch from underneath him, he didn't move, but held my gaze for a few moments longer, as if looking *through* me would somehow pass his thoughts into my head. When the shitty attempt at telepathy didn't work, he lifted an arm so I could roll down to the floor to get away from him.

"Forget it, I'm being… *fucking dumb*," I muttered, moving to the safety of the kitchen and putting as much space between us as I could without literally running away from the situation I'd thrown us into.

*What was I thinking? No one EVER says it back. I'm completely unlovable.*

I shook my head and blinked back tears.

"No, you're not," he sighed, still smiling as he stood on the other side of the island bench. He placed his hands in his pockets and rocked on the spot for self-control, like he always did when he seemed torn between reaching for me and giving me space. He shrugged, lip between his teeth, biting back a smile. "Honestly, Summer… I haven't heard that in *so* long. I guess part of me never actually expected to hear it again."

The confession took me by surprise. We'd only been together a few months and I already couldn't imagine *not* loving him. At least, the side he shared with me.

"I was too quick to say it," I said, waving my hand to the side of my face in hopes it could make the heaviness of my expressed affections to a mass murderer any less fucked up.

His shoulders slumped a little before he perked up. "No, baby. Not at all. I feel the same, by the way. *I swear*. I have for a while. A *long* while. But now I've missed a beat and it wouldn't feel right saying it back like this."

A different warmth spread from my neck to my cheeks, no longer feeling stupid for having told him how I felt, even if his words weren't exactly what I'd hoped for.

*Maybe he really is mine as much as I'm his. It'd be a first.*

"I need to get ready." I noted the time on the clock above the archway.

It was Friday, the second of the month. I would be heading out to Crave under the guise of a house call to an important patient and Logan was meeting up with his friends, meaning I would no doubt see him and the gang at some point.

"Okay," he sighed, seeming unhappy the conversation needed to end there. I rounded the bench and hugged him in an attempt to patch things up before we parted.

"Hey, d'you wanna join me in the shower?" I offered, grabbing handfuls of his jacket.

He raised an eyebrow at me and couldn't help but break his serious facade with a lazy smirk, knowing my invitation wasn't only to get ready to leave.

*This'll do the trick.*

I reached for his hands and quickly pulled him along to the bedroom. We still had enough time to improve his mood by putting my mouth to work before playing out the roles of our secret lives.

Logan and I sharing showers was one of my favorite parts of our time together. Whether we were hot from the gym before I started work, or after, when I'd be covered in someone else's bodily fluids by the end of the shift, we always found our way to the water together, and only wanted to be covered in *each other's* fluids if we could help it.

Our height difference made *most* positions in the shower tricky, or potentially deadly. I'd treated all sorts of injuries of couples trying to make it work, and for me, it wasn't worth the risk of broken bones and cracked skulls. I'd claimed the space as mine to bring him pleasure.

Logan would stand over me in the shower, head either tipped back under the water as he ran one hand through his hair or looking down at me to observe my work while his other hand gently gripped the back of my head.

I'd often look up to admire the rest of his anatomy as water droplets spilled down his sculpted body and onto my face.

The sheer sight of him made me work harder, using my lips, tongue and hands to ensure I'd soon feel his hard dick's intense pulse in my mouth as he braced himself on the tiled walls above.

The idea of us on our knees for each other made my spine so fucking weak and Logan always ensured I'd have my turn too. Though for me, we usually found ourselves on the bed, where he'd kneel at the end while I wrapped my thighs tight around his head.

I'd fall apart at the warmth of his mouth and slick tongue on my clit, and he'd keep a watchful eye on the way my back arched, listening to the way I moaned his name; the cue to glide his fingers deep inside me. He'd bring his face to mine so I could kiss him or he could bite at my neck as I came.

Once both our needs were well tended to, he dressed to meet his friends.

*That should have him thinking of me over the next couple of hours.*

I grinned as the front door clicked into place behind him.

While it was upsetting that Logan didn't want to include me in the gang while enjoying the fun side to the vigilante lifestyle, I was glad he kept up the act enough to not hang around to watch me dress in my poor attempt at a disguise.

I picked out the same black jeans like always and a long-sleeved, black cotton top with a few buttons under the neckline. It was still high enough that if I kept an eye on it, and covered up my tattoo, the remaining ink wouldn't be visible.

I usually didn't have too much to work with in terms of cleavage, but with the right bra and leaving the buttons undone, the plan was to give enough of an illusion that might tempt Logan into touching me, or have him burning with jealousy if we crossed paths during the night.

Unfortunately, the night had other plans.

# FIFTY

## SUMMER

The shift at the club was messy. Chaotic. I'd never seen anything like it in the years I'd visited both on Eric's arm and as the nurse sewing patrons out the back.

There were more people from out of town than typical. Gangs and enemies clashing more frequently than normal.

For the most part, the injuries weren't too serious, lots of cuts from bottles and knives. Bloody eyebrows and torn knuckles.

For the first time in as long as I could remember, I turned someone away, sending the man and his friends to a hospital as he'd been stabbed quite deeply. He needed more help than what I could confidently provide for him on my own.

It was a rare occurrence for me to give up on anyone, but with the extent of his injuries and the line of people needing my help growing each time I looked up, I needed to call the shots on what would be best and safest for everyone.

In the chaos of the night, I hadn't seen Logan or his friends. It was disappointing. I'd hoped to interact with him a little but there wasn't a spare moment between being sworn at and called names by drunken idiots, to hurriedly washing their blood off my chair, ready for the next to fill the space and demand I fix the problems they'd likely brought upon themselves.

When I turned to find yet another man being dropped in my space by the club's bouncers, I realized I couldn't keep track of how many heads and faces I'd stitched up by this point.

This guy was a bloody mess, further making me long for the order and quiet of the garage where I could work on one person at a time with breaks in between at my discretion.

He had a particularly nasty gash on the top of his head. Good thing his scalp was shaved or else it would have made things much more difficult to work with. As I leaned closer to him my senses were overwhelmed with the thick metallic scent of blood and the enormous amounts of alcohol he must have consumed in the club.

Making quick work to numb the area around the wound, I began stitching. But as I started, he complained the tugging sensation was making him nauseous. He swiftly rolled to the side of the reclined chair and emptied his stomach into a bucket that I kicked into place *just* in time.

Sympathy-spewing wasn't typically my thing, but the ceaseless aromas of blood, alcohol and now vomit, were making even my seasoned stomach turn. I felt like I couldn't keep anything clean enough and the air was too still, suffocating me in the small space in the back of the van with the odors of too many different bodies.

"I'll leave you for a minute to finish doing that." I patted the vomiting man gently on the shoulder before jumping out the back. I was quick to close the doors behind me, containing the sights and sounds of him being reacquainted with the food he'd eaten earlier in the day.

I stumbled around the side of the van to lean by the driver's door. Ben was on the opposite side, and I didn't want him pestering me while I felt so sick, not at all in the mood for his jokes while my insides churned.

My lungs were invaded by cigarette smoke as I took a few deep breaths. It normally didn't bother me, but I just couldn't escape the range of unpleasant fragrances Crave had to offer.

It quickly became too much. I bent over and braced myself to be sick by the van's front wheel. When nothing came, I hurriedly spat the saliva that pooled in my mouth, convinced it tasted like everything I could smell, and dry heaved again over that very thought.

*Classy.*

I was glad we were parked at the back of the club and I wasn't on display to the street, where more people were lining up and arguing with bouncers to try to get inside.

"Partying a little too hard tonight?" It was the familiar voice of the man I'd professed my love to just hours ago, muffled by his irresistible suit of lies.

"I wish," I let out a strained laugh and straightened up to lean on the van with my hands behind my back, embarrassed by being caught in the moment. "Tonight is too much, even for me. Everything is gross. The people are… a lot."

"It's *hectic,*" he agreed, folding his arms and resting his back on the wall of the club, a few feet in front of me. "The crowd inside is different tonight."

"You're not in there starting fights are you? While I always appreciate the money, I'd really like a break at some point."

I suddenly realized I hadn't seen Pyro for some time. Months, maybe?

*He's probably dead.* The thought upset me, but that was just the way things were in our world. People disappeared all the time, never to be seen or heard from again.

Logan laughed. "Nah, I've… got my eyes on more important things."

*Me, probably.*

Fuck, I hoped he meant me.

I looked him over and smiled, still feeling a little off. My mask was starting to give me a headache as it dug into my temples, and my stomach was still reeling.

He continued, voice a slightly higher pitch as his words tumbled out, "There's a lot of talk in there that some big names are on their way. Too many try-hards are hoping to get their attention."

My shoulders pulled back. It was similar news to what Matthias had shared. Maybe it was only a matter of time before it was my turn to go missing.

"Don't let it bother you. You'll be safe," he promised.

"Yeah?" I teased, attempting to flirt after almost having lost what little I'd consumed for the day, "How can you be so sure? Going to make a habit of jumping from the roof with me in *those* arms?"

"If that's what it takes to keep the nameless nurse alive." The smile in his voice was audible, and the nerves about us interacting so openly seemed to dissipate entirely as he shrugged.

"I could get used to that."

"Yeah?" he turned my string of questions back on me as he playfully flexed his arms, "Planning on getting into trouble just to be wrapped in *these* again? You don't have someone at home who'd be opposed to you running around all night with dangerous vigilantes?"

Giggling, I tipped my head and purred, "Why? You wanna fill his position?"

Logan pushed off the wall and braced himself on the van with his hand beside my head, lowering his face to mine so he could whisper in my ear.

"I can name a few things that I want to *fill*. And there are *many* positions I'd like to see that little body of yours in, *nurse*."

My heart skipped a beat and I swallowed hard as my eyes locked on the black spaces of the mask concealing his eyes. As if I were possessed by his closeness, my hand reached up to gently trace his jawline through the textured fabric.

He leaned into my touch, and I contemplated just how far I wanted to push this interaction. Surely, his own words were telling enough – that he was willing for things to go further at Crave? At least in disguise.

"Vengeance… will you take me upstairs?"

My question was breathy, strained as excitement built in my body. Was I finally being presented with a chance to fuck Logan while he wore the suit?

He nodded firmly after a pause, seeming to have needed the moment to think about exactly what this would mean for us. To my complete surprise, he lifted the lower part of his mask, just enough to expose from his neck, up to his mouth. His hand moved to the back of my neck, and he leaned in to kiss me.

My head floated in the blanket of cologne as familiar lips pressed hard onto mine. He'd never kissed me with such an intense force. It was as though he'd come to accept something that was holding him back, and whatever he'd settled on drove him to be more unrestrained with me.

*Oh shit, he's finally going to tell me!*

My breathing grew heavier and my hands roughly squeezed at his shoulders. He moved his arms around my back, pressing my body into his before lifting me from the ground to pin me against the side of the van.

Without breaking the kiss, I tightly wrapped my legs around his waist to hold myself in place. My hands slipped behind his shoulders, gently brushing the top of the stitches in his suit where I'd seamlessly sewn it back together while his gloved fingers made quick work of undoing the buttons on my shirt.

"*Ow,*" I moaned as he roughly grabbed at my breasts, "No, *don't stop.*" I demanded in a whisper when he paused.

"Okay," he chuckled anxiously, hands gripping my butt in preparation to carry me, "But we should take this somewhere you can scream my name without attracting an audience."

"Your name?" I moaned again, his hot lips left scolding trails along my collarbone and back up to my mouth, "Vengeance? Or Lo–"

"Oh, *fuck!*" The surprised shout came from my bodyguard. We'd been caught – lips locked and groping each other. Ben must have heard our talking come to an abrupt end, and had peeked around the side to see who was bothering me.

Logan released his grip, and I slid down the side of the van until my heels settled on the gravel. He sighed, the sound heavy with disappointment as he turned his face away to replace the mask.

"Everything okay here, boss?" Ben demanded in the best defensive stance he could muster at the shocking sight of me in a partial state of undress with a vigilante.

"I'm fi—" I was cut off by my body bending in half, expelling the vomit that had earlier evaded its eviction.

*Oh god, what the fuck is wrong with me?* I questioned my organs as another wave made its way to the rocks at my feet. *Is it the blood? The vomit? Maybe both.*

"*Whoa!*" Logan jumped back with his hands raised. "Hey, are you okay?" He grabbed my arm to pull me away from the pool at my feet and to straighten me up. With my face in his hands, his thumbs softly brushed over my cheekbones, and he tilted my head back to get a better look at my features. His breathing was quick, stressed.

"I haven't—" I started a little defensively, worried he thought I'd stumbled back into old habits during a particularly stressful night of work.

"I know," he said, "It's just… your eyes. Even when you're playing pretend, looking into them helps me focus."

"What?" I giggled in his grasp like a lovesick teen. "Really?"

"Yeah," Logan lowered his voice, "The way you look back at me makes everything else disappear… then I can hear nothing but your heartbeat. And when I hear it, I know you're safe." He cleared his throat, and although his face was covered, I could tell he'd dropped his gaze from mine, "If you're okay, then I can be too."

"I've got that much of a hold over you?" I tried to flirtatiously shrug the heaviness of his confession away in hopes it would take the heat from my skin with it. "I never would have guessed the *nameless nurse* could mean so much to a ruthless vigilante."

"Well, you do. You have *no* fucking idea." A small, nervous laugh passed through the fabric, the last thin veil of disguise between us. "You're *everything* to me, Summer."

I would have bet anything Logan could hear the pounding organ in my chest skip again at his confessions. They were some of the most romantic things anyone had ever said to me.

*Who am I kidding? They ARE the most romantic things anyone has ever said to me.*

Had I not been feeling like more bile was about to surface, I would have pulled him into the back of the van and told Ben to either stand guard or fuck off while I showed Logan exactly what those words made me want to do to him.

"We're leaving." Ben announced before I could respond.

"No, I've got a guy in there." I gestured to the van as I reluctantly moved from Logan's warm hold and fumbled to replace the buttons of my shirt.

"I don't give a fuck, we'll dump him on the curb. We're leaving."

He was just doing his job. If it were up to me I would literally work myself to death.

I sighed, "*Fine.*"

"Catch you next time, nurse?" Logan asked, following my steps as I walked around the front of the van and climbed up into the passenger seat. Tony would sit in the back and deal with the patient when the time came. "Maybe we can finish what we started?"

"She's got a *boyfriend,* gimp suit," Ben growled in warning, continuing his threatening behavior towards the masked man.

"Maybe," I said, giving the vigilante a wink. Ben reached across my lap to slam the door closed.

I started to feel a little better on the drive home, especially once the man in the back had been removed and we were no longer smothered by the awful, stale alcohol and vomit blend. I suddenly craved the smell of Logan's cologne to remove what lingered in my nostrils.

"Ben," I started, "Can I… tell you something?"

"Anything, boss. You know that. But you'll have to pay me more."

I rolled my eyes. "Logan is Vengeance." I confessed quietly as we took the long, dark roads to my house.

"Yeah, we figured. But we're gonna keep fucking with him until he admits it to you."

I smiled. "How long have you known?"

"Since the night he found us to get you out of Crave. He was worried about you. Eager to keep you safe from who we guessed was *Simon*, looking for you."

It was bizarre hearing that name spoken out loud after so long – *Simon*.

One of Eric's top Finders who'd been initiated before Danny and I, and only a year or two older than us. He was a surprisingly sweet man despite what the job entailed. But then, most of us seemed that way.

There were several Finders on Home's payroll. As many as Eric wanted or needed that he could trust in his circle at any given time.

Their role was to be on a constant lookout; seeking those who stood out in ways that could assist The Collection, people who had skilled sets of hands like mine, or others who were willing to sell their souls for a place in our family. They were also appointed to find trustworthy resources for crime scene clean ups, and were particularly good at making things disappear. People, namely, when they had to rid Home of those who'd been caught breaking their contracts. It was a little ironic.

They were obviously out trying to *find* me that night, to return me to Eric.

And while I hated the idea of one of my old friends being on the hunt for me, I was glad it was someone who might actually present me in a living state to the boss. Not everyone at Home appreciated that Eric played favorites, and I'd been at the center of so much of his attention, whether I wanted it or not.

Ben continued as I was lost in thought, "Logan said your title, you know? I don't think he knew that's what those Finders were saying. But *Stitch Up* was floating around the club that night."

I felt sick again, but only because I wasn't ready for Logan to learn that. I'd only shared enough of my past with him for us to function.

If he thought I was incapable of handling him being Vengeance, then he didn't need to know I was brought up in one of Bedlam's worst crime factions.

Could I tell my boyfriend I'd been branded with my title at nineteen and set on my path to become queen of Bedlam's underworld? How would he react to the knowledge that my abuser was my king, and our minions scoured the depths of the city's darkness to add more valuable pieces to Eric's precious Collection?

Could I tell Logan that I was a villain? One of the worst? And that the horrors and sacrifices that came with my title had worn me down to nothing? Surely a man who went by the name *Vengeance* would have a difficult time accepting his girlfriend was that much of a monster.

"He's a good guy," Ben admitted, elbowing me. "Not that we'll let him know it."

"He sure seems that way."

Logan kept proving to be nothing *but* a good guy, and that made my mind more of a mess. I hated feeling this way. One minute, fine and accepting of Logan and all that he was. Then the next, upset at the double lives we were both leading.

Something was making me more irritable about our situation than normal. Maybe I was still embarrassed about having told him I loved him without the reaction I'd hoped for – wanting a simple return of the sentiment, only for him to *almost* go so much further than that and seeming to settle on revealing his true self before we were interrupted.

*You're probably just tired. You took on way more people than you normally do for one shift at the club.*

Ben glanced at his phone. "Looks like he's pulled up at the house."

"*Shit.* Do I still have spare clothes in the back? I wasn't expecting him so soon." It took us longer than normal to get back with having to leave our extra passenger at a safe place to be treated.

"Yep, the bag is in the back. He's probably just worried after seeing you were sick." Ben pulled over to the side of the road and Tony hopped out, they waited outside to give me privacy to change.

Thankfully, Tony had cleaned up the back of the van. The space smelled strongly of bleach and disinfectant. I inhaled deeply to settle my stomach. It was instantly calming.

I removed my mask and replaced my shirt; dressed for the role of innocent girlfriend.

# FIFTY-ONE

SUMMER

## JULY 12TH

When we pulled up, Logan was waiting at the door, rather than having helped himself inside. Although he'd seen and been in the van at the club, as far as my *normal boyfriend* knew, it was for picking up patients, bringing them to my house or for taking me to house calls.

*Another item on my ever-growing list of things to hate about us.*

I had to keep track of that lie too. It was quickly becoming infuriating to think about.

"I finished up early for the night with the gang," he explained when I walked up the driveway to meet him, "I thought I'd come straight home."

In my mind, I translated his words to "I saw you leave sick and got home as fast as I could to make sure you're alright." It was sweet, until I reminded myself he *should* have been able to tell me *exactly* that instead of making up stories.

*What is wrong with you tonight? Maybe it's just making you mad because you used to do the same with Eric.*

I'd often twisted his words to make them sound how I wanted them to. *Needed* them to. It was a habit I absolutely did *not* want to bring into another relationship.

“It was a long night,” I mumbled, unlocking the door, “very tricky stuff.”

“You know, you always do your makeup so nice for simple house calls.”

*Crap.* I hadn’t thought to remove it.

*What’s the fucking point? He knows who you are. He just had you pinned to the fucking van with his hands in your bra.*

“Summer, if I didn’t know any better, I’d say you were living some kind of double life.” he teased, following me into the hall.

I spun on my heel to glare up at him, “Yeah? Like *you* can fucking talk, Logan.”

I hadn’t planned on confronting him. In fact, I had very much enjoyed our interaction at the club and thought it may have been an inch of progress in the right direction.

But now we were back at home and playing dumb games, I could no longer deny that I wanted *more.* I wanted *him.* Logan, Vengeance, I didn’t give a fuck, I just needed the truth.

He tensed at my tone. “What do you mean?”

Still feeling sick, I was quick to anger, and about to blow everything if I wasn’t careful.

“That’s how you want to play tonight? Accusing *me* of a double life?” The laugh that escaped my lungs was devoid of amusement, and the look on his face told me I’d gone too far with the bad mood. I needed to pull back. “I… I feel like there’s still more you haven’t told me… about who you are.” I said, biting my tongue to shut up.

What I’d said wasn’t *too* bad, but now I’d officially started an argument for no reason and had to find a way to end it fast.

Logan gulped, his eyes darting from mine. “I’m sorry you feel that way. But you know *plenty* about me.”

He’d evidently come down from the adrenaline at the club we’d both had pulsing through our systems at his willingness to take me to the rooms.

The long drive home could have given him too much time to find clarity. Now we were away from the temptation that Crave’s hypnotic aura bestowed on even the strongest minds, he must have decided to keep me in my stupid, safe bubble and away from his secrets.

Why couldn’t he see that I didn’t need protection from them in the first place?

"Like what?" I demanded, "What do you and your friends get up to all the time? I hear that you're *out* and dealing with *business* but you're always so quick to change the subject with me. It's enough to make me think–" I cut myself off and bit my tongue harder.

*Fuck! Shut up. Are you fucking insane? You're going to ruin everything!*

"Think what?" he clipped, jaw flexing.

"Think that you might *be* someone else. There are so many vigilantes out there, they could be anyone. What if *you're* one of them? You *could* be. Your friends are cool, but *strange*. You *never* let me hang out with them for long. Harrison and I get along well but you always come up with reasons to keep us busy when she tries to make plans with me." I accused, annoyed at him with how much his friends actually seemed to like me, but never given the chance to build deeper friendships. Even with Harrison seemingly on the verge of discovering my identity, if she were my friend, I'd be in far less danger if we were on the same side before she put all the pieces together on her own.

Shaking my head, I leaned on the hallway table with my arms folded and continued to lash out at Logan when he chose to stay silent, "You like to joke about *me* being Gifted but I'm not *fucking stupid*. I've noticed things about you."

"Summer, stop." he pleaded, pupils widening to an alarming size.

But I couldn't, I was giving him the perfect opportunity to come clean. *Again*. If he could just tell me now, our lives would be so much easier. I was *his*. I had been for months as I played along with his lies. The least he could do was tell me something real in return.

"Tell me you're not the reason I miscarried," I challenged, ignoring his flinch, "Surely I'd deserve to know if you were Gifted after going through that? Think of the life of lies and disappointment you'll be condemning me to if you don't tell me now."

"You think I'm Gifted, Summer? Superhuman? That I'm out fighting crime with the gang when I'm not with you?" he laughed, but it was laced with hurt at the blame falling squarely on him for both my pain and the loss of a future he still seemed to be subconsciously chasing.

"Yes. I do." I said firmly, eyes welling up at the sound; his laughter made me feel stupid, even though I *knew* I was right.

"Babe, while that sounds awesome, I swear, I am just a regular person, with a boring life."

*Ouch. Drop it.*

"*Boring?*" I was way too fucking moody to let *that* slide. "What we've got here is boring, is it?" I didn't mean to sound so upset, but my voice was thick with hurt.

I understood his words were flippant from being mid-argument, but aside from our secrets, life for me was actually starting to feel like it was worth living since he'd come into it. He still had no idea what my life had been like in the past, and the ways I'd tried to end it to be free of my misery.

*He doesn't know that because you haven't told him.* I was a fucking hypocrite. I still had plenty of my own secrets.

"Not the parts with *you* in it."

I couldn't take that as a compliment. Not at all. He had just *fucking lied* straight to my face. *Again.* My shoulders slumped in defeat as I turned for the bathroom.

"Summer," he started after me, "Please. Baby, this isn't like you. Are you okay?"

"I'm *fine!*" I spat my words so he could feel the same pain at watching someone he cared for being dishonest and having no choice but to accept it.

"You're *lying!*"

*Oof, so he's allowed to call you out, but you have no right to do the same? It's a real talent of yours to end up in fucked up relationships like this.*

The thought sparked a fresh round of rage in me. I was good at arguing. Good in the sense that I could keep going without backing down until I was out cold from having pushed Eric too far. What was one fight with Logan compared to that?

*God, help this man if he thinks I was stubborn before this.*

"And I hope you're not!" I shouted back. I kicked my shoes off in the walk-in robe, instantly dropping inches in height.

As if he had some kind of epiphany, Logan blinked hard and asked, "Is all of this about what happened earlier tonight? I'm *sorry* I didn't say it back."

Did he really think that could suddenly erase everything we'd said to each other since I got home?

I took another deep breath to calm my anger, remembering that I had actually *chosen* to be in this relationship and I didn't want it to end – but it only left me with more hurt.

I was done. Too tired and too upset to even begin trying to fix us.

My phone buzzed in my pocket and I glanced at the message. The bodyguards hadn't left and could hear us arguing. Tony was on his way in to check on me.

"It's not about that, it's about being *honest* with me!"

Tears spilled from my eyes. I was becoming an emotional wreck, as I so often had since Logan came into the picture. I still didn't have a strong understanding of what a normal relationship entailed, and with our sharing always being so one-sided, it left me feeling like I was the weaker of the two.

*It's not fair. Might as well be with Eric if things are going to continue being this unbalanced.*

"Listen," Logan begged, grabbing my arms tight when I turned, catching me before I could slam the bathroom door in his distressed face. He leaned down so that our faces were level, giving me no choice but to look at him, "I wouldn't lie to you, Summer… *I love you.*"

Silence filled the space between us. I bit my lip, hard, and my eyes dropped from his. They were the words I'd wanted to hear. That I'd *desperately* wanted anyone to say to me in return. But not like this.

It was wrapped in another of *Logan's lies*, making it feel like it couldn't possibly be true at all.

"If that's true, then tell me who you are." I demanded, sniffling in his grip. "What's your Gift?"

Logan's eyes glistened as he let go of my arms. Was he heartbroken I'd ignored his expression of love for me? Did he really mean it? My chest ached as he took a step back.

"Tell me, Logan." I pushed, folding my arms to hold myself together. "It's the only way we can make this work. Tell me, or we're done. I *trust* you. Can't you trust me too?"

He shook his head, blinking tight with frustration, "Summer… there's nothing I can tell you."

I gawked in complete disbelief. "After all this time. And *everything* we've been through – that's what you're sticking with?"

He looked down, slipping his hands in his pockets and swallowing hard. "It has to be. This isn't a *gift* anymore. It's a fucking curse. I love what we have. Summer, you're everything to me. I don't want this to end. I–"

"You need to leave!"

He let out a heavy sigh that almost made me reconsider my demand. "Are you sure? Ben texted to let me know you weren't well earlier. I really think I should stay with you."

Ben hadn't messaged him, I was with him the whole time and he knew Logan was the vigilante he'd caught me with. *More* lies.

God, I wanted him to stay. To work everything out and to tell him everything about myself. To do *whatever* it took to get him comfortable enough to come clean with me so we could be as normal together as our lives would allow.

But he was proving to be as stubborn as me, and I couldn't stand the idea of being around him if he were going to keep treating me like an idiot who didn't already know his secrets.

"If you can't be honest with me, then you need to *leave!*" I shouted as Tony entered the bedroom. The door was open, and he could see us in the walk-in. No chance of him walking in on all the fun ways we could be making up, instead of how we actually were – completely falling apart.

Tony cleared his throat behind Logan. "You heard the boss. Time to leave."

It hurt to send him away, but I needed to draw the line somewhere. This wasn't a sustainable relationship, the cracks were already constantly growing bigger. What would it take for him to tell me the truth before everything completely collapsed?

Could his secret be so important that it didn't matter if we became more of his collateral? Did *I* not matter enough to be allowed to know him completely?

"I'll be back to check on you tomorrow," he promised, looking as shocked as I felt at the way everything between us had so rapidly dissolved.

"Don't bother, *Vengeance*." I said coldly, slamming the bathroom door in his face.

I burst into tears once I believed the sound of my crying was out of his Gifted hearing range.

I hated myself for snapping at him. I'd forced him into a corner and he bit in defense. He wasn't ready. But at this rate, he never would be.

"We're leaving now, boss." Tony called from the other side of the door, "Do you need anything before we go?"

When I opened the door, I found one of the two men who had, in their own way, replaced my brothers. The two I liked, anyway.

I reached out for him, and he quickly wrapped his thick arms around me.

"I fucked up," I cried, "I got too attached and told him that I love him. What was I thinking? No one ever tells me they love me and mean it."

"That's not true," Tony said, hugging me tight, "We tell you we love you all the time. We mean it."

"You both tell me you love the paychecks and that the work is easy." I countered with a weak laugh, my head buried against his neck.

He pulled me away, holding my shoulders in his firm grip as he looked me over, "Need us to beat him up for you?" he joked, like a big brother would.

"We all know who he is, even if *he* won't admit it. That wouldn't end well."

"Then do you want us to stay?"

"No. I'm okay." I lied, not really wanting to be alone, but also knowing the bodyguards weren't the company I'd crave throughout the night.

When Tony and Ben left, I turned the hot water on and sat at the bottom of the shower with my head on my knees, curled up there for what felt like forever. I wanted to hide in that enclosed space and to not confront the world and the problems I'd left on the outside of the steamy room.

When the skin of my fingers became deeply wrinkled, I put myself to bed, feeling like a fucking mess and wishing for the night to be over.

I eventually fell asleep, but tossed for hours, stomach still giving me grief and too uncomfortable with Logan's warmth missing from the space beside me.

Hours later, a faint *click* woke me. My entire body tensed with an uneasy feeling. The sound was too similar to that of a gun being cocked in a dark corner of the room where a contract was being signed. Goosebumps tumbled over every inch of my flesh as I sat up in bed, alone.

Logan hadn't come back, and I felt more lonely in my empty house than I ever had before I met him.

Still, something about the sound set off my internal alarms enough to make me worry that maybe I wasn't alone at all.

"Logan?" I whispered to the dark, bunching the sheets around my body, equally desperate for *and* dreading the blackness that surrounded me to respond in some way.

When it didn't, I rushed for my phone on the bedside table and checked the cameras for movement in and outside the house.

Nothing.

*Just ghosts.*

# FIFTY-TWO

## LOGAN

*Where am I?* The sheets were different. The room behind my eyelids was bright. It couldn't have been her room. *Is it mine?* Either way, I needed to start my morning ritual. A deep breath in. No blood detected. Still, I had to check my hands.

I rolled over, prying my raw eyelids open one at a time to take in my surroundings. I'd only woken under this ceiling a handful of times in the last six months. It was a relief to see; I didn't always wake up where I'd fallen asleep.

I lifted my arms, inspecting my palms and fingers for any remnants of death. Clean.

*So... she's alive?*

I let out a slow breath. With no immediate evidence that Summer had been slaughtered, I felt for her in the space beside me. The sheets were cold, but that was typical with her. She sometimes didn't make enough heat for me to sense her without my other skills kicking in.

But my little nurse wasn't there.

The bed was empty.

I was alone.

My heart skipped a beat in a way that made me feel sick.

*Where is she?*

I scrunched my eyes shut, thinking back to when I'd last seen her.

*Her house. She kicked me out. Or did she dump me?*

God, I'd fucked up. I swallowed over the thick lump of guilt in my throat.

*First,* I'd fucked up by not telling Summer I'd loved her since too-soon after I met her. *Then,* I'd fucked up again by stupidly denying an identity she'd already discovered.

My chest ached over the thought of those blue eyes, full of tears as she glared up at me; the man who'd do anything for her, but was unable to tell a simple truth to save us. She deserved better than to be made to doubt herself or to feel dumb when I was the one in the wrong.

I stretched, hoping the pain would ease if I moved. I'd forgotten what it was like sleeping with so much room to myself. While my shoulders appreciated the ability to spread out, I would have preferred to roll over and be greeted by the mess of ebony hair from detangled braids. One night without her and I already missed her peacefully sleeping face, half buried in the pillows while I listened to her pulse. There were two other pulses in the apartment, but neither of them sounded like hers.

After our argument, I would have given anything to be woken by Summer rolling into my side, body melding to mine to siphon the warmth. It was rare that she would ever be the first to wake between us, but on the few times she had, I'd stir to her lifting herself to sit on my abs, leaning over my chest to kiss my neck and face to wake me.

There was a sound in the living room; the TV turned on. In the rare instances I was away from Summer, work, not with the gang *and* not climbing the most wanted list, I was here; the two bedroom apartment that I shared with my sister. She was happy for me to help cover the rent when I showed up, broken and on the run after Millie's case went cold.

*Millie... what would she think of me now?*

We were married for as long as we'd been officers in Bedlam; before my life was ripped into a downward spiral when I found her corpse on our bed. She had no idea what I'd done that led to her death, though I was sure she'd learned all of my secrets in those final, graphic moments. I should have known it was a matter of time before my call to set the scales straight in Bedlam would catch up to me. But I was too young and cocky. Too sure of myself and confident in my abilities to decimate the demons of the underworld without repercussions.

I paid for my mistakes with Millie's life, my happiness and our future.

I was stupid to think I could keep my vigilante activity a secret for the entirety of our marriage, but then, here I was again, in a new relationship that I'd destroyed by trying to preserve it.

Like any vigilante pushed in horrific ways to become the villain they'd always feared would consume their identity, I'd sworn I'd never allow myself to love anyone like I'd loved her. I'd also vowed never to kill again. Both had proven to be completely impossible. My rank amongst the country's greatest monsters could attest to that. The burn for vengeance wasn't something I could ever be in complete control of, no matter what I tried.

Then Summer came into the picture, forcing me to see that I was simply destined to keep repeating the same cycles of my past.

*Summer,* I sighed, *What the fuck am I meant to do with her?*

Rolling over, I opened the drawer of the bedside table, wondering if my sister was keeping out of my room. I'd unintentionally set a new trap with the third ring box in the drawer. The items, unsurprisingly, weren't arranged the way I'd left them.

*Nosey bitch.*

I slammed the drawer shut and laid face down in my pillow, blocking out the light that poured through the window above my bed.

*How does she fit into all of this?* I roughly spun over to glare at the ceiling again.

My mind was a mess with the possibilities. Summer knew my secrets, but hadn't run. She hadn't told the world the secret identity of Vengeance. She'd tried to get me to admit it, gave me an ultimatum and called me by the name I'd hoped she'd never speak. But I still couldn't do it. Not even to save us.

The kiss at the club and agreeing to take her upstairs kept playing over in my head. The exchange before the bodyguard's interruption was enough of a rush for me to give up on hiding from her. And maybe more shockingly, abandon my reservations about fucking in the rooms.

But I'd come to my senses by the time we met at her house.

I would *always* be a threat to Summer, whether I was the one to kill her or she faced the same fate as Millie. She may have known I was Gifted, but she had no idea I was also her worst nightmare. I wasn't the vigilante she'd playfully labeled me at Crave. Vengeance was a *villain*. One of the worst. Surely, revealing my identity would only put her in more danger? I loved her too much to even consider it.

*Probably should have at least told her that outside of a fucking argument.*

I hated that I hadn't responded fast enough when she told me she loved me, but the admission took me by complete surprise.

I'd wanted to tell her the same for months, holding back for fear I'd been rushing things again or that she didn't feel the same. We were having too much fun together, and I didn't want the heaviness of how I felt to weigh in on her still fairly-newfound freedom.

Freedom from a past life I *still* didn't have a clear picture of.

Summer shared so much more than I ever dared to, and yet, I was still lost in the dark when faced with the rabbit hole of her never-ending surprises.

Unlocking my phone, I re-read the texts from Reid; my partner at work before I'd lost my mind, and one of the few ex-colleagues in Bedlam who knew I was Gifted. He and Celeste were the only ones I kept in contact with after I'd obliterated most of our co-workers in a single blackout.

He'd messaged me when I drove home, informing me of a new lead on Celeste's death. I'd hoped it would have been a good distraction from the argument as Summer and I cooled off, but he'd been slow to share the information. Bits and pieces trickled in throughout the night, making for a broken and barely restful sleep.

Reid texted that someone named "Stitch Up" had information we needed to extract. When I responded that I had no idea where to start searching for a hero, vigilante or villain by that name, he sent me a vague description. We were looking for a twenty-eight year old female, pale complexion, dark hair, skilled surgical assistant. Ex-patient of Hartford Asylum.

The description gave painfully clear hints that the next person we'd be questioning for information would be *her*. Summer was either a false name, or one of several my girlfriend was known by.

Reid mentioned that Stitch Up might have kept a backpack containing her asylum uniform. It was too specific a clue to ignore.

After driving back to her house in the early hours of the morning, I snuck in while she slept. As I slipped through the shadows undetected, I regained enough control over my actions to pause. Crouching down beside the bed, I watched over my girlfriend. *Fuck*, she was beautiful, even in that state.

With the way she cocooned herself, tangled in the sheets, I could tell she was naked beneath them. No doubt cold and missing the warmth that burned under my skin in constant preparation for the darkness to overthrow my senses and destroy our prey.

Her hair, still a damp mess, spread across her face and pillow. Her eyelids were red, raw from crying over how upset she'd been with me.

My eyes burned at the sight of her, and my mind was torn in different directions as I tried to understand where the outburst with such intensity had come from. Was it only from being hurt at my inability to be honest with her? That would have been a reasonable explanation, but now with what little I'd learned from Reid, I wasn't so sure.

She had a secret identity, a title fit for the underworld, and a set of skills that could save herself or her cohorts if they were to find themselves in sticky situations. Maybe I'd watched too many movies, but someone like that suddenly appearing in the lives of a group of vigilantes had all the makings of a spy. Which would make me the dumbass, falling for another woman so far out of my league. I should have known that I couldn't have been so lucky to land "the girl" twice in a lifetime.

Was Summer simply getting nowhere with her own mission, losing patience with me as I stood in the way of her goals? Did she need my admission for reasons other than transparency between us?

Had I pissed off one of the major crime families and they'd sent her my way to gather intel to take back to them?

I believed I'd hidden well enough for the last few years. But with my signature moves traveling with me as I disposed of the guilty, there was a chance someone out there could have put the pieces together.

Though, if Summer were a spy or hired to infiltrate our gang, *she* would have known better than to become so attached to me.

She may have had many secrets, but words and bodies spoke separate languages. Sometimes they said the same thing simultaneously. Her heart raced, her pupils dilated, and the air anxiously caught in her lungs when she'd told me she loved me. She could have told me she *hated* me, and I still would have known the truth.

Her feelings for me were genuine – a stupid move for a spy, and my little nurse was far from stupid.

While in her room, kneeling beside her in the dark, I closed my eyes and listened for her pulse. Almost always forty-three beats per minute when she slept, though it would change a fraction as she sniffled with the occasional unsteady breath, still settling from having cried so much.

There was no one around that required her to uphold any kind of act. The presence of the bodyguards – their sweat, cologne and the faint smell of cigarettes – had long left the air of the house. The tears that soaked Summer's pillow were shed in private.

It was almost impossible to fight the urge to take off the suit and climb into bed with her. That strange pull she had on me seemed to have amplified in my short time away. My intense desire to protect her at all costs almost won out over my need to confirm Reid's troubling clues.

The temptation to hold her tightly from behind and whisper all my secrets in her ear as she wriggled close to absorb my warmth was insurmountably strong. But I had to be stronger, and instead, went against all faith and trust she'd built in me to further break into her safe space, finding the bag in her wardrobe beside her favorite heels.

The backpack was now in bed beside me, guarded from my sister. This wasn't something I could share with her for her own safety.

It contained the uniform Reid mentioned, with Stitch Up embroidered into the orange fabric. The confirmation from finding it filled me with more dread than I anticipated.

Hartford was for the *worst*. Meant only for the criminally insane – the baddest of the bunch that couldn't be fixed. Villains were only placed within its walls to stall their plans to destroy the city, the country, or the world. There was never a real hope of rehabilitating any of the psychopaths that were sent there.

I knew my girlfriend was broken, but *Hartford* broken? Not even I had expected that.

*Like I can talk, I belong there myself. I bet there's a cell waiting with my name on it.*

Summer mentioned being locked up briefly in her past, but I'd assumed it was for the underground work she did in the "cult." Though, I now knew it had to be some kind of mob if she went by a title like "Stitch Up." She'd created a clever cover story, one I still didn't have a clear picture of.

The fact she'd been locked up in a place like Hartford shouldn't, *and didn't* change my perception of her. If anything, I wondered more about what her ex had done that led the woman I loved to such a fucked up place.

*Is she far more dangerous than I ever suspected?*

If Reid were going to accuse anyone of being Celeste's murderer, he needed to be absolutely certain before telling me. He understood that once a name was embedded in my mind, there'd be no turning back – I'd kill them.

*Will it be Summer? It can't be... She probably just knows something that'll give us another lead.*

Light poured through the door to the balcony, warming my room and indicating that I'd been waiting for hours for more information.

I dragged my ass out of bed and showered, too exhausted to have bothered to carry out my routine the night before. I shaved. *Everywhere.* Always prepared for the chance I'd create a crime scene away from the shed, unable to risk leaving traces of my DNA amongst the mess.

*Everything will be fine. She deserves to know who you are.*

I should have known an argument like this was bound to happen eventually, things had been going too well between us for so long. Something had to build up and explode, but I hoped things would settle down again once this thing with Reid was dealt with. Then Summer and I could move on like normal.

*Normal.* I laughed to myself as I wrapped my lower half in a towel and left for the kitchen in search of food. *It was never normal to begin with, and now I might not have a choice but to admit that I'm a villain.*

# FIFTY-THREE

## LOGAN

"Goddammit, would you at least wear clothes out here?" Tommy grumbled when he turned to see which one of us had come from the hallway. He'd assumed his usual position – reclined on the couch and pissing time away on his phone.

He and my sister were apparently "off again" and with me back in my room for the night, he'd evidently been banished to the living room to sleep on the furniture that barely held him comfortably as he sat, let alone slept.

As I rummaged through the cupboard, my sister's door opened and light footsteps skipped down the hallway.

"Why are you here?" Nova asked with a sparkly frown. "I thought you'd all but moved in with Summer?"

"You'd love that wouldn't you? Rent paid and me out of your way to do fuck knows what in my room."

"Is she here?" she asked excitedly, leaning back to look down the hall like she expected Summer to appear and join us in the kitchen.

"No. She kicked me out," I mumbled, already giving her more information than I should have. Nova was hard *not* to talk to. I hated to admit how much of a half-decent friend my annoying little sister could be.

"What the fuck did you do?"

"Why do you instantly assume *I'm* at fault?" I slammed a bowl a little too hard on the counter.

"Come on, Logan. Of *course* it was your fault," she scolded, and Tommy laughed from the couch.

"She asked who I was. Straight-up called me Vengeance. She wanted me to admit it."

"So you told her?" – her eyes narrowed as I shook my head – "You're *going* to tell her?"

"No. I don't know. Maybe."

"You're fucking useless," she sighed and began filling the dishwasher, "She needs to know. She *does* know. This is your chance to have a normal life with someone you're crazy about and you're too fucking stupid to take it."

"Normal," I scoffed. "I'll be out again tonight. She and I need to talk."

"Ooo!" She bounced around the narrow kitchen as I loaded the bowl with more cereal than it could hope to contain. At least with Tommy always staying over, there was a wider variety of food in the house. While he wasn't Gifted like us, he ate almost as much.

"Don't start," I flicked a piece of cereal at her glittery face. Her overly good mood without ever taking all the details into consideration always pissed me off. "I need to work out what I'm going to do with her."

"You mean moving in together? Living happily ever after?" she teased, hopping up to sit on the bench across from me, "There's no way you two can move on without your identity out in the open." She clapped her hands and swung her legs at the thought.

"Have you been going through my stuff again, Nova?"

"Maybe. It's pretty. Would have cost every cent to your name. I thought you were saving for a new suit?" She grinned up at me, relief softening her features. It didn't take a mind reader to know how relieved she was at the thought of her brother choosing a life with the woman he loved over more of the same, solitary confinement I believed I'd been forever condemned to.

"What's going on?" Tommy asked, turning on the couch to face us, always one step behind. He wasn't stupid, but had to compete with Gifted siblings who had a constant sense of what the other was talking about.

"Summer's going to be one of us!" she squealed, dropping from the bench to join him on the couch, kissing him as she sat on his lap.

*On again, apparently.*

"For real? You're *finally* gonna tell her?" Tommy instantly caught Nova's contagious excitement. He'd liked Summer from the moment they met, not that he showed it. He was as bad as his ex-wife when it came to keeping secrets, and found it easier to stay quiet instead of trying to keep up with all of our lies.

Summer, being too clever for her own fucking good, worked that out far earlier than we'd hoped. I'd had to put an end to all group interactions after the night she'd confronted him.

"He's got no choice!" Nova beamed, "No more secrets. We'll all be able to hang out and get to know her. Just as it always *should have been*." She may have been speaking to Tommy, but her words were firmly aimed at me.

*She's right,* I admitted only to myself, not allowing my sister to know that her way was the only way forward. *I can't be with Summer and never allow her to get to know my family. That can't work. I need to tell her everything.*

"And he'll be doing better than just telling her!" Nova whispered. My life choices were apparently up for discussion, right in front of me as I tried to eat in peace.

She pointed to the engagement ring Tommy gave her eight years ago that she wore no matter the current status of their relationship. He bobbed his head slowly, catching her meaning but smart enough to keep his revelation quiet, knowing I'd launch the carton of milk I poured from at the side of his head if he were to make any smartass comments.

"Don't," I warned Nova as she pounced off Tommy's lap to join me in the kitchen again, "I was caught in a moment when I bought that. I think I need to take a step back and work out what's going on between us first."

"Why? Everything's gonna be fine once you open up to her. We love her. Don't ruin this."

"I'm not *ruining* anything," I started to argue, not knowing if that was entirely true. "We had a fight last night. Pretty bad one, I guess. She told me she loved me before I left for the club and…"

Nova rolled her eyes and angrily threw a towel at me. I was grateful the knives were out of reach, she wouldn't hesitate to throw one of them at me if she believed I deserved it. "Maybe it's best you hold off with a *ring* until you can work up the guts to respond to something like that."

She was right. I shouldn't have been so quick to rush into anything.

I'd been trying not to live my life on repeat, but had almost entirely made up my mind about Summer the moment I watched her shoot that patient in the neck. It sparked an intense desire to claim her, not just in *me*, but the darker parts of me, too. But it was too soon to spring something like a ring on her, and now I wasn't sure if she was a threat to us or not.

"Reid texted me last night."

Nova huffed as I poured my third bowl of cereal. "Don't try to change the subject."

"I'm *not*. He gave me a description of someone who'd have info on how Celeste died. Matched Summer to a T. She even has the Hartford uniform that he said she would."

That shut my sister up. For a second.

"Hartford? The looney bin?"

"Yep." I answered through another mouthful, watching as the information turned over in her sparkly head.

"Logan, I've always said she looks familiar. I have a feeling she might be–"

"Don't!" I growled, "Don't tell me *anything* about her. You need to stay out of it. I told Summer I didn't want to know about her past until she's ready to tell me herself."

Even with the possibility of Summer being a danger to us, I still wanted to keep my word. For all I knew, things between us would be patched up soon, and I didn't want her to think I'd gone behind her back to learn her secrets. She could have confronted me at any time, but didn't seem to feel the need to until I stupidly got too carried away at Crave. She'd given me space to be myself, and I still wanted to do the same for her.

"You're sure?" Nova pushed, "I think it might help."

"I doubt it," I countered, not wanting to hear her gossip, "I'll wait for what I need from Reid and I'll work it out."

"She's probably just a witness. Or maybe she stitched Echo up at some point, it's not impossible." Nova saw the best in everyone – the complete opposite to what I was capable of.

"I kind of have a bad feeling about it. He's meant to text with more details, but he's taking his time."

"A bit unusual for Reid to be *texting*. Doesn't he usually call you when he needs us for something?"

"Usually, yeah." I didn't think anything of it. There could be a million reasons why a cop couldn't speak out loud and needed to text instead.

"In the meantime, what are you planning on doing with your hot little nurse? You're going to fix things with her, *right?*"

"Messaging her now." I grabbed my phone from the bench to text Summer. "Gonna take her out tonight, we don't do *normal* things like that often enough. All we do is sleep and fuck."

"Sounds like you really have met your perfect match."

I bit back a grin. Summer was perfect. Maybe a little *too* perfect.

"You're probably right. She might have helped Echo," I sighed, "She's met more people than I could hope to keep track of. Maybe she can help us." I regretted saying the words the second they left my mouth.

"Oooo, your first mission together?" Nova teased, clapping her hands again. "She'll be joining the gang in no time!"

I rolled my eyes, "I'm still not involving her in *that* side of our lives yet. Maybe never. It's too dangerous for a human."

She rolled her eyes back at me. "You're *so* boring. Though it'll be good for Jackie to have someone when we leave her behind… So the ring… If all goes well tonight, will that be making an appearance anytime soon?" Nova missed Millie almost as much as I did, and I knew she desperately wanted Summer to be someone she didn't have to keep my secret from like she had in the past.

"Soon." I shoveled more cereal down. "I guess we'll see how she takes the admission that I'm wanted for mass-murder first."

"Oh, come on. She loves you. You love her. We *all* do."

"I do. It's just too soon, you know? Besides, I can't imagine she'd say 'yes' anytime soon. If I'm going to tell her everything, it might take some time for her to accept the truth… if she still wants to be with me at all."

"Too soon?" Nova giggled. "That's unlike you. What happened to Mr. Headfirst, diving into everything? Maybe Vengeance really did devour what remained of your romantic side. You told Millie you loved her on your first date. And I told Tommy I loved him like, a week after he asked me out."

We had our father to thank for that. He said the Harrisons were cursed, falling too hard and too fast. Mom was the level-headed opposite to balance him out and kept him from floating too far away with his fantasies.

"Look how well that turned out."

"Tommy and I still love each other, we just got too caught up in what we couldn't have." Her eyes sparkled a little more from tears that threatened her good mood.

"Exactly. Wouldn't I be setting myself up for the same failures as I did last time?" I set my bowl down, suddenly sick with the memories of intense disappointment with Millie and the sight of Summer covered in blood in my bed.

"Only if you go into this *expecting* the same things. Summer is different. In all the right ways. You've said yourself there's something about her. You need to learn to accept what you have and enjoy it while you can." She gave me a small smile and walked back to the couch to curl up on Tommy's lap.

"So you're going to tell her?" Nova confirmed as they both looked at me.

"That I love her or that I'm Vengeance?"

"Both?" she pushed.

"Both," I nodded, unable to contain the smile at the weight it would lift from all of us.

I left them in the living room to go back to my bed to try to sleep again, but I couldn't get comfortable enough to drift too deeply, too anxious about what the night could bring.

# FIFTY-FOUR

## LOGAN

Summer responded to my text when she woke up. As I dressed to meet her I decided to wear the suit under my clothes and left my mask in the bag with her Hartford uniform. I took them with me when I left the apartment so that *nosey Nova* wouldn't snoop.

I didn't want to be caught without the suit if Vengeance needed to make an appearance on our date. Though, I prayed I wouldn't need it, it could only end in death. It certainly wouldn't be the greatest timing – with me now set on starting the next phase of our lives together.

There was no turning back now. Summer wasn't going to accept anything less than complete honesty from me.

It was the middle of the night when I arrived at her house. I parked on the street and silently crept along the outer side of the fenceline. There was barely a blindspot in all of Summer's security cameras. I had to be quick with tossing the bag over the fence by the furthest garage, and rushing back to the gate so my movement was the only one to show up on her phone.

As I stepped under the harsh lights and lifted my hand to knock, she opened the door.

*Fuck me.*

The woman in front of me looked so… *alive.* Her black dress clung to every inch of her torso, I didn't have to use my imagination at all. I swallowed over my jealousy at the thought that others would see her like this, so much of her on display yet so covered up. Her makeup was flawless. I'd known for months she was oddly talented with the few beauty products she kept in her bathroom, but hadn't questioned until now that maybe it was all part of her training and disguises.

"You look… *unbelievable.*" The words escaped with a heavy exhale. I couldn't hold it in. I took her hand and spun her on the spot, taking in every inch of her to check there were no outlines of knives or other weapons strapped to her body.

She smiled. Happy. Confident.

So. Fucking. *Hot.*

"So do you," she blushed. I loved having that effect on her. The color flushing her cheeks stole the air out of my lungs. I smiled back, hoping it hid my exhaustion from barely getting any sleep without her by my side.

"We might take your car? I'll drive."

"Okay," she agreed.

It wasn't the first time we'd done things this way, so she didn't question it. Part of me wished she had. I couldn't have my car being seen at any potential crime scenes if the worst case were to occur, and as each second ticked on, I became more fearful of the fact there'd be a chance my beautiful girlfriend might not make it home.

We made our way to the garage and in the split second it took her to retrieve the car key from her small bag, I snatched up the backpack and threw it onto the backseat as she climbed in.

"So where are we going?" she asked after we sat in silence while I drove, clearly trying to hide her relief that we were on speaking terms.

"Well that depends, I guess." I said, pulling onto the highway.

She bounced in her seat. "Depends on what?"

I wanted to forget the information from Reid. I wanted to turn my phone off and enjoy the night out with her. I wanted to tell her that I loved her and everything we had together, no lies attached. I was ready for her to know me. *All* of me.

My phone vibrated with a message.

**Echo was poisoned by Stitch Up. Corpse dumped by bodyguards.**

My heart sank at the words on the screen. I quickly locked the phone so Summer couldn't catch a glance at what I'd just discovered.

Closing my eyes for a moment, I forced the darkness away for just a little longer. I needed time to question her before things got too out of hand. But I knew myself well enough to understand that *he* had already decided that Summer was going to die. I no longer had a say in the matter.

My girlfriend was capable of poisoning someone. She had a garage full of drugs and vials of unknown substances. After reading most of the labels, I'd seen she had poisons that only needed small amounts to take out a human, maybe not much more for a Gifted being.

"Is everything alright?" Summer's whisper was concerned, maybe she sensed the change.

"God, I *really* wanted it to be." I sounded cold, giving away my thoughts – but sheer disappointment was gutting me as I tried to convince myself that the woman I loved could never be responsible for my friend's death.

*I'm such a fucking idiot.* I shook my head of more blackness threatening to engulf my vision. *Did I really think I could ever have a normal life with someone like her? She's more of a monster than I am.*

"Logan, what's wrong?" Summer gently placed her palm on my leg. Where I typically would have found comfort in the small gesture, I instead fought off the idea of tearing her hand clean off her wrist.

*Don't slip away. You won't get any answers from her if she bleeds out in the car first.*

Swallowing my repulsion at her touch and the disgust in myself for being so fucking weak and blinded by whatever spell she'd been pulling over me for months, I simply gave her a little of the truth.

"What's wrong, *Stitch Up*, is that *you* killed Echo."

# FIFTY-FIVE

## SUMMER

I woke to a text from Logan.

**Take the night off, I'm taking you out. Wear something nice.**

After how we'd left things the previous night, I was in a weird headspace of not wanting to deal with him and desperately wanting to see him. I needed to give him the chance to decide whether he was ready to tell me he was Vengeance or to continue with his lies. If he chose the latter, we needed to give up on this whole dumb charade.

*Is what we have worth him being honest with me? Is he willing to throw it all away on a secret I already know?*

I messaged the bodyguards to arrange for a night off.

**Have fun** – Ben replied with a winking emoji.

**Use protection** – from Tony. While seeming like a joke, I knew he meant it after our trip out of town.

I sighed at my ceiling and rolled out of bed to start psyching myself up for the night, already assuming that Logan wouldn't be revealing his alter ego and we'd be breaking up.

*Wear something nice,* I recalled from the message. *Still, people can be broken up with while wearing pretty clothes.*

Keeping the waves from the braids in my hair, I put more effort into my makeup than normal. The finished look would have been worthy of one of the hundreds of tutorials I'd made in the past; showing off the absurdly expensive products Eric insisted I use to hide my tiredness and exaggerate my youth.

If Logan wanted to keep up the farce and doom our relationship, I wanted to give him a reason to regret it when he looked back on the night.

I slipped on a short, matte black body-con dress with long sleeves. It clung to every inch of my skin. I loved how it looked on me, but I'd never worn it with the almost-completely-removed tattoo visible with the low neckline. It was also quite low in the back, and some parts of the scars closer to my spine would show. Though for once, I didn't care. I didn't even bother with covering up the tattoo.

Retrieving my favorite shoes from the bottom of the wardrobe, I turned for the bed to put them on, but paused at the walk-in door. I looked down at the space where I'd grabbed the heels – empty except for the row of shoes. I couldn't recall when I'd moved the backpack, and couldn't remember where I'd put it.

My mind had been such a blur from obsessing over Logan for the last few months, I was evidently losing my defensive traits, barely looking for escapes and not noting every detail of my surroundings.

*I'll look for it later.*

As I opened the front door, I found Logan, reaching to knock. He didn't look real; too perfect in dressy clothes. He wore a dark gray, buttoned up shirt, black pants and shoes. It made me glad with my choice of dress for the night.

I beamed up at him, quickly forgetting how I felt during our fight at the familiar sight of him and the scent of his woody cologne.

*For now, at least. You can't forget what you've argued over just because he looks this good.*

"You look… unbelievable," he sighed, taking my hand and spinning me around to get a better look at me from all angles.

"So do you."

He smiled, but it seemed heavy with exhaustion, like something was eating away at the back of his mind. The argument and my desire to know the truth likely still played over in his head, just as it was for me.

"We might take your car?" he said, tipping his head in the direction of the garage. "I'll drive."

"Okay."

Logan was a little distant as we made our way down the sloping hills to the main roads. He constantly checked his phone and seemed to be lost in thought.

"So, where are we going?" I asked, after a few too many minutes of silence, feeling a little better now that we were at least acting *kind of* normal around each other with his secrets all but revealed to me.

"Well that depends, I guess."

"Depends on what?" I asked, excited to learn what we would be getting up to on a rare night out that didn't involve his work or the gym, and thankful for the sake of my stomach that we were moving in the opposite direction of the grunginess of Crave.

Logan didn't respond, instead he retrieved his phone from his pocket again. His eyes skimmed over a message for only a moment before he squeezed them shut, opening them again to scan the road around us. He took a deep breath and sped up, erratically weaving through the late night traffic.

"Is… everything alright?" I asked, placing my hand on his leg. Whatever the message contained had immediately made him tense.

"God, I *really* wanted it to be."

His tone had changed. Cold.

It lacked the usual warmth and smoothness, making the hair on the back of my neck stand up and goosebumps tumble down my bare legs.

*Like months ago… At the cinema?*

"Logan, what's wrong?" I searched his face for answers. Something was setting off his mood, and I didn't know how safe we were in a moving vehicle while he suffered one of those "shifts."

The next words that came from his mouth were both shocking and made absolutely no sense.

"What's wrong, Stitch Up," he growled through his teeth, "Is that *you* killed Echo."

I flinched at my title.

*He knows?*

The accusation was out of this world. I'd never heard of this person, both in this life or at Home. With a name like Echo, I could only assume it was one of his vigilante buddies.

"Wait, is that… Celeste? Jackie's wife?"

"Fuck, Summer! You should know, *you killed her!*"

How he thought I was capable of killing anyone – let alone a Gifted – was beyond my ability to comprehend while we tore along the freeway, barely dodging cars and swerving in and out of lanes.

I needed more information without making him snap. It seemed I was now, *again*, trying to avoid tipping the scales against me.

The excitement of the date rapidly dissolved, replaced by feeling as sick as I had the night before. Not even twenty-four hours ago we were kissing and planning on moving up to the rooms, only to now find myself being accused of murder.

"Baby, *please*," I begged, but he wouldn't look at me. "*Please* tell me what's happening. I don't know where this is coming from. Why do you think I killed her? I don't *kill* people, I *help* people."

"Grab the bag in the back," his voice had turned gravelly, colder still. He hardly sounded like the Logan I knew at all.

I unclipped my seatbelt and spun to feel around the backseat, patting blindly until my hand settled on something behind him. My backpack.

"You know what's in it," he spat.

"Of course I do, it's… my uniform from Hartford. How did it get in here?"

I rummaged through the items in the bag; the few necessities I'd always stored inside in case I needed to run for my life. My uniform was tucked down the bottom. It was one of the only undeniably identifying pieces of my past. If I ever needed to flee, it would come with me. I couldn't allow anyone who stumbled upon my house to know which villain had once occupied the space.

When I touched the orange fabric, I pushed down the memory of the events following Danny and Mikey's deaths. I'd been resuscitated in one of the worst asylums for the criminally insane that this country had to offer.

My uniform was one of the few things in my possession when I'd been released. I should have destroyed it, but had stupidly kept it as a reminder of what I'd freed myself from.

Everyone at Home was taken to Hartford after Nessa anonymously called in that the bodies of her husband and child were being kept in our building. Eric, of course, had conveniently left for the night after our last interaction in his bedroom.

After cutting a deal with some cops, I'd been released earlier than everyone else, giving me my one true chance to flee from Eric and the inescapable Home.

The list of injuries Eric left me with threatened to resurface as I stuffed the suit back into the bag and the sudden realisation of my situation hit me like a fucking avalanche. This was all too-perfectly executed. I'd fallen for someone new, my life was on track, I'd been slipping through the Finder's fingers.

*Oh, fuck.*

"This is *all* Eric's doing. I swear, whatever evidence you think you have on me, it's not true. It's all gotta be from him."

Logan glared at me, features sharp with insulted rage as though I were treating him like a child.

"I got my information *directly* from Reid," he growled.

The name was familiar, but I couldn't place it.

*Maybe a cop they have contact with? Who else would have this kind of information on me to share with him other than Eric himself?*

"Your *information* is fucking *wrong!*" I braced myself with one arm on the dashboard and turned to him, trying again to read his expression, to see if *anything* I was saying was getting through to him. Was his mind already made up? Were the scales firmly tipped against my favor?

"Yeah, *sure,*" Logan scoffed, "But the suit along with the story he's given tells me otherwise."

Holding my head in my hands, I tried to breathe as we moved too fast around the other cars. The erratic driving was making me nauseous. Logan swerved again and sped up before sharply pulling off to an exit.

"Where are you taking me?"

"Somewhere I can work out exactly who the fuck you are, Stitch Up. And what you did to Echo."

I flinched again at the name. Logan calling me Stitch Up hurt more than when Nessa said it with the intention of causing me pain.

Eric was too good. I honestly couldn't blame Logan. My ex had proven time and time again that he was a master of deception. People were nothing but pawns for his end game, and right now, my boyfriend was just another in Eric's plan to get me back.

*Would he really have me killed by an uncontrollable vigilante?*

If Eric truly orchestrated this whole thing, he must have known I wouldn't survive Vengeance and the signature mess he made of his victims. It was extreme, even for my ex.

I thought Eric would simply find a way to drag me back against my will. Wasn't I meant to be a perfect piece in his collection?

My body and skills were far too precious for him to lose, and I was certain he'd want me back in working order.

*Working order by anyone else's hands,* I countered with myself.

We sped along dirt roads through tall pines, complete darkness surrounding us on all sides. The headlights of my car were the only light source as we moved deeper into the forest.

I was tempted to tear the steering wheel from Logan's grip so we'd crash and I could try to run, but I was smart enough to know I'd be the one worse off in that scenario.

More waves of nausea rolled over my insides at the bumpiness of the unpaved road as we raced towards our destination.

*You might actually die out here,* the words popped into my head. *Thanks, brain. Couldn't fucking work that out.*

We pulled up to a moonlit clearing in the trees. A large, abandoned shed stood alone in the space. It wasn't unusual for the area. Growing up with preppers in the mountain state, I was aware things like this were hidden all over the woods. I'd found plenty on my jogging routes. It was a whole other thing to be brought to one to be murdered in, though.

"Get out," Logan demanded. "Don't bother running, Summer. I'll take you out before you can get too far."

My blood ran cold when I turned back to him, literally almost jumping out of my seat when I looked up at the black and red mask of Vengeance. He unbuttoned his shirt, revealing the rest of the suit.

*Fuck, I really am going to die out here.*

Logan made quick work of removing the rest of his clothes and exited his side. He was at my door before I could blink, opening it for me when I refused to follow the order.

*If I'm going to die, I'm going to do it being my un-fucking-bearably difficult self.*

I glanced through the windows for any path of escape through the trees, but it was too dark.

I spun on the spot, keeping seated as I looked up at Logan. "Not offering me a hand this time, Vengeance?"

When he didn't respond I rolled my eyes and slipped down onto the course dirt to walk to the shed, surprising even myself with my calm behavior. Maybe I'd already accepted my death at this point. I'd accepted it several times before, I should have been a pro at it by now.

*Maybe because it's actually going to happen this time?* My mind offered. *Fuck you.*

Logan opened the door and I stepped inside.

"Such a gentleman," I purred with narrowed eyes, hoping he couldn't see my hands shaking like leaves as I tried to hold them still by my sides.

The shed was dark and eerie. There were no windows, and only a few lightbulbs on strings illuminated our surroundings with a sinister glow. The entire floor space was about the same size as my largest garage and reeked of bleach. My nostrils burned when I tried to take deep enough breaths to smother the building panic in my chest.

There were ropes on the floor, and I thought perhaps Logan might be planning to hang me from the wooden beams above. I silently hoped whatever he chose would be that swift.

Unfortunately for me, my boyfriend made me sit on an old wooden chair that he retrieved from one of the rotting workbenches along the walls.

*Classic villain.* My limbs trembled as he tied me up in the center of the room. *Is that a sore spot I can use to my advantage?*

Though Logan was restraining the woman he believed to have murdered his friend, he handled my arms gently as he secured them. It made being held in this particular position a little easier, but didn't settle my nerves over how this might end.

I cleared my throat. "In all the time I knew who you were, I learned you were capable of some pretty awful things, but I never took you for an *actual* villain."

Logan's hands paused with the knots he was tying behind my back.

"What makes you think I am now?" He moved on to tying around my waist from behind, tone sour and confirming that I'd hit the nerve I sought.

"Well, you've made the girl fall for you, taken her out to the woods, tied her up and plan on killing her – I'd say you actually tick more boxes than my ex. At least you'll finish the job," I shrugged, subtly pulling at the ropes binding my wrists. Unsurprisingly, they were tied too well.

"Made *you* fall for me?" His masked face appeared over my left shoulder. "Are you fucking kidding? You popped up in my life out of nowhere, Summer. *Your* timing was a little too convenient if you ask me. And you think *I'm* a villain?" he chuckled darkly and set back to work, "That's a bit hypocritical don't you think? You killed Celeste. She could've been a hero. Explain how that makes you one of the good guys?"

"I've *never* pretended to be good." My eyes burned when he moved around the chair to stand in front of me. "I've always *tried* to be. All I've ever wanted is to help people. I've never done *anything* like what you're about to do to me."

He let out an exasperated sigh and lowered his voice, "Baby, I *need* you to start telling the truth. The sooner you admit it… the sooner he'll finish this."

I glowered up at him, not appreciating the pet names at a time like this. "There's nothing you're going to get out of me that you don't already know."

"I guess we'll find out."

His voice was normal again, more smooth and sweet than gravelly like it had been in the car. It sickly gave me comfort. I loved Logan's voice, and it was hard not to think about all the sweet things it had said to me over the past few months; the nightmares it had pulled me from, the way it hummed mindlessly to songs I couldn't recognise while we showered.

I held onto that in my mind – the Logan that seemed to love me back. It would get me through whatever was about to happen between us.

*There's no point. You're not going to survive this.*

As he stood above me, I cursed how hot he looked in that suit. Part of me was devastated he'd *finally* revealed his identity now and not earlier when I could have had a chance to fuck him while he wore it.

As if Logan could read my thoughts while I took in every inch of him, he said, "We could have been so happy, had you not murdered my friend."

"I don't believe you," I shook my head and wriggled my wrists closer to the knots of the ropes around my body. I knew he'd tied them too well for me to have no chance of escaping – I just didn't want to give up so easily. "I asked you if you were a vigilante. I'd given you so many opportunities to come clean with me. Your identity was *always* more important than us."

Seeming stung by my words, he folded his arms and leaned on a bench against the wall.

"You can't talk, nurse. You've got plenty of dark secrets too."

"The only thing I intentionally kept from you was the title Eric gave me. Now you know it – you should look it up. Where's your phone?" I leaned back in the chair, feeling a little more confident now that we were arguing and he wasn't tearing my body to pieces. "A quick search and you'll have the full, fucked up *Summer story*. At first, I kept it from you because I was trying to figure out if you worked for him–"

"You thought I worked *for your ex?*"

"*You* showed up out of nowhere for me too, Logan. And a vigilante handing me over to Eric would have been rewarded in ways you can't even imagine."

"I would *never,* Summer. Even with you destroying Jack's life, I would *never* condemn you to more of what he did to you," he tipped his head down to what remained of my tattoo and roughly rubbed the sides of his head.

"As things got more serious between us… I only kept it from you so that…" I stopped and looked down, feeling so fucking stupid.

"So that, what?"

"So that you wouldn't leave me to find him. I thought if you knew his name, you might've…" I looked up at the roof and blinked back tears. "*Cared* enough about me to add him to the disturbingly long list of people *you've* murdered. And," I giggled, mildly hysterical as I shook my head for the drops to fall from where they pooled under my chin. "I love you so much that the thought of *anything* happening to you while you hunt him down was too much to bear."

Logan's shoulders drooped. He ripped his mask off, threw it to the bench and placed his hands on his hips in a defensive stance he'd never used with me.

*He's trying to act tough but this is destroying him.*

"But you didn't, did you, Logan?" I pushed, keeping the conversation going so I could live a little longer, "You never really cared for me."

"I did," he said without hesitation before he sighed. "I was *fucking stupid* falling for you. I should have known you were too good to be true, Summer."

Another anxious laugh slipped up my throat. "I'm *exactly* who you think I am. Maybe a little more fucked up. But I swear, you've got this all wrong. You need to let me go."

He shook his head in an odd way, as though he were trying to sharply expel a disturbing thought with a twitch.

"I've got enough proof for Vengeance to kill you. We should have known it was suspicious for you to show up so soon after Celeste died."

The weight of Logan's disappointment in how things were ending between us seemed too crushing – mentally and physically. He kept shaking his head and frantically blinking, and the way he spoke about himself was odd, like he was referring to a whole other person and he had no say in what was to become of me. But we were alone. No one was coming to save me.

Eric putting me in such a terrible position was still unbelievable. He must have had eyes everywhere to learn that Logan and I were together. And me, moving on with someone else could have been unbearable enough for him to finally dispose of me in spite of his obsession and the need for damage control in Bedlam.

"None of it's true," I cried. "This is all Eric and his fucking cruel games. He's using you to get to me. *Please* untie me, Logan. You know how much being held like this scares me!"

Logan's eyes welled up, but he didn't move. "I'm sorry, Summer. I wish we could believe you. You have no idea how much I don't want us to do this to you."

"*We?*"

"Was I next? My sister?"

My skin crawled as his voice changed mid-sentence, adding to the nausea over my impending death.

"Your sister?" I scoffed in disbelief. "The one I *still* haven't met? Do you *really* think I'm capable of hurting anyone? With everything I've shared with you, Logan? Do I seem like a killer?"

He sighed and shook his head sharply again, it was more like a spasm. The sudden jerking motion made me wonder if his internal scales were somehow affected by each word I spoke. It seemed to work that way on the night I told him about my job. Back then, he appeared to have decided on the spot that I didn't need to be killed.

*At least not immediately. Five months after dating and falling for each other, sure.*

"Babe, let's go home," my whisper faltered, "I know who you are. I always have. We can start over." I started strong but my suggestion turned into panicked begging the more I spoke. "Please, I'll tell you everything you want to know about who I am! All of it! There's no reason we can't move on from this!"

"It's been decided, Summer. I was only here to get you to confess before he takes over," he swallowed hard, looking up and away from me. "It was the best I could do to make sure he doesn't draw this next part out with you."

"What the fuck is that meant to mean?"

"Your Vengeance's now."

"Wait!" I screamed as he reached for his mask. Logan froze for a beat before turning to me. "Don't I get a last request? *Anything* before I die? A dying wish?"

"What, like, a *fucking* fairytale?" he almost laughed, but it was choked by sadness, the sound making my eyes burn more. "I don't grant wishes, nurse." Logan scowled at the mask and turned it over in his hands.

A weak smile pulled at the corners of my mouth. "If I meant anything to you, Logan… I want you to kiss me goodbye."

Complete devastation marred his features and his sad eyes met mine as I sat completely defenseless, tied to the chair in the center of the room.

"It won't change his mind…" he whispered, "I am… *barely* in control as it is."

The dim light of the shed was playing tricks on my mind. It made Logan's eyes appear to switch between lighter and darker shades each time he squeezed them shut. It was as though the simple act of blinking was painful, and while he was threatening me with death, I still couldn't stand the sight of him in pain.

"I don't need to change your mind," I sighed, taking a final pass with blurry eyes at my surroundings, confirming there was absolutely no chance of escaping my fate. "You know, after all the shit I've been through, I think I might actually be ready to die. I didn't kill Celeste, *I swear*. But I deserve this for the other things I've done."

I didn't believe in an afterlife, but the possibility of being in the same, eternal state as Danny, just as I'd deserved two years ago – it all made me think that maybe Logan removing me from the picture was for the best. The thought of never having to see Eric again was a bonus.

Logan got down on one knee to the side of my chair, our faces just inches apart. Upon closer inspection of his features, his eyes really had changed. His pupils were so wide they almost entirely consumed his hazel irises. The points of his nose and cheekbones were angled in ways that had me second guessing if the dim lighting was to blame, or if it were something more.

*Does he have any control over what makes him look this way? Is he a shapeshifter? Possessed?*

Being Gifted, either of those things could have been true.

"Tell me why you killed Celeste. Jack deserves closure."

My hands pulled at the ropes, instinctively trying to reach out to hold him. He noted my small movements, gently shook his head and blinked away. Maybe he wanted to do the same.

"I'll tell you why, if you answer me this," I bargained.

Logan squeezed his eyes closed and balled his fists, taking a deep breath in, struck awfully hard by the false admission of my guilt to keep him talking and stalling the inevitable.

"What was your favorite part?" I sniffled, speaking quietly to the side of his face when he refused to look at me. "Five months, Logan. Surely something stood out in that time? For me it'd be blacking out and waking up safe in your arms. I've never trusted *anyone* as much as I trusted you then. And I knew you were Vengeance for months by that point."

He opened his eyes and finally turned to look into mine. "The hallway… That'd make my top three," he admitted despondently. "You, telling me you love me would have been a solid first… *if* it were true. Or the half-second when I thought we were gonna be…" he trailed off, cleared his throat and shrugged. Another sad smile tipped the corners of his mouth. He sniffled and inspected his gloved hands. "Closely followed by watching you shoot Alan in the neck. He was alive for most of what we did to him, if that's any indication for you to know what you're about to experience. I can't control him, Summer."

*We? Him? Maybe his Gift has something to do with a divided mind?*

I tried to decipher the last mystery of my boyfriend's Gift as my stomach threatened to relieve itself of it's contents. I didn't need the graphic details of my imminent death, I only needed him to get it over with.

*Could he be carrying some other version of himself that he's slipping into?*

*Will that side of him be the one to kill me? Is Vengeance not just a disguise, but a separate part of his psyche?*

It would explain how the sweet man I'd grown to love could be capable of committing such horrific acts. Maybe he couldn't do them on his own.

"I *do* love you, Logan," I said, firmer than I had on the couch, just one night earlier. "So fucking much. All of this was real for me. Remember that when I'm dead and you learn the truth?" I leaned across the small space between us to kiss him.

He didn't instantly pull away like I feared he would. Instead, he immediately held the sides of my face to kiss me for longer. The warmth from beneath the fabric covering his hands seeped through to my cheeks and neck.

The final connection between us was soft and mournful. We were two severely broken people, accepting that our time had been cut unfairly short. Too caught up in keeping secrets to allow ourselves to truly be known by the other who loved them in ways neither of us believed we deserved.

We were as bad as each other. As damaged as each other. Surprisingly similar with our grim backstories and both of us wanting nothing more than to move on from our dark and villainous pasts to live as normal a life as we possibly could. Part of me couldn't help but love all of that about us. Until now, of course.

*I'm so sorry, Logan,* I grimaced against his lips, *You'll be feeling this tomorrow. Maybe then you'll wish you'd tried harder to believe me.*

I encouraged him to part his mouth by opening mine, gliding my tongue along his lower lip. When he responded I nearly caved with my desire to keep kissing him. But I was about to die, there was no time for shit like that.

I bit him. *Hard.*

My teeth sunk deep into the soft flesh of his lip. The sweet taste of his hot blood flooded my mouth. I released my grip as he pulled back, and swiftly head butt his face, letting out a pained wail over the instant ache from the impact.

Dizziness overcame my senses. I hadn't been able to hit high enough on my own head, though the satisfying crack of his nose on my skull told me I'd done well.

Logan sucked in a sharp breath – then nothing.

Once the room steadied, I swept my eyes up from his chest to his face, still beside mine. He'd barely made a sound before it suddenly cut off.

The silence was chilling. Not normal for the amount of damage. His lip should have been enough to have him howling in pain, but there was no sign that it bothered him.

As I looked into his eyes, I was met with what I could only describe as an *entirely* different version of my boyfriend.

The blood that poured from his nose and lip was the only sound in the room, dripping over his chin in a staggered stream to the floor between us.

His chest heaved. He was taking heavy breaths, but the motions made no noise and they weren't a reaction to pain at all.

He was pissed off. And *he* wasn't Logan.

*He's gone. You're alone with Vengeance now.*

The sharpness to his features was exaggerated, his eyes entirely consumed by black, dead like the shark I'd once compared him to – their only purpose to devour the soul before them. He stood *silently* beside me, bodily movements not making a sound on the rough and dusty flooring. He turned from me and took soundless steps back to the bench to retrieve his mask.

As he pulled it over his head I noted the shape of his physique had changed. Not so much taller, but bulkier. The muscles of his arms, chest and legs all seemed to have expanded within the suit.

I couldn't refrain from gasping at the sight. The Logan I knew might as well have not existed. A wave of nausea crashed into my stomach, as though his very presence was unnerving. The dreadful sensation amplified with each step the embodiment of my death took toward me.

"We meet at last, Summer." His voice was the deep, distorted growl of a hellish canine pulled straight from a nightmare. "It was only a matter of time before you proved to be worthy of death at my hands."

"*What the fuck are you?*"

"The end."

# FIFTY-SIX

## SUMMER

My hands violently shook behind my back and my lip trembled at the overwhelming sense of complete doom that washed over me. Even with the mask and suit to hide his appearance, Vengeance emitted an aura that set off all internal alarms. I was pummelled with the desperate need to run, to avert my eyes and get as far away from this horrific being as the fucking planet would allow. But I couldn't.

*You're prey, cornered by an apex predator with no escape.* My reactions suddenly made sense – the goosebumps, the adrenaline. I felt so awful for all the hares my brothers and I trapped on the farm, imagining that this was exactly how they felt in the moments before Dad or the dogs disposed of them.

Vengeance stood only a few feet from me, arms folded and eyes locked onto mine through the mask. He jumped straight to his questioning, "Let's start with why you killed Celeste. Who wanted her dead?"

My head started to feel a little fuzzy. It stopped and started over and over, causing me to squeeze my eyes each time I blinked, trying to rid myself of the odd sensation. It was like water, beginning its swirl in an enormous sink towards the drain, only to have the plug replaced. Then pulled again the moment it settled.

"I don't know, I–" my skull snapped to the left, and my body tried to follow. The chair I was bound to almost tipped over.

It took a moment to realize what had happened.

He'd *hit me.*

It took an extra second before my cheekbone ached and the skin stung where it instantly split from the force. My tied hands instinctively reached for my face to help ease the pain. I didn't even make a sound at his action, utterly *shocked* that Logan would *ever* lay a hand on me in such a way.

*Okay... I'll give him that one.*

"Hit me again and I'm *fucking* done with you, Logan!"

"He's gone, Summer," the distorted voice taunted. "It's just us now. Start talking and I promise I'll make your death painless."

"How kind of you."

Another hit. Apparently this villain had no patience for sass. I threw my head back to breathe through the pain. When I spotted the beams again through watering eyes I wished I'd been hung instead.

In that moment, I could see why Logan might have chosen to be a cop. Vengeance would have been incredibly useful for drawing out confessions. His threatening demeanor and sickening presence would be enough to get anyone to confess their crimes, no matter the consequences.

Too bad for me, I had nothing to confess about Echo's death, and I didn't know where that left us.

*Does Logan hate the idea of heroes so much because he tried to be one?* He'd probably tried to use his Gift for good before things took such a terrible turn and he'd murdered so many of his colleagues. I wondered again what so many of them could have done to meet their end in such a brutal massacre – the same brutality I was about to experience.

"Hitting me won't give you answers I don't have."

He stood tall and folded his arms again. "You'd be surprised at what humans will spill once I loosen their tongues – and teeth."

I gulped as he paced in front of me, my ears straining to hear the silent steps. The leaves softly rustling outside were screaming by comparison to Vengeance's soundless stalking.

"You and Echo," he paused to look at me over his shoulder, mask pulling at his brow in what I could only guess was a scowl. "There's an undeniable connection. I can sense it. Maybe you killed her without knowing who she was. Still... You've done wrong, Summer."

I tried a new approach – I wasn't above begging. "Let me go. We can work out what happened to your friend. I'll do whatever I can to help you, I swear. We'll find who killed her, together, Vengeance. But you have to believe *it wasn't me!*"

My head turned again, sending my mind into a disoriented spin. Blood dripped down my cheek. Vengeance was apparently beyond reason and in no mood to be the *good guy*. Deep down, I knew he wouldn't be; this particular vigilante wasn't known for giving chances, only taking lives.

*Isn't this what you wanted? This was your goal all along – getting Logan to reveal his identity.*

I took a deep breath, accepting that I'd gotten what I'd wished for as another hit connected with the other side of my face.

He was *fast*. I couldn't see them coming, only feeling the pain when my flesh eventually registered the impact. Surely I could only endure a few more blows before I ended up dead.

I took another breath before feeling the sudden urge to vomit. He'd moved from my face to my body. The force with which he hit my abdomen was enough to send what little water I'd drunk since waking onto the floor at my feet.

*He's going to kill me and destroy my favorite fucking shoes.*

"Fuck, Logan! *Stop!*"

He hit again.

"Something's wrong with you," the monster snarled, face inches from mine. He smelled like… *nothing*. I couldn't detect the cologne that had only just filled my car. "What are you, Summer?"

I blinked at the mask, the small action sent a sharp pinch across the right side of my face. "I'm a fucking nurse!"

His shoulders bounced and the shed filled with an ominous rumble. The sound echoed, which made no fucking sense. We were in a small structure, not a cavernous space that would be needed to produce such spine-chilling tenors.

*Oh my god — is that his laugh?*

"And such a brave little nurse you are, Stitch Up." Vengeance teased, lifting my face. The knuckle under my chin radiated with more heat than Logan's skin ever had. "He's always so sad when he wakes up. This time I might understand why."

"Don't kill me! I'm more useful if I'm alive!"

"I don't doubt that. But your crimes will see that you won't leave this shed."

*Fuck this, I'm not going to sit around and wait to die.* I readied my mind to use one of The Surgeon's tricks he'd taught me to endure mine and Eric's alone time.

I took another breath, then another.

Another. *Another*.

And then, I slipped away.

It was a survival tactic to live through interrogations from The Surgeon's training of his youth, and one of the reasons I swore my old friend had been a spy before Eric found him, though he never admitted it.

I had a sense that my body was still under attack, but at least I didn't have to sit through *all* of it. In the dark, quiet and hollow space of my mind, I hoped that I would be dead soon so the pain of losing the Logan I knew would pass.

Even as I continued to take hits by his hands, I struggled to believe what I'd seen.

*He's more than one person?* I tried to make sense of it all, but was interrupted by being knocked over. It almost brought me back, but the light of the shed flickered and everything quickly turned black.

I wasn't the perfect student when Surge taught me these things, always more interested in learning how to heal people and floating around after Eric that I hadn't paid enough attention to the lessons to stay "under" when being knocked around quite so hard.

"Get up, Stitch," a voice spoke in my ear. It was familiar, but my head ached too much to work out who owned it, "You can't stay here, girl. Get the fuck up!"

# FIFTY-SEVEN

## SUMMER

An intense heat burned through my skull as I held the right side. My eyes fluttered open, and it took a moment to focus on my surroundings and who was kneeling over me. Harrison. Or was she someone else?

"Hey!" she said, tightly holding my face in her hands as I blinked up at her sparkly features. Glowing eyes pierced mine and the stars on her skin shone a bright purplish-blue. "She's alive!" she called through tears. I didn't know how long she'd been sitting with me, but she was completely distraught.

I could barely see past her as my sight adjusted, but we appeared to be outside.

The voices of Tommy and Logan came from inside the shed. Though it still wasn't *Logan*. Vengeance was insisting to my boyfriend's best friend that I be killed, and that he needed help finishing the job. Something was wrong with me.

"Harrison?" My voice croaked as she pulled me up to sit.

"It's Nova," she introduced herself by her real name for the first time and wiped away tears.

Now *that* was a name I'd heard in circles swirling the underworld. I should have known who she was, but had never seen the vigilante with my own eyes until I saw her at Logan's work.

She wasn't just an enhanced human, she was more like a Goddess, someone with a Gift worthy of the title 'superhero' but had instead slipped into the vigilante crowd.

"We've just found our contact within the police is missing," she hurriedly explained as we sat facing each other, with me still struggling to suck in air. "Logan told us he was going to see you. We tried to find you at home, but you were already gone. When your bodyguards showed up, they helped us track your car."

*Thank God for those two.* Tony and Ben would have spotted the strangers arriving at my empty house on their access to my cameras. I was going to have to up their pay. Again. Ben would be thrilled.

"What does that mean?" I asked, starting to feel my freshly refilled lungs betray me with one of my signature panic attacks now that pain was registering across my entire body.

"Someone is after you, Summer. We're trying to work out who. They've either set you up to have Vengeance kill you or at least have you in a position to track you down. Jackie's working on it," she reassured me, like I was going to hang around and be thankful for their help in discovering who. I already knew it was Eric.

"Fuck. Can I have my clutch?"

She grabbed it from my car, only a few feet away from where she must have dragged me. I had a small emergency stash of my favorite "mystery liquid" in case I got caught drowning in my own mind away from home.

As I injected it into my neck, she watched me, expression troubled. To her, I was probably just a pathetic human having a meltdown, but I didn't care, I refused to let everything go dark again. Especially now with both Vengeance *and* Eric after me.

"You need to get out of here while we calm him down. Can you drive or do you need me to take you?"

"I can drive." The meds had kicked in and I was alert enough to get out of there.

"I'm so sorry, Summer," Nova said, taking my hands and looking at the shed where things were being thrown and arguing was still going on. Her voice broke as she whispered in their direction, "He'll *never* forgive himself."

I didn't care at this point, I just needed to get out of there. I gave her hands a squeeze before letting them go.

I got in my car and drove. *Fast*. Probably too fast for someone who'd been knocked out and was now high.

After only a minute of putting as much distance between myself and the vigilante group in the forest, I was nearly blinded by a light flashing in the rearview mirror.

*Nova?*

I almost felt worried for Logan, then quickly reminded myself he had just tried to kill me.

*Vengeance tried to kill me. Not Logan.*

Were they one and the same? Different sides of him? I couldn't think straight after such a decent hit to the head.

The thought that Logan could hurt me seemed impossible. Maybe he'd been a fantastic actor for the last couple of months… But I refused to believe that I could be fooled so easily.

I didn't know enough about his Gift, but surely some parts of what we had were real amongst all the deception?

It wasn't too difficult to get back to the highway, and after following the long road between the pines I was soon headed in the direction of my house. I had nowhere else to go. Vengeance could find me here, but I was still too shocked and coming down from the meds to come up with a smarter plan.

As I pulled into the garage I scrambled out of my seat, becoming tangled in the seatbelt as I ran for the door. When I reached my wardrobe I stripped down, feeling fucking ridiculous in the dress after how terrible the idea of a normal date between us turned out. I opted for more practical clothes; jeans and a white shirt.

I could depend on them. It was something I could control while all the other pieces of my life started to fall apart, crashing and shattering around me as I tried to make sense of the shards.

My phone rang in my pocket when I entered the bathroom.

"I'm ten minutes away," Tony said the second I answered.

"No. Don't come here. I'm safe." I wasn't going to risk his life by having him around if Logan showed up as Vengeance and Tony got in the way.

"Boss, please–"

"Stay. Away. That's a fucking order, Tony. I don't want you here."

His sigh was heavy as I checked my face in the bathroom mirror, surprised at how well I'd taken the hits from someone who was clearly in the "Gifted murderer" category.

*Maybe some good part of him held out on me? No. Don't be fucking stupid.*

"Fine. But I'll be keeping an eye on you," he promised before I hung up on him.

Bruising had already begun to appear under my eye and my skin was torn horizontally along the right cheekbone. My hairline was bloody, and I gasped at the gash when I parted my hair on the right, a little ways back from my hair-line. A large purple mark had formed on my forehead where I'd probably broken Logan's nose. My mouth still had traces of his blood in the corners of my lips.

*What the fuck were you thinking? Getting involved with someone like him. Look at how it ended. It's a fucking miracle you're not dead.*

With trembling hands I cleaned the wounds and stitched them with some sutures I kept behind the bathroom mirror. A perfect line on my cheek, three extra stitches at the end. I'd done them out of habit, mindlessly sewing while lost in thought about *what the fuck* had just happened.

Stitching in my hair was a complete pain in the ass, but I did well not to get too tangled. There was no fucking way I would shave part of my head to make it easier, especially with it being so close to my face.

I tossed the needle into the sink when I was done. That had distracted me for a few moments. Now, what could I do to distract myself for the rest of my life?

My eyes burned again and more tears slipped down my cheeks. Was I meant to forget him? Just like that? The man who's cologne hung in the air of the walk-in. Who had more than a few of his shirts hanging in my wardrobe, his jacket beside them. The only person I'd entered a relationship with and willingly shared most of my secrets. The only man I'd consensually given all of myself to.

Did that all mean nothing? It just needed to come to an abrupt end and fade away?

I felt robbed. Raw. Paralyzed with the shock of spending nearly six months of my freedom falling for someone who so suddenly felt like a complete stranger.

*You knew what you were getting into before you started dating. And if Logan is somehow separate to Vengeance, he's probably feeling the same about Stitch Up.*

With my back against the wall, I dropped to the tiled floor. I needed to calm down to see things clearly, but I couldn't. Not here. The memories of Logan trying to save me from drowning in this very spot were replaying themselves over in my head.

*What do I know?*

I needed a mental list for clarity.

*Logan is Vengeance. Absolutely no doubt about that.*

*I am in love with a complete fucking psycho who just tried to murder me.*

*Well, part of him. I don't know...*

*My identity as Stitch Up is known... Maybe?*

Logan said the name, but didn't allude to knowing much more.

*Eric's true identity will be revealed to him soon. I'm certain he's behind all of this. If that's the case...*

Panic fought through the remaining drugs in my system. I needed to occupy my mind or else I'd slip into the darkness.

*Inventory.*

It was a stupid idea, but always helped me feel in control.

I checked every bottle, needle and bandage in the garage. I even counted the plastic bags for the trash cans.

When I ran out of things to organize in there, I went to the kitchen to count the abysmal number of water bottles I kept in the fridge and the couple of half-empty vodka bottles that I'd be best friends with later, Eric's timeline permitting.

Moving back to my bedroom, I glanced at the space on the wardrobe floor where my backpack had been. I pulled my phone from the pocket of my jeans and checked the security system's history.

*So it was him in the night.* Logan hadn't set off a single camera or alarm, though his code to get into the house had been used a few hours after I'd kicked him out. It was impressive. Fucking terrifying, but impressive.

*Serves me right for letting another fucking villain into my life.* I blinked to hold in more tears.

Reluctantly stepping back into the bathroom, I opened the cupboard above the sink. Pills, sutures, needles, pads, tampons.

*Hmm.*

I hadn't needed the last two for a while. Only twice and in regular succession since the time I'd redecorated Logan's room. The app on my phone that I used for tracking my workouts and other bodily functions revealed that it had been even longer than my original guess.

*Shit.*

"Nope. Fuck that." I said out loud, willing the thought out of existence. I'd been late plenty of times. *Most* of the time. I didn't take good enough care of myself and my job was incredibly stressful. My body was hit or miss with the most basic things, periods included.

*Not quite this late though.*

"Nope," I argued with no one, a little less confident this time. Six weeks was a long time, even for me. Or had it been longer? The haze I'd been caught up in since meeting Logan made it hard to pick dates and times accurately.

*As if I'm not in enough of a fucking mess as it is.*

I slammed the cupboard closed with more force than I intended, livid with myself. The mirror cracked in the bottom left corner, sending jagged lines through the glass that fanned out in a spiderweb of shards.

My reflection was distorted, and each piece of the splintered glass forced me to look at the broken girl from slightly different viewpoints, as fractured as the mirror she was staring into.

I turned on my heel and stormed back out of the house.

My mind literally couldn't process this new information without completely imploding.

I needed coffee.

# FIFTY-EIGHT

LOGAN

## JULY 13TH

Blind. Again.

*Fucking, Nova!*

My eyes burned from the whiteness that surrounded me in all directions.

*She is literally going to send me completely fucking blind!*

It would take a few minutes for the light to disappear, and far longer for my vision to be restored. Probably a little less perfect than last time. *Again.*

*I was fighting with Tommy.* I remembered that much. *Is that why Nova went all "super" on me?* Maybe I'd tried to kill her ex-husband.

I could sense I was kneeling on the ground; the hard surface pressed against my knees, though I couldn't see either of those things. It was the only safe place to be when blinded by the light.

Years of experience had proven that wandering around and trying to kill my sister only led to more damage to myself.

Holding my head in my hands, my skull felt like it could split open from the brightness that bounced from all angles, though the pain wasn't as bad as I'd endured in the past. It gave me hope that I hadn't slaughtered anyone. Vengeance usually took most of my energy when he tore people apart with our gloved hands – those headaches as I came down were far more debilitating.

Footsteps brushed the ground beside me. Light. Dragging a little on the dirty floor. All of my senses seemed to get temporarily fucked up by the light, though the others always came back in waves before my sight was restored.

*What's left of it anyway.*

"You won't *believe* what you did this time, Logan." My sister's voice was a mix of sadness and absolute fury.

"H-how bad?" I was almost too scared to ask. The movement of my mouth prompted me to run my tongue over my bottom lip. I could taste blood, but I couldn't tell if it was mine until I could see. It *tasted* like mine. It fucking *hurt* enough to be mine.

I tried to think back to what happened before being blinded.

Summer. Spinning her around in that dress.

*Summer. The texts from Reid.*

My breathing hadn't calmed from the fight with Tommy and now the thoughts of what I might have done to my girlfriend sucked the air straight out of my lungs.

*Did I kill her?*

It was another thing I couldn't confirm until my eyesight recovered. Maybe it would be better to stay blind. What I did to people during my blackouts was often too much for me to handle when Vengeance slipped back into the darkness and I resurfaced to see the mess he'd made.

The thought of what I might have done to her was already making me sick and I hadn't even seen the carnage yet.

"*Bad.*"

Though I couldn't see Nova, I imagined how she'd look in the moment. Standing over me, arms folded, ready to give me another lecture on something I wished every day I could have any control over.

The stifling, metallic smell of blood registered on my senses. *Her* blood. Everyone I'd murdered had their own distinct scent, and I'd been covered in enough of Summer's blood in the past to know she'd bled somewhere in the white space.

I inhaled, detecting the vast amount that had been spilled. It was far more than she'd lost in my bed.

*She's dead.*

"You *fucked up*," Nova continued as I remained unseeing on the ground, waiting to hear the awful details of what I'd done, like I had many times before, "I hate to be the one to tell you this, Logan… Reid is missing. Daniels thinks he's dead."

That information took me by surprise. But I couldn't respond, I needed to hear more before I decided how much of a complete and unforgivable monster I'd been this time.

*Did I kill Reid, too?* I was confused at where this was going, unable to remember seeing him for months. We'd only communicated through phone calls and the few texts he'd sent me since he visited from Bedlam to let us know that Celeste's case would likely go unsolved.

"Reid didn't send any of those texts! If you'd just *waited* until Jackie traced his phone, you would have known that!" she shouted, grabbing my blinded face tight in her hands, "Summer was *innocent*. She was set up, you *fucking* moron!" her voice broke as she cried. "And Summer. Oh my God, you should have seen what you did to her!"

My hearing must have cut out along with my sight. I couldn't understand anything else that Nova screamed at me. My lungs felt like they were being squeezed by hands stronger than mine, choking me from beneath my ribs. I couldn't fucking breathe. I didn't *deserve* to breathe.

*I killed her. She was innocent. How is that even possible?* Vengeance should have been able to get a truthful confession out of Summer, and false confessions didn't work on him.

Visions came to me in small flashes – Summer bound and screaming. Blue eyes overflowing with tears.

Vengeance and I didn't share my body at the same time. He'd lend me some of the abilities as I needed them, but it wasn't like he and I could have an internal chat and share stories. At best, he could give me small pieces of what I needed from his memories while he'd been the main driver, but not much more.

I flinched with horror, pulling my arms tight against my chest at the flash of my fists connecting with her ribs. Summer had been tied up… and I'd *hit* her.

*Me*, the man who'd done so much to protect her, had been the villain that destroyed her in the end. I was no better than her ex. I was *worse*. I'd succeeded in killing her. Snuffing out the light she brought into my life in her own strange way.

Summer was guilty of many things, but innocent of what I'd accused her of. Surely that meant I could spare myself the pain of existing without her and be at the top of my own hit list? This time, *I* was the one who'd done wrong. I had to put an end to this before I took out the rest of the people I loved.

Then suddenly – sight.

It came back from white to normal-ish in about a minute.

Looking around the space for the first time, I found we were still inside the shed. Once I gained my bearings, I slowly stood to inspect the damage with my vision, blurrier than I could recall from earlier in the night. A broken chair, ropes, blood, vomit.

*God, what the fuck did I do to her? Tell me it was quick for her sake?* I pleaded with the evil in my mind.

"Where is she?" My voice croaked as I swallowed over the bile that rose at the subtle scent of stomach acid. The sound of a heartbeat played in my head. It made no sense for Vengeance to share that noise with me. I didn't need to know Summer's heart pumped that fast as she met her end. He knew how I felt about her. It was cruel for him to let that pass between us.

"She drove home," Nova said as Tommy tossed her a knife from his pocket. "I'm going to go check on her now."

"What?"

"She. Drove. *Home*."

"No. That's *impossible*."

The sickening sound of Summer's skull hitting the ground came back to me. No one could live through that. *Maybe* a Gifted, but I'd been able to kill my share of them too.

"What's impossible, Logan, is *you*. Those blackouts of yours nearly cost you *everything* this time." She was understandably mad. She loved Summer, not as much as I did, but enough. Not that it looked that way in the moment, having just tried to murder her in the place I'd brought many others. None of them had ever made it out alive.

"You turned on Tommy again," she hissed, sparkly eyes bulging, "You left me no choice but to blind you. Had you killed Summer, I would have fried your fucking brain!"

Nova had been blinding me since we were children. Mostly through her unexpected outbursts as a toddler. But over the last few years, she'd worked out how useful her Gift was at keeping mine in check. When we lived apart I'd done so much damage I realized I couldn't, *shouldn't* rather, ever be too far from her to put me down if I ever became that out of hand again.

I peered outside the shed's door to find that Summer's car had gone. It left me no choice but to believe my sister's words, though they made absolutely no sense.

"Go home and clean yourself up," she ordered, "You're going to fix this."

"Fix what?" I almost laughed in disbelief, "*You can't be serious?*" The look on her face told me she *was* serious. "What I've done is completely unforgivable." I glanced at the blurred pool of my little nurse's blood, "She's done with me, Nova. There's no coming back from something like this."

"You need to *try!*" She raised her hands when I opened my mouth to argue, signaling she was done talking to me. One of the few things my sister and I had in common was our inability to put up with each other's shit, and she'd apparently had enough of mine for one day.

We left the shed behind. Tommy, feeling safe enough to remove his sunglasses now that his ex-wife had left, took me home in his car while Nova took hers to find Summer. I was surprised she trusted me with him again so soon.

I had blacked out and thought I'd killed my girlfriend when I came to, what did that say about me? I was insane. Unstable. Completely untrustworthy.

*Could Summer ever forgive me?* I had no right to even ask. I'd fucked up beyond belief, jumping to conclusions and torturing her. *If I'd just waited... But I didn't have a choice.*

If she really had been set up, someone would've had to have known my Gift well enough to understand it wouldn't allow me to stop once I had that information from Reid. Was their intention to have me kill her?

When we arrived at our apartment I immediately moved for the bathroom. I felt dirty, disgusted by my actions. Both as Vengeance for not following the rules I was unwillingly bound by, *and* as Logan for what I'd done to the woman I loved.

I ran my gloved hands under the water at the sink, watching in horror as more of Summer's blood washed from them.

*Unforgivable.*

Everything Vengeance stood for was questionable after attacking her.

Removing my mask, I inspected the damage to my face.

"I know I deserved it," I tried to joke when Tommy appeared in the mirror behind me, but my tone held no humor, too consumed by confusion over what I'd done. "But maybe try to go easier on the face next time?"

"I *wish* I'd done it. You *did* deserve it this time." They were harsh words from the friend who'd tried to help me for years with coming to terms with what I carried in my mind.

Squinting at the mirror, I noticed my nose wasn't just swollen, but broken. Before it could have too long in a bad spot with my fast healing, I wrenched the cartilage to the side.

*Fuck, that's gonna hurt when I wear my glasses. Shit where are they?* I tried to think of when I'd last used them as a fresh stream of blood ran over my beaten lip. The damage didn't look as it normally would if I'd been punched in the mouth.

*What the fuck, are those teeth marks?*

Tommy had never resorted to *biting* me before, it was incredibly out of character.

"What?" I asked, unable to take my eyes from the injury.

"Summer got in some of her own work before we arrived."

"*Summer* did this to me?" I had no recollection of receiving the injuries. The odd sense of being relieved that she was able to inflict something back on me as I tried to kill her quickly mixed with a hurt that I didn't deserve to feel.

I wouldn't have believed Tommy's words had I not seen the marks Summer's small jaw had gifted my lower lip in the blurred reflection.

Knowing her track record, she would have been the one to headbutt me too. And by the feel of the damage on my end, I knew she'd be hurting.

"You told us yourself, she's too good for you," Tommy sighed, shuffling on his feet. Something was on his mind.

"There's *more*?"

"Vengeance is… acting up," he said with an amused frown, "He's never really… *spoken* to me like he did back there."

I took my gloves off and began gently washing the blood from my face. "He *spoke* to you?" Vengeance wasn't known for holding conversation. I knew he could speak and he was able to draw confessions out of people by questioning them when he needed to, often quickly turning violent to loosen our victim's tongues.

"He told me I needed to kill Summer for what she did to Celeste," Tommy explained as he leaned on the doorframe. "That he sensed something strange about her. He believed it was the reason he couldn't get her to confess."

"He tried to palm the job off *to you?*"

"Well… It *looked* like you – *Vengeance* – had already done the job when we got there. But the two of you could still hear Summer's heartbeat. Nova took her outside until she woke up." He shook his head, probably not wanting the images I couldn't recollect to linger in his mind. My stomach churned as I recalled the amount of blood splattered across the concrete floor. "He… shoved her…"

"Shoved her?" I asked with a strained laugh, internally praying my sister would find Summer *alive.* "Well I'm glad he didn't jump straight to skull popping," I spat in disgust as the sound of Summer's heartbeat played in my mind again.

"Like a demonic toddler throwing a tantrum. He seemed pissed off that he couldn't do it. He couldn't get the confession he needed."

*Because there wasn't one to extract in the first place, you fucking monster.*

I didn't always want Vengeance to hear my thoughts, especially when my thoughts were about *her.* But I hoped he could sense how much I wished I could put a bullet through the pieces of my head that he occupied.

"I'm sorry," I said, turning to face a blurred Tommy. "I don't even know what I tried to do to you this time for Nova to blind me–" He cut me off by shaking his head and pushed himself from the frame.

"Make things right with Summer. Then I'll forgive you," he said with a small smile and left.

I sat at the end of my bed. Numb. Confused. Wrapped in a towel with my mind spinning and still trying to make sense of the hours that had passed. Trying to fill in the gaps with the little Vengeance would share with me.

My Gift wasn't one that anyone would be proud to have. I didn't just kill people, I eviscerated them. They were left unrecognizable by the time I'd finished. And I'd nearly done that to *her*.

I'd done too much *wrong* when I was meant to be setting things right.

*Could I blackout permanently?*

The first time I'd lost control, Vengeance had such a tight hold on the mental reigns it was a miracle I ever resurfaced. What if I stopped fighting him for control? What if I gave it willingly? If it worked, I might never see Summer again. But then, wasn't that what you're meant to do for those you love? Keep them safe – even from yourself? I'd always known I could be the one to kill her, and I'd selfishly put my feelings first. I needed to put her life above everything else.

My mind was made up.

I straightened my posture and focused on the heat beneath my skin, enticing the darkness to take me with the promise of *forever*.

My vision dipped in and out of the blackness, a stark contrast to my sister's light.

A vibration snapped me from my path.

My phone.

It was a text from *her*.

**Need to see you. Tonight. 9pm.**

I steadied my breathing, fending off shadows to type the only word I could remember how to spell as I read her message over and over.

**Where?**

*Need to see you... Why would she bother after what I've done?*

**Crave. Rooftop.**

Nova entered the apartment, checking in on Tommy in the living room.

"Logan?" she called, no longer sounding mad at me as she found me in my room. She instantly recognised my mood. "Oh no, Logan. Not again. It's not like after what you did in Bedlam. Summer is still here." She sat beside me, instantly in tears as she threw her arms around my neck. "Don't let him take you. He'll only leave again and you'll be left to face what he's done."

She referred to the time I'd shown up at her door after I'd lost my mind.

I'd tried to let the courts and justice system do their work, but the men who killed my wife in retaliation for who I'd slaughtered weren't so much as questioned for their role in Millie's death. And I blacked out.

*Everyone* was at fault for justice not being served.

Being at work at the time of hearing the news, I'd slaughtered everyone in the precinct. The event took me from a dangerous vigilante, whispered about in the underground circles, to one of the "most wanted."

There was no one around to stop me. Nova was two states away, trying to resolve her broken marriage with Tommy.

The sensation of removing the eyes of my boss was still permanently imprinted on the skin of my hands. The tension of her optic nerve and the sound as it finally snapped tore me into a moment of clarity.

As she screamed, still conscious in my grasp and begging me to stop, I found myself surrounded by the dismembered corpses of my friends and colleagues. I'd regained enough control over the bloodlust to escape and seek out my sister.

Fortunately for me, I'd left such a mess of my victims that Detective Logan Harrison had been named one of the many deceased. Another victim of the deranged Vengeance, giving me the rare opportunity to start anew.

Reid was off duty at the time, and lucky enough to not be on my path of destruction. It took him over a year to reach out to me after what I'd done. And when he did, it was only when he needed help disposing of those that he and his new partner couldn't deal with on their own.

Nova soon joined with helping me rid the earth of the worst of us, though I'd become one of them myself. Tommy got as fit as he could in a bid to protect her from me and others. It was a good distraction for the two of them, it gave them something to focus on other than their failing marriage.

Celeste and I had occasionally worked on cases together in Bedlam. She joined the gang after leaving the city behind, and brought along her wife to help us with intel we otherwise wouldn't have been able to access without Jackie's skills.

Our fucked up little family was complete until Celeste died.

Part of me had hoped Summer could be a part of that family too.

The more I learned about her, the more she seemed to fit into our group. But I'd selfishly decided that loving her meant I had to keep her at arms length, separating her from the parts of myself that scared even me. Living two lives again like I'd done with Millie and never learning from my mistakes.

"I'll be okay," I lied to Nova, "Just struggling with the idea that I'd…" I couldn't breathe again, unable to speak at the thought of hurting Summer.

"You didn't though. She's *alive*. She's safe at home, I saw her." Nova held out her arm to reveal Summer's perfect stitching up a long cut on her arm. The sight of the immaculately tied sutures made my eyes burn.

*She wouldn't have been able to do that if she were dead.*

"She contacted me. She wants to meet tonight."

I didn't know how to feel about Summer wanting to meet. Did she want to properly end things between us? I didn't deserve to have her tell me something like that in person.

Nova smiled and pulled my glasses from her head, handing them to me, "Oh my God, Logan! That's wonderful!" She seemed to know something I didn't. I couldn't imagine anything good could come from seeing the woman, so skilled with throwing knives, so soon after I'd tried to kill her. "Trust me, you two have *a lot* to talk about."

She bounced out of the room to see Tommy and to fill him in on her visit to Summer. I dressed and collapsed in the center of my bed, drifting in and out of an exhausted state of unconsciousness.

My little nurse appeared in visions behind my heavy eyelids; beautiful and happy one moment, then the image twisted into blood with the sounds of her begging me to stop beating her the next.

*I need to see her. This can't wait until tonight.*

The second I stood to leave for Summer's house, Nova burst into my room.

"I got a message from Summer! It looks like one that went to all her patients."

"I didn't get anything." I checked my phone, quickly coming to the conclusion that it meant Summer didn't want *me* to know. Nova held out her phone for me to read the message. "She's leaving?"

"I don't think it's by choice, Logan. You have to believe me. Something was off about her. A *few things* actually. I don't believe she'd leave right now."

"Wouldn't you try to run after what I did?"

"I'm *sure* she wouldn't. I don't think she's running from *you*." She spoke with a heavy certainty that I desperately wanted to buy into. "Jackie's still working on finding out more. But Logan, I think whoever sent you those messages wants Summer scared. Alone. Without your protection."

*It has to be her ex. Just as she tried to tell me.*

"We need to find her. *Now.*" I told her, charging out of the room to grab my suit from the bathroom.

# FIFTY-NINE

## SUMMER

I grabbed an iced coffee that wasn't *too* awful. Though it was far too sweet.

*At least it's not his.* My heart ached as I left the coffee shop, drink in hand and miserably trudging down a quiet street of small storefronts. Most of them were closed, it was still too early. Thankfully, not too early for coffee.

I needed to be out of the house. I needed the distraction. I didn't want to think about Logan and what had just happened between us. It was too confusing.

Logan was two people? A split mind? Did the man I love even exist? Was I hurt by the *other side?* Or was it *all* a trick, and I was simply beaten by my Gifted boyfriend?

*You've been sick... a few times,* the words popped into my head. They prompted me to bat the thought away with my hands like a lunatic.

I didn't want to look for all the "signs." I needed answers. Yes or no. No guessing like last time, when it was too early to know for certain if it was just heavy bleeding or something more until the bloodwork came back. I could prepare for it this time, and not turn a king bed into a bloodbath.

There was a drugstore between myself and my car. Open twenty-four hours.

*One of the reasons you left the house. You can't go home without them.*

It took every ounce of strength to get my feet to the door, then more to force myself *through* the door. I could only imagine how I must have looked, stopping and starting on the street and internally arguing with no one, shaking my head between sips of the iced coffee whose sweetness only added to my nausea.

I couldn't keep fucking around, I was running out of time. How close would Eric be? Would he be waiting outside when I was done? At my house when I got home?

I imagined how insane the conversation with Eric would be.

*Me, walking out of here with a pregnancy test. Off to confirm whether or not the Gifted psychopath who beat me also knocked up the most precious missing piece of The Collection. Imagine the look on Eric's face as I tell him that his Stitch Up is carrying another man's–*

I snapped out of the fantasy and vomited up half a coffee's worth of liquid on the side of the road. I couldn't stomach the thought of the word "baby." Not now. Not after Logan hurt me.

*This is temporary.*

Even if I were pregnant, it couldn't last. Just like last time. Logan was Gifted, I wasn't. It'd end the same sad way it did for all couples like us.

*Well, not exactly like us.*

As sad as it was to admit, this wasn't, again, something Logan and I had tried for. I couldn't miss it once it was gone. I could be fucking mad at myself, though.

I, of all people, should have known to be more careful and to not put myself through this again.

While I might have been late, this thing had two weeks max before I would be completely rid of any and *all* traces of Logan from my body.

While I thought I needed that knowledge to get me through this ordeal, surprisingly, it hurt to think about it.

Making my way directly to the aisle of pregnancy tests, I chose two with the highest accuracy rates and paid for them. Out of all the things I kept in my house, these tests weren't one of them. I'd only ever purchased them if a patient let me know in advance that they might be needed. Even then, I'd usually refer them directly to Reynolds.

The young guy at the counter gave me a troubled look that I couldn't figure out until I remembered that I hadn't bothered to cover up the damage to my face. I'd closed the wound, but had left the house in a hurry without thinking to put makeup on again. I was bruised, stitched up and likely oozing blood from at least one of my wounds.

Back at Home, I was contractually obliged to ensure any marks Eric left me with were to be covered at all times. Whether they be hickeys or handprints, I needed to hide what went on upstairs.

I never would have guessed I'd some day need to do the same with Logan.

"Not that it's any of my business–"

"Then don't say anything," I snapped and raised an eyebrow, not in the mood for being friendly.

He ignored me and continued anyway, "My sister was treated the same before she found out she was pregnant," he gave a subtle nod to my cheek, "It didn't stop. Kid's don't change monsters."

Blunt. To the point.

How else could you communicate something like that to someone you thought needed to hear it? It was a ballsy move, and not a topic that should be danced around. He was just trying to help, like I had done with everyone I'd come into contact with for my whole fucking life.

*Look where that got you, Summer. Beaten again. Pregnant again, but to a different monster this time.*

I nodded, "I won't be letting that happen."

He forced a smile and handed me a small bag containing the tests.

*He's like an omen, or a warning. I can't allow Logan to be in my life in any capacity now.*

We were over. We had to be. It didn't matter how I felt about him, or how he might have felt about me. Logan *hurt* me, even if it were only a *part* of him, that crossed a major fucking line.

I'd escaped Home to avoid dying on that line years ago, and I'd left without looking back. If I needed to, I could do it again.

As I left the store I decided then that I wasn't going to tell Logan about the tests and whatever the result might be. It'd be over soon anyway, and I stupidly still cared enough about him to not put him through another loss with me.

*Am I STILL protecting him? He'd be devastated if he knew...* More thoughts to shoo away like flies.

When I got in my car, I slouched in my seat, unsure of whether to start driving or to sit on the sidewalk and vomit some more before I had to endure the motions of a moving vehicle. That's when I saw them – in the cupholder of the center console beside my half-empty drink.

I picked up Logan's glasses and put them on. I'd seen Vengeance now. He literally changed Logan's physical form. I could only guess his eyes were somehow affected by that process 'cause my boyfriend really was blind as fuck. I could barely make out my hands on the steering wheel through the thick lenses.

*Ugh, is he stumbling around right now? Unable to see anything? How can he see without them sometimes?*

I folded the glasses and hooked them on the front of my shirt, glancing in the rearview mirror at the backpack on the seat.

After punching in the code for the front door, I ran straight for the bathroom.

A text from Ben appeared on my phone as I set it on the vanity.

**It's too early for you to be out. Everything OK?**

**I'm FINE.**

I used both tests and set them by the sink before closing the lid on the toilet to sit on it. My legs were about to give out from the nerves.

As I sat, alone and waiting, I realized I'd never taken a regular pregnancy test before. Not knowingly, anyway. I'd probably been tested during the monthly employee drug and blood tests at Home to ensure we were always at peak performance.

Those "botched removals" I'd told Logan about weren't made up chit-chat, Eric had at least two pregnancies between us destroyed before I learned about them.

*For your own good.*

But how was this any better? Beaten by my boyfriend and now waiting to see how long our combined DNA had left in my body before it would be violently rejected.

*Still, I kind of wish he was here.*

I wrung my hands and cracked my knuckles while tapping my boots on the tiles.

A knock at the front door snapped me from the thoughts. I gulped, grateful to be spared more memories of Eric's abhorrent treatment of my body, but terrified that he may have already been at my door.

"Fuck."

*Eric? Or Logan?*

I checked my phone to see if the cameras had picked up anyone.

*Nova?*

I tucked the tests into the top drawer under the sink, still not ready to read the results.

The second I opened the door I almost toppled backward as the sparkly woman threw herself at me, hugging me with one arm, "God, Summer. I'm so glad you're okay!" She still looked as sad as when I'd left her behind at the shed.

"Thanks?" I croaked in her tight grip.

"I know it's the worst timing, I'm so sorry," she pushed past me, leaving me no choice but to accept her into the house, "It's a bit bigger than I can handle on my own and I thought you'd be the best to come to for help."

"Yeah… Of course." I nodded when she showed me the cut to her forearm.

My mind was in too many places at once. How much could I trust her? She was one of Logan's gang. One of his closest friends. She knew what he was and I believed anything that transpired between us would be relayed back to him.

*Is he here too?*

"Are you alone?"

"Yes." she said, blinking at me with big, teary, faceted eyes.

"Come through to the garage." I unlocked the door and held it open.

My manic inventory-taking meant my tools were prepared and ready to go. I washed my hands at the sink by the shower, trying not to acknowledge the memories in this space. I scrubbed hard, hoping it would wash away the anxiety of the tests awaiting my return.

*One thing at a time…*

Nova sat upright in the chair, wriggling her slender body to get comfortable while I wheeled over on the stool.

She silently watched while I quickly cleaned her arm and stitched her beautiful, starry skin back together. She mentioned something about Tommy and Logan fighting, and that she somehow got caught in the middle, cut with glass.

I didn't know why people bothered lying to me. I wasn't stupid. This was another self-inflicted wound, and I'd bet what was left of my sanity that she was cut with a knife.

It was too bad I'd likely never see the gang again. I'd have loved to have found out who in the group was stabbing their friends so they could come pester me for a stitch-up.

"You're like magic," she grinned, admiring my quick work and clearly never having ever seen herself in the mirror to say something like that about me.

"Thank you," I said quietly, still numb and mind foggy with the headache that throbbed from the gash I'd sewn. The events at the shed only occurred a few hours ago, but with me trying to detach from the reality I'd found myself in when I got back, time had been passing in slow motion.

"He's safe."

"I don't care."

"Yes you do," she gently pushed, nodding down at the glasses hanging at the neckline of my shirt. I ripped the frames away from my chest and tossed them at her.

"He lied to me, Nova."

Using her real name felt good. Like one heavy lie had been wiped away and things could only get lighter.

"Because he *loves you.*"

It was nice to hear her say it, but it was too late. I was running out of time.

"I can't afford to believe that."

"You should. Ugh." She rolled her eyes as I handed her a clipboard with a form for her details. She slipped the glasses on her head and took the pen I forced into her hand. Being a new patient, I wasn't letting her get away with not doing the paperwork, self-inflicted injury to spy on me or otherwise.

"We all begged him from the start to be honest with you," she explained, scribbling on the paper. "From the moment he met you, he knew you were special. I've know him a loooong time, he's never been quite like this with anyone. He's been miserable for years, until now…"

Nova bent her body to get a peek at my face as I looked down. It didn't matter how many nice things she was saying – she couldn't change my views on the man who nearly turned me into a pile of bloody goo.

"Well that made two of us. But it's over."

"You don't mean that," she whined. "I would *never* condone what he did to you, but you've got to understand he would *never* hurt you if he wasn't completely convinced of what he was told."

"But *he did!* Tell me how I'm ever meant to be okay with what happened?"

"It wasn't *him*, Summer. You've seen it for yourself now, that's *not* Logan."

"Then who the fuck was it? Because it *was* Logan to some degree."

"His body, yes. But not entirely in here," she tapped her temple with her index finger and tossed the paperwork at me.

"Doesn't that make him more dangerous? Unstable?" I wheeled over to the desk to dump the clipboard beside the computer, gently rubbing my aching cheekbone as I rolled back to her.

"He tries his best to control it. Sometimes he loses the battle," she shrugged sadly. "Sometimes… he slips up."

"This was a pretty fucking big slip-up."

"It was," she agreed, sighing as she looked around the room and squinting at the cabinets. "His Gift is… complicated. We still don't really know what *it* is. Only that Vengeance is… *primal*. Out for blood."

"Was he born this way? Half monster?" I asked, wondering what kind of demon spawn Logan could create with the right partner. "I can imagine a serial murderer as a toddler would be a fucking nightmare."

Nova giggled, then turned sad again.

"Logan has always been *Gifted*, obviously. But Vengeance came later… It's the steep price we pay for having what's left of the Logan we knew and loved." Her smile faltered, and her eyes grew more glassy.

"Later?"

"I don't think I should be the one telling you this."

"Nova, please… If you really think Logan is worth another chance, I need to know. *Now*. What he is, and if he's safe to be around."

*Don't be dumb. Eric is coming and that test will tell you you've got days left, at most. There's no need to worry about what kind of father he could be and that you might be stuck sharing custody with a serial killer. There won't be a baby at the end of this.*

But Nova gave me a firm nod, and started telling me things that would only leave me more confused. "Vengeance, the dark *thing* he carries, only appeared a few years ago. Logan's Gift before that was always intense, but much simpler… *persuasion*."

My stomach dropped.

"What? Like mind control?"

Had I been under some kind of Gifted spell for months? Were my actions and feelings mine, or planted?

"Not quite. He can't like… turn people into mindless zombies or anything like that. You slept with the loser all by your own choosing if that's what you're worried about." She giggled, but she had no idea of the relief her words brought me. "He's always had the ability to coerce the truth out of people. I can too in a way, but I think that's just because people like me," she shrugged smugly, but then the expression faded to pained and the stars in her skin flickered blue. "But when Millie died… It broke him. Losing her fractured Logan. Unlocked a dark part of his mind. Most of his Gift and these new abilities seemed contained within this *other* side. As much as I wish Vengeance didn't exist, I think it's the only reason he's still alive. Vengeance saved him, in a way."

It was more devastating than I'd originally thought. Demon possession would have been a happier explanation to Logan's "other side" – not mind fracturing grief over someone he loved.

*Are we the same fucking person?*

Surely Logan understood me more than anyone else ever could? Especially after all I'd shared about Danny.

"What does it feel like?" I asked, "When Logan uses his Gift on people?"

Nova's eyes dropped from mine, "When Logan is in control… it feels… calming. Almost *good*. But Vengeance…" she shivered.

"It feels like you're drowning in your own head?"

She nodded.

"Wait… are you telling me that at any point, he could have forced me to tell him *anything* he wanted to know?"

Could Logan have learned my identity months ago? Eric's secrets? My drug suppliers and the codes for the house? My real name?

"Oh yeah, you'd be spilling secrets faster than the blood that was pouring out of this," she lifted her arm, pointing to her sutures. "If he *wanted* to."

"So, why didn't he?"

"The man you fell for is *real*, Summer, and he loves you. I know he fucked up and never said it properly, but I promise that's just him being a dumbass and scared of living his life on repeat."

*Well, that makes two of us.*

"It's hard to believe he's not as good as you say when you put it all like that."

"He's *always* tried to be one of the good guys," she smiled softly. "It was a useful Gift, originally, for his job. He and his old partner – Reid – they were quite the team. He had every reason to believe his friend when you were accused of killing Echo."

*So does this really mean we could still make it work?*

The aches in my body said *no fucking chance*, but her words made me want to say *yes*.

She looked at me with glassy eyes. "You have no idea how good you two could be together. He's such an *idiot*. Come with me to see him? He'll explain this all better than me."

"I can't. I'm not ready." I wiped my eyes as Nova sat on the desk chair and glided it over to hug me as I curled up on the stool.

"It's okay," she reassured me through my sobs, her own voice strained while she tried to comfort me. I was falling apart as reality set in – I couldn't start over with Logan even if I wanted to. I was out of time. "You're alive, that's all that matters, Summer. You don't have to forgive him, but I hope you'll at least get to know him for who he really is. It's hard *not* to love him when you know *all* of him."

I sat upright, rubbing my eyes as Nova flicked sparkly droplets away from hers.

"I'm sad I didn't get to know *you* better."

"I don't doubt you'll still be seeing plenty of me," she promised, not dropping the idea that Logan and I could possibly get over this insurmountable hurdle. She stood to leave and asked, "Can I use your bathroom before I go?"

"Sure, use the one in my bedroom. Door across the hall," I said absent-mindedly.

*Is forgiveness an option?*

Logan and I were both miserable and broken before we found each other. We'd survived the bizarre scenarios thrown at us in our short time, and I only seemed to have fallen for him more through each of those events. Maybe that was what it meant to love someone. I still didn't know. And now, I didn't have the luxury of hanging around to find out.

I waited for Nova by the front door to let her out. She beamed at me. I was glad one of us could manage a smile on a day as fucked up as this.

"You should call him," she said with an excited bounce. "He loves you so much, Summer, you really have no idea. And I *know* you love him. There's *no way* it can't work out between you two."

"I won't. It won't," I promised as she left.

"But you *should.* And it *will.*" She quickly disappeared, bounding down the driveway back to *crazy town* where I should apparently forgive my sweet boyfriend's broken mind for trying to murder me.

*The tests.*

I ran back to the bathroom, and when I reached for the top drawer, it was slightly ajar.

*Did I leave it like that?*

Surely Nova didn't go snooping through private things? I reached for the handle, hand trembling and scared of what waited inside. I had a murderous boyfriend and a psycho ex, but these tiny pieces of plastic were by far the most terrifying things in my life.

My stomach swirled, as if to give me the answer it knew I wasn't ready to see.

I peeked into the drawer and immediately slammed it shut.

*Nope. Uh-uh. That can't fucking happen.*

It was all suddenly too much; the events at the shed, Logan's Gift, the undeniable news from the tests. I dropped to the floor of my bathroom and cried, holding my head in my hands. I was certain it would explode if I let go for even a second.

My chest heaved with unsteady breaths and the sounds of panic filled the bathroom. I wiped my face more times than I could count. I hit the back of my head over and over against the wall in an attempt to knock the results right through my skull and onto the bathroom tiles. I wanted to kick the image away – to not have to accept it as truth.

I allowed myself a few minutes to put the pieces of my fragile mind back together before pushing off the floor to stand on wobbly legs.

*It'll be gone soon. Two weeks, tops.*

But it couldn't be, I was already far beyond that point. Denial was setting in nice and early, moments after seeing the results with my own eyes.

I pulled my phone from my back pocket to text Logan.

*I don't care what the fuck he is, I need him. I can't go through this alone.*

**Need to see you. Tonight. 9pm.**

It'd give me time to pull myself together without his influence and cologne fogging up my thoughts. I needed to rehearse what I wanted to say to him, and had to decide whether I believed he was dangerous enough for me to show up on my own and leave the bodyguards behind.

Three dots appeared, followed by his reply.

**Where?**

The single word pissed me off. He owed me so much more than that.

**Crave. Rooftop.**

I don't know why I rushed to message him so instantly. It showed how weak and stupid I was. After everything he'd done to me, I was clearly having trouble forgetting the better moments between us. Many moments being those that led to the undeniable "Pregnant" across the small digital screens of both tests.

Maybe if I saw him as *Logan* again I could convince myself to tell him about the tests and let him decide if he wanted to be present while this one failed. Then we'd put an end to our relationship and go our separate ways to spare us any more pain.

*Eric. Fuck. If he really is coming, I might not make it to meet Logan.*

After the text exchange I quickly set my house into what I could only call a "lockdown." Meeting Logan might end in Vengeance finishing what he started, or I could be snatched by Eric before returning to my house.

The cabinets containing the medications were sealed for long term storage and locked, the lights turned off.

They looked so strange. Familiar, but *wrong.* The garage resembled walking through a supermarket in the last moments of the store being open, giving the sense that you had to get out fast or else you'd soon be surrounded by darkness and trapped for the night.

The shelves of drugs taunted me when I walked to my desk. They offered me so many outs. Each bottle's contents in the right dosage could gift me freedom from my unknown fate.

The sickness in the pit of my stomach threatened to bubble up my throat as I weighed my options. I'd survived an overdose in the past, it was messy and not a guaranteed escape.

*And now that I'm temporarily hosting a half-Gifted parasite...*

I huffed and dropped into the chair at my desk, where I recorded my last video for treating Nova and entered her details into my system.

I added a bit more to the recording for Logan in case I disappeared between now and our meeting time. I wasn't sure if he'd ever see it, but it was a good backup incase I died, or worse.

I secretly hoped he would never find it. It showed my weakness for him; my mind was a mess between who I'd fallen for and the monster that almost ended me.

I briefly mentioned the... *tests*. I couldn't think of the words for what we'd created – not until I had a chance to learn exactly what it was.

If I were to believe for a moment that Logan and I had successfully created a baby, I might want it. I might want *him* and *everything* that came with loving my broken vigilante. But these were fantasies about a future that would always be impossible between us.

Would the news crush him like it had in the past with his wife? The miscarriage with me? Would this be something he'd want me to keep if by some miracle, the tests and timelines were accurate?

I ended the recording and text my patients;

**Closed. If I don't reopen within six months – assume dead.**

The message was delivered to all of my contacts, except for Logan. I knew he'd be at my door within minutes if he sensed I was in trouble, and I wasn't ready to face his troubled eyes after having been stared at by an unrecognizable side to him.

The hardest message to send was to my bodyguards – the codeword we'd agreed on for them to lay low. They'd be irate with themselves for not showing up earlier.

I missed them already.

"Mom," I cried to her voicemail, "I might be leaving again. Please answer? I need you. I'm... pregnant. Fuck. I don't know what to do. I just *need* you." I hung up and pulled my knees to my chest. Crushed again by the rejection that I should have been so used to by now.

The house was too quiet, like the calm before a storm. Silence pressed at my senses as I sobbed in the safe space I'd created.

I knew Eric better than he knew himself, and if he were coming for me, he wouldn't let me escape Home alive for a second time. My options were likely to be his forever again, or die refusing.

*Have you forgotten everything your parents ever taught you? You know what to do – RUN.*

I rushed to my bedroom and grabbed my backpack, stuffing it with a few more necessities; spare clothes and Logan's jacket.

I left my Hartford jumpsuit hanging in the wardrobe. As I touched the embroidered name, a shudder wracked my limbs. If I didn't leave now, where I might be headed was much, much worse.

I stashed one of the tests in my pocket, leaving the other in the drawer, not really sure why I decided to take it. Maybe I needed proof until I could have it properly confirmed.

I could have hidden – there were places in my house I could fit to play my last game of hide and seek with the Finders, but I could bet Eric's patience had been spread thin enough. Everything I'd worked so hard for could be destroyed if I played hard-to-get now.

I brushed my fingers along the length of the hallway table, glancing at my face in the mirror as I moved for the door.

The bruising on my face and forehead had set in. Vibrant shades of black and purple had formed around the cut I'd stitched, and the imprint of where I'd connected with Logan to break his nose. It was a move I now regretted if he were the one dealing with the pain, and not the embodied insanity that he allegedly shared his mind with.

My eyes prickled as I stared at my reflection.

"Should I go to him?" I spoke to the broken girl. She may have mimicked my movements flawlessly, but I barely recognised her. "Let him explain himself before I run?" I didn't know if I were unable to see the color red anymore, or perhaps I'd become so used to the flags waving in my face that I'd learned to block them out, but I couldn't wait until later – I needed him now. "Will he run with me?"

As I stepped up to the keypad, a car door slammed shut outside. My heart skipped a beat, thinking Logan might have felt the same and he couldn't wait until our meeting at Crave. But then, another door closed, and two sets of footsteps grew in volume as they approached my house.

*Fuck. The gate's open.*

It was unlike me to forget to close it, but then it was also unlike me to be suffering a major head injury.

Another noise made me startle. Soft footsteps above me. Someone was walking on my roof. Then another – the handle to the door in the laundry that led outside began to rattle.

I held my breath in my throat. A panic attack would only have me blacking out around people I couldn't trust.

*Should I fight? Grab knives?*

Either of those options would lead to my immediate demise if the house were surrounded and I started throwing sharp objects in defense.

I braced myself for the knock.

To my complete and utter dread, it came, echoing down the long hall.

"Come out, come out, Stitch Up."

There was no need to check who the cameras had detected. It was Simon. Will would be with him. The two were inseparable on their Finder missions. Their closeness and senses of humor reminded me of my bodyguards, and I think it played a part in why I'd hired the cousins in the first place.

I counted to five and tapped in the code to open the door, quickly raising my hands above my head.

"Hey, boys," I addressed them casually, like I hadn't been missing from Home for two years and was about to be forcibly dragged back into hell.

"There she is!" Will exclaimed with a wide grin at the sight of me.

"Boss needs you back home, Stitch." Simon's friendly smile held a little less enthusiasm than that of his comrade.

It was a relief to see them, though they were nothing more than friendly faces to soften my recapture.

"I assumed as much," I sighed and set my hands on my hips, gripping my sides tight so they wouldn't see how much I was starting to tremble.

"So. How are we gonna do this, girl?" Will asked, cocking his head mischievously. He was almost an exact copy of his friend, a little more tanned with dark hair and a mustache. He pulled a cigarette out of a pocket in his jacket lining and lit it. "The easy way, or the hard way?"

"Preferably the *easy* way," I laughed in a bid to show some confidence, "I'm… pregnant." Admitting the truth out loud for the second time didn't make it any easier. My features scrunched as the words left my mouth, and nearly made me spew up the rest of the coffee I'd drunk earlier. "So, you know, you might want to…" I nodded to the freshly lit stick between his fingers.

The two men glanced at each other over the tops of their sunglasses, revealing their tattooed titles on their necks.

"Does the Boss know about this?" Simon mimicked my stance with just as little confidence. His voice had turned shaky over the bomb I'd dropped at his feet, moments after being reunited. If they missed me at all over the last two years, they would have already been regretting those feelings.

These guys were tough, being some of the best in The Collection. It was satisfying, almost funny to watch them squirm at my announcement. Eric didn't like surprises, and Finders certainly didn't like being the ones to inform him about said surprises.

"I highly doubt that. I only found out about it – not even an hour ago. Here."

They both pulled guns from behind their backs when I reached around my side. They knew me well enough to know I wouldn't cause them harm, they were like brothers to me in the early days back at Home, but even they weren't taking chances with Eric's favorite stray being backed into a corner.

A red dot appeared on my chest at my sudden move, to which I rolled my eyes and used my free hand to flip off whoever had me in their sight, somewhere far in the distance. I tossed Simon the positive test that I'd tucked into the pocket of my jeans.

"Oh, *shit,*" he groaned when he caught it and inspected the result, angling it to Will as they put their guns away.

"Go call the boss," Simon told Will, who quickly disappeared down the driveway and back to the street. "I don't even know what he's gonna do with you now." He smiled and shook his head. "The fuck are you playing at out here, Stitch? Does the father know? I hope he's not planning on being involved," he laughed, the sound slightly more strained than before.

"He doesn't know. It's not serious between us." Every word of the lie hurt to speak, and the thought of disappearing without so much as seeing Logan one last time made my eyes sting.

Simon sighed, putting his hands in his pockets as he took in the details of the front of my house. "It's for the best, Stitch. Can't imagine he'd want to know what becomes of it once we get you back to Home." He'd already assumed the same that I had – Eric would promptly order the removal before it could interfere with our image. "Will the guy be missing you, though?"

"He might, yeah. Things were rocky between us at the best of times, but he'll eventually notice I'm missing."

Logan would know something was wrong the moment I didn't show up at Crave.

Simon blew out an exasperated breath. "Right, so we have a loose end to tie up."

"Boss says you can pack a bag and then we're outta here," Will called, walking back to us from the street.

"That's it?" I laughed, "Your guy hiding up in the mountain, he's not been ordered to, you know…" I pointed to the dot on my chest.

"Nah," Will grimaced, "The boss said he already knows. He's making alterations to your contract as we speak."

*How the fuck does he know? Maybe he's been keeping a far closer eye on me than I thought. Could I be showing other signs I don't know about?*

"Let's go, then." I picked up the bag behind my feet and followed them down the driveway.

Simon held the back door of the car open for me, ensuring it was shut tight the moment I slipped onto the seat. I didn't bother testing it, I already knew it couldn't be opened from the inside. My doors were always locked, no matter the standing between Eric and I.

I looked to my house as we peeled out of the street, already missing the life I made within its walls.

*I hope I turned the stove off,* I thought sarcastically. I'd never once used it since the house was built. I didn't know how to turn it on without burning the place down.

Several black cars appeared behind us. By the looks of the numbers, my property, and maybe the whole street could have been surrounded.

Simon handed the pregnancy test to me, not that I really wanted it now that it'd served its purpose. I didn't want to even think about it. I'd slammed the drawer shut after seeing the words and had barely looked at the one in my hands since I'd stuffed it in my jeans.

It *had* to be wrong.

*Both of them?*

It was *unlikely* that two tests from different batches could display the same result and *both* be wrong. But I couldn't have been as far along as they claimed. One or two weeks, tops, that was the absolute rule.

Everything else between Logan and I had been based on lies, why couldn't my eyes be lying to me now? I looked at the digital screen that clearly stated the number of weeks that had supposedly passed.

*Can I really be s–*

"You have no idea how good it is to see you again, Stitch," Will said from the driver's seat. "Home hasn't been the same without you. Especially Family Dinner. You always made those nights more entertaining."

He meant well, but I would have rather died than be taken back to all that would be awaiting my return in Bedlam.

"Gonna need your phone, Stitch," Simon reached his hand over the back of the passenger seat, clicking his fingers at me to be prompt.

I slammed it roughly onto his palm, accepting that my connection to the outside world was taken from me. Again.

# SIXTY

## SUMMER

We entered the lobby of a hotel thirty minutes from my house — a Finder at each side. I was tempted to scream for help, but it would only result in witnesses to my distress being shot and me in more trouble than I already was.

Simon and Will escorted me to Eric's room. I'd proven to be a flight risk after running away and disappearing for years, I wasn't to be trusted with even the simplest tasks.

As the elevator doors closed the reflective surface revealed the bruising on my face was growing darker by the minute.

*Eric will be pissed you've damaged his property.*

I shuffled anxiously in my place. The palm tightly gripping the strap of my bag was breaking out in a cold sweat, along with most other parts of my body at the idea of meeting face-to-face with him in this condition.

The walls of the elevator crept closer with each floor we climbed and I could already feel the heat of his disapproving gaze and hear the sharp words he would pierce me with. My stomach twisted in knots over the memories of how I used to act in order for Eric to forgive me, to take me back in a way, though we never technically separated.

As I glanced at the men on either side, upper arms pressed to my shoulders, I wondered what went through their minds, and anyone else's who knew the truth behind my disappearance. What did people think when Eric's devoted lover of so many years needed to be *dragged* back to him? And at gunpoint, no less.

It certainly didn't assist the loving image he tried so hard to portray to the world.

Simon held the door to the room open, quickly closing it before I was barely out of the way. Even one of Eric's top men didn't want to be present for this particular reunion. He was smart to avoid the boss for as long as he could, having missed the opportunities to grab me in the past. Particularly now that I'd finally been recaptured, gestating the proof of my disloyalty.

The room was silent. The lights were off.

In front of me was the high back of an armchair. To the left, the shadowy shape of a bed. I assumed the bathroom would be somewhere in that direction too. It was unlike me to not take note of every inch of my surroundings, but in this instance, there was no point. I was with Eric now, and there'd be no way out. To be with him meant I was in both complete safety *and* imminent danger.

To my right was a wall, mostly consumed by glass, not quite floor-to-ceiling like the icy facade of Home, but I was sure this room was picked for its similarity.

Moving further into the space, I spotted him.

Eric sat in another armchair beside the window, facing the one I'd seen from behind. His eyes were already devouring every inch of me as I came into view.

With the sun setting on the opposite side of the hotel, the last of its rays made the mountains in the distance glow a deep orange that illuminated one side of his face.

The Collector liked to set the mood for business deals, and this meeting between estranged lovers was no different. It was a fitting hellscape for signing away what remained of my tortured soul.

"There's my girl," he grinned devilishly as I took my place in the matching chair. There was excitement in his tone, but no warmth. No love for the girl who'd been missing for years; only relief that an irreplaceable possession was finally being returned.

I took in what features I could in the low lighting, unable to form a response from the shock of seeing him with my own eyes after so long.

He appeared a little more gaunt than usual, but he sometimes got that way when he became stressed and wasn't getting enough sleep. I was likely responsible for both of those things.

He was fairly pale, though not deathly like me. There was a good amount of warmth to his tone, and I'd seen he was able to get quite tanned in the past if he ever allowed himself enough time away from work to be out in the sun.

He hadn't aged a day in the two years I'd been absent, though he'd grown a short, neat beard. I'd never seen him with facial hair, and I couldn't deny that it looked *good* on him.

To anyone that hadn't been broken by this man, Eric would undoubtedly be gorgeous.

His eyes, piercing mine from across the coffee table, were a shade of green I'd not found on another human being.

There was a time where I would have done *anything* to find approval in those eyes. I would have thrown myself from the top of Home if it meant Eric would tell me he loved me. But he wouldn't. I'd tried, and he *still* didn't say it. In the ten years I'd dedicated to him, the words never came from his mouth, though they left my lips plenty.

He smirked at my complete lack of verbal expression and inability to hide that I was still so enchanted by his presence after being without him for so long. Though, it wasn't from the adoration he'd come to expect of me – that had been substituted with pure terror.

The last time we'd seen each other had been a fucking disaster. Worse than it had ever escalated between us. My limbs trembled at the thought of picking up from where we left on that night.

"I have a contract for you," he teased like a mischievous God. A piece of paper appeared, and he slipped it across the low table between us. Returning to his comfortable position, he reclined in the chair, gaze continuing to hungrily pass over my body. "I need you back, Sumar."

*I need you back,* echoed over and over in my mind, and I was scared a small part of me would read into that too much. All I'd wanted from Eric for years was for us to return to the way things were between us in the beginning. Before he turned cold and cruel.

*I need you back, I need you back.* The thought of him *needing* me in the sense that I'd once needed him was almost enough to erase months of one-on-one therapy.

*Jesus, woman. Be a little fucking stronger than that.*

I shoved his words out of my head. It was just more of Eric's bullshit to keep me in line, and I was fucking *done* with him. Though, the only way out of this room alive was tied to the wretched parchment awaiting my signature.

When I leaned forward to pull the paper closer, the unmistakable click of a gun sounded from the darkest corner of the room, somewhere by the other side of the bed. My mind snapped out of the words on loop. There was no need for theatrics, I understood I had no choice but to sign. It proved that nothing had changed. *Eric* hadn't changed.

*I have, though.*

And he must have known it; I wasn't threatened the last time I'd signed a contract.

I rolled my eyes and scribbled the name Eric bestowed upon me at sixteen – *Sumar Sál* – and slammed the pen on the table when I was done. I roughly pushed the paper his way before slouching with defeat.

I hadn't bothered to read the contract. Negotiation wasn't an option unless I were willing to provide more services or offer him more time. All I knew was that whatever was in that agreement would make me *his*.

Seeing my name on the paper brought on the nausea again.

Sumar Sál. *Summer Soul.*

The name I'd thought was pretty and had been proud to carry after he'd stripped me of the one my parents gifted me at birth. Though he never offered me a deeper explanation into why he'd chosen it, Eric assured me it was both perfect and suited me well. I'd avoided using it in full at all costs since my escape. It was a direct line back to him if it were to pop up in the wrong places.

Using *Summer* held its own risks, but I couldn't use my birth name, that was no doubt being monitored too. I'd tried a couple of other fake names but found I wasn't responding to them when called, and that only added to me looking suspicious. Keeping up with "Katie" for therapy was about as good as I could do. I was a runaway villain, not a trained spy with a dozen alter-egos.

"Are you unwell, boss?" I asked, finally finding my voice. I didn't really care about his well being, but I needed to gain insight into what new night-mares he had in store for me.

Eric's lips twitched with the threat of a smile. "Don't play with me, darling.

Not yet. You'll address me as you used to. And, no. I've found better people to tend to my needs in your absence."

He had to be lying. He only wanted me.

*Don't get too cocky, you suspected he was seeing someone else before you escaped.*

I swallowed over the classless response on my tongue, refusing to bite like he wanted. Now wasn't the time to ask whether Eric had resorted to fucking *actual* corpses.

He enjoyed spitting venomous words every chance he got, eager to watch as I writhed in agony. He wanted me to cave, to beg for his forgiveness and behave however he needed. He wanted me in line. Back in my place – *Collected.*

Unlucky for him, I'd grown a spine since I left. I just hoped it wasn't made of paper.

"I've already made adjustments for your… *condition*," he forced the bitter words through his teeth, as though he were already tolerating me and my wildness like he used to. "I am *deeply* disappointed in you. But… I guess this is what happens when feral creatures are left to their own devices. You can keep it, *for now*, if you wish,"— he continued through my eye roll – "But you shouldn't waste your energy and *that* body on the offspring of someone so unworthy."

*Don't fall for his lies. Nothing comes so easy with him. There'll be a hidden motive in there somewhere.*

How much did Eric know about Logan? Or Vengeance? Surely enough, having found a way to use him to almost kill me. But I didn't ask, not wanting to accidentally confirm any of Eric's theories about who I'd been with and what I'd done in my absence.

I did, however, have a question that I needed answered.

"So I can keep *this* one? But the times *you* got me pregnant were a different story? Did you really believe *your own* offspring weren't worthy of being carried by me?"

Eric paused, all movement frozen at my query.

He was unaware that I knew. It was nice to have the upper hand. Rare, but nice, despite the horrific topic. Even in the low lighting, I could see his jaw clench as he tried to come up with an answer for me.

*I've still got it.*

I could still get under his skin, only these days I wasn't doing it with the intention of getting him under mine.

"Yes," he finally admitted.

That fucking stung. I'd loved him so much. To have had his children would have undoubtedly only made me love him more. I believed that one of the *many* reasons it went against my original contract was so I didn't get the wrong ideas in my head about our arrangement. Had Eric allowed us to try for a family, I would have believed he felt the same for me. He had all the time and money in the world to make it happen, but he didn't.

Eric permitted me a moment to let his single word sink in, testing the poisoned waters to see what would harm me. To see if I were still the weak-minded girl he'd brought into our Home, or if I had grown up since he last saw me. Part of me couldn't wait for him to learn how much I'd changed.

When I didn't bite, he continued, "I wanted our original agreement to be reinstated. Instead, you've signed yourself over for just four months."

*Four months? Shit, maybe I should have read it.*

"If you choose to keep *it*, it won't be born under my roof." His tone was even, but his scowl oozed disapproval. "Your short time at Home will ensure that you'll be out of sight before it causes our image any trouble. If it survives…" he sighed, and the fingers of his right hand twitched. He flicked his left wrist to cast away the need to toy with his watch.

*You've upset him.*

I blinked and swallowed hard, commanding myself not to react to his subtle cues.

*Doesn't he know Logan is Gifted? He wouldn't be so bothered if he knew this pregnancy is going to be over soon.*

"You'll be permitted a brief leave of absence between contracts to deal with your mistake in private before you return–"

I couldn't hold in my laugh, "Return? You think I'll *return?* Once this contract is done, I'm *gone*, Eric." Did he really believe I wouldn't take the opportunity to leave?

"Do I need to remind you," he snarled, "That you committed yourself to me *for life?* I received only seven years of service in exchange for everything you ever asked for. Once it's removed, you'll come to your senses and return to your position by my side." He lifted a hand to silence me when I started to argue. "No more of this until we're at Home. Maybe The Surgeon will talk some sense into you."

I gripped the arms of the chair and gasped. "Surge is still at Home?" His contract was meant to end not long after I'd escaped.

Eric's gaze dropped from mine, features twisting with a small smile, "We *renegotiated* his contract." My guess was that The Surgeon had traded more of his life for the continued protection of his family. He'd likely never leave. That's how Eric collected some of his people for life. "I was informed we have the matter of the father to deal with before we leave for Bedlam?"

"He's just some guy. He doesn't mean anything, we're not even together. He doesn't know about… what's happening." I couldn't say the words in front of Eric, unsure if it were the deeply embedded fear of disappointing him further or for my own shattered mind's sake. "If we leave now I'm sure he'll give us no trouble."

I was torn between not wanting to face the man who tried to kill me, and desperately needing to see Logan before I disappeared. Eric wasn't one to back down from destroying people, and with what I was potentially growing, in his eyes, Logan had ruined the perfect idea of forever Eric had imagined for us. Leaving without a goodbye was for the best.

"No, I think you should end things properly. Break the boy's heart so we can have our happily ever after," he laughed to himself.

"Four months, Eric."

"I think the time apart has been good for us, Sumar." He dropped the tension in his shoulders and relaxed a little more into his chair, completely ignoring me, like always. "Two years apart to cool our tempers and start anew."

He didn't mean to start again from day one, when things were actually good between us. Eric was drowning in too much of his own darkness for us to feel that way about each other again. He likely meant to start from before the day he undoubtedly had my best friend murdered and I gave my best attempt at leaving him *forever*.

"So, you don't plan on putting my head through a mirror again, Eric?" I asked, tone sickly sweet as I grinned and tipped my head playfully. He hated it when I acted like a tease while bringing up the awful things he'd done to me.

"Have you got more names you've been dying to add to my skin in my absence? How's the belt collection going? I bet you've still got some with my nail marks on them."

He clenched his jaw again, "We got carried away in the end. Things will be different soon."

"I would hope so," I snickered, glancing out the window at the mountains I was about to leave behind indefinitely. "I can't imagine you would think to hurt someone who's pregnant. Though, you might still surprise me."

"The father?" he ignored my comments, steering me back to breaking things off with Logan.

"I've already arranged to meet him at Crave. Nine. Tonight."

"Perfect, it's on our way. For now, rest. We've got work to do the moment we get you back to Home." Eric nodded to the bed.

"What? I don't get my own room?" Any confidence I'd gathered instantly faltered at the idea of being so confined with him.

"We've never had separate rooms when traveling together," he snorted as if my question was the stupidest thing I'd ever said. He was in for a real treat with me going forward if that's what he thought.

"But we're not *together*."

"Not yet." He stood, and the man in the shadows of the room appeared, taking Eric's movement as his cue to leave. "But you'll be mine again soon enough."

"Four months, Eric," I said firmly. "Then I'm gone."

He gave a small laugh and handed the man my contract as he exited the room, leaving us alone together. He unbuttoned the sleeves of his shirt and rolled them up.

Looking down at me with narrowed eyes, he examined my features, "What on Earth have you been up to?" he shook his head and pressed his fingers under my chin, gently lifting my face. "The bathroom. Now. I need to inspect the damage to my girl in the light."

Standing from the chair, I moved obediently across the room. I'd just signed away my right to refuse, but I hoped he only planned on inspecting my face.

# SIXTY-ONE

## LOGAN

The TV was on, but I couldn't take in any of the gore splattering in front of me. Was the volume even on?

I leaned forward, tapping my thumbs on Summer's coffee table at either side of my phone, watching as the seconds ticked by. Each time the number changed, it was a new minute where she could reach out to me, and I wouldn't dare miss it.

We'd rushed to Summer's house in hopes to find her before she fled. But by the time we arrived, she was gone. The house felt eerie. Hollow. As though it had secrets it wasn't sharing with me. It taunted me from the moment I entered the code to let us all in.

There wasn't a heartbeat on the property, and while I hated that Summer wasn't here, my limbs were still tingling with the relief that we hadn't discovered her body and she hadn't succumbed to any of the injuries I'd inflicted since Nova left. We'd scanned every inch of the land for clues of her whereabouts.

The bathroom mirror was broken. It would have sent me into a spiral, but there was no sign of a struggle and Nova reassured me it'd been that way when she'd visited.

Tommy and I had even broken into the shed in the backyard in hopes the contents could give us some clues about where she'd gone. Adding to my ever-growing confusion over my girlfriend's identity, all we found were stacks of unopened boxes containing brand new knives.

There were only a few things missing from inside the house, my jacket included.

I hoped it was a good sign, that wherever she'd run to, she'd taken it with her and not disposed of it in hatred towards me. I may have deserved to lose it after what I'd done to her, but she didn't know why it meant so much to me.

*Because you didn't tell her.*

With eyes unfocused, I stared at my phone, sitting beside my mask on the table, my foot tapping uncontrollably as more minutes tick by.

She'd only messaged that she wanted to meet me and where.

Then, nothing.

Summer wasn't responding to anything else, not texts or calls from any of us. Against Nova's protests, I was certain Summer would be on the run. I couldn't blame her. She'd been severely betrayed by the person she only just professed her love to, and her ex was clearly coming for her. Why wouldn't she flee?

*Think, Logan. Her car is still here.*

My eyes blinked to the wall on the right, the garage was on the opposite side. I gulped over the thickness in my throat. I didn't want to think like a cop right now.

*Maybe the bodyguards came for her? Fuck, what if she's out in the woods?*

To compile on top of the growing sense of dread, I was tormenting myself; replaying everything I could remember from the shed over and over in my mind. Tommy and Nova had arrived just in time. Summer would have been minutes away from an unrecognizable mound of blood and organs. She knew it too, after I told her what I did to the man who cut her in the garage.

*But I didn't.*

Was that a good enough excuse to hope she'd ever talk to me again?

*And Tommy said Vengeance couldn't do it. What the fuck is that about?*

Why had Vengeance taken so long to get the process moving? He didn't usually play with his food before redecorating the room with it. Figuratively, of course, he thankfully wasn't a cannibal.

*Like that makes him any better.*

I wrung my gloved hands as another minute disappeared.

While my actions had my stomach threatening to redecorate *this* room, I had to admit I was impressed that Summer had the strength to get up and leave after what these hands had done.

Pain built behind my eyes. Each time I closed them I was met with more distorted visions; Summer begging for me to listen, telling me I had everything wrong. Vengeance also seemed to be in the mood to torture me for *his* mistake. Her heartbeat played on repeat in my head, adding to the throb along my temples.

In all the months we'd tried, we'd never found anything of value in our search for Celeste's killer. It seemed the first sign that Vengeance's judgment became unbalanced with the information from my trusted friend, his mind about my girlfriend was wholly made up.

Even with Summer's truthful begging, enough for him to sense her innocence, he had still tried to beat a confession out of her.

What drove him to veer from the known? The predictable? Did he feel as tired as I did? Was he sick of failing? Fed up with letting my friends down? Or did he simply decide the accusation was the icing on our morally gray cake?

*Everything* I knew about Summer was a gray area. We'd known she'd done enough wrong to be disposed of soon after I'd met her. But maybe, deep down, deeper than even Vengeance could reach for answers, Summer was truly good, and this was something he could never understand.

*If I had just let her explain… Or told the others what Reid sent…*

But I couldn't, and I didn't. And now she was missing.

*What if she's not missing? Could he have already come for her?*

My friends were busy while I sat with my thoughts. The untouched dining table was now covered in laptops and the gang were working hard to find *everything* they could learn about her in hopes they'd find clues as to where she could be.

I still didn't want to know anything personal. I wanted Summer *here* to tell me her darkest secrets. It wasn't fair to take that option away from her after all I'd done and kept from her. I'd demanded that anything they shared with me had to be on an absolute need-to-know-to-keep-her-safe basis.

Still, Vengeance lent me his superior hearing as they whispered about cameras.

"I can check that!" I called to them, opening the app Summer had shared with me for the codes to her house, annoyed I hadn't thought to check sooner. Had so many of my detective skills slipped away?

I'd previously explored all of the app's features and learned it stored about a week's worth of short clips from movements caught outside. To no surprise, the sensors picked up nothing when I'd snuck in the night before. To even less surprise, and complete disgust in myself, I often checked the comings and goings of anyone who visited her property.

Summer seemed aware of my possessiveness, but still let me have access to it. I took that as a good enough excuse to continue with my problematic behavior. Though, I'd turned the notifications off so that I wouldn't be completely consumed by spying on her while I was at work.

My heart sank to the pit of my stomach as I watched a clip with a timestamp from ten minutes after Nova received the text. Two familiar men approached her front door through the open gate, holding Summer at gunpoint in broad daylight.

"She's been taken," I sighed. *That's why she's not responding.* "They probably took her phone."

"I assumed." Jackie said, "Already tried tracing it." Of course she had. This was just another day of standard work for her, though I was sure she would have been feeling as sick as I was that we were searching for one of our own again.

"Reid's?"

"Untraceable now. Last used about a half hour from here."

*She might not be far...*

"Show me?" Nova's sparkly hand appeared on my shoulder as she leaned over the back of the couch. Summer tossed something to one of the men on the screen. The video had no sound, so I could only guess the man quickly pocketed a weapon Summer was too smart to use while being outnumbered by men with guns.

*I should have been here to protect her.*

I hated myself for not acting sooner – for not immediately coming to her after leaving the shed to try to fix what I'd done. Taking the two men out would have been all too easy.

*It's an abduction. You know what to do. You haven't failed yet. Summer is still alive.*

"Jack?" I called while Nova and I rewatched the clip. "Flights to Bedlam?"

Summer could have been boarding a plane with her captors by now. The sound of Jackie's nails tapping on the keys was an odd comfort. So long as we had something to look for, we could take steps closer to Summer.

"Only one. 4am. No private jets have come or gone in days."

I exhaled a heavy sigh. The video was timestamped later than that. The benefit to living in the mountain range to the north of the state; only one small airport served this area.

I opened another video, one where a car the men had arrived in was visible on the street. Nova called out the details of the plates.

"Got something!" Jackie squealed after a few minutes of erratic searching. She was an expert at finding and digging through private information. It was Nova's dream job.

"What is it?" Nova demanded, rushing back to her chair to see what Jackie had discovered. I turned to watch them over the back of the couch.

"It's not stolen. Registered to a business in Bedlam called Ho—, no, no. That can't be right." Jackie's eyes widened. Nova leaned over her shoulder.

"I fucking KNEW IT!" my sister slammed her hands on the tabletop as if she'd just won a board game and were about to start rubbing it into all of our faces.

Jackie scoffed in disbelief. "You *knew*?"

"Just a hunch," Nova admitted, feigning a humble shrug as she grinned at the screen. "Didn't I always say she looked familiar? Now we know why! For fucks sake Logan you could have told us *that* sooner."

"Told you what?"

"You're dating *Stitch Up*. Of all *fucking people*. My God!"

"I've only known her as *Summer* until yesterday." I frowned at the three pairs of wide eyes on me, "I still don't really know what it means. Is it a code name or something?"

Nova shook her head, laughing like she couldn't believe she needed to explain this to me. "She's only one of the coolest and most untouchable villains in *The Collection*. The girl is a legend in the underworld from here to Bedlam."

"She's *not* a villain!" I snapped, "If she was, she'd be dead."

That I was sure of, Vengeance could sense villains from a mile away. I wasn't much of a believer in souls or auras, but they were the closest explanation I had for his ability to pick out the "bad" ones.

"She's one of Eric The-fucking-Collector's," Nova snapped back, "That's kind of a big fucking deal, Logan!"

She always said my name too many times and in the same tone when she was irate with me. Which was essentially every waking moment of every day.

"Yeah Eric, she mentioned him plenty, her ex," I muttered, wondering if I should have used more of Vengeance's skills on Summer to learn about him. It never felt right, and if I had too much information, I'd have been torn from her to hunt for him.

"Seriously? *Ex?*"

When I turned again, Nova was *pissed.* The stars in her skin glowed deep red.

"Yes seriously. How bad are we talking?" They all gawked at me as if I were completely insane. More so. "Sor-*ry* for not keeping up with all the names of these freaks. Just give it to me straight."

"Oh, it's nothing," Nova bit sarcastically, "He's *literally* the worst case scenario. He practically runs Bedlam City."

*Hmm.* He did sound familiar. *The Collector*. Maybe he'd gained more power and territory after I'd left Bedlam behind.

"Well… shit." I sunk into the couch. It turned out my little nurse was involved with monsters far greater than me.

*And I thought she couldn't handle me being Vengeance. Maybe if we were open about who we were, it would have been a cakewalk in comparison by either of our previous lives in the city.*

The details of Summer's past didn't matter to me, I just needed to get her back. Even if she hated me forever and wanted nothing to do with me, the least I could do was return her to the life she had made for herself.

"Yeah, *shit*, you fucking *idiot*." Nova didn't mean it, she was just highly strung since her visit with Summer. She wished she'd done more or hung around longer. I wished that too, but there was no point in blaming her when it was my fault we were in this mess in the first place. "We need to get her back. *Now*."

She was pushing for this as much as me. I was glad she and my friends cared about Summer enough to feel this way, though it only made me regret keeping her from them.

I sat up again to look at my phone; back on the table so I could tap my knuckles on either side of it while I waited for any information that could help us. Though I now knew it was useless waiting for her to contact me, I also knew Summer was smart, resourceful.

"Look at this," Nova said to Tommy, pointing to her screen. He stood between the two women, leaning in to get a better look, "There's so many articles on him. See? She's always there in the photos at his side."

"Photos?" I asked.

"Yeah," she called back, "Nothing official. Like gossipy paparazzi pics of the two of them getting in and out of cars at public events. Some at clubs. Walking in and out of the entrance of where they lived. All the articles are about him, rising to power within the city. She was the young thing on his arm. In public anyway. Her identity as Stitch Up and her work would have been kept for the underworld."

It wasn't unheard of. Bedlam was nothing but a petri dish of vile characters. Many of them lived extravagant lives and paraded around right under the noses of those who were desperate to put them away for their crimes.

Jackie quoted the article they were all reading from, "Appearing out of nowhere at just nineteen, Summer – no last name – has caught the eye of Bedlam's biggest business magnate, appearing to have already moved into Home."

"He'd kept Summer hidden for two years at that point." I filled them in with the little I knew about the woman who continued to grow more mysterious by the second, "He didn't show her off until she was old enough to not make him look bad."

Another minute ticked over. *Every* second counted with abductions. The only benefit we had was that we knew *where* Summer would end up – Bedlam. But it would be easier to intercept if she were being held somewhere in the Gray Mountains than to wait until she were in The Collector's territory.

"What a fucking creep," Nova muttered under her breath.

"So, that's what he was to the public, what about 'The Collector' part?" Tommy asked.

"He does just that," Nova explained, filling in her human ex-husband on the drama she would have learned through her Gifted gossip circles.

"I've heard about him a bunch of times. He seeks out the best and gives them an offer they literally can't refuse. They work for him as part of a team that continues to gain credit and notoriety for their skills, and he keeps looking better for having them."

"So, Summer with her stitching?" Tommy confirmed.

"Yep," Jackie sighed. "According to this Hartford paperwork, Summer is definitely Stitch Up. Though, she looks a little different these days, not as lively as these other photos."

Nova raised her voice, directing it my way, "As mad as I am at you for not knowing shit about your own girlfriend, you sure picked a cool one. I'm almost proud that you're dating someone *this* far out of your league."

*Stitch Up.*

That name floated around the club and I'd found it on her Hartford uniform. I guessed it was a title but hadn't realized it held so much meaning. I'd teased Summer about having an origin story, and she'd only shared parts of it with me.

"Oh *Jesus,* look at this!" Nova whispered to Jackie, "What a fucking mess. Overdose? Then… how?"

They exchanged troubled looks.

"Is this something I *need to know?*"

"Some of it is," Jackie answered, looking a little paler than normal. "Did she ever tell you how she got there – to Hartford? The file has her full account to the police. It's very… graphic?"

Nova scanned the text on the screen and grimaced. "Imagine how rough he would've been with her to achieve that."

"No, she didn't tell me." I told them, trying not to come to any conclusions about what they were reading.

Jackie narrowed her eyes and scratched at her neck as she peeked over the laptop screen. "Logan… have you seen her mugshot?"

"Wow, was she *dead?*" Tommy asked, pulling up a chair between them, a bottle of vodka in his hand. There was nothing to eat in Summer's house. During our time together, I'd wondered how she survived on so little and left so much of her house untouched.

Like Jackie, subtlety also wasn't Tommy's strong suit, "Is she undead?"

It made me laugh. I'd joked about how her name didn't suit her and that she looked like a zombie after not getting much sun for two years and always looking so tired.

"No, she's not undead," I confirmed.

"A vampire?" he laughed, then his voice lowered, whispering to Nova, "Then why the fuck is there so much blood *in* her mouth?"

"No," Jackie argued, "See the report? It's all *her own.*"

"Is *this* something I should see?" I asked, becoming frustrated at all the broken pieces of information I could hear.

I nearly jumped off the couch when my phone buzzed. To my racing heart's dismay, it wasn't Summer, but the group sending me the photo of her mugshot, taken when she'd been processed into the care of the asylum.

In the picture, Summer's eyes were closed, and her hair was a little longer. The photo was in color, the red was bright, but I still did a double take.

Her skin was deathly pale. Paper white.

A thick, dried stream of blood from her mouth ran down the left side of her face and her neck. Small splatters decorated her features; she'd probably coughed it up.

There was a line of it around her mouth and nose from where a mask had been, and some must have pooled under it.

A cut on the right of her forehead had also been bleeding, with "DNR" scribbled in black across the rest. My eyes traced the delicately inscribed "Stitch Up" tattooed below her right collarbone.

*Fuck, she's so pretty.*

Only *I* could think something like that while looking at what appeared to be a crime scene photo. Just like every time I saw Summer covered in blood, I wasn't entirely sure the reaction was only *mine.* My sight always sharpened as Vengeance used my eyes to take in the crimson as it oxidized on her flesh.

It was a disturbing photo, even by my standards. What business did those at Hartford have with taking pictures of people in this state? Couldn't they have cleaned her up first?

"I don't need more details," I said firmly, closing the photo so I didn't have to continue seeing Summer that way. It absolutely wasn't the last image I wanted to have of her.

Then, it suddenly dawned on me that I didn't have *any* photos of her at all.

Being strict about keeping a secret identity meant avoiding cameras and I had zero social accounts. We both had secrets to keep, and not a picture of us together existed from the six months we'd known each other.

"Why don't you rest?" Nova called. "You surely need to after…"

"My murderous, rage-filled episode where I beat my girlfriend and tried to convince my best friend to kill her when I couldn't?" I offered snidely.

"Sure," she sighed.

While we were pressed for time, rest didn't sound like a bad idea. The blackouts were exhausting despite me not being mentally present for them, and I hadn't gotten much sleep in the apartment before leaving to search for Summer. My skull pounded with a migraine and I could barely think clear enough to speak. If the gang found anything we could act on, I needed to be in a better headspace.

"I'll come get you if we find anything." Nova's promise followed me down the hall.

I removed my glasses, freeing the swollen bridge of my nose from the frame's restrictions and set them on the bedside table. I dropped to my side of the bed. Alone again, with my phone in one hand and my mask in the other.

Summer and I weren't meant to meet up until later in the night, though I now had no idea if she'd show. Maybe if she escaped her captors, she'd show up seeking protection, hoping I'd be there. It was wishful thinking, but it was all I had to hold onto for now.

I hated that she'd picked Crave as our meeting place. If Summer showed, I couldn't meet with her on the rooftop as *Logan,* I'd have to be in disguise.

There was so much I needed to say to her. I hoped she'd give me a chance to explain myself and prayed she hadn't already written me off as the monster I'd proven to be.

# SIXTY-TWO

## SUMMER

"Hello, Vengeance."

The unseasonably cold air of the night swept around us on the rooftop of Crave. I pulled the collar of Logan's jacket a little higher around my neck, but the wind still forced its way through the fibers and sunk into skin that barely held warmth on the best of days.

Logan, dressed in his vigilante suit, stood about twenty feet in front of me.

Though I wasn't entirely sure what to think of him, I hated the amount of space between us. It didn't at all resemble what the last six months had been, where barely a ray of light could find a sliver of space to pass between our bodies.

I clenched my fists at the urge to reach for him and stuffed my hands into the jacket pockets like he'd always done to give me time and space.

I didn't want either right now. I desperately wanted his warmth.

But Logan was Vengeance. Vengeance was Logan? It was something I needed to figure out before I left.

All I knew for certain was that seeing him, silently standing before me, made me more confused than ever.

His friends loved him, protected him and his secrets. They didn't seem like bad people who'd stand idly by, watching me date and fall for someone who planned to murder me. If anything, Nova's sadness over Vengeance's existence made me believe they truly wished the being he shared a mind with didn't exist at all.

I wanted to believe her, and I wanted to run to him. I wanted him and I to escape and live out our lives somewhere else, far away from Bedlam, even away from the mountains if that's what he wanted.

Maybe he'd beat people to near death and I could try to save his victims in some sick fairytale we'd create together. I couldn't allow myself sweeter fantasies. And though disturbing, I hated to admit I would take that opportunity in a heartbeat.

If what Nova explained about Vengeance was true and Logan wasn't the one to hurt me, did it *need* to be over between us? Would it have been possible to pick up from where we were, just a few days before he tried to kill me? Was I insane for even thinking that having a life with one "side" of him was possible? How fucked was my mind to think I didn't need as much protection from Logan as I did with Eric?

*In my defense, I probably have a concussion.*

My thoughts didn't matter. My love for Logan and the idea of us being together would have to dissipate – fast. I'd signed my contract and had no choice but to leave with the devil I knew. I belonged to Eric again. On paper, anyway.

Logan carried an unknown evil, and I didn't have the option to stay and learn exactly what that could mean for us long-term.

*Fuck, what if the thing I'm growing survives and turns out to be the same?*

I took a deep breath to calm my nerves. My body still ached from the beating and I was so fucking tired. Remaining in Eric's presence for the entire day before arriving at Crave had me constantly on edge and unable to relax. I hadn't slept, and probably looked more like a corpse than ever.

My heart ached more the longer I waited for Logan to respond. I wished he would hurry up and say something.

I'd called him by his vigilante name so that any number of Eric's people listening in wouldn't immediately have a name to hunt him down the moment I left.

Even after what happened between us, I still couldn't live with myself if anything happened to him on my account. If Nova was being honest, and the man I'd fallen for really did exist, I needed to protect him too.

"Hello, Stitch Up." The words that left his masked mouth made me flinch. It stung to hear him call me that again – almost as much as the stitches in my hairline had when I'd braided my hair earlier, forgetting they were in there.

"Thought I'd let you know," I started, shaking my head of the hurt from his greeting, "I won't be around anymore. I'm taking a new job down south. So, you know, don't bother stopping by when you pass through."

I picked my words carefully, ensuring it didn't sound as though things were too serious between us. Like we were a couple of near-strangers meeting up for sex whenever he could be bothered giving me a second look at Crave.

Biting my tongue, I contained the smile trying to twist the corners of my mouth at the memories the building beneath our feet held for us.

Logan cocked his head to the side.

*Is he not understanding?* My breathing quickened at the thought that he might speak too candidly and get us both killed. *Wait, would it actually be the three of us? Does that even count yet? Fuck, he doesn't even know what's at risk here.*

"Okay, so… that's it?" he sounded equally bored with me as I did with him. "You brought me all the way out here for *that?*"

*This might work, keep going.*

"Yeah. That's it."

I certainly didn't want that to be "it" but I couldn't mention my reasons for meeting, and was starting to feel the all too familiar sense of panic kicking in the longer we stayed out in the open.

*Am I making a huge mistake? Should I try to run from Eric? I'll die if I break my contract again. We all will. How do I tell Logan I still want him – that I don't want this to end?*

The words tumbled out of my mouth; "Oh, and I'm keeping the jacket."

Would Logan remember the discussion we had on the couch all those months ago? Our attention had so quickly turned to each other's bodies from talks of silly code words.

He took a step toward me before abruptly freezing on the spot. Was he pissed off about the jacket? I knew it was his favorite, but I didn't think he'd physically tear it from my body in the cold.

It was either that, or he understood what I couldn't say.

The silence settling between us again was unbearable.

*Give him a sign you're pregnant! Don't leave him without a reason to fight to get you out of Home!*

Eric made it clear he believed I would choose him and return to my position. But I wasn't that girl anymore, and I might not have only been making decisions for *me*.

*Logan may have fucked up, but he's the father. He deserves to know.*

I couldn't *say* anything. I'd be heard. Before I could lift a hand to point to my stomach, I startled.

"It's time to leave, darling." Eric's bored voice spoke in my ear. I didn't know if he could see us, but he could hear my side of the conversation through the earpiece he'd forced on me in the car. "End this or I will."

*Nothing like a good threat so early in our reunion to get things moving along.*

I glanced out across the rooftops, wishing we could go back to the night I'd been vomiting behind the van to work out what was wrong with me. Maybe I wouldn't have snapped at Logan and set us on this path.

*End this or I will. God, you'd be stupid to tell him. Maybe it's best he never knows and you disappear before you get him killed.*

"Goodbye, Vengeance," I said, turning to walk away.

"Hey! Nurse?"

I looked at him over my shoulder, not daring to face Logan completely and allow him to think we could continue this conversation.

"I lov—" he started, but stopped when I raised my hand just a fraction in surprise.

*Shit, he was about to say it!*

It didn't matter that I was dying to hear him speak those words, they needed to be cut off. Professing any kind of true connection between us would be a death sentence for him.

He cleared his throat and instead went with, "Don't get too comfortable in my jacket. I'm gonna find a way to get it back." The softly spoken words floated on the cold breeze to swirl around me at the other side of the roof.

I tried not to smile, but failed, then replied so quietly I wasn't sure he'd hear me, "Nice save. *Nine* out of ten."

When I turned again, I didn't stop. My feet found the will to leave, knowing he got my message, and I understood his.

I climbed down the ladder on the side of the building and dropped to the balcony he and I had once leapt from, then made the long walk through the halls of rooms and down the steep stairs to the lower floor of Crave.

It wasn't long after nine, and a week-night, leaving the club almost bare.

I avoided eye contact with Kit as he poured drinks, and Anna had her back to me as she busied herself with washing glasses. When I'd arrived earlier with Eric, they each had to quickly get a hold over their shocked expressions, both at me with *him* and at the state of my face.

Most of the people at the bar were Eric's men, and stood as I walked past them, just like they always had, back in the day – taking mine or Eric's move as their cue that business was done and our team was ready to head back to Home.

On the street, Eric waited for me in the backseat of his car. It was no surprise that I would be escorted to Bedlam by The Collector himself. He'd trust no one else with returning me to my "shelf" – the thirty-seventh floor of the glass building in the heart of the city.

I opened the door and forced myself in, ignoring *every* cell in my body as it screamed at me to run for my fucking life.

He extended his hand as I secured my seatbelt. "Good girl. Now, are you ready to return to our Home?" His sleeves were already unbuttoned and rolled up around his elbows, comfortable for the long drive ahead of us. I spotted "Stitch Up" amongst the many grayscale tattoos that weaved together to decorate the skin of his forearm.

When I took his hand, he squeezed mine. Cold, much like my own. No warmth for me to steal.

"Let's go," I said with the best, fake smile I could muster through the sadness tugging at my features.

As the car started, I turned to the window, hiding the tears as they pooled along my lashes. Everything and everyone I loved was about to be so far out of my reach.

The drive to Bedlam would take at least a full day, and with two drivers taking up the front seats, our only stops would be for them to switch places. Once we reached the city, I had no idea where to begin with trying to find my way out again. I couldn't escape the same way I had last time. I might've had reasons and people to come back to and live for if I could get out alive.

*You'll find a way,* I promised myself to dam the tears, *Logan loves you. He won't leave you to rot in Bedlam. If he finds the video and believes you, he won't forget about you.*

My free hand shot to my chest and I jumped in my seat. We were at the end of the street, and had barely rounded the corner when a flash of light filled the car and the distinct sound of a gunshot rang loud from a distance.

I'd been exposed to plenty of gun-related violence in Bedlam, but I hadn't heard a shot like that since I was a teen when hunting with Dad and the boys. It had to be a large caliber.

*Designed to take out large threats.*

My breath caught in my throat. There were no bears in the rundown industrial area worthy of a bullet that size. None of the other passengers reacted to the sound, though they complained about the light. Had they expected to hear it?

"Eric?"

"Yes, darling?"

"P-please… *Please* tell me that had nothing to do with you."

"Do you really believe I–"

"I absolutely know what *you would do*, Eric. Tell me!" My treacherous eyes dared to let me down in front of the man I most feared showing weakness to. Tears fell to the seat between us, and Eric eyed them curiously as they rolled across the leather. "Tell me that bullet wasn't for him!"

"You know what this place is like, Summer. That could have been aimed at anyone, the vigilante *you* chose to bring into our arrangement, or otherwise." He tightened the grip on me and rested his head on his other hand, propped up on the door to his side of the car. His eyes flickered from side to side as he mindlessly observed the rundown scenery in the dark, already deep in thought and no doubt contemplating his next move; the announcement of my homecoming.

I knew this man and his fucked up games all too well. The monster beside me wouldn't hesitate to remove anyone he believed to be standing in the way of Eric and Summer being together for-fucking-ever.

The man in the passenger seat lifted a mobile to his ear. Dropping it after a moment, he spoke over his shoulder, "Your recruit was successful, boss. The target is down."

My entire body flushed cold. I couldn't see my reflection, but I could bet the color had entirely drained from my skin over the simple sound of Eric's relieved sigh.

*Fuck this!*

If Logan wasn't already dead, he would be soon. He'd need me, and I needed him.

I tugged at the handle and shouldered the door, assuming it would be locked, but trying anyway.

"Summer." Eric warned, "Don't make a scene."

I spun, elbowing his chest as I clawed for the handle on his side. My fingers barely brushed it before his hand sharply cuffed my neck. He was on top of me in an instant, palm hard on my throat as my back painfully pressed against the door.

Eric snapped his fingers at the men and one handed him a syringe.

"No!" I screamed, clawing at his arms and trying to pull my legs up to kick him off.

Eric knew better than to hesitate, immediately piercing my neck with the needle and forcefully shooting the contents beneath my skin. The drug worked like a switch to my nervous system, my arms instantly grew heavy and dropped to my sides, putting an immediate end to the struggle between us.

Eric's green eyes remained locked on mine, his scowling features growing blurrier by the second. When my breathing slowed and eyelids drooped, he relaxed his chokehold and gently held my face, kissing my forehead as I lost my grip on consciousness.

"Get some rest, Sumar. Our Home is waiting for us."

# ACKNOWLEDGMENTS

To you, reader. Thank you for taking a chance on my first book. I hope you'll forgive me for the ending and come back for more.

To my editor, Molly, who not only squeezed me into her busy schedule at the last minute, but treated Crave with the love and respect everyone told me it deserved. I'd been worn down, and I didn't believe Crave would ever make it, but you restored my faith in editors and in my writing.

To my Beta readers. Sam, you've been one of my biggest supporters since the moment I handed you my manuscript. I never would have thought some of my best writing friends could be found through beta reads, but I'm thankful every day that I answered your request for readers.

Taylor, thank you for containing the need to kill me over this cliffhanger. Though, I think I might need to move out of driving distance from you as the series progresses. I can't wait for more 2am chats about everything I've hidden within the series.

Andrea, your critiques and comments made Crave far stronger than it was before you came into the picture. I will be forever grateful for the way you challenged my ideas and my characters.

To J Cherry, my baby author twin. Here's to hoping our second book launches go far smoother than our firsts.

To @samguydude, for being the first follower on my instagram when I had absolutely nothing to offer as an author except a couple of bad memes. Thank you for cheering me on since day one.

To my family, thank you for stepping up when I was so down and for giving me the time and space to get this story out of my head.

# ABOUT THE AUTHOR

Stevie Carter is an emerging Australian author of dark romance, sci-fi and urban fantasy. This is Stevie's first book in a series that was written in bulk, post-breakdown.

Stevie never intended on being an author and promised herself that the Stitch Up Series would be her only literary works. That promise was promptly broken.

She can be found hoarding notes for future soul-crushing stories, displaying halloween decor year-round, drinking iced coffees, working on her drawing skills and creating cute crafts.

Find more of Stevie's work, content warnings and what upcoming events she'll be attending: **steviecarterbooks.com**

Connect with Stevie:


facebook.com/authorsteviecarter
instagram.com/author_steviecarter
goodreads.com/steviecarter
tiktok.com/@author_steviecarter

Made in the USA
Columbia, SC
31 July 2024

39779288R00307